Like the
MOON,
Mr. Purple

Like the
MOON,
Mr. Purple

Arcádio M. Morada, Jr.

ARPress
ILLUMINATING IDEAS.
EMPOWERING VOICES

ARPress
45 Dan Road Suite 5
Canton MA 02021

Hotline: 1(888) 821-0229
Fax: 1(508) 545-7580

Ordering Information:

Quantity sales. Special discounts are available on quantity purchases by corporations, associations, and others. For details, contact the publisher at the address above.

Printed in the United States of America.

ISBN-13:   Softcover   979-8-89389-070-9

             Hardcover   979-8-89389-179-9

             eBook   979-8-89389-071-6

Library of Congress Control Number: 2024914305

This Work is Dedicated to

TATAY CADIO • NANAY BABING

DELY • RUDY

My Past

MAMENG • DIMPLE • ALFRED

ELSA • NILDA • PIPING • OTÊ

MERL • PRID • NITZ

PANCHO

My Present

ADAM JUNE

My Future

CONTENTS

PREFACE

God creates the human families and, in his infinite wisdom and mercy, grants them the ability to weave a hodgepodge tale of their niche and existence in their allotted time and space. The Morada Clan of Bicol, therefore, like every family in the world, does not own any monopoly on this blessing, privilege—or crucible. But let me tell my peculiar hodgepodge just the same. With the coronavirus pandemic raging and dissipating into 2022 as standpoint, I look back at the seemingly itsy-bitsy and insignificant events that make up the collective tale of my family (and some special people), and realize that, *Ah*, these events helped define us, make us what we are, and lead us silently to the iridescent twilight of our years. By all reckoning, these events have been our signposts, watersheds, and milestones, as much as our pillories and gauntlets, along this beaten and hackneyed path called life.

Sometimes, the path goes straight, bedecked with dazzling flowers, but also sometimes tortuous and strewn with thorny and horrible beings. Like all mundane paths, it teems with adversities and reeks of death. There are times when we stumble, when we incur cuts and bruises, when there is more gravel than gold nuggets, when there are more rivers to cross with no bridges, boats, or even stepping stones at all. There are times when we, unwitting and map-less, are off the rails or the wearied tracks, when we fail no matter how hard we try or how careful we are, whereas the worst is yet to come. But there are times of triumphs, too—of achievements, of glories, of countless blessings, however small they may be—for the best is yet to come, either. And the Divine Creator of Human Families has gifted us our very selves for each other's sake, rescue, and betterment. We struggle, go the extra mile, scale tall mountains, and emerge at all, because we have this Map called Faith—in God and each other.

Neither are we a perfect family, for sure, nor are our stories grandiose, but it's our imperfections and their simplicity that make our stories valid, cohesive, compelling, and relatable. Even before the pandemic, we told ourselves that someone had got to narrate and write them, or they would lapse and fade into insignificance and oblivion. Someone in this all-too-human family had got to make good use of the said God-given blessing and privilege, let alone crucible. That's how and why my role came in.

The role felt like a birthright, as much as a yoke. I am assuming, of course, that upon my own shoulders lay the task of telling the Morada Clan's story nice and right.

I am called many names. Family and friends call me Jun. A co-teacher once dubbed me Jun Muslim. My big brother Rudy fondly called me Doc. My better half, ever-sweet Mameng who ordinarily calls me "My Love," blurts out "Arcádio Mimay Morada, Jr!" whenever she wants my attention, whenever she thinks I'm in trouble, or whenever she is upset by, or bitter over, me. One time or another, people called me Arc, Arcade, Archie, Aracadio, Arcadrio, Acardo—*whatever*. At work in Texas schools, colleagues and students have referred to me as **Mr. Purple**, which initially sounded like saying bluebonnets are *kinda* purple. But later I saw firsthand that some bluebonnets are *truly* purple, even pink. I can live with Mr. Purple, but please don't call me Mr. Pink.

Of course, the focal point, the greater bulk of the narratives, is my being Mr. Purple, the teacher. This is not to say, however, that mine is the most important or most colorful in the hodgepodge. Taken individually, each of these stories has their own appeal and can stand alone without the others. Collectively, however, they are another living proof of the gestalt and the cliché that the whole is far greater than its parts.

It's my bio—disguised as a slew of anecdotes and occupational vignettes, a prose and poetry anthology, a collection of spiritual musings, Facebook articles, blog posts, and more. From some obscure corner of the Third World, here's the life of a nondescript guy with his love story, work exploits, bittersweet memoir, and family history replete with actual events and real people. Though some names of persons, places, things, or events have been deliberately concealed for the protection and privacy of all concerned, there is no tinge of fake news or historical fiction in these pages.

With one-word titles complemented by one-liner abstracts as portents of things to come, the 42 chapters of **LIKE THE MOON, MR. PURPLE** may appear to be topsy-turvy and ambiguous. A few chapters comprise narrative panels that may appear unrelated but are actually unified thematically. In other words, they are not arranged chronologically. In this miscellany with such mode and arrangement, the reader may start with any chapter and it won't matter, right? But let me share a little secret: one of my early reviewers said it is well and wise to start with **G-O-D**, the 26th chapter. You may find a lot more sense in that suggestion, too.

And why 42? That's another secret.

The secrets and the sense are for the taking, so—

Give it a go, and God bless you.

-Mr. Arcádio 'Purple' Morada, Jr
& The Purples

1

SUN

You started it all

Tatay[1], I had never appreciated you as a father in your whole mortal life. Worse, through the decades since your passing, I had never given much thought to you as a father. *Mea culpa*, my utter failing, my bad. Let me make up for these grievous shortcomings now, with much regret and love; this entire saga of the clan which you started, and I recount, is a testament to that mishmash of regret and love. I am doing this with lumps in my throat, butterflies in my stomach, and tears in my eyes.

To start it off, you are my eponym; I am your namesake. I don't know if you yourself ever questioned your own *tatay* bequeathing you this name, but in my case, there were a few times in the past when I asked myself whether our name was a boon or a bane.

"*Mabatâon an ngaran mo!*"[2] a friend in college, named Sit-sit Basiño, said in jest. "Who in his right mind tags his son *Arcádio* nowadays?"

"Hey, *Arcádio* is of Grecian origin," I said. "It means 'of Arcádia,' a place in Greece."

"In Greece—of old!" he said. "Ancient, antiquated, outmoded, obsolete!"

"Thanks for the malicious synonyms, my friend!" I said, capping the discussion. Sit-sit has gone too long ahead, but if he were alive, I should tell him: "Wait, who's talking! Can we both look in the mirror, *Rosite*— that's your real name, right?" Rosite and Arcádio should both be laughing at the truth.

As for our surname, a Spanish origin and a service-oriented meaning ("inn, dwelling, residence," Google points out) are enough to compensate and boost my ego and spirit. And in Texas, where they call me **Mr. Purple**, I tell Texans I'm not *morado*. Our forename and surname need not gender-match, because the result is

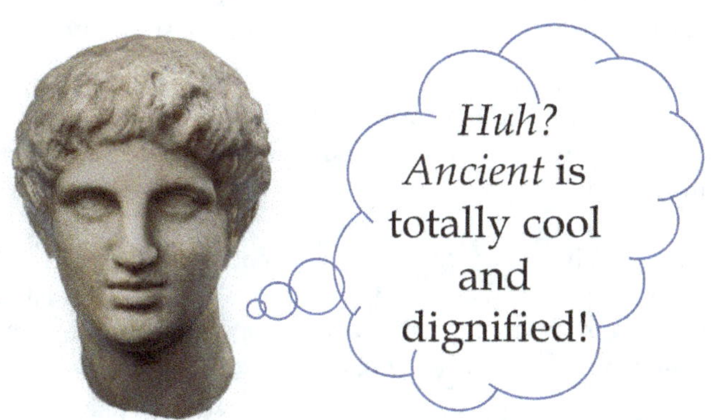

---

1   *Tatay* [**Filipino**, the national language of the Philippines], *Itay* or *Tay* in short form, means "Father." The female counterpart is *Nanay*, *Inay*, or *Nay*.

2   "*Mabatâon an ngaran mo!*" [**Bikol**, the language spoken by natives of the Bicol Peninsula, Southern Luzon, Philippines] translates to "Your name stinks!"

Los Fresnos Cisd 457 Def Comp Plan And Trust
Fbo Arcadio M Morado
600 North Mesquite
Los Fresnos Tx 78566
Re: LSW Annuity 556126X

TERM CONTRACT

STATE OF TEXAS
COUNTY OF CAMERON

NAME: **MORADO, ARCADIO**
I.D. #: **12256**

seldom trifling or inconsequential[3]. But in their strict and automatic adherence to grammatical gender in the Spanish language, Texans and Hispanics[4] in general insist on bestowing me that regal color.

There was nothing regal in your beginnings. You and Nanay were born in the boondocks of Albáy, Philippines, near the border between Camalíg and Jovellár towns. Your exact birthday, though, was anyone's guess, courtesy of Juan and Juana Morada, your parents, who might not have given importance to keeping official documents such as birth certificates. So, in need of your special date, they might have relied on memory, sans black-and-white proof, and told anyone who asked: April 15, 1915. They needed it when you were to enter school, which you did intermittently, by choice or circumstance. Walking long distances daily to more populated villages where schools stood wasn't an attractive come-on for schooling in the hinterlands of

---

3   Every time my name is written in official records or documents as **Arcádio Morado**, which has happened very often in Texas, having the "o" officially reverted to "a" can sometimes cost time, money, and/or effort, at one point even requiring a notary public to take effect.

4   The most recent incident happened on May 17, 2021, at Main Street Radiology in Jackson Heights, New York. A Hispanic lady deglamorized my name to a new level. I had come to the medical center to see a Hand Surgeon about some pain in both my thumbs. Now, the receptionist asked for my primary provider doctor's referral and my ID. "Good," I said confidently to myself, hoping for the best. The lady would see my name, how it SHOULD be spelled.

The receptionist then printed out some forms for me to sign. Shucks, I have a new identity—MORADA, ARCADIA. All the forms have it, in glaring black and white! Spanish language gender-noun agreement again?

I call her attention. The Hispanic receptionist, with one-centimeter-long mascara, flashes an apologetic smile, and rationalizes: "You know, sir, I *kinda* thought it's one of those names in the neuter gender, like Guadalupe, Andrea, and Trinidad, you know, can be male or female, whatever. So sorry!"

I am about to accept the apology, but realize: *Hey, lady, you just made me asexual!* I keep mum, but seethe in silence.

She types again and reprints, then I sign. The corrected mistake may not be as painful as the tenosynovitis of my thumbs for which I come here to be treated, but it is just as profound.

Come to think of it, I have a new rhyming, gender-bending name!

Camalíg and Jovellár during your formative years. Besides, when at last you reached Grade 3, your mother got seriously sick, because of which you stopped schooling altogether. Up to that point, however, you had learned to write your name, recognize and write numbers, as well as count and measure—basic competencies you needed to be of any success as a tailor. That's what you became.

An unschooled tailor you might have wished me to be, too. But you turned our lives around and aspired towards the stuff of legends. How and why? Wisdom might have convinced you to send me and my siblings to school, which had then become common in the Albáy hinterlands by the 1950s. Though I learned how to sew alright, you enabled me to discover worlds beyond sewing machines and threads and needles, and the easiest way to reach those worlds was through the schools. For sure, formal education was a slow, let alone pecuniary effort; but you came to believe that in the long run, it was the more important legacy you could bequeath your children, far more valuable than a few hectares of pristine land that you yourself and Nanay inherited from your forebears.

Alas, if formal education was so important, why had your first two educable offspring only reached high school, while the rest finished college with rigor? That was a rather disturbing question nobody bothered to ask you during your lifetime. On your behalf, may I offer my two cents' worth: You and Nanay found yourselves in a lifelong bind, in a tunnel, so to speak, with seven children tagging along and tugging. You saw the proverbial light at the end of the tunnel. Together, we struggled and followed the light, groping and inching through the dark. Then, you tapped two older children to help the younger, but the first of the two strayed away, leaving the second in charge.

For you, the tunnel was endless, the darkness limiting but becoming somewhat fun and inducive through which to plod. Your children became your school. Learning streamed from them to you, and once you got the hang of it, learning never stopped.

I remember the time you, in gentle humility, asked me, a junior high schooler then, how to figure out the board feet of the lumber from our ancestral land. So, I taught you how to multiply (the length, width, and thickness of lumber in feet), alongside with memorizing the multiplication tables. That done, you saw the need to divide numbers as an offshoot of multiplication. Next, the idea of fractions reared its head. And so on and so forth. I felt your sense of fulfillment, your joy of accomplishment. On occasions, though, I could get irritated by your insistence to learn even the most fundamental concepts, but much later I realized: Wasn't this what you enrolled me for at the Bicol University? Your insistence to gain knowledge might have started the subconscious in me, who first dreamed to be a civil engineer, to become a teacher.

You loved to sing, though not in front of a big audience; *big* means any number of people over 1 (which was yourself). You played musical instruments, too (harmonica, ukulele, guitar, accordion, violin), though learned by ear and played not as a virtuoso. Along with Nanay, you saw the need for music in our home and in our lives; for from whom did I inherit my love for music, if not from you?

One song you and Nanay ingrained in me when I was young was this plaintive and sentimental Bicol folksong:

Nenang

Nenang, nagtios an pusò ko, nagtios
Dahilán sa imo.
Nenang, minadulok sa atubangan mo,
Lilingya nin herak, lilingya nin herak,
An pobreng buhay ko!

Its melody, in gloomy minor mode, matched the lyrics in their sentimentality. I fell for the song; **Nenang** has never left me. In fact, right or wrong, it has defined my personality, style, and frame of mind. In 1975, I used it—paraphrased, renamed, and incorporated in my first operetta, "What Ever Happened to Magayón?" When the lover crooned the words to his beloved during the operetta's premiere in St. Agnes' Academy of Legazpi City in 1976, you were among the audience in the front row, silent and beaming, proud of your namesake and the song's transformation in my hands.

Ray a Bit of Your Sun

My love, must I always have to be far away,
Far from your heart's beating?
Am I meant forever by your heart forsaken?
Ray a bit of your sun, ray a bit of your sun
Before my life is done!

The germ of music emanating from you has permeated your granddaughter Carmela, nicknamed Dimple, whom you never met in life, and who is into the Arts. Her firstborn, Adam, born during the height of the pandemic, responds to music at eight months old, and babbles along with anybody who sings within earshot! You and I won't know how far-reaching that germ will further influence lives and generations. For this, I shall not be the only one forever grateful.

Unlike the pertinacious lover in **Nenang**, you were not a demonstrative person. Not thoughtful. Not outspoken. Nothing outward, but it didn't mean there weren't your heartstrings and the need to communicate. It's just that, since my faintest memories, you were a very reserved man. Nanay could attest to this if she were still alive. In the same manner, your daughter-in-law, my wife Mameng, can say that you and I are peas in a pod. Meaning, I am myself so reserved that often people find me as uncaring, unromantic, boring, thoughtless, numb, and worst, stone-hearted as can be. Well, I don't need to refute or dignify their observations. Enough to say that you are my father, and I am your son.

I think of you, so I am. A chip off the old block. The *manzanito* falls near the *manzano*. I am not *morado* because you are *morada*. We beat the same drum.

You were an epitome of patience and self-control. Not once had I seen you in any aggressive confrontation with others. In my conscious years, I had never been a witness to any violent altercations between you and Nanay. You didn't have any derogatory vice, nor unacceptable habits, not that I knew of. You might have been adept at hiding them to not inflict any influence or harm on us, your family. Being enigmatic was your lifestyle. Later, when your health failed, when you talked with great hardship because of stroke, "reserved" became an understatement. *Secretive* was your way to go.

It took months before you succumbed to the effects of the stroke. From distant Manila, where I worked, I came home in brief intervals to see you, as my other siblings who lived far away, with families of their own. On these few occasions, you never hinted at, let alone told me or any other sibling, what you needed to ease your sufferings. More than likely, you didn't want us to be burdened by your condition.

I never saw you go. Only Nanay and my two elder sisters stood by you on your deathbed. They didn't know if you were in pain, in painless suffering, or if you were looking for your missing offspring. They said you lay in long silence before breathing your last. August 1, 1991. I'm sure that silence did not mean you loved me—or my other prodigal siblings—less.

Never had you verbalized to any of us in the past the words "I love you." Not that I was aware of. True to your nature of restraint, of silence. And remember, we are peas in a pod; not once have I told you those words, either. But at long last, with shame, guilt, and happiness for having realized and owned up to a grievous mistake, today I'll say them to you with my whole mind, heart, and soul. Wherever you are now, I thank God for your fatherhood. I thank the Holy Family—Jesus, Mary, and Joseph—for the unholy but God-fearing family you begot. Without you and Nanay, there are no Dely, Rudy, Nilda, Piping, Jun, Otê, Merl, and Prid. Without you, there is no "I". Your enigma is what I am, and I am because you are. *TATAY, I LOVE YOU!*

Better late than never.

♥ From your like-father son, Arcádio Jr. ∎

Tatay

"*I shall not be the only one forever grateful.*"

Adam June, Tatay's great-grandchild, here looking
and moving forward to a brilliant future.

2
ROD
Mother knows best

The very first song I composed, circa 1963. I was in 5th grade at Sipocot North Central School, in Sipocot, Camarines Sur, Philippines. Of course, I could not write music then. What I had was the melody and the lyrics ingrained in my head until 1972, during college, when I thought I had the basic knowledge and tools to transcribe the song into its crude form, using pencil and a portable Singer typewriter. Personal computers were nonexistent then, as were any music apps and devices that could have helped me transcribe it this way more recently:

THE BIRDS

Words & Music by
A. Morada, Jr.

THE BIRDS

1. Swiftly and gently, the little birds fly.
   They float in the air; they go up to the sky.
   After a while, they come down to rest.
   And somewhere high up the tree lies their nest.

2. O Little Birds, won't you tell me why:
   I'm smarter than you, and yet I cannot fly!
   Do you, dear Birdlings, cry out in fear,
   As I do when Mother is not near?

**HE BIRDS** bespeaks a mama's boy. I am. I say this without equivocation. Whether the truth is pejorative or complimentary to my person, I leave it up to anyone's judgment. But let me pour my heart out first before they give their verdict.

Arcádio Morada and Flávia Mimay both grew up in Talôtô, a *barangay*[5] in the hinterlands of Camalíg, Albáy. In their teens, when they matched, he often confided to her his preference for sewing machines over plows. It was plain to Babing that farming in the boondocks meant of lesser importance to her beloved Cadió when they agreed to marry and start a family in 1935.

In the first years of their married life, Cadió's inclination to tailoring often consigned farm duties to Babing while he stayed in the house. Their first two children, Dely and Rudy, were born in this setup.

Dely was the first offspring, born in Talôtô, and I was the 5th, born in Jovellár, Albáy. Tatay Cadió and Nanay Babing must have decided that I should be his Junior as soon as they heard my first baby-cry and saw that I was a boy. In 1951, it wasn't possible to know a baby's gender in advance because no one had yet invented fetal ultrasound. Only a *parahilot*[6] was available for prenatal and birth procedures in remote Jovellár, where the couple settled after Talôtô—prompted by Dely's tragedy—in 1944.

To this day, no one could pinpoint with clarity and certainty firstborn Dely's mysterious affliction. Doctors ascribed it to peritonitis, but old folks maintained there was a supernatural touch to it. The story is often told that one afternoon in January 1944, towards dusk, while Cadió was on his sewing machine and Babing (in her 7th month of pregnancy with her 3rd child) was baby-sitting the toddler Rudy, she sent the six-year-old Dely on an errand to the next-door neighbor's house. The house was just a hundred meters away, but past a thicket of banana plants and a bamboo footbridge that natives believed to be haunted by otherworldly entities. Fine, done same such errand in the past. But as Dely walked home on the footbridge, she slipped and fell on the parched riverbed, seen by an old woman passerby, who later recounted the details of the accident. Dely stood up, staggered, and got home. Soon, she complained of abdominal pains that had Tatay Cadió and Nanay Babing rushing her to the Ante Memorial Hospital[7] in faraway Old Albay, Legazpi City, to no avail.

---

5   *barangáy* [Filipino] – village, the smallest administrative division in Philippine society.
6   *parahilot* [Bikol] – a native practitioner skillful in traditional medicine, healing, body-massage therapy, and delivery of babies.
7   Dr. Esteban V. Ante Memorial Hospital, 573 Rizal St, Old Albay District, Legazpi City, Philippines, established in 1930.

A tragedy one too many! The trauma it inflicted crystallized and prompted the decision to move from Talôtô to Jovellár and concentrate on the tailoring business. Jovellár was the most convenient choice to move away from crude farm life, the most logical step toward progress and civilization. It was also where the couple's 3rd up to 7th children were subsequently born.

So, I was the 5th child. Considering Dely's unfortunate childhood, mine was not a nice and ideal one either. Early on, ear infection and asthma, among others, maligned me. Given to brooding as a result, *maniwáng*[8] in construction and *maluyà*[9] in constitution, I was light-skinned, twinkle-eyed, and curly-haired, though. Most kith and kin visualized me as a silent-river-runs-deep-but-somewhat-harmless kid. The onus of that portrayal has stuck throughout my lifetime.

In 1957, we had to relocate again, from Jovellár to Sipocot, Camarines Sur. That's where **The Birds** gestated, and where I spent my growing-up years as a *baby boomer*.[10]

This baby boomer could break into song at will or by minimal prodding. Not that I could give Andy Williams or Perry Como a run for their money. Enough said that I inclined to music and could carry a tune. Asthmatic, true, but not too out of breath to sing. You should hear me belt out "Where Is Your Heart?" by Percy Faith from the 1952 movie **Moulin Rouge**. In 1964, my eldest brother Rudy enlisted my name in this amateur singing competition at the *saudán*[11] to croon the very question, but because of asthma, we went home before showtime—my singing career cut before it began. If one dares me, though, I sure can still emote with that song from memory. Only, look not for Andy or Perry.

Seriously, because I was the sickly mama's boy and papa's musical Junior, I had the edge over my other siblings in terms of preferential treatment (except, of course, Prid, our youngest, who arrived eight years after me). Nanay Babing often cut some slack in my defense whenever I got in trouble or whenever Tatay Cadió was on the lookout for *someone* who messed up something around the house. My younger brother Otê was always the usual suspect even if he didn't do it, or did nothing wrong at all. Nanay often looked the other way, condoned, or turned a blind eye, whenever I got concerned or involved.

But all things being equal, Nanay was the sterner disciplinarian, much stricter than Tatay. Now and then, even with my assumed entitlement, I would receive one or two lashes of the inanimate but wretched *tumagiktik*—the meter-long, dried and supple rattan rod. Once held by Nanay, it would gain a life of its own, a horrible and feared monster. Even its very name, an onomatopoeia, evoked fear by imitating its smacking sound on your buttocks. You did not grow up without experiencing the pain which the Nanay-*tumagiktik* tandem could inflict. In the Morada household, rules unfollowed or broken caused so much pain and agony through Nanay, the maker of rules, and the *tumagiktik*, the enforcer-aide.

Nanay used the rod to the fore when we were impressionable, less and less often as we grew in age. As a result, none of us became passionate rule-breakers or willful benders of the right. There was no vulgarity spoken inside or outside the household. There wasn't any deed or habit so foul the *tumagiktik* couldn't mend or break. Compassion and cooperation lay unwritten but understood and done. Nanay and Tatay wanted to nurture a God-fearing and law-abiding family, and that's what they got.

Nights were family Rosary time, in Spanish. By tradition, Nanay took the lead. She later saw to the older siblings learning the prayers by heart, and before school age, the younger ones could recite the prayers by

---

8   *maniwang* [Bikol] – lanky.

9   *maluya* [Bikol] – frail.

10   Pew Research Center, "Defining generations: Where Millennials end and Generation Z begins" by Michael Dimock, defines **baby boomers** as those born from 1946 to 1964, https://www.pewresearch.org/fact-tank/2019/01/17/where-millennials-end-and-generation-z-begins/.

11   *saudan* [Bikol] – town marketplace.

imitation. Even when I learned to recite the Rosary in English for ease, *Padre Nuestro*[12] and *Dios te salve, Maria*[13] still reverberated in my head, and *May*[14] Idang always came to mind. It was because the whole compendium of Spanish prayers and novenas Nanay had learned by rote herself from her own mother, May Placida Guiriba Mimay, who was of a much sterner, stricter, and more imposing Castilian stuff.

Not that May Idang was any Castilian by looks or origin; she was every inch as indigenous as any native Bicolano could be—short, brown-skinned, snub-nosed, kinky-haired, rounded nostrils, besides thick lips. From past accounts by relatives, I imagined the youngish Babing, knelt in front of the family altar, reciting the *Salve Regina*[15] aloud as her Nanay Idang stood by with *tumagiktik* in hand, ready to flick it on her at the slightest sign of forgetfulness or inattention.

Years later, I saw firsthand that method of discipline on Nenita, our adopted sister. Nitz was a bitty three-year-old when she came into the Morada household. We knew her *tatay*, Valentin Morada, as an itinerant handyman who could hardly make both ends meet in Sipocot. Not a relative though with our surname, Valentin approached Tatay Cadió and Nanay Babing one day in 1982, asking if they could take his toddler Nitz in as their own. They did.

As a new family member, Nitz imbibed the house rules fast—except for memorizing the Spanish formula prayers, which took a much longer time. Nanay used a *nigo*[16] of *monggo*[17] and a pair of old books to enable little Nitz to say the *Padre Nuestro* straightforward. If she forgot a word or stalled, she ended up kneeling in the *nigo* of *monggo,* hands stretched sideways, each topped off by a book on the palm. Everybody knew how *monggo* could burrow deep in your knees and the books could get heavier the longer you stalled. This setup did the job eventually.

And who might complain of the harsh discipline in behalf of the chastised sibling? If one did, it could turn and get placed on them. We could only cringe, watch, and learn from the mistake.

Discipline applied to whoever you were when you broke any rule of the house. One day in the summer of 1961, for example, I and my brother Otê were itching to swim in the *Dakulang Salog,*[18] an exercise forbidden but allowed with adult supervision. We connived with Raming, a cousin and Tatay's apprentice. We were to go by ourselves; he was to follow. If later Nanay were to discover the scheme, Raming was to present himself as our adult chaperon. So, with this arrangement, we proceeded and swam, to our hearts' delight, unchaperoned. But Raming, busy the entire day at the tailoring shop, never joined us. Worse, he had to confess our clandestine escapade and arrangement to Nanay. So, at reckoning, Nanay and *tumagiktik* waited at the door! (I got two lashes and Otê got five.) *Aray!* [Ouch!]

Another day, in the summer of 1962, six-year-old Merl and three-year-old Prid were playing house. Merl fancied dressing up a cardboard doll with colorful clothes, so she cut out this fabric that she took from the glass display cabinet in Tatay's tailoring shop. Sometime later, Nanay went looking for the fabric. I could imagine the surprise on her face when she discovered the dressed-up cardboard doll. She got the *tumagiktik*, of course, and soon I was counting the lashes, tantamount to the infraction. I stopped counting when Nanay chased poor Merl around the house and gave her more lashes than she believed the little fiend deserved.

---

12 *Padre Nuestro* [Spanish] – Our Father (The Lord's Prayer).
13 *Dios te salve, Maria* [Spanish] – Hail, Mary.
14 *May* [Bikol] – pronounced **my**, derived from *mamay*, mother; term of endearment for an older female, in this case, Grandma.
15 *Salve Regina* [Spanish] – Hail, Holy Queen.
16 *nigo* [Bikol] – a round and flat native winnowing basket.
17 *monggo* [Filipino] – mung beans.
18 *Dakulang Salog* [Bikol] – literally, big river; geographically, Libmanan River.

When it was over, Tatay Cadió hugged (of course, away from Nanay's view) the crying Merl and took her in secret to Main Theater, the neighborhood movie house, to assuage her pain. He understood the discipline, but it hurt him to see a crying child. He showed the same compassion by hugging the crying Nitz, who could not memorize the *Padre Nuestro* outright, after her ordeal with the *nigo,* the *monggo,* and the books. To my brother Otê and me after the *Dakulang Salog* fiasco, he said, *"Sa súsunod, magiribá kitáng márigos."* [We'll go swim together next time.]

Cadió had the complementary wife in Babing. To his indecisions, she put in quick action, few words, and stubborn will. To his doubts, she put in initiative, independent mind, and unflinching passion. Though unschooled, Babing was an exacting and uncompromising woman of substance, plausible goals, and endless determination.

On account of Cadió being busy and occupied as a struggling tailor in Talôtô, Babing took it upon herself to do the basic farm tasks during their early married life. She knew how to catch mudfish, *kasilí*[19], and fresh-water shrimps in the river that ran through their farm, how to plant upland rice, how to grow and harvest other seasonal crops, how to make home-made coffee from coffee berries, how to make coconuts into copra, how to make abaca hemp, how to weave *sinamay*[20], how to make *banig*[21] from *karagumoy*[22], *et cetera.* Among other native delicacies, she made the best-tasting *binôtong*[23], *tinaldís*[24], *molido*[25], and *tabrilya*[26]. God grew the head of a meticulous, hard-working homemaker on Babing's shoulders, and Cadió and his young household stood the better for it.

In 1967, we moved to Daragá, Albáy, where Tatay and Nanay saw to most of us become degree-holders and professionals through the 1980s. There, too, in 1988, when she was well into her 70s, she had a fall (reminiscent of her firstborn Dely's) which debilitated her body in a gradual and inexorable manner. She was trying to reach, from a second-floor window, a few luscious fruits of an overhanging guava tree. Slow but sure, her brittle backbone hurt and bent, giving her so much discomfort, thenceforth forcing her to lie on her side when she needed to sleep. Yet she suffered in silence—she never complained, refused medication during the early stages of the malady, and only agreed to go to the doctor, by her daughter-in-law (my wife) Mameng's entreaties and financial help, when it was near the point beyond resolve.

Seldom given to overt sentimentality, Nanay gave Mameng's shoulder a gentle touch. Maybe it was her way of saying thank you to this daughter-in-law and her readiness to help, for she was soon to leave for Texas to join me. Then she whispered in Mameng's ear. *"Indî mo man pagpabayaán si Manay Nilda mo."* [Take good care of your Manay Nilda, too.]

---

19   *kasilí* [Bikol] – fresh-water eel.
20   *sinamay* [Bikol] – stiff textile made and woven from abaca.
21   *banig* [Bikol] – sleeping mat.
22   *karagumoy* [Bikol] – a species of *pandan* (screwpine), *Pandanus simplex.*
23   *binôtong* [Bikol] – glutinous rice with coconut milk wrapped in banana leaves.
24   *tinaldís* [Bikol]– glutinous rice cake.
25   *molido* [Bikol]– ground pilinut (*Canarium ovatum*) candy.
26   *tabrilya* [Bikol]– home-made chocolate rounds.

Similar to her husband, Nanay was a master of impassivity and introspection. Whatever emotions she had, she was so adept at hiding them from us. When I was to leave for Manila for employment in 1978, she asked: *"Onó pakaráy an pigahanap mo? Kaipuhan mong rumayô para maghanapbu'ay?"* [What are you looking for? Do you have to go far away to earn a living?] When I came home to say goodbye and ask for her blessing before flying to Texas USA in 1992, she sent me off with an even more condensed set of words. Tatay had passed on just a year ago, and now her favorite boy, his namesake afflicted with wanderlust, was leaving for a faraway, foreign land. Distance could limit his coming home, and at the worst, she might not see him again. But what could she do? *"Kaipuhan mo talagáng rumayô?"* [Do you really have to go far?]

Those were Nanay's last words to me. Ever. In late July 1993, an overseas call from the Philippines sent me scampering home to Daragá, Albáy, from Brownsville, Texas, to bury my mother.

Do you, dear Birdlings, cry out in fear,
As I do when Mother is not near? ■

Nanay & her boy

3

DEEP-BLUE
One cold thing leads to another

Manoy[27] Rudy was ecstatic. "I received the refrigerator tonight, March 8," he wrote in Bikol. "So, in jubilation, I drafted this letter in haste to let you know. Let us celebrate! *Mas magayón*[28] if you could come to Colaclíng." Postmarked March 9, 1981, the letter arrived at my Manila boarding house on Friday the 13th, right after work.

Sure, *mas magayon*; so, early morning of the next day, I took the daytime train bound for Bicol. It was dusk when I disembarked at Colaclíng, a *barangáy* of the town of Lupí, Camarines Sur. My sister-in-law Manay Elsa and, of course, my brother Manoy Rudy were at their door to meet me. Missing was Pancho, their only son, who was attending college in Naga City, 50 kilometers away. His parents were both beaming, though, especially Manoy Rudy.

Manoy was turning 41, whereas I was 30. He married Manay Elsa, the couple having been together for 23 years now, whereas I was single and living alone in Manila. Manoy was more handsome than either me or my younger brother, Otê; he could have been a better-looking Junior in the Morada family instead of me. A custom tailor just like Tatay, Manoy Rudy was as industrious and responsible. He strove hard to be a good provider, diversifying his sources of income by putting up a *sari-sari*[29] store beside his tailoring shop, and it looked the joint business venture was booming. He even resorted to dealing in pigs and slaughtering them on Colaclíng market days. On the other hand, I never had my father's sartorial acumen, though I could run the sewing machine and apply a stitch or two. Manoy began no college, whereas I got through it and ended up teaching at St. Agnes' Academy of Legazpi City in 1974, then Xavier School, Manila, in 1978.

The idea of a refrigerator purchased in Manila and shipped to far-flung Colaclíng hatched a year earlier. In April 1980, while I was on summer break in my hometown Daragá, Albáy, Manoy Rudy came to visit. He talked to me and broached the idea, hoping for my help.

Manoy summed up Philippine summers in three words: *hot, humid, very.* Thus, he propounded that ice-cold goodies during this time of the year were so much in demand; he needed a big enough refrigerator to increase the supply. His meat business was getting lucrative and expansive; he needed a big enough refrigerator for cold storage. This was before the construction of Quirino Highway, passing through Colaclíng and making it more accessible. At that period, one could reach Colaclíng only through trains, railroad skates, or animals. So, because of its location and demography, just a few business establishments had refrigerators in Colaclíng.

---

27 *Manoy/Manay* [Bikol] – honorifics for an elder brother/sister or any older male/female in general.
28 *mas magayón* [Bikol] – more beautiful, nicer, better.
29 *sari-sari* [Filipino] – sundry.

I could enable him to a workable means of livelihood and secure a life-sustaining future for his family—if I helped.

But why buy the fridge from Manila, hundreds of kilometers away? Why not from Legazpi City, or closer still, Naga City? For sure, home appliance centers abounded in those urban areas, too. "Of course, but we don't have connections there," Manoy said. "In Manila, *you* do."

Got it. He needed help other than financial. The supposed connections Manoy iterated might have been my close contacts with Filipino-Chinese scions of wealthy business owners in Manila. He knew I worked in Xavier School, whose student body was mostly rich Filipino-Chinese who might be appliance store owners in the metropolis. With those close contacts, I could most likely ease transaction for his brand-new refrigerator transported by train to Colaclíng. His logic was that I could use my connections and clout to sift the lowest possible price, not to mention discounts.

It was a plausible idea, but inappropriate and unethical where I stood. "Schools anywhere may tolerate asking favors and taking gifts from their students, but not Xavier," said Ms. Jenny Huang Go, the Filipino-Chinese principal, emphasizing a school policy. Indebtedness mustn't corrupt a healthy student-teacher relationship. "When a Chinese does you a favor or gives you a gift, he expects something in return," Ms. Norma Sandoval, assistant principal, herself a Filipino-Chinese, once explained the policy rationale. "That's Chinese culture."

I did not convey to Manoy the Chinese culture bit, but I assured him my best to help. So, as he returned to Colaclíng in April and I to Manila in early May 1980, the refrigerator might have been, to him, a sure deal. To me, though, it was a problem I hardly knew how to solve.

Precariously, amid the pressures of work and in semi-conscious defiance of a school policy, I asked colleagues and students if they knew any appliance stores where I could buy a refrigerator, hoping with crossed fingers to hear replies such as "My Dad is the manager of this-or-that store" or "We own one" or "My Mom can introduce you to Mr. So-and-So who deals in this-or-that."

One such reply took me to Pacò, Manila. *Voilà!* A Westinghouse dealership made available and arranged for me, in installment terms and with a huge discount, the dream refrigerator of Manoy! I informed him posthaste. On July 12, he wrote back, *"Salamat sa Diós ta bagá sa ngonián magkákatotoó na!* [Thanks to God, this time it may yet come true!] Enclosed in this letter is money order amounting to ₱450. Let me know the payment terms till paid in full." (A good-sized fridge at the time could cost upwards of ₱2,000, about $260 by the prevailing peso-dollar rate of ₱7.70 = $1. My salary as a teacher at Xavier School was ₱650, or $84.)

Otê, my younger brother, came to Manila in August for a business of his own, met up with me, and returned to Colaclíng afterwards. (He lived with his parents-in-law just across the railroad tracks from Manoy Rudy's.) On August 25, Manoy wrote, "José [Otê] told me you weren't able to get the refrigerator because a big fire razed the store [where the fridge was to be bought]. Could you find another dealer? If not, please just return the money by mail, or [you can give it back to me in Daragá] if you are coming home for the town fiesta [Mary's nativity, September 8]." I could sense a brewing impatience in his words.

I didn't have time to go home that September. Meanwhile, throughout October onto November, I looked out with diligence for potential sources of the refrigerator, yet unsuccessful in finding satisfactory offers and discounts. Amid the rains and the *amihan*[30] of December 1980, I went to Colaclíng during the Christmas break to apologize, explain, give updates, and return the money altogether.

---

30 *amihan* [Filipino] – the northeast monsoon, a cold and dry northeast wind coming from Siberia and China and blowing down to Southeast Asia.

It was cold when I arrived in Colaclíng on December 28, but colder yet was Manoy Rudy or Manay Elsa's demeanor. In my suitcase was the 450 pesos, plus a melodion and an oldies songbook, both of which I always carried around like lifeblood. After lunch, Manoy asked if I could play some Christmas favorites and standard oldies for him and Manay Elsa. So did I, proudly, like I was playing for conjugal dictators President Ferdinand Marcos and First Lady Imelda Marcos in attendance. Then, the mood changed to jovial. In the middle of my mini-concert, Manoy told me to hold on to the money and to please keep looking for that elusive refrigerator. He requested two encore songs: "Little Things Mean a Lot" and "Blue Christmas."

Manay Elsa noticed that the melodion's rectangular case, made of hard cardboard with deep-blue felt lining, had a long tear near a corner, exposing the cardboard. She volunteered to sew and fix the tear before it could fray and get worse.

In January, a problem in Manoy's meat business arose and reared its ugly head. He had a rift with brother-in-law Domíngo, his partner in the business, who had invested his own substantial share in the capital. As a result, Domíngo wanted his money withdrawn from the partnership, a drastic move that could put Manoy in an unwanted position. It could immobilize the business.

Prid, our youngest sibling, relayed the news to me on February 5, 1981: *"Nápasadsád digdí sa Daragá si Manoy para magdisponér nin atík para pang-bayád kan utáng ka Mada. Daí pa daá so ref niyá. Anggót na. Ngatà bagá ta daí pa napápadará yan? Tapós na lamang an pista sa Colaclíng."* [Manoy scampered to Daragá to solicit money to pay off debt from Mada—Manay Elsa's sister, Domíngo's wife. He said there is no fridge yet. Manoy is pissed. Why have they not shipped one to him yet? It's already past Colaclíng's fiesta, which was in January.]

Piping, my elder sister, followed up through a letter on February 9: "You're in the best position to help. It's like this: Manoy Rudy came over and offered us his rice field [in Jovellár, Albáy] for a ₱2,000 lease. He said that if we are interested, we can take it, before he offers it to others." [Otherwise, if that rice field was leased to other people, the sure windfall including the bountiful rice harvest would go to them, of course.]

Back to Colaclíng, Manoy Rudy wrote me on February 12: "It's been two months since your visit to Colaclíng. I thought you would send the refrigerator soon, but up to now nothing. We have been waiting for a long time. It's already dry season, the best time to accrue money out of it. Why haven't you sent us [the refrigerator]? What seems to be the problem?"

And in the afternoon of February 18, a visitor from Colaclíng was waiting for me after work at the boarding house where I lived. He handed me a letter dated 2/17/81, from Manoy. "I presume you know the bearer of this letter, Padíng Pério. Our aim is to find out and understand why you haven't sent me the refrigerator. You well know how important that is to me. Please explain to Padíng Pério!" I could feel the wrath in the air.

Thank Zeus, I did not need to rationalize. Everybody knows the bird in Greek mythology called phoenix. At last, the appliance store in Pacò, which turned to ashes six months earlier, had now literally sprung to life, like phoenix dying in flames and reborn from its ashes. I told Pério that the deal was revived, and by March 5, the refrigerator would be ready to ship.

Finally! I heaved a sigh of exhilaration as I saw the upright box leave Pacò Station on March 7 in a crate aboard the freight wagon of the Bicol Express.

As the train rumbled away, I smiled from ear to ear. At last, the saga of the refrigerator was about to end. Manoy would claim it from the Colaclíng Station on March 8. On Friday the 13th, Manoy's ecstatic letter would reach me. On March 14, I would board the daytime Bicol Express for Colaclíng and arrive at dusk. All's well that ends well.

Hold on—

I need to mention that Colaclíng has another name, Del Rosário. This one evokes religiosity and the intercession of the Blessed Virgin Mary. We need this now, for something ominous and supernatural. Let's pray the Rosary for the rest of Manoy's story.

All's well that ends well? You ain't read nothing yet.

Domíngo might as well have been there, or probably not. But whether he was present physically or in spirit, there was a certain mood, a gravitas, an uneasiness in Manoy Rudy's house. I knew and had readily felt it since I arrived. I could sense something at the back of Manoy's thoughts and consciousness, lurking like a sinister shadow and inhibiting a purely joyful celebration. Like a sword of Damocles hanging over Manoy's head, it was ready to fall, only God knew when. Was it the business problem with Domíngo or the need for cash? Was it the ordeal of waiting and hoping for the refrigerator? Was it the exultation over its coming? Or was it me? Did my arrival complicate the situation? The sword was ready to fall.

As it was already dusk, the tailoring shop was close for the day, but the *sari-sari* store was still a beehive of activities. Manay Elsa tended the store, while Manoy Rudy took to the kitchen, concocting the most delicious pork *adobo*[31] with pig entrails I could never taste elsewhere.

There were many other entrées, mostly pork, on the dining table, now surrounded by a few family friends, apprentices, Manay Elsa, Manoy, and me. "My brother Doc has come by!" he said with utmost pride as he raised a bottle of beer. (He called me *Doc*, because in my younger days he wished me to become a doctor and treat my asthma.) "Maybe not lightning-fast"—everybody laughed, except me—"but my brother Doc made my refrigerator dream come true!"

"Some dream, Manoy!" I thought wryly, with a nervous smile.

More bottles of San Miguel beer and Ginebra San Miguel were chilled, ready for use. Spirits continued flowing, as well as pork kabobs for *pulutan*[32]. Again I unzipped the melodion's deep-blue case to provide music and entertainment. An apprentice got a guitar and gave my melodion an impromptu yet expert accompaniment. It would be a long night.

Past midnight we were ready for bed. Ruddy was the color of Manoy Rudy's skin after taking considerable amounts of gin. I was myself a little groggy from intoxication by six bottles of beer in four hours, so thereupon we called the party over. Manoy Rudy, Manay Elsa, and I went up to a small loft, the sleeping quarters, over the *sari-sari* store. She prepared my bed earlier, under a small mosquito net, whereas the couple occupied a bigger mosquito net a few feet away from mine. Mosquitoes were buzzing about, but the whole setup was cozy enough—or was I just too tipsy. I would be asleep in minutes. Just before I dozed off, I heard Manoy snore.

At about two o'clock in the morning—it was now Sunday, March 15—I woke up to the sound of moaning. Baffled, I went out of my mosquito net as fast as I could. By the light of a small night lamp, I saw Manay Elsa and heard her frightened and intermittent cries as she shook Manoy Rudy, who was moaning still.

---

31   *adobo* [Filipino] – a dish of pork or chicken simmered in a mixture of vinegar, soy sauce, and garlic.
32   *pulutan* [Filipino] – food accompaniment to alcoholic drinks.

"*Noy*[33], *si Manoy mo kangina pa naga-agurû! Indî na siyá nágigimatá!*" she said in between sobs. "*Noy*, your brother has been moaning! He doesn't awaken!"

Word spread like wildfire even in, and despite the cold wee hours. Some good samaritans hurriedly obtained a couple of railroad skates and, with weeping Manay Elsa, wheeled away now-pallid Manoy Rudy to Sipocot, the nearest town with doctors and medical clinics, about 12 kilometers to the southeast. Halfway, they would recount later, Manoy Rudy's body lay cold and inert, his pulse forever gone.

I could not now remember everything that transpired after the railroad skates left. All I could recall was that I stayed in the house, stood guard, and for a long time stared blankly, remorsefully, at the refrigerator. ∎

Manoy Rudy in his tailoring shop, which doubled as *sari-sari* store, in the early 60s, here shown with toddler Pancho on his lap, Manay Elsa on his left, and other relatives as tailors and hands.

Manoy Rudy's house as it appears to this day. Manay Elsa and Pancho don't live here anymore. Domingo and Mada took over the place and maintained the *sari-sari* store. Above the store, there still stands the loft in which I slept on that fateful Sunday, March 15, 1981. Outside the loft wall still hangs Tatay's tailoring signboard, which he bequeathed to Manoy Rudy when he retired from his own tailoring business in 1967. The house and the signboard are both symbols of resilience to age and neglect.

---

33 *Noy* [Bikol] – short for *Nonoy,* a term of endearment for a younger male.

4

NOTHING

Wednesday's child is full of woe

all it coincidence, happenstance, or fate. It defies explanation, whacks us senseless in our consciousness and rationality. While Manoy Rudy struggled for his last breaths on that fateful early morning of March 15, 1981, in Colaclíng, Camarines Sur, Manay Nilda was sound asleep on her birthday in Daragá, Albáy. She was 37.

Fast forward to March 15, 2017. Suddenly, I felt the urge and the need to write about Manay Nilda. She was 73.

Over seven decades ago this day, the young couple Arcádio and Flávia Morada welcomed a healthy baby girl, their third, into the world. They conceived her in the far-flung idyllic village of Talôtô, Camalíg, Albáy, where the young couple had a sizeable farm that provided for their needs. But in January 1944, their firstborn died there, her death so unforeseen and the memory so unpleasant, they moved the family to Jovellár, Albáy. A global war was raging at the time; life in Jovellár was as normal as could be—if you could call the occasional appearance of itinerant *húkbalaháp*[34] and the distant sounds of bombings, air raids, and gunfights normal. Cadió named the baby girl Nilda. It was March 15, 1944.

According to numerology, 15 is a number "of family and harmony, likely to be in the forefront of innovation in the home."[35] Numerology may not be rocket science, but who could assail the above number meaning for *not* being Nilda? For, as everyone would later see, she was to live a life far greater, nobler, and grander than her name. To her family, relatives, close friends, and acquaintances, she is fondly Manay Nilda, or simply Nilda, or merely—

Nil.

Nil came after Adelaida (Dely), who was born before—and died during—World War II, and Rodolfo (Rudy), who was born at its start. Fe (Piping), Arcádio Jr. (Jun), José (Otê), Emerlita (Merl), and Frida (Prid) later completed the brood. Most of us middle siblings were born in Jovellár, our two oldest were born in Talôtô, whereas the youngest one was born in Sipocot, Camarines Sur. And in 1982, we got Nenita (Nitz), from Sipocot, through adoption.

Tatay Cadió's tailoring business sustained a growing family before and after the War. Determined to provide well for us, he and Nanay Babing would hop from one place to another, where they deemed business

---

34   *hukbalahap* [Filipino] – an acronym derived from "Hukbong Bayan Laban sa Hapon," guerrillas fighting the Japanese.

35   Affinity Numerology, "Number 15 Meaning," https://affinitynumerology.com/number-meanings/number-15-meaning.php.

would be better and more lucrative. Thus, with the growing family in tow, they would move from Talôtô to Jovellár (Albáy), to Pilar (Sorsogon), to Legazpi City (Albáy), back to Jovellár, to Sipocot (Camarines Sur), then finally to Daragá (Albáy).

We children had to contend with such an itinerant life. My very first recollections as a child were of the early 50s sights, sounds, and smells at the pier of Legazpi, by which we lived. But the more vivid memories started in Jovellár.

I remember the tailoring shop in Jovellár in 1957. Tatay managed it, assisted by Nanay. We only had a couple of Singer sewing machines in operation, the first for Tatay's use and the other for Manoy Rudy's. Handsome seventeen-year-old Rudy, following Tatay's sartorial steps early on, already had a modest income and a girlfriend (Jovellár native and wife-to-be Elsa Ibañez) to boot. Manay Nilda had just finished elementary school, while Piping was in the primary grades. Because I was a six-year-old asthmatic, I stayed home, thus overprotected and pampered by Nanay, yet unschooled. Otê was a bubbly four-year-old running around the house and in between the sewing machines, and baby Merl was about to turn a year old.

Then, on March 17, 1957, Philippine President Ramon Magsaysay died in a plane crash, his death ushering in a political turmoil nationwide. The divided nation saw a national and local election of November 1957 wrought and drenched in blood. As in all Philippine exercises of the right of suffrage, there had been so much political violence and atrocities, even in our small hick town of Jovellár. One such incident happened right in front of our tailoring shop, altering the course and direction of the Morada family.

The local political protagonists and their loyal supporters had to take enough of each other. On Election Day, hatchets and machetes in hand, they ran after each other on the town's main street along which our tailoring shop stood. The ruckus caused a bloody scramble never yet seen in Jovellár.

All the violence proved traumatic to Nanay, who saw so much blood spilled. As a result, she had sleepless nights. Even if Tatay locked our house, she would insist that murderous people were outside, threatening to kill us, the children. Because of Nanay's nervous breakdown, it was not long before Tatay packed our things—and the children. The Morada family headed for Camarines Sur.

I was six years old; why we were moving on, or why we were going to Timbuktu or Zimbabwe, was immaterial to me. I can't even recall the hustle and bustle of transporting our worldly belongings from backwoods Jovellár to a crossroads town 140 kilometers away to the north. What I do recall was the passionate *Fascination*[36] and the ethereal *Bali Ha'i*[37] aired several times over on our radio box as we traveled to our new destination the whole ten-hour stretch of the moving time to Sipocot, Camarines Sur.

Yes, Sipocot, neither Timbuktu nor Zimbabwe. Soon, the sign MORADA'S TAILORING with embossed tangerine letters graced the facade of 638 San Juan Avenue, Sipocot. In no time was Tatay's tailoring business up and running again.

Several months after moving to Sipocot, Manoy Rudy eloped with Manay Elsa and started his own tailoring business and family in Colaclíng, about 12 kilometers away. Though Nanay's mental condition was getting stabilized, Tatay understood in silence that he needed to consign Nanay's responsibilities in the tailoring shop to Manay Nil. The oldest of the remaining brood, teenager Nil thus had to carry a significant burden upon her shoulders. She became not only Tatay's girl Friday but property custodian as well. Trustworthy and mature enough in Tatay's eyes, she handled anything and everything in the shop.

---

36   Jane Morgan's 1957 recording of the popular waltz song originally written by Fermo Dante Marchetti (music, 1904), Maurice de Féraudy (French lyrics, 1905), and Dick Manning (English lyrics, 1932).

37   Perry Como's 1949 recording of the popular song from the Rodgers and Hammerstein musical "South Pacific."

Meanwhile, toddler Merl grew finicky and sickly. She would not eat or only eat what she liked. The need for Manay Nil to stay put at home became even greater. Merl became such a delicate child that at one point, Tatay said, "Let's focus our undivided attention on this sickly child." Which, of course, meant Manay Nil *not* enrolling in high school to give more and closer attention to her ward.

Then, in 1959, Prid, the youngest, appeared in the scene. She was a cute and chubby baby that provided a refreshing respite in the Morada household and booming shop, which by this time already had an array of six sewing machines in operation, with several apprentices. Of course, Nil knew that with the coming of Prid, any hope of her own formal education got dimmer than before.

In the background, there was a looming threat. The ready-made clothes industry was on the rise and was giving custom tailors a stiff run for their money. By mid-1960s, more and more people would opt for the ease of buying ready-made clothes rather than go through the lengthy sartorial process. This did not bode well for small-scale tailors like Tatay. Together with Nanay and Manay Nilda, he saw the threat coming true. He could only do so much to keep the business afloat. It plummeted.

Before that happened, Piping graduated from high school and envisioned a teaching career. Tatay said yes to a grand future ahead of his 4th child as an educator. So, with Nanay beside him, he called Manay Nil aside, and said, "Let's send Piping to Normal[38] school in Daragá, Albáy." She said yes silently, no objections.

One day in 1964, Manay Nil clandestinely bought some Oil of Olay from the local drugstore. At another time, just as secretly, she bought a pack of Tampax tampons. "Are you experimenting?" Nanay castigated her verbally after discovering the secret purchases and threatened to throw the stash into the *imburnal*[39] beside the tailoring shop if the twenty-year-old bought such vanities without permission ever again.

Later that year, Manay Nil read in a national magazine about the cloistered nuns of the *Monasterio de Santa Clara* (Monastery of St. Claire) in faraway Quezon City. She wrote them, inquiring. When the Poor Clares responded with some paperwork, Manay Nil initially got cold feet but eventually mustered some courage to ask Tatay and Nanay's permission and signatures. Of course, the answer was an unblinking no.

The Junior finished elementary in 1965. In 1966, Tatay and Nanay—her mental state now stabilized—called Manay Nil aside, and said, "Let's have Junior join Piping and continue high school in Albáy." So, they sent me to Daragá and enrolled me in Bicol Colleges HS.

Tatay's tailoring business continued to plummet. So, in July 1967, Tatay and Nanay called Manay Nil aside and said, "Let's expect the inevitable. We need to move on to Albáy altogether!" Soon enough, the tailoring shop folded up. Tatay bequeathed his MORADA'S TAILORING signboard with embossed tangerine letters to Manoy Rudy for his own shop in Colacling. Then, Tatay, Nanay, and Manay Nil packed our things and the reluctant Otê, who just graduated from elementary school, and Merl, and Prid, who were both in the primary grades.

Move on the Moradas did, and found residence in Mapiñá, Daragá, Albáy. On August 31, 1967, while Piping, Otê, Merl, Prid, and I were in our respective schools—and only Tatay, Nanay, and Manay Nil were at home—a fire broke in Mapiña, consuming 28 houses, including our newly built, newly dwelt house. Though they escaped the fire unscathed, Tatay, Nanay, and Manay Nil agonized over the fact that their five scholars would later that day come home to a house burned to the ground.

---

38   Albay Normal School, later renamed Bicol Teachers College (1962), then Bicol University College of Education (1969).
39   *imburnal* [Filipino] – sewer.

Somehow, they saved a couple of sewing machines from the fire, one of which was Manay Nil's own. With most tailoring paraphernalia gone, however, there was no way to revive the tailoring shop. So, Tatay depended entirely on the income out of various crops from our ancestral land. (Remember that far-flung idyllic *barangáy* of Talôtô where he and Nanay originally came from?) Back where he started!

Piping graduated from the Bicol Teachers College in 1969, while I finished high school as valedictorian of my graduating class at the Bicol Colleges HS. In 1970, I took up Education courses in the same Normal school, which then had a new nomenclature: Bicol University College of Education.

No, Education was actually Plan B. Plan A was Engineering at Aquinas University[40], a local private school, through academic scholarships as per my high school credentials. But Plan A got invalidated, because of an academic catastrophe courtesy of Gene Andamon; through my swooping grade in Drawing 1, the professor concluded that I, in effect, could not draw *well*. Plan B reared its head.

In retrospect, Andamon was my angel and the Normal school, a blessing in disguise. There, I became Associate Editor of **The Mentor**, the school organ, and cultivated my passion for writing.[41] I had previously learned how to use the typewriter in Sipocot, being able to type about 60 wpm, but more than ever, there was now a great need for a typewriter of my own.

Manay Nil sensed the need; she would willingly trade her own Singer sewing machine for a Singer portable typewriter without saying words like, "This is mine, OK?" Nor did I hear her say, "Pay me later, once you get employed."

I used the typewriter through college. Eventually, like Piping, I graduated with a Bachelor of Science in Elementary Education in 1974 and became a full-fledged teacher at St. Agnes' Academy of Legazpi City. Meanwhile, Manay Nil remained as Tatay's girl Friday and the Morada household property custodian, minus her sewing machine.

In the meantime, Tatay, Nanay, and Manay Nil deliberated, "Should we enroll Otê in college?" Of course, in time, they did. He graduated from the Bicol University College of Agriculture in 1976 and later worked for the government through the National Irrigation Administration. There were by now three degree-holders in the family, with Manay Nil as stay-in girl Friday and property custodian.

I moved to Manila in 1978 to teach in Xavier School[42], taking along Manay Nil's Singer typewriter, yet unpaid. Then one day somebody stole the machine while I was at work. I relayed the news to Manay Nil, and she was heartbroken. In 1991, Tatay passed on, relinquishing Manay Nil's girl Friday title. But more than ever, she had to be the property custodian. For fourteen years, I taught in Xavier School before deciding to migrate to Texas, USA. Personal computers were just coming out. When I reached Texas in 1992, one of the first things I bought was an IBM PC. Manay Nil's Singer typewriter became a distant but unforgettable memory. Yet unpaid.

Ailing Merl had proven repeatedly that she was a certifiable survivor. Defying familial opposition to enrolling in college with her physical condition, she got into college, finished it and became a teacher like

---

40   In 2017, Aquinas University of Legazpi City, a Catholic university run by the Dominican Fathers/Order of Preachers (OP), was renamed University of Santo Tomas-Legazpi. Access information at http://www.aq.edu.ph/.

41   On September 21, 1972, Philippine President Ferdinand E. Marcos declared martial law, and curtailed press freedom in all publications nationwide, including campus press. Thus, my official capacity as campus writer was short-lived but I nurtured my writing passion, even if clandestinely. Later on, campus publication was allowed, with guidelines and restrictions.

42   Xavier School, 64 Xavier Street, Greenhills, San Juan, Metro Manila, Philippines. Access at https://www.xs.edu.ph/.

Piping and me. Prid herself had breezed through college and became an accountant. Then, in 1993, Nanay passed on. Manay Nil, of course, remained the property custodian. As always.

Manay Nil still lives in the old family house in Daragá. She has seen all of us go one after the other, like tailor birdlings from their nest. Age has dilapidated the nest, now half a century old. Yet that's where the property custodian still lives. That's where the maiden tailor bird still lives.

Alone.

So, the day was March 15, 2017, when I felt the urge to write this emotional tribute to her. It was a Wednesday. Manay Nilda was born on March 15, 1944—a Wednesday. Manoy Rudy was born on a Monday. Piping and Prid were each born on a Tuesday. I was born on a Thursday, whereas Otê and Merl came forth on a Friday and a Sunday, respectively. It's clear to see that in the Morada brood, Manay Nilda is the only one born on a Wednesday.

Do you still remember this old nursery rhyme we learned, recited, and sang in school?

> **Monday's child is fair of face,**
> **Tuesday's child is full of grace,**
> **Wednesday's child is full of woe,**
> **Thursday's child has far to go,**
> **Friday's child is loving and giving,**
> **Saturday's child works hard for a living,**
> **But the child who is born on the Sabbath day**
> **Is bonnie and blithe and good and gay.**

The learning-the-days nursery rhyme may actually be serious and foreboding, astrological, an augury of people's destiny, a vision of the future. I never thought about it that way, in the same way that I never thought about a favorite Matt Monro 1960s ballad as anything portentous. The ballad, penned by John Barry, and entitled **Wednesday's Child**, sadly echoes the nursery rhyme and sounds as if Barry knew Manay Nilda by heart. Go ahead, google the song, play or sing it, and as you croon the last line, tell the marines that you never felt goosebumps in your life.

Nil—I mean, Manay Nilda—is a Wednesday's child. Let the punditry begin on her behalf.

Things Manay Nil has gotten in abundance are our hands around her neck. She barely has anything else in life, apart from her fond rosary and her freedom to attend to her spiritual needs at Our Lady of the Gate Parish Church and her corporal and spiritual works of mercy through the Mother Butler Guild. She still lives in that lowly house, now decrepit, where Tatay and Nanay breathed their last, whose roof and walling have long been up to the mercy of every typhoon that comes prowling over our land—a lowly house which, miraculously like her, has withstood the test of the elements and time. Manay Nil doesn't even own a cell phone with which to communicate to her siblings, all of whom have their own separate lives to live and families to tend. She might not even know of, let alone see, this fond tribute I cooked up for her on her special day.

And yet—and this I say to all my siblings and their respective children and grandchildren—Manay Nil may have nothing to show in material life, but she certainly is wealthy in spirit, for she is worth her weight in gold. Manay Nil may have nothing to show by personal achievements, but she certainly has mountains of indulgencies and spiritual glories much more than the rest of us together could ever accrue. Manay Nil owes us nothing, but our indebtedness to her should hound us for the rest of our lives.

And yet, who came to her aid when she suffered a stroke and got hospitalized recently? It was only Nitz, our adopted sister, and her daughter Len, who were there by her side most of the time. The rest of us, blood brothers and sisters, nephews and nieces near or far, seemed out of reach and touch, busy with our own concerns. Who did pledge to sustain her with her monthly supply of maintenance medicine? Not one sibling or relative; it was my wife Mameng, sans prodding from me, who volunteered. If we are still always around for every other, then why are the rest of us salaried professionals and pensioners, seemed too poor to share or spare? I still believe that blood is thicker than water.

And yet, we owe her whatever we are today. Let there be neither any whiff of dissent nor ingratitude among us. No, gifts of Olay, Tampax, and other vanities are now a bit too late and anachronistic; what she needs are our time, our generous treasures, and the intangibles from our thankful hearts. Mameng's monthly monetary aid for her medical sustenance is just a pittance compared to Manay Nil's lifetime of unfulfilled and unfulfillable dreams. Let's give her *a* life. Rather, let's give her a taste of *the* life she missed, which we individually, collectively yet unknowingly deprived her, before it's too late. I still have faith in our innate goodness. We owe her. We owe. We.

To think that she is of family and harmony, in the forefront of innovation in the home! Numerology is not rocket science, let us remind ourselves. Nothing is everything. ■

Nilda

WEDNESDAY'S CHILD

5

IRON

There's more to Fe than Faith

"Fe!" Nanay Flávia's stern and exacting voice called Piping's attention as the teen was doing her homework one night in January 1961. She was in 6th grade, and I in 2nd. Nanay continued, *"Iatód mo si Junior sa eskwela kidamlág. Sing makausíp mo an maestra, sing nasa laúg na siyá nin kuarto bâgo ka umadón sa kwarto mo. Kung indî, pareho kamóng tatamaan nin tumagiktik! Dapat putulún an saláng gawî. Kákos pang paralo-ók!"* [Deliver Junior to his class tomorrow. Be sure you talk to his teacher and he is inside his classroom before you proceed to yours. Or else the *tumagiktik* would hanker for you, too! We've got to nip Junior's wrongdoing in the bud. He is too young to be truant!]

Indeed, I was.

The previous day, Mrs. Tesorero, my teacher, told us to bring some turfs of Bermuda grass to class, because she wanted to make the small vacant yard in front of our classroom verdant. Being a tailor's child living in a garden-less house in the commercial district of Sipocot, Camarines Sur, and knowing that I could never produce the assigned stuff on such short notice, I walked to school the following morning with flaccid feet, hesitant heart, and muddled mind. The road to school had a bridge over a railroad track. Instead of crossing the bridge and walking onward, however, I diverged—and hid among the tall *kugon*[43] under the bridge the whole day. In short, *naglo-ók ako sa iarróm nin tuláy!* I skipped school by staying under the bridge!

Years later, when I became a teacher myself, I vowed to be more conscientious so as not to give undue stress to my students and their parents by giving them reasonable and attainable homework assignments.

On a visit to Sipocot in 2016, I saw the old bridge alright, but now teeming, not with *kugon*, but with dilapidated houses on both sides and under. Thus, I failed to find the exact spot where, for hours, I stayed put to pass up school time in 1961. However, the town looked so intent on preserving the viciousness of that memory, for they had built a bigger and higher bridge alongside the undemolished old.

To while away the hours, I must have browsed over all the textbooks in my schoolbag, colored all available coloring books, and counted the coaches of all the passing trains as I waited for the end of the school day. I don't remember me eating lunch. Just around dismissal time in the afternoon, I waited for the first outflux of students walking home, then slipped into the crowd and walked along, making sure no one was from my class or grade level. The gambit seemed to work so far; everything looked fine, with Tatay, Nanay, and Manay Nilda as usual busy in the tailoring shop when I arrived, looking pretty unaware of any wrongdoing.

---

43   *kugon* [Filipino] – a species of perennial tall grass *(Imperata cylindrica)* native to southeastern Asia, Polynesia, Australia, Africa, and Southern Europe.

A little later in the afternoon, as I play on the street outside Tatay's tailoring shop, here comes Otê Moratalla (my classmate and son of our next-door neighbor, restaurateur Tió Fidél) who sees me and shouts, *"Oy si Arcádio! Nag-absent!"* [Look! Arcádio was absent from class!] Of course, Nanay hears him, and interrogates me with her ubiquitous *tumagiktik* in hand: "Where've you been all the time?" Before long, I am furiously crying in pain from multiple *tumagiktik* lashes—and vowing to Nanay that I would never skip school again.

The next day, Piping goes to school with me in tow—as per Nanay's instructions.

Or else.

From that niche in my consciousness with the hideous sign "Lessons Learned" incessantly comes this pathetic image of me wasting time under the bridge and consequently facing up to the misdeed. *(Sigh!)* Another memory piled in the niche dates back to 1964 and is about a big earthen jar, *tapayan* in the Bikol language. This time, however, the memory did not concern me, thank God. I remember well where the wretched *tapayan* stood in the kitchen before the gentle, soft-spoken Piping smashed it to pieces. Not on purpose, of course.

Ours was a typical old-style Filipino kitchen. There were two big earthen jars, *duláy* and *tapayan*, strategically placed. They both served as water reservoirs; the *duláy*, smaller, stored cold drinking water while the *tapayan*, stored water for *garó-garó*.[44] Our *duláy* was securely placed on the *banggera*[45], while the *tapayan* stood on the floor conveniently between the *banggera* and the *bangbangán*.[46]

That night in 1964, as teenager Piping was doing kitchen chores before dinner, she accidentally dropped a wooden *tuktukan*[47] smack in the middle of the *tapayan*. The impact of heavy wood against fragile earthenware, plus the swooshing of wasted precious water for *garó-garó*, still jangles in my ears to this day.

I was standing close by and saw what happened. Nanay was there, too, and for a while she stood transfixed, agape. *"Hesus, Maria, santisima!"* Coming round, she got the *tumagiktik* in a flash and furiously chased Piping everywhere the poor adolescent criminal went for cover. Under the dining table, behind the door, out of the kitchen, into the outhouse—you hadn't seen such a rapid-fire barrage of *tumagiktik* lashes in this household before. The sin was not just the abuse of, and disrespect for, domestic property; it was also the inordinate carelessness and lack of focus. Nanay had to discipline, and discipline she did, uncompromisingly. She didn't spare the *tumagiktik* and spoil the child.

We grew up with that kind of discipline. Not even Prid, the youngest and cutest sibling, was *tumagiktik-*exempt.

Nanay believed that molding children required iron discipline. If you nipped bad habits and proclivities in the bud, you ensured good growth. If children didn't know how to discipline themselves, the outside world would do it for them. Why not start inside?

That unfortunate *tapayan* incident while she was in high school in 1964 was Piping's last major infraction of house rules ever, as far back as my memory serves me.

---

44   *garó-garó* [Bikol] – washing, cleaning, and cooking purposes.

45   *banggera* [Bikol] – a shelf jutting out of the kitchen window, made of bamboo slats.

46   *bangbangán* or *dapóg* [Bikol] – native hearth; a big, wooden, four-legged cubical box filled with soil where cooking is done using earthen *kalán* or stove.

47   *tuktukan* [Bikol] – chopping board. Ours was the kind obtained from a tree stump—thick, bulky, and heavy.

Gentler times thereafter saw Tatay, Nanay, and Manay Nilda sending the soft-spoken Fe, the only sibling with a nickname much longer than her forename, to Bicol Teachers College in 1965, to be a molder of young minds.

Despite her shyness and silent disposition, Piping was a bright student. She graduated in 1969 and promptly found employment in Rapu-Rapu, an island in the Gulf of Albáy. There she would meet a co-teacher, named Eliseo, who would later become her lifelong partner and father of her children. They tied the knot in 1979.

Her name means Faith, and his, Paradise. What could be a better combination?

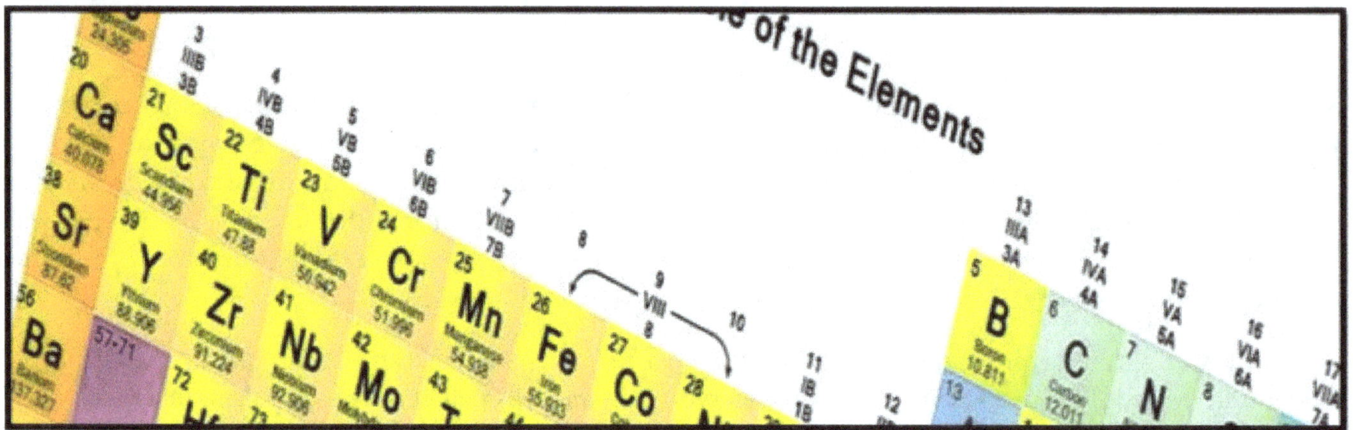

In the periodic table of the elements, you will see Piping. Go look for her.

Faith and Paradise soon activated six *rambunctious, rarely rowdy,* and *responsible* children—aside from being all *loving* and *lovable,* of course. (Any synonyms for *loving* and *lovable* that start with *r?*) Ryan came first, followed by Ritchie, Rose Anne, Ricky, Ruby, and Richard. Paradise was without doubt a fertile ground, and in no time was Faith's nest ready to *r-r-rumble* and *r-r-roar!*

The R brood is an altogether amazing success story. Ryan now works with the Philippine Bureau of Jail Management and Penology, as does his wife PV. Rose Anne is a civil engineer, whose partner, Rofil, is a military man. Ritchie is a nurse working overseas, in California, with his nurse wife Sol. Ricky is a certified sailor who got married before the pandemic to Sherry Anne, a teacher, from Legazpi City. Ruby, with a hubby named Patrick who's into sales, is the second nurse in the family, now also working overseas, in Singapore. The youngest, Richard, who recently got Cupid-hooked to co-worker Marian during the pandemic, has a career in hotel management. Already, Faith has seven (and counting) grandchildren, the latest from Ricky. What more can Faith ask?

Let us hear it from the mouths of the children of Faith 'n' Paradise.

S*i mama ang pinakabest of all the best moms in the world!"* raves Richard, the youngest. *"Si Mama ay super-mabait, maalaga, maunawain at gagawin n'ya lahat para maging okay kaming magkakapatid. Magluluto ng almusal, lunch at dinner namin…hindi kami nagsasawa sa luto ni Mama sa gulay na malunggay! Wish ko kay Mama… to stay healthy. We Love you, Mama! mwuah!"* [My Mom is the best of the best moms in the world. My Mom is super-kind, nurturing, understanding, and she will do everything to make all of us okay. She cooks our breakfast, lunch, and dinner… we never tire of her *malunggay*[48] dish. My wish for Mom… to stay healthy. We love you, Mom! *mwuah!"*]

Ruby sounds profound when she talks about her Ma. "I remember what you said in my childhood and even [up to] now: anything is possible if you put God first. You have lived your life this way, and you set an amazing example for the six of us. Encouraged us to follow our dreams and to never give up. Taught me to give my very best in everything. Believed in me always.

"I've seen you work hard for us. You've tried to give us everything that we need despite the tight budget. You've taught me to value money and to share.

"When I come to you for guidance on hard decisions in my life, you are always there to listen. Thanks, Ma, for everything."

"Mama, you know I love you," Ricky confides. "I always remember what you've said to me since I was young, that no matter what happens, you will always be by my side because you love me, you love us. You did everything for us. And because of your labor and sacrifices, we grew to become successful in our lives. When I was studying, even if you didn't have money, you still provided for my education, and I thank you for that, Mama. I love you so much. You're the queen of my heart. Whatever happens, you're the best mama in the world."

Rose Anne declares, "Mama is so soft spoken, the total opposite of Papa. She always remains calm despite our being *pasaway*[49] especially during our childhood years.

"Now that our family is getting bigger, with grandchildren Lucas [by Ritchie], Xander [by Ruby] and Baby Nash [by Rose Anne herself], I wish and pray that God may continue to shower Mama with more blessings, good health and many more years." [In and around the time of the pandemic, Zevi by Ryan, Kylie by Ruby, Yssabelle by Richard, and Zhamara Aeyllish by Ricky got added to the grand-brood.]

"Mama has superpowers! Wonder why?" asks Ritchie. "She can turn a simple dish into a sumptuous meal for all of her kids—whether it's a simple *tinapa* [smoked fish] or *tuyo* [dried fish]—but her side dishes of *'toyo-matis'* [*toyo* and *kamatis,* that is, soy sauce and tomato] with *manga* [mango] will just put those T-bone steak[s] to shame! She raised six kids and sent them to school (with help from loving uncles and aunties) and remained a loving wife to Papa. Mama is truly one of a kind. She can be your Editor-in-Chief for your book report, thesis papers; she can be your Guidance Counselor for anything under the sun. But most of all, she is our Beloved Mama who SMILES all the time no matter how hard life could be… LOVE from your favorite and *sabi mo 'pinaka-POGI'* [according to you, most handsome] son—Ritchie."

"My mama is one of a kind," Ryan echoes. "She is very loving, religious, and she never tires of reminding us to do only what is right. She is my conscience; every time I commit inappropriate behavior, she's always there to remind me and correct me. She is my role model, my strength. Despite financial constraints, she provided [for] all our needs. To be honest, I really can't imagine how my mother raised all of us. Perhaps she has magic!"

---

48   *malunggay* [Filipino] – often referred to as "miracle tree" *(Moringa oleifera)* for its nutritional as well as medicinal value; *kalunggay* in Bikol.

49   *pasaway* [Filipino] – naughty and stubborn.

anay Flávia's faith and stamina in the molding and well-being of her children only get matched by those of Fe regarding her own. Nanay raised 7, and Piping raised 6. Otê has 4, Merl and Prid have 2 each, while Manoy Rudy and I have 1 each. So, if there is one among us who can approximate Nanay's ferric perseverance, it is Piping.

I am convinced that Flávia and Fe came cut from the same cloth. Only difference is, they are opposite sides. Nanay relied on hard discipline, Piping soft, but both were certainly effective, and proofs abound.

For this, we give both Flávia and Fe high five. Motherhood is tradition. Nanay, the strict disciplinarian, may have gone to the Great Beyond, but Faith-and-Iron is fully alive here and now, holding on, and in her own way glorifying motherhood.

Five stars, three cheers, and two thumbs up! ■

"Mama has superpowers!"
-Ritchie

Piping, in 1969

The Calisuras
Seated L-R—Fe, Ruby, Rose Anne;
Standing L-R—Richard, Eliseo, Ryan, Ricky, Ritchie.

6

DIASPORA

Do you have to go far away to earn a living?

cene is all-too-familiar. Birdlings, newly hatched, chirp shrilly in the nest, open beaks pointing upwards, clamoring while waiting for food. From out of the blue sky, Tatay bird or Nanay bird comes and gives each chick a beak-ful of grub. Everybody is happy. For the moment.

Weeks later, birdlings are up and about, on the nest, wings almost feathered and fully grown, eager to fly away. Tatay bird and Nanay bird can only watch and see independence and insatiableness literally spring to life. Before the fledglings each embark on their first efforts to fly, they hear platitudes from either parent bird:

The world out there is so much different from your tiny home. There'll be obstacles and challenges. You will fend for yourself. Be mindful that when you choose to go, you are always welcome to come back as often as you can, as often as you want. Be mindful, too, that when the going gets rough, or when the going gets no further, home is always around.

The going finally arrives. One by one, the fledglings fly away... into the world.

Swiftly and gently, the little birds fly.
They float in the air; they go up to the sky.
After a while, they come down to rest.
And somewhere high up the tree lies their nest.

Yes, in time, by age and by use or abuse, the nest wears away. But it will be around as long as it can. The going gets on every which way, and it takes forever.

orever was 12 years, in my case. I had flown to Texas, USA many years ago, fending for myself with a family of my own. In 1944, six-year-old Manay Dely, our firstborn fledgling, fell down from a footbridge virtually to her death, while Manoy Rudy, second, flew over the Great Divide in his sleep in 1981. Manay Nilda became the nest's lifelong overseer after Tatay and Nanay themselves passed on in 1991 and 1993, respectively. The other fledglings stayed in, or close to, the nest. My elder sister Piping built her own nest close by, together with her lifelong partner Eliseo Calisura. Otê, my younger brother, flapped his agriculturist wings and reached his lovebird Edith Marollano's nest in Colaclíng, Camarines Sur, while younger sister Merl followed suit and found her own lovebird partner Henry Meralpis who lived close by Otê. The youngest, Prid, preened her dainty gossamer wings and flew diligently and sweetly with Tarlac lovebird Manny Vitug farther up to Caloocan City, in metropolitan Manila. Nitz, our adopted sister, lives close by the nest with her partner, Rowin Filarmeo. We hadn't seen each other all together in the eye for over a decade, my last homecoming being in 2004. Therefore, in 2016, I decided—with a lot of help and encouragement from my dear wife Mameng—to end 12 years of forever.

"We will rent a huge van that can accommodate all your married siblings and their spouses, plus Manay Nilda, Prid[50], Pancho[51], and the three[52] of us," Mameng verbalized her generous plans. "We will assemble in Manila. From there, we go on a tour of Luzon through Banaue Rice Terraces, Vigan, Baguio City, back to Manila, proceed to Villa Escudero in Quezon, then Bicol."[53]

"M-m-ma," I said, "we are talking of 12 people—"

"The tightwad in you talking, but don't worry," she said. Mameng worked and lived in New York with our daughter Carmela, while I taught in Brownsville, Texas. All accounting done, we were to spend about half a million pesos for the tour. *Indî ka mangubug-kubog! Ako an tayâ,* she said. "Don't cringe! It's on me!"

In the 1960s, I was a nestling in Sipocot, Camarines Sur, a sleepy town on the road to progress, strategically between two rivers: *Sadít na Salog*[54] and *Dakulang Salog*. My brother Otê and I would frequent *Sadít* more than *Dakulà* for our childish dips, but the latter, wider and deeper, offered more fun and adventure. Of course, we had to go with some babysitter, because one of Nanay's rules strictly forbade bathing in whatever river without adult supervision. At that point in time, it was the most enjoyable thing to do, especially during summer when school was out, when everybody was busy in Tatay's tailoring shop, and therefore when there was less probability of our absence being noticed. The fun was endless, but just as when we thought we could fool Nanay, her invisible radar would work, whereupon she would meet us at the door with her *tumagiktik*. The rattan rod was for whipping our butts till blue when we youngsters would break the rules of the nest, especially the one about swimming without a babysitter.

I love Sipocot as the town of my early days. It got its name, as tradition has it, when pioneering Spanish explorers asked some native fishers for the name of this place where there was always abundant *kasilí, baklâ, buyód*[55], and other local fresh-water catch. The respondents thought the foreigners were asking about their fishing nets (called *pocot*), and wanting to impress, they answered, *"Si, pocot."* The wrong answer to the right question stuck.

I wasn't born in Sipocot, though. Our original nest, where my first two siblings were born, developed in Talôtô, a *barangáy* in the town of Camalíg, Albáy. The town's patron saint is St. John the Baptist. However, what we consider our veritable nest, where most of us were born, took form in Jovellár, Albáy. The town's patron saint is St. John the Baptist. In 1957, Tatay moved our domicile to Sipocot, whose patron saint is—St. John the Baptist.

My earliest recollections of Sipocot included the dry but soon-to-get-wet month of May, when we expected to bathe outdoors in the first glorious downpour of the rainy season, known as *Agua de Mayo*, which

---

50 Prid's spouse Manny flew to the Great Beyond in 2015.

51 Manoy Rudy's only son, Pancho, represented his late dad. Manay Elsa, his mom, could not join the tour for age and health reasons. He and wife Lina of 37 years have produced 4 children (Ellaine Rae, Ellaine Mae, Janrio, Ellaine Garnette) and 3 grandchildren (Dj and Ella Sage by Ellaine Rae, and Kiere Zaskie by Janrio) to date.

52 Mameng, me, and our daughter Carmela.

53 The tour would cover an estimated 1,536.7 km.

54 *Sadit na Salog* [Bikol] – literally, small river; geographically, Vigaan River.

55 *baklâ* [Bikol] – a species of goby; *buyód* [Bikol] – fresh-water shrimp.

many oldsters believed to have healing properties.[56] Also, during this time of the year, the Sipocoteños[57] would celebrate *Flores de Mayo* (literally, Flowers of May) and the *Santacruzan*[58] festivals. The womenfolk, especially young girls of grade-school age, would bring bouquets to our church, the St. John the Baptist Parish Church, and place them around the white-and-blue statue of a beautiful lady. Or else they would sprinkle flower petals on the church aisles or areas around her. The beautiful lady was the Blessed Virgin Mary, or *Inâ,* the Blessed Mother.

Within the month of May, townsfolk groups would organize a special Novena to *Inâ*. Each major street of the town formed such groups. Ours was San Juan Avenue. We prayed the novena nightly, capped by the *Santacruzan* on the 9th. Beautiful maidens (or little girls) with their escorts, all pre-selected and dressed in their fineries, would take part in the *Santacruzan*. The ladies and their escorts walked under hand-carried bamboo arcs bedecked with flowers as the procession wound through town, while the *kantora*[59] sang Marian and other religious songs in Spanish. The procession was supposedly rooted in history[60], so the highlight was usually the most beautiful lady in the entire San Juan Avenue, representing Reyna Elena (Queen Helena of Constantinople), escorted by a little boy, Constantine (the Great). I don't remember role-playing exactly Constantine myself, but at least in one *Santacruzan,* I was an escort in *barong tagalog*[61] walking under some flowery bamboo arc with my partner, a beautiful girl/lady representing a biblical character or queen—*Reyna Mora, Cleopatra, Reyna Judit, Reyna Dolorosa, Reyna Sentenciada, Reyna et cetera.* To my young mind, the pomp and the pageantry of the *Santacruzan* in May were truly overwhelming and unforgettable.

My early schooling started in Sipocot. Not so early, though, because I started late, as Grade 1 at nine years old. This was on account of my being *apôon*, asthmatic. I was so sickly Tatay and Nanay had to delay my introduction to formal education via the school system. As far back as I can remember, I had trouble with *apô*, asthma, which would strike me almost daily in my early years. As a result, I developed a thin and frail physique and a loathing for strenuous physical activities. Nights I would sleep painfully through while seated on a rocking chair, because lying down definitely increased wheezing and coughing, and thus chest pain. So, in school, I would be sleepy and haggard most times. I hated movements, games, and climbing, as they tired me without fail. Consequentially, I learned to retreat to reading and introspection as defense mechanisms, and as a way of life.

Being *apôon* had its own perks, however. Almost always, I would be exempt from rough and arduous chores and responsibilities around the house. Even in school, teachers accorded me special lighter tasks (like correcting quizzes and tests, or arranging books neatly on the shelf). In college, the required military training every Sunday only saw me doing clerical work at the ROTC[62] office.

Now and then, Tatay and/or Nanay would go places with me in tow, brief visits that frequently turned out to be pilgrimages. To make offerings, or even to dedicate me to God or to *Inâ*, we would visit *Nuestra Señora del Pilar* (Our Lady of the Pillar, patron saint of Pilar, Sorsogon), *Nuestra Señora de Salvación* (Our

---

56   On several occasions, I would be compelled to bathe under the *Agua de Mayo* because of its "healing properties"—it would supposedly cure my asthma. It never did. In fact, most of the time it would trigger asthma attacks. But undoubtedly, it was such a joy to bathe in the *Water of May!*

57   Sipocoteños [Bikol] – natives of Sipocot, Camarines Sur; Sipocoteño/a – singular.

58   *Santacruzan* [Filipino] – a colorful procession/pageant parade through the streets of the town proper.

59   *kantora* [Bikol] – an adult female singer; or, collectively, choir of old ladies.

60   *Santacruzan* commemorates the search and finding of the True Cross—on which Jesus was crucified—by Queen Helena of Constantinople and her son Constantine the Great.

61   *barong tagalog* [Filipino]—embroidered long-sleeved traditional shirt for men, national dress of the Philippines.

62   Reserve Officers' Training Corps, a mandatory military education and training for college students for national defense preparedness, https://en.wikipedia.org/wiki/Reserve_Officers%27_Training_Corps_(Philippines).

Lady of Salvation, patroness of Albáy, in Joroan, Tiwi, Albáy), or *Nuestra Señora de Peñafrancia* (Our Lady of Peñafrancia, in Naga City, Camarines Sur). Tatay and Nanay, like most Bicolanos, honored *Nuestra Señora de Peñafrancia* as the patroness of Bicol, of the whole Southern Luzon. In solidarity with the entire Bicolano Christendom, my family would celebrate her feast day in September by going to Naga City where Our Lady is enthroned, by attending Mass, or by venerating Our Lady at home in prayer if circumstances did not warrant actually going to Naga. All this in a capsule was the religiosity, or rather faith, I grew up in.

To this day, I have no way of knowing how many times they offered or dedicated me to God through *Nuestra Señora* to pacify my raging lungs and ease my breathing. Through my *apô*, Tatay and Nanay unwittingly opened my spiritual eyes and brought me to the knowledge, mercy, and omnipresence of God.

ide by side, of course, with the spiritual was the mundane, my own physical development. I grew up in pubescence in Sipocot.

My every-Filipino-boy's rite of passage into puberty took place not in some medical center but at the *Sadit na Salog* in the summer of '65, before the appearance of pubes, before becoming freshman in high school. First, Tatay had to enlist me with a *paratatak*[63] (for fun, let's call him Tio Pitóy) who scheduled my cutting along with some other boys. When the appointed time came, I had to wallow in the river in my birthday suit for an hour. Then I was told to chew on some guava leaves, and approach Tio Pitóy who all this time stood waiting at the river bank, honing a stainless-steel razor and making sure it had no trace of rust or contamination, to prevent infection.

Each boy's baptism of pain begins and ends quickly. A guava branch shaped like 7, its sturdy base stuck to the ground, stands between you and Tio Pitóy. You approach the branch nervously. Tatay or big brother stands by for moral support. Tio Pitóy holds your organ, pulls your foreskin, then slips and lays it on the tiptop of the guava branch that is shaped like 7. He meticulously positions the sharp edge of his razor on top of, and across, your foreskin. Then three blows by a wooden rod on the razor do the bloody job. You don't dare scream, or be forever branded as soft and coward.

The first blow is painful but bearable, approximately equal to three *tumagiktik* whips, but you cringe and scream inwardly just the same: *aaaa!!!* The second feels like being whipped and stung by a manta ray, roughly equivalent to ten *tumagiktik*: *eeeeeee!!!* Finally, the third blow gives you the most pain like the Red Sea being torn apart—if we could pain-quantify such—by the staff of Moses, making you scream all the vowel sounds: *aeeiioooouhuuhuu!!!* At this point, you have no sense anymore to equate it to *tumagiktik* whips because you're crying on top of your lungs or you've fainted altogether. Howsoever you take it, Tio Pitóy at last laughingly declares, *"Tatak ka na!"* You're now sealed. "Jewish," so to speak. A marked, brand-new man. Being *supot* (uncircumcised) is now a childish epoch, a thing of the past.

As your cry of pain subsides and you regain your composure, you are told to apply the chewed guava leaves over your wound, then bandage. As a fitting dénouement, you hear Tio Pitóy say, *"Yan lang an kulóg na titioson mo, kumpara sa kulóg kan pangangakì nin kababaehan!"* [That's about the only pain your manhood has to endure; consider that women continually contend with labor pains!] He punctuates the cliché on gender inequality with a hearty laugh.

---

63   *paratatak* [Bikol] – literally, one who marks, seals, or cuts; a native practitioner of circumcision procedure.

The "Jewish" rite of passage over, you went home looking like some Scot in a kilt. Funny, but to be a man you had got to dress in drag your sister's, or mother's, skirt.

My "baptism" seemed like in keeping with St. John's watery reputation, or the traditional circumcision of Mary's Baby Boy eight days after birth. I did not mean to be risqué or distasteful by narrating it now. After all, John baptized people at the River Jordan, and Mary applied and honored Jewish tradition on his Baby Boy. But, hey, my baptism was of human and mundane pain, a rite nowhere religious. The rite of passage I had undergone in the summer of '65 just signaled I could now fledge. The fledgling in me was ready to go. In psychological terms, I was now an adolescent. I had come of age in Sipocot.

As adolescent, I started high school at Sipocot St. John Academy.[64] There, I had the best no-nonsense English teacher ever, Mr. Eustaquio Arenillo. He taught me, among other things, how to dissect this living thing called sentence. From there, he showed me the wonders of the written word, and the magic of the beautifully expressed thoughts. He showed me how to build the bridge to correct communication, or to rebuild and cross the bridge over troubled ones. He enlightened me about appositives, brevity, antecedents, cohesiveness, subjunctive mood, gerundial phrases, hanging modifiers, run-on sentences, and many other concepts besides, in just my freshman year. If you do not understand what I am yakking about right now, blame yourself and your own teachers, not him. I love Sir Arenillo dearly, and I always will be happy and thankful for his gifts to my intellect.

The sadder part was that we had to leave Sipocot and relocate to Daragá, Albáy, in 1967. Daragá is a town at the southern foot of Mayón Volcano. It was already a first-class municipality at that point in time, enhanced and made noteworthy by a church built in 1773 atop a hill overlooking the beautiful volcano. If you were *apôon* and you wanted to go up to the church, you had to suffer climbing the hill first, then wonder later at the magnificence of the volcano and the baroque beauty and architecture of the *Nuestra Señora de la Portería* Parish Church in front of you. The church is better known today as Our Lady of the Gate Parish Church, or simply Daraga Church. Home to Our Lady of the Gate... the Blessed Virgin Mary, *Inâ*.

Moving to Daragá also meant a change of school environment. Remember that in just one year I learned to love Sipocot St. John Academy as a freshman, so much so that I wished to stay more than anything. The transfer to Bicol Colleges HS in Daragá as a sophomore gave me a challenge greater than the fear of the unknown, affecting me greatly. I buried myself in books. All I wanted was to fledge, to learn more and explore the world like all Birds do, but the Owls and the Eagles of the school thought I was the Best Flyer, no small thanks to Mr. Anzano, Mr. Morcozo, Ms. Tonga, Ms. Vargas, Ms. Llanes, Ms. Ante, Ms. Guiriba, and Ms. Arnaiz, to name a few. With their collective competencies and guidance, after three years, I finished at the top of my graduating class. I was, of course, in cloud nine. As BCHS class valedictorian of 1969, I was ready to conquer the world.

Distinguished guest of honor, Senator Edgar U. Ilarde; Honorable Mayor of Daraga, Mr. Pedro Marcellana; President of Bicol Colleges, Ms. Bibiana P. Tabuena; Rev. Fr. Mariano Montero of Our Lady of the Gate Parish of Daraga; Officers and Members of the BC Board of Trustees; Parents, Fellow Graduates, and Friends.

---

64   Sipocot St. John Academy, re-established as Felix O. Alfelor Sr. Foundation College in 1986.

I am thrilled to stand before you on this our Graduation Day, very proud to be the one to tell you, on behalf of my fellow Graduates, how successful you have been in molding us into what we are today.

What we are today is dreams fulfilled. What we are today is expectations met, way more than what we have hoped for. Not only have you guided us to seek the best that we can be, you have also taught us to serve others along the way. You did not rest in our ambitions of academic excellence; you have instilled in us virtues and real values that are as important as intellectual pursuits. Your guiding hands have led us on the road to total personhood. Your limitless patience fostered the use of our heart as much as our head and hands. Without you, ours are but empty dreams. Through you, we are making hopes come true and tasting the dawn of success.

Words are not enough to express how grateful we are to the good Lord Almighty. He has showered upon us countless material blessings, talents, capabilities, and the interest in learning, but none of these deserve more than the praise and thanksgiving we now give Him for the gift of your presence.

To our parents and loved ones, thank you for your all-out support, financial and moral, which has buoyed us up through the years. You have always been there to help in whatever way you could. Sometimes we might not have recognized your efforts for our betterment and well-being, but you have been there just the same. Because you have always had our back through thick and thin, whatever crown or laurel we receive now, we should rightfully place upon your head instead.

To our dear teachers and school personnel, thank you for your selfless efforts, patience, guidance, and good example. The valuable training and experiences you have provided us with confidently ensure our brighter future. Long after we will have left our Alma Mater, long after we will have grown silver hair, none will ever erase what you have done to develop our intellect and capacities from our awareness. Sure enough, school life with you has had its darker moments, but the shining moments with you we will treasure for the rest of our lives.

To my fellow graduates, you, too, deserve my heartfelt gratitude. In our long years of togetherness, of sharing, of camaraderie, of adolescent ups-and-downs, we have been a challenge and a comfort to one another. The times we've shared were times of learning, living, and loving. They are memories that will become sweeter and fonder in the passage of time.

Tomorrow will be bigger, broader, and more complicated than today. As we leave off the joy and the pride of today's occasion, may we not forget that how well we apply what we have learned today determines our usefulness in the new beginnings of tomorrow. And so, my fellow graduates, let today be the start of our great tomorrow.

Thank you!

I aspired to be a civil engineer, knowing that I was good in science and math. I flew and flew even more with all the power I could muster towards the blue horizon, whence I saw Aquinas University, a private sectarian institution in Legazpi City. Well, after all "the valuable training and experiences" and inspiration incurred in high school, I thought the Dominican institution was a harbinger of a promising future.

No, our professor on the course Drawing 1 didn't think so; their single stroke for my grade quashed all hope and any promise at Aquinas, disempowering my scholarship grants there. Others said I did not flex my muscles and preen my feathers good or hard enough—because I moved to Bicol University College of

Education and ended up as a teacher. For a while, I preened my feathers at St. Agnes' Academy of Legazpi City, teaching elementary grades and writing my first operetta *"What Ever Happened To Magayón?"* on the side. Yet others continued asking, why did you end up teaching? Even to me, it was not clear at first that teaching was my calling.

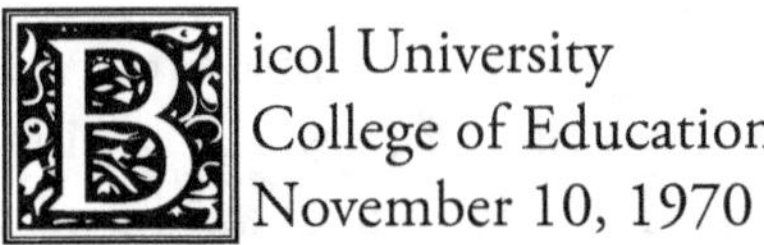

icol University
College of Education
November 10, 1970

Dear Manuel,[65]

I really didn't know how to begin. On one hand, leaving Aquinas University College of Engineering and moving to Bicol University College of Education painted a ridiculous and repulsive picture better left unposted. On the other hand, talking about it had been a dilemma: Should I open up a can of worms? I could have chosen not to write at all; but lately, over some mawkish poem, I reached the decision to reveal my worms to you, for these as they should be, are ought to be known. (And postponing might only mean grimmer story to tell.) Do not think that I have become a woebegone sentimentalist. I am still your rational, uncomplicated high school buddy. I simply need somebody's shoulder to cry on. My only close friend in Aquinas will understand, I'm pretty sure. I am not about to give you alibis and excuses.

How would you feel studying in a school you dislike, taking up a course you do not care about? My answer to that question immerses the ridiculous and repulsive picture into the can of worms.

The story began when Arcádio Morada, Jr., that timid, pimpled guy, enrolled at Aquinas University of Legazpi City, with the supposedly firm and sanguine dream to be an engineer.

Subsequently, because it was a dream, he woke up to reality and found himself where he is now—Bicol University College of Education. What a detour!

Yes, Engineering to Education. My former classmates could ask how come, and I might prevaricate by saying, "Anyway, they both start with E, don't they?" How come, indeed? I can't answer this without qualms, yet one thing is definite: I never willed this to happen. I never liked teaching. I'm not a gregarious individual. How can this painfully shy asocial individual be ever successful as a teacher?

I enrolled in AU with the dream and my high school grades as *puhunan*—capital. Therefore, it was matter-of-fact, pretty obvious, that the reason I am discontinuing my studies there is: *I failed to maintain my grades up*. They disqualified me as a scholar. I couldn't cope with my engineering subjects? Well, frankly, they were as easy as pie, except for one—Drawing!—enough to pull the others down. Everything got affected altogether—including my self-esteem. That was not the main reason for my failure, though. The reason was much deeper and complicated. It was psychological.

You must have noticed how other students made fun of our high school Alma Mater. They would describe Bicol Colleges thus: "Institution of Higher Earning," "*Bulok*,"[66] "Diploma Mill," "Home of Idiots!" You must have heard of these, too. Lucky you, living under a rock, if they did not affect you at all.

---

65   My high school classmate and friend Manuel Relorcasa, who became a lawyer and, last time I heard, worked in the Philippine national government as a Bureau of Customs officer. I don't know his present state of affairs, but he remains forever a friend of my youth.

66   *bulok* [Filipino] – rotten.

Those impressions I tried to change, but I failed. God knows how I tried. But how could I be at peace despite myself when all around me was hostility and indifference? How glad I could have been if I were numb!

But then I shouldn't blame those adverse impressions for my failure.

I tried to join some of the more radical students among us in their rallies and complain sorties not only so that I could belong.[67] Some acquaintances gave me warnings several times, which I did not heed. Looking back now, I don't know if student activism on campus was a smart thing to plunge into, but I didn't really feel uncomfortable in it. I did not join for the sake of joining. I believe I had some things in common with those who were walking in the streets of Legazpi City shouting and brandishing red flags, but I believe sacrificing my academic standing was not one of them. With or without good grades, I would continue to stand for my principles.

But then again, I shouldn't blame student activism for my failure.

Then consider my family's financial situation. Think about the 1967 Mapiña conflagration. Our properties, in one fell swoop, turned to ashes! Mine being a large family, we could barely cope up with the resulting condition. Indirectly, I'd say this affected me a lot. Was poverty not a factor in ruining one's ambition? Is transfer from AU to BUCE not a way of saving money, time, and effort? There's some truth to the fact that I moved because it is the most reasonable way. Economically, that is. Not emotionally, because now I feel I could not wear my face in front of my former classmates, teachers, and you.

But then, more so, I should not put the blame on poverty for my failure!

Many of our former classmates may now know my present state of affairs. Jesse, Silvestre, Fred, Henry, Buddy, etc. And you. May not my failure detract your friendship away. I consider you my best friend, so that during that seminar/talk I attended in AU sometime ago (call it homecoming of sorts), myself being a delegate of BUCE, I tried hard to talk to you. In fact, I requested Jesse[68] to inform you I was there. But that very moment when you came by the seminar hall, the speaker was in the middle of his interesting speech, and it would be so unethical for me to rise and talk with you. I gave you a signal to wait, but the speaker seemed to have the best time of his life, such that it took him eternity to reach his last point. When he was at last done, you weren't around anymore; perhaps you already had your next class period. Anyway, there will be other chances of coming back to AU, and other chances of seeing each other, even if short-lived.

Indeed, I still hope for a return. I doubt it, I repeat, if I can be a successful teacher. But I want to disperse the gloom and negativity before me; therefore, I will finish Education no matter what, and give myself a pat on my shoulder in 1974—count on me, for sure! Engineering remains a distant goal and incentive. Though perfectly illogical for me to still consider it at the moment, I will never lose hope I can find the way toward it again. It is something toward which I must work, despite the knowledge that I would probably never reach it.

I am not telling you alibis and excuses to gain, or gain back, your sympathy. Sympathize or despise—it's your choice. But listen to me first. Then, when everything is clear to you, you may explain to our friends how things went from bad to worse without my wanting. I have enclosed a mawkish poetry of mine, about the immature demise of my ambition, written amid confusion and frustration. Being a handiwork of my so-called talent, useless I hope not, the poem needs your patience and perseverance to read. Excuse grammatical errors,

---

67   Campus activism was starting to simmer in the latter months of 1969 leading to the so-called First Quarter Storm, from January to March, 1970, a period of civil unrest, mostly organized by students in the capital region of the Philippines and also nationwide, against the governance of President Ferdinand E. Marcos.

68   Jesse Armenta was a classmate and co-graduate at Bicol Colleges HS in 1969. We enrolled in Aquinas University at the same time. He later became a full-fledged lawyer.

nonsensical ideas, and confused figures of speech, if any. You can have the editor's task to correct it. May you understand me further by what is in between the lines.

<u>MY SWEET ENGINITA</u>

1

There was a merry time, my sweet Enginita,
You were so close to me.
I wafted like a song in this life opera,
As freely as could be.

2

Forgive me: by my youth I know I did deride
Your import in my life.
I, being so carefree, set seriousness aside,
My world with laughter rife.

3

You radiated in me the warmth of your touch
On the night we last danced.
The lively sonatas had so inspired me much,
For how my heart had pranced!

4

Then swiftly, like a bird, you turned cold and aloof,
Enough to pique my heart.
Were you not so flashy at my own nice behoof
I saw you not depart?

5

You ne'er knew by the dawn you had left your corsage,
Lying on the dance floor;
Then I took it, rejoiced. From a distant mirage,
I saw your face once more.

6

Thinking of none to fear, I was fast following
The trail on which you passed.
My sad and shaken heart was not loath believing
I could see you at last.

7

Somewhere I saw a patch of regal rosemaries
Where scents suffused the air,
Where huddled deities and attractive fairies,
Where the weather was fair.

8

These delightful creatures and their sheer loveliness
Had once more warmed my soul;
I never really knew such were omen's caress,
Wanting my mirth as toll.

9

As they attracted me, by this I was amazed:
A red scented sachet!
The quaint but pleasant smell right away had me dazed,
Turning gray the bright day.

10

And oh, my poor old soul, so enthralled, so dizzy,
Like walking in a maze;
Teetering in a world surreal and fuzzy,
I saw you 'yond the haze.

11

Milady, now that your importance I have found,
In a coffin you lie;
What has made your dear sweet soul disappear around?
Leave me now, I too die!

12

Talk, my Love, I hopefully beg for your mercy,
Your voice sweet and soothing,
Don't make this a goodbye so doleful and dreary—
Tears from my eyes falling!

13

Your deafening silence now, dear Enginita,
Crushes my feeble heart,
Devours, snuffs out my soul! In this life opera,
To be hurt is my part?

14

No, my dearest! I do not like to go this way;
I could, were you with me.
Not there in your coffin, lying full of dismay!
How do I revive thee?

15

My songs, they say, are no paeans but elegies,
Entertaining the dead;
My smile, my voice, so they say, auguries,
Nicer, better unsaid.

16

For what they say and think of me, I do not care,
Nonetheless, lachrymose.
To be near you, to be with you, is worth the dare
To let me dimmed by woes!

17

So please return, and live again, Enginita!
Take back for me your breath,
For you will hearten me in this life opera;
Your stillness means my death!

-Yours,

Jun

At any rate, I graduated from the Bicol University in 1974 with a Bachelor of Science in Elementary Education, with Concentration in Mathematics. St. Agnes' Academy of Legazpi City provided my first employment with a monthly salary of ₱120. Along came the age of self-sufficiency, or flying farther away and vying for it.

Manila beckoned, 500 kilometers away; the capital city of the Philippines had its distinct charm and spell, which I could not easily ignore. Nanay sensed this and asked, with reddish shades of loneliness, *"Kaipuhan mong rumayô para maghanapbu'ay?"* [Do you have to go far away to earn a living?] Unfortunately for Nanay, in 1978, Xavier School in San Juan—there goes St. John again—in Manila accepted my job application. In his own silent way, Tatay understood, if reluctantly, the longing for and the allure of the big metropolis on his Junior, for he never said a word about or against it. I guess Nanay knew, too, that she could not literally keep her brood forever in or near the nest. Especially her favorite, the mama's boy.

As a Math and Science teacher in Xavier School, I found residence in Little Baguio, a five-minute walk from Mary the Queen Parish Church. The church's white and blue facade displays an imposing M—for Mameng, a maiden I loved to go to church with. Just kidding! Though Mameng was a maiden I truly loved to go to church with, the magnificent M stood, of course, for Mary—Our Lady, Queen of Heaven and Earth, the Blessed Virgin Mother, *Inâ*.

Seriously, by 1981, I considered the next best thing to immortality: marriage. That year, I met my wife-to-be, Carmen, or Mameng, in San Juan, Manila. She was born and had lived most of her life in Barangáy 5, Centro, Camalíg, Albáy, whose patron saint is—*do you remember?*—St. John the Baptist. It was her first adventure trip to Manila, and she just got employed when we met. On a few dates, we put on hold our respective need for singlehood, self-sufficiency, and survival in favor of seduction. We were lovebirds in no time at all.

Only, there was one problem.

I worked among priests, religious sisters, and brothers in Xavier School. Ms. Lulú Domíngo, a secular nun of *Notre Dame de Vie* (Our Lady of Life)[69] based in Novaliches, Quezon City, who was the assistant principal for academics in Xavier, called me to her office one day in 1982.

Relaying a message from the incumbent principal, Ms. Jenny H. Go, Ms. Domíngo wanted to know if I'd like to be a religion teacher. "A what?" I replied, smiling, thinking I was just hearing things. "How would you like to undergo training to be a Christian Life Education teacher?" she reformatted her question. "Xavier wants to send you to Mother of Life." The Blessed Mother, *Inâ*, beckoning?

I did not know what Ms. Domíngo or Ms. Go saw in me that could pass for a religion teacher aptitude, but I said yes and they sent me with pay to Mother of Life Center[70] in Novaliches on a one-year formation/study grant.

I had so much to learn, so much more than I thought I already learned in college and in the outside world. Formation was like a self-overhauling of my faith and my whole being, spiritual or otherwise. Within a year, I belabored to look at myself in relation to others and my Creator, my God and my King, thoroughly and in closer perspective. I examined my "creed, code, cult"—my "head, hand, and heart."

Through the sisters of Notre Dame de Vie, several of whom were my formators in Mother of Life Center, I came to know and appreciate more and better the faith I was born in. They introduced me to the spirituality of, among others, St. Thérèse of the Child Jesus, St. Teresa of Ávila, St. John of the Cross, St. Emerentiana, and the founder of Notre Dame de Vie Institute himself, Blessed Fr. Marie-Eugène of the Child Jesus. (Pope Francis beatified him in 2016, while his cause for canonization is currently ongoing.) They opened the window to "[a] life of total consecration to God and to the world" to me. They prepared, guided, formed, and bound me to share in the difficult mission of evangelization of the Church.

While at Mother of Life Center, I composed my first Marian song, *The Queen Stands.* Several more religious songs came flowing out of my head, prompting me to presume I contracted an "avian virus"—nay, priesthood vocation. I strongly thought I had the calling to be a man of the cloth.

Obviously, I hadn't. Passion for Mameng won over passion for my presumed vocation. In 1986, Mameng joined with me in the sacrament of matrimony. "Of course, I love and serve God, too, by being a husband" would become my *raison d'*être every time people got curious about the turn of events. Perhaps, to other people, my marriage appeared more like non-vocation, or worse, sour grapes—that *is,* no novitiate or seminary accepted me. Fact is, I was so close to applying in Sacred Heart Novitiate of the Jesuits, in Novaliches, Quezon City, which I never did. Perhaps there was no calling in the first place.

The study-grant contract I signed in front of Ms. Jenny Go stipulated I was to stay and teach in Xavier for at least three years after the grant. Fair enough, because Xavier had paid my monthly salaries for one entire year without me actually working for the school. I stayed in Xavier for 14 years, from 1978 to 1992, nine of those as Christian Life Education teacher. But like any Xavierian imbued with *magis*[71], I fidgeted and looked for more.

---

69   Notre Dame de Vie Institute, now based in Barangáy Encanto, Angat, Bulacan. Access information at http://www.notredamedeviephilippines.org/.

70   Mother of Life Center is an educational institution which forms professional lay men and women for the catechetical ministry, religious education, Christian community leadership and other pastoral work. Access information about MOL at http://motheroflifecenter.wix.com/mother-of-life-center#!.

71   *Magis* (pronounced "màh-gis") is a Latin word that means "more" or "greater". It is related to *ad majorem Dei gloriam*, a Latin phrase meaning "for the greater glory of God," the motto of the Society of Jesus. *Magis* refers to the philosophy of doing more for Christ, and therefore doing more for others. Access information at https://en.wikipedia.org/wiki/Magis.

Fourteen years after flying to Manila on my own, I trained my eyes somewhere far beyond my nest, beyond the horizon. I thought I was now ready to fly over seas and oceans. Not that I had grown weary teaching in Xavier; Xavier, to me, is one of the best schools to be in, either as a teacher or as a student. So, in 1992, I flew across the Pacific Ocean, as neither engineer nor man of the cloth, but as a teacher. I was a family man flying to Texas USA, in search of greener pasture for my family of three, in furtherance of my diaspora, pursuing the American Dream.

At that time, Texas, like many other states, badly needed teachers. We were 25 teachers flown to Texas by Omni Consortium/Multicultural Education Consultants, a recruitment agency based in Houston (Texas) and Manila. Omni spread us out into the Rio Grande Valley. I was initially assigned to a school in the Pharr-Alamo area, in the parish of St. John the Baptist, San Juan, Texas, where the historic Basilica of Our Lady of San Juan del Valle magnificently stands.

The recruiting agency eventually took us to Brownsville, TX, where I stayed put and became a parishioner of Mary Mother of the Church Parish, Diocese of Brownsville. Though about 50 miles from Brownsville, the Basilica of Our Lady of San Juan del Valle, in San Juan, TX, seemed just a breeze away and easily became my favorite sacred destination in the Rio Grande Valley.

Initially certified to teach Mathematics 1-8, I taught Math 7 at Cummings Middle School, but subsequent certifications in Elementary Music and Religion enabled me to teach music at St. Luke Catholic School, Incarnate Word Academy, St. Mary's School, all in Brownsville, and last, Villareal Elementary School, in Los Fresnos Consolidated Independent School District, in Los Fresnos, TX.

While at St. Mary's, I took charge of the school's music ministry, a place and a job that inspired me to write several Marian and other religious and catechetical songs for children, including the **St. Mary's School Song**. In 2011, I published **The Purple Psalmody**[72], my book of musical settings of all Sunday psalms, dedicated to *Inâ*. One of my favorite settings was the *Magnificat* (entitled **My Soul Rejoices**) I wrote for her. With this closeness to *Inâ*, even in eclectic America, I wake up each day giving thanks for God's blessings and praying to live up to the creed, code, and cult of my spiritual life.

The hee and the haw of work and earning a living, as well as the demands of family life, might have forever distracted me away from the nest. Dimple, our only daughter, finished high school in Brownsville and aspired to get into New York to pursue her artistic dreams. She was eventually accepted with scholarships at St. John's University—John as in John the Baptist, as patron saint—at Queens, NY, at the same time enrolled for theater training at the American Academy of Dramatic Arts in Manhattan. In 2015, she graduated with two degrees in her name.

College responsibilities then over, Mameng said, "You have not seen your siblings in 12 years. Let's go home!" So, in June 2016, we packed four *balikbayan*[73] boxes full of Toblerone, Irish Spring, Néscafe, Nestlé coffee creamers, and other groceries, not to mention big bath towels. All these in tow, we went back home to the nest after 12 years of forever. My wife treated my siblings to a tour of Luzon on wheels, all expenses paid. It was surreal, like coming out of a long dream.

I've gone far and long enough to miss home. So, I was back to the nest and **The Birds**. [See **ROD**, page 6.] With *Inâ* and John the Baptist always with me, I've never really left home, have I?

Home is always around. ■

---

72 Arcádio Morada, Jr. *The Purple Psalmody*, United States: Xlibris, 2011, 350 pages, https://www.amazon.com/ Purple-Psalmody-Settings-Solemnities-Memorials/dp/1465379665.

73 *balikbayan* [Filipino] – repatriate.

Baby Boomers participating in a *Santakruzan* at San Juan Ave., Sipocot, in the early 60s. Ten-year-old Mr. Purple sat in the middle of the front row.

Teenage Mr. Purple walked proud as Valedictorian of his graduating class in 1969. He flew towards the blue horizon, aiming to be a civil engineer. After all the flying, he thought he had the best method of flight at his disposal, but he ended up as teacher. Why, and how come? It is an emotional and providential story by itself.

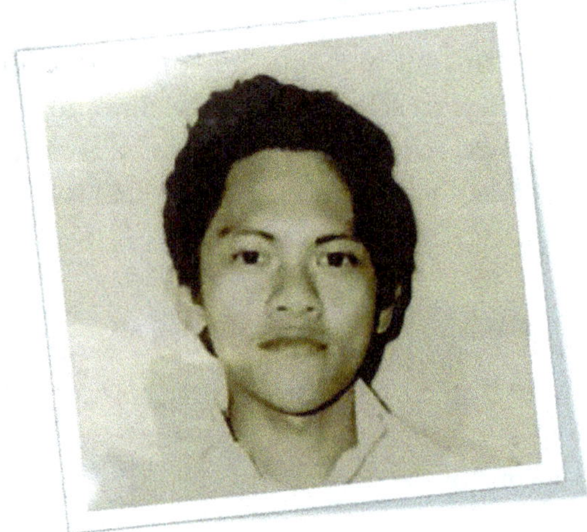

As a late bloomer, Mr. Purple graduated from college at 23 and got first employment at St. Agnes' Academy of Legazpi City in 1974, starting a career that spanned two countries, seven schools, and over four decades.

Mr. Purple, enjoying life and retirement at 71

7
BOND
Debt for the eyes is paid off in kind

The sky was overcast, and the day uneventful, except for some intermittent rains outside this boarding house where I lived, which was owned by the Tiomicos of Little Baguio, San Juan, Manila. I made no plans to go anywhere, after Sunday Mass at Mary the Queen Parish Church a walking distance away. It wasn't wise to be out, even with my sturdy black umbrella, for heavy rains were imminent. I locked myself inside my room and was about to lie down and read a book when I got startled by a knocking at the door.

"Happy birthday, Jun!" Tita[74] Nitz Chiyutu, the elder sister of my landlady, Tita Carmen Tiomico, greeted me as she raised a steaming bowl in her left hand. The pungent smell of ginger and onion emanating from the bowl kindled my spirit. "The weather may be less than good today," she continued, "but rainy days and *arroz caldo* are a perfect match."

Tita Nitz was an excellent cook, so the bowl of delicious *arroz caldo* was desirable and more than welcome.

"Ba't ka nagmúmukmók [Why moping around]?" Tita Nitz said. "Be up and happy! The latest James Bond movie is showing. Go watch and enjoy your day!"

"I'm broke, Tita Nitz," I said. "Sent most of my salary to Tatay for home improvement."

"Ay, kawawà! [Such a pity!] But you're a son with kindness in your heart, and lucky is your lady, whoever she may be."

After thanking her for the *caldo* and the compliment, and consuming the free bounty up to the last grain of rice, I turned to page 1 and read **When the Bough Breaks** in my bed for as long as it took to finish half through. At which time, I heard another knock at my door.

This time, it was Carmen. No, not my landlady.

Mameng, as everyone in the house called her, was another room boarder of the Tiomicos, but more than just a boarder. She was the new stay-in secretary of Tito Jess Tiomico, brother to Tita Carmen and Tita Nitz, whose business, Paramount Calibrators, dealt with large industrial weight scales and calibrating them. Tito Jess had the living room of Tita Carmen's boarding house double up as his business office.

---

74   *Tita, Tiya,* or *Tia* [Filipino] – a Tagalog honorific for aunt, also used to address with respect any older lady acquaintance; *Tito, Tiyo* or *Tio,* for the male counterpart.

"Happy birthday to you!" Mameng sang in fragments, then said in Bikol, "Tita Nitz told me." Mameng and I are both Bicolanos; I am from Daragá, Albáy, while she comes from the adjacent town of Camalíg. "Come on, let's go watch **For Your Eyes Only** at the Greenhills Theater. *Ako an tayâ* [It's on me]."

I didn't know what to do. "W-w-wait," I said. "This is such a surprise!"

"*Bukón toód ka sa biriglaan* [Aren't you used to spurts], so why not now?"

"It just isn't right—"

"OK, I get it. You're the gentleman, and I'm just being too forward. So, I pay for our tickets first, you just reimburse me when you can."

"No, thanks, Mameng, but..."

"I don't take no for an answer," she said. "So, you dress up and we watch **For Your Eyes Only**, or you mope in your room and I'll never talk to you again for the rest of our lives!"

I was ready to go in no time at all.

he movie, a blockbuster, had Sheena Easton singing the lovely theme song **For Your Eyes Only** and Roger Moore in his prime, playing Agent 007. But at the moment, even though I was both a music lover and a movie fan, the flick was simply the least of my concerns.

First, where to sit. The theater was full to the brim. I don't know the current state of Philippine movie-house affairs, but in 1981, movie theaters looped their main feature throughout the day from the opening at 9am till midnight, while people came and left anytime, allowing for staggered turnout. Halfway through the movie, a couple vacated adjoining seats near where Mameng and I were standing, which I gallantly swooped upon. First concern down.

Second, where to put my black umbrella securely. After some mental deliberation, I deemed it gentlemanly to place the big, long but foldable umbrella *between* my seat and Mameng's, a demarcation of sorts. There was, of course, the armrest between us, but the umbrella could count for added protection, security—and chivalry. Second concern down.

Third, what and how to teach in Guidance to my homeroom class tomorrow. I could teach Math or Science with my eyes closed, but Guidance was another story. Well, yes, I should better see Aida Dalupang, guidance counselor, for some teaching help and tips first thing in the morning. Third concern down, hopefully.

And fourth, this involuntary debt I just incurred today. I should pay Mameng as soon as money became available. *Nakakahiya.* (Disgraceful.) Till then, fourth concern would be down, bashfully.

While I was worrying thus, the movie came to its end. "What a gripping movie!" Mameng said; she always liked action flicks. "Exciting!"

It drizzled on our way back to the Tiomicos, from the jeepney stop to General S. De Jesus St. where we lived—in separate rooms, of course. Was I glad I had my black umbrella! Under its shade, Mameng and I walked too close to each other for comfort but walked together anyway, and with synchronized steps at that. Under its shelter, we walked safely in the rain. I never knew when else a thing so commonplace could be so sexy and heroic.

 woke up at 5:00 o'clock on the morning of July 7, two days after the movie, fumbling for pen and paper. *Tsk, tsk, tsk,* I could find nothing better than a used mimeographing paper with my Xavier School 1981 class list printed on one side and blank page at the back, but anyhow I wrote on the blank side. In less than 30 minutes, a letter incarnated. Then I tiptoed into the living room and carefully tucked the paper inside Mameng's office desk drawer.

Dearest Mameng,

Toód ako sa biriglaan, sabi mo sakô [You told me I'm used to spurts]. I accept and confirm that fact today. This may shock you, but I feel I must tell you this, otherwise I might land either in the mental hospital or in frustration and despair.

I have been telling you I have a problem. It's not financial, nor familial. Indeed, there's a problem, but it concerns you. That's why I couldn't have the heart to tell you. After 30 years, this is the first time I felt this way, and it's not funny at all. Of course, there had been some heartsy-fancies before, but they were all just passing feelings. This is the real McCoy, Mameng. I love you.

Don't laugh at me, or at my first genuine love. Or at my being corny, at this strange letter written on, of all things, the back of a used mimeo paper. If I tell you I have been having sleepless nights lately, that I feel very jealous whenever you talk with your male friends over the phone, if the very mention of that Miss Neneng Guráng[75] makes me mad, don't laugh. If I tell you why I act strange these days is that I think I love you—don't laugh.

My sister Frida is right. I am *pihikan,* choosy, but I'm sure this time here comes the right woman—you.

I hope you'll not get mad at me because of this revelation. I am hoping, too, that you'll care to let me know.

Lovelorn and lovesick,

 Jun

T he rest of the story is family history. Mameng eventually said Yes, OMG, and the bond materialized, triggered by Bond. Officially, Mameng and I got hooked in a ritual at Our Lady of the Gate Parish Church in Daragá, Albáy, on December 27, 1986—again, OMG! That first love letter on the mimeo paper has gotten enthroned on the very first page of our wedding album. And the first-date *utang* [debt]? "*Ay naku, hanggang ngayon, hindi pa ako binabayaran* [Oh my, he has not paid me back yet]!" she tells whosoever asks, feigning annoyance.

Well, my constant reply is, "Sweetheart, I have fully paid it off with my heart—for your heart only!" ∎

---

75   An old maid in the neighborhood with whom Mameng used to tease me.

8

IMPISH

He demands oryza sativa for dinner

I had it coming. My eldest sister Nilda, youngest sister Prid, my late brother Rudy's son Pancho, plus other siblings Piping, Otê, and Merl with their spouses, smiled at each other and formed a semi-circle in front of me, thereupon singing merrily as they brandished colored-paper cut-outs that spelled HAPPY B DAY JUN. This was the evening of July 5, 2016, at Vigan, Ilocos Sur, the first leg of our tour of Luzon. (We decided against going to Banaue Rice Terraces because of the rainy weather.) The five-day event, a Morada Clan Reunion after 12 years, was my wife Mameng's gift to me and my five living siblings.

So, my siblings and their spouses, in semi-circle, were brandishing letter cut-outs. Then they each took turns expounding on the letter/s they were holding. *They are doing a corny acrostic to roast me!* I thought as I laughed out loud, but deep inside, I felt uneasy. When my brother Otê's turn came, I feared the worst. He had the letter Y in HAPPY to expound in relation to me.[76]

"Y," he said. Prid echoed, "Y—*bakit* [why]?"

"Dapat kintâna, Manoy an angál ko sîmo [I should have been calling you *Manoy*]," Otê said. In my native language, *Manoy* is both a term of endearment and an honorific for an older brother. "*Pero pirmi mo akong pigaa-Y* [But you've always picked a fight with me]*!" Awáy*, pronounced *a-Y* in Bikol, literally means to fight, and *pigaawáy* means being picked on, fought against, picked a fight with, teased or bullied.

Everyone burst out laughing. *Are you kidding me, bro?* I thought.

This was so becoming of my younger brother José, whom everybody calls Otê. He is the irreverent joker in the family, although our parents derived his name from San José, you know, the husband of Santa Maria, in the Holy Family. But undeniably he was the quick-witted, the wisecracker, the comedian, with an impish sense of humor in our *un*holy family. Waggish.

He calls me Archie or Dolphy sometimes, usually pleasant or affectionate times.

Otherwise:

"*Querido* Cadió*!*" He makes *querido* sound more like "paramour" than "dear."

"*Viudo de Chary!*" Tia Charing was a flirty widow and neighbor.

---

76   Arcádio Morada, Jr., *tagaalbay*, "My Birthday 2016." YouTube video, 7:57min, https://youtu.be/52GnLDGFLvw.

"Novio de Pina!" Josefina was my old-maid mentor at the Bicol University College of Education. "I met your fiancée Pina accidentally last week. She said she missed you a lot. *Oy!*"

"Apôon! Nakita ko so litrato mo. Sa paghunà-hunà ko iká pinagá-apô na namán—mas halangkáw pa sa Mayon Volcano so mga habaga mo. Kaherák!" [Asthmatic! I saw your picture. I thought you were having an asthma attack, as your shoulders stood taller than Mayon Volcano. What a pity!]

"Always take care! Especially of your siren—please be kind to others!" *Siren* refers to the wheezing sound I make involuntarily during bouts of asthma.

"Medyo guapo!" [You're somewhat, but not exactly, good-looking!]

After a visit to the Manila Zoo, he tells me: *"Kahawíg mo palán an rhinoceros!"* [You look like the rhinoceros!]

"Ako nagkakaproblema sa oras na pigalitrato [I have a problem every time I have my picture taken]," he says. "I always look better than the last time!"

Who's more aged? *"Dobládo an pagkasubáng mo sâkon* [You are twice older than me]!"

"I passed the Career Service Professional Exam! 70.26. It should actually be 90.8, but the C.S. Commissioner thought it would be proper and respectful for me not to have a higher rating than you, because you're older than me." (I got 90.5 rating for the C.S. Exam for Teachers in 1975.)

Nice! Altogether true-to-form José!

ith a degree in Agriculture from the Bicol University, my bro Otê applied his chosen career in every situation. Coming home from school one day, he said, "I'm hungry! Is there any *oryza sativa* hereabout? I need to eat!" How could we have known beforehand that he was asking for rice?

I was already employed as a grade-school teacher at St. Agnes' Academy of Legazpi City, while he was in college, when he told our mother, "Nanay, I need money. I'm going to attend an agri-business seminar." Of course, Nanay's pocket was always open to every such endeavor.

Poor Nanay, she would eventually learn that "seminar" either meant "cine-nar" at the Lola Theater in downtown Legazpi City, or a clandestine trip to Naga City to woo midwifery student Edith Marollano there. Make no mistake, though: José Morada was as diligent a student as he was a persistent suitor. After he finished college and landed a stable job, the midwifery student indeed became Mrs. Edith Morada. On short notice, I had to take a leave of absence from Xavier School in July 1978 to attend Otê and Edith's wedding in Colaclíng, Camarines Sur.

Soon the kids poured forth as virtually swiftly as his jokes and witticisms. "I want to inform you," he wrote to me in November 1978 about his firstborn son, Joed. *"Si Edith nangakì na* [Edith just gave birth], normal—cesarean!" Married in July, the firstborn out in November. That was *really* swift, not just virtually, and this is not even a joke!

"So akì mi cute—mahilig sa music—kaya pinagpapraktis ko nang magkantá para X-mas simo pagpulê mo sa Disyembre." [Our baby is cute, likes music; therefore, I'm practicing him to sing as Christmas treat for you when you come home this December.]

Three more boys followed in quick succession. *Jingle lang ang pahinga!*[77] Otê or Edith had a fixation on the letter J. Joed, José Jr, Joséph, and Jesse each grew up to be handsome and successful boys in their own right, as good as—if not better a breed than—their father. The Morada seed is alive in the J strain. "The sons I don't have," I once told him in envy, with twitching eyes. "Playboys!"

Throughout the years, Otê had enjoyed employment with the Philippine government under the National Irrigation Administration, from which he retired in 2012.

In the intervening years, I have gone to Texas with my wife Mameng and our daughter Dimple. I have no boys, so the surname Morada is coterminous with me. (Again, my envious eyes twitch—and flash!)

Just as hard, I have been working and earning my keep, and retired in 2018 from government service in my Texas school district. But, thanks to Revlon, my hair is soft-black while his is all gray. *Woo-hoo! Na na na na boo boo!* Now, tell me who looks more aged?

Nanay always stood up for me, no offense. "Stop bullying your elder brother," she would tell Otê when she'd see us fighting, "or else—*tumagiktik!*" That's her rattan rod used for beating errant children among the Morada brood, which usually or always meant Otê. Being my papa's Junior, and my mama's boy, I got unimaginable power and favorable entitlement in the family all the time. No wonder why he could say what he said: *"Dápat kintâna, Manoy an angál ko sîmo, pero pirmi mo akong pigaa-Y!"* I guess, too, that in silent resentment, Otê gradually learned to fend for himself and do many things his way.

Otê was going into high school when the Moradas fell on hard times. Tatay's tailoring business took a turn for the worse as the ready-made jeans and denims craze monopolized the clothing market in the 60s and 70s. Piping was in college and I in high school, in Daragá, Albáy, while the rest of the family was struggling in Sipocot, Camarines Sur. Eventually, Tatay decided in 1967 to move from Sipocot and reunite the family all together in Daragá, Albáy.

In 1970, while in his third year at Albáy High School, Otê fell ill with typhoid fever. He missed school for two months and failed to take some term exams; thence he was practically dropped from the roster of students. Barely recovering from his illness, he felt he had to do something about his future. So, he scrambled off to school one day and asked to see the principal. Otê boldly told him he needed to get back to the classroom and finish the school year. He was ready to fail, but not for lack of trying. Astonished, the principal couldn't say no to this boy's persistence and determination. He wrote a note of re-acceptance and told Otê to hand it to his homeroom teacher the following Monday. Otê was back at school, and his classmates cheered as they welcomed him back. He finished high school in 1971.

By then, the papa's Junior and mama's boy was in the sophomore year in college. So, Tatay and Nanay called Otê aside and talked him into *not* enrolling in college yet, to let me finish first. More resentment! However, because of increased copra production and income from our ancestral farm in Talôtô in 1972, at last he stepped into the Bicol University. Initially enrolled in Arts and Sciences, he promptly found it not to his liking. The next year he moved to Agriculture.

That was it for him. To make the story short, he worked and humored his way through college and got his Agriculture degree in 1976. Worked for the government. Got hitched to a successful girl and produced four successful J-named boys of their own. Retired, enjoying the good life in rural Colaclíng, Philippines.

---

77   *Jingle lang ang pahinga* [Filipino expression] – The only break time is to urinate, in reference to jeepney drivers who work nonstop throughout the day, except to urinate.

I, too, am retired, but still struggling in rural Brownsville, Texas, and Woodside, New York, in America. Need I say more?

Happy Valentine's Day, my dear bro. From your Querido Cadió. Time zones and latitudes may have separated us, but I know we love each other dearly, and we miss each other as much. Isn't love grand!

Don't look at me. That's not hyperbole, and I'm not a bully. *Away!* ∎

Otê, at 65

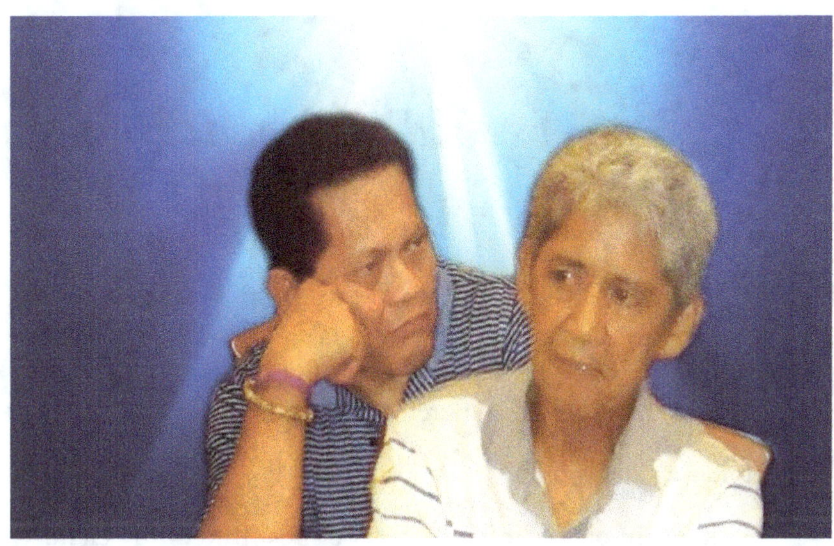

The bully and the bullied

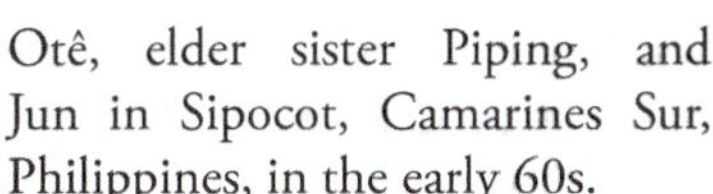

Otê, elder sister Piping, and Jun in Sipocot, Camarines Sur, Philippines, in the early 60s.

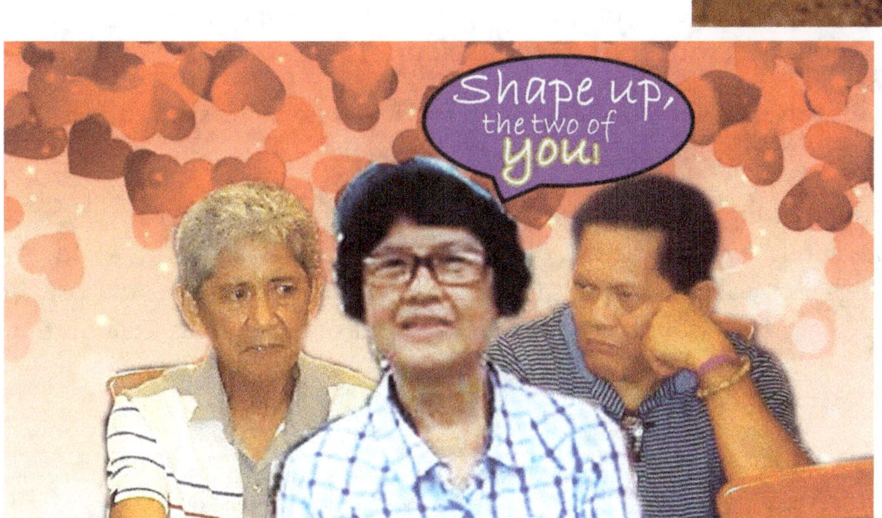

Otê, Piping, and Jun

9
ONE

A candid bifocal look at a miracle

Helen Keller once wrote, "[T]hose who have eyes apparently see little. The panorama of color and action which fills the world is taken for granted. It is human, perhaps, to appreciate little that which we have and to long for that which we have not, but it is a great pity that in the world of light the gift of sight is used only as a mere convenience rather than as a means of adding fullness to life."[78]

Hold on. Helen who?

Mark Twain once said that "the two most interesting characters of the nineteenth century are Napoleon and Helen Keller."[79] But the 19th century and the now-generation are two long poles apart, and never the twain shall meet, Mark. The millennials, in particular, may not have heard of her, unlike the oldsters among us who know Helen Keller as a famous American author, political activist, and inspirational speaker.

So what?

What set Helen Keller apart from the millennials and the rest of us bifocal mortals was her having overcome and risen from her multiple acquired disabilities. Yes, she became deaf and blind, and therefore mute, at barely two years of age. However, through the magnanimity of the gifted Anne Sullivan, a patient and dedicated teacher, Helen broke through the barriers of communication. She learned how to talk, read and write, finished college with academic honors—and became a world-famous achiever. Her wide-ranging interests, endeavors and achievements in many fields have made her in league with the most famous handicapped people in history. Helen Keller inspired future generations of people, with or without disabilities, to live life to the fullest.

That miracle of a disabled but full life was lived for 87 productive years. It was not a life spent in self-pity and human turpitude. It was a life of victory over seemingly insurmountable odds.

When Keller died in 1968, I was in junior high and my sister Merl was in 6th grade. As a nerdy type who would rather read than play sports, I was amply aware of Helen's demise and her significance to the world, for I had somehow read a few of her writings, especially her profound essay **Three Days to See.** I couldn't help it, but every time I thought of Helen Keller, there would always come to mind one anatomical connection between her and my sister Merl.

78   Helen Keller, "Three Days to See," The Atlantic, January, 1933. https://www.theatlantic.com/past/docs/issues/33jan/keller.htm.

79   M. Westwood, "Homework help: A brief character sketch of Helen Keller," Enotes. (undated) https://www.enotes.com/homework-help/brief-character-sketch-miss-helen-keller-706993.

Merl, nick of Emerlita, lived her earliest years during a tumultuous time in Philippine history. In 1957, the incumbent Philippine president, popular and well-loved Ramon Magsaysay, died in a plane crash. The ensuing presidential and local elections—at least in our small town of Jovellár, Albáy—turned out to be a contest of political personalities and their private armies, brigands, and hoodlums as well. The time was so fraught with lawlessness, instability, danger, and chaos that John the Baptist, the town's patron saint, must have been turning in his grave and crying out, "Repent!" Election-related violence was rampant, and a particular encounter between political antagonists on the main street of Jovellár was so bloody that it traumatized Nanay Babing, our mother, and caused her nervous breakdown. Merl was just a year old, having been born on March 25 a year earlier, but who knows what influence did all the election violence and Nanay's trauma have upon little Merl's impressionable mind?

Inevitably, Tatay Cadió had to make the hard decision to uproot the family from Jovellár and find livelihood elsewhere, at a river town in Camarines Sur named Sipocot. But Merl became finicky and sickly. She became malnourished because she would not eat, however good or enticing was the food served. Then her left eye swelled and protruded.

Tatay Cadió and Nanay Babing offered novenas and prayers, especially the devotion to Mary through the Rosary, in sickly Merl's behalf. When time permitted, they would travel to Naga City (seat of Our Lady of Peñafrancia) or Joroan, Albáy (Our Lady of Salvation), to dedicate the toddler to God and ask for the intercession of the Blessed Mother.

Frequent visits to the local doctors, and sojourns at the provincial hospital in Naga City, produced minimal effects and improvements, if at all, in Merl's left eye. At its worst, it would look like a rotting piece of red meat protruding from her left eye socket.

We turned to alternatives. A town quack prescribed laying some strips of fresh cow liver on Merl's forehead and letting them stand there awhile. (I could imagine little Merl's discomfort!) Another option was a *para-anito*[80] in Manangle, a remote village, to whom Tatay and Nanay desperately brought Merl for remedial measures. He had the reputation of curing people's illnesses by praying and chanting while walking on smoldering charcoal unshod—in behalf of the patient—till the embers died down. Well, the embers *did* die down and Tatay and Nanay went home mesmerized, but Merl's condition worsened.

In the end, after all available options were used and exhausted, doctors had to gouge out her left eye. The remaining eye, itself developing a cloudiness on the iris, got stabilized and miraculously saved, though the cloudiness lingered.

Just exactly how and why it happened, I honestly don't know. It was a delicate truth nobody dared to ask about until now. What medical explanation stared us in the face, waiting to be explored to save Merl's left eye? Looking back, I realize it was a mystery nobody among us could clarify. I was barely ten and had troubles with asthma. The people who could shed light on the matter—Tatay and Nanay—have long crossed over the Great Divide, whereas Manay Nilda was just a teenager upon whose shoulders lay most of the responsibility of running the household and caring for a sick sibling. In her 70s now, she could only supply hazy details, which I have recounted above.

So hazy were the details that they bordered on the weird. Take this account, for another example: A theory circulated that toddler Merl got infested with parasitic worms because of Manay Nilda's inability to mind her ward and prevent her from walking on dirty ground barefooted sometimes. The nematodes squirmed their way upward to the head. Eventually, they reached the left eye and damaged it irreparably. The parasites would

---

80 *para-anito* [Bikol] – "anito" practitioner. "Para-anito" refers to one who invokes "anito"—ancestor spirits, nature spirits, and deities in the indigenous and rural Philippines—to cure people's illnesses and heal the sick.

have done the same to the right eye, if not for the timely intervention of some eye specialist. The miracle of the right eye, her remaining window to the world, saved Merl's sight.

Or half of it.

It's the same miracle that has given Merl the fullness of her life.

For sure, Merl's childhood was neither a piece of cake nor a walk in the park. She grew up moody, sensitive and vulnerable to the slightest attention of classmates and bullies in school. Gradually, she would become overly conscious of her disability, often silent and withdrawn.

She was exceedingly and relentlessly bullied during her elementary and high school days. Curious or malicious stares of classmates on her empty left eye socket inhibited her. Taunts like *one eye* and *just one look* were common and sure to make her cry. On her very first day at the United Institute, a Presbyterian high school in Daraga, a classmate named Celmore Lozano nominated her *Muse* during the election of officers at the start of the school year—which humiliated and hurt her no end. These and other infinitesimal put-downs discouraged and so distressed her that the thought of suicide seemed inevitable. The school's adherence to the Bible gradually lifted her spirits and saved her. She remembered John 3:16 as one of the Gospel gems that inspired her to strive on.

College was an altogether different battlefield. Merl first wanted to be in the medical profession, and in fact she enrolled in and finished a certification program for health aides at Ago General Hospital (now called AMEC or Ago Medical and Educational Center) in Legazpi City. However, that innocuous thing called thermometer might have made her eventually realize that, if she was going to be a good health-aide professional at all, reading the tiny calibrations on the thermometer should be a breeze, a basic but crucial stuff. In fact, it was a major difficulty, letdown, and turning point. She got the certification alright, but never used it.

She then decided she wanted to be a teacher. "I want to enroll in Normal school," Merl said. Nanay had the first vocal dissenting opinion, because mothers knew best. Hadn't she realized yet that college was a completely different story? Besides, teaching is a social function, requiring all of a person's faculties and senses. "No," Nanay said. "In the long run, it's for your own good."

Nanay stuck to her point, trying to prevent her daughter from incurring what she thought would be future disappointments and failures if she went into college. With her physical infirmity, how could she be a successful teacher? *"Siring san ibang tao na may karimalásuan, ngâ ta indî ka na lang maghanap san makakaya mo, mag-ulát san káabutan mo?"* Nanay told Merl. [Like most people in similar condition, why could you not just strive for what you can do, wait for where destiny will take you?]

But Merl was not most people in similar condition. Nanay might even have made it easier for Merl to verbalize what she wanted to say all along: *"Nanay, abô kong mag-ulát na lang san káabutan ko."* [Nanay, I don't want to just sit around and wait for destiny to come by and take me wherever.]

So, the conflict raged on. Nanay was headstrong, even made more so by the rest of the family on her side, but Merl was insistent. No pun intended—she had a definite one-eyed vision. Merl wasn't just testing the waters. She went on a hunger strike and moped around to emphasize her point. No, she wouldn't eat till the Moradas allowed her to enroll at the Bicol University College of Education. The hunger strike lasted for as long as it took us to surrender.

We saw the determination, and Nanay capitulated. Perhaps it was for Merl's best interest. Our exacting and uncompromising mother succumbed to her one-eyed mismatch, again with no pun intended. Mothers know best, but it doesn't mean they cannot go wrong.

In short, in a nutshell, Merl finished college in 1982 and became a certified teacher. But expectedly, employment was scarce. In 1985, she eventually found it in a place called Badas, in the hinterlands of Lupí, Camarines Sur, and there fulfilled and enjoyed her calling. Meanwhile, she found a loving husband in local boy Henry Meralpis, with whom she has begotten two good-looking children, Lynn and Nhoy. Lynn placed 2nd in the 2017 Board Examination for elementary teachers in Region 5 and now works as a teacher in Lupi, while Nhoy is a musician, the keyboardist of 4th Corner Band, a local pop music band engaged in local gigs. Together as a family, the Meralpis have been very active in Church ministry in Colaclíng, Camarines Sur, their hometown. Merl has been into education for so many years now. She just retired from government service in July 2016. How's all this, Helen Keller?

Of course, Merl is no Helen Keller. Thank God she only has one disability, and maybe that's a blessing in disguise. Yes, she only has her right eye. But who knows, that single eye may have enabled her to help countless young children learn far better than other educators who have the luxury of two. After all, those who have eyes apparently see little, and those who are blind—or half-blind—apparently see more. That's what defined Helen Keller's extraordinary life. That's what made Helen Keller an amazing miracle.

And Merl? There, too, is a miracle in how she has lived her life and what she has become—despite one eye. In the final analysis, Merl is *a* miracle due to one. ∎

One-year-old Merl before the mysterious sickness struck, on lap of sister Piping, and with brother Ote.

Merl as she looks today

10
DESTINY
Youngest takes a ride for a fair head start

he may not remember it anymore, or she may not have known about it at all. Once upon an early morning many, many years ago, Prid didn't walk to school—she rode on somebody's shoulders. It was her first school day ever, in June 1965.

The explicit aim was to reach Sipocot North Central School ahead of anyone. Nanay Babing, our mother, gave the clear-cut instructions. Rogelio "Boy" Morada, a relative and apprentice in Tatay Cadió's tailoring shop, was to take our youngest sister upon his shoulders to Impig, where the school was, about two kilometers away from our house. Since our house cum tailoring shop was at mid-town along San Juan Avenue, and since at 7am vehicular and human traffic was mounting, Boy was to take the easier and shorter route along the town's railroad track, away from the prying eyes of potential inquirers. Curiosity might cause delay.

The implicit aim of the whole shoulder ride was just as clear-cut: to give Prid a head start. An advantage. A boost to good luck. A suggestion to greatness. A predisposition to destiny. A higher-level view of things. Nanay knew how it could be done.

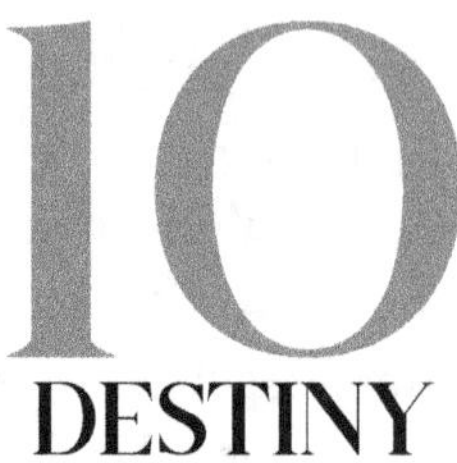n the 1950s and on to the early 60s, before the construction of Tara Bridge across the *Dakulang Salog,* the route that would more conveniently connect Sipocot to Naga City via Libmanan and Pamplona towns, there was not much vehicular traffic along San Juan Ave. especially at night. Every night was a grand time for playing *turubigan*. All you needed was enough water to make grid lines from one side of the paved street to the opposite side, and the other children of the neighborhood as playmates, and *voilà!*—you had the most enjoyable group game in the world, so simple yet unsurpassed in these modern times of computers and video games. My siblings, the Moratallas, the San Agustins, the Sarcias, the brothers Jaime and Levi, the Remots, Rufino, Roger, Armando, Catalino, and other contemporary playmates whose names I now hardly recall—we would play this game till our energies were spent or till our respective parents would summon us to get home or else.

At daytime, during weekends or whenever we were not in school, we would enjoy playing other traditional children's games such as *taratsian, pikot, dyolin, tumbang priso, darakupan, taraguan,* or even simply catching little mudfish fries in the canal and *imburnal* beside our tailoring shop. Other times we would while away the hours listening to the audio of the current movie showing in Main Theater, which was obliquely across the street from our shop. How so? The proprietor would hook up loudspeakers outside the theater to the movie showing inside, to arouse curiosity and entice passers-by. Thus, still fresh in my memory from the loudspeakers of Main Theater is this song from a 1958 Fernando Poe, Jr.-Berting Labra movie blaring all day: *"Lutong makaw, anong sarap ng lutong makaw!"* [How delicious is Macau Dish!]

Childhood in Sipocot was not all play and good times. On November 17, 1959, the threat of Typhoon Frida [Freda][81] was all-too-real. She came during the day with her destructive winds and rains. At nightfall, she raged all the more, prompting our neighborhood to seek refuge inside the Main Theater. The owner, of course, graciously granted permission to all families that needed a safe place to stay, including the Moradas, with Nanay in her 9th month of pregnancy. And so, we took shelter within the confines of the big building, confident and safe. Or so we thought. Deep in the night, as the storm continued to rage, we found out to our great dismay the winds were making the tall and wide brick walls of the theater vibrate precariously. It would have been a most grievous disaster had the walls and roof fallen on us! Thank God—He obviously had other plans. I would eventually migrate to America and write this snippet.

And thank God, that night Nanay gave birth to Frida.

For someone named after a raging typhoon, my youngest sister Frida—Prid, for short—is ever unassuming, optimistic, genial, soft-spoken, graceful, generous, and beautiful. Her position in the Morada family tree she could have taken to her advantage, but no, it never spoiled her, nor did she use it unduly to her benefit. She was never into sibling rivalry, nor would she hear of it. No wonder she was very close to, and well-loved by, both Tatay and Nanay, and all her siblings as well.

Hard times don't affect her, and she seems to have always emerged triumphant over them in her own good way and time. In 1967, the Moradas, in dire financial straits, moved to Daragá, Albáy. Just a month after moving, a fire razed our newly built, newly occupied house to the ground. More hardships stood in the offing, brought about by typhoons during the rainy season. We literally crawled our way to education despite the hardships. I can look back now and say I was the most, and Prid the least, affected. She remained as genial and optimistic as before.

We were a close-knit family in every little way. We enjoyed simple pleasures together. During silly playhouse times, I was *Boboy* or *Nog* to Merl as *Tia* and Prid as *Nay*, though I was older and bigger than both. On storytelling times in which I was the "master" storyteller, Prid was a great and ever-enthusiastic listener to the stories I culled from my readings in college, the movies I watched, and even the anecdotes I experienced during my first teaching job at St. Agnes' Academy of Legazpi City. During music times, in which I would teach Merl, Prid, and Pancho (my late brother Rudy's son) songs from music books and introduce them to the rudiments of music, Prid was ever patient and understanding, and so careful as not to incur my displeasure or ire, or to make my eyes roll, even if she (as she later revealed) could hardly understand what I was teaching. She would take such situations lightheartedly. Compassionate, conscientious, and adaptable, she has a hearty sense of humor. Otê, the family's irreverent joker, may be wittier and funnier, but Prid can make you laugh in her own natural and graceful way.

Prid's full first name is *Ma. Frida*. Ma. stands for Maria, the Blessed Virgin Mary of this world, dainty and sweet and full of grace.

When I took a job in Manila, 500 kilometers away from the family, Prid provided the light-heartedness and the humor I needed to ease my longing for home. By her many letters through the years, which I have compiled and kept fondly, distance was never a cause for despair. Take this first example, one of my favorites

---

81   Wikipedia, "1959 Pacific typhoon season," https://en.wikipedia.org/wiki/1959_Pacific_typhoon_season

in the pile, detailing in jest the night Edith, my brother Otê's wife, brought forth Joed, their firstborn son, into the world. She wrote it in a blend of English and Bikol on November 10, 1978, well into the middle of my first year of employment with Xavier School, Manila.

Biyernes na bangging madiklomon asin mauranon, kaming duwa ni Manoy Joe was walking outside and under the rain, fetching the midwife in the UI Compd. (A day before, during the check-up, Manay Edith & the midwife had a compromise for just the latter to go to our house to assist the baby delivery.) And so the story goes:

The midwife stayed for the night. The expectant mother expects to ulpot the bulging part in front, early morning pa. Mga alas 4:00 a.m. we heard pong! Nagputok na daa so panubigon, e di siempre burungkarasan. Nagkatirigpilô ko na pati so paraagong na midwife, malâ ta kataning ko siya sa pagturog. Sabi nimo niya, dai daa siya nangaturog. Tse! Bâgo pa-left & right so mouth air output niya. Like the way papa did it, aha, aha.

And so the story goes: Alas! Mga 7:00 a.m. na wara pang pag-ulpot ni baby. Ay, dificil baga, ano? Pigkokôdos na, so lobot lang kang aki an nagaluwas. Uyon so aki, pero sa mga bados, iyan an sisabing suwî. Kaharadit na kami. Iyo nimo. Pinakakán na so ina ki salág na malasado, dangog ko pagpakutal daa sa aki, asin si arikurong kan salag pinatatapok sa bintana na dapat dai makadutâ sa window sill. Pinainom na nin kinoromos na dahon nin kanyos asin so duga pinainom. Iyan an Rx ni mama dearest.

Pero wa epek pa rin. An nangyari next, pack up an mga crew members bound for provincial hospital at about 8:00 a.m.

10:00 a.m. the birth. Caesarian, men!

(Rough translation)

'Twas a very dark and rainy Friday, I with Manoy Joe walking outside and under the rain, fetching the midwife [from] the United Institute [a private school in Daragá, Albáy] Compound. (A day earlier, during check-up, Manay Edith & the midwife had a compromise for the latter to go to our house to assist in the baby delivery.) And so, the story goes:

The midwife stayed [in our house] for the night. The expectant mother expects to expel the bulging part in front in the early morning. But around 4am, we heard *pong!* The water bag ruptured, so everybody roused from sleep! I accidentally stepped on the snoring midwife, who was sleeping beside me. She later said that she had difficulty sleeping. *Tse!* How could she say that, when she was snoring, breathing through one side of her mouth, then the other. Like the way papa did, *aha, aha!*

And so the story goes: *Alas!* At about 7am, the baby had not come out yet. *Ay,* difficult, wasn't it? The mother heaved hard. Only the baby's behind was showing. Among pregnant women, it's called breech frank. We were so worried big time. Yes, we were. The mother was told to eat one half-done boiled egg, supposedly to make the baby easily extricated, and the eggshell to be thrown out the window, carefully so as not to touch the window sill or anything on its way. They also gave her the juice extracted from the leaves of *kanyos* [a native legume known as black-eyed peas]. Rx of mama dearest.

But to no effect. So, all the crew members packed up, bound for the provincial hospital at about 8am.

10am, the birth. Cesarean, *man!*

Prid finished college[82] in 1980 and eventually married Manny Vitug, a Tarlaqueño (from Tarlac, Philippines), in 1985, then moved to Quezon City, there to raise their own family. By 1992, she had two lovable kids, Kay and Jonie Boy, in tow, whereas I migrated to Texas. Two months after my departure, she wrote:

---

82   Divine Word College of Legazpi (south campus), corner J.P Rizal and Fr. J.L. Bates Sts., Albay District, Legazpi City, https://www.dwc-legazpi.edu/

(rough translation)

Were you to ask Jonie Boy, the top tune for him would still be *O Giliw Ko, Miss Na Miss Kita!* [*My Love, I Miss You So!*—a hit song at the time] Really, we are missing you. You know what, I dreamed that you came back home because of homesickness. *Ngeek!* You had $1,000. If I were a *jueteng* [an illegal numbers game] expert, I would have placed a bet. We could not see you off at the airport, for it rained hard on your departure. The kids got sick. Now they are fine. I am a very busy mother. In fact, I don't have time anymore for TV guesting or movies. "I'm a full-time mother, family is my priority [mimicking a celebrity interviewed on a Philippine talk show]."

Have you adjusted [to your new environment]? I hope you will write to us about the [fighting] cocks there. I mean, about the Texans.

We are fine, and hopefully Manay Mameng and Dimple, too. Kay is doing well in her studies, though her dad has so much expectation [from her]. As of the 1st quarter, she was 4th placer. Would you believe she is Most Behave[d] in her class! Her teacher even posted her picture near the door of her classroom. "She is good academically but shy in expressing what she knows." That's her teacher's comment on her [report] card.

Bye, bye, Manoy, & may God bless you always and [stay] always healthy.

Kung si Jonie Boy ang haputon mo, top tune pa rin niya ang "O giliw ko, miss na miss kita!" Really, we are missing you. Aram mo, nangaturugan ako saimo, uminulî ka na daa due to homesickness. Ngeek! May dara ka daang $1,000. Kung ako matibay tumayâ sa jueteng, tinayaan ko na. Dai na ako nakahatod simo, sa grabeng uran kan mahalî ka na. Nagherelang an mga akî. Ngunian okey na sinda. Very busy mother pa rin ako. In fact, I don't have time anymore for TV guestings or movies. "I'm a full time mother, kasi priority ko ang family ko, e."

O, ano, adjusted ka na diyan? Sana, suratan mo naman kami tungkol sa mga "manok" diyan. I mean, sa mga "Texans."

Okey man kami, I hope sa Manay Mameng man. (Si) Kay is doing good in her studies maski medyo grabe an expectation ni papa niya. As of the 1st quarter, 4th placer siya. Would you believe, most behave(d) siya sa klase nakapaskil pa nganî an picture niya sa may labasan ng room. "She's good academically but shy in expressing what she knows." Yan ang comment ng teacher sa card.

Bye, bye Manoy & may God bless you always and (stay) always healthy.

Then the Vitugs fell on hard times; Manny had a heart attack. Fortunately, he slowly and steadily recovered. Kay went to college, and occasional letters from Prid detailed family goings-on. Meanwhile, cyberspace and internet became the in-culture. Shortly after the worldwide web permeated humanity's social consciousness and stole from us the drive and eagerness to write letters manually, Prid's output dwindled to a trickle, and one of the last ink-and-paper handiworks she wrote to me, on December 5, 2001, was this.

(rough translation)

Pardon me if I just recently had the time to write to you. As ever, I'm very much preoccupied with so many things. I'm still with Philamlife with sideline as a bookkeeper in Bulacan [a province in Luzon, Philippines].

Manny's condition is OK, although he will now take his [maintenance] medicine & vitamins for life. Kay is in star section [best class] this year. Oni [Jonie] Boy says his sister looks "like books" already. Indeed, the moment she arrives home from school, she immediately studies and reads. The only chore she does around the house is washing the dishes. Great! By the way, Kay says if ever you ask what she wants for presents, I should say

Pasensiya na talaga kung ngonian lang ako nagkapanahon na makasurat saindo. As ever, I'm very very much preoccupied with so many things. I'm still with Philamlife saka may sideline as bookkeeper sa Bulacan.

OK naman ang condition ni Manny, although ang medicine niya & vitamins – for life na niyang iti-take. Si Kay nasa star section na this year. Sabi ni Oni [Jonie] Boy "mukhang books" na daw ate niya. Pag-abot-abot pa lang sa harong from school, study na naman yan o magbabasa. The only chore na naitatabang kaiyan ay maghugas nin plato. Grabe! Sabi palan ni Kay, if ever daw na maghapot kamo kun ano ang gusto niya, sabihon ko daw Harry Potter books. Maski nabasa na niya an 4 books kaiyan gusto pa niyang magkasadiring libro, child-like pa maski second year high na.

Si Oni Boy naman, iba na ang interest. Linkin Park fan na yan. Mga music na haboon ni papa niya. Well, sabi ko generation gap.

Kamo, how about you with Dimple?

Harry Potter books. She has read the four books [at that point in time], but she wants to have her own copies. So child-like for a sophomore high school student.

Oni Boy has a fresh interest now. He's become a Linkin Park fan. The music which his papa doesn't like. Well, I say generation gap.

How about you with Dimple?

Kay and Oni have now both finished college, each having their steady job. Dimple herself graduated in April 2015 from the American Academy of Dramatic Arts[83], and in June from St. John's University[84], New York—two degrees, in one fell swoop.

Remember Boy, the relative and Tatay's apprentice who carried Prid on his shoulders in 1965? Last time I heard, in the 80s, he moved to Laguna and worked in the Canadian Embassy. Pancho studied Engineering and worked for a while as Head Surveyor at Sunwest Water and Electric Company, based in Ortigas Center, Pasig City; in the time of the pandemic, he frequents Catanduanes, and goes home to his family and ailing mom as often as necessary. Otê finished Agriculture, rendered public service for years, and now has been a government retiree from the National Irrigation Authority since 2008. Merl is a schoolteacher in Lupí, Camarines Sur, while our elder sister Piping is also a schoolteacher in Albáy, the two of them now retired since 2008 (Piping) and 2016 (Merl). That makes me the third educator in the Morada Clan, myself having been a Math-Science-Religion-Music teacher, also retired since 2018, in Brownsville, Texas USA; in 2019, I moved to Woodside, NY, to be with Mameng and Dimple. Manay Nilda, Tatay's girl Friday, has been the unwritten property custodian of the Morada Clan to this day, even long after he and Nanay had passed away. And Prid? A single mom since 2015 when Manny passed away because of complications of diabetes, the youngest-named-after-a-typhoon girl majored in Accountancy and worked as Registrar for St. Francis Xavier Catholic School in Caloocan City for many years. In 2006, she passed the LET (Licensure Examination for Teachers). The 4th educator in the Morada Clan, Prid retired from service during the pandemic's sway in 2020.

The shoulder ride might have given Prid a head start. Perhaps an advantage, a boost to good luck, a suggestion to greatness, a predisposition to destiny. And, for sure, a higher-level view of things. Nanay knew how it could be done. ∎

Shoulder Rider, as she looks, multi-faceted, today

---

83   American Academy of Dramatic Arts, 120 Madison Ave, New York, NY 10016, USA, https://www.aada.edu/.

84   St. John's University, Queens Campus, 8000 Utopia Parkway, Queens, NY 11439, https:// www.stjohns.edu.

11
TEJAS
Friendly State becomes second home

You haven't heard of **Sam and Miguel**, have you? It's a Filipino movie not worth watching, pardon my opinion. But into my first year in the United States, in the year of our Lord one thousand nine hundred and ninety-two, I and my teacher roommates George Doloroso, Eugene Mangsat, Ernesto Ibarra, Adlai Saniel, and Rogie Legazpi at Borders Apartment #502 in Brownsville, Texas, enjoyed watching the shenanigans of two garbage collectors of Manila—that's the movie, in a nutshell. The worthless became appealing and worthwhile.

Indeed, it was the type of movie that I, a month earlier while still in the Philippines, could hardly indulge in, *bayadán mo man akó*, even if you paid me to watch it. In the first place, Regal Films, a Filipino movie company known at the time for producing inane song-and-dance movies, crafted it. Second, it starred Vic Sotto and Joey de Leon, co-hosts of a long-running noontime Philippine TV show, *Eat Bulagâ*, through which they regurgitated their goofy jokes and slapstick comedy and turned them into mass-appeal flicks through movie companies such as, of course, Regal Films. But as we huddled in the living room of our apartment in early September 1992, **Sam and Miguel** appealed to our emotions. Whoever rented the VHS tape was a patriotic genius. If the hill will not come to Mahomet, Mahomet will go to the hill.[85] The Philippines came to us through the VHS tape. Thanks, Mother Lily Monteverde and Regal Films!

We heard our tongue spoken. We gawked at the familiar sights and sounds of home. The streets of Manila, the vendors and their sundry ware, the ubiquitous jeepneys and buses, the snarling traffic, the slums, the crowds, the shopping malls, the people—in short, *our* Philippines. Wonderful!

It wouldn't take any stretch to understand why. In August 1992, I was one of 25 white-collar professionals, mostly teachers, who emigrated from the Philippines to work in the public-school system of the United States. Filipinos on a roll, our eclectic group came from the length and breadth of the Philippine archipelago. It was many firsts for most of us. First travel and first job overseas. It was likewise the first time to be separated from our immediate families, and our first immersion into a foreign culture and school system.

Culture shock was apparent the moment we boarded the China Airlines plane, Flight 826, at the Ninoy Aquino International Airport bound for Houston TX on August 18, 1992. On board were 18 Filipino teachers: Perlita Andres, Nemia Bagtasos, Emee Cabañero, Judith Cunanan, George Doloroso, Eleonor Felicilda, Ernesto Ibarra Jr., Rogie Legazpi, Eugene Mangsat, Nancy Martires, Ester Mejia, Arcádio Morada Jr., Leilani Olaires, Maria Oropesa, Armand Ramones, Maribel Reyes, Rose San Diego, and Vic Sinining. In particular, though it wasn't my first time to be on an airplane, the twin-aisle Airbus A310 was simply too overwhelming.

---

85   Francis Bacon, *Essays of Francis Bacon,* Chapter 12: Of Boldness, http://www.literaturepage.com/authors/.

During the stopover at Chiang Kai-shek International Airport in Taiwan, Rogie and Vic had to go to the comfort room to pee. "Hey, from here and now on," smart-alecky Ester said, "call comfort room *restroom*."

Okay, got it.

A few moments later, the two guys came out of the restroom—happy now, Ester?—and announced to the whole group in mock trepidation, *"Oy, ang urinal nila, alam kung tapos ka nang umihì!"* [Hey, their urinals know if you finished peeing!] They were referring to those urinals with infrared sensors that flushed automatically when you moved to leave, invented in the 1980s but at the moment still unfamiliar in the Philippines.

Our port of entry was San Francisco, California. The lines at the Customs and Immigration checkpoints were orderly such that we were officially *inside* the United States in no time at all. SF was, however, just a stopover because we were to fly to Denver, Colorado, and then board another plane for Houston, Texas, for the last leg of the journey. Meanwhile, there was ample layover time to enjoy at the San Francisco International Airport. Like jittery and excited children in Fantasia, we were scampering about and tinkering with Vendo machines in one moment, and the next moment posing for pictures of our arrival in front of whatever signs that had the words WELCOME, SAN FRANCISCO, U.S., or AMERICA.

The last stop was Houston, Texas. As our final connecting flight descended onto Houston Intercontinental Airport, the cityscape bedazzled our insular eyes, while the vast expanse of infinitesimal dots of lights over megalopolitan Houston mesmerized us. Alvin Tolentino, son of Ms. Florita Tolentino of Multicultural Education Consultants, otherwise known as OMNI Consortium[86] (our official job recruiter), fetched us from the airport and took care of us *mga bagong salta sa* America.[87]

Alvin Tolentino and company practically toured around downtown Houston as they took us to our temporary accommodations. We gaped and marveled at the skyscrapers, flyovers, and stack interchanges of the largest city of the United States in area. "Oh my God," I thought as I gawked, "America the beautiful, the awesome!" So emotionally overwhelmed was this Bicolano from the boondocks of Albáy that I could not contain my excitement when I called my wife Mameng for the first time since departure. Sobbing, she asked if I was actually in America because it sounded like I was just calling from Quiapo, Manila. "No, sweetheart," I said, "I'm in Houston, Texas now!"

The next five days saw us departing for South Texas in staggered numbers. Vic and Armand flew on Day 2. On Day 3, the rest of the group departed, except five—Ernesto, Ester, Maria, Nancy, and me. We stayed in Houston for five days. Perhaps Ms. Tolentino immersed us longer in the megalopolis on purpose, to allow us to acclimatize and rub off all the excitement, before taking us to the less-mesmerizing South Texas. So, on August 23, Alvin Tolentino herded us, still Houston-awestruck, to the Rio Grande Valley, our ultimate destination.

"Giddy up, Cowboys!" Ernesto said in jest, as we were boarding the small Southwest Airlines plane bound for the Rio Grande. "Old West, here we come!"

---

86   In later years, OMNI Consortium and Ms. Florita Tolentino would be embroiled in teacher-trafficking controversies. "Starting in 2001, the private contractor Omni Consortium promised 273 Filipino teachers jobs within the Houston, Texas school district—in reality, there were only 100 spots open. Once they arrived, the teachers were crammed into groups of 10 to 15 in unfinished housing properties. Omni Consortium kept all their documents, did not allow them their own transportation, and threatened them with deportation if they complained about their unemployment status or looked for another job." In 2004, OMNI Consortium/Multicultural Education Consultants faced charges of exploitation in recruiting teachers for Texas from the Philippines, https://inthesetimes.com/working/entry/16738/trafficked_teachers_neoliberalisms_latest_globalized_labor_source.

87   *mga bagong salta sa America* [Filipino] – newbies in America.

"Texas is *Tejas*," Ester said, volunteering a factual necessity for the moment. "It's a Caddo Indian word for friends."

"Immaterial!" Ernesto said. "All I can now touch, see, and smell is the almighty dollar! *Woo-hoo!*"

"That sounds ignoble!" Maria said, concerned and irritated. "We came for a higher purpose, ladies and gentlemen!"

"You should have gone to England, Mary, where the pound is mightier than the dollar!" Nancy said in her *provinciana*[88] accent. Everybody laughed, while Maria kept mum in her seat.

"Do you know that in the 18th century, during Spanish colonial rule," Ester said to pacify the situation, "Texas was known as *Nuevo Reino de Filipinas*, New Kingdom of the Philippines?"

"*Huh?* Really?" I said, unaware of the trivia. "Interesting!"

"And if you look at the map of Texas, the southernmost point is Brownsville—*tipotex*[89], as they call it. That's where we are going."

Brownsville is in the Rio Grande Valley. I conjured images from the Western movies **The Way West** starring Kirk Douglas and **Rio Grande** starring John Wayne as our small plane was landing at the Valley International Airport in Harlingen, TX. So, this was the semi-desert Valley, where cowboys, prickly pear cacti, mesquite trees, rattlesnakes—and jobs galore—were waiting for us. "What makes the desert beautiful," said *The Little Prince*, "is that somewhere it hides a well...."[90] Would that the well hidden in beautiful Brownsville ooze with the promised jobs we were after!

There is no place on earth too far or too remote for a Filipino. That may not always be true, but it is certainly true with Brownsville. As of the latest statistics, U.S. Census 2010 data,[91] about 525 Filipinos live in this city by the southern tip of Texas, eight thousand miles away from their motherland, the Philippines.

The Philippines is a country in the Southeast Asia/Pacific region. An archipelago of 7,107 islands, cultural and ethnic diversities characterize it, the bigger islands having their own unique cultures, traditions, dialects, and tribal subcultures. They cluster into three island-groups: Luzon in the north, Visayas in the middle, and Mindanao in the south.

Philippine culture reflects over three hundred years of Spanish colonization. The country had been under the colonial rule of Spain from the 16th to the 19th century, and evangelized by the Spanish friars, thereby becoming the first Catholic nation and the cradle of Christianity in Asia. As can be expected, Catholic religiosity and piety are predominant among Filipinos. They have Hispanic surnames, celebrate fiestas, go to churches constructed with Spanish architectural designs, and commemorate Catholic solemnities, feasts, memorials, and holy days. Other cultures, however, have their own vestiges of influence on Philippine cultural life. The *bayanihan*—spirit of kinship and camaraderie that the Filipinos are famous for—is from their Malay

---

88   *provinciana* [Spanish] – provincial, feminine gender; *provinciano*, masculine.

89   *tipotex* – acronym for "Tip of Texas," which refers to the city of Brownsville, TX.

90   Antoine De Saint-Exupery, *The Little Prince,* Chapter 24. Poetry Fountain, http://www.poetryfountain.com/littleprince/chapter24.html.

91   USA.com, "Texas Filipino Population Percentage City Rank," http://www.usa.com/rank/texas-state--filipino-population-percentage--city-rank.htm.

forefathers. Close family kinship is a Chinese heritage, and so are *pancit* [92] and *lumpia.* [93] Other religious faiths with smaller numbers are also prevalent, like Islam in Mindanao, representing 5% to 7% of the population. Wherever in the Philippines, hospitality is a common denominator in the Filipino character.

Foreign rule (Spanish, American, Japanese) and contact with multi-racial merchants and traders culminated in a unique blend of eastern and western cultures of the Filipinos. The Aeta or Agta (*Negritos*, as the Spaniards called them) were the earliest inhabitants, coming through land bridges from the Asian mainland. Then came the Malays from the Malayan Peninsula. The present day Filipino results from intermarriages of indigenous and different nationalities like Japanese, Spanish, American, Arab, Hindu, and Chinese.

Filipinos speak eight major languages: Tagalog, Bikol, Ilokano, Kapampangan, Pangasinense, Cebuano, Waray, and Hiligaynon. There are at least 120 dialects and 111 linguistic, cultural, and racial groups. Based on the existing Philippine languages, *Filipino*, the national language, developed; it is a standardized variety of Tagalog, enriched by the other Philippine languages. For over three hundred years, until the early 20th century, Spanish had been the *lingua franca.* [94] However, an overwhelming majority of Filipinos are fluent in English because of American colonial influence in the country's education system. Thus, the 1987 Constitution has designated Filipino and English as the official languages of the Philippines.

Filipino Americans are Philippine-born immigrants or naturalized American citizens who are of Filipino ancestry. Known as Fil-Ams, they live mainly in the continental United States. They make up the second largest group of Asian Americans and the largest group of overseas Filipinos. About 73% of Fil-Ams are naturalized United States citizens.

Filipino migration to the United States was first documented in the 16th century, with small settlements beginning in the 18th century. However, mass migration started in the 20th century after Spain ceded the Philippines to the United States.

Most Filipino-American communities are strongly middle class. Their representation is high in service-oriented professions such as healthcare and education. Enterprising Filipinos own businesses, like restaurants, oriental stores, or even recruitment agencies for white-collar professionals from the Philippines. Because of the need for teachers, especially in Math and Science, there has been a substantial number of Filipino teacher recruits in almost all states.

In 1992, the Omni Consortium of 2600 N. Gessner #264, Houston TX, headed by Mrs. Florita Tolentino, recruited 25 Filipino teachers for Brownsville, Texas.

Tipotex.

I t was hot, like the Philippines in summer, but not as humid, when the first group of 18 out of 25 teachers first set foot in Brownsville. "Every house is air-conditioned," I wrote in my very first stateside letter to my wife. "Everybody has a car, except us newly arrived Filipino teachers. There are a few public buses, rarely seen and on scheduled runs. You can't just go anywhere anytime you like, unlike in Manila where buses and jeepneys are available anytime and everywhere you go."

---

92   *pancit* [Filipino] – thin rice noodles with soy sauce, sliced meat, shrimp, Chinese sausage, chopped vegetables.
93   *lumpia* [Filipino] – spring roll made of thin crepe pastry skin called "lumpia wrapper" enveloping a mixture of fillings such as chopped vegetables, minced meat, and shrimp.
94   *lingua franca* [Spanish] – a common language used as medium of communication by people of diverse tongues or speech.

In another letter, I wrote, "Brownsville is a plain, no tall trees, no hills or mountains as far as the eyes can see. Man-made lakes known as *resacas* dot the place. They have two shopping malls, Sunrise and Amigoland.[95] No tall buildings, though. Most structures are cubical, like boxes. There are no slum areas like those that we have in Manila. Few pedestrians cross the streets. People are respectful and disciplined in offices, malls, supermarkets, restaurants, and movie-houses. '*Thank You*' and '*Have a nice day*' are common courtesies."

Food was cheap, especially produce and Valley-grown fruits like oranges and grapefruits. Electricity was cheap, too. Basic services were fast. It did not take long for us to find available living quarters and settle down, and landlines for our phones got activated in less than a day.

While acclimating and familiarizing ourselves with the new culture and environment, we spent the first week after arrival applying for jobs. We could not have been luckier, as we came at a very opportune time. Schools were opening the following week, yet there wasn't any reason to panic because many available teaching positions in the Brownsville Independent School District[96] were still unfilled, as announced on the Main Office bulletin board and the district website. The announcements also said that there was still a great need for Math, Science, and Reading teachers.

I was banking confidently on my qualification as Math teacher, having graduated with a bachelor's degree in education with Math as field of concentration, and previously taught the subject in reputable private schools in the Philippines. Interviewed at Cummings Middle School on Tuesday, August 25, I was immediately hired by Ms. Estella Aguirre (principal) and was told to report for work the following day. Most of the other Filipino teachers got similarly hired in various schools in BISD and a few in the neighboring Los Fresnos Consolidated Independent School District.[97] However, two ladies in the group, Maria and Nancy, had to struggle harder and wait for several more weeks before getting hired.

Amidst the frantic job hunting, a Hispanic American named Abel Ramirez Gonzalez[98] played a significant role. Abel had administered the FAST (Functional Academic Skills Test) to us in Manila back in April 1992, since it was a required test for foreign nationals aspiring to teach in America. Himself an educator all his life, Abel was Ms. Tolentino's operations manager in the Rio Grande Valley, on whose shoulders she placed the responsibility of securing employment for Filipino teachers brought to Texas by her recruitment agency. Right after our arrival in the Valley, the indefatigable, uncomplaining, ever-smiling, and accommodating Abel, with his son Xavier, daughter Erika and her husband Pat, would take us from one school to another as we sought interviews with prospective employers. No, jobs were not waiting for us with open arms; we had to strive hard and put our best foot forward, and Abel sweated it out with us, ever ready with his useful tips and hints. As we hunted for teaching posts, Abel encouraged, supported, sympathized, cried, and laughed with us all throughout. He had been our guiding force, the wind beneath our wings, so to speak. He went the extra mile around the Rio Grande Valley, boosting the morale of new arrivals and still-jobless Filipino teachers.

Being hired was short-lived bliss. For us who got in with little difficulty, first week on the job was no easy street, more like being under the sea when you didn't know how to swim. First day of classes was less than a week away. We hardly knew what students we would soon meet. With just a week on U.S. soil, most of us had barely assimilated the Texas public school system, let alone the cultural mores of Brownsville, the Rio Grande Valley, and Texas as a whole.

---

95   Amigoland Mall was closed down in early 2000s, because of declining clientele.

96   BISD, 1900 Price Road, Brownsville, Texas 78521, http://www.bisd.us/.

97   LFCISD, 600 N Mesquite St, Los Fresnos,TX 78566. http://lfcisd.net/.

98   Mr. Abel R. Gonzalez passed away on July 25, 2021. He is succeeded by his daughter Erika Ileana Gonzalez Garza as the President (CEO) of WECS, Worldwide Educational Consultant Services, Inc., which "specializes in providing fast and accurate credential evaluations and transcript analysis from foreign countries." http://wecseval.com/.

In America, or at least in Texas, parents don't spend a cent in sending their children to public school. From pre-kinder till high school, tuition, books, and bus service are free. Those who want can even avail of free breakfast and lunch, even snacks during free tutoring sessions on campus. The Texas Education Agency administers state-mandated tests annually, not only to evaluate student cognitive applications but teacher performance as well; therefore, test preparations for students occupy the top berths, unwritten, of most school curricula. Math, Science, Reading, and Language Arts get much emphasis and priority, as well as Sports (P.E.). Music, I would soon find out, received less importance, if at all. Morality and ethics subjects per se were non-existent. (In our younger days in the Philippines, we had *Good Manners & Right Conduct*, right from the 1st grade.) In this foreign culture of expansive privilege, two-pronged accountability, cognitive emphases, and broad liberality, would it be lambs or wolves coming to us as we waited at the classroom door on our first teaching day?

I wondered if it was just me, but I saw outright a bold, liberated, and tolerant America. In shopping malls and other public places, teenagers would kiss and make out in full view of everyone, yet everybody couldn't care less. It was very customary to hear '*How are you doing*,' '*Nice to see you*,' and other pleasantries, but so were cusswords and profanities. Right from the first day of classes, students could get so emboldened to speak out their minds that it was sometimes difficult to distinguish between forwardness and disrespect. To anyone with conservative, third-world upbringing like me, my first school days in America were a struggle and a re-examination of big moral issues.

Students at Cummings in 1992 were 95% Hispanic, the rest Anglos, Asians, and African-Americans. In one Math 7 class, I had 13 students, all Mexican migrants, who could neither speak, read, nor write English. We (they and I) simply could not communicate with each other, so my 50-minute period with them was truly dire hell. One day I thought I could use a little Spanish (*"la lección de hoy…"*) but it did more harm than good. From then on, they would mimic me and my accent, and my frequent get-back defense was to make them solve algorithm problems on several pages of their Math workbook, or give them several worksheets with kilometric exercises. *Hablo español un poquito; estoy produciendo un monton de idiotas.* (Sorry, no translation necessary.)

Seriously, I voiced out my concern to Ms. Estella Aguirre, the incumbent principal, who said she'd look into the matter. It turned out that the school counselor, who took charge of scheduling, presumed that *Arcádio Morada* was Latino, owing to my Hispanic name; hence, the Math class of Mexicans. And thenceforth, Lionel Richie's **Stuck on You** became my theme song.

There was a lighter side to being a newbie *pinoy*[99] teacher in America, too. Twice in a row, on the 2nd week of teaching at Cummings, funny things happened in my Math classes. One day, I was explaining the distributive property of multiplication when one boy came up and insisted on his own method, which his teachers taught him in Mexico. I told him that the strategy at hand was much better, more fit to his grade level, yet he still insisted. So, in desperation, I said, *"Bahalà ka sa bu'ay mo!"* [Do what you want with your own life!] At another time, in another Math class, after my explanation of another strategy, my Tex-Mex students appeared unconvinced, so I said, *"Ganyán talaga 'yan!"* [That's how it really is!] Of course, on both occasions, my students just gaped at me in wonder and surprise. Thereupon, the first group of students said, "What'd you say, sir?" The other group took the matter to the next level as they said, "We know it; you're throwing us bad words! We're gonna tell the principal!"

Vic Sinining's anecdote was classic. A flamboyant Visayan *pinoy* with a contrived British accent, BISD hired him to teach Language Arts in Hannah High School along Price Road, Brownsville. He was in the

---

99   *pinoy* [Filipino] – colloquial; a term of endearment, a demonym for Filipino/s; sometimes the female form, *pinay*, is used.

middle of his lesson when some students, fanning themselves with their hands, said, "Teacher, it's too hot in here!" So, Vic modulated the thermostat of the room's AC unit, then continued teaching. A while later, the students said, with their arms crossed on their chest, quivering, "Teacher, it's too damn freezing in here!" Again, interrupted teacher grudgingly went to the thermostat. Of course, after a few minutes later, the students said, "It's too hot! How can we ever have a nice temp around here?"

Vic said to himself, "This is too much! *Mga hinayupak na 'to, reclámo nang reclámo!*" [Assholes, ever complaining and complaining!] He then tried to translate his thought as he said in his British accent, "Why do you keep on…"—here he stalled, as he groped for the right word to use for *reclámo*—"Why do you keep on… reclaiming and reclaiming?" (In Filipino, *reclámo* means complain; therefore, *reclaim* seemed like a good-enough, rather perfect-sounding translation at the moment!) I could imagine the students gaping and snickering in amazement over the enhanced translation. Indeed, why did they *reclaim* and *reclaim*?

Students and co-teachers alike would, to my wonder, frequently ask about my favorite color. In no time did I find out that *morado* is purple in Spanish. In no time, too, did I become known on campus as Mr. Purple. That was how I wallowed in my newfound belongingness to the rainbow. Again, I sang Richie's song as the moniker stuck.

By mid-September, certain concerns were on top of all newly employed Filipino teachers' priority list: (1) taking up university courses to fulfill the academic requirements for teacher certification stipulated by the Texas State Board of Education, (2) acquiring official service records from the Philippines, (3) establishing credit, (4) owning a car, (5) looking for a separate apartment unit or acquiring a house for those of us whose families were to arrive from the Philippines shortly, and (6) learning how to drive and passing a driving test to acquire Texas driver's license. Those of us who never drove a car in the Philippines, like me, had to take a crash course in driving so that they wouldn't be literally left behind.

The Texas Education Agency needed our employment service records to determine our individual salaries. Initially, they allotted us the prevailing entry-level salary across the board, which at the time was $21,000 per annum. TEA had to know our previous employers and their accreditation status; our salary rate could go higher if we previously came from TEA accredited schools. Other factors, like Master's and Doctorate degrees, could catapult our rate up the salary scale.

Despite documents I turned in, however, TEA did not grant me any increment in my final salary rate for 1992. It concluded that Xavier School and St. Agnes' Academy, my previous employers, which were both reputable and accredited private schools in the Philippines, were not on the list of TEA's accredited schools. On the opposite side, those of us who came from Philippine public schools received enviable salaries because, to TEA eyes, any public schools anywhere in the world were intrinsically accredited schools.

Excuse me, TEA! I thought in exasperation. *Xavier School, St. Agnes' Academy—non-accredited?* This was unjust. Accreditation was tantamount to higher pay, which means mine would be much lower than those fellow teachers with the same years of experience in Philippine public schools. Xavier and St. Agnes were matter-of-factly high-performing institutions, duly accredited by the Philippine Association of Accredited Schools, Colleges, and Universities. I was utterly miffed.

If you felt your salary was problematic and frustrating enough, here's the rub. Try looking at the emotional side of the job you were being paid for. Just halfway through September, the dirty slip was already showing. Classroom management had become so difficult and stressful that I developed Monday-phobia, if you know what I mean. I felt no more joy and idealism in teaching during the day, nothing to look forward to when I went to bed at night. Several times I would call in sick, with no sickness, just the desire to stay in bed all day.

After I gained my Texas driver's license, I called in sick one overcast day, borrowed a friend's second-hand car, then drove the long stretch of Boca Chica Blvd, leading to the deserted and undeveloped Boca Chica Beach. There, I sat alone for hours, staring at the sea and listening to the waves, and recalling the only other time in my younger life when I skipped school—by hiding under a bridge. [See **Iron**, page 24.] I was then a student, and my teacher was the cause; this time, I was the teacher, and my students were the cause.

On account of their crucial age, most of my middle-school students were disrespectful, rude, and disruptive in class. They came to my class unprepared, fooled around during my lesson, disregarded classroom assignments and homeworks, passed love notes during class, and tattled during recitations. They spoke vile language, answered back, and given any chance, used stink bombs, bubble gums, or paper projectiles—even chalkboard erasers—to malign and humiliate the teacher. All these I experienced firsthand. Of course, there were sweet and nice and respectful students, too, just like everywhere else, but it was easy to opine why teachers in America got paid a lot more than their Philippine counterparts: Equal pay for equal work. Elsewhere, you worked in the vicinity of heaven. Here, you got paid more not only for teaching but also for suffering and surviving at the same time.

Students behaving thus, and salaries being inequitable, September 25, 1992, was a historic day, nonetheless. It was the very first time I got paid by Uncle Sam, through the Texas public school system.

Right after receiving my paycheck, I had a desperate, pissed-off, crazy idea. No, not to call in sick. I was planning, really contemplating, to fly back home to the Philippines for good, telling nobody, not even my wife. I booked a flight to Manila via Continental Airlines. Because of the short notice, I was told that the earliest available flight was on September 30, arriving in Manila on October 1st. Fare $643, confirmation number IWR2CH.

It looked like the absurd dream of Prid, my youngest sister, was coming true, after all. [See **Destiny**, page 54.] In a letter to me in October [see page 57], she revealed, "You know what, I dreamed you came back home because of homesickness. *Ngeek!* You had $1,000." (She might have been dreaming this while I was planning the runaway.) After paying bills and the plane ticket, I really had that measly sum left on hand.

Wait, I thought: How would I start a new life in the Philippines with barely $1,000 left in my pocket? Instead of Lionel Richie, this time I heard Maria von Trapp in the movie **The Sound of Music** sing in my ears, mockingly, "I Have Confidence!" Like her, I was so scared of the unknown. Like her, I asked *about my future*. Mine and that of my family, too.

On September 27, Sunday, three days before my scheduled clandestine departure, I went to St. Mary's Church early and prayed for discernment doubly hard. It was the eve of the feast day of St. Lorenzo Ruiz; he is the protomartyr of the Philippines and patron saint of the Filipinos. (In 1987, I wrote a song to honor him on his canonization that year.[100]) Also, Lorenzo Ruiz is the patron saint of all Overseas Filipino Workers. So, on the eve of his special day, the OFW in me was asking God, through the Blessed Virgin Mary, John the Baptist, and Lorenzo's intercession, to help me make sense of what was going on in my life.

The help I needed came most unexpectedly. A delivery truck drove by #502 Borders Apartment, flaunting, "Blue Bell Ice Cream!" Is that it? Sometimes the simplest thing is the antidote to the craziest idea! I strode to Sunrise Mall (a ten-minute walk from Borders Apartments), looked for the ice cream parlor, and bought a cone of Rocky Road. It melted my blues and crazy idea away; reason and common sense prevailed. *Nahimasmasan!* [Came around]. Later in the evening, I phoned Continental Airlines, canceled my flight reservation, and asked for a refund. I vowed to stay put and told myself: *God bless me, I will survive! I will live to tell the tale!*

---

100 Arcádio Morada, Jr., *tagaalbay*, "Lorenzo Ruiz, Santo!" YouTube video, 3:35min, https://youtu.be/ZHJGYIzuRro.

When I returned to my apartment after Rocky Road in the mall, my roommates were passing the hat for Nancy Martirez. She had been jobless for more than a month now. Her roommates decided not to charge Nancy her share of their apartment monthly rent. To pitch in, those among us from the whole batch who had their first paycheck passed the hat around for her survival in the U.S. Despite Abel Gonzalez's constant help, Nancy remained jobless and demoralized.

Ms. Tolentino's Multicultural Education Consultants, and all recruitment agencies for teachers to the U.S., should have seen to this: recruit teachers for America with at least a tolerable command of the English language as one of the foremost considerations. Nancy could hardly land a job up to this point because she, applying as English teacher *in* America, had a heavy Filipino accent. She was a Bicolana from Catanduanes province.

My carpool guy was Visayan and definitely had a heavy accent, too, but at least he did not come here to teach. He came as dependent of his wife, a nurse. If you were a Filipino professional in America, most likely you were a teacher or a nurse. And if your spouse was jobless, carpooling was a viable supplemental means of livelihood, since there was a constant stream of new *pinoy* teachers and nurses hereabouts. We, car-less newbies, depended on carpooling to and from school, the church, and the grocery store. Carpooling charge was $120 a month per person. More mobility, more pay.

Newly recruited teachers' hardships and challenges were a given. Early on, we had to grab every opportunity to engage in diversions from our hard knocks, stress-laden life in America.

One Saturday, October 16, our group's carpool guy transported us to South Padre Island for the first time, as his birthday treat. SPI is a narrow island along the Texas coast in the Gulf of Mexico. It connects to the mainland through a long bridge that looks like the EDSA-Ortigas flyover, only that it is about two miles (3.2 kilometers) long. The trip was significant because it was my first getaway in two months since I arrived in the United States of America. Up to this point, all we had was a subtropical workplace called Brownsville. The treat was a totally refreshing, wonderful time, a welcome break after two months of tiresome and emotionally taxing school work. Other carpools joined the treat.

The caravan drive going to the island, to us first timers, was an awesome experience. We had to pass through a semi-arid wilderness of prickly pear cacti and sandy plains stretching as far as the eyes could see. We watched as blackbirds and hawks flew as we drove by their habitats. The 27-mile well-paved road was a comfortable and scenic 30-minute drive. As we approached the Texas shoreline, we passed by a wide stretch of land submerged in shallow tidal water, where people caught crabs by using strings baited with, we learned later, raw chicken flesh. (*Sosyál na alimasag,* classy crabs! Wouldn't they bite for less than chicken dinner?) Then, as we ascended the flyover bridge, known as Queen Isabella Causeway, we could see the South Padre Island skyline. There were a few tall buildings[101], mostly condominiums, hotels, and inns on it. Though very narrow, about half a mile across, the island is a well-developed resort and tourist paradise.

Upon disembarking from our carpool guys' vehicles, the first thing that met us was the cold sea winds coming from the Gulf of Mexico. We noticed a lot of birds on the shore—seagulls. I thought, *So, these are the birds immortalized in the book* **Jonathan Livingston Seagull**, which I read in college in 1972. Some picnickers would hold morsels of bread in their hands, and the birds would caw and swoop up the bounty. It was a beautiful sight—seagulls a few inches above your head hovering and flying away with your feed.

---

101   In 1992, the Bridgepoint Condominium on 334 Padre Blvd was the tallest building on South Padre Island, with 29 floors, https://www.emporis.com/statistics/tallest-buildings/city/102206/south-padre-island-tx-usa.

Orâ sâdi sa Pilipinas [None like these in the Philippines], I thought. The wide stretch of chicken-hungry-crab-infested shallow salt water, the Queen Isabella Causeway, the barrier island called Padre, the Gulf of Mexico, the cawing seagulls—these were, for us, some of the new sights and sounds of America the Beautiful. Someday soon, our respective families would be here to enjoy them, too. By then, they would be the new *mga bagong salta sa America* who would experience culture shock and first impressions like we did.

On another day, Judith, Perly, Rogie, and I went to Amigoland Mall, courtesy of a new Mexican acquaintance. She toured us around downtown Brownsville. We went to the Brownsville Museum then proceeded to the mall, where my group had a grand time shopping for Christmas gift items at JC Penny and Dillard's. At lunch time, we clamored to eat at an elite restaurant in the mall called Wyatt's Cafeteria, where people in formal attires dined. Everything went fine except that about thirty minutes into our lunch, there were two American male customers who had a verbal argument that turned physical. Then one man pulled out his gun, whereupon everybody panicked and scampered around for safety. People instinctively dropped to the floor to seek cover under tables, chairs, or other furniture—everybody, except the *Pinoys*, us. When we realized we were the only diners still seated, we dropped to the floor, too, involuntarily. *"Ano ba ito?"* [What is this?] Rogie said, more amused than nervous. Really, Americans in gowns, tuxedos, and formal suits flat or crouched on the floor, under tables and chairs! Then, Perly, who was a doctor-teacher, said, *"Yung kamera! Litratohin natin!"* [The camera! Let's take pictures!] She fumbled for her camera, but mall security police arrived, mediated in the squabble, and quashed the fun. Gradually, everyone rose from the floor, regained their composure, and resumed eating. Everybody was too alarmed and shocked to smile—except the Filipinos. We were laughing our hearts out.

Remembering this incident could make us laugh afterwards, out of naivete or stupidity, while other experiences made us cry out of shame. It was one thing to see about the Philippines *in* the Philippines, and another to do it on the global stage.

One weekend, it surprised us to watch on TV a Tagalog movie with English subtitles. Entitled **Lucia**, it starred Lolita Rodriguez and Gina Alajar. Though it showed cherished familiar places in Manila such as the iconic Quiapo, the movie also sensationalized the garbage dumps and the scavengers at Smokey Mountain, the slums of Tondo, the whores of Ermita and Mabini. For a while we felt we were in the Philippines, but unfortunately the movie did not make us feel good inside, like **Sam and Miguel** did a few months back. **Lucia** showed the wretchedness, the poverty, the dirt, the slime, the hunger, and the sufferings of the poor *pinoy*. It was a movie by acclaimed director Lino Brocka but because of his untimely death in 1991, Mel Chionglo took over the helm. For the first time, I fully understood why Chairman Manuel Morato of the Censors Board would excise or ban movies like this: too realistic and honest for comfort, beclouding any redeeming value it might have. This was not doing any good for the global image of the Philippines. For the first time, I felt embarrassed as a Filipino. For the first time, I wanted to butcher those filmmakers who, in their desire to achieve stark realism, destroy my Filipino dignity in foreign eyes.

When I went to work the following day, a co-teacher approached me and said, "Is that how things are in the Philippines?" Suddenly, I became nationalistic, defensive, and emotional.

I couldn't help it, Your Excellency Fidel Ramos, President of the Philippines. I realized that regardless of whether you like it or not, anything Filipino in a foreign land carries the name and dignity of the Philippines, and once that thing gets stained by any means, it affects every Filipino, including the ordinary Filipino in you, Fidel.

Fast forward twenty-four years later, 2016. Rodrigo Duterte becomes the President of the Philippines. (He prefers to be addressed as "Mayor", never formally like Your Excellency or any of that sh*t, as he would call formalities). My co-workers in LFCISD seemed to take pleasure in saying to me, "I saw the Philippine president featured on CNN. He has a mouthful!" Suddenly I became nationalistic, defensive, and emotional, trying hard to not prolong the conversation. I might as well have been faceless.

But standing up for national dignity was the least of my concerns in 1992. Grappling with homesickness was rather on top of the list.

Welcome to the war. ■

CULTURE SHOCK *and* BROWNSVILLE FIRST IMPRESSIONS

Texas, Here We Are!

Abel R. Gonzalez
Ever indefatigable, uncomplaining, smiling, and accommodating

Touring Downtown Houston, August 19, 1992. From L-R, Eugene Mangsat, Ester Mejia, Nancy Martires, George Doloroso, Nemia Bagtasos, Rogie Legazpi, S. Boyles (owner of the teachers' temporary quarters), Ernesto Ibarra Jr., Emee Cabañero, Leilani Olaires (kneeling), Eleonor Felicilda (kneeling), Maria Oropesa, and Arcádio Morada Jr.

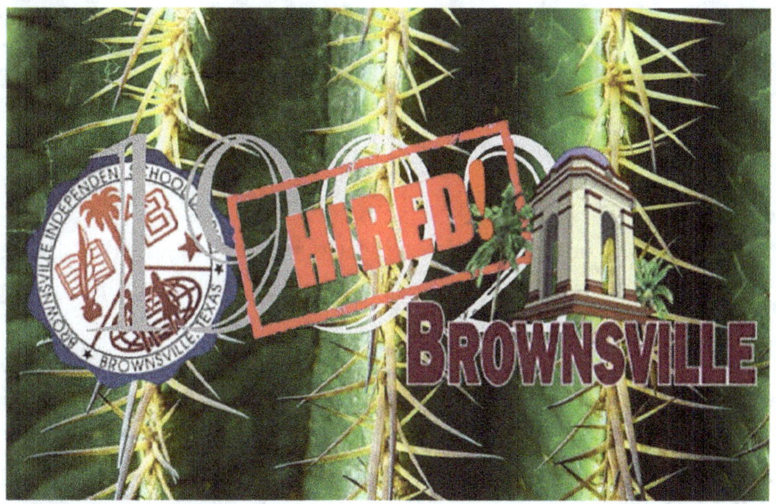

12

GUERRA
Absence and distance put up a fight

Miss you! You must be missing me too, but I say how you long for me won't ever be deeper and more intense than the way I feel as I am writing to you now. My eyes are welling up. Timely, and rightly so, because it's the start of *Semana Santa*[102] in the Lenten season of the Catholic Church, when reflection, passion, suffering, remorse, and prayer occupy our days. While the Christian world was commemorating Jesus' triumphal entry into Jerusalem today, Palm Sunday 1993, I got so homesick, I let off some steam by writing this inconceivably long letter to you.

"You" means you, my beloved Mameng, and baby Dimple—together, the sun of my days and the moon of my nights. At first, before my departure for Texas, I thought it would not be so difficult to be far from you, and I would not long for you that much. But that was wishful thinking. So far from the truth.

If a week passed without receiving a letter from you in Manila or my siblings/relatives in Albáy, or even from any of our friends and acquaintances anywhere in the Philippines, my longing for home became even more intense. I thought it was driving me crazy, and eventually killing me. That was more like it, closer to reality.

Postal letters and telephone landlines were the major channels of communication with you, the latter as the faster and more efficient. I wish there were other ways to get in touch with you faster, more efficiently, and less costly. My telephone bill for September 1992 was $260. For September 5 alone, the longest time we talked—37 minutes—I paid $42.35. But that's okay; I am not whining. I'm waging a war, and it's not a cheap war.

One time, we were talking on the phone, and you placed your receiver close to Dimple. I heard my baby babble. Would that present-day tech savvies, gearheads, and geniuses come up with gadgets that one day allowed us not only to hear the babble but also see who was doing it—for free![103] That would be the day! *Tsk, tsk,* we'd say 1992 was such a distant era, light-years away!

Without such amenities, writing letters for home and expecting letters in return had been my chief preoccupations to ease my longing for you. In one melodramatic letter, I wrote, "I had a dream last night. It was, of course, about Dimple and you. She was so cute, healthy, lovable, cuddly, kissable, and so smart for her age, and you were always beside her. *Bagá katotoó na nasa ampangán ko kamóng duwá ni Baby, ináaduk-adukán.*

---

102   *Semana Santa* [Spanish] – Holy Week.

103   Modern cell phones equipped with audio-video apps, were to take decades to come out, and Mark Zuckerberg was just eight years old, I suppose not even dreaming of Facebook and Messenger yet!

Dahil siguro ta kamó saná an lamán san isip ko kayâ akó pinangaturugan." [It seemed so real, you and Baby in front of me. I kept on kissing both of you. I might have dreamed of you because you were always on my mind.]

Through the letters from you, I could cull between the lines how you yourself were waging your own war not only against homesickness, but even more so against annihilation. You soft-pedaled me into thinking everything was fine with you, but I could see clearly the sacrifices you were doing to make ends meet after I left for the States, to survive on your own.

One Saturday in mid-September 1992, they aired the movie **Not Without My Daughter** on cable TV. The movie touched a sensitive chord, making me cry. I thought of your anguish as Dimple, at two weeks old, struggled for her survival because of sepsis at Lourdes Hospital in Mandaluyong, Manila. I thought of your sacrifices as you subsisted on *sergeant-at-arms* and *payless*[104] for weeks on end, in order to scrimp and save for Dimple's baby formula until you received the money that I sent from my first American paycheck in September. Yes, sweetheart, you'd do everything and anything for your little one; you couldn't simply live without your daughter. Neither can I live without Dimple. Not without my daughter!

Through our letters, we updated each other on current happenings in the Philippines and the U.S. What is the latest national news on the political scene? Who is the current box office star? What are the nice movies now showing here or there? Oh, don't forget to watch **Sister Act** and **Live Wire**. You should not miss them.

As you can see, I have brought the movie buff in me to the U.S., though nowadays I prefer to watch movies on VHS in the comfort of our apartment rather than on the big screen. My roommates and I would usually take turns renting VHS cassettes of Tagalog movies from the local oriental store. If you recall, I was still there in Manila with you when the movie **Sam and Miguel** was shown in SM cinemas, but we didn't waste our time on it. Wonder of wonders, when we watched it here in Texas, we liked it a lot!

Here in Brownsville, they call their movie-houses Cinemark. Oh, I miss SM cinemas, or Philippine theaters, in general. You stay in for as long as you like, repeat the movie for as many times as you like. That's not how it is here; they want you out of the theater after every screening. Besides, our theaters are so much better in quality, and bigger, than Brownsville's.

I went to Cinemark on the 3rd Saturday of September to let off steam. (Releasing pent-up emotions is becoming my way of life nowadays.) Clint Eastwood's **Unforgiven** was showing. One of my ESL (English as a Second Language) Math students at Cummings Middle School was with a group of Mexican teenagers playing rowdily in the Games Arcade beside the movie box office. Thank God, he didn't see me; the least I wanted to have on a fun Saturday like this was a distraction from an unruly and garrulous student like Mauricio Guerra.

The ads and posters of coming-soon movies in the theater lobby were too colorful and interesting to pass up. Just five minutes before screening time, I walked by the concessionaire and spotted another student whose name I could never ever forget: *Lyka Cantu*. She was with a group of girls her age, eating popcorn. She spotted me, too, whereupon she cupped her hands around her mouth and told the other girls in a hushed yet still audible voice, "That's my Math teacher!" *Patay malisya*[105], I pretended not to notice her and went on my way to the auditorium. In the corner of my eye, I saw and heard the girls laugh boisterously at what Lyka had just told them.

I could figure out exactly what funny thing she said. Two weeks earlier, in my Math class, after writing some lesson notes on the blackboard for the class to copy, I returned to the teacher's desk and sat down for

---

104   Euphemisms, concocted by our house help Belen, for Ligo sardines *(sergeant-at-arms)* and inexpensive instant ramen noodles *(payless)*.

105   *patay malisya* [Filipino] – feigning unawareness.

a while. Then, just as I was about to stand to continue my lesson, something momentarily held my bottom down. Surreptitiously placed earlier on my seat while I was teaching and not looking, a huge freshly chewed bubble gum held me down! The class burst out in utter jubilation.

I felt so mad and humiliated, but the class snickered even more. In my rage, I forcibly detached my pants from the gum, stood up, straddled to the Intercom device on the wall, pushed the button, and said, "Principal please!" Ms. Estella Aguirre came straightaway to my classroom, but of course, her presence was useless. The class protected its own. A code of silence, etched in stone, was in full-force control. Nobody snitched.

Oh, correction, somebody later did. I had this nerdy boy, fortunately, who always carried a blue Post-it sticky note pad everywhere on campus. Trinidad Martinez was one in the minority who had been friendly with me from School Day 1 but so cautious as not to antagonize the unfriendly majority by giving any hint that they were on my side and that they liked to learn what I had to teach. In the afternoon of the gum incident, I found two blue Post-it notes among my stuff on the teacher's desk. One read, "Gum—Lyka Cantu." The other: "B more strict—Trinity."

In an instant, revenge-and-retribution-hungry blood rushed to my head. *Gago* [stupid], *stop, do not confront the girl!* I scolded myself and held my horses. *You are the adult, the authority, the professional! Do not go down to her level! Instead, closely monitor her behavior in class, and be extra cautious so as not to give her any more open windows and options to misbehave.*

And now, at Cinemark. **Unforgiven** was such an agony to watch because all I could think about was Lyka Cantu. So much for fun Saturday!

Looking back now, I believe the girl was hugely contributory to my "September Crisis." I wrote to you about this in one of my October letters. Work stress and class management problems simply piled up to such an uncomfortable degree that I willed to abandon everything, to surrender to failure, to get back to the Philippines, while telling no one—my roommates, my employer, Mr. Abel Gonzalez, Ms. Florita Tolentino, not even you. Sorry, sweetheart. I feared the unknown, so scared to death on the job was I, but hesitant to tell you because if I did, you might dissent and prevent me from going back home to you, moneyless.

What if I did actually go home? Would it have solved my problems? What if I conquered my fears head on instead? I ask myself as I continue writing this letter, on this Holy Monday. As Christendom remembers the Cleansing of the Temple, I remember looking at myself in the mirror, smiling, and saying, *"Gago!"* I smiled because my feet were still on Texas ground, thank God, trumping difficulties and still earning dollars for me, you, and our daughter. I would have made the most devastating and shameful decision in all my life if I had succumbed to my emotions and flown back to my nest.

Between Manila and Brownsville, TX stretched thirteen thousand kilometers of space. Between me and you, that physical space translated to a desperate longing for home. To abate that longing was no easy feat. But remember: I could not go home, then home should come to me. Make haste, my dear wife and my baby. Papa's waiting!

Baby Dimple's 6th month birth anniversary (on November 26) coincided with Thanksgiving Day. I wished I were there to celebrate that milestone with you. All I could do, apart from making overseas calls, was praying for baby Dimple's well-being and good and abundant life. "Thanks, Lord, for our little darling. May you continuously shower your blessings on her. Please grant her a long and abundant life. May she remain as healthy and lovable as ever," I prayed.

Recall that after Dimple survived sepsis, we took our one-month-old darling to the Church of Our Lady of Mt. Carmel in Quezon City. We prayed for Our Lady's intercession in behalf of our Dimple for her constant well-being, just like what my own parents did when I was young and suffering from asthma. In America, as I celebrated Thanksgiving Day, my batch of teachers and I went on a pilgrimage to San Juan, TX, about 50 miles from Brownsville. We visited Our Blessed Mother at the Basilica of Our Lady of San Juan del Valle, where once again I implored her and St. John the Baptist to watch over you and Dimple and keep you both in their care at all times.

There was a cold front in the Rio Grande Valley during that Thanksgiving Day. It was chilly, like "inside the refrigerator," as roommate Adlai, another teacher, put it. Even at noontime, we had to be in jackets. Temperature was low (though not freezing) both at daytime and night. Undoubtedly, chilly times were upon us during our first Thanksgiving and first winter in America.

The Pilgrims at Plymouth thanked Divine Providence for their survival during their first year in the New World. We *Pinoy* Pilgrims at the Rio Grande did just that, too. In 1992, we replicated a piece of American history in our little, if insignificant, way.

It is now Holy Tuesday as I write this part of the letter. On this day, Jesus went with his disciples to the Mount of Olives, which was east of the Temple overlooking Jerusalem. Here, Jesus delivered the Olivet Discourse, an elaborate prophecy about the destruction of Jerusalem and the end of the age. Using parables, Jesus spoke about the end times events that included his Second Coming and the Final Judgment. He not only answered the disciples' questions, but presented practical lessons for those who lived at that period, encouraging them to be faithful, watchful, and prepared.

To me, the end times didn't have any immediate significance at this moment in my life. My personal sufferings preoccupied my psyche as I longed for home and for you.

Something would somehow mitigate such mundane sufferings and longing every time we *Pinoys* would gather around to party. Funny and blasphemous to even think of fun parties on Holy Tuesday! But really, during those first crucial months, we grabbed every opportunity, every occasion to socialize, to tell stories and work experiences, to share (potluck) and eat together. And, boy, where there were *pinoy* parties, there would always be food galore every time.

An Ilocano couple, *Manong*[106] Ros and *Manang* Ray[107], who by 1992 had been in Brownsville for 18 years, invited us to dinner one day. They owned a big house in a posh neighborhood called Brownsville Country Club, plus four other houses for rent. *Bigatin!*[108] The nice thing about this dinner was that they served us all-*pinoy* dishes: *pinakbet, dinuguan,* steamed fish, *kare-kare, menudo, et cetera.* It felt like home. After three months of nothing but American food, or what appeared to be *pinoy* cuisine, at long last we savored authentic *pinoy* dishes on a silver platter, literally. Afterwards, our gracious hosts even gave us a *pabaon*[109] of fresh vegetables from their backyard—*malunggay, ampalaya*[110], green papaya, eggplant, and okra. We returned to our apartment fully satisfied in the stomach and in the heart. We longed for the next party.

---

106   *Manong* [Filipino] – derived from the Spanish *hermano*; an honorific for an elder brother or any older male, commonly used in northern Philippines; female counterpart is *Manang*.
107   Mr. & Mrs. Rosauro and Raymunda Alibin of Brownsville, Texas and Batac, Ilocos Norte, Philippines.
108   *bigatin* [Filipino] – bigwigs.
109   *pabaon* [Filipino] – give-aways. provision (of money, food, or supplies) given to someone leaving or making a trip.
110   *ampalaya* [Filipino] – bitter melon.

Pinoy parties were neither trivial nor few and far between. Sometimes, they happened once or twice a week—a birthday bash here, a baptism there, an excursion somewhere. Notable was the "welcome party" tendered by the sisters *Manang* Bella and *Manang* Pura Luna, even if it was well into our 2nd month in Brownsville. We learned that the sisters, respected and respectable teachers both, had been education *bigatin* in the Philippines before migrating and working for almost two decades in Brownsville. The sisters chanced upon us at St. Mary's Church one Sunday, recognized the compatriots in us, then graciously invited us to breakfast, at the Valley International Country Club, on them. Again, the sumptuous merging of the stomach and the heart made for an unforgettable memory.

Someday soon, you'll meet *Manong* Ros, *Manang* Ray, and the sisters Bella and Pura. Wonderful people all!

Came December 1992. One night, as **Jingle Bells** played from my boombox on my study table, the telephone rang. I heard the receiver say, "Collect call from the Philippines. Do you accept?" But of course! Then I smiled from ear to ear as you responded "Hi, My Love!" to my "Hello, Sweetheart!" Aside from the long-distance kisses and the love-greetings, I told you with great excitement, "Christmas *na* Christmas *na talaga* [It's really Christmas] here in Brownsville. Wherever you go, you sense honest-to-goodness American Christmas. Genuine Christmas trees. Mistletoes. Poinsettias. Holly. Christmas lights. The colors red and green everywhere. Christmas sights and sounds. Of course, no snow and sleigh, no white Christmas in Brownsville. *Sana* [I wish], you and Dimple were here to experience with me my first American Christmas."

Such wordy sentimentality, despite the practical rule that collect calls should be short and snappy, like telegrams. But homesickness is not a practical war, either. In this war, the rule of the heart reigns supreme, regardless of time.

On the first week of December, Ms. Florita Tolentino, our job recruiter and owner of Multicultural Education Consultants in Manila, Philippines, treated us to an early Christmas Party at the Sheraton Inn Brownsville. She was leaving soon for the Philippines to give the FAST (Fundamental Academic Skills Test) on December 28 to teachers aspiring for U.S. jobs. During the party, Ms. Tolentino revealed that one Filipino teacher, not in our batch, had abandoned her job and was nowhere to be found. She is Josie Basco, a former Xavier School co-teacher. Tolentino related that even as early as the last week of September, Josie told her friends that she could not take it any longer—the job and the students were simply unbearable. Nobody knew where Josie had fled. She might be anywhere in the States except "the hell," as somebody among us put it, "that is Texas!"

Tsk, tsk, dalawa sana kaming Xavierian na nag-AWOL! (There would have been two former Xavier teachers who had gone AWOL!)

In mid-December, they showed "I'll Be Home for Christmas" on cable TV. I turned my TV off. *Duh!*

By December 16, Ernesto Ibarra, who occupied the first room with Eugene Mangsat and George Doloroso in our two-room apartment, was mad about our November phone bill. With due respect, considering that he previously agreed to use his name to register our Southwestern Bell telephone account, Ernesto was not fuming mad, just in-control mad. The reason was that, in the current phone bill, there were many unaccounted-for collect calls from the Philippines, no callers or recipients specified. "So, who's going to pay for these?" Ernesto asked. He knew all-too-well that as account-holder he had the responsibility to pay the bill in full, but he also knew for certain that Adlai Saniel and I, who occupied the 2nd room with Rogie Legazpi, were the frequent and customary recipients of collect calls on our apartment's common phone line. Therefore, Ernesto had the right to insist that Adlai and I should take charge of the unaccounted calls. However, I too had the right to protest and tell him I documented all my calls in a notebook—which I showed him as proof—and I would only pay for those which were specified on my list.

Before I go on, it is now halfway through the Holy Week, Spy Wednesday, as I write about Ernesto and our telephone impasse. Read on, sweetheart.

To stop the impasse, and to closely monitor subsequent collect calls from the Philippines, Ernesto had the telephone line in the living room and our room disconnected. The only line he left functional was the one in his room. Therefore, if Adlai or I wanted to make overseas calls or receive collect calls, we had to do it in *his* room. Nice! Adlai and I could still make calls, but who would, with *guardia sibil*[111] present and listening? I could not blame him, but two wrongs could not make a right.

Consequences? I could not call you on Christmas Day. Terrible! December 27, I could not even call you on our anniversary. Horrible!

The only solution was a separate phone line. On December 28, I called Southwestern Bell, which instantly activated my phone line, only for my use, inside my room. Too late for Christmas day and anniversary, however, and too early for New Year 1993.

Veni, vidi, vici! I came, I saw, I conquered. That sounded very presumptuous, like a swift, conclusive victory. It was anything but. *I came* to Texas. *I saw* America was not a bed of roses or a pleasant pill to swallow. *I conquered* not, but tried hard to survive this land of promise the best way I could—in 1992. Now the year was exiting. So were two teachers among us. Compared to the misfortunes of Vic Sinining and Maria Oropeza, my telephone blues were so insignificant, like poppable pubescent pimple in the face.

Vic, of "reclaiming" and *Pinoy*-British accent fame, took flight to Oregon during the Christmas break, abandoning his job, never coming back. We were told that whatever he would do and wherever he would be on campus at Hannah High, the poor guy was always the butt of malicious student jokes. We could only guess as to the ordeal that prompted Vic to do what he did.

Grapevines had it that one of Maria's students repeatedly asked to go to the restroom. Too young to be incontinent, and Maria had already given the boy permission four times. When the little brat approached her for the 5th time, the straw that broke the camel's back broke Maria's, too. "You can pee your pants, but I am not letting you go!" she said. So, the boy did what he had to do, as per suggestion—and more. He put his sweater and school stuff in the puddle of his urine. Maria, of course, had the shock of her life.

The next day, the principal summoned Maria to his office. The boy's parents were suing her and the school. However, the parents would drop the charges against the school only if it would fire teacher Maria.

In December, the school district asked Maria to leave. She left. Stealthily. We never heard from her again.

Naturally, Vic's disappearance and Maria's termination upset Ms. Tolentino. Their cases, besides that of Josie Basco, would have far-reaching effects in the hiring of Filipinos in Texas schools. They would now hesitate to hire more Filipino teachers, considering our compatriots' predicaments and courses of action. Bad news!

---

111   *guardia sibil* [Filipino] – literally, civil guard, in reference to the Spanish Civil Guard of old; derisively, someone who stands on guard, watchful or suspicious of others.

The good news is I still have my feet on Brownsville ground, struggling to stay firm, maintaining equilibrium—and surviving. If Maria, Josie, or Vic's shoes fitted me, God forbid, may God give me the wisdom to think and discern before resorting to acts that I would regret later. I will not sacrifice our future by giving up and going away from my job. Texas may be hell for some, but to me, hey, it's still *the* America that overflows with milk and honey.

It is now the evening of Maundy Thursday as I am writing this portion of my letter. I have just been to St. Mary's Church, for the beginning of the Easter Triduum. "The summit of the Liturgical Year is the Easter Triduum—from the evening of Holy Thursday to the evening of Easter Sunday."[112]

We still had classes up to today. Would you believe that, as late as Spy Wednesday, I was being observed on a 15-minute walk-through in my class by Ms. Lerma, my Math supervisor? How's that for close teacher supervision? Thank God, there weren't any gum-equipped Lyka Cantus, and the Mauricio Guerras kept their hands, feet, and mouths to themselves! I guess I impressed Ms. Lerma; she said so after the walk-through.

In the mass of the Lord's Supper this evening, I wished my students took the place of the apostles during the ritual of the Washing of the Feet. I knew for sure way over 12 individuals to handpick for that life-changing experience. I wished!

The rest of Maundy Thursday evening, I vowed to spend in silence. No unfit and unnecessary conversations, no TV (except Holy Week specials), no sleeping late. Tomorrow, Good Friday, I would suspend writing, devote myself to silent prayer and reflection, and on Black Saturday, I would join my carpool on the Stations of the Cross at the Basilica of Our Lady of San Juan del Valle in San Juan, TX.

Today, April 11, is Easter Sunday 1993, as I conclude this letter. I've just attended the Easter Mass at St. Mary's Church, thankful to God for the gift of salvation. Thankful, too, that in one month, you and Dimple will join me at last, as you said so in your last phone call. After all the pain, the tribulations, and the suffering that absence and distance wrought on us, we will be together again! No pain, no gain. No Cross, no Resurrection.

Likewise, after all the difficulties of my job so far, I am taking control of my professional life. With all the moral support which the Cummings faculty was giving me, especially Louie Leal and Shirley Bowman, I will strive to be better, not bitter. No problem is so epic as to render me a failure. I am good, and though I may not have the stuff of legends, I shall continue to pursue the American Dream.

As for the emotional department—*here we go again*—I shall quote a handiwork from my youth, **Ray a Bit of Your Sun**:

> My love, must I always have to be far away,
> Far from your heart's beating?
> Am I meant forever by your heart forsaken?
> Ray a bit of your sun, ray a bit of your sun
> Before my life is done!

---

112   United States Conference of Catholic Bishops, "Triduum." http://www.usccb.org/prayer-and-worship/liturgical-year/triduum/.

Oh, have you ever felt deep within you a longing,
Or must I still declare you are human to feel?
How can I live without your most precious affection?
With you I can go on; without you, how can I endure?

Yes, absence makes the heart grow fonder, to the point of death—I'm dying to have you and Dimple by my side, for without you, how can I endure? So, in that crucial meantime, write me a letter letter letter as often as you can, please. Call me, just call call call please. And have that Philippine Airlines plane flown to Texas pronto pronto pronto! *Sige ka, tibád sa sobráng kamunduán, agom mo magka-tililing tililing tililing!* [Beware, deep sadness might give you a crazy husband!]

Joke only, dear. Still, I pray to God that it would not happen to me. Our Lady and John the Baptist are always by my side. I will survive to tell the tale.

Promise. ∎

In 1992, I left my family (wife Mameng and baby daughter Dimple) in the Philippines for greener, albeit semi-desert, pasture that is Texas. Eventually they followed suit, after 10 months of juggling with the Philippine Bureau of Immigration, in March 1993.

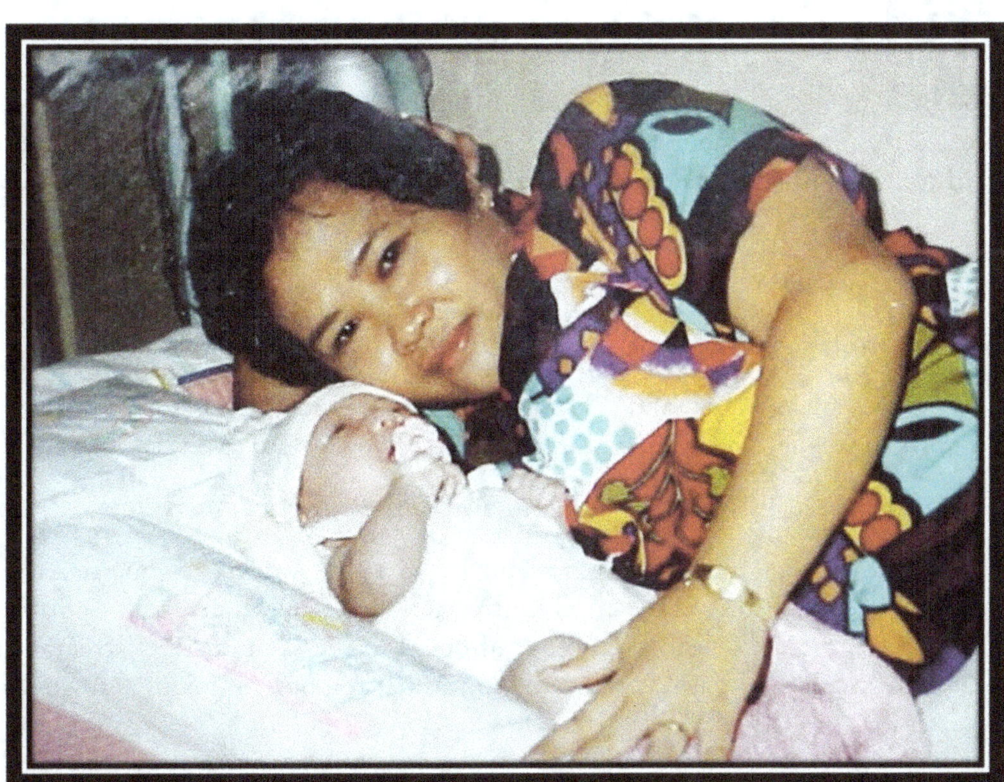

L-R: Rose San Diego, Maribel Reyes, Rogie Legazpi, and me, during Breakfast at the Valley International Country Club tendered by the sisters Bella and Pura Luna. "Who could say that I had a lot of problems with my students right now?" I wrote to Mameng on November 16, 1992.

13
GUARDIANS
Receive it / Share it

"When God tells us something, what do we do?" The visiting priest at St. Mary's, my parish church in the Diocese of Brownsville, posed this question at Mass. His homily was timely on Gaudete Sunday, the 3rd Sunday of Advent, described by Pope Francis as "Sunday of Joy." The visiting priest from Mexico continued, belaboring his question in his Hispanic accent. "How do we respond to the good news of Christ's first coming in the past, his coming to us in the present, and his final Advent in the future?"

In my silent confusion, mainly caused by the accent, I was paraphrasing his question my way: *How do we respond to God's message in our life?*

"By receiving it, and sharing it," the priest said, answering his own question as he continued his homily.

"On Gaudete Sunday and into Christmas, the Church presents to us the best models we can ever have on the ways to respond to God's message in Christ. Two models, two ways.

"The Blessed Virgin Mary and John the Baptist: *Receive it, share it.*"

In the Annunciation, Mary's receptivity to God's word is unquestionable, clear as day. The sudden appearance and greeting of the angel in front of her, of course, made her "greatly troubled." You and I would have reacted similarly, were we to be confronted in the same manner by such an apparition. But what sets Mary apart from the rest of us humankind was her response of joyful and wholehearted yes to God's plan of Incarnation through her.

> My soul rejoices in my God,
> my soul rejoices in my God,
> My soul rejoices in my God, my Savior!
>
> My soul proclaims the greatness of the Lord.
> My soul rejoices in my Savior,
> For he has looked upon his lowly servant.
> From this day, all generations shall call me blessed.
>
> The Almighty has done great things for me.
> And holy is his name.
> He has mercy on those who fear him
> In every generation.

He has filled the hungry with good things,
And the rich he's sent empty a way.
He has come to the help of his servant Israel,
For he has remembered his promise of mercy.

My soul rejoices in my God,
my soul rejoices in my God,
My soul rejoices in my God, my Savior!

-**My Soul Rejoices**[113], Song #87 from THE PURPLE PSALMODY
based on Lk 1:46-54

Of course, in Mary's mind and heart, there was never any doubt about God's omnipotence when she asked, "How can this be…?" She merely got curious about how God would accomplish it, since she was a virgin who had "no relations with a man."

Mary's virginity made her receptivity to God's message so pure. Her fiat—Mary's total and wholehearted yes, her absolute openness to the word of God—is so remarkable she is the quintessential Christian, a model to emulate. She received God's word totally such that it became flesh in her. So too must we be receptive to God's word such that we embody and live it.

If in Mary we have the best model on how to receive God's message, the priest continues, then John the Baptist shows us what to do next.

As Mary is the best example of pure receptivity, John the Baptist is the best example of pure voice. When asked to identify himself, John told the nosy priests and Levites, "I am the voice of one crying out in the desert, make straight the way of the Lord…" (Jn 1:23)[114] This voice, coming from a prophet, shared and proclaimed God's word.

"More than a prophet," the Lord said to the crowd, describing John in Mt 11:9-10. "This is the one about whom it is written: 'Behold, I am sending my messenger ahead of you; he will prepare your way before you.'"

"OK, Lord, got it," perhaps someone among the crowd bantered. "But, wait, Lord, I heard this guy is weird! He blurts out weird words, consumes weird comestibles, and dresses up in weird garments!"

Who are you, John?
What are you, John?
Are you the Messiah?
or Prophet Elijah?
Why do you talk
and look so weird?
Isn't it weird to talk and look like you do?

Hey, why be curious 'bout me now?
People, you worry 'bout yourselves!

---

113   Arcádio Morada, Jr., *tagaalbay*, "My Soul Rejoices." YouTube video, 2:36min, https://youtu.be/qOO5Tj7NDpI.
114   *New American Bible, Revised Edition* (2011), Saint Benedict Press, will be used throughout this work, unless otherwise stated.

The Lord is coming. Prepare his way!
Be good to one another now!

What should we do?
What could we do?
Is it not yet too late?
Don't you think it's too late?
How should we know?
Where should we go?
Can we not find divine helping hand in you?

Hey, someone greater than I am,
He is about to lead you now.
He will baptize you in his spirit.
You follow him more nearly now.

-Who/What Are You, John?[115]
from CATECHETICAL SONGS FOR CHILDREN (unpublished)

The Lord replied: "Amen, I say to you, among those born of women there has been none greater than John the Baptist; yet the least in the kingdom of heaven is greater than he."

John was the greatest prophet before Jesus, true, but he was as human as each of us. John was born without original sin, true, as Jesus and Mary were, but unlike them, he was, later on, subject to its effects. Simply put, John was mortal, like all of us, born of women. Therefore, anyone who is in "the kingdom of heaven"—though he might be the least in that realm—is still better or greater than John and anyone of us. What set John apart from all mortals was that he, in his particular time and place, prepared others for the kingdom of heaven by baptizing them and leading them to believe in the Messiah, thus serving as a model for believers of future generations. That's where his greatness lies.

John the Baptist was a staunch proclaimer of the Word.

John's mother and Mary were cousins. While Elizabeth was in her 6th month of pregnancy with John, the angel appeared to Mary and told her about the Incarnation. The angel also told her about Elizabeth's condition. So, in haste, she went to visit Elizabeth to help. As the cousins greeted each other joyfully, John leapt inside his mother's womb—responding as he received God's word while he was yet unborn. Receiving the message in his mother's womb, John later on proclaimed it out into the world.

Elizabeth was well aware of the grace that visited her. Joyfully she told her cousin Mary, "Most blessed are you among women, and blessed is the fruit of your womb!" In response, Mary sang her Magnificat: "My soul proclaims the greatness of the Lord!"

Mary proclaimed the Good News.

The priest concluded his homily, saying, "May we all imbibe the example and guardianship of Mary and John the Baptist in our lives."

---

115   Arcádio Morada, Jr., *tagaalbay*, "Who/What Are You, John?" YouTube video, 3:06min. https://youtu.be/ GHsJm0MII8g.

ith that said, it's easy to see why I believe in the presence of the Blessed Mother Mary and St. John the Baptist in my journey of 71 years—and counting—from Talôtô, Jovellár, Sipocot, Colaclíng, Daragá, Manila (Philippines) up to the Rio Grande Valley and Brownsville, Texas, and Woodside, New York, USA. My life and the respective lives of my family, which I have recounted here, are so intertwined with our spiritual consciousness of Mary and John that it is impossible to have written this entire Purple saga without mentioning them even cursorily. I believe their presence and guardianship have made this collective story of our lives less drab, more writeable, and therefore worthy to share.

Coincidence? Happenstance? Excessive presumption? Self-righteousness? Call it what you will, but I call it faith. ■

MARY & JOHN—Guardians of My Diaspora

14
PORTAL
Even when it's dark, there's light

You might not believe how public school children in America think in spiritual terms—at least in our little corner of the State of Texas called Olmito. Well, I myself had no idea at first; therefore, the following profound thoughts that came forth from the mouths of my young secular wards surprised me no end.

One afternoon, while driving home from work, I looked up at the sky and saw a most interesting sight. "Heaven-sent!" I said to myself. "That's so connected to my lesson for tomorrow!" Therefore, I stopped by the roadside and took pictures of it. The morning after, I flashed the captured sight on screen from our projector machine in class. I was going to use the image to introduce the African-American spiritual **Sun Don't Set in the Mornin'**. My music classes, kinder to 5th grade, were to sing the American folk hymn with differentiated activities, as planned.

"Tell me what you imagine, looking at this picture," I started it off.

Religious discussion was not the intent, nor would I interpolate and steer thinking towards that direction. I just let any thoughts pour out, which I wrote down, sifted, organized, and now enumerate, starting from the most obvious observations.

"Dark clouds," Osiris, a 1st grader, said. "A giant hole in the sky with light," Sarah, in kinder, said with confidence, echoed by many other students in the upper grade levels. "Light shining down on trees through a circle in the sky," 3rd grader Xiomara said. "Mad clouds!" Edgar, a 2nd grader, at times unfocused and inattentive, blurted out.

"Excuse me," I said. "Are we supposed to blurt out answers, to answer without being called?"

Next came the interpretations. "Sun is powerful!" Anahi, an energetic 1st grader, said. When classmates asked why, the girl said, "Because it makes a big hole through the clouds so we can have light!" "A fight between dark and light," Anne, a 4th grader, in a soft voice, said. Edgar the 2nd grader explained, softly this time, "The clouds are mad because they want the place all for themselves but there comes the sun!" "But even if it's dark," 3rd grader Addison said, "there's light in the world."

82

"It looks like a portal to heaven," Destiny's 5th grade mind expounded. "It looks like someone is coming, about to conquer the world!" Luis, a 3rd grader, said. "Looks like someone great is going to come down from above!" another Luis, a 5th grader, said in earnest, whereas at other times he always fooled around.

And then came the ethereal. "A person dies, and the light sucks him up and saves him," kindergartner Aaron said. "Someone is looking for people to play with because people are sometimes lonely," Jayden (1st) said.

Who's someone? It almost tempted me to ask, but I suppressed my tongue.

"God," 2nd grader Andrea, without hesitation, gave a name to the light. "God has been calling the people," Kayla (3rd) gave voice to the light. Therefore, "God is coming down," said Lizbeth (4th), as did Alina (2nd) who was sure that "God and angels are going to stop by and visit." "There is hope," Irma (5th) said, "Heaven is opening. God is coming!"

"Jesus is coming to sing a lullaby to everyone, because he wants everybody to feel better, even if the sky is full of clouds!" This was 5th grader Priscila's vision, which, in spite of its wordiness, has become my favorite of all.

"Mary and Joseph will sing a lullaby, too!" said Priscila's friend Emma.

We all ended up learning and singing the spiritual. Everybody's enthusiasm exhilarated and inspired me as I accompanied the singing on the keyboard. No one expressed dislike for the song, not even Glenn the 2nd grade Music-hater. The children were all animated as they crooned:

esus, son of David, have pity on me!" the blind Bartimaeus cried out loud as Jesus and his friends were on their way to Jericho. Many of them rebuked the blind man and told him to be silent. But Jesus heard him, stopped walking, and said, "Call him!" They did, whereupon Jesus asked, "What do you want me to do for you?" To which Bartimaeus replied, "Master, I want to see!"

Jesus granted his request. Bartimaeus saw the light of day. He saw Jesus and followed him. (Mk 10:46-52)

Jesus' friends at first wanted to disregard Bartimaeus' faith. They sure underestimated the power of his conviction. In the same manner, we sometimes underestimate the faith of our young public-school children. Modern culture, secularism, and legislations prohibiting prayers and religious activities in American public schools might have, with alarming success, retarded the growth of the mustard seed of faith in our young children. Yet they could not silence the children's voice of faith. God is light, and in him there is no darkness at all. (1 Jn 1:5) Like Bartimaeus, the children want to see. Our children in America are never too young to see Light.

At least the children in our little corner of the State of Texas called Olmito. ■

Like Bartimaeus, our children want to see. Our children in America are never too young to see Light.

AVOCATION
Till I bite the dust

he afternoon is cold, and you're alone. You turn the boob tube on. **Annaliza** greets you on the Filipino Channel, but you hate watching inane movies and telenovelas. A million other cable channels don't offer choices to your liking and interest, either, so... might as well do what you passionately love to do.

You turn your computer on and click your word-processer app. Nothing. Your brain is too hard put to transmit any word to your fingers. You turn to the internet and open Google's dialog box. You type the first thing that comes to your mind—"lonely boy." Hundreds of images of boys in various degrees of mental anguish appear in view. One particular image catches your attention, and you're instantly inspired. Then, with a little help from your photo-editing software, and with lots of imagination, the poor child is up and ripe for some reinvention. You redefine the poor child, thus:

<u>BALLAD OF THE LITTLE ORPHAN BOY</u>

See the little orphan boy as he walks down the street,
Dressed in dirty clothes, no shoes on which to lay his feet.
He's such a lonely picture of a life that has gone wrong.
How could he find his dreams without a home,
without a home?

His father and his mother were all gamblers, so were they.
From morning up to morning, they would gamble, day by day.
He would be left at home, nobody tending to his needs.
How could he find his dreams in such a place,
in such a place?

One night this little orphan boy,
He might have seen his parents home.
We never knew exactly what really happened there.
But all we know is that it burned with two people scorched along
While their little boy was on the street
with a match in his hand he was holding so strong.

So now the little orphan boy is out, as you can see.
But tell me, what's he out for, running after you and me?
He grasps his little stomach as he says to passers-by,
"Have pity, I've no breakfast yet!"
And afterwards he starts to cry!
Woo-oo-oo-oo-oo!
Shall we help?
Should we help?

Using your imagination, the boy metamorphoses into an orphan, a waif, an unwitting murderer. So much melodrama, the element in movies or telenovelas that you are shying away from, that you abhor. You then realize that this is life. Life is everywhere, whether you notice or not. And when you think your ordeal is over, it hits you with a moral question intended to appeal to your compassionate nature. *Aw,* come on, cut it, this is neither the confessional nor the pulpit—this is just the creative mind at work!

And as if the poetry is not enough, music follows in a couple of days. Where does creativity end and ennui begin? ■

UN'S UNE-ULY AUNT. This was the title of a post I wrote on my blog. I repeat—Un's Une-uly Aunt. You ask: Who? Whose aunt? What kind is whose aunt?

Those who know me personally can figure out the title in a snap. Those who don't... well, it sure looks like crap but, without doubt, striking. Puzzling. Intriguing.

Before unraveling the "mystery," may I digress and make a confession. *I lied.* In public, and globally, at that.

Two months ago today, I declared in anguished poetry on Facebook that I would not write again. Short of making a YouTube recording of my delirium, I wanted to say goodbye to an avocation that has given me immeasurable joy and fulfillment all my life.

<u>REST</u>

This is it.
My pen now halts to rest
Behind the jalousies of my mind.
It will from now on
purl no more for me.
It will from now on
set no more waymarks
Into the depths of my soul.

I do not regret.
My pen has served me
In hours of solemn solitude,
When nothing else I heard
But the persistent echo of my soul.
It has obeyed my commands
For reverberations.
It has put to wake
My hunger and dreams
With extreme satisfaction.
It has taught me perfect
Ventriloquism.
It has loomed and blended lines
Into ideas,
Pictures,
Sagas,
And
Personal histories,
Much more than I've hoped for.
It has provided milestones
For my own.

But all good things end.
I don't live in a vacuum.
I've created more sadness
than jubilation.
I have created more problems
than solutions.
Euphoria doesn't last.
In times such as now,
When voice falters,
When mind declines,
When emotion muffles reason,
When silence reigns,

My pen bids goodbye,
Though deep down it pains
To write goodbye:
Goodbye!

"Ono na namang kadramahan yàdi?" My wife Mameng, #1 fan and critic, wanted to know upon reading the distraught free verse. "What's all this melodrama about?"

Instantaneously, a few friends[116] showed up. Diana suggested, "How about 'until next time' instead... Perhaps taking a break from it for a little bit..."

Judith asked, "Why????" Mercedita more than echoed, "Why g'bye jun?" "What's going on?" Eleanor chimed in, as did Maria, who wrote: "Why do you bid goodbye?"

Indeed, I bade goodbye to writing, to end a passion, through that sulking poem. (*"Beautiful...,"* quipped Belinda; "[B]eautifully crafted," assessed Maria.) In it I whined, cried over spilt milk, and like a child, complained about a reader's frank and heartless feedback on a long article I previously posted on Facebook. He said, "I'm normally compassionate, not this time. Cut it clean and short—for your own good. No one has time to read your posts, idiot!"

My initial reaction to the scathing remarks beggars description. Dumbfounded, I deleted the comment outright, not only because of the name-calling. Truth hurts.

---

116   Angelina Mast, Sipocoteña, California resident

Ann Gutierrez-Ventoza, former workmate at Xavier School (XS), Manila

Bambi Lara of Los Angeles, California, former workmate at XS

Belinda Rios, workmate at Villareal Elementary School (VES), Los Fresnos TX

Diana Cepeda, workmate at VES

Eleanor Diaz, of Houston TX, former workmate at St. Mary's Catholic School, Brownsville TX

Ella Soriano, of Queens NY

Gina Rebancos, of Brampton, Ontario, Canada; former student at St Agnes' Academy (SAA), Legazpi City PH

Josefina Javier, classmate at Mother of Life Center (MOL), Novaliches, Quezon City, 17th Gen, Pilgrims

Judith Cunanan, of Harlingen TX, co-teacher, Batch '92

Leilani Umadhay of San Antonio TX, co-teacher, Batch '92

Lourdes Rocafort, of New Jersey, former workmate at XS

Maria Bulanon-Sarte, classmate at Bicol University College of Education (BUCE), Batch '74, former workmate at SAA

Masan Litonjua, former student at SAA.

Maura Tesorero, nurse/doctor and neighbor at Pompeii St, Brownsville TX

Mercedita Tabuclin, classmate at MOL, 17th Gen, Pilgrims

Nelia Ong, teacher and neighbor at Pompeii St

Salvacion Gaveria-Losantas, classmate at BUCE, Batch '74; former workmate at SAA.

Wilbert Yuque, former student at XS

The negative comment was one too many, reverberating loudly even in my sleep. It was the straw that broke the camel's back, the heap compounded by the deafening non-reaction and indifference of my online *readers* (translation: *friends*). Is this how they think of me?

Words of wisdom poured in to pacify my inner turmoil and reassure my flagging spirits. Wilbert wrote, "Just do what you do. People have the option of seeing less of what you post or entirely unsubscribing from updates you publish." This was seconded by Judith who said, "[W]hoever wrote that comment... is not even 1% of your readers. So, ignore. Let the good prevail! It's anyone's decision to read or not to read someone's posts. Don't be intimidated by anyone. Just keep on writing, my friend. Let your literary skills and your pen go to work again." In the same vein, Bambi said, "[K]eep writing. They who don't want to read your sharings don't have to, and whatever they decide to do is not your problem!" In three words, Leilani summarized, "Go for it!"

Lourdes suggested, "Ignore those idiots. They are not capable of comprehending what you're posting!" Ella weighed in: "No matter who you are, there's always a basher. Don't mind them because they're jealous and can't do what you can!" Ann regretfully said, "[N]o such ignorant soul should prohibit your passion..." Sympathetically, like all the others, Nelia avowed, "I enjoyed and will always enjoy reading your posts, Manoy. Don't let those haters win!"

Masan recommended, *"Sir, I-block mo sana su nagsabi saimo.* [Just block your detractor. That way,] We still get to read your posts..."

To further boost my morale, Diana said, "God has gifted you with a talent for expression through writing." Maria added, "Share the gift God has bestowed upon your creative mind." "Just continue doing what brings you joy," Salvacion mused. "Don't say goodbye, for you've inspired so many," Eleanor elaborated. "Your pen must not take a halt since it has served as your company while you're in solitude. That pen must continue to glide to create stories of your unreachable imagination and ingenuity. Through your pen, you have made inspiring songs, meaningful poems, and heartwarming stories that captivated and inspired others to write."

Bambi patted my shoulder, saying, "I appreciate your talents, Jun." "We appreciate you," Leilani patted the other.

In the meantime, past, present, and future got longingly expressed. Josefina opined, "OO NGA CLASSMATE NA MISS NAMIN MGA POST MO." [Yes classmate, we missed your posts."] "I miss your writing," Angelina revealed. And Maura predicted, "Gonna miss your writings."

Gina lamented, *"Sir, pawno na su mga fans mo?"* [How would your followers fare?]

I smiled. Comforted. Yet the turmoil continued, the spirits still flagged.

My shell is too brittle and too small for comfort. I project a pachydermal image with lame toes and onion skin. I'm a whiner, far too loud and too much, so much for so trivial a reason, so hard for so long. I always see the tiny black ship in a sea of white. I am an introvert; I am a pessimist—traits that rear their ugly heads in the things I write. That I often make a spectacle of my wretched self in passionate prose or poetry is what my detractors see.

I am always too wordy for comfort and clarity. (This post alone has 1,600+ words!) "No one has time to read your posts" can't get any closer to the truth. That I write long articles which turn off potential readers is what my detractors see.

To my readers, I harass and terrorize by forcing them to use the dictionary for highfalutin words against their will. That I'm not user friendly is what my detractors see.

To them, I am a despicable stickler for grammar. In this age of instants and short-cuts, I insist on the correct use of punctuations and words. My phraseology is alien and irrelevant to the cyber-generation. I feast on idiomatic expressions and figures of speech that netizens avoid, just as I avoid netspeak like the plague. To them, I am old-fashioned and arrogant, turning readers off. That's what my detractors see.

For two months now, I've fretted and trudged. Something was missing. With my wife, I took a jaunt to upstate New York, Washington DC, Philadelphia, Thousand Islands, and Niagara Falls, to derive some summer pleasures. Something was undeniably missing. We trekked down the cliffs of Watkins Glen and got ourselves dampened by the falling waters off the sides of its breath-taking canyon, taking a thousand and one selfies along the way. We enjoyed the view, and yet something was disturbingly missing. Then, to be thrilled to the bone, we rode the jet boat on the fearsome rapids of the Niagara Gorge. The jet boat ride thrilled us to the bone alright—but something was sorely missing.

Like the missing J's in the opening line. Obvious and devious. Puzzling and intriguing. Yes, Virginia, there is a Santa Claus, but there is no aunt, just jaunt.

Without J, the title defies logic and reason. Without my pen, I am lost and intractable. Put J in the proper places, and meaning falls into place. Give me the pen to write, and life becomes more colorful and livable.

In the long run, the words of my friends who showed care did not go empty, inutile, and unheeded. Not a scarecrow, I too have a brain; I just needed time to realize for myself that I was not beyond fruition. Therefore, here now Pinocchio returns. He vows to retrieve his pen, to write again, to ventilate his ideas and feelings through the single avocation he loves to do. May his nose elongate further if he so lies again!

To my friends who neither disdained nor abandoned me, but buoyed me up, despite my irrational emotions and kilometric scribblings, thank you very much.

To my detractors, who see my writings as nothing but lengthy babbles—well, it's your choice and, as Bambi said, it's not my problem. You are free to choose your pursuits and avocations, as I am free to express myself the way I see fit and to my heart's content. I vow to continuously improve my craft, to somehow even my output and your expectations, but there's no compromise between right and wrong. In all endeavors, good taste, ethical behavior, and God's precepts and righteousness bind you and me.

And to everyone, I vow to write till my pen runs no more—which is one way of saying to write till I bite the dust.

Contrary to what the Pinocchio in me said to not write again, which obviously is a big lie, I will. You can hardly end a passion, more so forget.

My pen will never again pretend to lose its will to purl, I promise. I have an endless ink supply, and nothing can deplete it. Nor by distraction prevent it—remember Jun's June-July Jaunt, my futile attempt to ignore the writing flare. The flare for writing may have momentarily gone dim on me, yet it brightens up at will. The flare, and my flair, for writing will stay deeply rooted in my being. You ain't read nothing yet.

THE FLARE AND THE FLAIR. I am not playing with words. I am playing on those two intangible ideas to help us understand writing a bit better. Be forewarned, though, that I am neither certified nor schooled in the craft, nor is this write-up a manual. However, I believe I have enough know-how to call a spade a spade; I strive to self-improve by practice and experience; and I am confident that by mustering a few insights and tips, I may move others not just to write but to write effectively and well.

To better grasp these ideas, let us liken writing to going on a trip. Everybody has had this experience, so certainly we know that in every trip we take, there must be the why, the how, and the where-to of it.

Suppose we want to go to New York. Perhaps for business or pleasure, to visit a relative or friend, to go on an educational/cultural tour, to watch **Wicked** on Broadway, to see up close the Statue of Liberty. There is always a reason for going. Nobody embarks on a trip without purpose, motivation, or driving force.

In the writing process, the fire, or the passion to write is the starting point (a writer is not weak-spirited). We need to have that burning desire to put our thoughts to visible linguistic symbols, to communicate our thoughts to others. With that passion, we rally our pen (and/or keyboard) to entertain, to inform, to instruct, or to persuade. That's the why—the flare.

How we want to get to New York depends on the means of transportation, plus other factors that affect the speed, length, cost, safety, comfort, or ease of travel. Some of us may choose to go by car, bus, ship, train, or plane. (Walking may look stupid and illogical as an option, but why not?) Whatever it is, the means of transportation we take determines how fast, how long, how easy, how comfortable, how enjoyable, or how memorable getting to New York will be.

In the writing process, we use skills and tools to accomplish our purpose. We are now talking about the rules of grammar, syntax, spelling, punctuation, the right choice and arrangement of words, style, brevity and conciseness, parallelism, figures of speech, idiomatic expressions, and other concepts that make writing more meaningful and effective. That's the how—the flair.

New York, of course, is the destination, the finish line. In the writing process, the finale is the written piece, the article, the hard copy, the brainchild—a visible incarnation of the inner workings of the brain. That's the where-to, the goal of every writer.

We may have a common destination, but the reason for going there and how much intensely we need to go vary from person to person. When we write, comparatively, our purpose for writing differs. A 5th Grade girl writes a "How I spent my summer vacation" composition for her Language class to tell a story. Her teenage brother writes a love letter to persuade, while her Dad writes a business letter to inform. Each accomplishes their respective writing goal according to their individual desire and capacity. Your flare and mine vary.

I drive my car; you travel by plane. I take longer; you're there in a flash. We differ in the way or manner we go. Writing follows a similar vein. Everyone expresses ideas differently, depending on the manner or mode at their disposal. In the wake of a tornado, for example, a boy tersely writes, "The winds uprooted the oak tree!" His sister, who also witnessed the event from a safe vantage point, is less frugal in her description, thus, "Like an angry giant of untold strength, the savage winds uprooted the old oak tree in our backyard!" Still another family member, their Mom, most flamboyant in her way with words, writes, "There is no denying the fact that these horrible winds that passed over us today were the hands of the angel of destruction, for in their wake the irreplaceable hundred-year-old oak tree in our backyard was humiliated and incapacitated like a seedling uprooted from its base! Too sad!" Your flair and mine vary.

When there is urgency to reach our destination, even walking due to unavailable or disabled transportation is better than not moving at all. We may reach the destination in an agonizingly long time, but at least we strive to inch forward; later, we can just run and skip and gallop or hitch a ride along the way. In the realm of writing, a friend and I may individually embark on a writing project, say, to write a novel. After some time, I may just be wrapping up my first chapter, while my friend is already making a hard copy of his brainchild. I need not lose heart, however; I can always correct and improve my writing task and speed. Your flair and mine are improvable.

There are many ways of getting to New York alright, but they are on a case-to-case basis. I lived in Brownsville, Texas, so there were many choices as to the routes I could take; land, air, and water means of transportation were available to me. Air and water means are the options for my brother José in the Philippines to reach the Big Apple. If Kree Whoever lives near Mt. Everest, reaching New York is his near-impossible dream. In the same manner, some people have all the skills and tools to write, others have limited competencies, while others have none. Writing can be effortless for you, hard labor for me, or painful torture for some others, not just because they have nothing to write, but more so because they don't have the flair to write. Your flair and mine, some time in our life, might not even be there.

Sharply said, if our flares differ in degrees of intensity, our flairs for writing differ in their degrees of excellence. To put it in another way, the beauty and effectiveness of our written pieces are directly proportional to the quality of our individual flairs. In a scale of 1 to 10 degrees (°), some of us may be ideally good at it (10°), most of us are less good (1° to 9°), while some 0° good—they do not have the flair at all, sorry to say.

Shucks, how so? Why may we not have it? How do we get the flair to write, in the first place?

We acquire the flair; it is not hereditary. It is a gradual process, taking years to develop. We might not have it some time in our life (that's when we have 0° flair), but we may still gain it if we so desire and work for it. However, we cannot acquire it overnight. It takes time to master linguistic skills and put them to good use.

We may learn the flair starting from our earliest social interactions at home, with our family, like when Mom introduces us to the wonderful world of ABC playfully using toys. More formally, we may learn the flair in school through our teachers. (*May*, of course, means conditional, depending on external factors and our readiness and openness to learn.) For example, I account for much of my being a stickler for grammar from my first-year high school English teacher—Mr. Arenillo (see page 33) of St. John Academy of Sipocot, Camarines Sur, Philippines. But I thank all my teachers, as we should without favoritism and exception, because every selfless effort they did in the classroom to enrich and promote our education—and our flairs—shouldn't go unnoticed and unheralded.

The flair is a developing process. Our zeal to read strengthens, supplements, and enhances our knowledge of the rules of grammar. You are a voracious reader because you know that, apart from its educational and entertaining values, reading helps you become a better writer. Through reading, you expand your vocabulary. Reading exposes you to new and varied ways of expressing your thoughts, and thus it widens your horizon. If you want to write, it matters that you read.

The flair is an ongoing process. My flair for writing did not start and end with sentence diagraming; rather, it has been ongoing, from my earliest years up to my highest education rung attained, and beyond. Our environment, our culture, our interactions with other people, our social life—these are other strong determinants of what and how we write, over and beyond school. I can talk about colonoscopy more effectively now that I already underwent one. A scuba diver can best describe the environment under the sea after diving. Lea Salonga can talk and write about the colors and nuances of musicals because she's been there. People in love write the best love letters. Of course, you can write through research alone, but better writers are those who write through their head, hand, and heart. You live it; you write it.

Some people argue it does not matter what language we use—English, Taglish, Spanish, Spanglish, hieroglyphic, cryptographic, technical, highfalutin, cyberspeak, whatever—as long as we get our message across. Other people, especially those engaged in social networking, argue that it doesn't matter whether we have grammatical errors or wrong uses of words in our online interactions, as long as we get our message across. Right?

Of course, the language we use matters. What use is a brainchild in Tengwar or Koyra Chiini if only J. R. R. Tolkien or the people of Timbuktu understand it? As for the argument that we can disregard rules of grammar and spelling in favor of brevity and speed in social networking—well, we can be brief and grammatically correct at the same time. There is always the danger of misinterpretation if we sacrifice rules of grammar, spelling, and punctuation for brevity. Besides, people will respect us more if in our online interactions, we—as a rule of thumb—don't forget good grammar, spelling, and punctuation. As **dramallama56** [a blogger] wrote, "Why do I care about any of this?? Well, here's why: I'M NOT GOING TO RESPECT YOU UNLESS YOU USE GOOD GRAMMAR. And other people won't either." We will do well heeding this advice!

The way we arrange our words to form sentences is important. A talented writer does so to express what he means in the best and most correct way and to get the best effect on his readers. Consider the following sentences:

- The ice turned the heat into liquid.
- The ice turned the liquid into heat.
- The liquid turned the heat into ice.
- The liquid turned the ice into heat.
- The heat turned the liquid into ice.
- The heat turned the ice into liquid.

Common sense dictates how to arrange the words to convey the right meaning. Unfortunately, lapses in common sense sometimes happen when we write, especially when our sentences are long, disoriented, and complicated. So, our writing effectiveness suffers. We organize our thoughts by properly arranging our words and sentences, and we increase our effectiveness manifold.

It is a rule worth remembering to carefully choose, use, and arrange our words when we write. The right use of words matters, as does the use of the right words and their best arrangement. "Knowing which word to use or how to write a phrase correctly can make a big difference in your writing."[117]

Every part of our written work should be apt and significant. My use of New York as our destination may seem random and trivial to the unmindful, but to the reflective mind it is the place of arts and culture; therefore, isn't that where we want to be as writers, physically and metaphorically? Our choice of words lends greater meaning and significance to our written work.

After all is said and done, we realize we give so much of ourselves when we write. When we immerse ourselves in this process, we subject our whole person to a task that strains us both physically and spiritually. We realize, too, that in the end, our handiwork is not just the sum of all our written words and sentences. If I am an effective writer, my total person will starkly peek in between the lines, and my voice will reverberate long after the last punctuation mark. So, considering all these, do we have what it takes to write? As in, do we have the why and the how to go to New York? As the famous song goes, "If I can make it there, I'll make it anywhere!" The workings of our brain need to incarnate. If we have the flare and the flair to write, we'll make it to our goal, right? Let's go prove it. Let's go write! ∎

---

117   Vicki Price, "Spelling is Still Impotent" (Florida Literacy Blog), https://floridaliteracy.wordpress.com/tag/bad-resumes/.

Mr. E. Arenillo, the very first
teacher who inspired me to write

16
HEART
Weighed and found wanting

Pandora's curiosity got the better of her. She had been asking, "What's in the box?" and nobody obliged. When she couldn't bear it any longer, she gave in to the lure of the box's key and lifted the lid. This, despite the god Zeus's warning not to open the box. This, despite her partner Epimetheus' admonition not to open the box.

Out of the box came the evil things the world would ever have.

Eve was no less inquisitive. God had warned her against eating the fruit of the tree of knowledge of good and evil. When the devious snake lured her into taking just a curious bite, she fell for it. This, despite God's order not to eat from the tree. This, despite her partner Adam's silent repudiation not to eat from the tree.

Out of Eve's own willful disobedience came the sinfulness and predisposition to sin that the world would ever have.

With the lure of temptation, Pandora and Eve disobeyed the warning. Both used their hearts, not their heads. Each of them did not have a pure heart.

We were born to, and inherited, the stigma of such an impure heart. The sacrament of Baptism cleansed it at first, and thereafter, the sacrament of Reconciliation cleanses it again and again, because the predisposition to sin exists throughout our lives. We are and always will be predisposed to sin. Unabated by our own free will, sin is the force that pushes us to death and perdition.

Pandora and her offspring had Hope. Eve and her offspring—ourselves—have the Christ. Fortunately. ■

I remember the day too well in the summer of '62. I was in the elementary grades in Sipocot, Camarines Sur. It should be vacation time, for there was no school, and everyone in the family was at home doing their chores. Outside our house, on the wall, was a sign with big, bold, embossed tangerine letters that read MORADA'S TAILORING, and inside, business was lucrative and booming. Now, Tatay was making measurements for the new customers in our living room cum tailoring shop. Manay Nilda, Manoy Olding, Boy, Enyong, and Jaime—apprentices, resident tailors, all relatives—sat behind their Singer machines, each busy sewing slacks, shirts, or denims. Nanay was into making button-holes and buttoning, while Piping, my elder sister, was in the kitchen cooking lunch with Nanay's instructions. The younger children, Otê, Merl, and Prid, were just as busy playing in a corner of the house, while I did "gardening." I was planting corms of *natóng* or taro plant in our marshy backyard.

From nowhere, this scrawny middle-aged lady, who introduced herself by the name of Tomasa, arrived at the shop looking for Cadió. She said that she'd been on the road for several hours now, too haggard to continue. Somebody in the past informed her that Cadió had a tailoring shop here in Sipocot, so she dropped by to say hi. Of course, Tatay recognized her and did not just allow her to say hi—he invited her to stay for lunch. That stirred matters in no trivial way.

For Tomasa turned out to be one of Tatay's flings in his youth. Young Arcádio was a handsome, virile man; it could be no surprise if she had ever fallen for him, or he for her. From her fiftyish looks, we could still see the tawny face of the young Tomasa in the old woman seated with us at the dining table. It was a pleasing face, flirty yet no mean, although now it was pale and famished. Life had not been very kind to her.

Tatay sat at the head of the table. On his right were Nanay, Prid, Manay Nilda, Merl, Piping, and me. On his left was Tomasa, directly across Nanay, followed by Boy, Manoy Olding, Enyong, Jaime, and Otê, who was directly across me. The opposite end of the table, across Tatay, was empty.

Tatay was lively, but cautious and gentlemanly throughout the meal. Nanay seldom spoke, apart from a few pleasantries. Our resident tailors who dined with us were in their most observant selves, while we kids were silent, owing to the stranger in our midst. We didn't know what was going on, or who the hell was that visitor on Tatay's left. I, for one, fidgeted because Manay Nilda, Otê, and I didn't occupy our usual seats, which were supposed to be next to each other on Tatay's left. The temporary disruption of the normal state of affairs irked us.

Who was Tomasa? She was unknown to us till after lunch, whence she continued on her journey. Right after she left, we children didn't stop pestering Nanay on Tomasa's identity till it was at last made known. "Your *tatay* and I were engaged, yet the nerve of that woman to still behave as seductive temptress when he was around," Nanay said, pointing her gaze at Tatay, who just flashed a meaningful smile. "We now know why Tatay chose you over her," one of us observed. "You are more charming!" Unmindful that Nanay was blushing, another one said, "And Tatay's heart wasn't for her." Tatay flashed another smile. "If Tatay married Tomasa instead, we would not have been here!"

That was the first and last time we ever saw the unexpected guest with a jilted heart. ∎

There is another story of a woman gate-crasher whose heart was more righteous and abiding. We do not know her name; the Gospel of Luke only tells us she was a sinful woman, nothing on how or why. Luke tells us she came over to the party hosted by Simon the Pharisee because she learned Jesus was one of the invited guests. For sure, Jesus hadn't met her before, but she had been looking for him with intent and love in her heart.

The sinful woman found Jesus seated at table. She wept and bathed his feet with her tears. Then she wiped them with her hair, kissed them, and anointed them with an ointment from an alabaster flask that she carried.

Simon the Pharisee noticed. He thought, "If Jesus were a prophet, he would know what kind of woman is touching him."

Of course, Jesus knew. He called Simon aside and rebuked him by first narrating the *Parable of the Moneylender.* (Lk 7:41-43) This moneylender forgave two debtors with unequal debts when they were both unable to pay. "Who of the two would love the moneylender more?" Jesus asked. Then he called the Pharisee's attention to his lack of basic courtesies which any host should accord a guest in their culture, vis-à-vis the woman:

- You did not give me water for my feet; she did.

- You did not give me a kiss; she did.

- You did not anoint my head with oil; she did.

"Now, who shows great love: you or this woman? So, I tell you, her many sins have been forgiven; hence, she has shown great love. But the one to whom little is forgiven, loves little."

He said to her, "Your sins are forgiven." ■

Love apples? I do, by their lonesome, or on cereal or oatmeal for breakfast. This morning, though, I had this Fuji that scowled at me even before I poured milk into my bowl of raisin bran. I had never come across as graphic and unamiable a Fuji apple as this one before, and so its impact on me was flabbergasting, today being the eve of Valentine's Day.

An incident in school the other day came to mind. I guess it connected to, and coincided with, this scowling Fuji.

Larizza, one of my 4th grade students, was scouring the yard in front of the Music Room during an off-period. "What's the matter?" I asked. She gave me a don't-disturb look and proceeded with her task. I approached her and noticed her cupped right hand. "You lost something?"

"No, Mr. Purple, I found these." She opened her right hand.

"Stones?"

"Yes, but not just. These are special."

"*Hmm.*" I nodded, trying to stretch my imagination of what made the stones special, but finding none. They were just ordinary pebbles of various shapes and colors. "Kindly tell me why they are."

We went inside the Music Room, and on a desk she arranged the stones in a row.

"Easy to see."

"Awesome!" I said, finding no sense in both her stuff and her words.

"Each of these stones is a heart."

"Oh, I see." I sorely needed a sorcerer's crystal ball. Larizza saw hearts in the stones. What I saw were hearts of stone. What I saw was the maturity and hardness of my heart. My adult eyes didn't see the wisdom in the child.

Now, as I recalled the incident involving Larizza, the thought of her hearts of stone brought me back to Fuji. At present, the diced apple lay mixed with raisins and a prune on top of raisin bran, ready for the milk.

"Na na na na boo boo, Mr. Purple!" Larizza taunted. "You don't see hearts? You don't have a heart!"

If apple stands for health and wisdom, then what this Fuji is saying is the same as Larizza's taunt. Though I strive for health through a diet of apples on breakfast cereal or oatmeal, I seldom see wisdom in apples or stones.

"You don't have a heart!"

Sticks and stones could break my bones, but her words hurt me. "You're mean!" I said in jest. God knows where the conversation might have led further to, had the wall clock not pointed to class time, while the school bell rang.

My wife, my daughter, or any person dear to me might agree with you, Fuji and Larizza. The two of you ask them, and they will for sure attest to the fact that I am, at the very least, impersonal, and at the very most, uncaring. I won't belie it or argue with you. People think I am impersonal and uncaring because I am shy, introspective, and withdrawn, most often mistaken for insensitivity and unfriendliness.

I can love, though, Larizza. I do a lot of loving. I love my wife, my daughter, my family, my relatives. My friends Mel, Gen, Olet, and Flor[118] have special niches in my heart. On a different level, I love my school, my students, my country, the Church, the saints, St. John the Baptist, the Blessed Mother, the Holy Family, and God, foremost of all. I am not the Tin Man; I am human, and I sure have a heart.

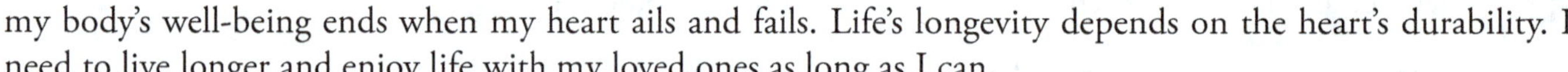

You should have met Tatay, Larizza. My father. He was much like me. To a great extent, I am much like him. We were peas in a pod. My Fuji apple self did not fall far from Tatay's Fuji apple tree.

Now, Fuji, let me talk to you. My heart is an apple, just as you are. I am trying to make it stand for health and wisdom as best as I can, because my body's well-being ends when my heart ails and fails. Life's longevity depends on the heart's durability. I need to live longer and enjoy life with my loved ones as long as I can.

My heart is comparable to you, Fuji, ever the sweetest among the apples that I have tasted. Taste is your upside, but you have occasional deformity and imperfection, too, such as your scowl this morning. My heart does scowl, too. My foibles, idiosyncrasies, and sinful ways are the scowls and downsides of my being.

Back to you, dear Larizza. My heart is finite and mortal. At my age, my heart is only as healthy as the absence of cardiac pills (at the moment I have 3) in my medicine cabinet. Someday it will reach its ultimate limit and stop functioning—God forbid! I wish it were indestructible, but my heart is not a stone.

Apples and stones can break my heart, but who cares as long as love lives there? Love is eternal. Love beats everything. ■

y heart, I now daresay, has been in the right place. One lazy Sunday afternoon back in 1982, however, a prophet named Isaiah might have insinuated where my heart could have been. I was leafing through the Bible for want of something to do when I chanced upon his book. In it, he said,

---

118   Mel-Greg Concepcion, Genelita Garcia, Fr. Floro Avenilla, and Flor Manalo – My and Mameng's best friends dating back from the 1980s.

"Then I heard the voice of the Lord saying, 'Whom shall I send? Who will go for us?' 'Here I am,' I said; 'send me.'" (Is 6:8)

I had encountered this innocuous text or its variations in other places and conditions countless times before (foremost was Dan Schutte's **Here I Am, Lord** hymn). I could have taken it for granted just the same. At the moment, though, I saw not just a modicum of significance.

Two days earlier, Ms. Lulú Domíngo, the elementary assistant principal of Xavier School where I worked as Science and Math teacher, called me to her office. She said, "Xavier wants to send you to Mother of Life Center." She explained that MOL was a formation center for catechists and religion teachers; that I was to live and study there for one school year and one summer; that I was to receive a salary as usual from Xavier School; last, that I was to teach Christian Life Education after the term. It was to be a study grant funded by German sponsors through the sisters of Notre Dame de Vie based in Novaliches, Quezon City.

The offer was not as enticing as my preoccupation at the moment. I was then applying for a male secretarial job in Saudi Arabia. With my résumé, clout, and connection in the recruitment agency (which was owned and operated by a Xavier student's family), I was 99% sure of getting hired and going abroad.

Then came the proffered MOL study grant. "Could I, in one year, grasp enough of my religion, let alone learn how to teach it?" I asked myself. I wanted to keep the offer out of my mind until I chanced upon this prophet Isaiah and his innocuous text. "Here I am; send me."

It touched me this time, and I took it as a personal epiphany—or so I thought. The die was cast. Without further ado, I went back to Ms. Domíngo and accepted the offer.

And so, in June of the next school year, 1983, I bade my family and my girlfriend Carmen goodbye. I told her we would not see each other for the duration of my live-in study grant. I was back at school, brushing up on my faith—besides learning how to best impart it.

The immersion into Mother of Life Center put to light one realization after another. I was lacking in the "creed, code, and cult" departments of my faith—knowing it, living it, and expressing it through worship. Although there was so much to imbibe in so short a time, my musical avocation had found haven, and the formators at MOL put it to good use. I led my batch of catechists, the 17th Generation, later to bear the name *Pilgrims*, in its music ministry. My job was teaching the group catechetical and liturgical songs for the Center's various feasts and celebrations. Ms. Nilda Rosas, a secular nun of Notre Dame de Vie, guided me but stayed as inconspicuous as possible. She gave me encouragement and free rein to choose or compose much needed music for the Center. It was this time when I started composing religious songs, which in three decades were to become my book, **The Purple Psalmody.**

Then, while forming me into an integrated faithful, Mother of Life kindled in me the thought of a much nobler ministry. The thought spread like wildfire throughout my whole being. I now wanted to be—a priest. A religious. A Jesuit.

Why Jesuit? Well, I worked in a Jesuit school. I hobnobbed with Jesuit brothers and fathers. Maybe because, as far as I knew, the Jesuits are the most service-oriented religious. Some priests are more devout in prayer, others in intellectual pursuits, still others in service. For me, the Jesuit is the happy harmony of them, the most astonishing amalgam of what makes a clergy, in equal and transcending proportions.

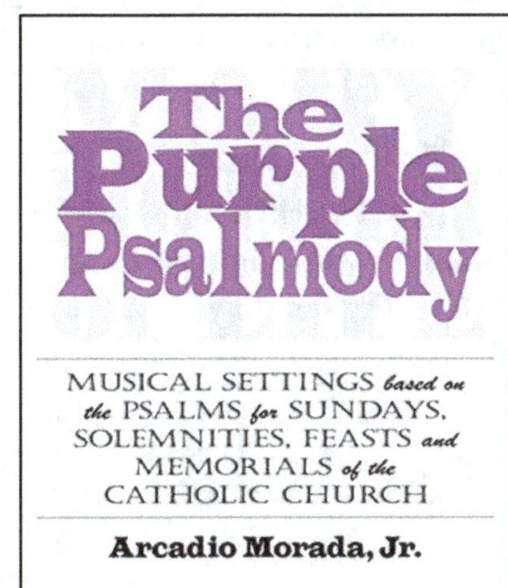

With MOL's blessing, I attended a vocation seminar at Sacred Heart Novitiate in Novaliches, Quezon City, hoping for more discernment. The experience was awesome and persuasive. At the end of the seminar, I was ready to apply as a full-fledged *seminarista*.[119]

In due time, though, my real calling reared its head. After MOL, I taught Christian Life Education in Xavier, as stipulated in the contract signed before the grant. In the meantime, Carmen—the girlfriend—was trying to figure out why I had not visited her since coming out of MOL. It was imperative that I wrote her a four-page letter of revelation, detailing why and asking for forgiveness. "I love you, but I love Someone else more... I am sure God is calling me for another purpose, at your expense. I want to be a priest."

There's a thick line between wanting to be and being called to be. Fast forward to 1986. Carmen and I tied the knot.

Hey, haven't I said I wanted to be a priest? I once had the avid intention and the ready heart of one who heard a call to the vocation. Or so I thought. ■

Dear Ms. M. Ramos[120], I am very sorry about the recent events on campus. As you know, the Xavier School Grade 3 Companions Club[121], with me as Moderator, got scrapped because of under-enrollment. The Recorders Club, my music club, meanwhile, claimed a big turnout.

I can hardly explain why. What I know is that I did campaign for both Companions and Recorders in my Grade 3 classes. For this reason, I did not see fit to still campaign in front of the student body during the big assembly in the gym last week. On the sideline, I encouraged most of the former 2nd grade Companions to rejoin the club in 3rd grade. It couldn't be right to think that I worked harder to recruit membership for the Recorders than I did for Companions.

If this development shocked you as Companions Over-all Coordinator, it disheartened me no end. It was a slap on my dignity as the only Grade 3 CLE teacher. When you came into the Teachers Room and said aloud, *"Alam ba ninyo na si Jun ay excommunicated na sa CLE? Walang gustong sumali sa Companions Club niya!* [Do you know Jun has been excommunicated from CLE? Nobody wanted to join in his Companions Club!]"—I experienced the most terrible humiliation in my professional life.

Granting that you got surprised and disappointed by the membership outcome, you could have talked to me firsthand. You could have inquired from me first, if you regarded yourself as a professional, mindful of work ethics. Why does Cita Carluen[122] have to be the first one to know and to confront me, saying, *"Sabi ni Ms. Ramos..."* [Ms. Ramos said...] Why do you have to call me *Jun Muslim*? If you did these in your desperation as Coordinator, if you did these in jest, may I tell you it's an overkill joke of the lowest order, spiteful and degrading.

May I clarify matters with you: I have no conflict of interests, or as Cita put it, "conflict of objectives." CLE and Music are two of my fields of interest. I love them both. Why should I betray one in favor of the other? Why should you accuse me of favoring Music in expense of CLE?

---

119   *seminarista* [Spanish] – seminarian, one who studies in the seminary or school for priests.
120   Asst. Head, Grade School Christian Life Education Department, Xavier School, school year 1985-86. She was also a nun of Notre Dame de Vie.
121   Extra-curricular club of the Grade School Christian Life Education Department, Xavier School, school year 1985-86.
122   Ms. Cita Carluen, Head, Grade School Pilipino Department, Xavier School, school year 1985-86.

Maybe it was a crummy joke. Maybe you needed to vent your immediate reaction. Last, maybe it was a powerful indictment of what we are. What you did could compel me to have a bigger heart for Music than CLE with you at the helm.

God bless you.

-Jun Muslim Morada ∎

Transfiguration Sunday, February 24, 2013. St Mary's Church showed a video of Bishop Daniel Flores of the Diocese of Brownsville in his bid to encourage vocations among the faithful at Mass today. Manang Ray, a member of the Angelicus—the Fil-Am Choir I formed and directed—said I should have been one of those young men priests-to-be in the video. Of course, I smiled in bashful acknowledgment, but deep inside, it embarrassed and annoyed me. I should have desired it during my younger days; now I bask at the thought that I was a priest-wannabe, less affective than priest-passé!

Besides, Mameng came into my life when I thought I heard God's call; she put my real calling fall into place. In fairness, she did not make my supposed dream fall into pieces. Mameng made me whole and integral. She helped me find my real ministry.

"I have called you by name: you are mine." (Is 43:1)

In hindsight, that was not God calling me into Holy Orders, but Mameng into Matrimony. With this redirected call, please allow me to make a list. My two beloveds, Mameng and Dimple. Brownsville, TX. The Angelicus. **The Purple Psalmody**. Unpublished volumes of religious, as well as secular songs. Teaching jobs at Cummings Middle School, St. Luke's Catholic School, Incarnate Word Academy, St. Mary's Catholic School, Villareal Elementary School. These came to be because I answered Matrimony's call. A transfiguration of sorts, isn't it? As the Angelicus sang our recessional song, **Transfigure Us, O Lord**, I thought, "In my case he did, in his time he did. Thanks, Lord!"

A different lifetime came to be, because I did not become a priest. ∎

IRS/MESDAMES[123]: On behalf of the members of our Association, I want to commend you for a job well done. Your hard work and dedication to bring the Philippine Madrigal Singers to Brownsville, TX, was noteworthy. The Madz, as the famous group is more commonly known, lived up to its reputation as the Philippines' foremost singing and cultural ambassadors. As a result of your efforts, we were on the receiving end of a wonderful cultural treat that was the Madz's concert at the Mary Mother of the Church Parish Hall last March 21, 2013.

Most, if not all who attended, had a wonderful time for arts and culture, as well as entertainment. They also experienced how camaraderie and the *bayanihan* spirit could work wonders in our community life. Brownsville became even more blessed and richer in esthetics and culture, by your enabling the Madz to come to this part of the Rio Grande Valley. You worked hard for it; we got the Madz down here. Therefore, you deserve our congratulations and gratitude.

---

123   An open letter to the Board of Directors, Fil-Am Association of Brownsville, TX, March 24, 2013.

A job well done—well, almost, that is—because there was a little, though important, aspect of the whole affair that was found wanting. This was the souvenir program. I believe in the dictum that printed matter should be perfect, because it stays and sticks. A printed material that's full of mistakes and mediocre workmanship does not do any good to any endeavor, much more so to a grand undertaking as the Madz concert.

We have gone through the pages of our souvenir program, and we found a cache of typographical and grammatical errors and defective workmanship. I could only think of two reasons. First, there was no time to edit and proofread, or there was no meticulous editor or proofreader. Second, the software used to make the pages was not good enough, or not used right.

The Filipino community in Brownsville does not lack for bona fide writers and editors who can help. All you needed to do was ask. I am sure, too, that many Filipinos here know how to use good photo-editing apps that can turn out professional-looking pages better than what we had. All you needed to do, again, was ask. Of course, time was not in your favor. There was just too little time for too demanding a job. But the proof of the pudding is in the eating; the proof of the souvenir program was in the reading. There is no excuse for a printed material full of typographical errors, grammatical misuses, and deformed pictures and graphics. There is no excuse for mediocrity.

That you asked for monetary sponsorships—and sold the finished product at the gate before the concert—made it even more exacting. It was, therefore, imperative to come up with something worthy, convincing, and right. Instead, what we got was, I repeat, wanting.

I did not write this letter to create enmity of whatever form between you as my officers and me. That's insubordination. I did not write this letter to attract attention to myself. That's narcissism. I did not write this letter to feign I know all the rules. That's arrogance and self-righteousness. I did not write this letter to criticize for its own sake. That's vanity. Rather—and I suggest you take it according to this light—I wrote this letter as a learning experience for us. Who knows, soon, any Filipinos and other races alike who read our printed material would say, "Hey, Filipinos are versatile!" Who knows, soon, we could come up with something we can stand for, not disown. Soon, as in, the next time around.

I am ready for the after-effects of this letter upon me. The least that you can do is to disregard it. The worst, to delete it. You might ostracize, unfriend, and ban me from future Brownsville Fil-Am events. A *persona non grata* you might brand me. But what will these accomplish—cover the truth? Truth shall set us free.

-Arcádio Morada, Jr. ∎

Peace is Flowing Like a River. I'm sure you know that old liturgical song by Carey Landry. Well, may I make a minor alteration—*Life is flowing like a river*, or shorter, *Life is like a river*. Even this modification is nothing new, as so many philosophers, prose writers, and poets have expounded on the simile in the past. The British author Aidan Chambers, for one, has an interesting musical twist, angle, accent, turn, or take on this.

Chambers writes he [or his personal life] is "... like the water flowing in the river...." Among many other musical terms, the flow descriptions he uses are *andante, furioso, tranquilo, lento, pianissimo, giacoso, lacrimoso, legato, staccato, vivace*. He always hopes to be *amoroso*. (Aidan Chambers, *This Is All: The Pillow Book of Cordelia Kenn*)

He might as well say that life is a musical river. Those of us who understand the Italian musical terms can see the ingenious analogies. I want to presume that Chambers was referring to me today. I could picture myself in the light of his flowing descriptions of a musical river.

I rise in vibrant spirits this morning, and drive myself to church for the Sunday Mass. Today is a holy day of obligation, not just a Sunday, but Ascension Sunday. Ascension is one of the few holy days of obligation of the Church in the liturgical year. That's where and when my vibrant spirits twist and turn. Like a musical river.

The officiating priest is not my favorite; he is a wholesome and intelligent but black man of the cloth whose African accent is a firewall between me and my understanding his tongue. Can it be that my auditory nerves are not functioning well, and I need a pair of hearing aids?

The liturgy planner must have been sleepy or in a foul mood at the time they planned for this Sunday, and so was the music planner. Churches could use readings for the 7th Sunday of Easter, but the missalette recommends the Ascension readings for this Sunday. Now, a minister reads the First Reading, followed by the cantor's Responsorial Psalm. Oh, they are using the First Reading and Psalm for the 7th Sunday of Easter. Fine, no problem with that. After the Responsorial Psalm, however, the Deacon stands up, goes to the lectern, and browses the pages of the Lectionary, suggesting that something is amiss. True enough, because the Second Reading and the Gospel are now taken from Ascension Sunday Mass readings! Hello, liturgy planners!

As for the songs and hymns used, to me they are more attuned to the 7th Sunday of Easter theme, not for Ascension. Sure, any music planner can dish out any liturgical music for any occasion. The chosen music, however, should be more in keeping with their mission to enhance worship by sticking to the liturgical theme of the moment.

Comes the cantor. In fairness, he is in control of his songs, and his dedication to his ministry is remarkable and admirable Sunday after Sunday. However, I am sorry to use this harsh and uncompassionate observation; it's apt time I should. First, he should have sung the right Psalm for today's liturgy as specified in the Roman Missal and the current missalette—his responsibility as much as the music planner's. Second, his long or sustained notes always become tremolos comparable to shaking pebbles inside a tin can. I apologize for this unkind analogy, but in all honesty, it can't keep me immersed in my prayers and meditations for long, no matter how hard I try.

No wonder, while in vibrant spirits when I entered the church, I come out in my unkindest self, raving and ranting, criticizing things around me as if I were perfect! Then I hear the American composer Carey Landry say, "Peace is flowing like a river!"

"Life, too, is flowing like a river, Carey!"

Mr. Chambers may have the final say: "Life is a musical river."

I realize, of course, that my mindset is what I become. I am a negativistic person, always looking at the dark side, always unmindful of the good. Yes, I laugh as heartily as I can, but I criticize heartlessly, too. I behave as one without a heart. Which has gotten me into troubles, misunderstandings, predicaments, and failed friendships time and time again.

I realize worshiping God should not depend on the priest, the liturgy planner, the music planner, the cantor, the choir, or the hymns in the liturgy. It should not depend on my mindset and me. True worship depends on the intensity of the relationship between God and myself. It depends on Faith, my faith in God. It depends on Love, my love relationship with God and his people. The bottom line is—though it's so hard to admit to myself—I go to church to please my person, not God. I go to church to see what I want to see in my environment and other people, not to see God. I go to church to prey on others, not to pray.

For these, I owe God—and everybody—an utter apology. ∎

ow or then, in big or small ways, I fall short of charity, of what Jesus told me today in the Gospel, that of loving one another. This time I won't speak on behalf of anybody—that I often violate this command in more ways and more times than I care to admit and to remember. *Mea maxima culpa.* My most grievous fault. As I rub shoulders with others in my desire for discipleship, I often don't and can't see that discipleship is "a commitment to God, to others, and to oneself."[124] I often point to someone as a person whom I love to hate, when to that person I could be the other way around.

As we rub shoulders with others, conflicts, envy, anger, jealousy, misunderstanding, and unhappy situations come up, which we later regret. But I do not need to slump forever—I can rise from the sinkhole others or I have created for myself. It is never too late to discover my attitudes that need to be changed. It is never too late to acknowledge my sinfulness. Despite the stigma of my impure heart, it is never too late to look at the brighter side. Despite an impure heart, it is never too late to love.

Oh, if I could only get to every individual whom I have victimized by my uncharitable behaviors throughout the years! If I could only find and gather everyone whom I loved to hate! If I could, I would say— Let's kiss and make up!

Distance, time, and space block me off, making it difficult to make up. But it is never too late! I will start with my wife. ∎

n a nutshell, I have collected my thoughts on you and me vis-à-vis over three decades of marriage. As with other marriages, ours is a compendium of good and not-so-good events. Let me start with the not-so-good.

It saddens me whenever you are disappointed in me. It pains me whenever you lambaste or tongue-lash me, and call me names. It discourages me whenever you do not give me a chance to explain my side because when you are upset your words are long, winding, and intractable, in this sentence's likelihood: *Your anger comes out of your mouth as a long northbound train from Neverland which nevertheless has a long way to go before the next station but which is traveling southward and so won't be reaching its destination in a million years or forever.* It disturbs me whenever you count to my face my so-called past sins, regardless of whether they connect to our argument at hand. It grieves me whenever you accuse me of things that I did not do. It disheartens me whenever you compare me and put me side by side with our daughter in terms of our common sins and wrongdoings *(syempre, kisay pa manunud!*[125]*)*. Because any of these agitates me, my reaction is consistently that of silence, the Cold Retreat, which I have perfected so well.

---

124   Msgr. Heberto Diaz, incumbent Parish Priest, Mary Mother of the Church Parish, Brownsville, TX. From his Homily (April 28, 2013).

125   *syempre, kisay pa manunud* [Bikol] – of course, inherited from whom else.

Not-so-good thoughts. They exhaust me. They give me sleepless nights. My middle name, though, is Patience, and I do not get mad. Well, maybe I do, but not *mad* mad. Even if I become sad and mad, it doesn't translate to hatred, because I love you. I will not be half the man that I am without you by my side.

I love it whenever we reconcile after a fight. We constantly do because, despite your veneer of toughness, you are such a loving and tender person. I just have to make the first move or make *lambing-lambing*[126], and the Fall of Bataan[127] follows for sure. I love it whenever you laugh with me as we talk; our mingled laughter is one of the sweetest sounds to hear. I love it whenever we garnish our conversations with glee now and then. I love it whenever we enjoy each other's sweet nothings, inane stories, gossips, and tattletales. I love it whenever you tell me you miss me, even if we just talked five minutes ago. I love it whenever I enfold my arms around you in a warm embrace. I love it whenever you portray my embrace as a fine woolen jacket on a wintry day and say that you enjoy a sense of security in my arms. Mostly, I love it whenever we exchange I♥you's, then we kiss and go beyond into *butingtingan*[128] and Blissland. I love it whenever our individualities disappear and our souls mingle as one. These moments I cherish. I will not be half the man that I am without you by my side. I love you.

Thirty-six years ago, we vowed to each other to be together through thick and thin, in sickness and in health, till death do us part. Through the years, I have never wavered in my belief that our marriage is made in heaven. Nothing can separate us, as nothing can separate us from the love of God, because we love, and God is love. Through the years, each of us may have had our spate of shortcomings and frailties threatening our togetherness now and then. We've never lost heart, though; we always end up kissing and making up (besides going into *butingtingan* and Blissland). We end up ever together, sharing each other, bound by love, grounded in love.

Heart is the matter. Love is what we are. ♥♥ ■

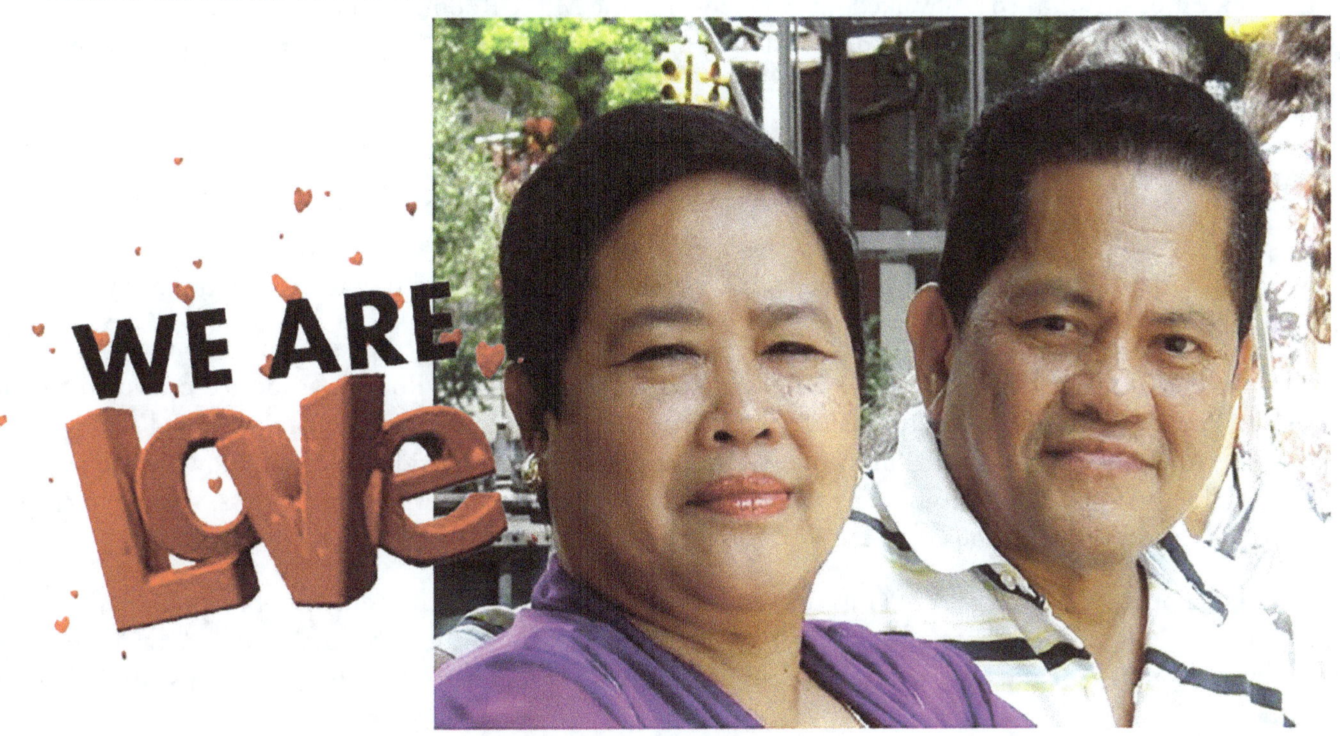

---

126   *lambing* [Filipino] – acts of affection and intimacy.

127   *Fall of Bataan* – In Philippine history, the day (April 9, 1942) when Filipino and American forces officially surrendered to the Japanese in Bataan, a peninsula of western Luzon, Philippines; used here as symbolical surrender.

128   *butingtingan* [Filipino] – from root word *butingting*; means meticulous attention to details; "*butingtingan* and Blissland" is a phrase used humorously here to mean the sexual acts of foreplay and making love.

17

ARK

Creatures great and small teach a life lesson or two

 had wished for heavy rains since last weekend. Dark clouds gathered indeed, yet only gave us intermittent and scattered rain showers. What the heck, I said in exasperation after one such. My lawn was browning and balding, the ground so compact and parched, my grapefruit tree in the backyard so stunted and discolored I wished the heavens poured more rains! Echoing the child Oliver Twist in the musical movie **Oliver!**, I said, "Please, Sir, I want some... *more*."

Sir almost choked and rotated his eyes. "More?" Translation: Be careful what you wish for!

Yesterday, the meteorologist on TV announced a storm warning. The impending storm gathered as soon as I left for school in my *karag-karag*[129] 18-year-old Honda Passport this morning. The rains fell at around 10 am. "Oh, c'mon!" I smirked as I walked my 2nd graders to the Music Room. "Just one of those short-lived gusts of rain, you'll see." Just one of those drizzles barely wetting the ground. "I wish there were more rains!" My little musicians patronized. "Yeah, more rains!"

St. John could not accede more. The Baptist was partial to water. If the Rio Grande Valley and the Rio Grande River were thirsting, the more the enigmatic John might say, "I hope that rain floods up the Jordan River!"

In an instant, flood watch and emergency alert flashed on my android phone. Really? Seriously?

At noon, the wish materialized. My 3rd, 4th, and 5th grade classes, scheduled to come to me after lunch, were the enthusiastic receivers of the wet tidings of great pour. The Music Room was located outside the main campus, accessible through a covered walk. As the students walked to the Music Room, they had a grand time getting wet on purpose and wading in the now-increasing puddles just outside the room. How they loved rains and puddles even better! I could have had a heart attack thwarting their every intent! By 2:35 pm, at the end of my last class, I was a nervous wreck.

Sure enough, there were more rains than expected. Enough to soak not only my browning and balding lawn, but the school's and those of Cameron County, or even of the entire Rio Grande Valley, I assumed. The rains were so persistent and intense that our dismissal procedure went berserk, lasting not the usual 15 minutes but 60.

More?

---

129   *karag-karag* [Bikol] – decrepit.

nother noteworthy flooding came to mind. It happened a few years ago, after weekend rains inundated my little Texas city of Brownsville and its environs, including Olmito, where Villareal Elementary School, my workplace, stood. To everyone's relief, the water did not rise too high and receded fast. Still, I found out when I came to school on Monday that water got inside my classroom and damaged many classroom paraphernalia. It turned out that this was the least of my worries.

First, two big tarantulas showed up from nowhere and flaunted their presence on my classroom wall. The show by nature elicited shrieks and screams from my students. By nature, too, that the teacher was at the end of his wits: what if any student got hurt during the commotion? Every grade level had to come to the Music Room within the day, and during the tarantula sojourn, at 8:30am, kindergartners were in my charge. Imagine toddlers in mad scramble!

Next, a group of squirrels came out from my closets or thereabouts (though at different times) and scampered around the classroom! Again accompanied by shrieks and screams, this time by the first graders at around 9:00am. Just when I thought, at 10:30am, that the very last animals had gone out of Noah's Ark to re-propagate their species, came the biggest surprise. One of the 2nd graders spotted a brownish creature, not the harmful kind, not much bigger than your thumb, curled up unmoving on my bookshelf: a garter snake!

My wards, shrieking and screaming, scrambled to the opposite side of the room as I called the janitor thru the intercom for the nth time. Blas came around in no time. "What is it this time?" Every hand pointed to the bookshelf, where the garter snake lay still, unmoving and unmoved. Of course, in no time too was the snake by Blas vanquished, its head crushed in an instant.

Well, I guess I was not a very good Noah, and I did not have my Ark to the right specifications. There was a moral lesson too: if you are a snake, don't be too ambitious as to read. Reading maketh a man full, but a reptilian crushed.

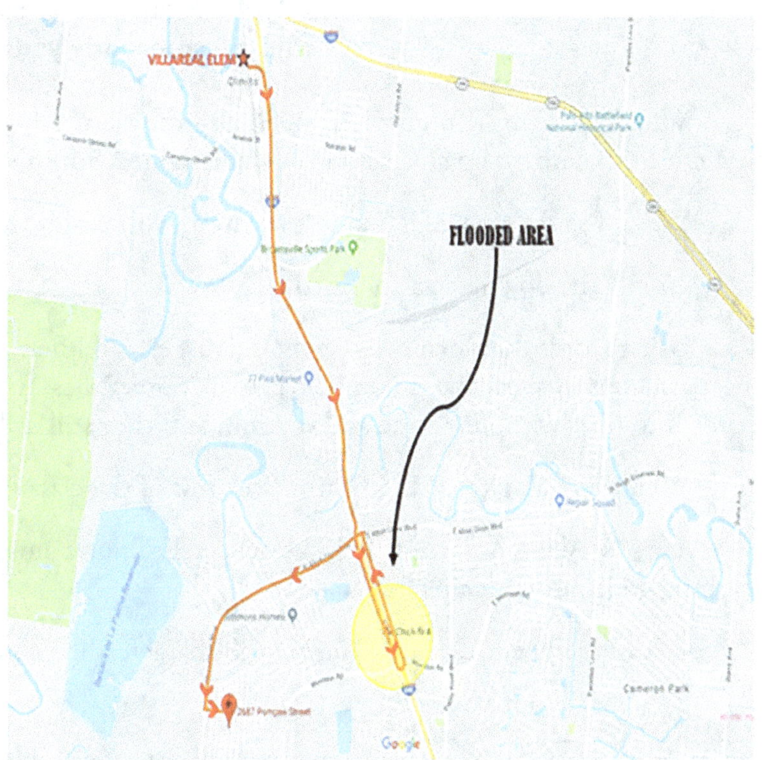

"Because of the heavy rains, faculty and staff are free to go!" The voice of Ms. Yliana Gonzalez blared through the intercom right after the dismissal procedure. Ms. Gonzalez was the incumbent Principal at Villareal Elementary. "It is obvious this inclement weather is not likely to improve soon. Be careful on your drive home." I thanked her in my mind and thought: I have to get home fast to evade the traffic and any street flooding, or whichever came first. Little did I know that both were ongoing at the same time!

On fine days, going home from work could take me 15 brief minutes. But now, as I exited the highway to take Alton Gloor towards my Pompeii Street abode, there was immobile traffic in around a foot of flooding on Frontage Road. There were three long bumper-to-bumper lanes of vehicles. It was impossible to break through the lines and maneuver getting to the rightmost lane to turn right at Alton Gloor towards my street. OK, no problem. I should cross Alton Gloor, make a left U-turn by Morrison Road toward the other side of the highway, get back to the Gloor, then turn left to it. I should be home in no time at all.

Oh me, oh my! There was flooding in Morrison, too! Scores of vehicles of every make got stranded, mine one of them. Only consolation was, I got stranded because of the other vehicles, not because of my old *karag-karag* 18-year-old Honda Passport. While newer but lower vehicles' engines conked out in the floods, mine waded through with no hitch. To make the story short, I reached Pompeii—but only after three hours!

More? Please, Sir, don't choke from surprise, and don't rotate your eyes. No more, no more, no more! ■

acchaeus. We can liken him to an elephant, a big and proud animal. Why and how so? As far as you and I know, Zacchaeus was a tax collector from Jericho in Jesus' time, wealthy, small in physique, short in stature, nobody's friend, and everybody's foe. Let's see further. Zacchaeus, a small and friendless man. The elephant, an enormous pachyderm, wrapped all over in wrinkles. Where is the connection?

They both must be interesting stories. People love interesting stories. Just what exactly are the elements of a story to be interesting? One which people can relate to. One which bespeaks truth in the readers' own lives. Has a striking conflict told in a striking style leading to a striking conclusion. Simple enough to be understood by anyone. Teaches a truthful, universal lesson. Zacchaeus' is an interesting story. What about this elephant's?

One day in Music class, I had my 4th graders chant the following poem as patsch[130] exercise and intro to my lesson on beat and rhythm.

Way down south where bananas grow,
A grasshopper stepped on an elephant's toe.
The elephant said, with tears in his eyes,
"Pick on somebody your own size!"

"What's a poem, Mr. Purple?" asked Zagith, a boy who was always a handful. Seriously? Thereupon, I thought fit to embark on an ambitious incidental teaching about poems.

"Well," I said, "a poem is a kind of writing with words that rhyme and follow a rhythm."

"*Huh?*" The boy made a confused face.

"Using words that rhyme—as *grow* and *toe*, *eyes* and *size*." I followed this up with my chanting of the lines and patsching to show the rhythmic pattern. "Sometimes, though, writers just put together specially chosen words into lines without rhyme and rhythm, and they still call it poem—free verse."

"Whatever," Zagith said. This time, the rest of the class showed wondering faces.

"Ask Ms. Alanis, your homeroom teacher; she knows more about what a poem is." Thus did my incidental teaching go kaput with a referral.

Back to the poem/chant. "Who are the characters in the story? Of the two, who's the bully? Who's being bullied?"

---

130   *patsch* [Music] – body percussion: to pat either the left, right, or both thighs (or other body parts) with the hands.

"In Music, too? Everybody's talking of bullies and bullying in school!" Ady said in his seat.

"October is Anti-Bullying Awareness Month, moron!" Joseph said.

"Watch your language, Joseph!" I had to intervene. "Ady and Joseph, what do we do before speaking in a discussion?"

Ady raised his hand, and acknowledged, said, "Sorry, Mr. Purple."

"Sorry, Mr. Purple!" Joseph said. "Sorry, Ady!"

"Aldair, in our poem, who's the bully? Who's being bullied?"

esus came to Jericho and intended to pass through the town. He, his disciples, and believers literally had a parade. The thief and cheat Zacchaeus had heard so many wonderful things about Jesus, the son of a carpenter named Joseph and his wife, Mary of Nazareth. He wanted to see him, but he could not, even how hard he tiptoed, because of the crowd of spectators in front of him. He then climbed a sycamore tree.

Jesus took notice, looked up, and said, "Zacchaeus, come down quickly, I must stay at your house." Jesus' disciples, his special friends, witnessed this. They grumbled, saying, "He is staying in the house of a sinner!"

Jesus and Zacchaeus talked with each other. Zacchaeus said, "Behold, half of my possessions I shall give to the poor, and if I have extorted anything from anyone, I shall repay it four times over." "Today salvation has come to this house," Jesus said in reply. "For the Son of Man has come to seek and to save what was lost." (Lk 19:1-10)

ow was Zacchaeus like the elephant? Or the elephant like Zacchaeus? How did they reflect on each other?

Elephants are enormous and proud animals. But this elephant underwent a transformation; it regarded itself as insignificant in the face of a minuscule antagonist, for reasons other than cowardice or idiocy. Isn't this called spiritual conversion?

Zacchaeus was wealthy—big time in the socio-economic standards of his era. But when he saw Jesus, he underwent a transformation; he humbled himself by being sorry for his past sins, intending to atone. To be with Jesus was a life-changing experience, a spiritual conversion.

In the eyes of Jesus, Zacchaeus deserved love and forgiveness. No matter how small, short, big, proud, or bad anyone used to be, transformation and conversion can always be had—if in Jesus' presence they realize and face up to their lowliness in sin.

What now, grasshopper? ▪

hen I was in college, in the early 1970s, I tended a couple of guinea pigs. They were so easy to take care of, so docile, shy, and likable. Bought from a pet shop in Legazpi City, they thrived and bred so fast it was difficult to give them names and remember. In a few months after purchase, I had an entire clan of squirming creatures in a wire mesh cage that needed immediate remodeling and resizing. I built and intended it only for two.

Voracious consumers, they ate *zacate,* a local species of grass. This grew in wild abandon along the banks of the *Golden River*[131] behind the Bicol University College of Education campus where I was studying at the moment. For practicality, I would reap a generous supply of this grass for a week's consumption. Every time I arrived with their supply, the cute pigs emitted their characteristic wheek[132] from afar, aware of my coming with their food.

We tended a few native chickens in our yard, too. Compared to the guinea pigs, the chickens were more self-supporting. Though sometimes we fed them their feasts of corn, rice grains, and growing mass[133], the chickens scrounged for grubs, insects, and other edible matter around our yard and elsewhere beyond our fence. They were fast and efficient food producers, but so were they fast and efficient poopers.

My siblings and I were a curious lot. We always looked forward to when roosters and hens performed their courtship and reproductive rituals. We held our breaths when the hens laid their eggs and hatched them. The hatchlings were an endless source of wonder and fascination for our inquisitive and impressionable minds. Watching them metamorphose from egg to "chickenhood" to fried chicken was a veritable and practical lesson on creation, reproduction, and survival.

"Napadârâ na su mga manok [Has anybody given the chickens their water yet]?" someone in the family would ask, and another one would fill a container with clean water. The chickens took turns drinking from it, before going ahead to their merry scrounging way soon afterwards.

Meanwhile, it was my job to tidy up the guinea pigs' cage and remove the unconsumed *zacate,* which was often contaminated with fecal matter and urine. Then I would replace a generous volume of fresh grass, and the eat-discharge cycle resumed. As I did this routine, it never crossed my mind that there wasn't any water container in the cage—my guinea pigs never drank or clamored for water. Yet they *did* urinate. On the flip side, though the chickens drank, I'd never seen them, even once, urinate.

One species drinks but never urinates. Another species urinates but never drinks. There's a predicament here.

In life, what looks obvious sometimes isn't. Translation: Or so we think.

In the first place, guinea pigs aren't pigs but rodents; they did not originate from Guinea. Despite their docile and likable nature, they are messy in their cage. No matter how often you clean their living quarters, it reeks of urine fast because, as guinea pigs urinate, they drag their lower bottom for territorial markings. This behavior often mixes urea with their food.

Do guinea pigs drink? Mine, because of my ignorance, did not, for I never gave them water. But the scientific-minded know that there's water in the grass. Only I refused to apply science or didn't realize it. On one hand, when a creature—man included—manifests not a particular behavior or ability, doesn't mean it doesn't have what it takes. We judge by reflection and presumption. Then, when a creature behaves in a specific

---

131   *Golden River* – geographically called Colabos Creek, in Daraga, Albay.

132   Wikimedia Commons. "Guinea Pig Feeding Wheek." Sound file, 8.2 sec. October 12, 2006. https://en.wikipedia. org/wiki/File:Guinea_Pig_Feeding_Wheek.ogg.

133   growing mass – enriched, processed commercial feed.

way, we are quick to label it based on our standards. We judge by reflection and perception. If you give a guinea pig water to drink, it will! Everybody has not seen chickens urinate—as humans do—because they only have one orifice for their discharge. So, their poops contain liquid waste—plain urine. It never crossed my mind.

In life, what looks obvious sometimes isn't. ■

Mudfish (*Channa striata*) is a species of the snakehead fish. We call it *haroan*, *aruan*, or *talusog* in my native language. "It migrates from rivers and lakes into flooded fields, returning to the permanent water bodies in the dry season, where it survives by burrowing in the mud."[134] You can find mudfish anywhere in the Philippines where there is freshwater: in rivers, lakes, lagoons, creeks, waterholes, even in canals, and *imburnal*.

Or in Mapiña.

Mapiña is an itch at the southern foot of Mayon Volcano. That's a figurative, or figuratively literal, way of describing our village whose name in Filipino means "pineapples aplenty." For our village at the foot of Mayon neither grows pineapples nor corns—only people who covet any fruits of value but realize sour grapes are more abundant and affordable. You can't be too willing or satisfied scratching it off, it being an itch at the foot. Just a kilometer from Daraga town proper, Mapiña connects two ways to the national road, along which the town's commerce and education centers abound. The two ways are the asphalted road of First Park Subdivision, and a footpath winding along and passing over the Golden River.

These are the contrived opening lines of my short story of local color, **Mudfish**, written in 1970. While I was in my adolescence in the late 60s in the Philippines, my family moved from Sipocot, Camarines Sur, to Daragá, Albáy. At that point in time, my parents had no other pressing wish but to have my siblings and me continue and finish our schooling. They believed in education as the only means of offsetting poverty, for we left Sipocot in dire financial straits. Daraga was a progressive town, so they settled the family there.

The Moradas found residence in one of those little villages on the outskirts of First Park Subdivision, named Mapiña. The village was close, within walking distance, to Daraga Elementary School, Bicol Colleges, United Institute, Albay High School, and Bicol Teachers College. I graduated high school from Bicol Colleges HS Department in 1969 and took up Engineering at the elite Aquinas University in adjacent Legazpi City. But in time I had to take a sudden detour to Bicol University College of Education (BUCE). From the vantage point of Mapiña, BUCE and the teaching course satisfied the need and call for convenience instead of ambition. Mapiña was situated right behind BUCE, separated only by a concrete fence, dense shrubbery, banana plants, some undergrowth, and a natural spring—the village water source. Oh, by the way, Mapiña was punctuated by the ever-stinky Golden River. In **Mudfish**, I describe the river thus:

---

134   *Wikipedia*, "Channa Striata," https://en.wikipedia.org/wiki/Channa_striata.

So, in July 1967, my family moved to Mapiña. In August, not much more than a month after the transfer, and a few hours after we had gone to school, a conflagration swept across the village. It razed 28 houses and obliterated them from the Daraga census and the face of the earth. To our great misfortune, the statistic included our new, dwelt-just-for-a-week house.

Everybody knew where and how the fire started. It did from our neighbor's house, the very one next to us, which was old and of light materials, nipa thatched roof, and wooden walling. The owner was a distant relative, an overbearing old maid. Before the fire, neighbors saw her sweeping her yard and gathering the dried leaves and other yard waste at the *barisbisan*[135], then setting them on fire. On a windy day as August 31, 1967, her chore to sweep the yard waste and get rid of it was more than efficient. It took less than an hour for 28 houses to be swept away, incinerated, as well.

The incident, or accident, reverted us to 1, "*balik sa uno*," so to speak. It was especially traumatic to Tatay and Nanay, then in their 50s, and Manay Nilda, my eldest sister, who saw the disaster happen. They could only do so much to save our properties as they could. It must have been so disheartening and unforgettable to see your belongings go up in smoke. Then Typhoon Welming came. Typhoons are so common and recurring in the Philippines, you could think Nature does not want to leave us alone, or lose its grip on us. More especially, Welming divested our ancestral land in Talôtô, Camalíg, Albáy, of life-sustaining produce of coconut (for copra), coffee, and abaca. We needed those so much as sources of income right after the fire. As a result, tension and hopelessness prevailed and overwhelmed our lives. Tatay and Nanay might never have expressed it to us children. From the bottom of their hearts, I knew they were hopeful and anguished, calm and delirious, strong and bitter at the same time. Of the siblings (Rudy, Nilda, Piping, myself, Otê, Merl, and Prid), I was the least resilient and the most vulnerable, the one who had been innermost affected. I questioned in silence. I doubted. Bitterness and pessimism consumed my whole being. I might not have degenerated into unbelief of the Almighty, but I guess I was on the brink of doing so. You can read this in **Mudfish**, too. (Here, the characters Puri and "I" are engaged in some metaphorical debate on mudfish and their habitat, while crossing the Golden River, thereby reflecting their respective subconscious.)

---

135   *barisbisan* [Bikol] – any point along the perimeter of one's house where rain flows down from the roof.

> "A clean pond isn't possible?" I asked
> "Of course, possible. Though, mudfish are not for clean ponds."
> Our eyes met in mutual repudiation. I felt he was making a fool of me.
> "You mean mud is eternal," I said.
> "You said it."
> "The basic rule in the universe is change."
> "Better to change *your* concepts."
> "Consider evolution."
> "Darwin didn't know mudfish," he said. "Mud is eternal—and universal."
> "Don't be naïve, Puri. Mud is subjective and conditional."
> "Mud is unconditional forever!"

How negativistic, this Puri, whose full name in the story is Purisimo Buendia. Read on.

> "Never hope," he said, "that God will spare mudfish good lives. This is not being sacrilegious."
> By now, dead infuriated I was. Two people have their longest distance between two points, and at this moment we reached ours. *Dear mudfish, I soliloquized. God has blessed you with enviable, sturdy life. You can live through conditions and circumstances few other species can withstand!*

What "I" said in soliloquy rings true of mudfish. God has blessed this lowly dark-colored fish with enviable, sturdy life. During the dry season, when water is scarce *(duh!)* and death is common, our snakehead friend burrows in the mud, refuses to give up, and stays alive. It lives through conditions and circumstances few other species can withstand.

By the way, **Mudfish** is autobiographical.

In 2014, I posted **Mudfish** as a note on Facebook. Beforehand, the manuscript languished for years in my stash of memorabilia files. Of course, I don't have any way of knowing how many of my family and friends were ever interested in clicking the link to a long and highfalutin story, let alone read. The title alone was grim and uninviting.

Let me digress and discourage you further by a few platitudes and poems. Sometimes, when it rains bad or sad things, it pours. Two choices: either we take cover under this umbrella called optimism, or get soggy and chilled body or soul altogether. Here's the first.

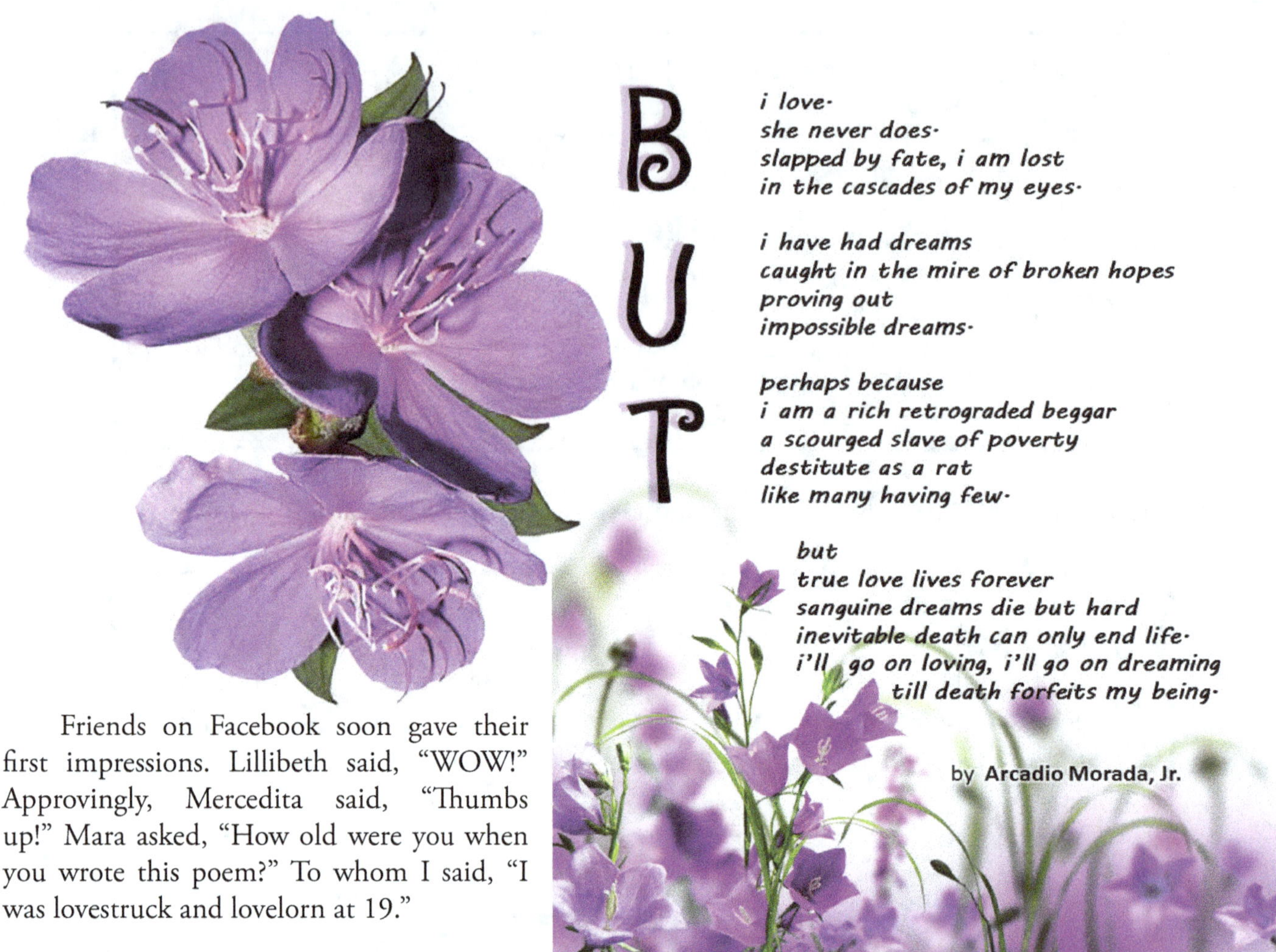

Friends on Facebook soon gave their first impressions. Lillibeth said, "WOW!" Approvingly, Mercedita said, "Thumbs up!" Mara asked, "How old were you when you wrote this poem?" To whom I said, "I was lovestruck and lovelorn at 19."

Mara said, "Wow, such a tender age. These days, young men write differently. Or perhaps they are not even interested in writing at all. I guess the youth these days have to learn a lot from the wisdom of the older generation. You have a lot of depth at a young age of 19. I wonder how many Arcádios have we in this present generation."

Discussion on my favor! Pride surging, I said, "I wrote that way because of too much emotional burden. I call it **IMIP** [**I**mpassionately **M**urky **I**nternal **P**lay], an abbreviation I coined in an earlier write-up. *Torpe, binasted ng crush, sinisisi ko ang aming kahirapan sa buhay noon. Maski sino siguro,* given those circumstances, *ay mapipilitang magsulat ng dugo, di ba?"* [Clumsy and too shy to make amorous advances, jilted by my crush, putting the blame on poverty for the sufferings in our life then. If you were in those circumstances, wouldn't you write with blood too?]

"Matindi pa yata sa IMIP ang pinagdaanan mo, Kuya," Mara said, somewhat patronizing me. *"Normal lang ma busted at maging torpe lalo na kung bata ka pa. Marami rin ganyan nung generation ko. Pero tulad mo, puro professionals na rin silang lahat ngayon at maayos ang buhay.* [Your experience could be worse than IMIP, Kuya.[136] It's but normal to be jilted and feel clumsy and shy when one is young. So many such people in my generation. But like you, all are professionals now, leading lives in order.] It only proves that poverty should stop no one from improving his life. And you did, Maestro! Imagine, *sinong torpe or na busted ng ex-crush ang nababasa ang mga sinulat mo on a global stage? Bihira yun... isa ka doon!"* [What *torpe* and jilted lover has his writings read on a global stage? You are! That seldom happens.]

---

136   *kuya* [Filipino]— an honorific for an older brother; conventionally used to address with respect any older male.

(Are you talking about me, Mara? Don't blame me if I act like an idiot with false entitlements!) "Thanks, Mara. You made my day. Have you read my story **Mudfish**, by the way? That's autobiographical, *mahaba nga lang*. [Very long.] But if you have patience and *tiyaga* [perseverance] to read through, you will understand my adolescent angst better. This story I wrote when I was just a teenager. I bet you might not believe I did it. For real, and it's there waiting for the reading."

Well, at least one *did* read! My faithful reader Rose, a Reading/Language Arts teacher in Texas, makes a brief review of my short story pronto. "After my Sartrean breakfast, I want to taste the Pavlovian dinner. *Mudfish* story entails hard core reflection of how man gets disillusioned by the 'powers-that-be' in the academe. It's also a reflection of how helpless another human being could be in convincing another to keep believing in what life offers. My childhood memory of mudfish was something light and gay, contrary to the gloomy and serious mood of this story. But, wow, the readers here need Deweyan mind to extract the genuine message."

"That's why the common reader does not appreciate my *Mudfish* story!" I said in a condescending tone. "It takes a reader like you, Rose, to confirm to myself that I had something to say when I was 19 years old. To be frank, in its long years of existence, nobody else has ever given it any review, much less a good one like yours. You are telling me now that there is value to my having written it at all. That's the reason, too, I've never attempted to send this story for publication, not only for fear of rejection, but worse for *ambiguphobia* (fear of being misunderstood). Now someone's talking. It took 44 years [that's how old this story was in 2014] to see it come true. Thanks, Rose. I owe you a cup of Starbucks coffee!"

"I thought you just wrote this, at least before you reached what people call the Age of Wisdom." Rose sounded incredulous. "You had this wisdom too early in your life. Rare genes. I wonder what happened to Puri? Starbucks, 8 pm, *Kuya!* Tell me about him. I'm guessing he has become an extreme existentialist."

"OK, see you there at 8 pm," I said. "Let's discuss **Mudfish** over a cup of Starbucks coffee!"

"Oh, no!" Rose said. "That extreme existentialist, or so I thought, has metamorphosed into a spiritual poet. After knowing the identity of Puri, we can now shift to psychology... an unfamiliar territory. But OMG *Kuya*, Puri had my sympathy all throughout the story because, to a certain extent, I could identify with him. See you then."

I'm sure not everybody knows of what she was talking. Only one way to find out. No, don't go to Starbucks. Read **Mudfish**, in Appendix A.

A word of clarification: Puri—not "I"—is the person, not the persona. My middle name, I want to rectify, is Pessimist.

In no time the following poem, **Mudfish**, came to be, which a year later became a song. In 2016, I posted the poem on my Facebook blog, **From My vantAge Point**. The poetry of my then young soul might have been impressive enough to my grade-school classmate and Philippine daily columnist Horace Templo. He said, "A very beautiful and inspiring poetry! I have my own several very personal interpretations. Your poem, Mr. Arcade, brings back many youthful and juvenile memories to me! Thanks a lot for sharing."

I said in immediate reply, "I'm humbled and honored at the same time. That *the* Horace liked a poem from my youth is worth giving that handiwork a second look."

False humility aside, I regard **Mudfish**—story, poem, and song altogether—as special. First, I wrote them five decades ago, yet somehow they still ooze some appeal. They draw and reflect a picture of me during a specific era of my life, talking to my alter ego. (My "brother" and I are one and the same person, me; and so, this collective handiwork is autobiographical.) Thanks, Horace, for telling me I own something to re-evaluate my life with, to be proud of, and to treasure for the rest of my life.

__MUDFISH__

1
Oh, I have a brother who calls himself
a mudfish, mudfish, all the time.
He is mad at me. I cannot keep from
dreaming goldfish, goldfish, oftentimes.
But, brother, you've to have some dreaming in your heart,
otherwise, you'd lose your mind.
Why not think of some limpid rivers
or some clearer, cleaner ponds
Where we can find clearer water, cleaner matter?
Where we can wash our dirtied scales,
Where to renew our wearied souls,
Where to forget we'd been in mud before.
Yes, brother, we can always get out of this mess called mud.
Mud is not a quicksand nor has it some hands to hold us down.
Though we may have the power to withstand this dreary mess called mud,
We can always get out of this mess if we try. Oh, let us

2
Face the fact, my brother, in this life
we can be happy only when we strive.
The world has rooms for us as long as we can
keep ourselves, our will, strong and alive.
But, brother, if our brain constrains us here to rot
and stay just down behind
There's no hope for some limpid rivers
or some clearer, cleaner ponds
Where we can find clearer water, cleaner matter.
Where we can wash our dirtied scales,

Where to renew our wearied souls,
Where to forget we'd been in mud before.
Yes, brother, we can always get out of this mess called mud.
Mud is not a quicksand nor has it some hands to hold us down.
Though we may have the power to withstand this dreary mess called mud,
We can always get out of this mess if we try. Oh, let us

3

Fix ourselves then, brother, and bound together
let us have some schemes unreeled.
We are going to leap into a place
where we can see our dreams fulfilled.
But, brother, if it happened that we
would land to one where life is as unkind,
We could leap to other limpid rivers
or some clearer, cleaner ponds
Where we can find clearer water, cleaner matter.
Where we can wash our dirtied scales,
Where to renew our wearied souls,
Where to forget we'd been in mud before.
Yes, brother, we can always get out of this mess called mud.
Mud is not a quicksand nor has it some hands to hold us down.
Though we may have the power to withstand this dreary mess called mud,
We can always get out of this mess if we try. Oh, let us

4

Try! ■

The commotion began while the 3rd graders were having their warm-up run during P.E. in the gym. They, particularly the girls, were shrieking, screaming, and scrambling as they passed by the rolled-up gate facing the railroad tracks outside Villareal Elementary School. This gym gate opened to a patch of grasses that stretched up to the railroad tracks past the school's wire mesh fence.

Every Thursday, until grade-level choirs got organized in October, I needed to be in the gym with P.E. coaches Aaron Weinberg and Richard Cheshire. This was a school arrangement that somewhat demoted me from Music specialist to P.E. teacher-aide. I helped the coaches supervise their classes, besides doing little chores for them. So, it was my task to figure out the commotion. I hoped it was not another baby rattlesnake straying into the vicinity as happened in the past week.

The culprit: two frogs mating at the threshold of the gym's roll-up gate. Well, not frogs in reality, but giant toads (*Rhinella horribilis*). One on top of the other, they appeared as a single entity from afar, but seen close up, the creatures were hopping in sync towards the inside of the gym. No wonder the children's commotion.

GIRL 1:   Poor mama! She must be so tired carrying her baby on her back!
BOY 1:   That's not a baby! That's a boy frog on top of a girl frog.
GIRL 2:   Riding?

BOY 2:	Oh, c'mon!
GIRL 3:	How do you know it's a boy frog on top?
BOY 3:	They're having fun.
GIRL 4:	They have warty skin—they're toads!
BOY 4:	Why toads do that?
GIRL 5:	Who cares?
BOY 5:	That's nature.

Out of the mouths of babes!

It was my imperative to root out the cause of the commotion. A stick, a broom, or a spade could suffice. Blas, the school janitor, was cleaning the restroom next to the gym, so I borrowed a broom. With caution, I approached the amphibious couple as the coaches made the students sit in their designated places. In one fell swoop, I had the toads (baby-and-mom, girl-and-boy, whatever) banished out of the gym. The unhinged creatures disappeared in the grasses faster than they came into the gym.

Outside, the post-noon sun was sweltering. The interior of the non-air-conditioned gym might have been so unbearable and inconducive to learning if not for the giant electric fans on the floor and overhead spinning full-blast.

The 3rd graders were now seated in silence as Coaches Cheshire and Weinberg started their lesson for the day: *How to do PUSH-UPS.*

"We need to do push-ups the right way," Coach Weinberg said. "This is to prepare you for the Fitness Gram." (The Fitness Gram was the required physical fitness assessment tool administered in Texas school districts by the Texas Education Agency.)

"UP! One, two, three, four!" said Coach Cheshire, his voice modulated louder so the students in the back row could hear. A student earlier chosen by Coach Weinberg showed how to do the push up in front of the other students. "DOWN! One, two, three, four! UP!"

"Your body should be straight as you go up," Coach Weinberg said. "Don't let it curve! Your arms should form 90-degree angles!"

"UP! One, two, three, four! DOWN!" Coach Cheshire modulated his voice higher and louder, because students in the back rows were fidgeting. "One, two, three, four! UP!"

"Do I have to watch this demonstration?" I asked myself as I stood in a corner of the gym. Blas smiled and said, "Can you do that, Mr. Purple?" Then, from out of the blue, Jewel Akens' **The Birds and the Bees**[137] flashed in my mind.

The birds, the bees, and the toads in heat... and the babes in push-ups, too!

Seriously? Unbelievable! ■

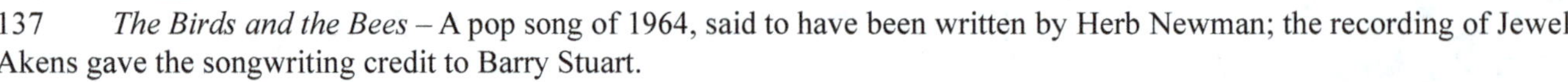

---

137   *The Birds and the Bees* – A pop song of 1964, said to have been written by Herb Newman; the recording of Jewel Akens gave the songwriting credit to Barry Stuart.

This particular day in 2013 marked the 3rd year anniversary of my having found Azkal—or Azkal having found me. The ash-colored schnauzer followed me while I was walking my poodle, Valentine, on the early morning of October 26, 2010.

The schnauzer appeared ragged, hungry, and thirsty, his fur caked with dirt from exposure to the elements, maybe from long periods of homelessness and non-bathing. Even then, he was so plump he moved as if a sausage walking. *Some lost dog*, I thought. He called my attention by barking at me and Valentine, although not in a harassing manner. Valentine barked back; I pretended not to mind. Then I gave Valentine's leash a jerk, and we continued on our way home.

"Leave us alone!" I shooed him away before I slammed the door of my house on him to scare him off back into the street. The dog had been following us, and even as Valentine and I crossed the threshold, the schnauzer was ready to jump in after us, if not for my loud command. "Leave us alone!" This second time stopped him in his tracks.

Forty-five minutes later, leaving for work, I found the homeless dog still where he last stood. Amazed, I stood transfixed in front of him, who sprang and, with no sign of inhibition, licked my shoe. *Hmm*, I thought this show of affection should not get me carried away. Before leaving, though, I went back inside the house and got him a dish of dog food and a container of water. The canine obliged by gobbling the feast. Amused, I relished the thought that I was doing something humane.

In the afternoon, coming home after work, I found the street dog still where I left him, waiting. "What's gotten into this Azkal?" I asked myself as I parked my car in the driveway. By now I gave him the name Azkal, derived from the Filipino phrase *"asong kalye"*—meaning street dog—which his homelessness had made him. Azkal met me as I stepped out of the car, licked my shoe, and wriggled his body around my legs. Touched, I made an awkward and wary pat on his head. That pat sealed my fate—and his!

Azkal dashed into the house ahead of me. Of course, the sudden intrusion surprised Valentine. He was barking over this sheer invasion of his territory. I pacified the poodle and carried him up in my arms. This was insane, but I talked him into accepting an itinerant visitor and giving him temporary shelter—one he himself had been in for the past four years now.

"Valentine, I want you to meet Azkal," I said, as if a nitwit admonishing the dog. "He needs help. I want you to welcome him to our home." Then I picked Azkal and gave the two dogs a bath. Again, I relished the thought that I was doing something humane.

The two got along well, fast. By now I gave the "temporary" visitor the nickname Ash, owing to his velvety ash-colored fur. Valentine's ears drooped while those of Ash stood. Between the two of them, Valentine was the grouchy, solitary, and more reserved one, while Ash was playful, friendly, and more mischievous. Despite their differences and idiosyncrasies, I started calling them "Boys!" (The sons I never had.) Valentine was the picky eater, while Ash ate everything given to him. No wonder Valentine was so lean, while Ash so plump, as if a giant sausage.

The following days were a period of finding Azkal's actual owner. They might have been searching like crazy, while in my eyes he became winsome and adorable with each passing day. For weeks, Valentine and I roamed the neighborhood where we found Ash, who walked along unleashed, but never out of sight. The aim was to find his former home. When homeowners stood outside as we walked by, it was routine to ask if they knew the owner of "that schnauzer." Of course, I always expected a "No idea" or "I don't know" answer, because a positive one could break my heart.

Ash was so easy to love. Three years of searching passed with no claimant coming forward to retrieve what they owned. Good for me because, to be honest, this dog's departure, aside from breaking my heart, could dishearten my soul. I tell you, no one and nothing can compare with our human propensity to love dogs. People don't own dogs; dogs own people. We do not call them man's best friend for nothing.

Mameng, my wife, bought Valentine as a puppy back in 2006, on—when else—Valentine's Day. Earlier than the poodle, we had no dog inside the house. ("Lucky" and "Charm" were past, dead dogs stationed their entire lives outside the house.) She only bought the puppy on the coaxing of her three charges. (My wife served as a nanny to Anthony, Trevor, and Bryan Searle, sons of Dr. Karen Brooks, a prominent Brownsville TX surgeon.) They convinced her it was a very good Valentine gift to Carmela, our daughter.

Mameng handed the baby poodle to Carmela in a small, cozy puppy basket. First time separated from his mother, the puppy was yelping hard as he looked for her. When Carmela touched him with fondness and sympathy, the puppy in effect said, "Here is my mom now! I am weaned from my biological one. Need to stick to this surrogate!" She'd been his unwritten but obvious master and mother thenceforth.

Valentine, Val for short, had become so attached to Carmela that he barked at any person who'd go near her. To him, anyone, including my wife and me, was a threat and potential obstacle to their bond. He growled, flashed his menacing teeth to whoever was the threat, and dashed in front of her to "protect" her. When she had to leave for college in 2010, Valentine would revert to his passive, solitary ways. But "happy days are here again" whenever she came home on vacation.

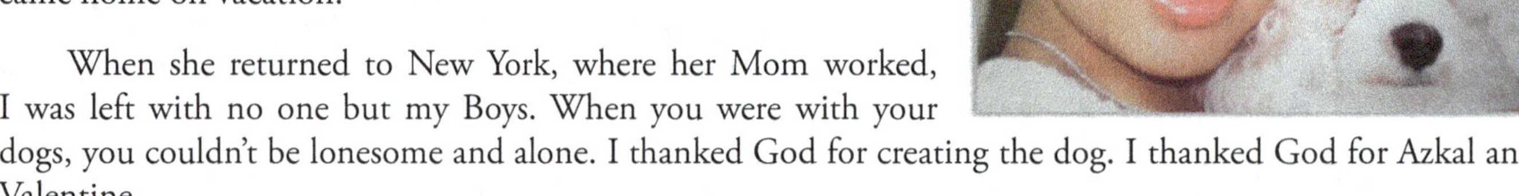

When she returned to New York, where her Mom worked, I was left with no one but my Boys. When you were with your dogs, you couldn't be lonesome and alone. I thanked God for creating the dog. I thanked God for Azkal and Valentine.

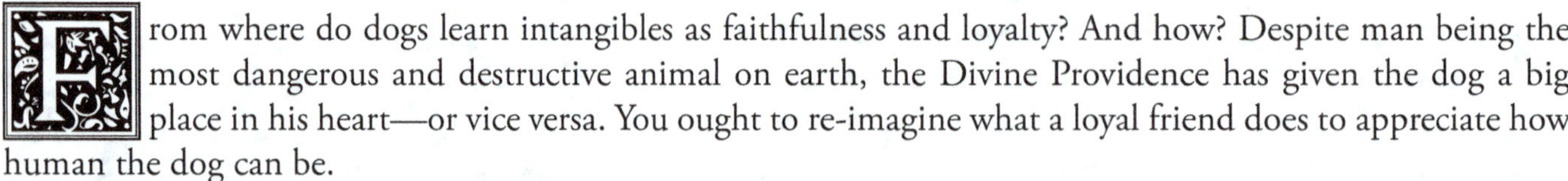

From where do dogs learn intangibles as faithfulness and loyalty? And how? Despite man being the most dangerous and destructive animal on earth, the Divine Providence has given the dog a big place in his heart—or vice versa. You ought to re-imagine what a loyal friend does to appreciate how human the dog can be.

Two friends sometime ago expressed taking to *the* dog which, crystal clear by now, was proximate to my heart.

Janet Monroe of Brownsville, Texas, a registered nurse, wrote:

> Today I came home from work tired but excited about something that I can hardly explain. I feel like there was something special that happened this time of the year that I just could not remember. When having dinner with my family, I glanced at my dog, and that same magical feeling came back to me. That feeling of immeasurable love, excitement, and

tenderness over this little creature filled my heart once again. Today marked the 4th year since the time little Clarabelle (as she was then known) became part of our family. We rescued her from Denver. A lonely dog, she came with nothing but an old blanket to comfort her on her journey to our home, and a wishful pair of big brown eyes seeking love. I told my little story again about her first day with us. I put her in her new bed with toys, a fresh blanket, and a pillow, but the entire night she never slept. Instead, she just wandered around the house as if looking for something. On the second night, she did the same, but this time I figured out that I had to put her old blanket in her bed. Sure enough, she cuddled with it and slept. Over the years, her clothes, blankets, and stuffs increased. I put the old blanket away with her stuff, but today I wanted to touch that blanket, like the first time I held her in my arms covered with it. I took the blanket out and washed it with my bare hands, because tonight I want her to sleep beside me, covered with the same blanket. I want her to feel that comfort from her favorite blanket and the person who showered her with boundless love all these years.

From General Santos City, Mindanao, Philippines, my friend Joe Hormigos is a school principal. He wrote once in reply to students under his charge interviewing him on "the most useful animal":

Racing in my mind were all kinds of livestock—all kinds of meat. My thoughts shifted to battle cocks—but that's useful only if you place a bet (*sabong*) and win. Well, I'm going for... the dog! Man's best friend. Domesticated to be our companion. When I got home that day, and was met by dogs, it was an affirmation of my answer. In dog language, they all expressed: My master is here! My master is here! And it's like we haven't seen each other in ages. The dogs do not know what kind of day I've been through, nor do they show any care for that. It's all about Now and that they're glad I'm home. If it's Love, dogs really give Love a splendid meaning.

To Janet I replied:

I love the way you wrote of your lovely and lovable Clarabelle! I guess your thoughts came both from the head and the heart. They flowed forth from your pen (or keyboard) without effort and so full of wondrous and exhilarating feelings. I have read none other writings of yours (till now), but I can say you write with passion, you write from the heart. My God, Janet, you are a writer!

I remember you saying that *'mahina ako sa ganito, sa math lang ako magaling,'* [I'm not good at this, I'm only good at math], referring to writing. I believe you have the flair for writing. And by writing on Clarabelle, you struck a common chord in us that is at once harmonious, sonorous, and pleasing. I cheer for man's best friend; I have a poodle, too, though not as knockout as Clarabelle, named Valentine—a handsome boy.

To Joe I replied:

I agree with you, Joe, on our dogs. Dogs for real give love a splendid meaning. That is why we humans endow our furry friends with so much love. But how come we don't give kitties and cats the same honor?

To both Janet and Joe, I replied:

Upon reflection, I can think of one explanation. This may sound blasphemous, and in no way attempting to be exact. The truth it points to is profound, so relish it if you please.

Do you know why "dog" is the inverted spelling of "god"? God loves us. No matter what, God's faithfulness to man is beyond doubt. Same way with your dog and mine—our furry friends, once they come to love us, never fail or disappoint us. Of course, it's wrong to put the dog in league or equal footing with God, so the mirror reflection—the inverted position—will do. Your dogs and my dogs, Valentine and Azkal, love their human friends without limits, a pure and indubitable reflection of God's love for man. ∎

April 14, 2013

THE EXECUTIVE OFFICERS AND MEMBERS OF THE BOARD
Fil-Am Association of Brownsville, TX, 2013-2014

Dear Sirs/Mesdames:

Peace in Christ!

It has been 21 days since I posted an open letter on the March 21 Philippine Madrigal Singers' concert in the Fil-Am Association of Brownsville page on Facebook. The letter was constructive criticism aimed to invoke change and improvement in our future endeavors. I addressed the letter to the Board of Directors, never meaning to malign a person or group of persons, or to tarnish the reputation of any individual. As the letter writer who believes in freedom of speech, I aimed for—and expected—positive actions from you as pillars of our Association. Instead, the letter created not only a stir but an uproar of the most disturbing kind. It has upset the hornet in its nest among you, and the hornet has been rattling its stinger since then.

The idea of posting the letter on our Facebook page was a last resort, a decision I had to make after weighing other options. Would I get the desired result if, for example, I just gave each of you a copy of the letter? Would I get the desired result if, for another example, I just gave the committee on souvenir program a copy of that letter? I didn't think so. Many members of our Association believe that some of you are—excuse the metaphor—the hornet which they should not disturb in its nest. They perceive the rest of you to be cautious so as not to displease the hornet on its pedestal, so nobody dares touch it with a ten-foot pole. By posting it on our Facebook group page, I hoped to help you see the truth, and motivate you to spring into collective action. And, excuse the figurative language again, the truth in the open letter was my ten-foot pole.

It took no time for three among you to misjudge my letter as derisive. A volley of insults aimed at me followed, courtesy of the Fil-Am Association Facebook group administrator and her circle of sympathizers. The tirades were:

- That I am arrogant, a know-it-all, and therefore,

- That I am MR. PERFECT, in all caps.

- That if I thought I knew something, why didn't I volunteer to help make the souvenir program? Where was I when it was in the works?

- That I am unreasonable. The committee had only a short time to prepare, so I should have been more understanding of their situation;

- That I was not setting a good example to the youth. *"Teacher ka pa naman... sana hindi iyan ang itinuturo mo sa mga estudyante mo"* [You are a teacher; I hope you are not setting an awful example to your students] or something to that effect;

- That I am narcissistic and egotistic;

- That I was not even present at the concert, that I considered myself too good for the Madrigals;

- That I could not afford the $20 admission fee, because I'm *only* a teacher;

- That being so, I should have just called and [the hornet] would have sent me a complimentary ticket right away;

- That if I was so interested in the truth, why did I single out the souvenir program? Why did I not complain of the venue, Mary Mother of the Church Parish Hall, as far inferior to UTB? The University of Texas at Brownsville was the Madrigals' concert venue two years ago;

- That I am proud and unspiritual.

That I am arrogant. First time I am branded and accused of acting superior to anyone! If advocating for truth is being arrogant, then call me one because what I say is true. If, in standing for the truth and the right, I am misconstrued as an arrogant self-proclaimed crusader, then the problem is not me. The problem is you, because the truth intimidates and scares you.

That I am MR. PERFECT. Would I be overjoyed if I were! But I am not. I am not know-it-all, either. Never did I say I know all the rules. Never said I can do everything. Yet, even if I do not know all the rules, even if I can't do everything, I know how to apply what I know to make good and right things. What my open letter did was to tell anyone, Filipino or otherwise, who ever read the souvenir program that the Fil-Am can do better than that. Just because I complained of imperfections, could some of you be so off track by calling me perfect—with sarcasm.

That if I thought I knew anything, why didn't I volunteer to help make the souvenir program? Now wait a minute! This ignorant observation came from one of you who could have known better. The Fil-Am president requested me to write the original draft of the Greetings for the souvenir program. After I wrote it, one intelligent head among you, well-versed in technical writing, improved the draft to make it less academic and more unmistakable, with my grateful permission. She then submitted the revised draft to the committee on souvenir program, who took it upon themselves to edit our joint-heads work to conform to their taste. Ask anyone to read the printed Greetings, and they'd say, "Oh, what a taste!"

That I am unreasonable. Of course, I know that there was little time to do the souvenir program. But the time you had, if indeed little, was enough if you only tried hard enough. Time constraints don't excuse you from mediocre work. You can't tell and expect people to understand that your souvenir program was fraught with typographical and grammatical errors because you didn't have enough time to edit. "There is an abundance of qualified human resources around you waiting to be tapped; the only key is prudence and humility to ask"— that's coming from our well-versed technical writer-officer. "Proofread the entire document and ask others to proofread. Minor mistakes and oversights rob a souvenir program of its professional quality." That's not coming from me, either, but from David Koenig, an Associated Press writer on his blogsite at Techwalla.[138] An extraneous comma on the very front cover of the souvenir program ("presents,") illustrates Koenig's truism. Your innocent-looking comma is a powerful indictment of the quality of effort you have exerted into making

---

138   David Koenig, Techwalla, "How to Design a Souvenir Program," Step 9, https://www.techwalla.com/articles/how-to-design-a-souvenir-program.

the souvenir program—that comma should not have been there. I beg to tell you that laughing that comma off is a disappointing sense of humor! That comma, though, is just the tip of the iceberg, and that I have the iceberg to prove it. I am hoping you will ask to see the long list of typographical and grammatical errors—which I will give you with pleasure if you so wish. Along with this hope is your patience to go over the list, the wisdom to see the iceberg, not just its tip, and the honesty to own up to it. Last, I hope by looking at the list, you will have the courage to pinpoint who is being unreasonable, even if the culprit is smack in your midst.

That I was not setting a good example to the youth. That I am narcissistic and egotistic. *"Teacher ka pa naman, sana hindi iyan ang itinuturo mo sa mga estudyante mo."* [You are a teacher; I hope that is not what you are teaching your students.] The same officer who said I did nothing to help now declares that I—she spelled out my name for the world—am a wrong example as a teacher. Wow, in my 36 years so far in this noble profession, I have never been so debased! *Isa po sa mga itinuturo ko ang magsabi ng totoo. Itinuturo ko po ang maging maingat at magalang sa pagsasalita. Itinuturo ko rin po ang paggamit ng tamang pananalita. Hindi ko po itinuturo ang mangmaliit ng kapwa. Hindi ko po itinuturo ang pagwawalang-galang sa kapwa. Hindi ko rin po itinuturo ang magmatigas ng kalooban kahit alam ko sa sarili ko na ako ay mali.* [One thing I teach my students is to tell the truth. I teach them to be cautious of what they say. I teach them how to say things in the proper way. Never do I teach my students to degrade or disrespect others. Nor do I teach them to be unyielding even if they know they are wrong.] I teach my students to aim for excellence and high standards. I teach my students good deportment. I teach my students to uphold their own dignity when others humiliate them. I teach my students the freedom of speech. If, in doing what I preach, you point a finger at me as being narcissistic and egotistic, that's your own opinion. But don't throw it to my face and act as if you were stating a fact, because the rest of your fingers may be pointing at you.[139]

That I was not even present at the concert because I consider myself too good for the Madrigals. Now, this behavior is egotism—if it were true! Truth is, I had a paid ticket. Why was I not there? We can use the Tagalog phrases *hindi ako nanood*[140] and *hindi ako nakapanood*[141] to explain why I was not there at the concert. *Hindi ako nakapanood* because (1) I was in charge of a school program that coincided with the concert time and ended at 8:00pm. Truth be told, though, I could still have attended even if late, but I chose not to go. *Hindi ako nanood* because (2) the venue was too disappointing, and (3) the souvenir program was too embarrassing. No offense to Mary Mother of the Church Parish, which offered the venue out of its good nature. For me, though, the Philippine Madrigal Singers deserved to perform inside the Church, not the Parish Hall. It was too small an auditorium and lacked acoustic considerations for renowned artists as the Madrigals. They needed a better venue for their audience to fully appreciate their artistry and excellence. But to say that I was not there to watch the Madrigals because I was too good for them was way overboard and too baseless an opinion.

That I could not afford the $20 admission fee, being only a teacher; that being so, I should have just called [the hornet] ***who would have sent me a complimentary ticket right away.*** This is the worst insult I have ever received as a teacher! First, thank you for your generous, even if artificial, offer. I understand nurses receive a bigger pay than do teachers. But despite my meager pay, I have more than enough to spend on my basic needs and with more to spare. Yes, you are a phone call away but I do not have and keep your number, and I don't need a complimentary ticket because, I repeat, I had one. *Ang husay mong mangmaliit ng tao; porke malaki ang kita mo, ang akala mo lahat ng taong maliit ang bulsa ay maliit din ang utak at dignidad.* [You're

---

139   How do you call a person who appeared in at least 20 pictures, not counting those too small and blurred, in the entire souvenir program? Go ahead, re-browse over your copy, see and count for yourself. If I am narcissistic and egotistic, what do we call this I-am-entitled-to-post-those-20plus-pictures-because-I-am-the-Souvenir-program-coordinator person?
140   *Hindi ako nanood* [Filipino] – I did not watch.
141   *Hindi ako nakapanood* [Filipino] – I wasn't able to watch.

adept at belittling people; because you earn more, you think other people with small pockets have small brains and dignity, too.]

That if I was so interested in the truth, why did I single out the souvenir program? Why did I not complain about the venue? According to the Fil-am Association of Brownsville Facebook group administrator's own declaration, the venue was far inferior to UTB, Madrigals' concert venue two years ago. Well, I DID. Days before the concert, I told three officials of our Association of my opinion on the venue. But I excluded this concern from the open letter because, though it was a shortcoming, I thought it was forgivable and time-specific. The problem with the souvenir program was different because of its far-reaching urgency and importance. Disprove to everyone that it's the best that your collective heads can do.

That I am proud and unspiritual. "Despite of (sic) your derogatory comments I found peace, understanding and discernment of the situation." "We are going to be bless (sic) more if we are humble. May the Holy Spirit guides (sic) us in everything that we do." My beleaguered friends would always end their insulting comments with prayerful invocations as the foregoing, as if to underline their great spirituality, and my brazen lack of it. Apart from their moral tone, one expression can synthesize these comments: *Your slip is showing.* Or: *Your words gave you away.* Here is the strongest reason the souvenir program, under our friends' care, got doomed to fail even before it got printed.

Proclaimers of these invectives were THREE officers of our Association. Another was a friend sympathizer who admitted having made the souvenir program herself WITHOUT your knowledge. This sympathizer was also the one who started the ball of insults rolling. Which brings me to these questions: As officers, don't your statements and actions, official or not, mirror our organization? As officers, do you follow any ethical standards in what you say and do, considering that you carry the name of our organization? What sanctions do you give when anyone of your own tarnishes the good name of the officers' circle and the organization?

Despite the foregoing personal attacks against me, done on Facebook, I kept my cool and self-control. If I answered back tooth for tooth, I would only dignify indignities hurled at my personhood. The points I raised in the open letter didn't matter. Truth and objectivity didn't matter. What mattered was emotions and the want to get even. So, the attacks turned personal and vitriolic. And because they turned that way, the attacks on my person affected my family, especially my wife and daughter. Even my relatives in the Philippines who read the volley of insults via Facebook hastened to call and tell me they, too, got hurt.

It has been 21 days and so far, these are the actions that the Association has meted out to me. ONE, the Association, through its Facebook group administrator and her sympathizers, has patted itself on the back and condoned the souvenir program committee's inefficiency. They even congratulated it for a job well done! TWO, the Association has stricken the open letter and the ensuing comments off its Facebook page. And THREE, and most appalling, the Association has blocked me from its Facebook page, in effect declaring me *persona non grata* thenceforth.

You can delete my posts, for all I care. Yes, I don't have a monopoly on the truth, but this much I can say—my open letter spoke the truth. You may have deleted it, but the truth stayed in the minds of those who read it. You may say as well that only one member of the officers' circle did the deleting, but this much I can say, too. Your silence means you are condoning it, and your inaction means either you don't care for the truth, or you shiver at the thought of disturbing the hornet's nest. With your silence and inaction, our organization had given its approval to the group administrator's action. With your silence and inaction, you are saying my letter was nothing but lies and nothing of immediate or important concern.

To top it all, you struck off my name from the Fil-am Association of Brownsville Facebook page. Or I guess the administrator of our Facebook group did. But under command responsibility, you all did it. Now I can't even access the page of my organization, much less post pieces of my mind on it! Now the administrator can continue maligning my person till she is blue in the face, without me being able to defend myself. By what authority can one officer do this? Did you allow this at all? "Stop making the matter worse, *i-delete mo na lang!*" [Just delete it]—did anybody among you issue this directive?

I am one of our Association's members of good standing, and most of you can vouch for my own humble contribution to it. Let alone the fact that I have paid for a lifetime membership. So, as any member of this honorable group, I demand the right to speak up and be where I belong. Nobody has the ultimate privilege to cast me off just because the truth slighted their ego. Just because they can't handle the truth.

The Fil-Am Association of Brownsville Facebook page is our group page, led by our circle of officers upon whose authority the group page exists. It does not exist under a dictatorship, under one personality, and with members who will only do its bidding and favor. If the administrator will say that the FB page is her private creation, so she can do whatever she wants, then let it be and let her keep her cabal. But let us demand that it should not carry our Association's name, or we should altogether strike it from the face of the—well, Facebook—earth.

Disregard this letter—we have other media and avenues. I will not stop seeking redress for my grievances. I will not stop till I get the justice I deserve.

Silence means condonation. Inaction means approval. Or prove it otherwise.

Let me end this with a famous prayer by the American theologian Reinhold Niebuhr, for all of us. "God, grant me the serenity to accept the things I cannot change, the courage to change the things I can, and the wisdom to know the difference."

-Arcádio Morada, Jr. ∎

The other day, my students and I came upon a green caterpillar inching its way up the tree in the small playground at the back of the Music Room. Against the gray-brown bark of the rugged tree trunk, the vibrant green of the caterpillar caught our attention. It had been crawling on the gravel and now it was wriggling up the tree—to our curiosity and delight.

The creature must have fallen off the tree sometime, and now it was trying to negotiate its way back to the luxuriant foliage in its instinctive search for food. Caterpillars being voracious leaf eaters, our green friend knew where it was going: up and up only! The children in play tried to distract it away from its journey, but it understood its destiny. Nothing, not us, could sway it away from its purpose. Nothing, not us, could alter its route!

In time, this caterpillar becomes a chrysalis, then a lovely butterfly. The start is so different and unrecognizable from the ultimate destiny. Every phase is a major change in its development. It comes full circle when, as an adult butterfly, it lays its eggs. To every egg that becomes a butterfly, metamorphosis is always a journey worth taking.

armela, you are undergoing your metamorphosis, your own phases of change, though in a much slower way. It has taken you 24 years—and counting. Like the caterpillar, you understand where you're going. You perceive your direction. Sure, you know where your journey is taking you. I am more inclined to call this evolution than metamorphosis. As the lovely butterfly is the caterpillar's own end, your journey is still on, and changes are being made of your own accord.

In league with the caterpillar, you have been such a wonder to behold. Chubby and delightful, you were such a darling toddler, worthy of inspiration for my song, **Small**.

Small is beautiful,
Small is wonderful,
Small is heaven sent for us all.
Small is lovable,
Small is flexible.
Big has to start with something small.

Who we are, what we are, where we are
Don't matter at all.
In God's eyes, in God's love,
We are all adorable.

Small is marvelous,
Small is fabulous,
Small is heaven sent for us all.
Small is lovable,
Small is flexible.
Big has to start with something small.
Big has to start with something small.

At the outset, in 1992, we nicknamed you by that delightful muscle deformity on your right cheek. "Dimple" was a straightforward choice, of course. Your actual forename, though, takes much more brain to understand and contextualize. Few people realize *Carmela* is not just the fateful conglomeration of Carmen, Mel, and Arcádio. (Mel-Greg Concepcion, my co-worker in Xavier School, Manila, Philippines, and a dear friend of your Mom and me since the 1980s, is one of your baptismal godfathers.) Realize further that your forename is an offshoot from a title of the Blessed Virgin Mary, Our Lady of Mt. Carmel, whose shrine in New Manila, Quezon City, Philippines, we often visited. Mom and I sought Our Lady's intercession when, as a two-week old baby, sepsis struck you. Of course, you could not have been here on your journey's 24th year had sepsis thwarted that cute baby's life!

Heaven sent you to us in May. Add the digits of 26, and you get the symbol of harmony and balance, the ability to decide, as well as abundance and power. Numerology aside, you are such a jolly person, flexible, adjustable, and adaptable—you get along well with people. You exude charm and joy, and you are such a joy to behold. Oh, to be born in the merry month of May!

At an early age, you inclined towards the arts. Singing, performing, and dancing in front of people endeared you to them. Growing up, you were often the center, the life, the color, or the chief attraction of parties and gatherings. You never showed stage fright; you exuded confidence. Early on, you manifested theatre was your life.

There was pronounced opposition to it at the start. Your Mom and I wanted you to look at, and look for, other options. Our family friends, the Dimaguiba[142], tried to help dissuade you. But your eyes remained fixed, your vision lucid. As that caterpillar, you saw where you were going. You knew the direction. We could only watch you and give you the needed prayers and support. You set your mind, heart, and soul for one explicit goal.

There was no turning back. That caterpillar might have zigzagged because of distractions, or missed the direct path sometimes, but it never wavered in its goal. You never wavered in your convictions, either. Up, up, up was the way to go!

And now that you have realized your vision, joy is in your heart. Success means joy in what you do. Your heart rejoices because you love what you do and you do what you love. We pray you succeed in your career in other aspects—for example, the monetary part of it. As much as satisfying your soul, we want you to line your pocket and gain material foothold and financial success, too. We will pray for your way to the bank.

Don't worry. Evolution is a slow and sure eventuality. In consonance with evolution, success is a ladder, an ongoing and never-ending one. You don't achieve it overnight, to reach the topmost. One step at a time, you scale that ladder to kingdom come. You have scaled the ladder at a significant height so far. The next step higher is waiting to be had.

The green caterpillar was right to aim for the foliage at the top of the tree. It was a journey worth the effort. There will still be struggles and challenges, but you can never go wrong aiming for your success! It's there waiting for the taking. ∎

Philippine presidential election 2016 had come and gone. Rodrigo Duterte won by a plurality vote of 16 million, with a platform of change. On June 30, he was inaugurated as the 16th President of the Philippines. That early, the Filipino people experienced the colors and nuances of the Duterte presidency. Cussing was the new official language, and vulgarity the new official normal of the Philippines. Extra-judicial killing, though illegal by any moral yardstick, was the unwritten current Code of Kalantiaw.[143] Bounty hunting became a profitable business, with everyone a potential hunter and hunted. Northern Philippines became happy and grateful *in aeternum;* they could now inter their beloved son Ferdinand Marcos—or, as doubting critics say, his wax replica—at the *Libingan ng mga Bayani* (Cemetery of Heroes), courtesy of Rodrigo Duterte. Vice President Leni Robredo would soon realize how difficult it was to be the second highest official of the land, unrecognized by the first. China would stay adamant in claiming Philippine sovereign territories that it thought was its own, with not just small help from the occupant of Malacañang of the South. Philippine media and the President would, from the looks of it, not see eye to eye. The Catholic Church, too, would be on a bitter spit and spat with the newly elected head of our land.

In view of these events, not a few among us would join the colony of bats. You know, those who believe in themselves and the principles they stand for, and yet are blind, tongue-tied or voice-less in the face of the overwhelming current moral issues. Take this feisty lady senator who had always been a vocal barometer of

---

142   Dimaguiba – a group of Fil-Am professionals in Brownsville, TX, who bonded and through the years became long-time friends: Marlene Aranda, Rey and Prescy Calara, Tim and Maribel Colglazier, Ron and Edith Lane, Jun and Mameng Morada, Don and Ging Relayson, Ely Scheiber, Nap and Mau Tesorero, and Clyde and Lou Trovela.

143   Code of Kalantiaw – a set of laws enacted and enforced in 1433 supposedly by one Datu Kalantiaw of Panay Island, Philippines. The punishments imposed by the Code were extremely brutal and not relative to the severity of the crimes. Many Filipino historians, however, maintain that the Code of Kalantiaw was a blatant hoax.

sensitive political issues in the past—mum about Duterte till she died. Take this former President of the Philippines, whose silence nowadays is inversely proportional to his unsolicited comments for presidential policies in the past—mum about Duterte. Least but not last, this cabal of editors and columnists of a few dailies who had spared nothing in their criticisms of former President Benigno Aquino III—mum about Duterte. We hope they are just looking for the right time to open their eyes and voice out their stand in the best interest of the entire nation. We hope, too, that they are not the Bat in my retelling of Aesop's fable, **The Birds, the Beasts, and the Bat**.

long time ago, when the world was young, a debate arose between the Mammals and the Birds. They wanted to resolve which group the Creator had endowed more and better favors.

The Mammals said, "We are superior, no doubt. The Creator has equipped us with special inborn qualities. We dominate the land!"

The Birds had minds of their own. "The Creator who created the Mammals and us too, has not equipped *all* Mammals with special inborn qualities, and not all animals equipped with special inborn qualities are Mammals. We dominate the air!"

"The Creator has blessed us!" said the Mammals. "We have the privilege to govern and decide!"

"The Creator has blessed us more!" said the Birds. "We have the right to be and the right to have!"

"*Huh!*" the Mammals said as they thumped the ground with their limbs. "Such presumption! We are far superior to any winged creatures on earth!"

The Birds flipped and flapped their wings in rebuttal. "Such arrogance!"

Thus, the debate continued with no sooner resolution in sight.

Now, as the word war raged on, there appeared out of nowhere an animal called Bat. The Birds approached Bat. "Here is your chance to do a noble deed, Bat. You've got to defend your race. Join us in the coming Big Battle. You will be a hero. Besides, we will win—we have the cleverest martial strategy of all time!"

"Why should I join the Birds?" Bat asked with a smirk. "I'm not a bird. Don't you realize I'm covered with hair? I inherited the intelligence and the magnificence of the Mammals!"

"You fly, as we do. No Mammals can."

"I'm a mammal, can't you see?" Bat gnashed his teeth. "Leave me alone! This is a pointless war, of which I want no part. I'm not a warlike species!"

Therefore, without Bat, the Birds faced the Mammals in the Big Battle.

In the early stage of the war, the Birds were winning. The Mammals approached Bat. "Here is your chance to do a noble deed, Bat. You've got to defend your race. Join us as we wage the Big Battle. A hero you will be!"

"Why should I join the Mammals?" Bat asked with a smirk. "I'm not a mammal. Don't you realize I have flight and access to the sky? I have inherited the agility and swiftness of the Birds!"

"You have hair for body covering, as we do. No Birds have hair."

"I'm a bird, can't you see?" Bat gnashed his teeth. "Leave me alone! This is a pointless war, of which I want no part. I'm not a warlike species!"

Therefore, without Bat, the Big Battle continued. This time, the scale tipped in favor of the Mammals.

Instead of vanquishing the Birds from the earth, however, the Mammals had a sudden change of heart. Amid the widespread loss of lives, the Mammals realized the uselessness of war and the senselessness of the violence. And so, in truce, they said to the Birds, "Let us stop this nonsense! Let there be love and harmony throughout the earth. Let us redeem ourselves through peace."

The Mammals then put a stop to making their hair stand on end, while the Birds plucked their flying colors. In unison, they agreed to start a new life on earth. Mammals and Birds clasped one another in brotherhood, humility, peace, jubilation, and celebration. "This is the best way to live in happiness forever!"

And Bat? He was not on anybody's mind. During the Grand Celebration, he was nowhere in sight. He was hiding in some dark cave, hanging upside down. Aloofness would mark the rest of his days. He was both a bird and a mammal, and neither one of them. ■

verybody knows the story. Somebody came to town, met with adulation and joyful celebration. No, I'm not referring to Yankee Doodle, who came to town a-riding on a pony. I'm not talking of Shrek and his best friend and sidekick Donkey, either. The story is of the King who enters Jerusalem riding on a donkey.

All creatures great and small,... the Lord God made them all.[144] I apologize for being pejorative of the donkey, which follows.

Many people, not only the smart-aleck, despise the donkey or ass as the embodiment of stubbornness, stupidity, and cruel jokes. Anybody will mind if called a jackass, a jenny, or a mule. (A jackass is a male donkey, a jenny is its female counterpart, while a mule is the offspring of a jackass and a female horse.) Most mules are *baog*, sterile in Filipino; they have the correct "parts" but cannot reproduce. For this reason, if you mate mules, you get nothing. We may as well castrate them, and no harm done. "Castrated mules" exercises redundancy.

In modern parlance, a mule is a person who smuggles or delivers illicit substances (such as drugs) into a country. Many months ago, China executed a Filipina for being a drug mule.[145] She got caught in Shanghai carrying a significant amount of heroin in her luggage. Trafficking drugs for a hefty sum from drug cartels was a blatant violation, a stupid risk she took, hard to condone. She did not deserve such a harsh fate, in fairness, for such criminal stupidity.

Have you heard the Indian story of the Lazy Donkey? Heard of the donkey who wanted to be a dog? Ridiculous and stupid, sorry. Using the stereotypical connotation of a jackass, even Abraham Lincoln was to have told a tale to deter favor seekers during his presidency, thus:

Once there was a king who went out hunting after his minister assured him it would not rain. On the way to the woods, the king passed a farmer who was working the land with his donkey. The farmer warned the

---

144   Cecil Frances Alexander, "All Things Bright and Beautiful," Hymns for Little Children (1848), https://en.wikipedia.org/wiki/All_Things_Bright_and_Beautiful.

145   Paterno Esmaquel II, *Rappler*, "Filipina drug mule in China executed," July 3, 2013, https://www.rappler.com/nation/32801-filipina-drug-mule-executed.`

king that it was raining soon, but the king just laughed and continued on his way. A few minutes later, rains poured, which soaked the king and his minions to their skin. Upon his return to the castle, the king fired his minister and sent for the farmer. He asked the farmer how he knew it was going to rain.

"It was not me, your Majesty. It was my donkey. He always droops one ear before the rains fall."

Aha! The king bought the donkey from the farmer and appointed the animal his minister at court.

Outright, that was not a stupid thing to do. The king's mistake only reared its ugly head afterwards. "Because ever since then," Lincoln was to have concluded the tale, "every jackass in the kingdom comes applying for an office in the king's court."[146]

Then the vulgar donkey jokes. No small thanks to the English language for putting so much disrepute and dishonor upon the ass—the point or object of our asinine jokes and irreverent idiomatic expressions.[147]

Q: What happens when you are carrying a donkey and you chuckle so hard you drop him?

A: You're laughing off your ass.

Q: What happens when you buy a mini-donkey?

A: You are getting a little ass.

Q: How do you compliment a donkey?

A: "Hey, nice ass!"

Q: What do you call a donkey that was born with a brain injury?

A: A dumb ass.

Q: What do you call a donkey with a PhD?

A: A smart ass.

Q: What do you get when a donkey eats a porcupine?

A: A pain in the ass.

Such idioms may appear colorful and risqué, and may sound inappropriate and offensive to many people!

I am not writing these things to assail goodness and propriety, or to condone irreverence. I am just raising a point: how far we have gone in tarnishing the image of the lowly donkey in our midst.

For the donkey is not every inch negative.

The donkey is an animal known for its even temper, patience, endurance, and sure-footedness. Joseph the carpenter and the Virgin Mary traveled from Nazareth to Bethlehem, a distance more or less 80 miles over rugged and inhospitable terrain. Mary, riding on a donkey, was heavy with the Child. It must have been the donkey's even temper, patience, endurance, and sure-footedness that carried the mother of the King, unsullied and unscathed. The Nativity story could never have been complete without the donkey.

---

146   *Variety Reading,* "Lincoln's Donkey," http://varietyreading.carlsguides.com/forwards/lincoln.php.
147   *Jokes4US.* "Donkey Jokes," http://www.jokes4us.com/animaljokes/donkeyjokes.html.

There's wisdom from this donkey story, too.[148] Once, a farmer's donkey fell into a useless well. Realizing that the donkey is old, and the well needs to be covered up anyhow, the farmer shovels dirt into the well to bury the animal alive. Of course, the piteous donkey brays, asking for help. It cries even more so when it realizes what the farmer is doing. But then, to the farmer's amazement, the donkey stopped crying.

A few shovels of dirt more, and the farmer discovers in astonishment the donkey's scheme. With every shovel of dirt that lands on its back, the donkey takes a step up after shaking off the dirt. Soon enough, the donkey steps over the edge of the well and scampers away.

Moral of the story: Life is going to shovel dirt on you. Stop crying. Shake it off and step upward. You can surmount the deepest wells that way. That's for us, homo sapiens; the donkey is just incidental!

The donkey was first domesticated in the East (Egypt or Mesopotamia) around 3000 BC. It was common in Palestine. Relatives of the horse in the *Equidae* family, donkeys have worked together with humans as beasts of burden and companions for millennia.

Now back to the Baby King. He got older, and he had to march to Jerusalem on a donkey. Why not a horse? In contrast to the horse, by tradition the animal of war, the donkey is an animal of peace. A peace-loving king might come riding on a donkey, while a king hell-bent on waging war rode upon a horse. When the King entered Jerusalem on a donkey on Palm Sunday, he wanted to give the message and impression that he came in peace, as the Prince of Peace.

The prophet Zechariah said: "Behold: your king is coming to you, a just savior is he, humble, and riding on a donkey, on a colt, the foal of a donkey." (Zech 9:9) Likewise, King Solomon rode to his coronation on a mule that had once belonged to David (1 Kgs 1:33-44).

Jesus is the King; he broke traditions. Kingship was one of them. Traditional ideas of kings are power, wealth, pride, warlike disposition, and readiness. But he shied away from limelight and honor. In fact, he always warned his disciples after performing miracles not to tell others. But, on Palm Sunday, he rode on an ass to enter Jerusalem. The people lined up the roadway, saying in jubilation, "Hosanna to the King!" They waved palm fronds and their cloaks and then strewed them on the road as he passed—which was a tradition to shield a king from the dirty road. Did the King want celebrity status despite expectations to the contrary?

OK, he wanted to show us in symbols that he is royal—a king, yes, but a different kind. A King rooted in service and humility. A King whose first consideration is not his own self but his constituents' welfare. Our welfare.

After the royal entrance to Jerusalem, a sequence of horrors hounds him. He sweats blood in Gethsemane. Judas betrays him. The Romans arrest him. Peter denies him. He undergoes a mock trial. Pilate condones his crucifixion, and he dies on the cross alongside thieves. His persecutors humble Jesus too lowly. For what? The way of the cross is his way of fulfilling his kingship. His way of telling us that the King loves us and that our welfare is foremost in his mind.

The way of the cross defines our salvation. The horrors the King experienced led to our redemption. We glory in the thought and benefits of salvation because he first broke traditions and sacrificed himself for our sake. Even for those who were waving their palms at his entrance to Jerusalem.

---

148   *Heart & Soul Network*, "The Donkey in the Well," http://www.heartnsoul.com/donkey_story.htm.

Remember the animal on which the King rode. At that exact moment in time, the small and lowly ass of our disreputable expressions, stories, and jokes must have been much bigger than the biggest elephant, whale, or dinosaur that ever lived. ■

Most of the time, or every time for most of us, his voice is not audible. We don't hear him. God could speak to us today—why not?—but he speaks in most cases through his written word. He has given out ways to lead us to hear him. The Holy Spirit, the events and circumstances in our life, the various ways other people touch us—these are enablers and "amplifiers" to perceive him talking to us. By comparing what we "hear" to the truth in his written word, the Holy Bible, we come to recognize his voice.

How do we come to recognize the voice of someone we think we know? Through constant communication and intimacy. That's how we know we are talking to a member of our family, for example, even if only through the telephone when they are absent or out of sight. We know their voice though over wide seas half the world away.

We recognize someone's voice if we belong to them or their circle. Jesus gives a perfect analogy himself:

We can imagine here a big gathering of sheep, hundreds of thousands, into one paddock or fold. They brought them in for shelter, protection, and safekeeping for the night, arriving in smaller groups or flocks one after the other, each flock led by a shepherd. The keeper in charge of the paddock welcomes and lets them in. As the sheep of one shepherd mix and mingle with the other shepherds' sheep, we can imagine the resulting chaos and confusion. We ask ourselves how on earth will a shepherd retrieve his sheep in the morning, missing none?

Simple—by using his voice. In the morning, the shepherd just calls out his sheep by name. They come to him because they recognize his voice, then he leads them out!

Communication leads to familiarity, and familiarity to intimacy. If we want to recognize God's voice talking to us, we need to be familiar with Jesus and belong to him. We can only recognize the voice of God when we strive to be familiar with, and belong to, Jesus Christ as our God and King. ■

 looked at my reflection in the mirror this morning and thought of dyeing those silver strands in my left eyebrow. For some time now, they have exposed to unsuspecting people my probable age, so at the back of my mind I resent their silvery presence. I plucked them off sometime, but of course they regrew. For every silver hair an aging person like me pulls out, it seems two or more appear in its stead or around it. So, now I resort with compulsion to dye them to achieve the same illusory effect. Well, I realize I was just trying to hide signs of aging. Other people, most of them ladies, go to Belo Medical [an esthetic salon] on purpose to diminish the onslaught of age and promote aging with grace. And, hey folks, most of us look toward aging with subconscious reluctance.

A nephew texted me on my sister Prid's husband Manny being confined in the ICU of the Philippine Heart Center. He said Prid needed moral and financial help. I said a prayer for his healing. My wife Mameng, ever her generous self, did what had to be done, as family and as Christian; she sent help and reminded me of my hypertension. Take care of your heart for me, she said in effect. I do, sweetheart, as the doctor and the oatmeal have been my constant companions for over ten years now. Diseases never to come to you or me, I prayed.

(My brother-in-law Manny Vitug succumbed to complications of diabetes on March 1, 2015. *Eternal rest grant unto him, O Lord, and let perpetual light shine upon him. May his soul, through the mercy of God, rest in peace. Amen.*)

Over news and social media a few months ago was Bob Saget having died in his sleep in an Orlando, Florida hotel room at 65. His **Full House** fans were beside themselves, whining, and bemoaning his "untimely" demise. To be exact, just what is the "right" time? At 95 or 105? I am not an avid fan of him or of his TV series myself, but I could imagine him traveling toward his foreordained destiny among other deceased celebs and stars. I said a prayer for his soul's repose.

Black is the color of death, and no one personified it in a more horrifying manner than 'Jihadi John.' He'd been in the news as the Executioner in black. Believed to be Kuwaiti-born London computer programmer Mohammed Emwazi, the masked ISIS militant with a British accent, had no qualms at beheading Western hostages. Oh, decapitation was not the only, nor the most gruesome, atrocity his group had done in Syria and Iraq. With impunity they had raped, mutilated, executed, crucified, burned, or buried alive enemies of their ideology and faith. Jihadi John and his ilk were wilder than the wildest of wild animals in their modern-day crimes against humanity. I agonized after watching an online video of how they scorched to death a captive Jordanian pilot inside a cage. Every time the ISIS executed their hapless captives, I prayed for enlightenment, remorse, conversion, repentance, and forgiveness, though impossible they might appear to be.

Speaking of wild animals, far more prudent but just as revolutionary is this animal, scientific name *Turritopsis dohrnii*, a thumb-sized jellyfish in the Mediterranean Sea and the waters of Japan. Discovered in the 19th century, scientists had studied them in the 1990s. They found them to be by far the only living creature that can revert itself back to a former stage of its life. Meaning, that in the face of stress, aging, disease, or physical injury in its mature life, this living organism can transform itself back to youth! How revolutionary can you get! Enthralled scientists call it the immortal jellyfish. I'm dumbfounded, and what I can say is, *Hey, be my shrink, Mr. Turritopsis—can you please guide me how to do it?*

That foolish call gives me away. I realize I am fussing, out of my subconscious mind, about my mortality. I'm fussing about aging, disease, or physical trauma as the *eeny-meaney-miney-mo* cause of my death, God forbid! Without admitting it, I am Juan Ponce de Leon once again in frantic search of the Fountain of Youth. I am civilizations throughout the ages looking for the philosopher's stone, universal panaceas, and elixir of life.

The good news is, there is such a Source of Life Eternal. The bad news is, humanity, including me, has looked for it in the wrong places. Where might we find the Source? The bad news is, the answer to this question sounds very far. The good news is, it's very you-won't-believe-it near!

I was born into the faith that teaches the answer to the question. My parents, my teachers, and other people around me, religious or not, have taught me about the Book, the Good News, the Bread, the Way, the Truth, and the Life. I need not look any farther and further. The Book, the Instruction Manual of Life, shows the true Source of Life Eternal. Death is the way of all flesh, but the Book tags the Way to immortality of everyone in faith. Just like the paralytic hovering by the Pool of Bethesda, the Source heals everyone who waits and listens and believes. More than that, everyone who believes and follows the words of everlasting life gets to live it.

The Book is inviting me now. The Book is inviting us now. More than ever. There is no way for someone to say they have exhausted and understood its wisdom to the fullest. No way for someone to say they have seen the wonders and riches it describes. Let's heed the invitation. "Open me and read the words of everlasting life."

Jesus'. ■

18
TWO-FACETED
This I or i of mine

noops, peruse this piece of writing, and what comes to mind? *Tsk, tsk, tsk,* you smirk as you shake your head. Someone incurred myriad problems to have written this song that follows. Take a second look and judge for yourself.

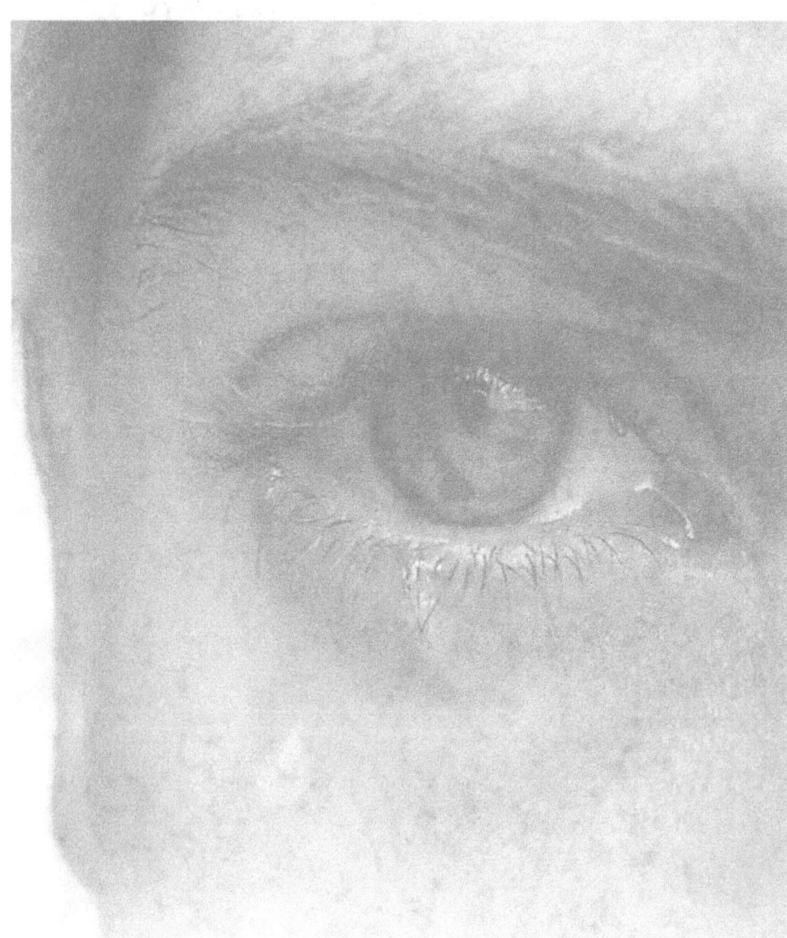

<u>RESIGNATION</u>

How will I ever find
A better place under the sun?
Other people say that life
Is like the wheel and like the tide.
Yet to me my life is nothing
But a storm of loneliness.
Yes, it's a wheel that never turns
And it's an ever-ebbing tide,
Always low.

So, I cry alone tonight,
feeling so low, feeling so tight.
There's nobody near to love,
no one loves me, no one cares!
A flightless bird, a willow tree,
a stranger hopelessly alone!

Someone said I have to sing,
To fight, to rise when I do fall,
To go on, to love and taste
Whatever joys others may share.
But to live is playing games
Where I don't win and always lose.
Times when I tried were times I failed
And felt how much others have left me
Afar.

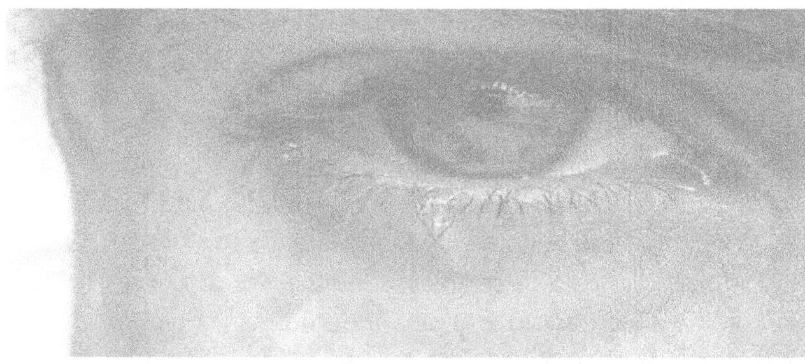

You deduce a slew of terrible things must have depressed the writer. He sounds as if carrying a very heavy load upon his shoulders, and he is near the edge of his own ravine. He sounds so anguished that he is even contemplating death. You pray for the person. Hoping that he is not suicidal, you know that suicide is the 10th leading cause of death in the United States, and that 123 Americans die by suicide every day. You hope against hope that depression won't result in annihilation, and that the person will see the absurdity of his intentions.

We, too, experience being troubled and depressed now and then, although with varying degrees or intensities. It is a fact of our day-to-day stressful lives.

"Don't worry," my surgeon said before he did colonoscopy procedure on me.

"Expect me in your class within the next 10 days," Mr. Pablo Leal, Villareal Elementary School principal, announced his classroom observation plan for me, but don't worry.

Bills need to be paid, to avoid fines and eventual Credit Bureau reports, but don't worry. The lawn has been waiting to be mowed, but don't worry. The leaking faucet needs repair, but don't worry. There is infestation of mice and cockroach in the garage, but don't worry. Ash, my schnauzer, is incontinent because of old age, while Valentine, my poodle, shows signs of mites, but don't worry. Everything will be fine, yes, they will. Don't worry.

"Don't let your hearts be troubled," read the good deacon at Mass last Sunday. There is always a solution to our troubled hearts. "If we have faith in God, a lot of problems can be solved, or at least can be accepted or understood." (Fr. Jerry Orbos, **Philippine Daily Inquirer,** May 18, 2014).

That person who wrote our song in question—he needs to have more faith in the Absolute Being, our Omnipotent God. I know. For *I* am the one who wrote it.

Sorry, my bad—*i* wrote it. *i* was ready to call it quits and go. Time proved me wrong. ∎

I and *i*

The person sitting next to you has some things that [s]he can do well. There are some things that [s]he can do better than anybody else in the whole world…. The person sitting next to you is an inexhaustible sort of existence. Within him are energies that have only been partially awakened. Nine-tenths of his possibility has not yet been touched off…."

Those are Dr. Ross L. Snyder's words. He (1902-1992) was an eminent religious educator from the Chicago Theological Seminary, and these words are from his **A Meditation: Focus Person**, as quoted by Rev. Walter E. Johnson.[149]

Man is an embodied self, an incarnate matter. He is a being in the world, in time and space, in physical existence. The world thrusts him into circumstances in which he has no choice or control—his culture, heredity, environment, sexuality, family, talents, class, *etc.*—which affect his physical, social, and psychological being. Despite these limits or determinants, his is "an inexhaustible sort of existence," one that we can never contain in a nutshell nor explain in full using symbols and words. A thousand and one doors are wide open to him for what he can be and do. He is dynamic, a struggle for perfection amid imperfections, a continual realization from abstract to concrete. Though limited by his incapacities, he has his share of God-given capacities ("things that he can do well," "things that he can do better than anybody else"). If he goes beyond these limits by accepting and responding to them, in front of him opens up a universe of possibilities.

I look at nothing else and focus nowhere else for a good or wrong example: this *I* or *i* of mine. Matter of fact, far better and far worse examples exist, past and present. But neither do I want to mis-evaluate and underestimate nor condescend and cast aspersions on other people by dropping their names.

I am Filipino, not American or any other race. With Filipino blood running in my veins, I was born and had lived in the Philippines for four decades before residing in the United States for three decades now. Howsoever I may want to declare that I am an American citizen, it doesn't erase what my origins are; I am only an American by naturalization. Never can I be American by looks, by hook or by crook, because I am not Caucasian, my skin is brown, I am short and snub-nosed, I speak with an accent, and a host of other inescapable and undeniable Filipino reasons.

I was born into a conservative, authoritarian family. It has reared me in its strict discipline, but with an abundance of familial love and guidance. Spanking was a means to a good end. This *I* or *i* of mine is a product of such discipline grounded in love.

I spent most of my education under the Philippine public-school system. Though my parents were themselves unschooled, more because of external than internal reasons, they saw to send me and my siblings to school and make us finish it. With the value they placed on education, my parents guided me to love schools; in due time, I developed a fondness for the disciplines, mathematics and music in particular. Through a line of exceptional teachers who fed me the basics and needed boost for success, I—albeit reluctant at first—came to pursue and finish an education career myself.

If only I had multiple bodies and more financial means! If it were only possible to be in two places at a particular moment! I might have studied engineering or music in a Manila school (over 500 km road distance from my hometown where I took my teaching course) to be a civil engineer or a virtuoso pianist. I could not build bridges, roads, buildings, and infrastructures now, because I chose to build children's minds instead. Impossible to be a virtuoso pianist either—too late now to have what it takes to be one—because I preferred the skills of playing lessons to little children to form their minds instead. For my life career, I chose education over engineering and performing arts.

I strove to excel in math in college, burning midnight oil to comprehend Spherical Trigonometry, Calculus, and other such highfalutin math stuff, graduating with math as my field of concentration. Although I did not become a virtuoso pianist, I had the patience and perseverance to self-study music up to being able

---

149   Ross L. Snyder, "A Meditation: Focus Person," quoted by Rev. Walter E. Johnson, http://www.revwalterjohnson. com/My-favorites/index.html#a-meditation.

to sight-read any piece of vocal music, explain what the figures and symbols are, and sing it outright. Even if I never learned to play the piano with significant skill, I composed and published a sacred music book, and accumulated two unpublished volumes of my own songs, two unpublished operettas and a cantata—and still counting—because tinnitus and music ring in my ears. From accepting my incapacities came forth other possibilities of what I could be, which I pursued to the best and fullest of my capacities.

This *I* of mine has opened other doors. Once a part of a school paper's editorial board, I own several short stories, essays, and poems that may never see print (so I mount them on a website of my own for the world to see). I could do 60 or more words a minute on a manual typewriter, and nowadays my fingers dash more than that on a keyboard. I can play the recorder (musical instrument) so well as to lift your spirits or lull you to sleep. Give me any sentence and I can diagram it for you and explain its syntax—or haven't you heard I was the Class Grammarian of my high school graduating class? *Konprontasyon*—a play on student activism—a brainchild in my senior year of college, won First Prize in the Bicol University College of Education One-Act Play Competition in 1974. "Awit Sa Kaunlaran" [Hymn to Progress], a musical brainchild, won 2nd Place in a Bagong Lipunan [New Society] Songwriting Contest in Albay in the same year. My sacred music entitled "Among You" was selected and sung in the Composers Forum during the National Pastoral Musicians Convention in Detroit, Michigan, in 2011. Under my leadership, the Fil-Am Choir of St. Mary's Church in Brownsville, TX, has ministered to Sunday Masses since 2009. They sing responsorial psalms from my first (and, I hope, not the last) published book, **The Purple Psalmody**. This compendium of not-so-trivial achievements is just one-tenth; nine-tenths of my possibilities are still untapped.

I never enjoy a cigarette between my lips nor its smoke in my lungs, or a swallow of a drink tasting as bland as, or harder than, beer. I am a home-body, more so at night, hence I am not a bar-hopping night-owl. My idea of gambling is playing solitaire, and Las Vegas and Atlantic City are not in my list of places to go. An avid movie fan, I stash good movies, through the years accumulating a modest DVD/Blu-Ray collection which can be the envy of my kith and kin. Reading and writing are lifelong hobbies.

BUT—

This *i* of mine is a debacle in sports. A very poor conversationalist. A nervous, passive leader. Asthmatic. Very timid in front of girls and crowds. Afraid to be on stage or on the spot. Never can draw well. Never can sing worthy of notice. Lazy letter-writer. Prefers to be in the backdrop or sideline. Afraid of the dark and the deep. Easily moved to tears. Constantly sleepy. Finicky at meals. Melancholic and melodramatic. Inveterate procrastinator. A lousy lover (my wife says). And so on. And so forth.

This *I* or *i* of mine is human—and man. I am the person sitting next to you. Or the *Y* or *y* of You. Both *y* and *i* should have no regrets about being. I don't know if You agree, but *i* sure have regrets, and *I* don't. ∎

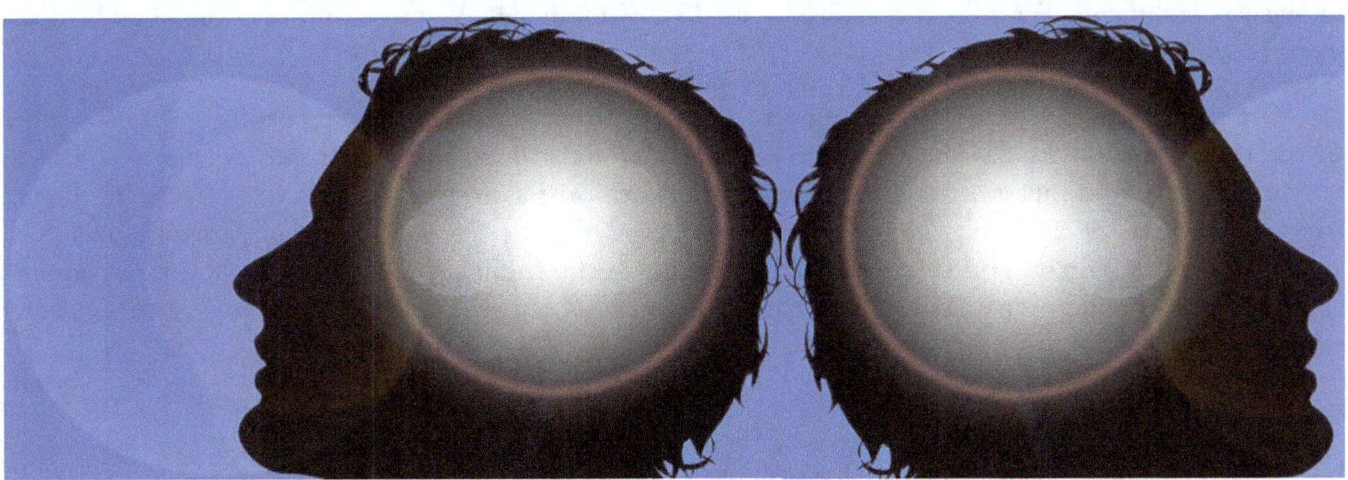

19
DYSFUNCTIONAL
The sons—not the Father

The good priest at our New York side of the woods (Woodside, NY) had a mouthful to say about, you know, bearing our own crosses. He might have somehow heard of me having a troubled and troubling week! No kidding. I've had this gaping wound on my left big toe for a week now, inflicted by a female *kasambahay*[150], that has left me in pain and my family in anguish. Another female *kasambahay*, who might have meant no harm, daubed and doused alcohol on the wound—by accident, she said. It made me shout expletives which you wouldn't want to hear, and which, of course, hurt the douser. For a week now she had not spoken to me, so for a week now I'd felt as troubled as she'd been. Limping with my troubling foot, I went to listen to the good priest during Mass at my side of the woods.

Bearing one's own cross is as Christ-like as can be, the good priest said. It is the way to follow Him. "Consider a president's anti-immigrant cum pro-white stand, for example, as a cross to bear." "*Uh-oh*, what a cross!" I said to myself, as I heard murmurs and unsolicited comments from the congregation. "Jesus must be a Democrat!" "That's blasphemy!" "This is going too far!" "*Shh!* Listen!" A parishioner in the back pew stood and walked out. "Well," said the good priest, "if we have the heart of a Christian, if we are what we say we are, we bear our cross without a grudge." Right?

The people fell silent. It was simmering inside my chest.

Politics aside, the good priest said, "When someone does us wrong, the good Christian in us says, 'Forgive and forget.' The other Christian (as opposed to the good Christian) in us says, 'It takes time to forgive, let alone forget.' Peter the disciple said, 'Lord, how many times shall I forgive my brother when he sins against me? Up to seven times?' Jesus replied, 'I tell you, not seven times, but seventy-seven times.' Jesus tells us that forgiveness is difficult. Forgiveness may need a lifetime of forgiving. We must continue forgiving until the matter settles in our heart."

The good Christian in me says, "Forgiveness is hard to find, yes, but not impossible." And the other Christian in me counters, "When others do me injustice, and I demand punishment, people are quick to tell me I don't have compassion, and I am vindictive. When others do me injustice and I forgive and forget, where is my sense of right and wrong? Where is my sense of justice? Should the good Christian in me be compassionate and forgive Hitler, for example, for his sins against humanity, so others would not perceive me as heartless and vindictive and unchristian? What do I care about Hitler? About Trump? About my *kasambahay* who caused me pain?"

---

150   *kasambahay* [Filipino] – house mate, a person who lives with others in a household.

And then I recalled a day earlier overhearing my *kasambahay* #2 (the alcohol douser) talk to my *kasambahay* #1 (the wound inflicter)—that I should be more Christian and forgiving. Christian and forgiving, my foot!

Should I forgive my female *kasambahay* #1 for wounding me so others would not perceive me as heartless and vindictive and unchristian? The scale between her action and Trump's and Hitler's may be different, but the same principle applies.

We are not cave dwellers. We are Christian—compassionate, forgiving, and not vindictive, because that's what Jesus said: "Forgive." But God gave us the Ten Commandments, too, his code of crime and punishment. This code does not say we may commit adultery or kill or steal or insult and slander; anyway, if the other guy is a Christian, he will be compassionate and not vindictive, and he will forgive us.

My left big toe hurts, and I'm limping. The gaping wound will take time to heal, and so does forgiveness. In the meantime, Jesus says to me through the Gospel, "Whoever wishes to come after me must deny himself, take up his cross, and follow me." (Mt 16:24)

I pray, "Help me, Lord, to be a good Christian—not the other Christian. To forgive. To see the way you see. Help me, Lord, to see the beauty of the Cross."

The good priest, continuing his homily, interrupts my flow of thoughts and prayer. He talks further about God's kindness, mercy, and generosity. OMG, I'm sorry, I'm so dysfunctional; it's so hard to weigh things over here on my side of the woods! ■

Where is the mother? We know what mothers are and what they can do. While our mothers feed and clothe us, they—the "light of the home"—own the uncanny ability to put up with our ridiculous behaviors; they redirect and care for us as long as their physical bodies allow. They make sure that our happiness comes before their own, and they accord us unconditional love. But within this family, where is the mother?

The father is well-to-do, even in the metrics of our time. He owns vast tracts of land for grazing and farming. His tenants harvest wheat and bread from his fields, grapes and wine from his vineyards, besides spices and olives. Apart from sheep, he owns pigs, goats, mules, oxen, horses, and camels. He is wealthy beyond compare.

And yet…

He has a young son who comes to him one day, saying, "Father, give me my inheritance. I want to go far and live as I please, to live a life of my own."

Prodigal Son photos courtesy of http://www.freebibleimages.org/photos/prodigal-son/

I want to be free,

Like the birds that fly,

I want to be free, like the wind

Without rules to live by.

Who cares if I go

tumbling,

gambling,

fumbling,

crumbling!

It's nice, it's cool to be free!

-I Want to Be Free (verse 1)
from CATECHETICAL SONGS FOR
CHILDREN *(unpublished)*

This is ridiculous! Despicable! In whatever culture, anywhere, what the son is asking is tantamount to asking for his parent to—die right at the moment!

And yet, the father speaks not a word. His young son's preposterous demand must have stilled him for a moment, shocked him, but he goes on anyhow to divide his estate between his two sons. He gives the younger his share.

Whereupon the younger son sets off to a faraway country. He lives his days in profligacy, spending his money in extravagant ways. He shows no regard for his family or his future until he has nothing more to spend and famine creeps through the land. Because he lacks education, of course he needs to work for his sustenance through menial jobs, even as lowly as feeding swine.

Anguished realization after another makes him come to his senses. "In my father's house, servants live more luxuriously than I have forced myself to live. Pigs eat enough and more sumptuous meals than I do now! This is what freedom has brought me. This is what worldly things have brought me!"

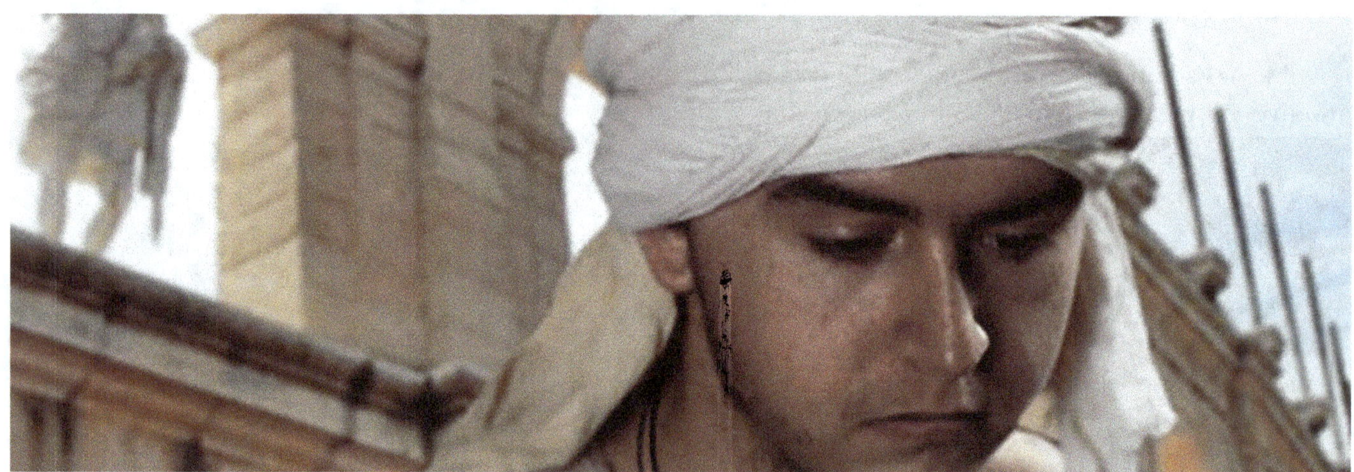

So, you want to be free,

like the birds that fly?

You want to be free like the wind

Without rules to live by?

But freedom is

doing and following

what you ought

to be doing.

Yes, nice, it's cool to be free!

-I Want to Be Free (verse 2)
from CATECHETICAL SONGS FOR
CHILDREN *(unpublished)*

"So, then I will rise, and to my father, I will seek forgiveness. For I have sinned against heaven and against him. He does not deserve a son like me, and I don't even deserve to be called his son, but I'll go, anyhow."

What kind of father is this? Isn't he as much dysfunctional as his son? Isn't he as much a problem as his son? The son insulted him by asking for his inheritance, as yet he was still alive, but he never so much as gave him counsel and thwarted his desires. He anguished as he watched him leave and go astray, yet he never said a word of wisdom to redirect him to a righteous life.

Never, really?

He is a father who will do everything to help him turn his son's life around, to make it right. If only he were here! He has been praying for his return. And now, wait, isn't he that ragged man approaching?

He whoops as he runs towards the approaching ragged man. "My son is back! I need to welcome, embrace, and kiss him!"

Father and son meet beyond the gate. "No, Father," the son says, "I don't deserve your embrace and kisses, for I have not been a dutiful son to you!"

The tenants, the servants, and the villagers bear witness to this moment of great joy. They hearken to the body language and utterances of the two partakers in this emotional scene.

"You are my son," the father says. "I lost this son, but I found him at last!" Then, to the servants, the old man gives orders. "Get the finest robe and put it on him! Fetch the most precious ring and put it on his finger! Look for our most exquisite sandals from Jerusalem and put them on his feet. Roast a fattened calf, then invite the entire village. We'll make a grand welcome feast for my son!"

What kind of father is this? This father forgives the past and welcomes an irrepressible son back to his fold. He forgives the past and welcomes a dead son back to life. He forgives the person who his son was and welcomes the person who he will be. That's the father he is, full of mercy and compassion, full of kindness and love.

As dysfunctional is the other son. He is as disrespectful as can be. Displeased and irritated by his father's actions on his younger brother's arrival, he sulks and refuses to enter his father's house. This forces the old man to come outside and plead with him. He argues with him and answers his father back, in front of the entire village. In his irritation, he doesn't even address his father Father. He is making a scene at his father's expense.

The feasting stops and everyone gapes at the unfolding spectacle. Again, they hearken to every gesture made and word uttered in this emotional scene.

"Look," he says. "I've been a good, uncomplaining son. Through these years, I slaved for you and not once did I disobey your orders. Yet you never even gave me a young goat to feast on with my friends. But when that son of yours returned, who swallowed up your property with prostitutes, you slaughter the fattened calf!"

The villagers say in hushed tones: "How dare the elder son humiliate his own father! How dare he accuse his father of slaving him! How dare he accuse him of favoritism!"

"Son," he says, "you think I am the problem. You think the fault is mine because I've never praised you for doing a good job. By your reckoning, you think this celebration is lavish. By your reckoning, you think I am wasting my time and effort making this commotion when I couldn't even give you a modest goat to feast on with your friends. But, Son, you've been here with me always. Everything I have is yours. I lost your brother, but I found him at last. Doesn't that deserve a celebration?"

God is the Father, we are the sons dysfunctional. You and I are the older or the younger. We are so rich and so blessed in God's fold, but God still gives us free will to choose. It's a choice to stay within or outside his fold. It's a choice between life and death. While many of us choose to stay away, we need not fret. Our loving and merciful God welcomes us back and gives us new life if we return to him. He enfolds us back in his arms despite our unworthiness.

Remember, we are the dysfunctional—not the Father.

After we grasp the profundity of that truth, my question returns: where is the mother? Forgive me if I still think a mother could have mattered and changed the course of the story. But Jesus is the original storyteller, not me. There is no point in my propounding an opinion and raising a question. His parables—for instance, this one (Lk 15:11-32) upon which my retelling is built—are simply told but deep in meaning and full of wisdom. He is neither verbose nor highfalutin. The simplicity, integrity, symbolism, and truths of Jesus' parables are unquestionable. ■

20
MAGAYÓN
Spirit of the show, from inception to fruition

gnes of Rome, feast day January 21. "She is one of seven women who, along with the Blessed Virgin [Mary], are commemorated by name in the Canon of the Mass."[151] She died for her faith at 12 or 13 years old. Venerated for ages in Christendom, she is the patron saint of young girls and those who are seeking chastity and purity. But I am not now to speak of Agnes, nor am I to write about her physical beauty or the beauty of her soul. For at the moment, I am inclined to dwell on another beautiful lady, this time of Bicol folklore, in Agnes' behalf.

In 1975, as a faculty member of St. Agnes' Academy of Legazpi City, Philippines, I penned an operetta about the legend of *Daragang Magayón*[152], entitled **What Ever Happened to Magayon?** It was our production for the Feast of St. Agnes that school year (1975-1976). The show, performed by elementary school students with no background in acting and singing, turned out a success, and was four times re-shown to the public. As of this writing, the members of the cast, now all grown-up, are scattered worldwide, as are the director (Ms. Naomi Ravalo) and the writer (me).

The operetta unfolds into an ancient Malayan setting, peopled by native royalties with titles of *datu, rajah, lakan, apo,* and *sultan.*[153] Its characters are typical Malayan, in the customs and traditions of old. It centers on Magayón—the young, tall, and beautiful daughter of an aging datu who dislikes all her noble suitors, most especially a rajah with an attitude.

One day, amidst a luxuriant forest, she meets a handsome prince from Moroland, who woos her. Awakening follows. The two later discover that the world is a wonderful place to live in because they are in love and meant for each other.

But other people's plans get in the way, especially those of the rajah with an attitude. Because of him, the story ends in a tragedy. However, Nature takes over and makes things right. Magayón, though gone, is present for all the world to see, for all generations past, present, and yet to come.

Magayón's story tells how the Mayon Volcano came to be. It's a legend, of course.

In the 1980s, I made revisions to the libretto, adding a PROLOGUE (see Appendix B) and more songs. When in 1992 I migrated to the USA, I took the extant libretto along and placed it in a chest of memorabilia,

---

151   *Wikipedia.* "Agnes of Rome." https://en.wikipedia.org/wiki/Agnes_of_Rome.
152   *Daragang Magayón* [Bikol] – literally, "Beautiful Maiden"; the heroine of the Bicolano legend of Mayon Volcano.
153   *datu, rajah, lakan, apo, sultan* [Filipino] – rulers, chiefs or monarchs in early Philippine history.

(The original program cover , designed/created by Mr. Fidel Siapno)

where it lay hidden for some time, forgotten.

In a recent St. Agnes alumni homecoming, some of the original cast and their classmates expressed their dream to re-show the operetta, whereupon they duly informed me of the plan. Noel Andres Perdigon, my former student, spearheaded these dreamers. It gave me honor and joy to know that after four decades, Magayón could reemerge from dormancy, not just with beautiful memories but more so beautifully revived culture and esthetics as well.

The idea about presenting the legend of Magayón (and Mayón Volcano) as a cultural show germinated in November 1975. During a teachers' meeting in St. Agnes' Academy, the grade school faculty and staff were brainstorming about potential activities for the upcoming school foundation day on January 21, 1976. Naomi S. Ravalo, one of the faculty, broached the idea of a cultural musical show, which she offered to direct herself.

She said that one of us—her index finger pointing to me—was going to make the script, that we were both excited about the whole prospect. Nervously, I was willing and ready to burn the midnight oil and slug it out. Many co-teachers shared our excitement, but the task, said the few who did not, was just too big to complete within too short a time. **If There's a Will, There's a Way!**

For every problem, there's a solution.
If there's a will, there's a way!

Look at the little ant:
in spite of its size,
it can lift a mountain
that is a grain of rice!
If you'd tell me, it's a creature
that is far from being nice,
I would tell you it's a trifle
that is daring and wise.

And there's the tailor bird,
Pay eyes on him:
Uncomplaining it sews its nest

146

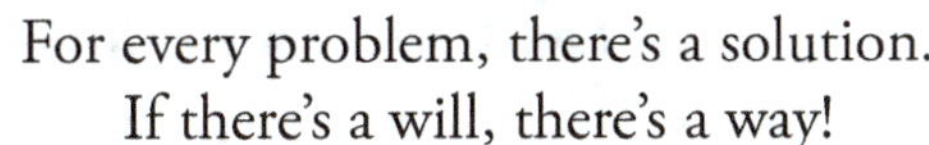

to suit its whim.
If you're wond'ring how he does it,
how on earth he keeps it trim?
Better ask who ever taught
this trade to him.

How many men are there
whose own bones they break,
They create their own storms,
not knowing what else to make.
Have they ever looked at bamboos?
With the winds, they sway along,
Growing taller for tomorrow,
always ready, brave, and strong.

For every problem, there's a solution.
If there's a will, there's a way!

I could make it, I said, and I did. A few days later, to Naomi's astonishment, I showed her the first draft of my operetta, **Whatever Happened to Magayón?** (Later, realizing the negative connotation of the word "whatever," I switched the title to read, **What Ever Happened to Magayon?** A minor change took the meaning to a whole new level.)

Of course, Naomi knew I was a college writer, as she was. We both served in the editorial staff of **The Mentor**, our campus paper, during our respective times. We graduated from the same university with the same degree, though she was two years ahead of me. What she did not know was that since elementary school, I had been composing songs as a passion. She just didn't know either that both the script and the music of *Magayón,* my favorite Bicol folklore, had been latent in me. With her as initiator and catalyst, everything toward the operetta's completion fell fast into place.

Naomi came from a cultured family; I was a neophyte teacher in my second year of teaching. Upon first reading, she approved of the script right away, but the music was another thing. When I presented and sang to her a few of my songs, however, she liked them without hesitation, too. "We definitely had to show your operetta," she enthused.

By December, with help from a few other teachers, we completed the selection of the cast, hands down. Reycelle Manuel (Magayón), Ronald Salazar (Rajah Buhawen), Jimmy Herras (Gat Malayo), Philip Perez (Datu), Evelyn Perez (Dawani), and Irene Encinas (Daliwawa) made up the main cast. Arlette Lana (Narrator/Sorcerer), Marisan Mejillano (Priestess), and Agnes Mahinay (3rd wife) played supporting roles. Thirty-four other kids from 4th to 6th grades sacrificed their Christmas vacation for daily rehearsals. With support and encouragement from the SAA administration, staff, and parents, our operetta was on its way to success. It was to be enhanced further by the excellent piano accompaniment of SAA high school music teacher, Mrs. Celeste Ronda. Since I only composed the melodic line of the songs, Mrs. Ronda provided the musical arrangements, incidentals, and embellishments needed to add flavor and color to my music.

We premiered **What Ever Happened to Magayón?** on January 15, 1976, with the SAA school community. It was re-shown to the public on January17-18. St. Agnes' Academy and parents sponsored its March 13 and 14 runs, at the Bicol Colleges HS, my secondary-school Alma Mater, in Daraga, Albay. After one show, Ms.

Josefina Lucena, my former professor at *Student Teaching 1* in college, wrote me a note that raved: "It was wonderful! I'm so proud of you!" Another former college mentor, Ms. Anicia Habitan, also watched one show, and could not contain her excitement as well: "I won't be able to conceive of that idea of presenting *Daragang Magayón* that beautifully! What creativity! Had I known it was that beautiful, I should have asked my students in Children's Literature to watch it. Thank you!"

Scene 1 presents Magayón, an old datu's daughter, and the problem that her youthfulness creates. Beautiful and very tall, she's in an age where one considers herself a woman-not-yet while everybody around says she's a girl-no-more. Why noble suitors swarm around her like bees is, therefore, a question incomprehensible to her. All such suitors she dislikes, especially a powerful rajah who gets so impatient that he vows to win her by hook or by crook.

That threat becomes a problem. In **Scene 2**, the aging Datu calls his advisers, wise men of the tribe, to a meeting. The critical-minded, the brave, the passive, and the ridiculous convene.

-From the PROGRAMME NOTES, January 17-18 shows

It is during that meeting when the Datu and his advisers proclaim, *"If There's a Will, There's a Way."* It was also during one fateful faculty meeting in November 1975 when Naomi Ravalo and I declared that in less than two months we could showcase culture in our school's foundation day celebration through an operetta.

That we did, and the rest is SAA history. The proceeds from the show helped build the SAA gymnasium almost five decades ago. So, you see, we had the show in Agnes' behalf.

If There's a Will, There's a Way was just one of the 18 musical numbers I composed for this show (21 songs in the revised edition). It was the song that captured without doubt the spirit of the whole Magayón affair, from its inception to fruition.

Before the euphoria of the show wore off, Sr. M. Asuncion Bonafe, OSB, Directress of St. Agnes' Academy, wrote me a thank you note, saying: "Your operetta will be long remembered by all the graders. Thank you!"

Well, after 46 years, what could I say but, "You're welcome, Ms. Lucena. You're welcome, Ms. Habitan. You're welcome, Sr. Asuncion."

If there's a will, there's a way! ■

21
FORMED
Four days in the Life

ecember 7, 1983. We are expecting here in Mother of Life Center an eminent visitor, Josef Cardinal Hoffner of Cologne, West Germany, together with our Jaime Cardinal Sin and a few Filipino bishops.

Ms. Beckers[154] is very excited. She has motivated us to prepare well for this event. For two weeks now, we've been brushing up on *Simbang Gabi*, a choral gem by Lucio San Pedro. Another musical piece we have practiced to perfection is *Bagbagtu*, a medley of indigenous songs we sang during the visit of Austrian priests last July. Three among us from *Sambahayan*[155]—Jack (Wanchakan), Olet (Avenilla) and Pitz (Valencia)—have been memorizing a poem on the Three Kings, a literary piece we presume Ms. Beckers values so much. They will recite this in front of the Cardinals and company, complete with actions and costumes. Someone among us giggles and says in a soft voice, "The three gentlemen look so very corny!" "*Shh, baka marinig ka ni Miss!*" another one says with much caution. "Hush! Miss [Aida Perpiñan, the Directress] might hear you!"

In addition, Jack, Arlene (Natocyad) and Tina (Remigio) are to do a tribal war dance from the Mountain Province, accompanied by gongs imported from Baguio City. You will laugh if you only see Jack now; he is wearing the traditional *bahag* (G-string) with his dark gray underwear showing. Another classmate says, *"Naku, si Jack! Magpapakita rin lang ng briefs, yong luma pa ang pinili!"* [My goodness, this Jack! Why does he choose to exhibit his old briefs!] Kidding aside, we are ready for our visitors' arrival and sojourn.

In the meantime, most of us are hoping and praying in silence for a remarkable, if not flamboyant, performance. *Holy Spirit, enable us to represent Mother of Life Center in the best way possible!*

ecember 6, yesterday, started in the usual manner. Wake-up alarm at 6:00 am. Holy Eucharist at 6:30 am with Fr. Servulo San Martin, whom we, with fondness, call Fr. Buloy. (The good priest is our professor in New Testament twice during the week, and every time he comes for his class, he celebrates the Eucharist to begin our day.) Breakfast at 7:30 am. (For this morning, Ms. Navales and her crew treated us to a feast of eggs and sausage.) After breakfast, house chores/task/duties. Fr. Buloy's class at 8:30 am, lasting for a couple of hours. At 11:30 am, lunch. Noon break starting at 12:00. By 1:30 pm, Ms. Perpiñan's Guidance & Counseling class, which consumed most of the afternoon. Individual silent prayer in the chapel at 6:00 pm, and then supper at 7:00 pm.

---

154 Ms. Mathilde Beckers, a secular nun of Notre Dame de Vie, established the Mother of Life Center in 1967.

155 *Sambahayan* [Filipino] – the male students' quarters at Mother of Life Center.

Ordinary and uneventful day, right? Wrong. Just after supper, Ms. Perpiñan clinked her drinking glass and, in a serious tone, announced that there would be an important meeting in the classroom after dishwashing. We asked ourselves in apprehension, *Naku* [Oh, my], are we in trouble? What's in store for us from our directress?

So then, right after dishwashing, we waited with nervous and deafening silence in our seats, in the classroom. The expected directress materialized in the person of Ms. Nilda Rosas, who is in charge of the Center's music ministry. Ms. Rosas announced that the matter at hand was so serious Ms. Perpiñan instructed to meet us in the Multi-Purpose Room upstairs instead. *Naku! Lalong ninerbiyos kami* [My, the more we had the jitters] as we trod up to the MPRoom. *Ano kaya talaga ito?* [What could this really be?]

When we reached the dimly lit Multi-Purpose Room, an old woman with a cane, looking out the window, startled us as she said: *"Mga bata! Mga bata!"* [Children! Children!] Of course, we gaped in amazement. Just what is happening? *Sino ba ang matandang ito?* [Who is this old woman?]

The woman whooped again, louder, *"Mga bata! Mga bata!"* Then from the outside the "children" dashed in: Ms. Perpiñan, Ms. Vicky Reyes, Ms. Rosas, Ms. Osit, and Ms. Cristeta Navales, all dressed in children's outfits! And the old woman? None other than Ms. Beckers herself—who else!

That was the surprise. The Staff, to teach us about St. Nicholas whose feast day is December 6, thought it wise to impart the information in the most dramatic and imaginative way. Since people knew St. Nicholas to be a generous person, especially to children, the Staff had prepared candies, chocolates, and cakes for us. What we thought of as a serious meeting turned out to be—with our collective heavy sigh of relief—a wonderful teaching-learning moment and a fun-filled "children's" party! We had great fun!

Dear Staff, pray tell us, what other novel ideas are you cooking up for us? Being formed in Mother of Life is getting more exciting day after day!

Tomorrow, December 8, we will go to the Manila Cathedral and be ushers and usherettes during a special Mass, which Cardinals Hoffner and Sin will concelebrate. Then we will go to Radio Veritas where Ms. Rosas and Flor (Manalo) will receive their respective prizes for winning in the *"Sino ang Katekista?"* (Who is the Catechist?) Contest. In the evening, we will have a para-liturgy in honor of our Blessed Mother, plus, of course, *yehey*, a grand agape—*"engrandeng kainan"* in simplest terms! (Thanks, Ms. Navales, and your coterie of kitchen assistants!) Tomorrow, as every Catholic knows, is the feast of the Immaculate Conception.

Happy feast day to Our Lady, to Mama Mary, to Mother of Life! Happy feast day of the Immaculate Conception to everyone!

March 25, 2015. Today, Solemnity of the Annunciation, I re-dedicate this hymn to Our Lady. I once did, when I was young and fresh from Mother of Life Center. My formation into catechetical ministry, religious education, Christian community leadership, and other pastoral work involved living in the Center for one year (school year 1983-1984). A full year of supervised pastoral work in the institution that sponsored me (Xavier School, 1984-1985) followed. Last, a summer integration work back at the Center in 1985 capped the formation curriculum.

I composed this song and finished it right on March 25, 1985, at the start of the summer integration work. In this song, I intended to encapsulate everything that I have learned in my formation at MOL. In between the lines, I incorporated my faith, my personal thoughts on Mary, and how I have come to love her through the years. Mary is my guardian, my Star, my Intercessor, my Model of faith.

This song is over three decades old. Yet the passion with which I sang it in 1985 is still very much present in me as I am singing it now. My jubilation in singing it now is as great as when I first wrote its lyrics and melody. As I sing, I hope I have not failed in my mission and calling. I hope I have not failed you, Mother of Life!

<u>MOTHER OF LIFE, WE HONOR YOU TODAY</u>[156]

Even as we come from different walks of life,
We commit to you in answer to a call.
Diverse may be our ways of living,
Yet in unity, we're striving,
To be true and faithful to the call.

Under your protection and your loving care,
Help us learn to know the Way, the Truth, and the Life.
O perfect handmaid of the Lord,
O Virgin Mother of the Word,
Teach us Jesus, Center of our Life.

<u>Chorus</u>:
Mother of Life, we honor you today!
Full of grace in every way,
Teach us your fiat, your loving fiat.
Teach us to live like your Son.
Mother of Life, most faithful and most pure,
Mother of our Savior,
Here in your dwelling, give us your blessing,
Mother of Love, Mother of Life!

As we do our mission in the years ahead,
Ever be the Star to guide us to be one,
One in all our undertaking,
To proclaim and go on spreading
To the world the Good News of your Son.

---

156   Arcádio Morada, Jr., *tagaalbay* "50 Generations," YouTube video for Mother of Life Center on its 50th Anniversary in December 2017, https://youtu.be/ceNpnON1ecc.

Glory to the Father, glory to the Son,
Glory to the Spirit, with Mary we sing!
In our trials and jubilations,
In our prayers and celebrations,
Thanks and praises to our God we bring!
(Chorus)

Coda:
For greater life! ∎

Established in 1967, Mother of Life Center (MOL) is a Catholic inter-diocesan Formation House and Graduate School for future catechists and missionary disciples of Christ for the Philippines and for Asia. It is located in 123 Susano Road, Barangay San Agustin, Novaliches 1117 Quezon City, Philippines.

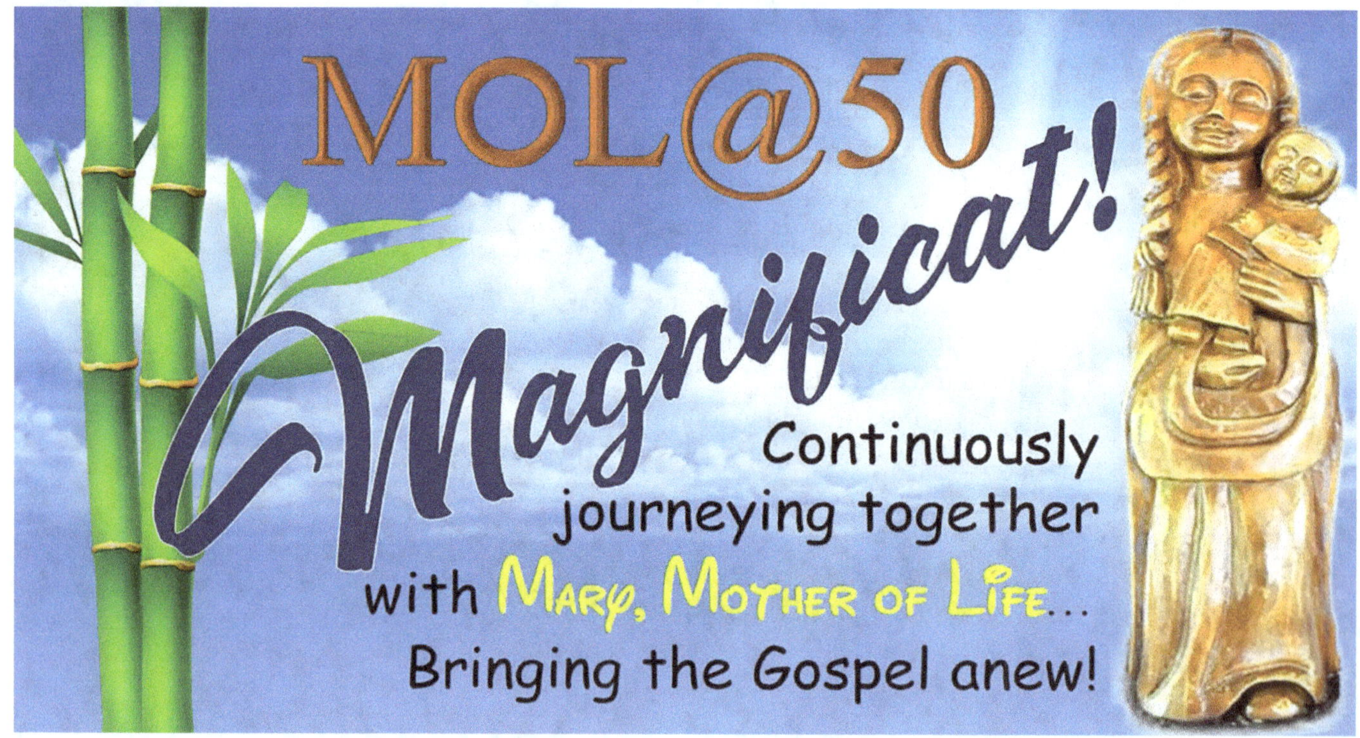

22

LUX

For God's greater glory

hen I left Xavier School for the United States thirty years ago, friends and colleagues called the move adventurous, unpatriotic, or regrettable. Five Texas schools and countless gray hair on my head later, I look back with fondness at Xavier School and say, "Hey, guys, AMDG!"

AMDG is the abbreviation for *Ad Majorem Dei Gloriam!* This is the Latin motto of the Society of Jesus, a religious order of the Catholic Church. It means "For the greater glory of God." That is Ignatian spirituality in a nutshell.

I'm referring, of course, to St. Ignatius of Loyola, founder of the Society of Jesus, whose anniversary (July 31) is the school's quintessential feast. Based in Greenhills, Manila, Philippines, Xavier School is under the management of the Jesuits—the well-known nomenclature for the Society of Jesus.

IGNATIUS[157]

He was a man of wealth and fame, a vain and brassy fellow
A fearless soldier of a king, so off to war, he did go.
But then he found the unexpected
when his right leg was hit and shattered.
His worldly dreams were shattered, too.
He realized he'd rather fight for Jesus.

Ignatius, Ignatius
Founder of Christ's army
Society of Jesus, so it came to be.
Helping men to fight against the evil in the world,
Guiding them to turn to God and go back to his fold.
Ignatius, Ignatius
Brave soldier of Christ.
Brave soldier of the King
Brave soldier of Christ.

-from CATECHETICAL SONGS FOR CHILDREN *(unpublished)*

---

157   Arcádio Morada, Jr., *tagaalbay*, "Ignatius," YouTube video 2:25 min., https://youtu.be/B5aXjaNRIUw.

During my early years as a Texas teacher, one fastidious 5th grader accosted me and asked, "You came from the Philippines, right?" Such innocent introduction to the malicious jaw-dropper that unexpectedly followed: "Do Filipinos live in trees?"

Of course, I know that this mindset, verbalized so often by my stateside students, is more out of naïveté than racial prejudice. I have learned to not get intimidated and to live with it, for I live and teach in a country where most people don't, or barely, know the Philippines. "Boys and girls, give me a break," I responded.

A few years ago, though, I gave myself the break to humor another generation of students (with the same mindset) and give them a dose of their own medicine. They wanted to pinpoint the Philippines on the world map, longed to hear sample Filipino words, and enthused to find out how Filipino schools and students looked. I was expecting the jaw-dropper to come any minute. Well, I said with less enthusiasm, "*Maganda* means lovely. *Maunlad* means progressive. Just go visit **www.xs.edu.ph** and see for yourselves!"

The *oh*'s and the *wow*'s and the OMG's that followed were enough attestations for "Xavier School, our pride and glory." At the back of my mind, I was condescending, thus: "Now, who lives in trees?"

Indeed, I have always looked up to Xavier as the school to emulate, to match, to beat. The school to be in, either as a student or as a teacher. Xavier is incomparable, way above any elementary or high school in the Philippines. I can even proudly say, even in these United States.

That's not stretching the truth.

Let your light shine… *Luceat Lux!* ∎

"**G**od said, let there be light," I remember an uncle on a family drinking spree once said, "but I prefer lite beer over booze!" Alright, I got the joke, but his homophones did not hit me as hard as those that I just encountered today. For today was a Sunday, and one reading at Mass mentioned the words "Be holy." At the back of my mind, God forgive me, I was thinking "holey" instead. To make matters worse, during the Consecration of the Bread and Wine, I was trying to see—again, God forgive me—any cognitive relationship between *holy* and *holey*. At first, I saw none.

"Be holy, for I, the Lord your God, am holy." (Lv 19:2)

How can one that's holey be holy? More muddling, how can one be *wholly holey holy?*

This is not, I realized, a useless play with words. There's something profound to be learned here, which I now want to share with you.

First off, I love what the famed Jesuit composer John Foley wrote: "When God built the human heart, he made it with a hole in it."[158] If I may embellish it, I want to imagine the ideal human heart with not just one but lots of holes in it.

Of course, in reality, we do not want holes in our heart, for they don't equate to comfort and physical well-being. In spirit, however, the number of holes in our heart determines its richness. More holes, more openness to let love in or out. The hole in our heart, Foley wrote, is "an openness that can let others in if we don't block it with selfishness, and if we grow into it."

---

158   John Foley, SJ, "The Temple of God," Spirituality of the Readings, 7th Sunday of Ordinary Time, Year A, February 23, 2020, The Sunday Website at Saint Louis University, https://liturgy.slu.edu/7OrdA022320/reflections_foley.html.

Selfishness shuts the doors of our heart on others. Since God is kind and merciful, the doors that let love in are kindness and mercy. We open our heart to relieve the physical and spiritual sufferings of others. First, the physical needs. To feed the hungry, give water to the thirsty, clothe the naked, shelter the homeless, visit the sick, visit the imprisoned or ransom the captive, and bury the dead. Then, the spiritual needs. To instruct the ignorant, counsel the doubtful, admonish sinners, bear patiently those who wrong us, forgive offenses, console the afflicted, and pray for the living and the dead. These are the corporal and spiritual works of mercy. They are the doors to grace, holiness, and perfection.

God is holy. God's heart is wholly holey for everyone. Is our heart as wholly holey?

To be holy is to have a wholly holey heart.

My friend, co-worker at Villareal Elementary School, and fellow movie enthusiast Isabel Flores and I often brainstormed and compared notes about shows on streaming networks. She asked me once, "Have you watched the series **The Kindness Diaries** yet? It shows a rich man's acts of kindness...." There couldn't be any timelier and more welcome question than this, I told myself; at that point in time, I was busy looking for illustrative stories of being "holey holy" for a future write-up.

Thanks, Isabel. You are heaven-sent!

Now let's have the true events in the life of—

Leon Logothetis, a successful broker, an Englishman living in Los Angeles. Definitely rich, he once was depressed and felt disconnected from life. Then he reached a turning point when he saw a homeless chap with a sign that read, "Kindness is the best medicine." He got so inspired to reconnect with people that he gave everything up. "From a distance, the world seems like a big, bad, scary place—war, poverty, corruption, hate," so goes the introduction to Season 1 of his docu-series. "But I believe that up close there is enough good, enough love, and enough pure kindness to make the world go round."

Indeed, to make the world go round, Leon traversed the globe. He was to rely entirely on the generosity of others for food and shelter, and mainly his 1978 Chang Jiang motorbike for travel. At first, it was primarily receiving kindness from others to meet his goal, but gradually he gave back. He repaid special acts of kindness with unexpected and life-changing gifts. (This is a spoiler alert.)

Let us follow Leon Logothetis on his extraordinary journey of letting God's light shine by opening doors of love, hopes, and dreams in his heart. Wholly holey holy!

Leon starts off from California on his Chang Jiang. In Colorado, he meets a fellow Englishman and his wife. The couple are very active and involved in caring for the handicapped, elderly, and homeless. They happily open their door to him for the night. Leon later finds out that amid their humanitarian works, the wife has medical bills and he has a son getting married in Scotland—an occasion which they can't possibly attend. Before leaving the following day, Leon pays for the couple's round-trip tickets back to Scotland for their son's wedding. The gift of love.

In Pittsburgh, Leon meets a homeless African-American who invites him to stay for the night in his "camp." The guy has nothing but still offers Leon little amenities he has for his comfort and well-being.

Although he himself needs help, everything the guy speaks about is helping those he feels are worse off in life, despite himself literally living on the streets. Before he continues on his journey the following day, Leon gives the homeless man a house and pays for his education for a certificate program. He later on becomes a chef. The gift of security.

From New York, Leon and Chang Jiang board a ship bound for Spain gratis. There he meets two impoverished but talented musicians performing in the streets of Barcelona for meager donations. Leon befriends them, and they invite him to stay with them for the night. He learns they are Nigerians and dream of becoming successful musicians to better provide for their own families in Nigeria, whom they miss so much. Their own music video in the works, they say, can bring them to the next level in their music career, but the undertaking involves so much money. Sure enough, before Leon leaves the next day, he helps them pay for their music video. The gift of inspiration.

Traveling eastward, Leon meets a fencing teacher in Italy, who willingly allows him to stay with him and his family in their apartment for the night. He tells Leon that he got his love for the sport from his own fencing teacher, and that now it's his turn to teach it to the young. The teacher dreams of transforming his students into Olympic materials for Italy. He bewails that not very many indulge in the sport because of the expensive equipment that goes with it. Later, the Italian teacher gets the surprise of his life when Leon grants him his wish. Before leaving on his journey, Leon gives him funds to pursue his dream. The gift of transformation.

In Eastern Europe, Leon meets a farmer who shows him his farm—and his large family. He supports his family with one cow. This farmer gives Leon gas for Chang Jiang, a place to stay for the night, and food to ward off his hunger—from the kindness of his heart. Touched, Leon buys him another cow! They can get by with one cow; imagine what another cow can bring. The gift of abundance.

Onwards to Turkey, Leon meets a Muslim who turns out to be the first Turk—and the first Muslim—that ever climbed Mount Everest! The guy welcomes him to his abode, feeds him, and lets him stay for the night. Leon discovers that the mountain climber heads an NGO (non-governmental organization) that does rescue works on a voluntary basis. He, too, learns that their mission has rescued over 1,800 people in various kinds of peril. Knowing this, Leon buys the Turk complete equipment for 25 of the NGO's volunteers. The gift of service.

The political conditions in Iran and Pakistan do not let travel through the two countries, so Leon and his motorbike have to be flown by cargo plane to India. In New Delhi, he gets face to face with extremely poor but genuinely cheerful people. He meets a *tuk-tuk* (rickshaw) driver who believes in his great faith that "Guest is God" and "Humans help humans." He earnestly shares with Leon his hut, his bed (which accommodates 5 people), and his meal. Full of gratitude, he gives the family a new *tuk-tuk* for sustenance. The gift of tomorrow.

Leon realizes a simple but profound truth. "True generosity isn't about giving when you have a lot. It can be about giving when you have so very little for yourself."

In another extremely poor part of India, Leon meets a tobacco-chewing father of two young boys. The Hindu orients Leon further on the Hindu religion—through the Ganges River, the holiest river throughout India. He offers the no-money traveler a place to stay and the river to "cleanse his soul." He swims with him in the 5th most polluted river in the world but nonetheless the center of every Hindu religious life. Leon learns the father has high dreams for his two sons and hopes to send them to school, which unfortunately costs so much. He witnesses how one man's love for his faith and family gives him the strength he needs to persevere in a place where so very many have so very little. Leon says to the unsuspecting father, "I will pay for the education of your two sons until they are 18 years old. The ability to give two kids an opportunity to educate themselves is truly an honor. I feel such joy inside my heart." The gift of education.

Bhutan is a landlocked country in Eastern Himalaya between India and China. Leon painstakingly reaches Bhutan, where a kind-hearted man accommodates him. Leon learns later that the man is in charge of an orphanage. Here the children love to play sports and to study in a school environment, but unfortunately the orphanage has limited sports equipment and no safe drinking water. Yes, bottled water is available but only reserved for guests like him. Of course, before Leon leaves the next day, he gives the children lots of sports equipment, two water purifiers, and a new library equipped with 1000 new books. The children and the orphanage staff flash a picture of happiness. The gift of joy.

Arriving in Cambodia, Leon meets a widow and her little boy living in a makeshift hut with three walls and no door. She is struggling with HIV and can barely feed her son. Faced with such abject poverty and disease, Leon can't control his tears from flowing and gives them a new house to protect them from the elements. The gift of protection.

In Vietnam, Leon meets a surgical doctor who, aside from accommodating him for the night, has been treating old people of their blindness—for free. His decision to pay 100 of such surgeries—for the better sight of others—comes out naturally. Such an incredible act of kindness is scarce, especially in a place such as this.

"There are many people in today's world [who] think that true riches are about how much money you have in your bank account. Yet… true riches are really what you have in your heart."

Leon crosses the Pacific Ocean to Canada from Vietnam through a container ship, of course, for free, through humanity's kindness. Back in North America on white man's land! He is refused accommodations as happened several times before, but finds it in an animal shelter whose caretaker's acts put back humanity's kindness in perspective. In return, he gives the animal shelter new beds, medicine, toys, collars—everything that the dogs need, makes them happier, and gives a "forever home" quicker. The gift of loyalty.

Back in Los Angeles, he looks for the very first person who gave him free gas at the start of his incredible worldwide journey. How to repay his kindness? Leon fully pays for this man's round-the-world tour, hotels paid for, flights paid for, besides lots of spending money. Plus $1000 to give to someone and change their life. The gift of gratitude.

Kindness is the best medicine. In Leon's words, "Life is what we make it. It is the things we can control that ultimately define us. Every day make the decision to choose. When you do, choose kindness."

That's how we let God's light shine and become wholly holey holy. ∎

There is a lovely but fabricated story about light, worth retelling, to drive home a point.[159] In the winter of 1864, the US Civil War raged between the Union Army led by General Ulysses S. Grant and the Confederate Army led by General Robert E. Lee. Out of the blue, a feast of light gave a respite to the darkness of the night and the horrors of the war. It so happened that one of Lee's generals, Maj. Gen. George Pickett, had received the good news that his wife gave birth to a baby boy. To celebrate the event, his fellow Confederates built enormous bonfires along the front line. Of course, this did not escape the attention of the enemy, Grant and the Union Army. He ordered fast a reconnaissance to find out what was happening. When afterwards he was told that the bonfires were in celebration of the birth of Pickett's baby, he ordered his men to build bonfires too. Both sides had seen nothing of this nature before. For miles and miles, there was not any shot fired, any fighting done, any war engaged. Only spectacular light. Not for long, though.

---

159   Civil War Talk, *Forums*, https://civilwartalk.com/threads/did-picketts-men-celebrate-his-new-baby-with-bonfires-at-petersburg.20414/.

When the bonfires died off, darkness and horror engulfed the battle lines once again. But this wonderful story is not true; it did not happen. Someone only fabricated the story. Historians point to Pickett's wife as the fabricator, to sensationalize things. It was *a false and short-lived light.*

In 1901, twenty-two years after Thomas Edison invented the light bulb, the Livermore, California, Fire Department hung and turned on a light bulb manufactured by Shelby Electric Company. It is still there and still gives off light.[160] It has outlived its maker, for the bulb company did not last long because nobody reordered. The light bulb has been the town's most important and famous property, pride, and major tourist attraction. Guinness Book of World Records for 2013 mentioned the bulb's 112th year of existence. The light bulb shines on and on as if forever. But of course, there will come a time, when even this light bulb will see its own end and get busted. This is *a true and long-lived light.* Lasting, but not forever.

Even the sun, our major source of light, will not shine forever. One day it will stop shining, although not in our lifetime. Yes, the sun will in time burn out, having used up half of its hydrogen fuel in the last 4.6 billion years since its birth. It still has enough hydrogen to last for another five billion years. The sun is a *ten-billion-year light.* Unimaginably long, but not forever.[161]

The man had seen no light, although no fault of his own, because he had been blind from birth. But now on his eyes the Man smeared clay, moistened earlier by His saliva, then told him to go wash his eyes in the pool of water. So, he went and washed, and came back able to see. (Jn 9:1-7) Face to face, he now sees Jesus, the Light. *The True Eternal Light.* ∎

I had no salt. My neighbors across the street, Maura and Nap Tesorero, had arrived from the Philippines the other day and had given me a couple of female *alimango*[162] from Pangasinan as *pasalubong.*[163] I was preparing the ingredients for a lunch of my favorite dish of crabs in coconut cream garnished with *malunggay* leaves and *siling labuyo*[164], when I noticed the lack. Maura and Nap's respective cars were not in their driveway. If they were home, I could have just asked for a spoonful, and this could have solved my problem outright. So, I dashed off to Walmart, for in my pantry there was no salt.

The dish was a hit—at least to me. It was super-delicious, invoking memories of homemade cooking by my kin in my native land. Truly, the Philippine crabs tasted better than ever. Their orange *aligi*[165] was the devil's temptation to the core. With rich coconut cream, every corner of their shell, every claw and leg, and every segment of the crabs' body were an occasion to sip—and a true feast of cholesterol! However, the addition of *malunggay* and *siling labuyo* gave the whole concoction a healthier side.

But what if there was no salt anywhere available? Could my favorite dish have been as delicious? Would I have still loved to eat the *alimango* and *malunggay* and declared my dish a hit?

This is the nature of salt. Salt enhances the taste of other things, so they will appeal better to our taste buds. You can eat insipid crabs with *malunggay* for all you care, but they'll have more gustatory appeal with a dash of salt. On the other hand, nobody wants a dinner of just salt. Salt is not self-oriented. Salt serves.

---

160   Snopes, "Livermore Long-burning Lightbulb," https://www.snopes.com/fact-check/watt-a-lightbulb/.

161   *National Geographic,* "Sun," https://www.nationalgeographic.org/encyclopedia/sun/.

162   *alimango* [Filipino] – giant mud crabs, *Scylla serrata.*

163   *pasalubong* [Filipino] – homecoming gift.

164   *siling labuyo* [Filipino] - *Capsicum frutescens,* generally accepted as the world's smallest hot pepper, cultivated in the Philippines.

165   *aligi* [Filipino] – the roe of fertile female crabs.

So akin to light. Light is not self-oriented, too. We see and appreciate a lovely flower because of light. Light reflects from the flower to our eyes. But even if we have eyes and there are lovely flowers, we see nothing without the presence of light. We perceive things because of light. As light is not the primary object of our perception, light is useless by itself. It becomes useful only if it enables us to perceive other things. Light serves.

It is at this point that I want you to meet my friend Bambi.

Mrs. Bambi Lara is a retired teacher. Many years ago, we were co-teachers at Xavier School. *Ad Majorem Dei Gloriam!* She taught high school and I elementary before she moved to California and I to Texas. We weren't much acquainted with each other personally and socially, but I knew for a fact that she was tall in stature, regal in bearing, and pleasing in appearance. She handled English and Literature.

We lost contact for a long while, till Facebook reunited us. I now see snippets of Bambi's personality, and she must have gradually known, too, that I am an introvert, a pessimist, and a whiner at heart. She was a teacher well-respected and well-loved by everyone.

More than just a teacher who taught English grammar, composition, and literature, Bambi was likewise a wondrous inspirer of dreams.

Ask Willie.

Willie T. Ong, doctor and writer, was one of those countless students whose lives crossed with Bambi in Xavier. His story says it all, "Who Inspired You to Dream?" In his *Philippine Star* column MIND YOUR BODY on February 3, 2015, he related how:

- Bambi, as a teacher, inspired him to believe in himself and strive to work his best using his full potentials;

- Bambi, as a teacher, inspired him to write and become a writer through her teaching strategy called "Friday paper";

- Bambi, as a teacher, became his "mentor, guidance counselor, and inspiration rolled into one";

- To Willie, the doctor and writer, Bambi is "the most wonderful and inspiring teacher he has ever known. A teacher who believed in him when he didn't believe in himself";

- Willie, the doctor and writer, will always be grateful to Bambi, his high school English teacher.

"And so," Willie affectionately said at the end of his column, "to Mrs. Bambi Matias Lara, who is now fully retired after devoting 45 years of her life to teaching, here is my latest essay. It's my Friday paper, Ma'am. And it's for you."

Wow! Was I touched by this former student's affectionate recollection of his teacher! This was something that needed to be known by the world, if not yet. So, on Bambi's post on Facebook mentioning and sharing Willie's endearing article, I said as comment, "Very inspiring, Bambi, and, of course, *kakainggit* [enviable]. Stories of triumphs in our noble profession come few and far between now and then. But while the rest of us only bask in our modest achievements, here you are with your crowning glory indeed! You're so fortunate to have such appreciative person coming forward and affirming your lasting influence on him—and what a very touching way of expressing his gratitude! (I'm very sure, though, that he is not the only one.) Both you and Doc Willie represent the best there can ever be and therefore deserve congratulations.

CONGRATULATIONS!

Bambi is a true salt and light in the world. To be a true salt and light is to improve the lives of others so that they draw towards the goodness of God. By the words of his former mentor, Dr. Willie Ong himself is "heaven's gift to so many because of all your philanthropy and care for the disadvantaged!"

We rejoice at the knowledge that the salt-and-light who was Bambi, served on Willie the student, has now been transformed in the service of Willie T. Ong, M.D.

The Lord bless and keep you, Bambi and Willie. Please do not tire of using your gifts in God's service, for God's greater glory. May your tribes increase!

Luceat Lux! ■

-from **Xavier School Hymn**
composed by Dolores Avelino

23

PAIN
The kind that refuses to go away

What did this letter of acknowledgment entail, let alone expect? Between the lines, it said I should be well prepared in mind, body, and soul to show, after four years of Normal education, my competencies as a teacher applicant. The letter writer even asked Mrs. Patria G. Lorenzo to vouch for my credentials and moral character as a matter of course. Mrs. Lorenzo moved my tassel left-to-right on my graduation day a few weeks earlier, in her capacity as Dean of the Bicol University College of Education,

The interview went finer than fine. Sr. M. Consilio, a nun of the Order of St. Benedict (OSB), maybe in her forties then, soon became my very first supervisor. (The M in her name, I learned later, stood for Mary, as in *Mary* the Blessed Virgin.) The nun was the no-nonsense grade-school principal at St. Agnes' Academy of Legazpi City in 1974, always dignified in her habit but one who never forgot to smile.

Sr. Consilio put me in charge of a Grade 1 class for that very first year of employment. In the succeeding years, the school saw me fit to teach Music, Science, and Math in the upper grades. The school's method of instruction then was "Individualized Instruction," I.I. for short.

Being a fresh-graduate teacher, I had to do much learning and adjusting to cope with the demands of I.I. But more stressful was dealing with Sr. Consilio's stern disposition and strict discipline, which she imposed upon and expected from the faculty and staff. As regular as clockwork, she checked lesson plans, complete with compliments, corrections, comments, or annotations in red. Classroom-and-teacher supervision was topmost in her list of administrative tasks, for the paramount goal of the school should be student success and empowerment. In my honest opinion and recollection, she required to see that her coterie of subordinates measured up to her standards. Sr. Consilio made sure we nurtured, enhanced, and aligned our competencies with the school's mission statement.

In Latin, *consilio* did not mean "on purpose" or "designedly" for nothing.

At the end of that school year (1974-1975), Sr. Consilio announced she was leaving. The Order of St. Benedict higher-ups reassigned her to another Benedictine school for the next term. This saddened the entire St. Agnes family—students, teachers, administrators. Our pain and their gain. But not before making a mark

St. Agnes' Academy
Legaspi City G - 103
Philippines

March 8, 1974

Dear Mr. Morada:

We received your letter of application for a teaching position at St. Agnes' Academy. Kindly come for an interview on March 26 or 27 at 9:00 a.m.

Please take along also a letter of recommendation from Mrs. Patria G. Lorenzo.

Thank you.

Sincerely,

Sister M. Consilio, OSB.
Grade School Principal

on my person. From the good nun I learned so much, things schooling never taught me. The stern yet rational nun was never wanting in her constant reminders towards the adherence to Christian principles and lifestyles of the St. Agnes grade school hierarchy and family.

One such reminder she gave towards the end of that school year, to be exact on March 5, 1975, written on the chalkboard in the Faculty Room. The boardwork struck us for its honesty, simplicity, and capacity to draw anyone into self-examination and reflection. It pricked me, so to speak, and moved me to write a song entitled **Our Song**.

Someone ought to have etched this reminder in stone for everyone who works with children. Everyone, including, among many others: parents, grandparents, social workers, pediatricians, dentists, child psychologists, camp directors, sports coaches, librarians, day-care owners, priests, teachers.

Practice what you preach.

Where had all the years gone? A few years ago, after teaching in 7 different schools in the Philippines and in Texas USA, I went to visit my hometown, Daragá, Albáy. I heard that the good nun was back at St. Agnes as the incumbent high school principal. Legazpi City was just a 15-minute ride away. I was so excited at the prospect of a re-connection with my very first supervisor after several decades.

Without delay, I sought an audience with her. When the appointed day and time came, I garbed myself in a nice but simple attire, so as not to give the wrong impression. I made sure that I had at hand AKO BAGA IKOS (I'm like a cat), a binder of my early musical compositions; **Our Song** was one of them. The intent was to give a visual on how Sr. M. Consilio, OSB, Principal, influenced me during my very first year as a teacher.

The imposing figure that met me at the door, and now seated behind the principal's desk, still looked familiar in her nun's habit, although with the stark signs of aging. Her face still looked strict, but with a telltale disparity—it was now too frugal to smile. After we exchanged pleasantries, I introduced myself.

"Refresh my memory," she replied. "It is vague with age, after all these years, so I hardly recognize you." So much for not wanting to give a wrong impression! Oh yes, I endorse a reason for the unrecognition: I had kinky hair, and I sported an Afro hairstyle in 1974. No kidding.

"You said I once wrote this on the Faculty Room chalkboard? *Hmm*, strange! I might have, but I don't remember either. Sorry for having given you so much pain." She flashed a faint smile. So much for idealism!

This time, the chalkboard was blank. The handwriting was on the wall.

The other day, I was so immersed in the business of preaching that I at the moment forgot the practicing. Oh me oh my, this was not 1975 but 2015. Four decades of teaching, four decades after Sr. Consilio. Forty years of her boardwork in my mind and in my song. Where have all the years gone?

In my peripheral vision, I saw the 3rd grade girl looking at me with piercing eyes, and tears were falling from them. As I just dismissed the music class and the students were lining up to go back to their homeroom, I called the girl aside and asked, "Why are you crying?"

"I did nothing, but you yelled at me," she said without hesitation. "You told us we should respect each other in class, but you yelled at me!"

I was dumbfounded, and I said what teachers always use as a defense mechanism in circumstances of this nature: "Natalie, I did not yell at you; I raised my voice."

Tell that to the Marines. The child's heart might be fickle, but not unreasonable or hypocritical. Natalie was reminding me of Sr. Consilio. She was reminding me of the adage that is as old as the teaching profession itself. I realized I was myself apologizing. In an instant, her face reflected a change of heart. I never had a hug more heartfelt than what she gave me.

Wasn't this too late in the day for me? Wasn't it too late at this point in my teaching life to realize it was so much easier but less gratifying to write on water than to etch in stone? After work, I went straight home and started recording the song I should have done in my first year of teaching. The song I should have sung at the back of my mind before every class all these years. I have three more years to practice what I teach before retirement. Might be too late the hero, but let me do it! Let me sing **OUR SONG**![166]

Oh God, do we ever reflect at what we do
to these children of ours?
We give them so little really,
these children of ours.
We tell them, Wait, I'm busy!
Be quiet, I'm talking!
Pick it up! Study! Practice! Go and do!
But we aren't quiet, we don't pick up,
We don't go and do.
We aren't quiet, we don't pick up,
We don't go and do.

---

166   Arcadio Morada, Jr., *tagaalbay*, "Our Song," YouTube video, 2:49min, https://youtu.be/5nXbrFbv4u8.

We aren't quiet, we don't pick up,
We don't go and do!

Oh God, do we ever reflect at what we do
to these children of ours?
We give them so little really,
these children of ours.
We tell them, Hey, don't gamble,
Speak nice words, Be courteous,
Never smoke, never drink, never lie till you die!
But we ourselves gamble, we are liars,
We speak filthy words.
We always gamble, we are liars,
we speak filthy words.
We always gamble, we are liars,
we speak filthy words!
Oh God, do we ever reflect at what we do
to these children of ours?

These children of ours, I gave them just about my whole life. But after forty years of teaching, it feels as if I have done so much and accomplished so little. You were right, Sr. Consilio. There's so much pain. ∎

One day, in the year of our Lord 1989, at the corner of EDSA and Ortigas Avenue in Manila, there was a hive of excitement and activities transpiring. It was the exact spot where the EDSA Shrine would later rise, a small Roman Catholic church. It was the same spot where three years earlier, the People Power Revolution, the peaceful uprising that amazed the world, had occurred.

By then I had lived through 38 Easter seasons. I had been an educator for 15 years to the day. It was my 6th year as a Christian Life Education teacher at Xavier School in Greenhills in San Juan, a city in Metro Manila, Philippines. This teaching assignment was an offshoot of Xavier School's sending me on a study grant in 1983 to Mother of Life Center, a formation house for catechists and religion teachers. While there, I took and finished a course that enabled me to make an in-depth look into my faith—my doctrinal, prayer, and worship, as well as moral life. With that context, therefore, anyone would expect from me a better and wiser understanding of what happened to two of Jesus' disciples on the road to Emmaus. (Lk 24:13-35)

Let me refresh memory. In the afternoon of Easter Sunday, Cleopas and another disciple of Jesus were walking towards Emmaus, an ancient town located a few miles to the northwest of Jerusalem. They met a stranger—the risen Jesus, who just appeared from out of nowhere. Just three days after the Crucifixion, they did not recognize Jesus. Instead, with candor, they spoke to him of their sadness at recent unfortunate events that befell their Master. After arriving at Emmaus, they persuaded the stranger to come and eat dinner with them, and during the meal's course, at the breaking of the bread, they recognized him. It was then when Jesus vanished into nowhere.

So, I supposed to have a better and wiser understanding of what happened on the road to Emmaus. You could bet I had and expect me to know the story at heart. But there can be a chasm between doctrine and application. A chasm between learning and witnessing. Between what you know and what you do. Between what you preach and what you practice.

On that unforgettable afternoon in 1989, I was on my own road to Emmaus. On an after-work errand via public transport to Cubao from Xavier School, I had to alight by the corner of EDSA and Ortigas. The hustle and bustle at the EDSA Shrine construction site had been going on for some time now, becoming so familiar to commuters and pedestrians nobody cared or noticed anymore. But there was something that could not escape everybody's attention, including mine, at that very moment. An emaciated man in dark sullied rags holding a tin can was lying right at the curb, barely conscious, foaming at the mouth, while humanity passed by, yet unmoved and uncaring. Although a few individuals stopped and gaped at the unconscious man for a brief while, they soon proceeded to their own concerns and selfish undertakings.

I noticed him myself and, though as much in a hurry as the others to fulfill my errand, stopped likewise to gape at the man's unconscious form. He was still breathing and one hand twitching. I presumed he was epileptic and must have had one of his seizures. The worst was over, thank God, but he was alone. I thought, *"Kawawa naman!"* [Pitiful!] And just as the other pedestrians did, I moved on to my private concern, leaving behind the epileptic. A paramedic, a doctor, or a policeman might come before long to help. Someone would soon come and attend to the man.

Meanwhile, while on the bus to Cubao, voices rang in my ears, not those of the bus driver or conductor nor of the vendors plying their ware inside the bus. The voices I was hearing were those of my formators in Mother of Life Center. In sarcasm, they might as well be saying, "Congratulations, you just missed your own Emmaus! You met Jesus in the epileptic, and you passed him by as though you didn't care!"

When Jesus rose from the dead, he took another form. That's why Mary Magdalene did not recognize him. That's why Peter did not recognize him. Include in the line-up, Cleopas and his companion, too. I, a wannabe loyal disciple in the 20th century, struggling to be faithful to my catechist call—was that why I could not recognize him, too? He took another form?

Of course, Jesus took another form! "Amen, I say to you, whatever you did for one of these least brothers of mine, you did for me." (Mt 25:40)

I've trodden other roads to Emmaus thenceforth, and I'm not proud to say this. But this road has remained in my consciousness like a flesh-eating virus, a thousand-foot tidal wave, an abysmal ocean, an inescapable black hole. It will, I guess, forever be an ache in the deepest recesses of my heart.

Poet Margaret Sangster wrote, in *The Sin of Omission*, "It's not the thing you do, dear, / It's the thing you leave undone / Which gives you a bit of heartache / At the setting of the sun."[167]

And [Jesus] said to Cleopas and companion, "Oh, how foolish you are!" (Lk 24:25a) I might as well have been that nameless other guy!

In 1989, at the corner of EDSA and Ortigas, where the EDSA Shrine now stands, an epileptic was Jesus personified, whom I did not recognize. So unwise and regretful to have passed up the chance! *Mea culpa.* Ardently I pray I may always recognize You in others. Let your face shine on me at every chance I meet You in others. ◼

---

167   Margaret Elizabeth Sangster, "The Sin of Omission," Poeticous, https://www.poeticous.com/margaret-elizabeth-sangster/the-sin-of-omission.

he lady ticket collector at the main door of the Jacob Brown Auditorium, with a courteous demeanor, stopped me and gently asked for my entrance ticket. My nose was in the air as I flashed a smile. I said, "I am the director of St. Luke Catholic School Children's Choir." She let me go ahead.

When a stage hand alerted the choir members backstage minutes before their performance, I walked as a peacock towards the stage along with them. The taut stage guard stopped me and asked where I was going and why. I said, without batting an eye, "I am the director of St. Luke Catholic School Children's Choir." So, he let me go ahead. After the warm standing ovation for the 12-minute choir performance, the president of the Board of St. Luke Catholic School, as master of ceremonies, made an enthusiastic acknowledgment speech. With aplomb, he summoned onstage "the person who directed the whole thing, Ms. Adriana Besteiro, and Mr. Morada, assisting!"

Huh? Nose snubbed, peacock's tail feathers clipped!

The embarrassing confusion turned hard to appease. The morning after the concert, Fr. Juan Nicolau, incumbent pastor of St. Luke Church and founder of St. Luke Catholic School, called on Sr. Helen Rottier, SLCS principal. He congratulated the choir and heaped praises on the SLCS faculty and staff for a job well done. To express his utmost thanks, he was requesting a repeat performance of our concert piece, **Fun Songathon**, right after the 10:00 am Mass on the coming Sunday. Sr. Helen accepted the accolades on behalf of the school and the choir. "With pleasure, Father!" the school secretary heard her say. Then he asked to talk to Adriana Besteiro to iron out details.

Wait, was he looking for the choir director—or the choreographer?

Sr. Helen should be the first to know. She forwarded the call to Adriana Besteiro.

Let me make the context broader. It was in early February when Sr. Helen invited me to her office to talk of a recommendation by the SLCS Board on me. She explained the Board wanted to know if I could prepare a front act by the choir, a thank-you number, for **The GARIBALDI Concert** in May. This was to be the school's biggest gala fundraising show of the year, a benefit concert featuring Garibaldi, a Hispanic singing group well-known at the time in Mexico and Texas.

I agreed to produce a musical number, of course, as both Sr. Helen and I enthused at the prospect of the choir performing in the concert. The excitement was more significant for me, having formed the school's children's choir at the start of the school year with her encouragement. Honed up by our weekly Mass singing stints and various intermittent performances on campus, the choir was ready and eager for a different audience in a different venue. A great opportunity was in the offing.

I began searching for the fitting concert piece. Browsing through my music resource files, with much luck, I found an old choral piece from St. Scholastica's College Music Department (Manila) from 1975. The piece was significant enough but lacked relevance and the recommended length of at least ten minutes. It was then with urgency that I combed through music stores in Brownsville and out-of-town, looking for more resources. At last, I concocted a medley of fun and concert-quality children's songs that could entertain for sure—as a token of thanks. To add relevance, I inserted Disney's "I Just Can't Wait to Be King" (from **The Lion King**), then composed an introduction, a thank-you song, and a coda myself. Through my computer and various music apps, I recorded musical scores that added up to over ten minutes of digital music accompaniment.

My efforts in putting the entire project together elicited an enthusiastic and positive response from Sr. Helen when she first listened to the choir sing the medley in April. More intense and frequent rehearsals followed. We wanted to give our St. Luke community and clientele, not to mention the public attending, a run for their money. The children should satisfy the paying public's craving for entertainment, simultaneous with esthetics and culture. More rigorous rehearsals! The entire time, I held the baton.

With the medley having taken shape, I needed a choreographer. That's when Adriana Besteiro came into the picture. As one of SLCS's primary grade teachers, Ms. Besteiro was a very imposing Hispanic lady, both in outward size and inner disposition. Sr. Helen talked to her, and Adriana said yes, no problem.

The choice was excellent, judging from the results.[168] No one could deny Ms. Besteiro's contribution to animate the medley. As I stayed on the sidelines while she did her stuff, she appeared more visible during the choreography rehearsals, such that anybody could have likely thought she was the director. Never had I given her the baton.

The rest is history.

After the choir performance, my wife Mameng, who was in the audience, turned from proud to upset. Why not? She'd seen firsthand the hardship and effort that I undertook to come up with that front act. I had had to go to school early and come home late, then spend nights and weekends orchestrating the medley accompaniment. Yet, despite the endeavor spent with the choir, they only recognized me as—*gasp*—the assistant to the choreographer! As the logical reaction, my wife and I dashed out of the auditorium—walked out, you might say—right after the president of the SLCS Board's "acknowledgment" speech.

Where did things go wrong? "That guy does not even know your first name," my wife said in a taunting voice as I was driving us home. "Thank him for acknowledging you even exist!"

I am a shy person to the painful extreme. It's my reflex to shy away from recognition and being put on focus or on the spot. I might not have wished to be acknowledged, if at all, on such an occasion with an enormous audience as the gala Garibaldi concert. Given what happened, how I wished they knew to whom the recognition was due.

Yet I moved on, had to, as did Sr. Helen. In 2000, I learned that the Diocese of Brownsville assigned the secular nun as the new principal of St. Martin de Porres School in Weslaco, TX. After St. Luke, I found successive employments in three other schools in the locality (Incarnate Word Academy, St. Mary's Catholic School, Villareal Elementary). Meanwhile, our paths crossed again when one fine Sunday in 2014, I met Sr. Helen at the parking lot of St. Mary's Church in Brownsville, after Mass. A whole gallery of nimbus-cloudy SLCS pictures flashed in my mind.

The ever-smiling and soft-spoken Sr. Helen said, "I blame myself for not having corrected the mistake." She hugged me, while I wondered why she brought up the topic. "But understand that St. Luke Catholic School will be forever indebted to you for what you have done—you started the music program and set up the choir. May you continue to use your talents for the greater honor and glory of God."

Amen to that, and thank you, Sr. Helen. It should have gratified me. But, no, the feeling was akin to *consuelo de bobo*[169] with a tender slap on the face.

---

168   Arcádio Morada, Jr., *tagaalbay*, "Fun Songathon," St. Luke Catholic School Children's Choir, YouTube video, 11:46min, https://youtu.be/FXrh7wRWpHg.
169   *consuelo de bobo* [Filipino] – literally, "consolation for the idiot;" in other words, "mock consolation," https://filipiknow.net/pinoy-idiomatic-expressions/.

Several months later, I heard the news that Sr. Helen left for the Pearly Gates.[170] God bless her soul! The nun's "I blame myself" confession came to my mind, as if by a force majeure.

It's been decades, Sr. Helen. Fr. Nicolau founded SLCS in 1992. I joined St. Luke in 1994, when you were the principal. I started the music curriculum and the children's choir. That Garibaldi concert happened in 1995. I am not sure whether Mameng still remembers the event, let alone the ignominious acknowledgment speech and the walk-out. The wound inflicted upon my dignity healed in time, of course, but a pain refuses to subside and go away.

It's the courteous lady at the door and the taut guard backstage, forever thinking of me as that proud, shameless, snub-nosed, and featherheaded liar. ■

St. Luke Catholic School Children's Choir, 1995

<hr>

170   "Sr. Helen Rottier, 74, faithful sister of St. Joseph of Carondelet for 54 years and sister to seven siblings passed away at Nazareth Living Center in St. Louis, MO, on May 19th, 2015, at 8 p.m.," https://www.legacy.com/obituaries/brownsvilleherald/obituary.aspx?n=helen-rottier&pid=174917956.

24

BLESSED

Gaze, head, and heart toward Mary

"Our Lady of Guada-*who?*" One might think this naïve and offensive question came from someone outside the Catholic Church. Some diehard Protestant or another Christian fundamentalist sect, right?

Wrong.

A Catholic I am acquainted with asked this question, one who prefers either to treat his own faith in jest or to stay ignorant by choice.

Indeed, it is disheartening to know and realize that some Catholics, even those among us who profess a knowledge of the Blessed Mother, actually "choose to ignore her."

That's how Deacon Luis Zuñiga described those who call themselves Catholic yet do not see Mary's role in our salvation history. In the homily the Deacon gave during our celebration of the Immaculate Conception last Monday (December 8, 2014), that's how he described them who do not consider the blessedness of having Mary as our Mother, the Mother of the Church. Our Advocate, Protector, Model of Virtue. Most Gracious Lady, Mother of our Creator, Co-Redemptrix. (These are just a few of the many titles ascribed to the Blessed Mother.)[171]

Who does not feel blessed by her presence? If the angel Gabriel regarded Mary as the "favored one" (Lk 1:28)—full of grace—why can we not accord her with esteem, honor, and veneration? How incongruous it may sound that we believe in Jesus the Son and Redeemer, yet ignore the mother who brought him forth!

Even some devout Catholics sometimes frown upon news of Marian apparitions and quickly dismiss them as frauds or fanciful tales. For reasons, though, because Marian apparitions (or the supernatural appearances of the Blessed Virgin Mary) may come from doubtful sources and questionable circumstances.

But the legit or genuine Marian apparitions, those approved and recognized by Church authority, the Holy See, are a different story altogether. Take the apparition of Our Lady of Fatima to three shepherd children of Portugal in 1917. Or that of Our Lady of Lourdes to Bernadette Soubirous of France in 1858. And, of course, that of Our Lady of Guadalupe to Juan Diego in 1531. These apparitions are the strongest argument why Catholics, and other Christian sects besides, should stop ignoring and instead start turning their gaze, head, and heart toward Mary, Mother of God.

---

171   See http://www.catholic.org/mary/title.php and/or http://www.roman-catholic-saints.com/titles-of-mary.html.

By all accounts, when Juan Diego, age 57, reported the apparition of Our Lady of Guadalupe on Tepeyac Hill in Mexico in 1531, he did not receive a lot of attention in Rome, since the Church was busy with the challenges of the Protestant Reformation of 1521 to 1579 and perhaps very few Cardinals in Rome had ever heard the details of Mexico and its environs. Yet, just as a large number of people were leaving the Catholic Church in Europe as a result of the Reformation, Our Lady of Guadalupe was instrumental in adding almost 8 million people to the ranks of Catholics in the Americas between 1532 and 1538. The number of Catholics in South America has grown significantly over the centuries. Eventually with tens of millions of followers, Juan Diego had an effect on Mariology in the Americas and beyond, and was eventually declared venerable in 1987. Juan Diego was declared a saint in 2002. Furthermore, the Basilica of Our Lady of Guadalupe on Tepeyac Hill in Mexico is now the third largest Catholic Church in the world, after Saint Peter's Basilica in Rome and the Basilica of the National Shrine of Our Lady of Aparecida in Brazil. Recent reported apparitions such as Medjugorje have also attracted a large following.[172]

Let us accord our Blessed Mother with the esteem, honor, and veneration she deserves. On the Feast of Our Lady of Guadalupe (Dec 12) and every time we need to, let us thank God for giving us Mary, Mother of Life, and let us proclaim in our most jubilant collective voice her being the **HIGHEST HONOR OF OUR RACE!**[173]

♪♫ HIGHEST HONOR OF OUR RACE

#42 *from* THE PURPLE PSALMODY*
by Arcadio Morada, Jr.
Based on Judith 13:18bcde-19

Antiphon:
You are the highest honor of our race,
You are the highest honor of our race!

1.
Blessed are you, daughter,
by the Most High God,
Above all the women on earth;
And blessed be the Lord God,
The creator of heaven and earth. (*Ant.*)

2.
Your deed of hope will
never be forgotten
By those who tell
of the might of God. (*Ant.*) ■

---

172   **Visionaries and Mystics** (website), "Marian Apparitions," https://visionariesandmystics.blogspot.com/2010/04/marian-apparitions.html.

173   See audio-recording, "Highest Honor of Our Race", http://yourlisten.com/Arcadio.Morada/highest-honor-of-our-race; or YouTube video, *tagaalbay*, "Highest Honor of Our Race," https://youtu.be/5Y4t1BLTgdQ.

he very first biblical passage that contains the promise of man's redemption also mentioned the Mother of the Redeemer. "I will put enmity between you and the woman, and between your offspring and hers; They will strike at your head, while you strike at their heel." (Gn 3:15)

Catholic Encyclopedia explains Mary's Immaculate Conception, thus, "The person of Mary, in consequence of her origin from Adam, should have been subject to sin, but being the new Eve who has to be the mother of the new Adam, she was, by the eternal counsel of God and by the merits of Christ, withdrawn from the general law of original sin."[174]

The Immaculate Conception, according to the teaching of the Catholic Church, was the conception of the Blessed Virgin Mary in her mother's womb, free from original sin.

We commonly confuse the doctrine of the Immaculate Conception with that of the Incarnation and the virgin birth of Jesus, though the two deal with separate subjects. The Catholic Church teaches that Mary's parents conceived her through normal biological means, but God acted upon her soul (kept her soul "immaculate") at the time of her conception.

Although the Catholic Church has widely held the belief that Mary was sinless or immaculate since Late Antiquity, the doctrine was not dogmatically defined until 1854, by Pope Pius IX in his papal bull *Ineffabilis Deus*. The doctrine of the Immaculate Conception states "that the most Blessed Virgin Mary, in the first instance of her conception, by a singular grace and privilege granted by Almighty God, in view of the merits of Jesus Christ, the Savior of the human race, was preserved free from all stain of original sin."[175]

The Catholic Church celebrates the Feast of the **Immaculate Conception** on December 8; in many Catholic countries, it is a holy day of obligation or patronal feast, and in some a national public holiday.

Protestants reject the doctrine because they do not consider the development of dogmatic theology to be authoritative apart from Biblical exegesis.[176] ■

I myself have so much more to learn about the Feast of the **Presentation of the Lord.** I assume it is true for many fellow Catholics, too. The Presentation is familiar to me mainly as the 4th Joyful Mystery of the Holy Rosary. Other than that the holy family and a couple of oldsters named Simeon and Anna got involved in the story, I barely know anything about this feast of the Catholic Church.

Yes, the Presentation of the Lord is a Catholic feast, but one which is rooted in Hebrew tradition. Just in case you may want a refresher, as I do, Luke 2:22-38 is a big help.

- **"When the days were completed for their purification according to the law of Moses, they took him up to Jerusalem to present him to the Lord..."** (Lk 2:22)

The feast of the Presentation (February 2) commemorates a day of purification, renewal, and hope. Forty days after Christmas, we commemorate Mary's obedience to the Mosaic law by submitting herself to the ritual of purification at the temple, as commanded in Lv 12:2-8. "When a woman has a child, giving birth to a boy, she shall be unclean for seven days, with the same uncleanness as during her menstrual period. On the eighth day, the flesh of the boy's foreskin shall be circumcised, and then she shall spend thirty-three days

---

174   *Catholic Encyclopedia*, "Immaculate Conception," https://www.newadvent.org/cathen/07674d.htm.
175   *Papal Encyclicals Online*, "Ineffabilis Deus: The Immaculate Conception, Pope Bl. Pius IX – 1854," https://www.papalencyclicals.net/pius09/p9ineff.htm.
176   *Wikipedia*, "Immaculate Conception," https://en.wikipedia.org/wiki/Immaculate_Conception.

more in a state of blood purity; she shall not touch anything sacred nor enter the sanctuary till the days of her purification are fulfilled." (Lv 12:2-4)

Mary and Joseph, as devout Jews, observed religious customs faithfully. One of these was for any Jewish couple to take their firstborn son to the temple in Jerusalem after the mother's days of purification. (7 days after birth, then 33 days more, since Jesus was a boy.)

It would have been a different story if Mary's baby were a girl. Then this would need her to have a longer purification period and to keep out of the temple—for 66 days! (Lv 12:5)

- **"Every male that opens the womb shall be consecrated to the Lord..."** (Lk 2:23)

The ritual of circumcision (7 days after birth) does not coincide with, and is not the same as, the presentation (40 days after birth).

Circumcision is the Hebrew baby boy's admission to the faith of his fathers. Presentation in the temple is his formal dedication to the service of the Lord. Mosaic law bound Mary after forty days from Jesus' birth to appear in the temple with two offerings (doves or pigeons)—as a sin offering and a burnt offering.

Before Moses led the Hebrews out of Egypt where they were slaves, God sent many plagues to convince Pharaoh to let the Hebrews go free. One of these plagues was the death of the firstborn. But he spared the Hebrew children. Because of this, the Hebrews would make an offering on the 40th day after their first son was born. Every firstborn son belonged to God. So, while they were at the temple, Mary and Joseph would ritually "buy back" the baby from God.

"Firstborn son" means the "male that opens the womb," not the "first of a series of children born." The Protestant objections to Mary's eternal virginity based on references to Jesus as "firstborn" of many children get negated as totally without foundation.

- **"... [A] man in Jerusalem whose name was Simeon."** (Lk 2:25)

As they arrived at the temple, an old, holy, and intelligent man named Simeon met Mary and Joseph. (Simeon had studied much about the prophets of Israel. It was during his studies that he learned of the coming of the Messiah, after which he spent many years praying for the Messiah to come. On one such time of prayer, Simeon had heard the voice of God, who promised him he would not die without seeing the Messiah.) The moment Simeon saw Jesus, he took the baby in his arms, blessed the Lord, and said in effect:

"I can now die in peace because my eyes have seen the Savior of the world!"

While all this was happening, Anna the Prophetess was also in the temple. Herself old in age, she had been a widow for many years and spent her time in the temple worshiping, fasting, and praying. When she saw the baby Jesus, she praised God and spoke of him to all who were awaiting the Messiah. ■

August in New York; so I am inviting everyone to a pilgrimage with me. Virtual. Every time August comes, I take this pilgrimage in spirit all these years that I have lived in the United States. This pilgrimage I had taken firsthand a few times in the long-distant past, in the company of family and friends. Every time nostalgia gets me down, I take this virtual pilgrimage with a vow to make it a physical one soon. It is a pilgrimage fraught with Filipino indigenous spectacle, religiosity, and culture. It is the pilgrimage to *Nuestra Señora de Salvacion* in Joroan, Tiwi, Albay, Philippines.

The devotion to Our Lady of Salvation started with the sculpting of a wooden statue of the Virgin Mary in Joroan. Joroan was a barrio historically considered part of Buhi, Camarines Sur, but is now a parish of Tiwi, Albay, of the Diocese of Legazpi. Joroan has been the home of the original sculpted image, while a replica is in the parish of St. Lawrence, in the municipality of Tiwi.

The sculpted image shows Our Lady carrying the Child Jesus Christ in her left arm; her right arm is grasping by the wrist a man who is about to fall into a hellmouth. In addition, an angel kneels by her left foot with a basket of burning hearts offered to Christ, whose stretched left hand accepts them while the right hand holds a burning heart.

According to tradition and historical records, the image of Our Lady of Salvation was sculpted from a severed *calpi* tree that refused to wither and die in Joroan in the 1770s. Because it was a coastal town, Joroan was then vulnerable to Muslim attacks on account of its location. Every time the Muslims attempted to burn the native houses, no fire would ignite. The natives attributed the miracle to Our Lady. For this and a host of other subsequent miracles, the whole Bicol Region, if not the entire Philippines, has venerated *Nuestra Señora de Salvacion.*

In 1975, Bishop Teotimo Pacis of the Diocese of Legazpi formally declared the Virgin Mary with the title of Our Lady of Salvation, as the heavenly patroness of Albay. In 1976, the Diocese celebrated the Bicentennial Jubilee of its patroness. On August 25 of that year, the Catholic Church, through Jaime Cardinal Sin of Manila, crowned Our Lady of Salvation and proclaimed Joroan a Diocesan shrine.

It is this shrine I want to visit now. Come with me to this virtual pilgrimage of a lifetime. Who knows, I may never go this way again.

Joroan, Tiwi, Albay, in August is festival-like. It is a month of thanksgiving Masses, devotees in constant coming and going, days of praying and diversion, days of faith and religiosity. The center of all this excitement is, of course, the image of the *Nuestra Señora de Salvacion.* She is garbed in rich attire as she stands for the arrival and veneration of the faithful pilgrims.

Land and water transports are the only means of going to Joroan from the adjoining towns of Albay and other provinces. Arriving in Joroan after a scenic bus trip, we proceed to the shrine to present ourselves before Our Lady, thank her for the journey, or implore her aid. Our fervor, faith, tenderness, and piety are evident as we go before the altar and prostrate ourselves before her image. We pray with devotion. We do not come out of the church until we experience either a spiritual satisfaction borne by faith and trust, or hunger (for lunch). In either case, we go outside the church, after bidding Our Lady a temporary goodbye. We then dine in one of the *turo-turo*[177] which proliferate outside the church.

Back inside the church, we hear once again the sound of fervent prayers. We gape at the sight of devotees who go the entire length of the aisle toward the Sanctuary on their knees. The constant coming and going of the faithful, all absorbed in their devotion, hypnotizes us. We marvel at the innumerable candles burning in strategic places, in different sizes, lengths, colors, and shapes.

Next, we pray as we inch our way to the aisle that leads to the altar. Our pilgrimage is no pilgrimage without at least getting up close to her image. It is the one thing that matters, the highlight of our visit, the crown of our devotion. We love our Blessed Mother far more than our actions and words can say. Other faiths

---

177   *turo-turo* [Filipino] – from the root word "turo" or "to point at/to", a modest eatery where you point to the dish you want.

belittle ours because of these outward signs of piety, but altogether, this is us. This is tradition. This is Bicolano devotion imbued with a great love for her, as well as great hope for Our Lady's help and protection.

From early morning, the church bells do not stop ringing for Eucharistic celebrations. Throughout the day, the faithful come, celebrate the Holy Mass, and go. After every Mass, you see them come out of the church in renewed faith.

Outside the church, hordes of vendors are plying their ware of inexpensive clay cars and kettles, religious articles, and toys for the pilgrims (and for the children left at home). As a child, I would ask my parents to buy any of these goods after all the praying and venerating. Alas, for now, I would have loved to buy and bring *koron* (clay pot) and *badil-badil* (clay gun) to New York if this pilgrimage were real!

Our pilgrimage is not complete without the side trip to the Baño. That's a medicinal hot spring, where we can wash off the grimes and dried sweat and stench we have accumulated during our sojourn in the shrine with other pilgrims. After bathing, we may want to go to Naglagbung, a spring of boiling water, to see liquid "hell." According to the old folks, they could "hear" at Naglagbung the wailings of the deceased who are suffering from the flames of hell, similar to the suffering of the rich man in the parable *The Rich Man and Lazarus*. (Lk 16:19-31)

Our pilgrimage is complete. Better be, because soon, September beckons. It is the month for another great Marian devotion in the Bicol Region, the devotion to Our Lady of Peñafrancia in Naga City. I don't know about you, but after this virtual trip, my love for the Blessed Mother becomes ever stronger. I believe that through her intercession, I can be as close to her Son as can be.

Pray for us, Our Lady of Salvation, our Mother, *Inâ*.

Aba Ginoong Maria,[178]
napupuno ka ng grasya,
ang Panginoong Diyos ay sumasaiyo,
bukod kang pinagpala sa babaeng lahat
at pinagpala naman
ang iyong Anak na si Hesus.
Santa Maria, Ina ng Diyos,
ipanalangin mo kaming
makasalanan ngayon at kung kami'y
mamamatay.
Amen. ■

---

178   The song is my musical rendering of the catholic prayer **Hail, Mary** in Filipino, http://yourlisten.com/Arcadio. Morada/aba-ginoong-maria# (for audio); https://youtu.be/O1e8WSgjEpI (for video).

25

ACOLEO

The Seasons in our Salvation history

ADVENT. A time of waiting and hoping. Most people think of it as the season of waiting for Jesus' coming—not entirely wrong, but not entirely right either. Of the waiting, the Big Book says, "Be watchful! Be alert! You do not know when the time will come." (Mk 13:33) So, one needs to be prepared. A simple and often ignored reminder.

Well, including me and many among us, I presume, everyone rivets the reminder to their mind only when Advent reoccurs. But it always stays unheeded during the other seasons of the Church year—**A**dvent, **C**hristmas, **L**ent, **E**aster, plus the **O**rdinary Sundays between Christmas and Lent, and Easter and Advent. **ACOLEO.**

Just yesterday, I wanted to put a warm, Christmassy atmosphere around my house, so I thought of putting up a decorated tree, a *belen*[179], a Filipino lantern, and Christmas lights.

Everything was going smoothly and joyfully; I was enjoying the whole chore up to the Christmas lights. For this job, I used a ladder and a heavy-duty staple gun that weighed two pounds for attaching the wires to the periphery of my roof. I followed a simple, step-by-step pattern, too. (1) Set the ladder steady. (2) Ascend with caution. (3) Staple a couple feet of wire. (4) Set stapler aside. (5) Descend with caution. (6) Scoot the ladder to the next undecorated edge of the roof. Everything was going hassle-free as I scooted the ladder until the stapler gun (which I placed on one of the upper steps of the ladder) went plummeting on me! I ducked, yet a moment too late—the 2-pound metal stapler gun swooped and landed on the left side of my face just below the eye!

Christmas-preparation job rudely interrupted, I stopped and sat in my driveway for a while. As I was nursing the black eye, a van with a mocking plate number **CRY-4457** passed by, of which I took a snapshot with my camera. Don't ask me how I did. I presumed the owner was Filipino—a compatriot! (Using your keypad, this should come out straightforward: **CRY-4457** is **CRY-HILP**—that is, HELP in accented Filipino).

Wait, seriously, if you're up in or around Brownsville, or maybe even anywhere in Texas, you may have noticed the proliferation of vehicles with **CRY-** on their plates. I have, over the past weeks, recorded this interesting collection, among others:

CRY-2229
CRY-9653
CRY-8463
CRY-7867

---

179   *belen* [Filipino] – nativity/manger scene.

CRY-3696

CRY-5683

CRY-4457

(Come on, use your phone keypad and figure out what the plate numbers say!)

At first, I could not figure out any significance of these trivial numbers, until today. Today is an epiphany of sorts; I am connecting dots.

Advent is a time for waiting... with hope and longing... for our Savior. In this **CRY-TIME**, I am a human being needing to be saved. I am the boy who is wont to **CRY-WOLF**. A **CRY-BABY**, I am so accustomed to **CRY-LOUD** yet **CRY-DOWN** my opportunities to be with my Savior by choosing to do **CRY-PTIC** evil most of the time. Yet today, on this first Sunday of Advent, I realize once again the need to **CRY-STOP** and **CRY-HILP** [read with Filipino accent]. I'm needful of salvation, and I long for my Savior.

I need to prepare and to be always prepared for his coming, not only with external Christmas decorations but more so in my heart and soul—internal. And today Advent comes as a hammer hitting me literally on the face!

"Be watchful! Be alert! You do not know when the time will come."

REPARE YE THE WAY OF THE LORD! That's the rousing song from the rock musical *Godspell*. In seven words, it echoes the prophet Isaiah, and paraphrases the admonition of repentance from John the Baptist to each one of the faithful in the Church.

John the Baptist said:

Repent, for the kingdom of heaven is at hand!

(Mt. 3:2)

The prophet Isaiah foretold John's ministry over 700 years before his own time.

> **A voice proclaims: In the wilderness prepare the way of the LORD! Make straight in the wasteland a highway for our God! Every valley shall be lifted up, every mountain and hill made low; The rugged land shall be a plain, the rough country, a broad valley. Then the glory of the LORD shall be revealed, and all flesh shall see it together; for the mouth of the LORD has spoken.**
>
> (Is 40:3-5)

The sacrament of baptism cleanses us of original sin. But our inclination to sin remains and, powered by our free will, buffets us with actual sins throughout life. These are the obstacles that make our highways crooked, the bumps, hills or mountains that make our valleys rugged. John the Baptist enjoins us to straighten and flatten them back for the Lord's coming.

I remember a profound scene in the contemporary movie **God's Not Dead**, where a surreal conversation transpired between an old mom (who had dementia) and her pragmatic and unrepentant son.

SON: *(talking to her unresponsive mother)* I don't even know what I'm doing here. I mean, it's not like you even know who I am. You prayed and believed your whole life, never done anything wrong, and here you are. You're the nicest person I know. I am the meanest. You have dementia; my life is perfect. Explain that to me.

MOM: *(suddenly starts talking to herself)* Sometimes the devil allows people to live a life free of trouble 'cause he doesn't want them turning to God. Your sin is like a jail cell, except it's all nice and comfy, and there doesn't seem to be any need to leave. The door's wide open till one day, time runs out, and the cell door slams shut and suddenly it's too late. *(Then, as if from a sudden re-awakening, she faces him.)* Who did you say you were?

We, you and I, are the unrepentant son, and we might do well to listen to Mom. We might do well to heed John the Baptist. Prepare the way of the Lord. Repent. For one day, time runs out, and the door slams shut and suddenly it's too late. ◼

Twenty-six school years now seem just a flash in the pan. Two of these as math teacher at Cummings Middle School in Brownsville Independent School District, Brownville, TX. Ten years as math and/or music teacher in various private catholic schools in the Diocese of Brownsville. And fourteen years as Music specialist at Villareal Elementary, a public school in Los Fresnos Consolidated Independent School District, Los Fresnos, TX.

In my 24 years as a music teacher, December was always the most stressful, yet the most fulfilling, most gratifying, and most memorable of the months of any school year. Why? Because of this beloved entity called "Christmas program." Every music teacher, by job description and expectation, has to mount one.

My catholic orientation and formation would always poise an unwritten requirement in all those Christmas presentations: to celebrate joy and show reverence for Christ as the reason for the Season. After all, when we strive to present any worthy and genuine Christmas program, and call it that, we talk about God (_Christ_mas) directly, and the Baby Jesus indirectly (Christ_Jesus_mas).

Christmas can never be without Christ. A Christmas program without Christ is not a Christmas program.

A few past Christmas programs, precious memories by now, include the following titles. "The First Christmas," St. Luke Catholic School, 1995; "And Mary Danced For Joy," Incarnate Word Academy, 1997; "Christmas with the Angels," St. Mary's Catholic School, 2000; and "Jingle Bell Jukebox—the Flipside," Villareal Elementary School, 2014. Let me dwell on this last one as the object of my throwback.

I've never had a Christmas program without Christ. Christ is ever the key feature. In ready-made secular _holiday_ programs as "Jingle Bell Jukebox—the Flipside," I always find logical ways to insert the sacred Christmas story into the program script. The program in the end always says "Merry Christmas!"—not "Happy Holidays!"

Putting up a Christmas program is no simple task. Here's the what-and-how of my Christmas 2014 presentation at Villareal Elementary School.

You can't expect to be an excellent singer overnight, so _practice, practice, practice!_ That's the rule of thumb I drum up in my choir classes (1st grade to 5th). _Ad nauseam._

I organize the grade-level choirs in September, two weeks after the school opening. In the initial meetings, the choir members and I discuss our ground rules, goals, and expectations. We then brainstorm on the year's scheduled performances. The next two or three meetings (we meet once a week) are spent in activities to establish routines and improve singing skills, mainly vocalizations. By the first week of October, half of choir time is introduction and initial practices for the Christmas program. There's usually one-fifth casualty around this time—three in a group of 15 members quit, saying at my back: "Boring!" This is the ongoing means of separating the chaff from the wheat. Well, the chaff comprises those who miss the point that singing by itself is fun, or those who are not interested to sing in the first place; they sign up for choir for other reasons than wanting or needing to stretch vocal cords and perform. The ones who stick around are the wheat, those who usually have the seed of what it takes.

I scout for prospective Christmas programs as early as right after the year's Christmas program. By that token, I googled "Jingle Bell Jukebox the Flipside" last December 2013. After acquiring the program kit with script and accompanying CD, I evaluate if material is usable in its entirety, or needs modifications to suit my students and school condition. I usually change the script and use or discard suggested songs, and look for substitute songs to my liking from other sources. Sometimes, I produce a totally different script altogether.

I plan to use four of the nine songs in the program kit of "Jingle Bell Jukebox—the Flipside," not only because they appeal to me. More importantly, I always have my current choir students' competencies in consideration. We are a school with a small student body but not lacking in talents to tap. I reckon three of the four songs are good production numbers (*i.e.,* sung by all choir groups). The fourth song I deem good for solo, though the composers wrote it as a two-part song.

By the end of October, everyone (up to the youngest members, 1st graders) has memorized and taken to heart all the production numbers. By November, I finish scouting for other solo numbers or more production numbers. Soloists get auditioned, and I complete the repertoire. I am not an instrumentalist; so, I generate the music accompaniments using music apps, or get/buy karaoke versions, if available. Google, YouTube, or iTunes are excellent sources.

After Thanksgiving break in late November, I rehearse soloists, speakers, and narrators on alternate schedules. After-school rehearsals become more frequent; choirs, soloists, speakers, dancers have their own weekly turns to meet with me. Which means after-school work for me is every day, and I get to go home at 5 pm or later till December. (Teachers leave from work at 3:50 pm.) Boy, do I have a life! And I don't get paid for overtime.

Meanwhile, a Nativity coordinator, the efficient Rosita Vela at present, recruits Nativity scene participants from the general school population. She chooses from volunteers those who are to roleplay Mary, Joseph, the magi, the shepherds, and the angels. The choirs learn choreography/movements for the production numbers. With the help of other faculty and staff, we complete dances or other musical numbers. This year's addenda are "Run Run Rudolph!" by the Cheerleaders (care of Ms. Janie Calvillo and Ms. Lupita Solis); "My Little Grass Shack" (hula dance) by the Villareal staff; and "Turkey Dance" by the 1st Grade members and "Rockin' Around the Christmas Tree" by selected 2nd and 3rd Grade choir members. Another choreographed movement number ("Snow Dance") by the girls of the 5th grade choir will later materialize, at the eleventh hour, with the help of Melissa Shafer.

By the second week of December, we are ready for the general rehearsals. These usually happen on the three days preceding the day of the show. I need to be formidable during these three days. Aside from having to manage more or less than a hundred squirming and ready-to-burst-out-singing choir kids this year, I get to prepare a 100-slide PowerPoint presentation that runs along with the script. The school likewise expects me to mount a two-page programme/invitation with insert sheet, and assemble and disassemble the school's portable sound equipment for the general rehearsals and the actual show. I do this, on account of Villareal not having an auditorium for school programs. The school cafeteria serves as the venue for large gatherings. Since the portable sound system doesn't put up and dismantle itself, whoever sponsors a program has to take care of the sound equipment to give way to student dining throughout the day. It's an arduous setup, but, hey, I'm not complaining.

I am not, because I always have the accommodating Melissa Shafer on my side. Our unwritten professional partnership dates back several years. I don't remember how it came to be; it just somehow fell in place. I get everything ready as overall coordinator; she directs—and acts as host and/or narrator of the program. This, despite her own professional duties working with dyslexia students, as Robotics and Chess Club sponsor, Reading specialist, yearbook sponsor, campus technology consultant, among other responsibilities. Boy, does she have a life!

Her positive outlook keeps Melissa and people around her going. You cannot be near her and not get intimidated, infected, enthused, and inspired by her own positive approach and outlook on life. Not only once have work difficulties and problems tempted and pushed me to retreat into my little shell and comfort zone. But she was always there to say, "You can do it!" I believe her, because when she says that, I see excellent results!

As earlier mentioned, "Jingle Bell Jukebox—The Flipside" is a secular holiday program. No problem. In the script, especially towards the end, I seamlessly incorporate the Nativity tableau, giving the impression that it is a vital and logical part of the secular presentation. In addition, Melissa and I ask the school Principal to do the job as narrator for the Christmas story, which the incumbent, Ms. Yliana Gonzalez, willingly accepts. The Principal's narration of the Nativity story undoubtedly makes it the most expected part of the show. It starts with "In those days…" and ends with the choir singing, *"Gloria in excelsis deo!"*

Once the sacred scene unfolds on the actual performance day, as narrated by the Principal, all secularism flies out of the school window, so to say. The Nativity tableau easily becomes the gist, the highlight of the program. By the way, Villareal Elementary is a public school.

The proof of the pudding is in the eating. On December 18, we performed in two shows, the first for the school, the second for the public. Villareal Elementary School administrators, teachers, staff, parents, and the public witnessed the secular holiday program "Jingle Bell Jukebox—The Flipside" metamorphose into a true-to-reason Christmas program.

And they said: "Wonderful!"

Glory be to Christ—the reason for the Season! ■

Most of us go to the movies, so here is a simple quiz. What is common among these 10 male movie actors? Jeffrey Hunter, Max von Sydow, Robert Powell, Willem Dafoe, Jeremy Sisto, Christian Bale, Jim Caviezel, Andile Kosi, Diogo Morgado, and Cliff Curtis.

I have been so avid a movie fan myself that I may have up to now spent an enormous fortune satisfying the hobby. As far back as I can remember, movies have been a staple fare of my existence. Growing up in my small rural hometown of Sipocot in the Philippines, I remember there were two movie theaters right across the street where I lived. It was in those dilapidated, bed-bugged buildings where I watched the cinematic delights of my youth. Disney's **Toby Tyler**, the English-dubbed **Marcelino Pan Y Vino**, and the Greek-mythology fantasy of **Jason and the Argonauts**, to name a few.

There are special movies that stay in your head long after you viewed their last scenes and credits. They get embedded in your consciousness, waiting to be drawn from memory at will. An epiphany sometimes happens, as with 10 movies with the abovementioned lead actors. I've drawn these 10 movies from my long cinematic timeline—from the 1960s to date. Of course, this movie timeline limits and confines my list only to those I've watched. And in more than a century of movie-making, there's an entire universe of movies of every conceivable genre out there.

Four of the actors are American, 2 English, 1 African, 1 Swedish, 1 Portuguese, and 1 New Zealander. Different nationalities, but they played at different times the person of Jesus.

Yes, the 10 of them portrayed Jesus.

There are many other notable Jesus movies, aside from the 10 in which the aforementioned actors starred, but my special list excludes them because of the following reasons. (a) They were before my timeline. (b) I have not watched them. (c) They are musicals, which I love watching but which I consider being in an altogether different plane. (d) They are cartoons and animations, not live action movies.

Jeffrey Hunter starred in **King of Kings** (1961). Max von Sydow, **The Greatest Story Ever Told** (1965). Robert Powell, **Jesus of Nazareth** (1976). Willem Dafoe, **The Last Temptation of Christ** (1988). Jeremy Sisto, **Jesus** (1999). Christian Bale, **Mary, Mother of Jesus** (1999). Jim Caviezel, **The Passion of the Christ** (2004). Andile Kosi, **Son of Man** (2006). Diogo Morgado, **Son of God** (2014). Cliff Curtis, **Risen** (2016).

My personal notes on these Jesus actors. Hunter was the matinee-idol Jesus. Distractive big-name Hollywood stars in cameo roles surrounded von Sydow's Jesus. Morgado's unclothed body was too chubby for comfort in his crucifixion scene, so they kept the camera focus on his whole body to the minimum. Dafoe portrayed a Jesus based on a controversial novel which propounded an utter blasphemy and which was not Gospel-based. Kosi's movie is a critically acclaimed African fable, a reinvention of the story of Jesus where Jesus is black. Caviezel's portrayal is the most realistic, let alone gory, using Latin (the language of the Romans) and Aramaic (the language which Jesus might more than likely have used during his time). To me, Bale is the more or less perfect Jesus, if not for his youth at the time he made his Jesus movie. And to me, by far the best Jesus movie ever (actually a 6-hour miniseries) is Franco Zeffirelli's **Jesus of Nazareth**, with Powell as Jesus.

That's as far as my eyes could see.

Jesus is not fiction. He is a real person in history, born in the 1st century in a country inhabited by a race of people that descended from Abraham, the first Hebrew. He was born when the Romans occupied the Holy Land, when oppression was rampant and God's chosen people, the Jews, prayed and hoped for the Messiah. Jesus was born of earthly parents, Mary and Joseph, both from the lineage of King David. Jesus not only lived and observed Jewish laws, but taught others how to live a Jewish life, too. Later, Jesus was proclaimed King of the Jews both in adoration and in derision, charged, and imprisoned with an offense against Jewish law. Then the Romans crucified him. He died and got buried in a Jewish cemetery according to Jewish custom and tradition. Without doubt, Jesus was born, lived, and died a Jew.

As a Jew native to a Middle Eastern country, specifically Israel, how did Jesus look?

Throughout the ages, painters have had a field day putting into canvas their perception of Jesus, but no one could say with certainty how our Savior looked. There are no extant pictures, paintings, or portraits of him which historians could consider authentically his. Nor does the Bible give any physical description of Jesus. Almost none, that is, for in 1 Sm 16:11-12, the prophet Samuel mentions "ruddy" to describe David, who descended from Abraham, who later became King David from whom Jesus likewise descended. Merriam-Webster defines *ruddy* as "1: having a healthy reddish color, 2: red or reddish." Therefore, was there any possibility of a black Jesus? I'm not a racist, but I am not inclined to think so.

Another thing. I apologize for my limited scope of experience, but I can say actors from just about any country have portrayed Jesus in movies. Just about any country—except Israel. When will filmmakers produce a Jesus movie in which a true-blue Jew plays Jesus?

Over two thousand years ago, God showed himself to man by becoming man. He chose the country of the Jews as the land of his birth. But that Good News was not solely for the Jewish nation. God saw that the

Good News was for the non-Jews as well, to the Gentiles. For that's what our God is—the God of every nation! He is everyone's. In the manger, during the Nativity of Jesus, that's what our eyes have seen.

That is the Epiphany at the Nativity.

Merry Christmas and a blessed New Year to everyone! ■

 hey had sinned against God. In those days, "…all the princes of Judah, the priests, and the people added treachery to treachery, practicing all the abominations of the nations and defiling the Lord's house which he had consecrated in Jerusalem." (2 Chr 36:14)

In 605 BC, the Chaldean king Nebuchadnezzar, king of Babylon, besieged Jerusalem. The Babylonians vanquished the Jews, destroyed Jerusalem including Solomon's magnificent temple, and deported them in 597 BC, 587 BC, and 582 BC, respectively.

Their conquerors took scores of the Jewish people to Babylon, even the wealthy and educated, as captives and enslaved them in exile. The Jews suffered and longed to return to their beloved Jerusalem to rebuild the temple of the Lord.

Redemption came in the person of Cyrus the Great. This Persian king subdued the Babylonians in 539 BC. After the fall of Babylon, Cyrus the Great allowed the Jews to return to their homeland, after 70 long years—and rebuild their temple.

The biblical accounts of their captivity and exile bespeak great loneliness and longing. This was what I wanted to project and communicate when I set Psalm 137 to music in 2011. The result is the musical setting **If Ever I Forget You**.

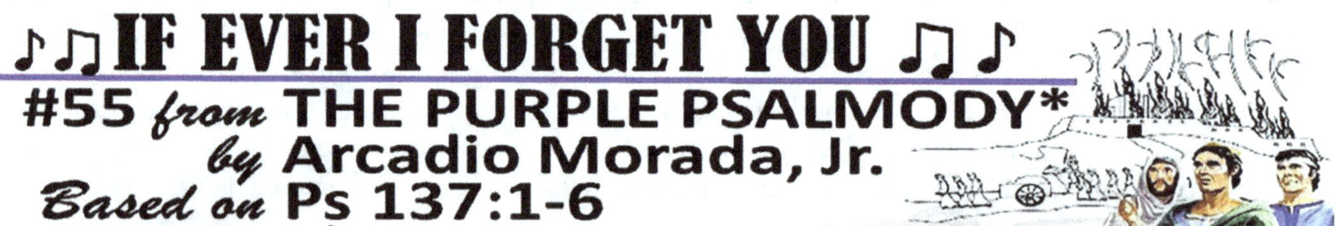

Antiphon:
Let my tongue be silenced
if ever I forget you.
1
Are we not God's chosen people,
Captives in this land called Babylon?
Here we weep as we recall the past
And the things God has done for us. (Ant.)
2
Here our captors mock and revile us,
Ask of us the lyrics of our songs.
'Sing for us the music of your God,
Joyously, fervently!" they say. (Ant.)
3
How can slaves and captives sing with joy

> And with fervor in their captors' land?
> Oh, if ever we forget you,
> Our own dear Jerusalem! (Ant.)

It is one of the saddest melodies I have ever composed.[180] ∎

o, [and] from now on do not sin any more. That's what Jesus told the adulterous woman. (Jn 8:11) Like sharp spears, the words aim more pointedly towards me, too. Not that I am prone, if at all, to flings and extramarital affairs. Rather, that feeling comes from being guilty of sin in whatever form, whatever size. The guilt of sin gets written all over my face, more clearly than I could admit.

I rebuff. I may be sinful, but how could I go sin no more? This is what wretched me harbors at the back of my mind:

"Oh, yeah, Jesus, get real! I am sorry, but isn't this telling me to eat my meals, and brush my teeth, then eat no more?

"I am born to sin; in sin I am born; to sin I am predisposed. Temptation is everywhere. Satan is everywhere. Where and how can I go and sin no more?"

Well, I realize I'm bad, to say it mildly. Wicked, to put it bluntly. I am a split personality. My compassion is skin-deep, and my actions are often tainted with malice. I'm adept at putting on a light show when there's pitch darkness deep in my heart. I appear good outside when, in fact, I am horrible inside. People don't see the dirt in my thoughts, in my motivations, even in my intentions. I appear sociable within sight of others, but nefarious when others are not around. How's that for a Dr. Jekyll and Mr. Hyde?

Monsignor Heberto Diaz has an apt description for me in his letter to St. Mary's parishioners in this Sunday's Bulletin: I have this "unswerving ability to become lost in sin."

Very true! In fact, I am degreed in sin—MA in E, courtesy of Dark University. E for Evil.

Yes, I will sin no more, though I know there are pitfalls along the way. I will try as much as I can. If I fall, I will stand, because I know Jesus reaches out his hand to me and why he does that is too great a love and a mystery for me to understand. God's mercy endures forever. "Infinite mercy," Msgr. Bert calls it. Today, in the first week of Lent, is not a whiny Sunday, after all my negative rantings. Today is a hopeful Sunday, one filled with joy.

Coming from another Mass, another place, and another priest, my wife Mameng relates to me her parallel points for reflection. The good priest from the TV Mass on Filipino Channel presents a profound food for thought for this season of Lent.

- **M** for Mortality—I am mortal; *the wages of sin is death.* (Rom 6:23)
- **E** for Eternal life—God's love makes me eternal.
- **R** for Repentance—I repent and remain in God's love.
- **C** for Conversion—Change my heart, repel evil earnestly.
- **Y** for You and me—We are all in God's plan of salvation.

Lent is the season to re-examine ourselves and our own spirituality. Lent is a time for M.E.R.C.Y. ∎

---

180   Arcadio Morada, Jr., *tagaalbay*, "If Ever I Forget You," You-Tube video, 3:19min, https://youtu.be/C5ChkQ0zAuQ.

Just before Jesus dies on the Cross, he utters these bewildering words that are so unsettling for those who don't know the context. *"Eloi, Eloi, lema sabachthani?"* which means "My God, my God, why have you forsaken me?" (Mt 27:46)

Indeed, why does he sound in utter desperation and agony?

♪♫ MY GOD, WHY? ♫♪
#82 *from* THE PURPLE PSALMODY*
by Arcadio Morada, Jr.
Based on Ps 22:1, 4, 13-14

Antiphon:
My God, my God,
Why have you,
Why have you
Abandoned Me?[181]

1. All the people laugh and scoff at me.
Many of them wag their heads and say:
"Let the Lord whom he relies upon
Deliver him, if he loves him!" *(Ant.)*

2. They divide my clothes among themselves,
Scourge me, then they pierce my hands and feet
"Let the Lord whom he relies upon
Deliver him, if he loves him!" *(Ant.)*

3. Yet the Lord will come quickly to help;
He has not disdained my misery.
Then I will proclaim his holy name,
Give honor and glory to him. *(Ant.)*

A few days before uttering those words, Jesus was going to enter Jerusalem with his disciples. Donkey for humility or horse for might and power—on which animal did Jesus choose to ride while entering Jerusalem on Palm Sunday? The Romans and other Gentiles who missed the context of his act might have laughed, scoffed, and wagged their heads. Jesus was riding on a donkey, *huh*, funny! Few of them realized, if at all, that Jesus was fulfilling prophecies of old. In the same manner, when Jesus uttered "My God, why have you forsaken me?"—he was fulfilling prophecies about the Messiah written over a thousand years old. Read the prophet Isaiah, chapter 53:4-5. He made these prophecies when people or any authorities anywhere had not even used crucifixion as a mode of capital punishment and execution. Then King David echoed these prophecies in Psalm 22.

Let's go read Psalm 22. Just so we stop thinking that, near death, Jesus was mouthing meaningless words. Just so, we start believing that Jesus is the Messiah. ■

---

181   Arcadio Morada, Jr., *tagaalbay*, "My God, Why?", YouTube video, 3:33min, https://youtu.be/P7tJ2YeKWNQ.

homas was neither the first nor the last. The following list is an interesting compendium of people, both famous and infamous, throughout past and contemporary history. Conquerors, statesmen, philosophers, writers, scientists, playwrights, composers, musicians, artists... you name the persuasion, and for sure find its role model of skeptic vision or wisdom. Many of them simply did not believe, might have had some faith at the start, but one reason or another might have caused an incipient disbelief. Some of them neither had faith nor disbelief to start with. Still, some others, like Thomas, had their belief system controlled by evidence or proof as its *raison d'être*. Of course, I am talking about doubting Thomas. He was one of the 12 apostles, who would not believe the divinity of Jesus till he had touched any physical evidence after the Lord had risen from the dead.

When Thomas first heard of Jesus' resurrection, he questioned it pragmatically. "Unless I see the mark of the nails in his hands and put my finger into the nailmarks and put my hand into his side, I will not believe." (Jn 20:25) When the risen Christ finally met him, the Lord said, "Put your finger here and see my hands, and bring your hand and put it into my side." (Jn 20:27) Then, Thomas said to Jesus, "My Lord and my God!" (Jn 20:28) He spent the following years traveling and spreading the Gospel. He died on December 21, 72 AD, in Mylapore, India.

Some people in the list lived before the time of Thomas—and Jesus. In the old dating system parlance, we call that era "Before Christ," or BC. "1 BC" meant 1 year before the birth of Christ. The time after the birth of Christ is AD, "Anno Domini," in the year of our Lord. Therefore, AD 1 meant 1 year after the birth of Christ (not After Death). Nowadays, though, for secularism, or to negate the influence of Christianity and the mention of Christ in the dating system, BC is now called "Before the Common/Current Era" or BCE. AD is CE or "Common Era."

I strongly adhere to using BC and AD! The least I can say about this new dating system: it is appalling!

Now back to Thomas and his ilk. Here is my list of them doubters, agnostics, atheists, skeptics all—before and after Thomas, before and in the year of our Lord, BC and AD.

Heraclitus, Aristophanes, Democritus, Aristotle, Epicurus, Voltaire, Benjamin Franklin, Thomas Paine, Marquis de Sade, Johann von Goethe. James Madison, Napoleon Bonaparte, Charles Darwin, Abraham Lincoln, Edgar Allan Poe, Karl Marx, Walt Whitman, Samuel Clemens (Mark Twain), George Bizet, Friedrich Nietzsche. Thomas Jefferson, Thomas Edison, John Adams, Sigmund Freud, George Bernard Shaw, Jose P. Rizal, H.G. Wells, Marie Curie, Frank Lloyd Wright, Vladimir Lenin. Bertrand Russell, Robert Frost, Albert Einstein, Joseph Stalin, James Joyce, D.H. Lawrence, Irving Berlin, Jawaharlal Nehru, Alfred Hitchcock, Pearl S. Buck. Mao Tse-tung, Aldous Huxley, Ernest Hemingway, Walt Disney, Howard Hughes, Ayn Rand, Jean Paul Sartre, Sergei Prokofiev, Richard Rodgers, Katharine Hepburn. Adolf Hitler, Oskar Schindler, Albert Camus, Gene Kelly, Burt Lancaster, Isaac Asimov, Marcelo Mastroianni, Richard Burton, Linda Ronstadt, George C. Scott. Carl Sagan, John Lennon, Bruce Lee, Bill Gates, Mark Zuckerberg, Warren Buffett, Ted Turner, Frank Sinatra, Billy Joel, Barry Manilow. Sarah McLachlan, Elton John, Mick Jagger, Brad Pitt, George Clooney, Natalie Portman, Bruce Willis, Woody Allen, Angelina Jolie, James Cameron. Jodie Foster, John Malkovich, Ian McKellen, Julianne Moore, Jack Nicholson, Donald Sutherland, Kevin Bacon, Guy Pearce, Joaquin Phoenix, Ray Romano. Antonio Banderas, Larry King, Amanda Bynes, Robert Redford, William Shatner, Stephen Hawking, Samuel L. Jackson, Chris Rock, Meryl Streep, Daniel Radcliffe, etc.

Fame, fortune, and reputation appear to be the common denominator. The famous, the infamous, the rich, the brilliant, the artistic, the charismatic—they are in the list. Pharrell Williams, "Happy" singer, describes them as "Pompous!" He has another description of them, "Arrogant."

I leave out many names, chosen and sifted for brevity's sake. So, the list is not complete. The gang isn't altogether here.

And, surely, Thomas has never been alone.

I am fortunate and blessed to have been born into the Catholic faith. More than feelings, and by my own free will and reasoning, I have been in the faith despite chances and lures of conversion to other belief systems. As contained in the Apostle's Creed of my faith, I believe in the Trinity, the Church, the communion of saints, the forgiveness of sins, the resurrection, and life everlasting. I believe in a loving God who calls for me to love him and others in return. I believe in a merciful God who forgives my transgressions and enjoins me to forgive others just the same.

I believe in Jesus, and I feel fine I am not in Thomas' company. ■

Ash and Val, my two dogs, may seem inappropriate as subject for an Easter musing. Looking closely at their names, however, may actually drive home a startling aptness: Ash and Valentine. Mortality and Love. Suffering and Sacrificial Offering. Passion and Resurrection. Death and Rising. Good Friday and Easter Sunday. Lent and Easter!

They also led me to what I now consider my favorite image of the season: 3 sunflowers in a blanket of green.

As I walked Ash and Val on Good Friday, we stumbled upon this three-some in a grassy patch on a vacant lot among hundreds of other yellow wildflowers. Stunning in their golden brilliance amid a blanket of green, the flowers were a feast for the eye and for the soul. I had been looking for an inspiration for my Easter musing all week long, and now, here before me, these flowers appeared resplendent in their stark simplicity and commonality.

In the night's darkness, they await longingly the rising of the sun in the East. Looking up to the sun, they rely on the sun; they follow the sun, till they wither and die.

They remind me of our being Easter people. People of the Resurrection.

In the darkness of death, the Easter people wait for the rising of the Son in glory. Their faith in, their love for, and their hope in the Son enable them to withstand their own Good Fridays and the darkness of their own passion and death.

Here are three exceptional Easter people. Poor in spirit all. Shining examples of simplicity of faith and commonality with us because they were once among us, real flesh and blood as we are. They lived on this earth one time or another as we have, reminding us we are all Easter people. They remind us to look to the Son for the beauty and the brilliance of the Day of Glory.

orenzo Ruiz was born in Binondo, Manila, in 1594, from a Chinese father and Filipino mother. He studied Spanish and the fundamentals of the Catholic faith from the Dominicans who were in charge of the parish of Binondo. He became an errand boy of the friars, a sacristan, and when he was older, an "escribano." [scribe]

Lorenzo got married, and the union bore three children. Raised in a Christian atmosphere himself, he directed his family towards an abiding trust and love of God. Lorenzo was a devout Catholic: he attended Mass faithfully, set himself to receive the Holy Communion every first Sunday of the month, and loved the Virgin Mary. He joined the Confraternity of the Holy Rosary and spent some of his precious time in spreading the devotion to Mary.

Lorenzo was a simple, cheerful man. All he dreamed of was to fulfill his obligations as a husband and father. But one day, he had a quarrel with a Spaniard. When the Spaniard was found dead shortly after, the authorities accused Lorenzo of homicide. No one knew how true the accusation was, but Lorenzo feared for his life. He sought to escape from the arm of the Spanish authorities in Manila.

It so happened that the Dominicans were then preparing to embark on a mission in some place in the Orient. Lorenzo volunteered to join the group and, with a heavy heart, bade goodbye to his loved ones. The friars, aware of the trouble he was going through, did not hesitate to take him. Lorenzo's intention, however, was to remain in Macao and there earn a livelihood for his family.

The expedition, however, did not go through Macao, but sailed directly to Japan, where Christianity was under siege. At that time in Japanese history, the Tokugawa Shogunate was hunting down Christians, putting them in prison, and executed them if they did not renounce their faith. Realizing that he was on a jump from the frying pan to the fire, that he headed instead for another trouble, Lorenzo felt dismayed. But after some reflection, he abandoned his plan to go to Macao and became a missionary himself.

A few days after their arrival in Okinawa, the Japanese authorities discovered the missionaries, including Lorenzo. They arrested, imprisoned, and tortured them. After two long years, they transferred them to Nagasaki to face trial. The place for the trial was not a tribunal hall but a torture chamber, as it was customary for the interrogators to torture the prisoners while they were being questioned.

When Lorenzo's turn came, they asked him, "If we grant you your life, are you willing to renounce your faith?" Lorenzo gave them a quick and straightforward answer. "I am a Christian and this I profess, and although I didn't come to Japan to become a martyr, I am now willing to give up my life for God. You can do with me whatever you please."

The Japanese sentenced Lorenzo and his companions to death. The place of execution, their Calvary, was Nishizaka Hill, Nagasaki. Muzzled and hand-tied, they were marched barefoot to the place of execution. To inflict more sufferings to the victims, the Japanese administered death slowly and painfully. They subjected Lorenzo and his companions to bizarre and horrible punishments. They hanged them heads down inside small pits and only their limbs appeared above the ground. To slow down the flow of blood, they bound Lorenzo's body slightly with a rope. Once in a while, the torturer would make a slight cut on his flesh, to determine if he was still alive.

Lorenzo remained in this condition for three days. At the end of the third day, September 29, 1637, he died from exhaustion and pain, as did all of his companions sooner or later. The Japanese burned their remains and threw their ashes into the sea.

In December 1981, soldiers of the Salvadoran Army's select, American-trained Atlacatl Battalion entered the village of El Mozote, where they murdered hundreds of men, women, and children, often by decapitation. In a place called La Cruz, the soldiers raped many of the women. One of these was a young woman, an evangelical Christian. The soldiers had raped her many times in a single afternoon and subsequently tortured her. Despite the atrocities being committed against the young woman, however, she clang to her belief in Christ—and sang hymns all throughout!

To say that it was a gory and horrible scene was an understatement. Not content with what they had so far done, the soldiers shot her in the chest, but the young woman, momentarily interrupted, kept on singing. What nerve, what audacity this Christian woman had! Stupefied and tiring of this ordeal she had put them into, the soldiers got their machetes and once and for all cut off her head. Of course, the singing stopped.[182]

essica was a healthy teenager. She had not been to her pediatrician for a long time. When she was a sophomore in high school, she experienced some tiredness and pain, so her mother took her to the doctor. When they received the call with results of her examination, the news was devastating. Jessica had acute lymphocytic leukemia. The prognosis was not good.

At the time of her diagnosis in May 1995, Jessica was raising funds for a summer mission trip to Mexico. She continued with her plans, even as she began treatment at Doernbecher Children's Hospital in Portland, Oregon. The treatment was effective, and she went into remission quickly, while still making regular trips to the hospital for tests and continuing therapy. As summer approached, however, she suddenly began having problems again and sought for medical care. They found a drastically compromised immune system that resulted in an infection which swept through her body and was resistant to antibiotics.

Jessica had leukemia! She knew that death was a possibility. She had to face the prospect that the life-threatening disease might cut her life short at age fifteen. Yet the hope of resurrection was clear in her testimony, as expressed in the October 13, 1995, entry of her journal:

> **"**
>
> God is in control of all things!
>
> He has a plan for me that is being carried out as I write this.
>
> Angels are watching over me.
>
> What have I to fear? Death?
>
> That is only one more step to HEAVEN!
>
> GOD IS IN CONTROL!
>
> **"**

---

182   Mark Danner, *The Massacre at El Mozote*, New York, Vintage Books, 1994, pp. 78-79.

Jessica's struggle with leukemia lasted eleven months. Finally, after eleven days in pediatric intensive care, the doctors said they could do nothing more. They disconnected her from all life support, and at age sixteen, her earthly life ended. The date was April 5, her mother's birthday. It was Good Friday.[183]

Jesus endured pain and humiliation on Good Friday. The sufferings of Lorenzo and his companions, of the tenacious young woman in El Salvador, and of courageous Jessica—these are but shadows of Jesus' Good Friday in our world. They should inspire us to be more resilient and receptive to the crosses in our lives. They should not distract us from the real meaning and value of suffering in our life, because, as Jessica wrote, God is still in control. God is in charge of the universe. There may be violence, brutality, debilitating illness, injustice, and sin in the world—no doubt about this. Yet there is also grace and peace and hope and forgiveness and redemption and Easter to look forward to. That is what Jesus' resurrection brings.

The promise and hope of the Resurrection—this is what we celebrate as Easter people. Ash… Valentine. Lent… Easter! ◾

---

183   Anne Jeffers, "Living in the Reality of the Resurrection," EASTER PEOPLE, March 7, 2013, http://sldunn. wordpress.com/.

26

G-O-D

unseen hands draw everything in place

y kindergarten music class wanted to sing the **Alphabet Song** one day. After my short intro on the keyboard, everybody sang ABCD EFG. This cute smart-aleck girl, named Hailey, never given to silence, sang **Twinkle Twinkle Little Star** instead.

"The matter, Hailey?" Pedro, one of her 19 classmates, said in a complaining tone.

Annoyed, I cut off the singing altogether and stared at the boy. "I thought we were going to sing the ABC," Pedro said, short of apologizing.

The cute Hailey rebuffed in a most cocky manner, complete with a shrug. "What's the problem? They're the same. **Baa baa black sheep**, too."

What's in a name? It's the tune that counts. We were singing one of the world's most recognizable tunes, albeit with different lyrics. Did everybody know?

"No," Pedro said with a desperate face and tone.

"I can even sing **Mary Had a Little Lamb**." Here comes smart-aleck Hailey again. "Same as ABC, too!"

"You're kidding," I say as I smile. "We'll see." I start the keyboard intro once again for ABC, and the girl sings. "Mary had a little lamb / Little lamb, little lamb / Mary had a little lamb, little lamb, little lamb / Mary had a little lamb / With fleece as white as snow." All she did was adapt Mary to ABC.

"Who's Mary, anyway?" Jay Sebastian asks. This classmate sits near the shelf of percussion instruments, always eyeing on the vibraslap which I guess he plans to play later, during our Pick Your Instrument game.

"I learned in Sunday school Jesus is the Lamb of God, and Mary is Jesus' mother," Ismael, who often sits at the back of the class, says. "So, we sing of *this* Mary when we sing **Mary Had a Little Lamb**."

"That's a good point." I acknowledge Ismael's logic. "I love it!"

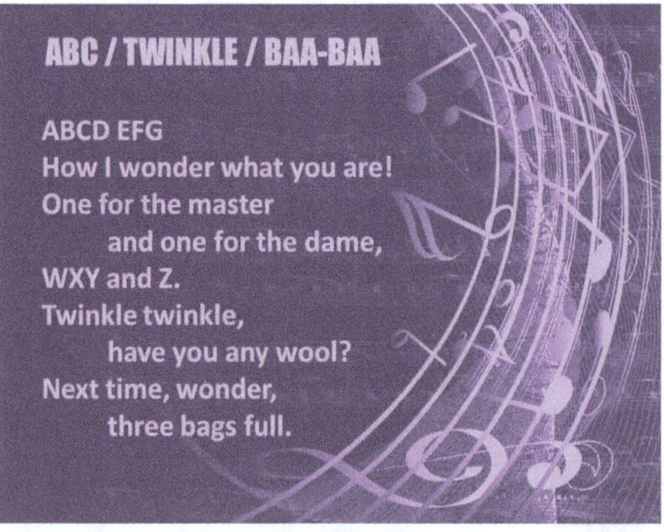

"Let us go back to singing," the problematic Pedro cuts in again.

I divide the class into three groups, and start them into singing together ABC, TWINKLE, BAA BAA BLACK SHEEP, while Hailey sings MARY HAD A LITTLE LAMB! Of course, we're in a kinder class, so I don't mind the chaos that ensues.

Cool! Smart-aleck, messy but clever! Three songs—I mean, four songs—in one!

God enables things, in his infinite wisdom, to align and fall into place. In our ignorance, we call it coincidence. We don't notice the alignment, but God is in control of everything, and they're there. They fall into place, whether we notice it, or whether we go for it. It takes scientific, philosophic, theologic, or simplistic—the purity and boldness of a child's—eyes, to make us realize that. Yes, God enables things to fall into their rightful places. Even those that may look incongruous and clashing at first.

All my kinder kids can sing the ABC as proficiently as they can say the 26 letters in the English alphabet. Everybody knows that. There may not be any kindergartner, though, who can figure out what G-O-D gives us if A=1, B=2,… Z=26. It requires the skills of one-to-one correspondence and computation. Do the Math.

I'm no kindergartner. God gives me 26.

I am just an ordinary Filipino in an adopted land, working so hard to live and earn my daily keep. It had been twelve long years since I last set foot on my beloved native land, yet I hardly noticed. When the opportunity presented itself in the summer of 2016, I and my wife Mameng along with our daughter Carmela packed our bags and flew to the Philippines posthaste. It was not only a coming-back-home but exploring-your-homeland trip as well. It turned out to be our most memorable homecoming to date. One of the trip's highlights that made it so was *El Nido*.

El Nido is Spanish for "the nest." Nothing usual on this exotic archipelago of limestone islands at the West Philippine Sea off the coast of mainland Palawan. Spanish colonizers gave it the name owing to the abundance of edible nests of the birds *Aerodramus fuciphagus*, known around these parts as *balinsasayaw*. Balinsasayaw build their nests on the sheer cliffs of the islands, making them even more difficult to get. El Nido locals have, for centuries, defied hazards and danger by harvesting the nests for income, providing the key ingredient for the expensive delicacy known as bird's nest soup. The nests are most-sought-after and prized in the urban world.

Getting to El Nido costs a fortune for the common Filipinos, through even the most basic or cheapest tour package, because of its inaccessibility. For that reason, many of my countrymen find themselves incapable of going there, let alone experiencing it, in their lifetime. So, given the resources and the chance, one should go! Mameng and I thought we might never have another chance to go that way again if we didn't go now. And so, with our hard-earned money, we did.

God enables things to fall into place, remember? Everything felt as if paradise. El Nido is paradise. Garden Cottage #26, the quarters assigned to us at Miniloc Island, El Nido, was modest luxury—an oxymoron—to our vacation-hungry, stateside, workaholic bodies. The thatched-roofed cottage, constructed with indigenous Filipino materials, is deceptive in its simplicity. We find provisions for luxurious amenities inside, such as a fridge, amid a lush, tropical forest at the bottom of a limestone cliff, just behind the cottage.

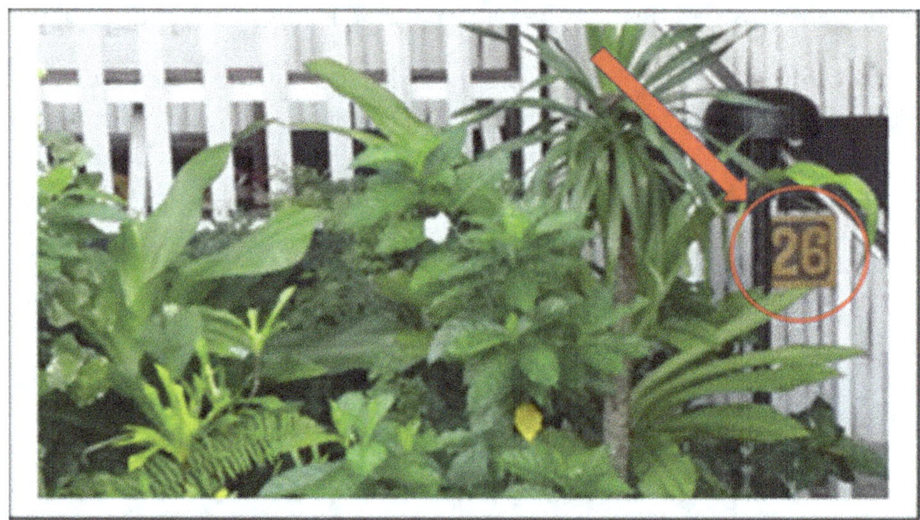

Even if what we got was the cheapest tour package available, yet we, as the other guests, were virtual kings and queens pampered by nature and men. The Resort-people, mostly natives, were so accommodating and amiable. Three days was not enough to savor the good things the islands offered. We were hungry for more.[184]

El Nido ladies sang vernacular songs to welcome you as soon as you disembarked from the Airswift plane coming from Manila. From then on, your only means of transport was by boat. Boat rides were so comfy and enjoyable. The white beaches were rustic, but exceptional. We swam, we snorkeled, we kayaked. I never thought island-hopping could be so much fun. We explored a cave whose entrance was so low and small you could only get in by inching your way lying on your back. I had my first kayak ever (at my age, honestly) at the Small Lagoon and at the Big Lagoon. I also snorkeled and marveled at the colorful coral formations at the bottom of the deep, crystalline waters of the lagoons. Carmela and I got to swim up close and personal with 1.5-meter-long jack fish during their feeding frenzy; they were so close I cringed at the thought they could nibble me instead of the feed pellets because of our intrusion. The view on top of Snake Island was incredible! Every meal was seafood galore. Each day was over with you thinking you'd love to see more of nature or do wonderful things more. But, given our limited time and resources, we could only take so much of good things. We hadn't even tasted any bird's nest soup yet! The same ladies who serenaded us on arrival now sang *bon voyage* as we dragged our leaden feet while boarding the chartered airplane back to Manila.

---

184   Arcádio Morada, Jr., *tagaalbay*, "God's Gift of El Nido," YouTube video, 11:26min, https://youtu.be/XLCig4mpj6s.

Back to the metropolis, we found ourselves billeted at this lodging establishment called Asiatel Inn, Room #26, for ₱1,200 a day, with (we learned later) no running hot water. Civilization as we knew it. Back to reality!

Flying back to Texas was a step further into reality. Reality meant getting back to 2687 Pompeii—the street where I lived in Brownsville, Texas. More signs of reality were driving back to work and teaching music to my Texas students. Reality was having kindergarten students who, time and time again, loved to sing ABC cum TWINKLE cum BAA BAA cum MARY. Four-in-one.

I was to retire in 2018, after 26 years in America.

And, oh, have I mentioned that my wife's birthday is February 26? My daughter's is May 26. Manay Naita, Mameng's sister, one reason we had to go *balikbayan* (back to homeland) in the first place, was born on January 26. Three other relatives, Polô, Ambê, and Erwin were born on January 26. Can you beat that?

I finished my manuscript of this book, copy editing, and proofreading, exactly on January 26, 2022! G = 7, O = 15, and D = 4. God gives us 26, you see. ■

Bird's-eye view of Miniloc Island Resort, El Nido. The sheer limestone cliffs in the background tower over the cottages and the Clubhouse below. The Resort is reachable only by water transportation. (Photo courtesy of elnidoresorts .com)

27
YELLOW
A puny gesture calls history to mind

"For you, Mr. Purple," the 1st-grader said as she handed me this tiny bouquet of yellow flowers she had picked from the playground at recess time. The gesture was so puny and innocent, yet earnest.

My first impulse was to say: "What..." However, what came out of my mouth was, "Oh, how lovely!"

The little girl then dashed off to join her classmates in their play, but not before receiving a heartfelt "Thanks!" from me in grateful appreciation.

I kept the tiny bouquet in my grip even after reaching the Music Room. By instinct, I got my cellphone and took a snapshot of the flowers for posterity. Three yellow flowers. Puny. Sweet. Significant.

I posted the picture and story. Aida Alcazar Naz, a colleague from as far back as the Normal school in 1970, got inspired and remembered a piece of Alfred Lord Tennyson's mind:

> **Little flower—but if I could understand**
> **What you are, root and all, all in all,**
> **I should know what God and man is.**[185]

"Mr. Purple, see how God works even in three tiny flowers," said Cleofe Perez, a former co-teacher at Xavier School, Manila. "I miss that."

Teacher-BFF Lillibeth Boncato said, "An innocent token with a deep sense of strength. Love it!" Felicitous words from our friendship that dates back over 20 years. Beth and I came to America in 1992.

I couldn't agree with Aida, Cleo, and Beth more. The hand of God is manifest even in little daily experiences in our life as teachers, such as this girl with her puny bouquet of yellow flowers. The flowers so cute and her gesture so innocent! All I needed to see was a receptive heart and a discerning mind—and a personal connection to history that happened over 30 years ago.

---

185   Alfred Lord Tennyson, "Flower in the Crannied Wall," poem (1863). https://www.poemhunter.com/poem/flower-in-the-crannied-wall-2/.

In retrospect, I can now say with certainty and wisdom: what a year 1986 was! It was in 1986 when I got involved in two opposite events that were to become landmarks and milestones of my life. The first, a cutting loose. The second, a coming together.

he 1986 EDSA Revolution was the cutting loose of the hapless Filipino people from the reign of a dictatorial regime. At last, we yanked ourselves away from the clutches of an ignominious dictator named Ferdinand E. Marcos.

The beginning of the end of the Marcos dictatorship was, many Filipinos believe, his own doing: the assassination of his nemesis, Ninoy Aquino. The harshest critic of Marcos and the biggest threat to his political power, Ninoy was coming home from a three-year exile in the United States. No sooner had he stepped on the tarmac of the Manila International Airport than bullets from the AVSECOM (Aviation Security Command) men knocked him down, dead, on August 21, 1983. It was only a matter of time when the Filipino people, overburdened by the yoke of Marcos' abuses, would at last muster courage and see the light.

The light that enabled us to see materialized on February 7, 1986—the presidential snap elections. Marcos' rubber-stamp COMELEC (Commission on Elections) declared him the winner, whereas the citizens' watchdog NAMFREL (National Citizens' Movement for Free Elections) proclaimed Aquino's wife Cory the rightful one. From then onwards, Marcos' rule careened downhill.

On February 22, Juan Ponce Enrile and Fidel Ramos, key personalities of the Marcos cabinet, held a historic press conference in Camp Aguinaldo at around 6 pm. Their cabal of rebel soldiers flanked them as Enrile and Ramos announced their defection from the dictator's hold. The news was all over, on TV, on radio. It spread like wildfire.

At that point in time, Mameng and I lived across the street from Xavier School (where I worked) in a compound where other co-teachers also lived. Lulu Magtibay (for many years taught in New York and New Jersey, but came back to the Philippines, and now deceased), Lourdes 'Odette' Rocafort (now living in New Jersey), and Doming Litong (now in Houston, Texas). The five of us became unwitting participants in a patriotic drama that was about to unfold.

On Radio Veritas at around 9 pm, the Archbishop of Manila, Jaime Cardinal Sin, admonished all Filipinos to come to the aid of the beleaguered Enrile and Ramos. We responded to the call; Odette, Lulu, Doming, Mameng, and I trooped to Camp Aguinaldo through Ortigas Avenue and Epifanio de los Santos Avenue, more popularly known as EDSA. We were not alone, though. Countless other people from all walks of life heeded Sin. Men, women, children, young, old, rich, or poor, traversed the streets of Manila and converged *en masse* at EDSA in what was to be the beginning of the EDSA Revolution.

On the morning of the following day, February 23, news spread that Enrile, Ramos, and their men holed up in Camp Aguinaldo. They needed all the help and support they could get—moral, emotional, food, water, and other stuff. Again, heeding the call, my co-teachers Doming, Odette, Lulu, Mameng, and I walked the distance at dawn towards the Camp. A sizeable crowd of people—*er*, community—was already around and near the gate of the Camp when we arrived. Most of them wanted to get near the rebel soldiers and give them the foodstuff that they brought along. A miracle was unfolding in the meantime. A great mass of humanity (at some point reaching about two million strong) gathered in a place where there was no animosity, resentment, tension, or belligerence. Festivity, brotherhood, *bayanihan* (communal unity) spirit, generosity, and neighborliness were not only felt, but seen. The world would come to know it as the miracle of EDSA.

Someone much later coined the name *People Power Revolution* to describe this peaceful movement by the Filipino people. We showed a repressive regime that enough was enough, through non-violent means. We showed the world that if we acted as one in large number, we could topple a hated regime and cause a dictator's fall.

Later that day, Marcos would appear on television with loyalist generals, hinting at a possible artillery strike while announcing plans for his upcoming Tuesday presidential inauguration. Whether a ruse or a contingency plan, it seemed not to matter at all because more and more people continued to gather at EDSA. At that exact moment, Mameng and I were amid thousands of Filipinos at the corner of Ortigas and EDSA, across the imposing POEA (Philippine Overseas Employment Administration) building. This innocuous corner would later become an iconic historical spot. We were standing where the EDSA Shrine would rise in 1989. It was a wide vacant grassy lot where presently a multitude of people stood, waiting. We didn't altogether know what we were waiting for or expecting. Some said Marcos loyalist forces were coming by land, others said by air, some others saying they could come howsoever. Now and then, someone would lead the singing of patriotic songs, especially *Bayan Ko*. Groups of religious men and women led prayers. There was no pandemonium. No tension and fear of the unknown. No religious hostility or segregation. There was only festivity. Camaraderie. *Kapwa Ko Mahal Ko* (My Kindred, My Love) spirit. Free water, bread, *sitsirya* (snack food), anything edible for the tired body. Rosary and eclectic prayers for the spirit.

Then they arrived. At around 4:00 pm, a large contingent of Marcos loyalist Marines came rolling in their tanks and armored personnel carriers. Their target was the rebel group's refuge—Camp Crame and Camp Aguinaldo. The loyalist Marines could not get to the camps without passing through the mass of humanity at EDSA. When they tried to advance, the people would not let them through. They stood in the way of the tanks, and they would not budge. I was about 20 people away from a tank myself; the sheer density of humanity did not allow me to get closer to the tank. Some military officers threatened to open fire at us if we would not disperse and give way. But the people stood their ground. We answered by singing *Bayan Ko* even more passionately, offering food and cigarettes to the soldiers, and enjoining them to pray along. *"Lahat tayo Pilipino!"* [We are all Filipinos!] someone in the crowd bellowed. The Marcos loyalist soldiers tried to press on, but we met them with louder singing and more intense praying.

Eventually, the Marines left and returned to where they came from without a shot fired. There followed jubilation, free food galore, and more festivities. We went home that evening tired in body, but ennobled in spirit.

During the next two days, movement shifted to the areas near Malacañan Palace. It was undeniable, however, that the victory started at EDSA, and the people had already won the struggle. It was just a matter of time before Marcos would flee to Hawaii, which happened on February 25, 1986, ending his authoritarian rule.

After everything that happened, I say with great pride that the Filipino people showed to the world the stuff we are as a nation. I say with great pride the Filipino people are a loving and lovable race. We are not a nation so bankrupt in morality as to do nothing when pushed to the wall. I disagree with a U.S. official who said that the Philippines is a country of "40 million cowards and one son of a bitch."[186] I say with great pride the Filipino people have shown to the world a template for the struggle for freedom and democracy. And I say with great pride that Mameng, our friends Lulu, Odette, Doming, and I were hands-on partakers of that struggle. We were there at EDSA in February 1986. You bet your bottom dollar we were!

---

186   Luis V. Teodoro, "Cowards and SOBs" (Vantage Point, blog), September 23, 2011, https://www.luisteodoro.com/cowards-and-sobs/.

bout a year earlier, there was another revolution raging, albeit personal. Not the cutting-loose, but the coming-together kind. On May 23, 1985, I gave Mameng, my girlfriend then, a willful and courageous "quiz" intending to start a colorful and titillating era of my life.

The multiple-choice quiz ran this way:

I love you and I'm ready to take full responsibility for you.

(a) Come to me and let's get married. Period!

(b) Crumple this letter, throw it into the trash can, and forget everything.

(c) Go to your engineer or whoever sonofabitch can give you a ₱5000 monthly salary and house and lot.

(d) Follow your sister's advice—Be practical!

Whoa, wait! I can guess what you are thinking. I beg you to put the situation in context by reading the letter, here in its entirety.

23 May 1985

Dear Mameng,

This may be my last letter—the one to end everything between us or to start a new life together. I know you are fed up with how I'm running our relationship, how I'm treating you. But you must also know that I'm fed up with your impatience, with how you show your lack of understanding of my personality.

You think I'm taking you for granted. You think I'm irresponsible and thoughtless. You say you've become impatient waiting for my promised letters, and yet you say that my letters are full of lies! Okay, so you think you can't bear me any longer. You were so angered by my thoughtlessness that you said your GOODBYE. Well, then, I can't hold you off any longer, can I? It's final, you said. But let me have the last words.

I love you, and I'm ready to take full responsibility for you. Come to me and let's get married. Period! Go to your engineer, or whoever sonofabitch can give you a ₱5000 salary and house and lot. Follow your sister's advice—Be practical!

Multiple choice. Take it or leave it. Now or never.

On the other hand, you can crumple this letter, throw it into the trash can, and forget everything.

Sincerely,

Jun

ecember 27, 1986, marked the day Carmen Monsalve chose (a) and became Mrs. Carmen Morada. Well, the choice looks more right than wrong, because we've been together for over three decades now.

36 years ago:
Me: Sweetheart, the pen doesn't work!
Mameng: Just sign it with your heart.

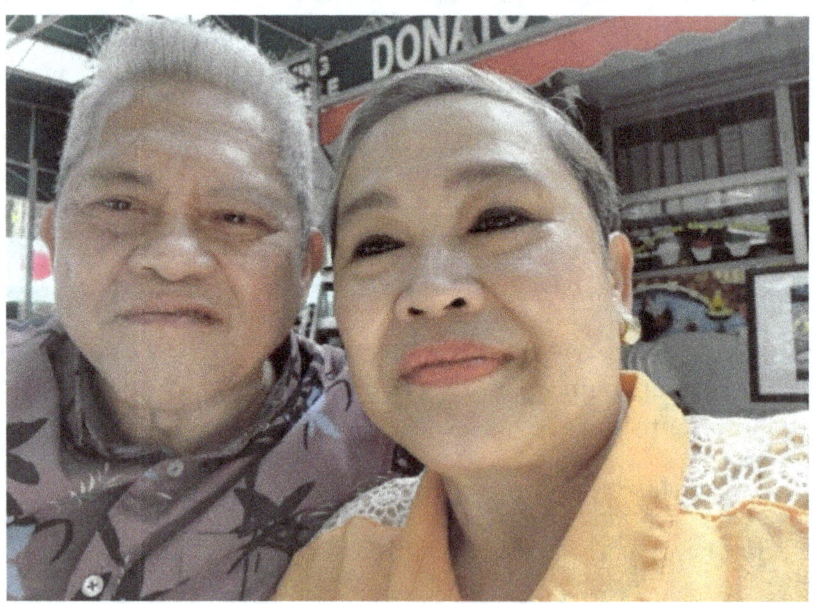

Now:
Me: Never thought that the ink was blood, sweat, and tears!
Mameng: Happy wife, happy life!

Mameng should have known by now that there was a Choice (e), which is as yellow and true as if I had written it in black and white—

(e) I don't promise you a rose garden. ■

EDSA 1986

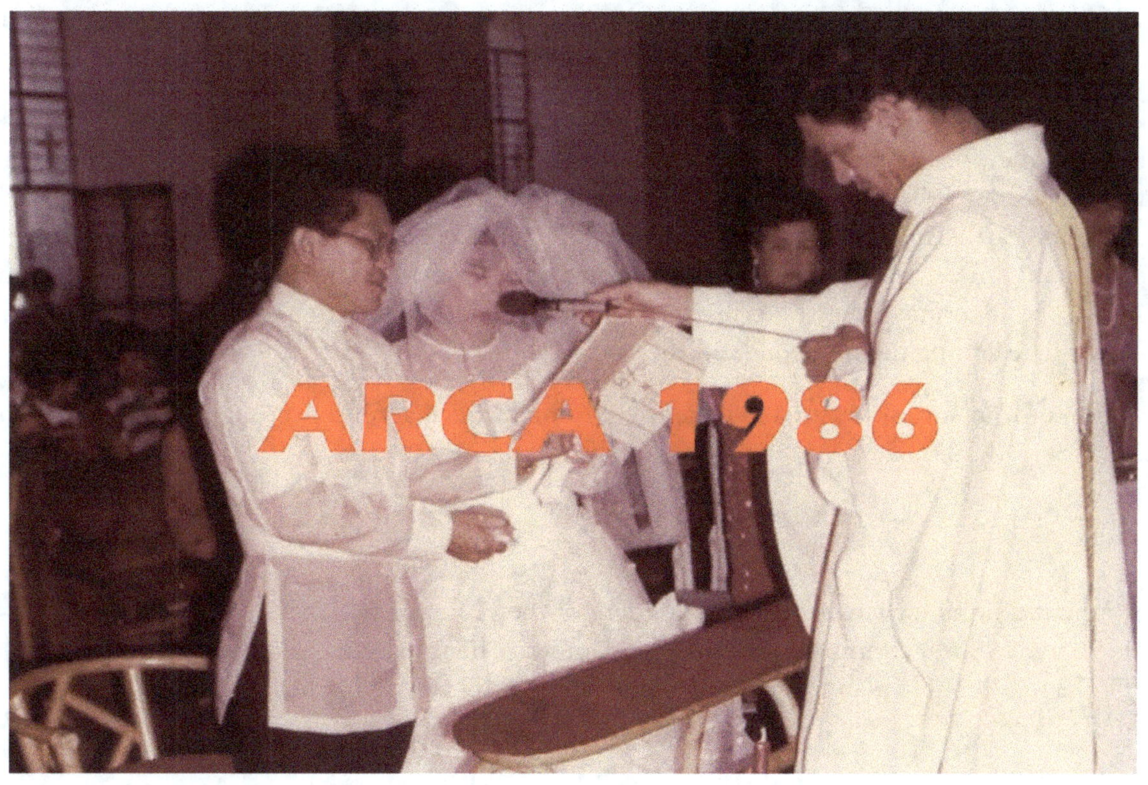
ARCA 1986

28

CONTRASTS

The line in between is thin, the difference immense

here was a story that floated in mischievous, irreverent, and loyalist circles in 2005 right after the death of Sin. I mean Jaime Cardinal Sin, Archbishop of Manila and catalyst of the Philippine People Power Revolution of 1986. When the good Sin died, so the story goes, he got delivered straight to heaven, met by St. Peter at heaven's gigantic door. Thereupon he heard a vast choir of angels singing in jubilation and beheld another gigantic door opening to a limitless room. Far ahead in front of him shone a bright Light so intense yet so soothing to the eyes, as two archangels ushered him toward the Light. On both sides of him, throngs of the saints and the righteous departed were in glorious applause of his arrival.

As he approached the Light, he looked around him. Here, there, and everywhere his eyes panned, he saw people whom he knew in life—family, friends, acquaintances, teachers, nuns, Mother Teresa, fellow priests, in particular Oscar Romero. There were many famous people he never met, movie stars, journalists, social workers, doctors, even statesmen as—OMG! He thought he saw an apparition, which he never expected to be there at all! Someone familiar and infamous! How in heaven's name did *he* get here?

With that question in mind, the holy man of the cloth in mortal life approached the Light, now transfiguring into none other than Jesus Christ Himself, on His kingly throne! The God whom he believed in and worshiped on earth! And Christ welcomed him with outstretched arms—could there be any more glorious sensation than this? After the handshake and the hug and other pleasantries, Sin collected the simmering thoughts from the innermost recesses of his heart. At last, he found the strength to say: "Lord, if I may ask, why is Marcos here among the righteous and the saints?"

And the Lord, in his immeasurable patience, wisdom, and magnificence, said, "My one and only Sin, why not?"

erdinand Edralin Marcos, the 10th President of the Philippines, ruled with iron and tainted fist from 1965 to 1986. A cunning politician and kleptocrat, he ruled the Philippines under martial law from 1972 to 1981. He planned and schemed, along with his wife Imelda Marcos, to perpetuate himself and his family in power. "His regime was infamous for its corruption, extravagance, and brutality."[187]

In 1969, Marcos became the first Philippine president to win a second term. However, not all Filipinos rejoiced at his presidency, and the month following his reelection included the most violent public demonstrations

---

187   *Wikipedia.* "Ferdinand Marcos," https://en.wikipedia.org/wiki/Ferdinand_Marcos.

200

in the country's history. Three years later, facing growing student protest and a crumbling economy, Marcos declared martial law, a state of emergency which gave military authorities extraordinary powers to keep order. Marcos' excuse for declaring martial law was the growing revolutionary movement of the Communist New People's Army, which opposed his government.

We now know that the actual date of Proclamation 1081 was September 22. Because of Marcos' penchant for numerology, however, he antedated it to September 21. Seven was his favorite number, and 21 is a multiple of 7. September 21, 1972, thus, became a sad and sorry date in the annals of Philippine history. Martial law was such a deplorable mark in our life as a nation that its impact and repercussions are still felt even up to the present.

Ruling by decree, Marcos curtailed press freedom and other civil liberties, closed down Congress and media establishments, and ordered the arrest of opposition leaders and militant activists.

Through martial law, Marcos confiscated and appropriated by force and duress many businesses and institutions, both private and public, and redistributed them to his own family and close friends. Marcos silenced the free press, making the state press the only legal one.

Marcos' family and cronies looted so much wealth from the country that to this day investigators have a hard time determining precisely how many billions of dollars they stole. Estimates have propounded that Marcos alone stole at least $10 billion from the Philippine treasury. The Swiss government, at first reluctant to respond to allegations that Marcos held stolen funds in Swiss accounts, has returned US$684 million of Marcos' wealth to the Philippine government.

In the 2004 Global Transparency Report, Marcos appeared on the list of the World's Most Corrupt Leaders. The list showed him second to the late President Suharto of Indonesia. According to the same list, Marcos amassed between $5 billion to $10 billion in his 20 years as President of the Philippines.[188]

Along with Marcos, Defense Minister Juan Ponce Enrile, General Fidel Ramos, and General Fabian Ver were the chief administrators of martial law from 1972 to 1981, and Marcos' closest advisers. General Ramos was the Chief of Staff of the Philippine Constabulary, and General Ver, the Chief of Staff of the Armed Forces of the Philippines. Enrile and Ramos would later abandon Marcos' "sinking ship" and seek protection behind the 1986 People Power Revolution, which ousted the strongman. The Catholic hierarchy, with Jaime Cardinal Sin at the helm, and Manila's middle class, were crucial to the success of the massive crusade.

Jaime Lachica Sin was the Roman Catholic Archbishop of Manila from 1974 to 2003. Of Chinese-Filipino descent, Sin became known mostly because of his instrumental role in the People Power Revolution that toppled dictator Ferdinand Marcos. His flock, however, knew Cardinal Sin for his good sense of humor. In jest, he called his residence "the House of Sin" and smiled at the ironic combination of his name and title, Cardinal Sin—"deadly Sin."

In a Catholic country plagued by a dictatorship from 1972 to 1986, Cardinal Sin often suppressed his smiles. He criticized the Marcos regime for its indifference to the plight of the poor. While advocating an independent church, he supported intervention in "the morality of politics." Thus, he caught the ire of

---

188   Transparency International, "GLOBAL CORRUPTION REPORT 2004: POLITICAL CORRUPTION," page 13, https://www.transparency.org/whatwedo/publication/global_corruption_report_2004_political_corruption.

President Marcos and the First Lady many times over his criticisms of the government's human rights violations and over Imelda's extravagant expenditures.

The cardinal became very vocal about the violence and cheating which characterized Philippine elections in the 1970s and 1980s. In the 1978 elections for delegates to the National Assembly, he issued an open letter "calling on church members to report any instances of fraud." His involvement became more active in 1986 when President Marcos called for snap elections for president and vice-president. Marcos needed a new mandate to convince the world of the legitimacy of his regime.

Cardinal Sin played an important role in unifying the opposition. He convinced Corazon Aquino to run for president against Marcos on the February 7, 1986 snap elections. (Corazon was the widow of Senator Benigno S. Aquino Jr. whom Marcos jailed. He went to self-exile in the United States, but upon his return to the Philippines in 1983, he met his death by assassination.) During the snap elections, the government's Commission on Elections (COMELEC) and the volunteer group National Movement for Free Elections (NAMFREL) reported conflicting counts. However, the Marcos-leaning legislature proclaimed the Marcos ticket victory in haste, based on COMELEC tallies. The people protested.

Some 300 officers in the military rebelled against Marcos and Chief of Staff Fabian Ver. The minister of national defense, Juan Ponce Enrile, and General Fidel Ramos, led the rebellion. They asked Cardinal Sin to protect the rebel army against the president's reprisal by mobilizing civilian support. The cardinal made an appeal by radio, and the people, Catholic and non-Catholic alike, heeded his call. They went by the millions to stand guard by the gates and fences of the military camp where the rebel soldiers, Enrile, and Ramos stayed. When Marcos sent government tanks and weapons to crush the rebellion, the people's prayers, smiles, and protests prevented the government troops from firing. With his family and a few close associates, Marcos fled the country in desperation. The rebel government installed Corazon Aquino as President.

The Friday I was organizing and writing this story was, as usual, the most awaited day of the week for many students in my school. This was on account of the 45-minute period of "free play" during P.E. Fun Friday! Well, always fun, but not always the entire period. The P.E. coaches, Mr. Weinberg and Mr. Cheshire, often gave short health lessons before letting the children engage in whatever games they preferred to play in the playground. Sometimes, however, the coaches might reduce or cut their playtime because of disciplinary reasons, or otherwise.

On this particular Friday, for instance, the health lesson for all grade levels was *Gun Safety*. The children watched a video without the slightest complaint—or "you talk, no play!" If you interrupted the proceedings in whatever way, the coaches could revoke your playtime. At the end of the video, the lesson asked the children to recite a corny rhythmic verse on gun safety: "Stop, don't touch, leave the area, tell an adult!" I could sense that the children obliged and patronized the coaches just to get over it. The ruse worked because the coaches and I (as a Friday P.E. assist) allowed the children to go to their free play without much ado. You could not see any happier children than our Friday students—except for this 2nd grade boy. Mr. Weinberg called out his name and told him to go back to class to do an unfinished worksheet and test.

The others would have fun while he worked. I could see the child muttering and making a face as he proceeded to his classroom. "It's not fair!"

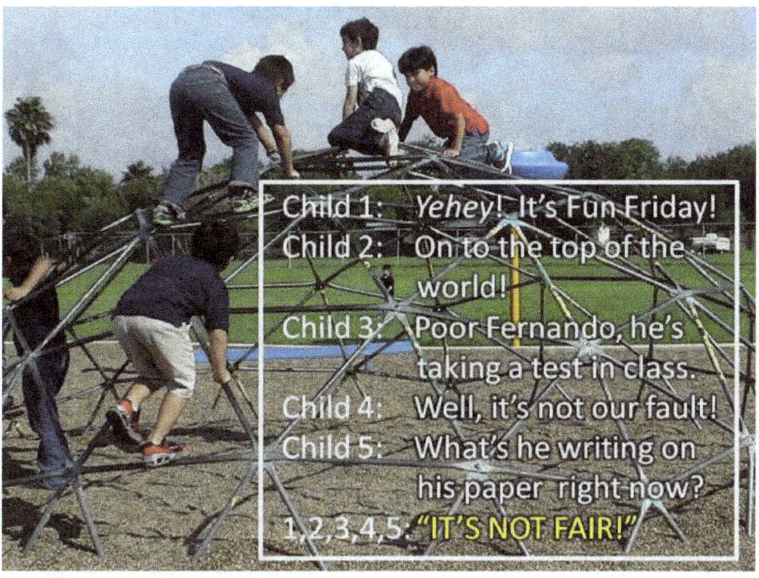

We could imagine Cardinal Sin muttering and making a face, too. "Lord, it's not fair!" No offense to the good Sin, for that's the direction our ordinary human mind would surely take if the story were for real. However, Sin was not ordinary, and whether the story is true is not the point. The point of this story is what the landowner does in the parable of the vineyard workers. (Mt 20:1-16)

Jesus told of a very rich and generous landowner who goes out one morning and hires workers to work in his vineyard. He designates the first group of workers early in the morning and promises them a good wage. He keeps hiring others as the day progresses, each new group having to work fewer hours than the group before them. Just one hour before the end of the workday, he hires the last group of workers, then tells his foreman to pay everyone a full day's wage. But this leaves the workers who toiled the whole day somewhat bitter. "It isn't fair!" they say. "We worked the whole day and bore the heat of the sun, while this last group worked just one hour. It's unfair that everybody receives the same wage!"

Jesus, through this parable, is addressing all good people who are morally and religiously bearing the heat of the day. Jesus is assuring us, too, that rich rewards await us for doing this. But, as the parable makes it understandable—and here is the catch—we can have everything and enjoy nothing because we are watching what everyone else is getting.[189]

God is the vineyard landowner, and we are the workers. Similar to the brother of the prodigal son in another Jesus parable (Lk 15:11-32), we do what is right, but we are watchers and moralizers at the same time. We are such that we become bitter and envious when the Father shows generosity to others, more so to our brother, the prodigal. We can have everything, yet we enjoy nothing because we are watching what everyone else is getting from the landowner, God the Father.

When we or any of his children approach him in sincerity and truth, our God gives us our just reward, regardless of the time of day and our circumstances. Someday, when our heavenly turn comes, we will be told, with the vast choir of angels singing, "We are so glad you made it here!" For such is the stuff that makes up heaven—a generous God and the communion of his angels and saints.

Me, myself in heaven? Why not?

---

189   Fr. Ron Rolheiser, "Embittered Moralizing—An Occupational Hazard for Good, Faithful Persons." In Exile, 25th Sunday of Ordinary Time A, September 21, 2014, https://liturgy.slu.edu/25OrdA092114/reflections_rolheiser.html.

Our generous God, in his immeasurable patience, wisdom, and magnificence, welcomes all—be it Sin, Marcos, or us, me and you.

 am not saying that Marcos, or Sin, is in heaven, nor can I say downright that the good Sin would react that way to deplorable Marcos' presence there, if ever. What I'm saying is, both Sin and Marcos had had their opportunities to be with a loving God when they were alive, as you and I have right now. The question is, did they take them before their respective reckoning? Only they knew the answer. And only we know our own answer when our turn comes.

"Seek the Lord while he may be found, call upon him while he is near. Let the wicked forsake their way, and sinners their thoughts; let them turn to the Lord to find mercy; to our God, who is generous in forgiving. For my thoughts are not your thoughts, nor are your ways my ways—oracle of the Lord. For as the heavens are higher than the earth, so are my ways higher than your ways, my thoughts higher than your thoughts." (Is 55:6-9)

We may never understand how the wages from the vineyard owner were just. We may never understand God's generosity, considering personal events and circumstances in our life. But love is the key, and God is love. Love transcends human questions and transmits divine answers.

Before long, we realize that the mischievous, irreverent, Marcos loyalist story not only shows a picture of our own humanity. It portrays far more unequivocally the kindness and goodness of our loving God. ∎

 was walking Ash and Valentine at dawn today. The morning was so commonplace I did not expect a profound epiphany to stare me in the face—and a profound change to strike me at the heart. It happened as we approached and passed by the Christmas ornament at 2663 Pompeii St, Brownsville TX. (Google the address if you want; it is not a figment of my imagination. A street view of it will show a satellite photo taken a few years ago. The house, of course, looks more rundown today.)

I pass by this house with its lone Christmas ornament four times a day, two when I walk my dogs, the other two when I go to and from work. So, I see the ornament several times every day, day in day out, to the point of it becoming "invisible" to my senses. Besides, its ordinariness, its drabness, and its stark contrast to the Christmas ornaments of the neighboring houses make it even more unimpressive and unnoticeable.

It sits upon an unmanicured lawn along the street where I live, in front of a brown tile house. Were it not for this Christmas ornament, you could surmise the house is uninhabited at the moment. But no, there were occupants in the house because at other times I had seen lights emanating from within this house.

But not this time. Now everything is dark, this house and the two-story houses on its right and left sides are unlit. So, from a distance, as I turn the corner toward Pompeii from Venice St., the ornament emits a light that looks so bright and surreal.

Most of the houses in my neighborhood, as in any other during this happiest season of the year, display and show off many exterior ornamentations. Christmas lights of different shapes, sizes, and colors adorn roofs, windows, and trees. Reindeer, Santa, Christmas trees, snow globes, and Nativity scenes in varied materials, shapes, colors, and forms highlight the front yards of houses here or there. Collectively, they vie for humanity's attention, and add to the celebratory mood and spirit of the season.

The ornament in question is a manger scene with Mary, Joseph, and the Baby—figures made of opaque plastic equipped with light assembly inside each. Aside from the three figures, there's nothing much to see

except uncut grasses, drab house, austere surroundings. *The owner of the house lacks artistry for putting up such an ornament,* I thought, the first time I saw it a few weeks ago, right after Thanksgiving. *Worse, the owner of the house is deficient in creativity, imagination, and resourcefulness,* I criticized. *Worst, the owner of the house did not have the wisdom and spirit of the season,* I judged. *This manger scene leaves much to be desired,* I concluded. But now, at pre-dawn and with the lights of all the neighboring ornaments turned off overnight, the manger appears so pleasant to behold as I, Ash, and Valentine walk closer to the manger. Mary, Joseph, and the Baby are more resplendent in their simplicity and singularity than ever. I feel something surreal.

And the epiphany strikes. This lowly manger is Christmas, isn't it? God's Son coming amid darkness, adversity, drabness, austerity, ordinariness. God's Son coming amidst the artificial glitter and shine of the world.

And then the change of heart. Why am I looking for other things besides Mary, Joseph, and the Baby— aren't they enough to make Christmas *Christmas*? What else am I looking for?

No, the owner of the house at 2663 Pompeii Street, Brownsville TX does not lack artistry, creativity, imagination, and resourcefulness—I do. No, the owner of the house has the wisdom and the spirit of the season—I don't. He may not be the most creative person on the street where I live, but he knows how to make Christmas be Christmas. He may not be the wisest guy around, but he is full of wisdom, for his ability to show the genuine spirit of Christmas. Christmas is not for the senses, but for the soul and the heart.

I thought I knew more of my faith than the house owner at 2663 Pompeii. No, it's obvious I don't.

I personify Ash. The owner does Valentine. ■

ust we always hear the voice of the wind
Dispelling the voice of the Star
Which, according to tradition and the Book
Illumined the Incarnation of Justice, Peace, and Love?

Open our hearts, unravel their tangled fibers.
Must we always be inspired by the Season of Joy?
Or must we rather hear the voice of mortal souls
Resonating with the voice of their hearts
Which, because of depression and misery,
Drowns out the Season of Joy?
Look at them, decipher the codes in their dreams and despair.
Must the Season never be tinged with gray and hopelessness?

Whatever our answers, we keep this in mind:
In that moment of adversity and aversion—
Whiff of dung for a Baby's first breath,
Lowly swaddling clothes,
Manger for a cradle,
Hay for a bed—
The Mother never complained.
The Father never cursed.
The Baby King smiled.
Henceforth, the Paragon of Light and Radiance. ∎

-PARAGON
from POEMS FROM MY YOUTH (unpublished)

nwitting participants in an ordinary yet another spiritual experience were these three girls in my choir class today. Well, count me in too, because I did not know I was complicit in the unfolding of a spiritual reality that would strike me later in the day.

The three girls belonged to the 2nd Grade choir class. They were three of the faithful choir members from 1st Grade to 5th who have managed so far to stick it out this far, springtime, in the school year. This small group of students stayed in the choir despite the enormous attraction that was P.E. You know, in my school, in every grade level, Music and P.E. held classes back-to-back, and every Friday was Fun Day. During their scheduled time, every grade level went either to P.E. or choir—it was a free choice and a no-hassle decision. Up to 80% of the students in each grade level would rather go to P.E. and free play in the school playground than go to choir and sing. (1 student among the 20% was male.) You can say that if they remained in the choir up to March, the students must be interested in music for real. If they stuck till May, the end of the school year in our school district, they must love to sing for real. Faithful to Music. Intrinsic music lovers.

A few minutes before every choir period ended, I usually took my singers out into the playground next to the Music Room. I did this to give them a chance to stretch. And taste what they would have been doing if they had chosen P.E. on Fridays instead.

Spring is everywhere. Here, there, and everywhere are patches of wildflowers, most of them yellow, white or pink. And here comes the first girl trotting up to me and saying, "Flower for you, Mr. Purple!"

The flower in question is yellow (smooth hawksbeard, *Crepis capillaries*). "How sweet of you, Hailey! Why are you giving me this?"

"For letting us out to play! Thanks, you're the best!" (To any of these students, you're the best teacher if you let them play outside—they hunger for diversion and physical activities.)

"Thanks, too, for the flower. Go ahead, play. You only have a few minutes." She runs away to the swing as the second cute girl approaches and shows me two pink flowers in her hands (pinkladies, *Oenothera speciosa*).

"Mr. Purple, what are these things in the middle?" Anahi asks with a thick Hispanic accent. "They look icky!"

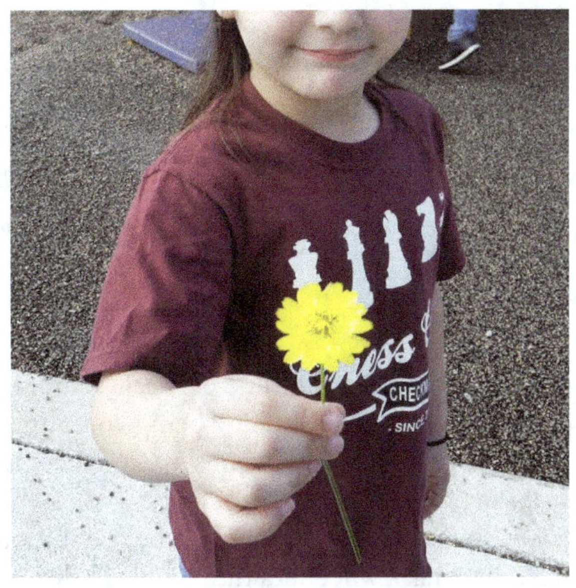

"I believe they are the male and female organs of the flowers." (Hold on, why did I have to say it this way?)

"*Ew!* You mean... *ew!*" Anahi says, with a tone and facial expression that looks as if she just ate the fruit from the tree of the knowledge of good and evil.

"You can ask your science teacher if that sounds incredible to you," I say, swallowing saliva. Anahi calls the third girl and beckons her to come. Felicia approaches us.

"What's the problem?" the new arrival asks. Felicia is a cute Hispanic girl who's shy but loves to be on stage and sing. To be in the choir is one way for her to do what she loves.

"Anahi is just curious of these pink flowers." I pick one from Anahi's hand and, with the yellow given to me by Hailey beforehand, position them near Felicia's right ear. "Colorful. Aren't they lovely, tucked behind your ear!" I take a snapshot with my handy cellphone.

Felicia flashes me a leery look. "My mom said that's poisonous. The pink one."

"I don't know if that's true; I'll have to check," I say as I pull the flowers away from her ears.

"It can kill, my mom said. I don't want to touch it, or you to place behind my ear."

"OK." Then to the rest of the choir in the playground I say aloud: "You have two minutes! Use it wisely!"

At last, it's time to go and I blow my whistle, which hangs by my ID on my school lanyard. Everybody lines up in front of me. Hailey, Anahi, and Felicia come up and give me a collective hug. "For what's this hug?"

"You're the best, Mr. Purple!" Hailey says. "Can we stay a minute longer?" Anahi and Felicia both clasp their hands in mock supplication. "Please, please, please, Mr. Purple, you're the best!"

"No, we have to go. You'll be late for your next class!" I say. "End of discussion."

There is a thin line between compliment and flattery, but the difference between them is immense. Of course, I enjoy being complimented as *the best*, though only my mother could attest to that. The rest of humanity could take it with a grain of salt, let alone agree. On various occasions coming from many people from different eras of my life, they too have called me creative, talented, ingenious, smart, promising, wise. *Delicadeza* or propriety dictates I can't tell you more or whether these descriptions are true or false, but that's where lies the trouble to dichotomize compliments and flattery. They can both be true, or they don't have to be lies to be called flattery. I am not saying these are lies or they gratify my vanity. I couldn't be sure either if they were compliment or flattery at the time people spoke them to me.

To balance the good things said or written here of me, friends and family have likewise called me, among many other things:

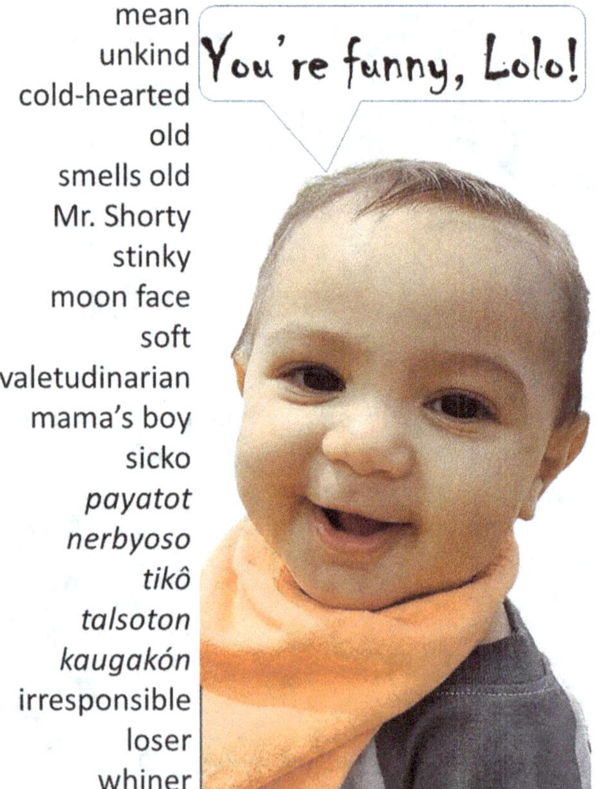

(I reserve the right to skip translation of the Bikol words.)

We don't even have to know whether the praises or attention showered on us are true or false. A compliment, of course, is something true, but lying is not a condition for flattery. Compliments and flatteries can both be true. What separates flattery from compliment is the motive behind it.

The giver of a compliment says it without vested interest. Behind a flattery can lurk the giver's ulterior design.

The girls wanted to manipulate me to ingratiate themselves. They wanted to manipulate me, hoping I was to give them extra time to play. They wanted to manipulate me to gain my trust, for me to give them what they wanted. The unwitting girls, without doubt, gave me a flattery.

Psalm 145:8-13 is giving sincere praise to God for what he is and his wondrous deeds. This psalm, I realize, is one of the responsorial psalms that I put into new music settings included in **The Purple Psalmody**, published in 2011. It's the same psalm which the Fil-Am Choir of Brownsville was singing this Sunday of the week of my experience with the three you're-the-best girls. The psalm enthuses God is gracious, merciful, slow to anger, of great kindness, good to everyone, and compassionate toward all his works.[190]

We are works of God's hands.

The Virgin Mary praised God with grace and humility. *Magnificat anima mea Dominum!* "My soul proclaims the greatness of the Lord, my spirit rejoices in God my savior! For he has looked upon his handmaid's lowliness; behold, from now on will all ages call me blessed!" (Lk 1:46-48) When we

- give him thanks;

- bless him;

- discourse of the glory of his kingdom, and speak of his might;

- make known his might to everyone and the glorious splendor of his kingdom;

- realize and help other people realize that God's kingdom is for all, and that his dominion endures through all generations;

- do all this sincerely, with no ulterior motive—

then, we give God praise and thanksgiving. We give glory to God. We give God compliment.

Through it all, we glorify God. ■

♪♫♩ **I WILL PRAISE YOUR NAME** ♫♪
#48 *from* THE PURPLE PSALMODY*
***by* Arcadio Morada, Jr.**
***Based on* Ps 145:1-2, 8-11, 13-14**

---

190   Arcádio Morada, Jr., *tagaalbay*, "I Will Praise Your Name," YouTube video, 3:53min, https://youtu.be/0zhpRKhPjHQ.

29

PISCINE

Inside the net of salvation

So he said to them, "Cast the net over the right side of the boat and you will find something." So they cast it, and were not able to pull it in because of the number of fish. (Jn 21:6)

To be exact, how many fish were there on the net? Reading John further, we find out just how many.

So Simon Peter went over and dragged the net ashore full of one hundred fifty-three large fish. Even though there were so many, the net was not torn. (Jn 21:11)

How many times have we heard this gospel reading in the past? We had it again in today's (Sunday, April 14, 2013) Mass, prompting this thought at the back of our minds, "Here we go again!" Hearing it for the nth time makes our mind non-porous, or closes it with a block that impedes further understanding its nuances. But in the hands of an able and insightful priest, as Msgr. Heberto Diaz of St. Mary's Church, a familiar gospel passage gains a new perspective.

Msgr. Bert says, "We are all inside the net..." Right away, it strikes me as something novel. Jesus doesn't pick out whom to save—he saved everyone. We are inside the net of salvation. Everyone's effortless redemption? Hold on—should we just wait, be complacent, and do nothing while waiting for the Fisher to haul us in his net? What can I do, what can we do, to deserve to be inside that net?

Each of us is among those "153" species of fish. Most of us accept outright and with joy our being piscine inside that net. Others, not knowing any better, accept being inside the net with reservations. A few species will try to escape by jumping off from the net, being piscine by instinct. Not to be outdone, a few among us will try to use our razor-sharp teeth to gnaw at the net. Through their action, they are trying to escape from the confines of the net into the darkness of the ocean's depths. The net is there, redemption is ours, but so is our choice to stay inside the net.

And love is redemption. Jesus asks us, "Do you love me?"

I recall Tevye, in **Fiddler on the Roof**, asking his wife that same question. Golde answers, *Do I what?* Not that she is deaf, or unable to understand. She's only trying to tell him the obviousness of her answer. In their years of togetherness, her actions have spoken much louder than the word yes.

Same as Golde, each of us has a ready answer, and we think it's obvious, too. Hopefully, our actions match our declaration of love for Jesus, whose net of salvation has caught us in his glorious clasp.

♪♫ DO YOU LOVE ME? ♫♪

from PSALMS & OTHER LITURGICAL SONGS Vol. 2
by Arcadio Morada, Jr.
Based on Jn 18:15-27, 21:15-19

REFRAIN: (Cantor, with Choir)
Do you love me?[191]
Yes, I do!
Feed my sheep.
Do you love me?
Yes, I do!
Tend my sheep.
You know that I love you,
You know everything.
Do you love me?
Yes, I do!
Feed my sheep.

(Cantor) 1. When you were younger,
You used to do what you wanted,
And go where you wanted.
But when you grow old,
You will stretch out your hands,
Someone else will lead you
Where you do not want to go.
(Refrain)

(Cantor) 2. Remember back when
The people asked if you knew me,
Three times, if you knew me.
But without scruples,
You said you didn't know,
You said you didn't know,
And you said you did not know.
(Refrain)

Coda: *(sung at the same time)*
(Choir) I love you!
(Cantor) Follow me! ■

---

191   Arcádio Morada, Jr., *tagaalbay*, "Do You Love Me?", YouTube video, 3:07min, https://youtu.be/VhfBCO0s6x0.

30
REMEMBER
Extracting meaning from inhumanity

The book's cover is frayed, and the pages are brownish and brittle. How can they not be, when the book has traveled over ten thousand kilometers of space in half a century of time through diverse seasons and climes? The odyssey started from its purchase when I was in college in 1972, to my first job in Legazpi City (1974). I took the book with me on employment in Manila in 1978, through my study grant and sojourn at Mother of Life Center in Novaliches, Quezon City in 1983. My migration to Brownsville, Texas in 1992 couldn't be complete without it, and my retirement move to Woodside, New York, in 2019 capped the journey. Through all this time and distance, the paperback has been with me in my "baul," my treasure trove of earthly bric-à-brac.

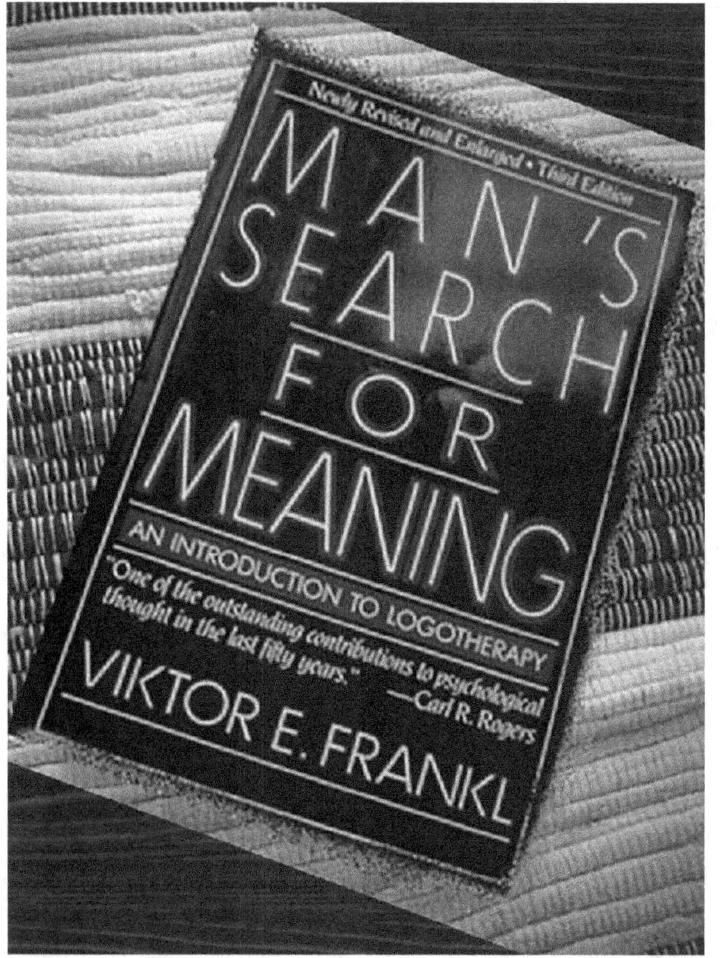

The book in question is the 1971 edition of Viktor Frankl's **MAN'S SEARCH FOR MEANING: An Introduction to Logotherapy**. I bet my bottom dollar you won't want to read that yourself. You'd say it sounds serious, boring, and "not of my time." Well, I couldn't blame you. You couldn't be more correct.

It has been my constant companion, manual, guide, and beacon of sorts, but I won't put it that way. Truth is, through most of my three decades in the U.S., I had left the book in the backdrop, relegated to the storage bin. It doesn't mean, though, that I've downgraded, or worse forgotten, whatever significance it has had for me.

Only thrice after college had I retrieved or reread it. First, when I critiqued it as reflection paper for a Mother of Life course (1983); second, when I used that reflection paper for a page on my personal website in 2013; third, on March 12, 2014, when my mobile phone flashed a newsfeed notification for a Facebook post of Donna Belle that was at once nostalgic and piercing to the heart.

Let me put this in context. Donna Belle is the daughter of Rosite Naa Basiño. At the time, she wasn't my FB friend, but Rosite was. In August 2012, I came across his name while browsing, and right away I added him as a friend, along with a message. "I thought you were the Rosite who was my classmate at the [Bicol University] College of Education. Sit-Sit, we called him, and we graduated in '74. Sorry if you are not him. But your picture looked like him!"

I remember, in 1972, in Economic Geography, we had a course requirement in which we had to discuss with thoroughness the economy of the different geographical regions of the world. This entailed so much researching, drawing maps, and typing a voluminous quantity of researched materials. Sit-Sit and I were a team. We compiled, he drew, I typed. (I had a portable Singer typewriter then; word processors were just a haze in dreamland.) That was the first and last time we worked together.

At the end of the course, we both got an A. On March 15, 1972, he handed me a package wrapped in newspaper. *The* book. He said, *"Sa gabos... salamat!"* [For everything, thank you!]

The first time I looked at the gift, I nearly snickered and frowned. I never saw an object more uninviting. I controlled malicious reactions, though I presumed he saw my disappointment. "You read it," he said. "No regrets!"

Well, at last I did as suggested, two months after, in summer, when I had nothing better and fun to do. When I *did* open the book, something fell from it. By accident or without intention maybe, Sit-Sit had inserted the receipt from the purchase of the book. He bought it from Prieto Book Store in Legazpi City, now long defunct, for ₱2.75. If we consider that the minimum jeepney fare at the time was 10 cents, the book did sure cost him a fortune. The date on the receipt was—

I dashed to the storage bin and retrieved Frankl's book. The receipt was still there, folded and inserted into the pages. Right away, I unfolded the receipt and looked for the date of purchase: March 12, 1972. Forty-two years ago... Today!

Do you now understand why that newsfeed from Donna Belle was nostalgic and piercing to the heart?

By the way, according to Rosite's timeline (yes, he still has an active FB account), he passed away on November 3, 2012.

Was today his way of reminding me of the meaning of life?

The book comprises two parts. In the first, Viktor Frankl recounts his experiences in Nazi concentration camps during the last world war. Out of the incredible suffering and degradation, both physical and psychological, which he himself had experienced as a Jew, he developed his theory of logotherapy. He expounds on this theory in the second part of the book.

Frankl lists three phases of man's psychological reactions to prison life. First, during and after his admission, the inmate experiences shock because of his abrupt immersion into an altogether different, frustrating way of life. Then, during the phase when he is well-entrenched in camp life and routine, apathy and/or emotional death characterize his psychological reactions. He blunts his emotions and then feels that he does not care anymore. Third, during and after the prisoner's release and liberation, he experiences "depersonalization," bitterness, and disillusionment. "Depersonalization" is a moral deformity caused by the sudden release of mental pressure. He is bitter over his fellow men's superficiality and lack of feelings. That suffering never ends disillusions him.

Frankl's theory of **logotherapy** ("logo" means "meaning") says that we can discover meaning in life in three different ways: by doing a deed, by experiencing a value, and by suffering.

The first, the way of accomplishment or achievement, is obvious enough. The second is by experiencing something, such as a work of nature or culture, and likewise by experiencing someone, i.e., by love. Third, whenever an unavoidable experience or unchangeable fate confronts anyone, an incurable disease, for example, just then the chance to actualize the highest value, the meaning of suffering, presents itself. What matters is the stance we take toward suffering.

Nothing in the world could, in the most effective way, help one survive even the worst conditions as the knowledge that one's life has meaning. There is so much wisdom in the words of Nietzsche, whom Frankl is fond of quoting: "He who has a why to live for can bear almost any how."

While reading through Frankl's book, one can always get a sense of spiritual exhilaration, as I did. In the first place, he assures me I as human, as any other, have that capacity of resilience against all odds, that I can endure no matter what. Any human being can learn to live with the discomforts in life—he can get used to them—provided his life has meaning. Suffering ceases to be suffering at the moment it finds a meaning.

Man's chief concern is not to gain pleasure or to avoid pain, but to see a meaning in his life. That is why man is even ready to suffer on the condition that his suffering has a meaning.

I always frowned at the thought of pain and suffering, hated people who hurt and put me in places and positions where I suffer. But now I realize that what I need, what every man needs, is not a tensionless state. You and I need a striving and struggling for a worthy goal. What you and I need is not a discharge of tension at any cost, but the call of a potential meaning waiting to be fulfilled.

I need to achieve. This is one of my fundamental needs. It is through accomplishing something that I put my worth to the test. It shows how I make use of, and transcend, my being toward a goal I set out for myself.

I need to experience a value—something or someone. I need things of grace and esthetics to nourish my soul. Art and culture supply countless such things to me. I need people to love. Without others, without somebody to love, my life is just a worthless heap of flesh.

I need to suffer. No, I don't mean ascetic or masochistic suffering. It is that suffering which comes in the ordinary way in our daily life. Great or small, intense or superficial, each suffering colors one's life and gives it more meaning. The more sufferings one has, the more colorful his life will be. The extent of suffering which a situation presents does not matter; what matters is the approach which one takes toward such suffering.

I remember the day our house burned to the ground in 1967. Tatay and Nanay and my eldest sister Manay Nilda were the only people at home; we the other children, were in school or out for familial errands. Yet advanced in age, my parents and sister could only watch as fire consumed most of what our family had accumulated over the years. People of lesser spirits might have been disillusioned and might have wallowed in bitterness and self-pity, but not my parents—they faced the ensuing suffering in a different light. If only for the persons they loved, there was enough reason for living and carrying on the business of life.

Last, and most important, I need God. Everyone needs God, the Absolute. God is the goal toward which I lead my life. He gives its most profound meaning. My parents, despite the unwanted calamity, still regarded life as meaningful because of their faith in the Absolute. They believed, as I do, that God is the meaning of life. That was why the resultant suffering was, for them, not a very heavy cross to bear.

As written in Psalm 56:9, "My wanderings you have noted; are my tears not stored in your flask, recorded in your book?" I believe no sufferings are in vain. Therefore, as Viktor Frankl says, "The crowning experience of all... is the wonderful feeling that after all [man] has suffered, there is nothing he need fear anymore...." ∎

My interest in the Holocaust took root when I was an elementary-grade child in Sipocot North Central School in Impig, Sipocot, a small rural town in the Philippines. I remember watching a Holocaust movie at the town plaza in the 1960s; the movie's title escapes me now, but the horrors that I saw were enough to arouse my interest. However, it was in college when that interest took to heart much more intensely. Through the years, a potpourri of movies, documentaries, books, and other reading or audio-visual materials on the topic would engross me with much curiosity and fondness. "Obsession" is the exact word which my daughter at a recent time used to describe my predilection to anything, and everything, that concerns the Jewish undoing. I am obsessed by the Holocaust.

This obsession is such that any mention of whatever German always conjured images of Hitler, the Nazis, and the pogrom they perpetrated upon the hapless Jews. Tita Tess' daughter was getting married to a German national, and I was invited to the wedding. Is he a Nazi descendant? Was his father a Hitler Youth? Count me out! Do I, by any chance, want to live in New Braunfels? No way—that's a German city in Texas! Wait, you say you detest everything German? Why did you accept your study grant at Mother of Life Center, knowing that the funds came from German benefactors? I know, but I accepted the grant because I wanted to ask the German nun who established the Center if she was a Nazi. If not, what did she do during the war when her fellow Germans were doing their detestable crimes against humanity? I meant no disrespect.

Ms. Ruth Alanis, my co-teacher at Villareal Elementary School, and her 4th grade students were reading "The Girl Who Survived" this week. The book's subtitle caught my attention right away: *A True Story of the Holocaust*. Sparks began and the *H* siren screamed in my subconscious, so I begged Ruth to lend me a copy. I had to read this book! And sure, I did.

Bronia Brandman was a Jewish girl of eight years when Hitler and the Nazis invaded her country of Poland in 1939. The book tells of her unforgettable and incredible but true story.

Seventy-seven years ago, in May 1945, the Allied Forces defeated the Germans and ended the war in Europe. They ended the war, but they were too late to save the lives of 6 million Jews, 1 million in Auschwitz-Birkenau concentration camp alone, who fell victim to Hitler's megalomania. Contrary to Hitler's wicked wish of a Jew-free world, there had been survivors who rose from the darkness of their days to recount the horrors and refresh our memories. Bronia Brandman is one of them. Let us hope and pray that execrable things as Hitler's Final Solution never happen again.

 wished the Nazis, through their savagery and inhumanity, had not only done away with the old, among other groups, but their tendency for dementia as well. Although I am old, I don't have dementia, thank God! Though I am obsessed with the Holocaust, I am neither German nor Jew. I swear this statement is a disclaimer.

Wait, I'm sane to a T at the moment. I have just finished watching this movie entitled REMEMBER with thespians in their twilight years: Christopher Plummer and Martin Landau. Of course, we remember Plummer as the strict but lovable Capt. Von Trapp, in one of the most popular movies of all time, *The Sound of Music* (1965). He has had a slew of other notable movies to his name. By contrast, I recognize Landau in supporting roles in classic films *North by Northwest* (1959), *Cleopatra* (1963), *The Greatest Story Ever Told* (1965), and *They Call Me Mr. Tibbs* (1970). Plummer and Landau are two excellent actors despite their age, and in REMEMBER, they are just outstanding! I say this not because I have a kinship with them at my age of 71, or because I know nothing of acting or dramatic arts. In my life, I've had artistic propensities and inclinations myself.

In the movie, Plummer and Landau play two Holocaust survivors whose families the Nazis wiped out at Auschwitz concentration camp. Their story begins in a nursing home in New York. The two elderly residents plot to exact vengeance vigilante-style on Rudy Kurlander, real name Otto Wallisch, who was *blockführer* at Auschwitz during the Holocaust. Landau's saner role devises the scheme, carried out to subdued and subtle perfection by the demented role played by Plummer. The problem is, there are four Rudy Kurlanders in the U.S. and Canada. Thus begins Plummer's harrowing mission to find and kill (with a handgun) the right Kurlander, through the long-distance guidance of Landau from the NY nursing home. Interspersed amid the search-and-kill operations are Plummer's bouts with dementia.

"Do you still know you have a wife and a daughter in New York?" asks my wife, as if quoting from the Book of Lamentations. "I'm the only one calling every time!"

"Where's my pair of eyeglasses? Has anybody seen my eyeglasses? I'm going crazy!"

"Mr. Purple, it's on your head!"

"When did you last see your cellphone?" the Los Fresnos CISD police asked, after a missing cellphone report from my Music classroom. "Have you tried calling your number using other phones? If it's somewhere nearby, of course you'll hear the ring." We used another phone and dialed my CP number. "No, we can't hear any ringing, so my CP is nowhere nearby! Someone stole my cellphone! Can you put it on the blotter now?"

After two months, tucked among audio-visual aids in the storage closet next to the Music Room, the cellphone shows itself up in its black glory, though fully discharged. After charging, it showed a mute setting. Oh, well, how could I be so...?

"Dad, where's my bunch of keys?"

"What do you mean *where*—did you give it to me?"

"Of course, I gave it to you before I went to the bank, before you came home to the apartment. How else could you have opened the door? Go find it by retracing your steps."

"OK, I entered the apartment. Then I washed our laundry at the laundromat and bought a few groceries. I placed the groceries in the fridge in your room. That's it! I went nowhere else!"

"Dad, my keys! I need them for work."

I run my fingers through my hair as if attempting to pull it. Damn keys! To tell you the truth, I don't remember. Why have I become so forgetful? I go to the laundromat and ask the caretaker for lost-and-found keys. I ask the grocery store cashier if she saw the same. No, they saw nothing because nobody turned in the same.

After hours of worry and agitation, my daughter says in exasperation, "Dad, you placed my bunch of keys near my bed! How could you not have remembered placing it there?"

Sorry, I forgot to remember. Oh, thanks for making me remember the movie REMEMBER with Plummer and Landau! Where was I?

A month ago, I was in the Philippines with my wife and daughter. The weather was terrible. We just wanted to stay either in air-conditioned hotels or at the beach, whether day or night. Whenever we ventured outside, it was hot and humid. A hammock by the seaside was a godsend. I had frequent asthma attacks; it was unfortunate that my inhaler didn't work. My wife and I had pneumonia. My daughter was coughing too, so at bedtime we were a triadic symphony of lungs in revolt. But, asthma or no asthma, El Nido Palawan is a paradise! (Google it.) Nature, limestone islands, and islets; secret lagoons, caves, white beaches; jackfish a meter long and other tropical creatures swimming, unfazed, by your side; snorkeling and kayaking; corals untouched by human hands; seafoods galore at the clubhouse, etc. etc. You should go there in your lifetime. It's worth the money and the effort—and the terrible-weather sacrifice. A whole new world, priceless. You'll not regret it!

The movie REMEMBER—where was I?

Zev, Hebrew for wolf, is Plummer's character name. Zev encounters the first Kurlander; he is not Otto Wallisch. He finds the second Kurlander, but he turns out to be a homosexual Jew, himself a survivor from Auschwitz. The third Kurlander is dead. Zev finds this out from his Canadian State trooper son—who turns out to be a neo-Nazi. Zev pees in his pants and shoots the neo-Nazi dead alongside his German shepherd. Then the fourth Kurlander—hey, seriously, do you suppose I should tell you what happened to him and thus give the movie away? Well, if I do, you'll miss the thrill of the twist, and the satisfaction of watching the movie yourself!

So, I'll just keep my mouth shut and instead meditate on my immediate future—

I'm still too deep into vacation modality. In two weeks, school begins. No big fuss, because I teach music. Music is the math, the language, and the elixir of the bored soul. (That's my own *consuelo-de-bobo* concoction;

you don't have to take my word for it). This weekend I watch Isabella, favorite singer in my school choir, star and shine in *Alice in Wonderland* at the Camille Playhouse in Brownsville. Promising young artists preen their plumage and practice their craft in this local thespian house. The younger generation is readying to take over and assume control. Reality bites, and so does dementia.

In the meantime, I love movies, Holocaust movies in particular, and I don't have dementia (yet). You don't either, I presume, but as a warning and reminder, you must watch REMEMBER before it's too late. Now. ■

emember, too, the savagery committed closer to home by the race who swore in their Declaration of Independence "that all men are created equal." Recall the inhumanity committed by the same race who thought they were just and conscientious. I have just finished watching **12 Years a Slave,** and I'm moved, affected, transfixed, stunned to the max. You do not watch this movie and pretend to stay unscathed for two hours. The power of cinema is such that it redefines you in the interior. It transforms you into a person with a newer outlook on things while you are immobile on your couch. And I tell you I am one film buff who's very hard to please.

Halfway through, I couldn't even pause the DVD player to eat my dinner at the dining table. I had to continue watching and eat in the living room while at it.

The horrors of slavery bared before my eyes made me cringe, as graphically as innumerable other movies with that topic have done before. Still, I cried—as a horrified child—literal tears of sympathy and hate. Human trafficking is another curse that everyone must help eradicate, I declared to myself with clenched teeth. I screamed with Patsey while she received those unspeakable inhumanities and lashes she did not deserve. I hurled expletives at Michael Fassbender as the slave-breaker. Though I have little liking for Brad Pitt, I liked his redemptive role here as a traitor to his just and conscientious race. Tears welled from my eyes as I rejoiced with Chiwetel Ejiofor as the unfortunate Solomon Northup when at last he reclaimed his freedom and his home. And I agreed with the Academy of Motion Picture Arts & Sciences when they conferred on this movie the Best Picture honor at Oscar Awards 2014.

Steve McQueen, the director, is black. It's no wonder why he had to do this movie. It must have given him no small measure of exhilaration and personal vindication. Move over, Steven Spielberg—though you're still my favorite director! I admire your **Amistad**, I do, but forgive my current assessment. Compared to **12 Years**, your own slave movie is a walk in the park.

Cinema suspends reality for a while. One sign you're back is the urge to check out notifications on Facebook. But, hey, where is my phone? For two hours, I forgot it existed altogether! I looked around, in my room, garage, guestroom, restrooms, even under my bed. It was nowhere to be found!

Patay![192]

I panicked. I had walked Val and Ash before watching the movie. No, I was sure I did not drop or misplace it along the way, because I had dawdled on Facebook before watching. But my android phone—where, where, where? For the second time, I looked through the various corners of the house.

Found it, OMG, at the last place where you would put your phone in, or where you could by accident put your phone in—*refrigerator!* A humiliating trip by the morrow to the nearest T-Mobile phone store flashed

---

192   *patay* [Filipino] – literally, dead. Used in expressions, it can mean *"I'm dead," "I'm a goner," "I'm devastated!"* It may also mean, *"I'm in big trouble!"*

in my mind: "Forgive me, sir/ma'am, but could you help me revive my refrigerator-stranded phone?" Whew! With much luck, I didn't need to go because my phone was so smart it still turned on, revived itself, and worked after being chilled for nearly two hours!

Here's the causal equation:

12YearsASlave+HabitOfTakingMyPhoneWherever+MicrowaveableTVdinner+MyAge=PhoneInFridge

Cinema suspends reality, but remember, man's inhumanity to man is real. *Do* remember. ■

I love movies, Holocaust movies in particular, and I don't have dementia (yet).

31
STUCK
The whys and wherefores of us

He was my professor at the University, in successive courses, Art 1, Art 2, and Economic Geography, circa 1970-1972. Bespectacled, stocky, and dark-skinned, he was no taller than me, who had by then my current height of five-foot-three. He being a chain-smoker, his fingers and teeth were nicotine-stained because of years of smoking. You knew he was in your vicinity because he reeked of cigarette smoke, *"araní maski arayô"*—so near yet so far. Most of us students gravitated around him nonetheless, because he was super friendly, he was good company, and he was "in", though married and with children. Outside the classroom, he treated us as if there was neither distinction nor dividing line between professors and students. Most significant for me was that I always got good grades from him.

She was two (or three?) years my senior, the elder sister of a female classmate of mine under his courses. Fair-skinned and petite, she occupied the post of editor-in-chief of **The Mentor**, the College of Education paper, one whose style of writing I liked. I was an aspiring campus writer myself, so I wanted to socialize and gain her friendship. By associating with her, I had the vested interest in learning more of the nitty-gritty world of campus journalism. The goal was to ease my way into a future application for a position on the paper's editorial board. Through her sister, I got introduced to her, while a few (in)significant literary pieces of mine got published under her watch. Everything was coming up roses in my campus life until I felt I was falling for her.

There was something in her that told me I did not just fancy her. I was longing for her presence. I felt a magnetic force between us when she was around, though I was not sure if she could sense it too, by any chance.

"Seryoso ka, o kapáy [Are you serious or crazy]?*"* Rosite, my close classmate-friend, said when I mentioned to him my blooming feeling for her. Then he cupped his hands on my ear and said, *"Batà 'yan ni Sir!"* [She is Sir's girl!]

"Huh? How do you know?"

"Everybody knows!" Sit-Sit said in disbelief. *"Asus!* You're the only one on campus who doesn't know."

Obviously. "You mean," I asked, pouting, "they are in a relationship?"

"Maybe more than just a relationship," he said. My hopes and fantasies of being a Romeo to her Juliet just went kaput.

The school days and years flew by fast. She graduated and left the University, maybe without even knowing I got a dampened crush on her. I graduated two years after her.

Fast forward to 1974, my first year of employment as a teacher. My employer required a transcript of my academic records. I went to apply for a copy of my transcript at the Administration Office of the Bicol University. At the registrar's office, my olfactory nerves sensed something familiar in the vicinity—my bespectacled, smoke-smelling professor.

After exchanging pleasantries, he asked me where I was working at the moment and what grade level I was handling. I said I was teaching 1st grade at St. Agnes' Academy of Legazpi City, and I loved it. "Good! Teaching is the noblest profession."

I should know by then.

"Have you had any word from her since graduation?" I asked, no malice intended.

With no tinge of inhibition or reservation as well, he said, "Yeah, I still write her letters, as she does me once in a while. We still communicate."

I felt an ancient longing in the chest resurrected and revived as I reached for something inside my attaché case, which was full of class records, student quizzes, and worksheets. "I hope you enjoy this." His hand quivered as I handed him a transcribed copy of my music composition and he saw the title—

"You mean, her…" He stalled. He was trying to conceal his emotions, but I could see that there was a storm surging deep inside him.

"Yes, Sir, no less than her poem." To me, it was one of her most moving handiworks, published in **The Mentor** during her senior year, a portrait of her deepest emotions at the moment. "A few days ago, I turned her poem into song. I just finished transcribing it last week. Very providential that I ran into you. You can have this copy for yourself, Sir."

"I didn't know you were a composer. Mr. Luna should be so proud of you!"

"No, Sir. He knew this as my hobby." Mr. Luna was my Music professor at the University.

He could not contain himself, as his eyes then gloated in awe over the strange piece of music with a fond and oh so familiar title in front of him. Still wide-eyed, he said, "I will ask someone to play this for me on the piano." And then in a joking tone: "Let me see if your hobby is worthwhile enough and your music is as good as her poem!"

"Sir, to anyone who knows our mutual friend, nothing can be better than her poem, except herself."

I handed him the music sheet. Then we bade each other goodbye. That was the last time I ever smelled his characteristic scent. That was the last time I ever saw him.

A few days later, a note came in the mail saying, "Jun, I cannot think of worse words to describe what you have accomplished. Your music is so not ordinary. Your song evokes the bitterest memories. The notes you wrote make up the saddest melody I've ever heard. I LOVE it!"

<u>BEYOND REALITY</u>

Words by TV / Music by Arcádio Morada, Jr.

1. There is too much of a gnawing silence
within my heart.
There is too much of the stillness
within my soul.
Within the wells of my mind,
there is no water at all.

2. How could I break that gnawing silence
within my heart?
How could I reach the roots of
what is within,
The roots of truth that my heart can't magnify
nor exalt?

Refrain1:
For you came near to me,
looked into my soul and left.
And that much to create a painful wound
and wildest dreams
Within my heart, that calls and seeks for you
Beyond reality.

3. I could have forgotten my dreams last night,
my dreams last night,
Buried my aching heart in cups of wine,
why not?
And fought the most tender passion
within my soul for you.

Refrain2:
But you came back again,
looked into my soul and left.
And that much to create another wound
and wildest dreams
Within my heart, that calls and seeks for you
Beyond reality.

Coda:
Look into my soul and leave,
And that much to create another wound
and wildest dreams
Within my heart, that calls and seeks for you
Beyond reality.

That was not the end of the story. A year after that chance meeting at the Administration Office of the Bicol University, I dabbled in Tagalog poetry. I wrote my own sentimental—you can say "mawkish" or "sappy"—words to the same music I had written for her poem. (I apologize to my non-Filipino readers for not translating. There is so much to lose in translation. It may suffice to say that the title means "Love Me".)

IBIGIN MO AKO

1. May sasabihin ako sa iyo,
nguni't ang samo,
H'wag kang tatawa't baka
mamatay ako.
Noon pa ma'y dati nang
hibang ako sa iyo.

2. Parang baliw kong inulit-ulit
ang nadaramdam.
Parang sakitin namang
'yong iniwasan.
Manhid ba 'ko, o di lang
marinig ang sagot mo?

Refrain:
Ibigin mo ako,
bakâ mabuhay muli
Ang puso kong baon
sa kasawia't siphayo.
Bakâ muling matutong magmahal.
Ibigin mo ako!

3. Wika mo pa'y kaytamis ng dila
ko sa pag-ibig
Nguni't hindi tunay ang loob
ng dibdib.
Puso ko ba'y sinungaling
kung ikaw ang pinipintig?

4. Lalo mo lang inihahatid
sa huling hantungan
Buhay ng pag-ibig kong
tunay at banal
Sa tuwing ibabaling mo
ang iyong tingin sa iba. *(Repeat Refrain.)*

Love me, leave me. That's the core of this story. I hope life has been kind to him. I hope life has been fair to her. As for the third corner of the triangle, if there was such, let us see what Mameng, my wife, has to say.

In time, my wife Mameng got hold of, and read, this story from me. No, not that I meant to hide it forever from her. She is my #1 fan, everybody knows. She relishes my writings and gives me the most heartwarming, or the most scathing, feedbacks even when nobody else does or cares to comment. But this time she declared a one-day Cold War. She didn't talk to me or minded when I tried to call her attention. At the end of that deafening period, she said, "I was so much disappointed in you!"

As if I was THE unfaithful. I said in defense, "Sweetheart, I was just a poet. It was just a song. I was not the paramour!" ∎

If I am known for anything, it's my hearty laugh. It is scarce, though, especially considering I've lived alone for over ten years now, since our daughter Carmela pursued dramatic arts in New York and her mom had to go live with her. But I had a good one today, early Monday morning, on my way to work, alone. My laugh turned from chuckle to guffaw as my wife Mameng narrated her "bad" dream of me last night. She, too, was on her way to work in Port Chester, New York, and while seated and waiting for the Metro North train to start off, she called me. This Texas Monday morning was gorgeous, whereas it was rainy in New York; but everything in her dream, she said, was as bright as day.

"Tell me the truth!" The clinking and clanking of the Metro North punctuated her narration.

Before I recount my wife's dream, let me first share another. Last Saturday, our daughter Carmela had a dream (of me, too), which she, so perturbed, hesitated at first to tell her mom. But she had to know. Mameng, in turn, hesitated to narrate Carmela's dream to me, but I, too, had to know. Why the fuss? Carmela dreamed *I died a horrible death!*

Now this one I should laugh off more intensely. I am as healthy as for one of my age. I don't drink and smoke. My cholesterol level and hypertension are under control. I don't have enemies that might want and design my demise with premeditation. No worries give me sleepless nights. On top of these, I try to always keep a cheerful disposition despite problems that come my way. No predicaments that my hearty laughter can't mitigate!

It's only a dream, Babe, and don't you worry.

Now, here's my wife's subconscious vision. She finds out I have another woman! Whoa! She follows me to a hotel in a tryst with this woman, and after confrontation, finds out I have another child (by this woman or another, she does not clarify). She gives one very precise and glaring detail—the venue of my unfaithfulness is Leslie Hotel. As bright as day!

Does anybody know where to find Leslie Hotel? In Brownsville or elsewhere in Texas? Are you sure, Babe, it's not Leslie Motel for one-night stands? Carmela might ask for the name of her step-sibling!

Ha ha ha ha ha! No predicaments that my hearty laughter can't mitigate. Besides, it's only a dream, Babe, so don't you worry! ∎

At some point in my younger days, the urge of the creative mind might have taken root. I don't know, to be exact, how or when. It was just there, incipient, ready to use and amuse.

avenous as a hungry animal looking for sustenance, I remember myself devouring every book and reading material on which I could lay my eyes. Of course, whence I took in, I gave out. That period, the 70s, was the pinnacle of my youth, the golden era of my life.

odles upon oodles of handiworks, mediocre or otherwise, got churned out of my head in collaboration with my heart and hand. Letters, essays, short stories, poems, songs, operettas. One among the heap was this gooey lovey-dovey

ong. It antedates you, my Love, by eight years—meaning, I composed it in 1973, before we met in 1981. Neither did I compose it with somebody as inspiration, nor did I intend it for somebody in particular.

re you think otherwise, here's the story behind its creation. The '73 Junior-Senior Prom of my University needed a song to use in a symbolic ceremony wherein my batch, the Juniors, was going to give roses to the Seniors. As I was active in the campus literary scene, the prom organizers tasked me to find the song best suited to the need. Finding none to my liking, I composed one—*aha*, A ROSE FOREVER was born!

Sweetheart, don't budge. Read on further.

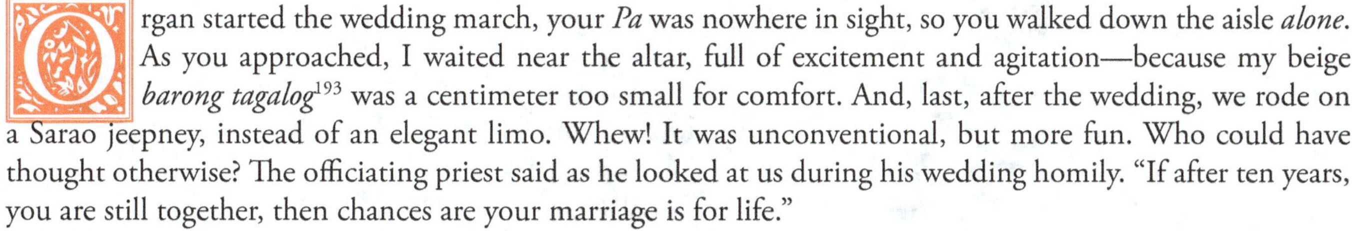

unny, but 36 years ago, this 2022, in the euphoria of the Philippine People Power Revolution, we tied the knot. It was an ordinary wedding turned unconventional by its bloopers and blunders. First, we didn't want to bother or burden our parents' pockets, so with our limited resources, we shouldered the whole affair ourselves. Upon arrival at Our Lady of the Gate Parish Church in Daraga, you stepped on the hem of your wedding gown, nearly tripping. Captured for posterity on video, your awkward position could have been more unglamorous if you fell flat on the threshold of the church. When the church

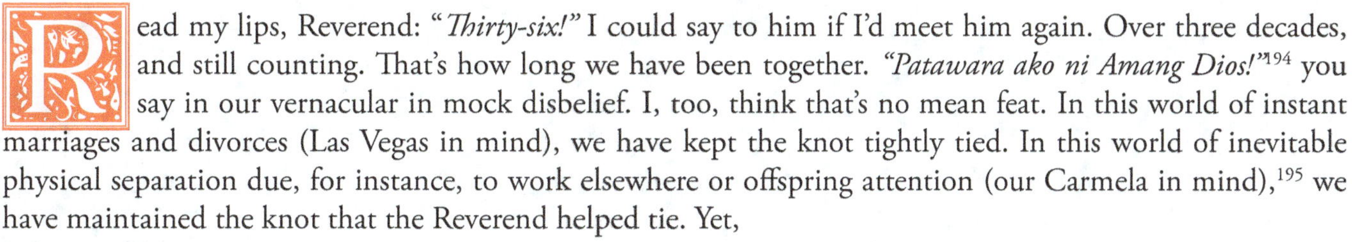

rgan started the wedding march, your *Pa* was nowhere in sight, so you walked down the aisle *alone*. As you approached, I waited near the altar, full of excitement and agitation—because my beige *barong tagalog*[193] was a centimeter too small for comfort. And, last, after the wedding, we rode on a Sarao jeepney, instead of an elegant limo. Whew! It was unconventional, but more fun. Who could have thought otherwise? The officiating priest said as he looked at us during his wedding homily. "If after ten years, you are still together, then chances are your marriage is for life."

ead my lips, Reverend: "*Thirty-six!*" I could say to him if I'd meet him again. Over three decades, and still counting. That's how long we have been together. "*Patawara ako ni Amang Dios!*"[194] you say in our vernacular in mock disbelief. I, too, think that's no mean feat. In this world of instant marriages and divorces (Las Vegas in mind), we have kept the knot tightly tied. In this world of inevitable physical separation due, for instance, to work elsewhere or offspring attention (our Carmela in mind),[195] we have maintained the knot that the Reverend helped tie. Yet,

---

193   *barong tagalog* (See footnote #61, page 31.)

194   "*Patawara ako ni Amang Dios!*" [Bikol] – God the Father forgive me; here used as expression of amazement and surprise.

195   Her mom had to stay with her in New York as she pursued college, while I stayed alone in Texas.

 ven as we inch toward our fourth decade, and our gray hairs show, we cannot boast of a perfect relationship, for ours is anything but. We have had our own share of differences, misunderstandings, heartbreaks, worries, struggles,

 erbal tussles. But we, especially you, never let a night pass without having our differences settled, misunderstandings clarified, tussles quieted down, heartbreaks patched, worries appeased, struggles smoothened out. Conflicts for sure abound; but

 phemeral are our pains and heartaches because we know how to say sorry to each other whenever sorry is apt. We know how to make the other laugh whenever one of us is sad or mad. We are the check and balance of each other. "I love you" comes out of our mouth as naturally as food into it, both of which we live by, without doubt. Shared hugs, kisses, warm shower, hot bed, and erotic caress till bliss are plusses in our happy marriage. As we celebrate our anniversary this year, we believe deep in our hearts that God made our union in heaven and "A

ose Forever" is but a minor detail about the love that we share. I declare that even if I didn't compose this song with us or you in mind, it nonetheless fits us to a T; it is for us and for you. I speak in authority as the one who made it. I now sing it for us, to you. God be our guide, God be with us, as we face the future and pray: *"That if all roses fade, I'll never fail to still give you my heart forever."*[196]

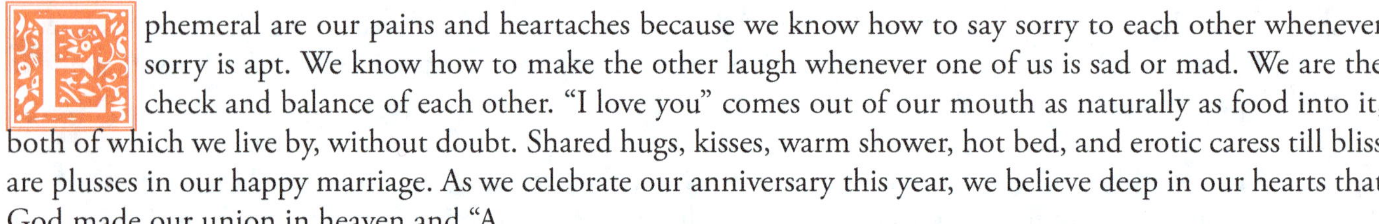

I'll give you a rose forever,
A rose that will stay by time.
What it has to say, please remember:
"Smell my fragrance of ideal care!"
I'll give you a rose forever,
With devotion and fervent pray'r
That if all roses fade,
I'll never fail
To still give you my heart forever! ∎

 rowing old had better go with growing up hand in hand. Aging coincides with maturity, and wisdom is directly proportional to age. If not, that's when we grow old, but look immature. We marvel at the sight of precocious children but shudder when the old do not act their age. We don't grow "down," unless we are roots or our body parts self-destruct.

---

196   Arcádio Morada, Jr., *tagaalbay*, "A Rose Forever," YouTube video, 3:17 min, https://youtu.be/BIFU9rL4fdU.

One sign, or rather advantage, of growing up is knowing that we stand at a vantage point. From this point, we see ourselves and our past endeavors with fresh eyes, often with hopeful certainty that things in our life have improved and become better somehow. We build this vantage point on our experiences, knowledges gained, and righteous judgments. We embody wisdom as we grow up and old.

Let us take the flair for language—and me—on focus.

Not that I have such a flair to brag, let alone flaunt, impress, and impose upon others. I can never call myself an excellent public speaker, not even in my wildest dreams, because I am not. (In fact, I shrink at the prospect of having to enunciate to an audience no matter how small.) Neither will I declare myself an excellent writer, for I have only scarce published proofs to show. Therefore, instead of "flair for language" being a signpost of growth, may I use the phrase "sense of language" or the way of expressing oneself. It sounds less boastful and intimidating.

I'm a hardcore sentimentalist. I keep souvenirs, records, or reminders of the lows and highs of my life, accumulating a significant trove of curios at my age—71 as of this writing. Familial as well as love letters; personal, business and/or professional correspondence; journals, events calendars, logbooks, scrapbooks; index card notes, school projects and compositions, college research papers; internet resources and gems, printed emails—name it, I collect and keep it. That dry leaf I collected while praying for further discernment in the garden of Sacred Heart Novitiate, Quezon City, in 1983 is still between the pages of my Bible today; it is a solemn reminder that once upon a time I thought I heard the call to be a priest. A carbon copy of that impassioned letter to Ms. Ramos, a nun and fellow religion teacher who called me *Jun Muslim*, is among many others in my volume "Professional Correspondence"; it is a constant reminder of how one's immaturity— whether hers or mine—could rear its ugly head. My trove of curios may be as good as trash, but to me, any written handiwork or keepsake from any era of my life is a personal treasure. It is a record of a point in time which will never happen again. It is a record worth keeping.

So, for now I retrieve from the trove this emotional piece that I wrote as a ballad in early 1975—forty-seven years ago!—when I was in the prime of youth. You may call it quintessential Arcádio at that stage of my life. A social-media friendly reminder, though: Read on but abandon ship if it proves too shallow or deep a water for your mind. Trash it if it feels too bland or pungent a fruit for the taste. If we have little time to read long narratives, such as this, leave it.

THE BALLAD

Now I wonder: how did I, why did I, what moved me to, write this? So here I do a critique of myself. Here I poke fun at, and mock, my own creation. I look at myself from my vantage point of 71 years, with a new vision of the world to see. Here is that handiwork, circa 1975, critiqued in 2022.

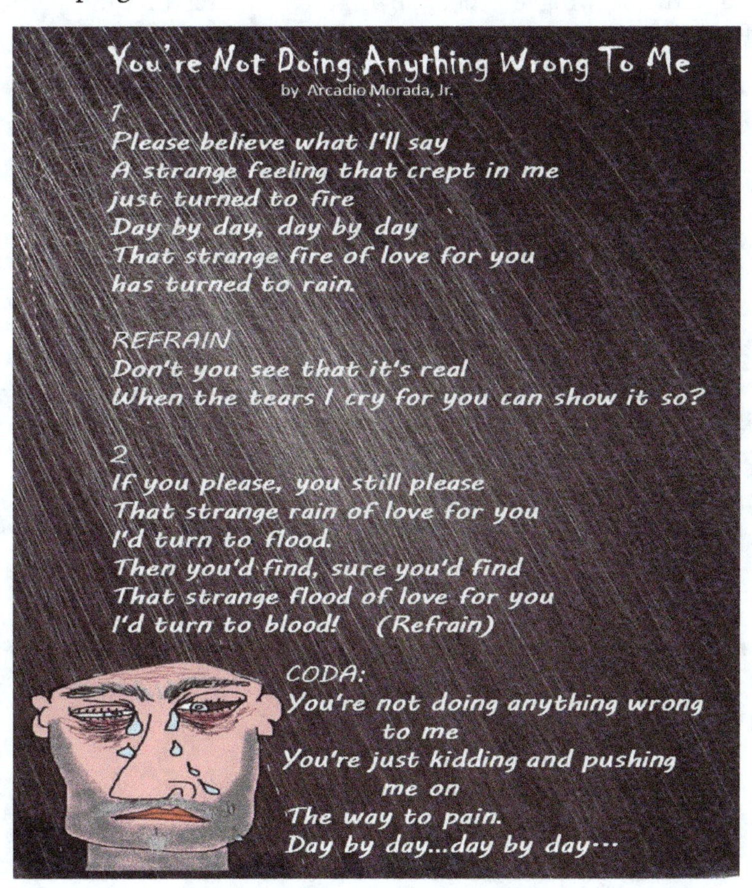

You're Not Doing Anything Wrong to Me

I reckon this title is the corniest ever among my youthful creations. Such double-speak: a masochistic denial of suffering, yet a mawkish acceptance of fate! (Nosebleed, anyone? Sorry, I offer no translation: this description is as simple as I can get.)

Please believe what I'll say

An invocation that whatever I will say is the truth and nothing but the truth. On the technical side, the ballad is in the minor mode, thus "sad." Add in "dark" and "foreboding." I've had a predisposition to minor mode, even in my youth. So now I relate the truth, in my typical gloomy way.

A strange feeling that crept in me just turned to fire

"You" (the subject of my ballad) and I must have met, resulting in sleepless nights. I wonder in silence what attractiveness "you" possessed that so struck my fancy and passion.

Day by day, day by day
That strange fire of love for you has turned to rain

It's warm season in Crush Land. I'm in heat. (No, not the adrenaline rush!) Climate veers to dry season, and the coming of the rain is just a matter of time. "You" spurns me, and in silence I cry from foolish expectations. Love is corny and foolish.

Don't you see that it's real
When the tears I cry for you can show it so?

The proof of the raining is in the dropping. This crying supposes to be a lonesome and secret exercise, but here I insinuate that "you" must see the proof. Unloved, I want "you" to feel guilty.

If you please, you still please
That strange rain of love for you I'd turn to flood

Want more proof? A sudden downpour causes flash floods. I cry a river, what more proof does "you" need? Oh, and by the way, "flood" is not as far as "your" No can take me. Watch out!

Then you'd find, sure you'd find
That strange flood of love for you I'd turn to blood

Uh-oh, suicidal. A bloody threat! Reeling under what pundits call a quarter-life crisis, those in ages between 20 and 30 are most likely to have suicidal tendencies, say psychiatrists. (I was twenty-something when I wrote this song.) The doctors even report cases of children below the age of 10 commenting on and contemplating suicide.

Don't you see that it's real
When the tears I cry for you can show it so?

Back to refrain: The melodic contour/direction of this part of the ballad enhances its emotional impact. It suggests passion and pathos, leading to the climactic Coda. Again, an indirect summon to guilt.

You're not doing anything wrong to me
You're just kidding and pushing me on the way to pain

Here, the masochistic denial of suffering and mawkish acceptance of fate get confirmed and sealed by substitution. (Nosebleed once more!) I am now putting the entire blame on "you" for being so unfeeling and sadistic.

Day by day… day by day…

The pain continues, little by little, engulfing my being. *Whew!* Unrequited love is a tiring and tiresome exercise. Cross my heart and hope to die.

THE WIFE

How did my young persona in the cusp of adulthood use his sense of language to get his message across, to stress his point? I'm amazed by the way he used figures of speech and symbolisms that were simple and common, yet effective and forceful. In musical terms, I love the way he used soaring notes and *sustenatos* to emphasize the passion he wanted to impart to his listener. Too unfortunate I'm not Caruso, Pavarotti, Domingo, Bocelli, or Groban[197] to give justice to his song.[198]

But the 64-dollar question is, is "You"—the subject of my passion—a real, breathing Mona Lisa with a tantalizing smile that could invoke rains and floods and blood on me? From my vantage point, I assert that "You" was just a product of youthful vicarious experience. (Webster Dictionary: "vicarious *adjective* vi·car·i·ous \vī-'ker-ē-əs, və-\: experienced or felt by watching, hearing about, or reading about someone else rather than by doing something yourself.") I didn't have to live the ballad to compose it, did I?

How can I reconcile this with "Please believe what I'll say" invocation used to start the ballad? It's called poetic license, folks, not lying. It's very much the same as the "I'd turn to blood" threat, which in reality was just a bluff. I might get depressed now and then, but not to the point of self-annihilation, so I declare I didn't, and still don't, have suicidal tendencies. Besides, my Christian upbringing will never let so. I am not lying through my teeth.

---

197   Enrico Caruso (1873-1921), Italian operatic tenor; Luciano Pavarotti (1935-2007), Italian operatic tenor; José Plácido Domingo Embil (born 1941), Spanish opera singer; Andrea Bocelli (born 1958), Italian opera singer; Josh Groban (born 1981), American singer-songwriter.

198   Arcádio Morada, Jr., "You're Not Doing Anything Wrong to Me," Audio file. https://yourlisten.com/Arcádio.Morada/youre-not-doing-anything-wrong-to-me.

"You" was just a figment of my imagination, I reiterate. I affirm the ballad is not a product of firsthand experience. It is nothing but an imaginative expression of someone on a precarious threshold—a teenager no more, a full-fledged adult not yet.

For sure, "You" was not Mameng, my wife of 36 years now. Yes, Mameng too, the moment I first laid eyes on her, made me experience that "strange feeling that crept in me" which "turned to fire." The big distinction was that she said yes when I told her so. Besides, the ballad antedates her by six years, we having met only in 1981.

On top of everything thus explained, a conversation happens over and over between my wife and me.

"Seriously?" she asks in disbelief. "You never had, or never courted, anyone before me?"

"Cross my heart and hope to die!"

"How about Kooky?" She makes a face at me.

Who's Kooky, anyway? Well, Kooky is a pseudonym for a real person, not vicarious. Kooky and I attended same university, took up same course, earned the same degree; then we got employed in same two succeeding schools before I met and married Mameng, and migrated to Texas USA.

"I never courted, let alone fell for Kooky!" That's my constant rebut. How I wish she'd take my word for it!

Like the song, I invoke the truth and nothing but the truth. "Please believe what I'll say!" No poetic license, nor lying through the teeth. Cross my heart and hope to die. End of conversation.

Or is it? ■

 still have not wavered in my belief that our marriage was made in heaven. In many respects, heaven has blessed our union from the start. Romeo had his Juliet, Samson his Delilah, Anthony his Cleopatra—but, sadly, they were all ill-fated and doomed. Happily, I have Mameng.

There's an art to it, whatever, but there's an art to how we tick. I hardly know how it's done. Call it a fascinating and happy mystery none of us knows howsoever it crept into our being and engulfed our consciousness for the past three decades of our togetherness.

<u>THE ART OF LOVING YOU</u>

1. The sun would shine,
Why should I care?
All songs I sang
Seemed out of tune.
Flowers bloomed
But pink and red*
Were the words I was longing
to hear them described.
I would say that God was cruel
 [for] Giving curse of loneliness.
Nights would come as often as
I thought all my life was a bore!

But the sun never shines
Without purpose at all.
It cherishes the life
I held as a bore.
How I wonder that all flowers
Bloom today, as I wanted them to.
And I shout, "God is kind!"
He has taught me the art of loving…

2. Now I sing
A life song
With feelings quaint,
And so sublime.
Hear the words
And melody
Of a love that will never
Grow old by time.
Mock the wish
But not the hope.
Spurn the song
But not the heart.
Turn your back
But not your soul
And the reason which
I'm living for.

Yes, the sun never shines
Without purpose at all.
It cherishes the life
I held as a bore.
How I wonder that all flowers
Bloom today, as I wanted them to.

And I shout, "God is kind!"
He has taught me the art of loving
You!

Late in the day, I gathered my nerves and recorded the song. The audacity is unmistakable in the finished product,[199] shared on YouTube: this guy is a trying-hard. In Filipino, *"ang kapal ng apog!"* Truth be told, mine may not be the most winsome voice in the world, but I couldn't care less. For me, the whole try is a testament to that mysterious art that makes us click.

I wanted the world to know. First off, I posted it on Facebook at past two in the morning of February 26, your birthday. This was because, even if I had finished recording the song at dusk, making an accompanying video and uploading it on YouTube consumed the better part of my night. The video, which I conceptualized as something simple yet heartwarming, wasn't that easy and short to make. I thought it might make you happy and your day super special, and that could be a just reward. Now feast on the rest of the story.

To be downright honest, I did not conceive this corny lovesick poem—and the "life song" that followed its creation—with your person in mind. I mean, I wrote this in 1972 when I was midway through college, when you were in high school, and we were well-nigh in different galaxies. At that point in time, I was what you could call a dork, a nitwit, a bookworm—whose urgent concern in life was to finish school and start a career. Girls were second-class citizens and a collective nuisance, and I was a late bloomer.

Then we met in 1981, while I was teaching at Xavier School, Manila. In other words, it antedated you for nine years. Your emergence in my life changed its course and my story. I thought at first it might dishearten you to know the truth, but that's the risk I'm willing to take. You won't have a soft spot for a person lying to you on the inspiration for his song, and my conscience won't delight in that, either.

Time passed, fifty years after the song. Within that time, Doris Day crystallized *Que Sera Sera* in **The Doris Day Show**, while Gladys Knight popularized *The Best Thing That Ever Happened to Me* with The Temptations. Within that time, too, Anne Murray sang *You Needed Me*, Diana Ross and Lionel Richie's duet of *Endless Love* was a hit. You and I got married, and we had Carmela. We migrated to the United States, and Kenny Rogers belted out *Through the Years*, long before our 36th anniversary in December 2022, amid the pandemic. Sadly, Day and Rogers have passed on, although Knight, Murray, Ross, and Richie—the four of them in their twilight years—are still crooning their songs. And the redemption to your favor struck me a day before your birthday.

As a habit, I write a letter or dedicate something to you on your birthday. Tomorrow would be your birthday, but today I had to babysit our grandson Adam. I had writer's block. I didn't know what to do, let alone what to write. I panicked. Only a day before your birthday, and I still had nothing to show I cared. I being so stressed, my bladder acted up super. On a trip to the bathroom, I collided with a stack of banker's boxes; out from one of those came **AKO BAGA IKOS**—I am a Cat, "a collection of secondhand coupon bonds disguised as songs"—nothing but handiworks from my youth.

The sides are fraying, and the pages are getting fragile and brown. From 1972 to 1975, I had typed every painstaking page after page using a Singer portable typewriter (now long gone because of a thieving roommate, back in the 1980s).

---

199   Arcádio Morada, Jr., *tagaalbay* "The Art of Loving You," YouTube video, 4:05min, https://youtu.be/XdxE2a2Mwsg.

Yet in these pages is a sentimental journey back in time that I indulge in every once in a while. They are testamentary to my early fascination with words and music. Call me a man of the past, but I am not what I am now without the handiworks from these pages.

"Well, what have we here?" I asked myself. As I flipped through the pages, a sentimental journey, so to speak, unfolded. These were works from my golden age, my Renaissance. It was a time of adverse financial problems in my family, of failure in my studies, of student activism during the Third Quarter Storm. From that crucial time of my life oozed forth many poems, songs, letters, essays, short stories, and other written handiworks as if from an inexhaustible source. The compendium came along with me in my migration and pursuit of the American Dream. Now stashed in banker's boxes, they were open for the reminiscing—as this moment when I had writer's block and could not think of what to write for your birthday.

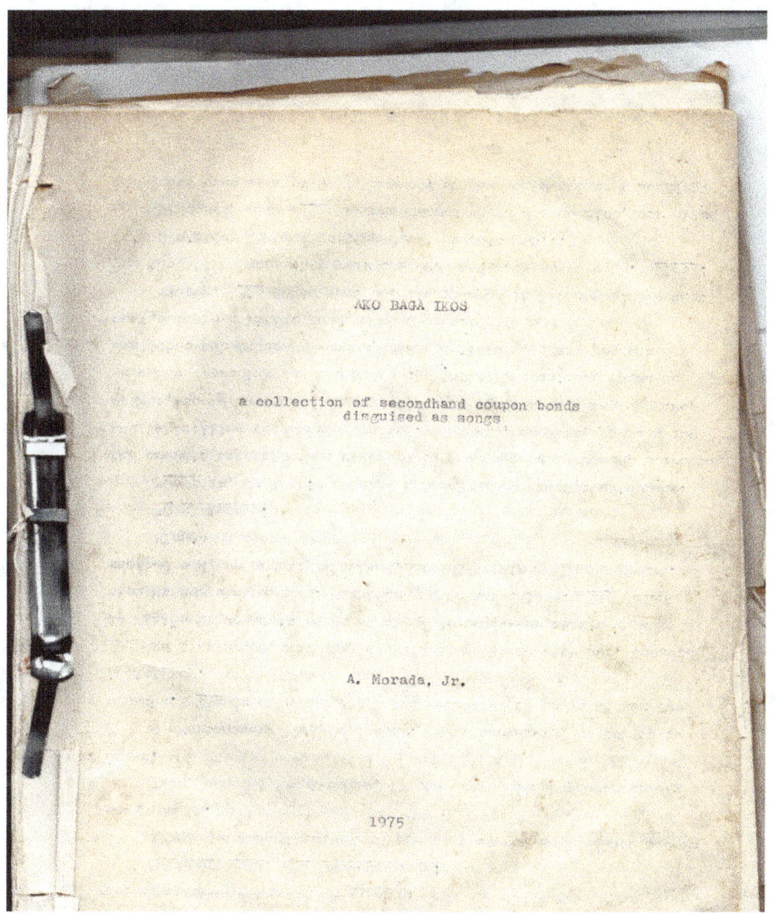

"The Art of Loving You" on page 40 caught my attention. That corny, sappy, lovesick poem, senseless at the outset, was now making perfect sense in the light of you. Unedited,[200] the text of the poem now makes everything true about my life with you. You have been my companion for a long time and most of my life now. You know every facet of me, and I know yours as well. Written roughly half a century ago, this corny, sappy, lovesick poem/song now looks especially made for you. I'm downright stuck on you.

Oh, yes, Sweetheart, with everything falling into place, the "You" in "The Art of Loving You" has turned up to be none other than you. The song had been waiting for its fulfillment in you. You had it coming. It deserves no one but you. And tops, my life has become happier and richer because of you. ∎

---

200   Except for the word "red" in place of "gay", which several decades ago carried no negative connotations.

32

HONEYMOON

A wonderful place is this world we live in!

The tour was our first in a long, long while. I mean, we have gone to a few places, but not alone by ourselves, not just the two of us. Neither have we gone out of Texas often (only to New York in July 1994 and the Rocky Mountains in December 1995). In our over three decades in these United States, we have only gone to San Antonio, Corpus Christi, Dallas, Austin, New Braunfels, Galveston, Houston, or thereabouts. (OMG, we have not even visited Disney in California or Florida, and Carmela is now twenty-something!). Throughout this time, we traveled with our daughter and our close friends in tow. So now, without Carmela (who couldn't come because of work in Manhattan) and friends to share in the fun, we decided it was high time to go by our twosome.

Nor was it an expensive tour, per se. In fact, we couldn't call it *bongga*[201] or planned. Her gracious employer at Port Chester, New York, gave my wife Mameng a 7-day paid vacation. Incidental was my birthday falling within that week, and I was in New York on my annual visit with my wife and daughter. So, the tour was both her birthday gift for me and her own chance to unwind!

It turned out to be much more than that. We never thought it was to become our second honeymoon, three decades after the first!

The tour starts at Flushing, New York. Inside an air-conditioned bus called **Covered Wagon**, we occupy our seats before departure in a cacophony of Asian tongues. Among Chinese, Korean, and Indian nationals, as well as tourists from Bangladesh, Myanmar, and a sprinkling of other Southeast Asian countries, Mameng and I are the only Filipinos.

Departing from Flushing at 7:30 am, the tour bus winds its way through the traffic of Queens and Manhattan, then several cities of New Jersey. Around 10:00 am, we reach Philadelphia. We are to stay in Pennsylvania's largest city for an hour or so. Our first stop is Independence National Historical Park, to see many historic sites such as the Liberty Bell and Independence Hall. In the annals of American history, Independence Hall is a notable place connected to the Declaration of Independence and the United States Constitution.

Towards noon, we leave for the U.S. capital city of Washington, D.C., to see prominent government structures and landmarks. First is the National Air & Space Museum, where we marvel at the history of flight. Then we visit great memorials to two iconic U.S. presidents—Washington and Lincoln. (The U.S. Capitol Building is under construction/repair, therefore out of the itinerary.) Of course, we don't miss out on the White House and a cruise on the Potomac River to view famous landmarks such as the Pentagon.

---

201   *bongga* [Filipino] – very stylish, lavish, ostentatious.

234

The iconic sites of Washington D.C. consume much of our afternoon, and by 6 pm we are tired and starving for dinner at a Chinese restaurant in Baltimore, Maryland. After dinner, we head to the hotel, the Wyndham Grand in Baltimore.

Something *grand* comes to mind, at another place, context, and time. Once upon a time in the Philippines, Tatay (my father) allowed me to tug along with him to a big-time *sabong*[202] in a local cockpit. That was the first time I saw a *Gran Encontrada*, a grand meet, in which game cocks from surrounding towns and villages came to compete. Of course, there were big-time losers and winners.

Now the day is over, the night is young, and though Mameng and I aren't, *Gran Encontrada* is sweeter the second time around, you bet! As our friend Doming Litong says, *"Yan ang gran encontrada na walang natalo!"* [That's the grand meet where nobody lost.]

Much earlier in my life, I composed a song that—recalled after 40 years to this day—gives me now a tingling sense of *déjà vu*. Without having experienced platonic, much less erotic love at that point in time, the youth in me wrote an hour-and-a-half-long operetta. Grade school children in Legazpi City, Philippines, performed that operetta in 1976, giving flesh to my libretto and 18 songs. One of them was **What a Wonderful Place**. (A little warning, though: I wrote this song when the words *gay* and *queer* had simple meanings.)

1.   What a wonderful place is this world I'm living in!
Flowers are blooming as they've never bloomed before.
The sun shines bright, and the air's so still
While the birds are singing so gay.

2.   What a wonderful place is this world I'm living in!
I've got somebody who cares.
But most of all, it's a wonderful place
All because I am in love.

REFRAIN: It's not so very queer to see that I am happy all day.
I like to sing and sing, come on and sing along with me.
Let's sing and sing and sing along, and share my glee!

3.   What a wonderful place is this world I'm living in!
The trees are growing as they've never grown before.
There is life in most everything I see
And my troubles are all gone away. (Repeat 2.)

-from the operetta **WHAT EVER HAPPENED TO MAGAYON?**

The song antedated the day I met Mameng for 5 years, our paths having crossed in 1981. Presently emerging from our hotel room ready for the second day of our tour, my wife is practically singing the song. Oh yeah, I am singing too! *Déjà vu!* Remember, it's our second honeymoon!

---

202   *sabong* [Filipino] – cockfight.

WISH TO BE AMISH

From Baltimore, Maryland, **Covered Wagon** goes northward and takes us to Lancaster, Pennsylvania, the home of the Amish community, an 18th century culture in our modern world. The Amish originally came from the Netherlands and settled in Lancaster County when William Penn was promoting religious and cultural freedom. Their way of life today is in close resemblance to that of their forefathers 300 years ago—simple, non-materialistic, slow-paced, quiet, unbound by technology. The Amish focus their collective lives on service of God, family, and community. They dedicate themselves to peace and humility, and to preserve their values, they avoid the ways of the modern world.

The tour immerses us into an Amish village. We go inside an Amish house, taste Amish pastry, buy Amish houseware from their stores, admire and touch their garden flowers, shoot selfies among their corns. An Amish boy delights us, so we invite him to join us for a souvenir picture. The boy, shy and polite, declines—were we not told earlier that they don't, they never, indulge in these modern vanities?

It's surprising yet exhilarating to see that despite our so-called modern conveniences, the Amish can keep their way of life. They avoid using anything technology- or electric-powered, such as television, automobiles, cell-phones. The men sport beards, the women wear blouses and skirts in drab colors. They dress as simple as can be, without personal ornamentation. They exude peace and humility, yet are thoroughly productive. In their simple ways, they are dynamic and progressive.

The Amish use buggies as their primary means of transportation. In an Amish house, the boys sleep in one room, the girls in another. Amish gardens are so remarkable in their simplicity. The Amish try to be self-sufficient. A luxuriant Amish cornfield tempts Mameng and me to pluck a few ears of corn for the taking. Instead of malls and department stores, they have stands.

All this knowledge gives me goosebumps. Theirs is a simple, wonderful life! Theirs is a wonderful place! I think I want to be Amish. Won't you?

HERE SHE IS HERSHEY!

You're reading right, yes, the famous chocolate! We don't blame the people of Hershey, Pennsylvania, for calling their city *The Sweetest Place on Earth.*

By mid-morning, the tour takes us to Hershey, PA. Here we marvel at an exciting animated journey of the Chocolate World, Hershey's virtual kingdom. We learn where cocoa beans come from and their journey from the tropical rainforest to Hershey, PA. We see, touch, hear, and smell the delicious transformation from bean to the famous chocolate. Wonderful place!

Like children, we leave Hershey with much hesitation, but not before buying a few bars of their goodies and a giant Hershey Kiss for Carmela.

WAT KIN WE DO AT WATKINS GLEN

The afternoon sees us in another wonderful place: the *Watkins Glen State Park.* A glen is a narrow valley; that's just what's in store for us in this most famous of the Finger Lakes State Parks, towards northern New York State, westward of Ithaca, NY.

A small river runs through this narrow valley. Within two miles, the glen's stream descends 400 feet past 200-foot cliffs, generating countless waterfalls along its course. The gorge path winds over and under waterfalls and through the spray of Cavern Cascade. We walk along rim trails overlooking the gorge. We trek down the cliffs of Watkins Glen and get ourselves dampened by the falling waters off the sides of its breathtaking canyon. Of course, we take a thousand and one selfies along the way for posterity. What a wonderful place!

ROCHESTER RIVERSIDE

What a day! We are full of the wonders of God's creation, as well as man-made ones. (Remember Amish lifestyle and the Chocolate World.) **Covered Wagon** drives us to Rochester, NY, a distance of more or less 3 hours of travel time to Buffalo, New York. Across the U.S. border from Buffalo to Canada lies another wonderful place in the superlative sense—NIAGARA FALLS! But that's going to be for the next day, the tour guide tells us. The prospect fills us with anticipation!

The tour billets us in another excellent hotel (Radisson Hotel Rochester Riverside) for the night. Meanwhile, assistant physical therapist Carmela works her butt off in Manhattan. It's a wonderful place, and we're having a wonderful day, honey. Don't blame us; we told you to come!

Inside the luxurious Radisson Hotel room, and while lying in the warm king-size hotel bed, I wink at my Mameng and my wife winks back at me. It's seduction time, and the moon is yellow.

"W e're at Niagara Falls!" So goes Mameng in our native dialect as I take a video of her with the world-famous falls in the backdrop.[203] With a naughty grin, my dear wife next says, *"Ta yâding agom ko, inúragan na!"* [My husband is so perversely persistent!]

Both of us burst out laughing. Then she says, barely audible, *"Pígparapásasabí sâkon!"* [He wants me to say this.] *"Orâ kuno tsaka-tsaka!"* [No translation provided; you don't want to know!]

At last, she says with confidence and authority, *"Mgá tagá-Camalíg* [Residents of Camalig, Albay, Philippines], *didi kami sa* Niagara Falls *sa* U.S. side. OK?"

It's more than OK. I marvel at the innate beauty and grandeur of the Falls—as I did three decades ago, for the real, the true, the innate Mameng. Spontaneous. Genuine. Frank. Uninhibited. Fluid. Full-blown as a flower in bloom. Bright and warm as day.

But that's going way ahead of the tour. Let me start from the beginning.

B y 6:30am, Mameng and I are more than ready and eager to begin the itinerary of the day. "Tomorrow is the most exciting part of the tour," the Chinese tour guide said with enthusiasm before we **Covered Wagon***ers* retired to our respective hotel rooms the preceding night. "Warning, if you're not in the lobby by seven, the bus leaves without you!"

---

203   Arcadio Morada, Jr., *tagaalbay*, "Mameng at the American Falls," YouTube video, 1:03min, https://youtu.be/BA8JvmfyRlQ

He said the threat in such a nice way that he sounded without malice, with only the tourists' good in mind. Which proved effective because by 6:30, everybody is waiting by the hotel lobby, ready to go. We are one of the very first ones.

So here we are, energized and full of expectations around the purported exciting activities of the day.

"If we leave by 7, we catch the first trip of the *Maid of the Mist*. After that, we explore Old Fort Niagara, then after lunch, we go to Terrapin Point on Goat Island, the closest point you can ever get to Horseshoe Falls.

"And the highest point of the day is the jet boat ride along the Niagara Whirlpool Rapids!"

Of course, by the skin of my teeth, I hardly understand the tour guide's English because he is Chinese, and I'm not racist. His many declarations abovementioned—oh, I just put the pieces together, no stretching, so to speak. And the pieces fit well!

MAID OF THE MIST

By 9:30 am, we arrive at Prospect Point, Niagara Falls State Park, and descend to the Observation Tower; at the base of this architectural wonder is the *Maid of the Mist* dock.

We don the blue raincoat provided each tourist. Blue becomes the color of the day! Blue, in its positive sense, is symbolic of freedom, strength, optimism, loyalty, faith, power, protection. In her raincoat, my Mameng personifies blue!

"Hear the crashing waves. Hear the thundering roar of 600,000 gallons of water falling right before your eyes. See the breathtaking views. Soak up every drop of powerful spray aboard the Maid of the Mist. It's the only way to experience one of the world's most amazing natural wonders…" (quote from *maidofthemist.com*)

After the *Maid of the Mist* boat tour, we watch an IMAX movie. "Niagara: Miracles, Myths, and Magic" is a very exciting and informative docu-drama in which we see a remarkable dramatization of the legend of **Lelawala**, the Maid of the Mist. After the show, the tour allows us to explore the view around Niagara Falls. We do this from Prospect Point Observation Tower. Likewise, we go up close with the American Falls at the foot of the tower, at Crow's Nest, and thereabouts. The sights and sounds of the Falls are wondrous and ethereal. A most amazing wonder of Nature is right before our—and the camera's—eyes!

OLD FORT NIAGARA

Towards noon, **Covered Wagon** takes us to Old Fort Niagara. "Fort Niagara is a fortification originally built to protect the interests of New France in North America. It is near Youngstown, New York, on the eastern bank of the Niagara River at its mouth, on Lake Ontario." (Wikipedia.) They built the very first edifice in 1678, expanding to its present size in 1755. Within the fortification, a succession of Native American, French, British, and American soldiers lived and worked from the 18th to the 20th centuries.

THE JET BOAT RIDE

By mid-afternoon, we are ready for the "highest point of the day" as described by the tour guide. Remains to be seen. Well, looks as if he's serious, and we garb in red, as on a trip to hell and back!

OMG, what a ride! The rapids are so spine-tingling! I will remember this till the day I die![204]

THE HORSESHOE FALLS

After that ride at the Whirlpool Rapids, everything else is anticlimactic, right?

"Follow me to Goat Island," the Chinese tour guide says, and we do. We don't see any vehicles, so only pedestrians, not land transportation, ply on the island. It is an exhausting walk after that jet ride which drained us of our emotions and strength. But we follow regardless.

Oh, we see the Rainbow Bridge from a good vantage point. The Rainbow Bridge connects the U.S. and Canada sides.

Good view, but that doesn't make this long walk to Goat Island that rewarding. Reaching Terrapin Point on the island makes it so. The climax of the day is to get up close and personal with the WATERS OF THE RIVER[205] at the Horseshoe Falls at Terrapin Point—

"You are just a few feet away from the edge. You can sense the mist on your face. The raging waters drop onto the rocks below with such sonorous and powerful force that you wonder how life can survive if an intentional or accidental fall occurs. You cringe at the thought, but then who in his right mind will dare plunge into these waters?

"Here in misty white against azure sky is Nature in her breathtaking magnificence. Here manifest in a straightforward, spectacular, and rambunctious display is God's omnipotence."

These are my meditations—inevitable once you are at Terrapin Point, the closest you can ever get to the U.S. side of Horseshoe Falls, more famously known as Niagara Falls.

Your works are wonderful indeed, O God!

hen you reach the highest point, there's nothing else to do but descend, right? After the previous day's excitement, I don't know if the tour can keep its momentum and thrill, or maybe it's high time to say "No Way Jose" but down.

But first, a piece of Geography. There is this small river in northeastern Minnesota called North River. So, who cares? Well, no one, I presume. However, just in case you dare to care, the North River is the source stream for the Great Lakes. From this tiny water fountain starts the whole caboodle of water that makes up Lake

---

204   Arcádio Morada, Jr., *tagaalbay*, "At the Whirlpool Rapids, Niagara Falls," YouTube video, 4:50min, https://youtu.be/bqU9boQSTRc

205   Arcádio Morada, Jr., *tagaalbay*, "The Waters of the River," YouTube video, 2:41min, https://youtu.be/mONpH8_wbFk.

Huron, Lake Ontario, Lake Michigan, Lake Erie, and Lake Superior—*en masse*, the Great Lakes. They drain into the Atlantic Ocean through the St. Lawrence River, or *Le Fleuve de Saint-Laurence.*

A total distance of 3,058 kilometers stretches from the North River to the mouth where St. Lawrence meets the Atlantic. (By comparison, the Philippines stretches 1,850 km from its northernmost point to the southernmost.)

The statistics boggle the mind. The earth has a total volume of 1,386,000,000 cubic kilometers (km^3) of water. 10,633,450 km^3 of this total is the quantity of fresh water in the world, which includes ground water—to a great extent inaccessible to humans. Now, the total fresh surface water in the world, found in lakes and rivers, is 93,113 km^3. 22,671 km^3 of this quantity is in the Great Lakes.

Hold on, help! I am gasping for air, trying hard to visualize 1 cubic kilometer of water. Harder still, such that I'm drowning, to imagine 22,671 cubic kilometers!

And now this: The Great Lakes together make up the largest body of fresh water on earth at—hold your breath—6,000,000,000,000,000 gallons! That's 6 quadrillion gallons, my gosh!

No wonder so much water drops at Niagara Falls in one second! Picture now, if I can, the quantity of water flowing in one day from North River in Minnesota to the mouth of St. Lawrence River in eastern Canada. That quantity boggles my little imagination and is too hard for me to understand!

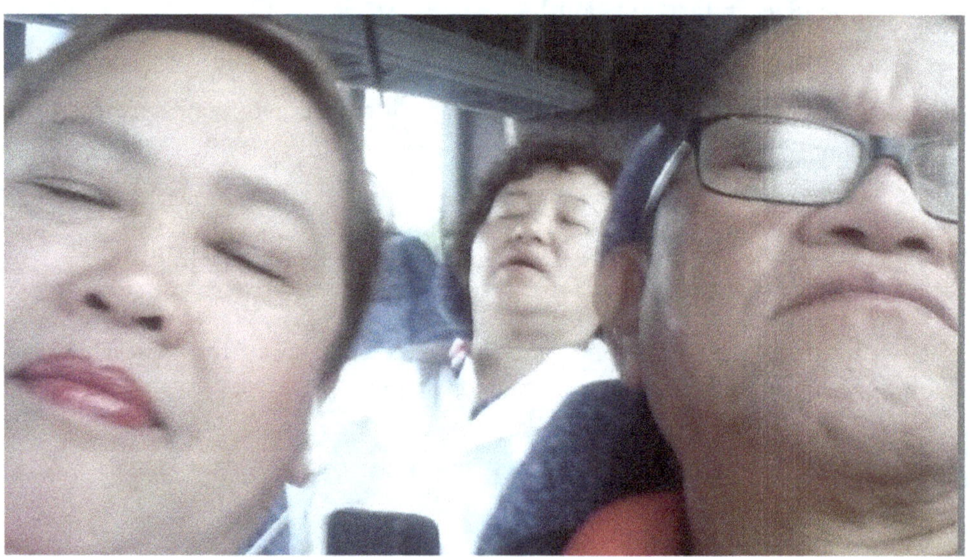

These things occupy my mind as we prepare for the last leg of our 4-day tour. Seen here sleeping, I am rather processing ideas in my mind. With that Chinese photobomber in between my wife and me, we are a quintessential picture of the tour: Asians in desperate search of summer fun slumbering in between itineraries. Because the preceding day was for me the climax of the tour, everything that follows is bathos. There's only one place left untraveled and untouched (by us!) in the itinerary: **Thousand Islands.**

Remains to be seen if our Thousand Islands sojourn is bona fide anticlimactic.

Usual time of departure is 7:00 am, with the tour guide's effective threat to be there at the lobby of Rochester Riverside Hotel, or else "the bus leaves without you!" From Rochester, the bus goes northeastwards, and in due course, the road parallels a body of water, which I later learn to be the St. Lawrence River, *aha, Le*

Fleuve! **Covered Wagon** then winds its way towards Alexandria Bay, NY, our last destination before heading home to Flushing, NY, and before calling off this entire tour.

Back to Geography. We know rivers flow towards the sea. The Great Lakes (H-O-M-E-S) may look distinct from each other, but in reality they are a compendium of rivers interconnecting and draining towards the Atlantic Ocean. St. Mary's River connects Lake Superior to Lake Huron. The Straits of Mackinac connect Lake Michigan and Lake Huron, in effect making them one lake. St. Clair River and Detroit River connect Lake Huron to Lake Erie, in turn connected to Lake Ontario by the Niagara River. At length, Lake Ontario flows into the Atlantic through the St. Lawrence River. Both the United States and Canada share in the rich bounty of these waters on their journey to the sea.

Alexandria Bay is a coastal town along the U.S. bank of *Le Fleuve de Saint-Laurence.* When we arrive at this sleepy town, the engine of **Covered Wagon** conks out and entails repair. OK, while we enjoy the Thousand Islands Cruise, let the engine resuscitate!

The Thousand Islands make up an archipelago of 1,864 islands straddling the Canada-U.S. border in the St. Lawrence River as it emerges from the northeast corner of Lake Ontario. They stretch for 50 miles (80 km) or so downstream…

The 1,864 islands range in size from over 100 km² to smaller islands occupied by a single residence, or uninhabited outcroppings of rocks that are only home to migratory waterfowl. (*Wikipedia*)

The native peoples called this region the Garden of the Great Spirit. (*visit1000islands.com*)

We inch our way by the islands. One by one, the islands (that is, the few covered by the tour) unravel before our eyes: their natural charm, their watery environment, their wonderful individual histories. There is so much on which to feast your eyes. There is so much for which to thank the Creator!

Toward noon, we receive the alarming news that **Covered Wagon**'s engine is not road-worthy yet. "You may explore Alex, NY." That's the tour guide enjoining us. "Take pictures. Walk around town!"

Well, what else can we do? Alexandria is neither 5th Avenue where to shop in style, nor Times Square where to marvel at current artistic and cultural scenes on display. It's not even Canal Street where to choose the eatery we fancy. On the streets of Alexandria, we sure walk around, not knowing what else to do or where to go. In the long run, tired and hungry, we come to this eatery serving forgettable specials.

At last, after 3 hours of mechanical work, **Covered Wagon** is up and ready to go! We heave a collective sigh of relief. We snap our last picture of the day with whom else but our Chinese tour guide, Aaron Luan. Young, strict, and sometimes misunderstood, especially by the Indians at the rear part of the bus, but altogether amiable, likable, lovable, and wonderful. Mameng and I thank the nice guy and promise him we will recommend this tour, with him as the guide, to our friends back home.

The past four days have shown us so many (Asian) people with which to do things together. So many places to marvel at and visit. So much water to travel on and to see. Yet so little time to get awed further by and explore. We are on our way back to Flushing, New York, by 3 in the afternoon. By 8:00 pm, we arrive in Flushing, and we pass the threshold of **Covered Wagon** for the last time. It's raining. And that's our denouement! ■

33

TRUST

At life's imminent edge, the last and only resort

You don't avoid things just because you're scared of them!" Cody told Norman Bates. I am not Norman, neither am I a friend as close as he was to Cody; but pangs of conscience struck and draped me as if she was talking to me instead. Oh, sorry, you don't know Norman Bates? He is the deranged character in Alfred Hitchcock's 1960 iconic movie **Psycho**, and at present I was watching its prequel series **Bates Motel** on TV.

Face the music, Cody might as well have been saying in more relevant terms. That ought to be me paraphrasing because I am as ardent a Music teacher as Walter White is a Chemistry teacher. Analogy ends there, because Walter has the big C. Cancer of the lungs. Anxious to leave his family behind with nothing financial, he comes up with an exceptional, if not reprehensible, way to provide for his family with something after his imminent demise. "When we do what we do for good reasons, then we've got nothing to worry about," Walter White says to someone in **Breaking Bad**, another TV series I was binge watching.

"Never give up control," Walt says to a fellow cancer patient. "Live life on your own terms."

Uh-oh. Walt might have been saying that to me, too.

While at this, let me introduce you to another character, a Russian spy by the name of Rudolf Ivanovich Abel. He was a real person, though, not fictional, like Cody and Walt. But his message is as profound and true-blue as theirs, if not more striking. His story was told in the historical movie **Bridge of Spies** by Steven Spielberg.

With Abel having been arrested and tried in America as a Russian spy, a lawyer named James Donovan interviewed him for his defense. Donovan said, "Apparently, you're not an American citizen." Abel replied, "That's true." "And according to your boss, you're not a Soviet citizen, either." Abel said, with a faint smile, "Well, the boss isn't always right, but he's always the boss." So, Donovan asked, "Do you never worry?" Abel said, "Would it help?"

The lawyer then said, "I have a mandate to serve you. Nobody else has. Everybody else has an interest in sending you to the electric chair." Abel agreed. "You don't seem alarmed," Donovan said. Abel just shrugged his shoulders and said, "Would it help?"

Would it? Abel might as well have been posing the question to me. Which brings me to this epiphany:

Cody or Walt or Abel might as well be my wife Mameng talking one time or another. "You face whatever problem head on, dear! Be more honest and open to me because I'm family and I know what's good for you.

Don't rely on what you read online as gospel truths downright! Go see the doctor. Worrying does you no good. Worrying won't help!"

Of late I had been, you know, worrying sick and scared of the end. My mortal end.

Let me contextualize. Around the first week of October 2016, I started feeling a certain discomfort on the left part of my head above the ear. Taking notice but disregarding the pain, I thought it was just passing, so I slept over it, thinking it was going away as stealthily as it came. But the next day, the discomfort was still there, occupying my consciousness, making me worry. At work, at night, day in, day out, over the weekend, over October, it had remained. I remember taking Tylenol once or twice to ease that little pain, but it kept coming back after insignificant relief. My worrying did not diminish, let alone stop.

What if I had a brain… tumor? What if I had the big C—as Walt had? If I expired, what would happen to my loved ones? How many years… months… weeks… days… have I remaining alive? No, I thought in anguish, I can't tell Mameng, I can't tell my daughter, they're going to worry, I don't want that happening.

I googled online for brain cancer, looking for answers. OMG, many topics on this dreaded malady and its symptoms popped up on my computer screen, as if it was the most natural and common illness on earth! OMG, I needed to go to the doctor and verify whether my symptoms were for the real big C! But no, I couldn't bear to know the truth. I needed to forget it, to think of other things aside from worrying.

I am a cinephile, so I turned hard to Netflix or my Blu-ray player to divert my attention. This was how I chanced upon **Breaking Bad**, **Bates Motel**, and **Bridge of Spies**. For a while, the worrying let up, but for sure it came back.

I turned to prayer. I always devote some time to prayer, but I can't remember any other period in my life when I prayed in so fervent and relentless a manner. "O my Jesus, Who said, 'Indeed I say to you, whatever you ask from my Father in heaven, it shall be given you.' Here I am, asking Thy Father in Thy name, for my family's safety and well-being, especially my wife and my daughter in New York. Keep us always in your love and care, away from harm, temptation, danger"—here I swept the rosary crucifix across the left side of my head—"and disease." Sometimes, without awareness, tears came flowing from my eyes.

Donovan said to Abel, "The death sentence is not a foregone conclusion. Don't worry." The steadfast Abel said in reply, "I'm not afraid to die, Mr. Donovan. Although it wouldn't be my first choice. What's the next move when you don't know what the game is?"

Yes, I didn't know what my game was, either. I wanted to be steadfast as Abel. I tried to be one as long as I could. Monday before Thanksgiving, I dashed to Dr. Ronaldo Factoriza's medical clinic at last. The Filipino doctor in Brownsville was optimistic but couldn't assure me, so he referred me for CT Scan, and to come back for the results on Wednesday, right before Thanksgiving.

At the Imaging Clinic, I asked the technician if he had any unwanted news for me. He said he saw nothing of interest, but that I should not rely on his word because he was not the expert.

I could not sleep, anticipating the results. I prayed even harder. "God grant me serenity to accept the things I cannot change, courage to change the things I can, and wisdom to know the difference. God, please grant me the most significant Thanksgiving Day of my sorry life!"

And then the results.

ife is poetry, and this piece won't be over unless I write of life vis-à-vis poetry. No kidding, for poetry, as life, is how you make it—long or short, among other attributes. When I was in college, I was too ambitious to try reading the English translation of **The Iliad**, Homer's ancient epic Greek poem. *Epic*, as in super-long. I mean, it has over 15,000 lines! I loved poetry, but I concluded I could not stand it at such length. Who could dare read, let alone write, a poem that long? But, mind you, **The Iliad** is not even the longest poem ever written. That distinction goes to **Mahabharata**, a Hindu epic poem comprising 200,000 verse lines! *Wow!* As in *What?*

The opposite end of the pole is the world's shortest poem. The debate still rages on as to the shortest poem ever written, but the answer for sure lies in what the world of creativity calls minimalist poems. These are very compressed and concise poems that get their message across mostly by visual rather than verbal means. Minimalist poems make up at least one word, or even one letter or character.

My minimalist poem, *Poem,* here partly shown, is my first example:

A poem is a skeleton
with flesh and blood.

Another minimalist from my trove of poems:

Staring squarely
at you
reminds me
how lascivious
my eyes
and how
changeable
my weather

Then this one from my tired and worried mind:

FOOUND
THE L ST!

My shortest poem, though, got composed with much thought and emotion in anticipation of Wednesday's CT Scan results. Here cries the poem to grieve with and bemoan.

END.

Tuesday night was chilly, but Wednesday morning was in the 80s. Without fuss, Dr. Factoriza divulged the results: *No lump. No tumor. What shows here is sinus on your left lobe... there's water where there should be space.*

Huh? Really? Sinus and liquid inside my head had been causing my pain? He prescribed a slew of pills to take. Inside me, my soul was jumping for joy. Give me **The Iliad**, or even **Mahabharata**, and I'm willing to read it through, cover to cover. I'm in pure nirvana!

I'm still high, so high that I keep hearing Walt, who was in remission on the episode I just watched. He said, "So you're all gonna have to be stuck with me for a while longer."

I guess I will say that too. My family, friends, colleagues, co-workers, and world: "You get stuck with me for a while longer!"

Life is poetry, either short or long. In my mind, in my head, my own life was on its end, but the Giver of Life gave it a new lease and length. So, without hesitation, with joy in my heart, and with gratitude and praise to God coming from my mouth, I change my shortest poem. It is now written, with much thought and emotion likewise, on the most memorable Thanksgiving Day of my life. Of course, it should be crystalline that its title is *What Now?* Here flaunts my revised shortest poem to cheer on and relish.

, AND

The colonoscopy procedure went with no glitch. Everyone and everything were ready for the 'cardinal procedure,' as coined by Rose Bugtong, a Reading/Language Arts teacher-friend. The secretaries, the attending nurses, the doctor's assistant, Dr. Jaime de la Garza; the rolling bed, hospital robe, TV, warm blanket, gadgets, vital signs monitors, plastic bag for my personal effects, and plastic container for my dentures—were all in place. Within three hours, I was to undergo a procedure to figure out whether I had those colon polyps that could wipe my mortal existence off the earth's surface.

I had to strip naked and divest of my belongings ON (even the underwear) and IN (including dentures) my body, which I tucked altogether inside a plastic bag. "Yes," the attending nurse said, "everything needs to be removed." The last to go was my purple wrist band. What attribute does my personal symbol have that could affect the exploring of my bottom? So naked, albeit alone, with nothing else but a blue robe to preserve my decency, I waited and wondered. (I just realize now, the robe covered my frontal possession but exposed my glorious back if I stood. Colonoscopy is thru the anus, *duh!*) Oh, if my friends could see me now! And as I waited and wondered, there was plenty of time to wax sentimental, emotional, and spiritual with the following thoughts.

First, I am old. No denying it now. The Filipino saying *"Kalabaw lang ang tumatanda"*[206] could not offer me any consolation anymore. If the shoe fits, wear it. I am wearing the shoe now, and the best proof that it fits me just right was the reason I was here in this hospital room. "Everyone over 50," states the brochure Dr. de la Garza gave me earlier, "needs to be screened for colorectal cancer." Where did my youth go? Where has my middle age gone? I never noticed them go. Or minded. The doctor gave the brochure to me to tell me in effect that I am no longer young or middle-aged. Now I was too hesitant to confirm and verify the fact that I have passed the threshold of the old.

---

206   *Kalabaw lang ang tumatanda* [Filipino] – Only the water buffalo gets old.

Corollary to the thought of aging is mortality. My mortality. "Every year in the United States," so points out the same brochure, "50,000 people die from the disease." Though not from colon cancer, my dad passed away at 75, and my mom at 76. If either age is the average family norm, then I have a few more years to go! Is this time enough for me to do what's still to be done, to carry out what I still want to do, to go where I still want to go? Our dear Fil-Am choir colleague Nanay Flor is in her 80s, still going strong, singing, traveling as often as she can, and living life in the best possible way.[207] Or maybe I can live to be over a hundred years myself and become the Guinness record holder of the oldest living Filipino. But then the thought of mortality always lurks everywhere when you're old, especially when you're alone and given to thinking. Even, and much more, in this hospital room now.

I see the watch on the wall, 8:00 am. There at St. Mary's, it's time for the first-Saturday Mass for the Blessed Mother to start. I pray a petition prayer to the Lord through Mama Mary. *Lord, grant me a successful procedure and a speedy recovery.* I think of tomorrow's Mass.

The attending nurse tells me to lie supine. He covers me with a warm blanket because, he says, it's going to be chilly. Then he pokes and secures an intravenous needle into my right-hand vein. A while later, he pushes my rolling bed through a labyrinth of short hallways to another room where, he says, Dr. de la Garza will do the procedure. In the room, another nurse, a Filipina named Bella, introduces herself as in-charge of sedation and asks me a few medical questions. *(Come join the Fil-Am choir,* I am tempted to tell her.) The doctor's assistant, who introduces himself as Eusebio, comes and secures several little tubes on square pads stuck on my chest; now I am connected to the vital signs monitor where I see my heart-beat line (thanks to God, no flatline). He gets a tube connected to a green outlet on the wall and tells me to insert the two-pronged end to my nose. In the end, Eusebio tells me to lie on my left side while Bella connects the sedative to my IV.

This is it, I say to myself.

In circumstances like this, we find ourselves in every respect at the mercy and magnanimity of other people. Into their hands lie our safety and well-being. Did Bella feed me the right sedative? What if Eusebio used the wrong outlet for the wrong gas? What if anybody, by honest mistake or inefficiency, did the wrong thing for the right purpose or the right thing for the wrong purpose? Flatline! Mameng and Dimple were not about to hear my voice on their smartphones again. And I was not to direct and sing with the Fil-Am choir again. But that's stretching reality way too far. The fact is, I trusted people and never doubted they were doing their job right and well.

I lie sedated and wait. For how long, I don't know. I see Eusebio detaching the tubes and saying, "It's done." *Huh?* It's finished? Why did I sense nothing—neither the doctor nor his probing hands or any tube with built-in camera inserted into my large intestine through my bottom? There's only one way to find out: touch ground zero—hey, it's greasy all over and around my anus! I wipe the grease off under cover. The attending nurse wheels me back to my room, where my belongings wait for me. In a jiffy, I'm out of my blue robe and into my own clothes. Dr. Jaime de la Garza comes in and shows me the result: a picture of one polyp. "Benign," he says, "which I burned." Thank God! And thanks, Doc! I call my friend Nap—whose wife Maura brought me here earlier—to inform him I am ready to go home. Later, I thank the couple for their great help.

My 'cardinal procedure' is over, but Rose Bugtong has yet to explain the cardinal bit. Colonoscopy is successful. I'm unscathed, and I feel wonderful. I call Mameng's smartphone and inform her, and Dimple shouts for joy. A bowl of oatmeal with berries and apple becomes my breakfast at 10:00am. I turn my phone on and reads Fil-Am choir secretary-general Mara Ugalino's text announcement: "Choir practice tonight, 8:30pm at the Nicart's. We sing tomorrow!" I'm normal, and I'm back to normal. ∎

---

207   Nanay Flor, whose full name was Florencia B. Ropeta, passed away on Monday, Nov. 11, 2013, eight months after this piece on my colonoscopy was written.

ou know the experience. You've been under the knife, one time or another. Or you've been up there among the clouds, defying gravity thousands of feet above the ground on an airplane. Haven't you? In either case, you find yourself at the mercy and magnanimity of other people—and God.

I can remember a surgery and a procedure so far done on my person. When I was 22 years old, my parents rushed me to Ago Hospital in Old Albay, Legazpi City, because my right earlobe got so swollen as a ripe cherry tomato. The attending physician cut through the earlobe, extricating the pus and benign tumor that had formed in it. Four decades later, I underwent colonoscopy procedure that detected and removed a benign polyp inside my large intestine. I may consider myself lucky to a great extent, if only for the number of times I had surgeries or hospital procedures and their positive results. The Hippocratic oath of the medical profession covered the efficiency and propriety of those surgeries and procedures, ensuring my safety and well-being.

Or did the oath protect me for real? Despite the oath, don't doctors sometimes make mistakes and commit malpractice? This question may sound too harsh and too much, but the fact is, anyone needing surgery goes through it with total trust in humanity and God. We trust God is working to heal us through those special people. We trust God enables them to cure us.

Today, I bade goodbye to my wife and daughter in New York. I needed to return to Brownsville, in Texas, by an early morning flight. Of course, there was the usual pain of departure and separation. But two incidents made it even worse and worrisome.

Two nights earlier, my family wanted to welcome the New Year with champagne, so my daughter and I went to this wine store along Roosevelt Avenue in Woodside, New York. Amid the frigid weather, the busy humanity, blaring car horns, and the rumbling 7 Train, I smelled the powerful scent of sampaguita flowers from nowhere. What's sampaguita doing on a wintry day in busy Woodside? When later I asked, Carmela said she smelled the same.

Then last night, the first night of the New Year, I got tasked to mount three frames of Carmela's graduation pictures on our apartment wall. For no logical reason, the glasses on two of the frames broke into several pieces. To me and my wife Mameng, this did not bode well, especially that on the following morning (today) was my trip back to Texas. With our Filipino superstitious upbringings, these incidents of the preceding nights were depressing and macabre.

Presently, I am on the last leg of my trip back to Texas, from Houston to Brownsville. As the plane cruised over 30,000 feet above the ground, I sat transfixed, looking out through the window of the plane. When my first flight left New York four hours ago, it was still dark; so there was nothing much to do, giving me so much time to play with my electronic devices to pass the jitters away.

But now, in the light of day, I waxed profound. While up there, suspended in mid-air, I do nothing else but meditate—and pray. My life and that of every other passenger on this plane are altogether at the mercy and control of the pilots, their crew, and the technology at their command. We hope and pray they use it with flying colors, no pun intended. What they say, we do. Where they go, we go. They make mistake; we die! Cross my heart, and hope to d—

Oh, God, my God in whom I trust, into your hands we commend our safety and salvation. Lead the crew's human hands to bring us to safety and well-being. Through You alone leading them, we can reach our destination safe and sound.

Sure enough, before long, familiar land, trees, houses, rivers, and *resacas* appeared. At the moment, no sweeter sound can be than that of the landing gear touching the runway. Worry is a useless emotion. I should be more trustful, or trustful enough.

"No evil shall befall you, no affliction come near your tent. For he commands his angels with regard to you, to guard you wherever you go." (Ps 91:10) Aren't doctors and pilots angels too?

I turn off my phone's airplane mode. I call my wife to say I'm on the ground and my entire body intact. Not dead and euphemized by wreaths of sampaguita flowers and their scent. Not disintegrated as broken pieces of glass from two picture frames. Of course, I don't say it that way. Superstitions make us worry and shatter our faith. Trust in God amplifies our faith and brings us at peace.

Thanks, Lord, for the angels in my life. And for a wonderful life lived so far. ∎

34
REPOSE
Grief follows joy ever in a cycle

 ays before Super Typhoon Haiyan, otherwise known as Super Typhoon Yolanda, hit the Philippines, a Bicolano friend from my home province of Albay wrote a prayer on social media. "Lord, spare us Bicolanos, spare our province from the nth calamity that's Philippine-bound. Please, Lord."

Yolanda made landfall on November 8, 2013, as a Category 5 storm. It brought massive destruction to the Visayas, Philippines' central region. Haiyan/Yolanda was the most powerful storm in 2013 and one of the most powerful typhoons of all time.

"The typhoon's fury affected more than 14 million people across 44 provinces, displacing 4.1 million people, killing more than 6,000 people and leaving 1,800 missing. In addition, Typhoon Haiyan damaged 1.1 million houses, destroyed 33 million coconut trees (a major source of livelihoods), and disrupted the livelihoods of 5.9 million workers. Overall damage is estimated at $5.8 billion."[208]

Another friend, Eli Nicart, who comes from the Visayas, is distraught and writes on Facebook:

> **My heart aches and my stomach is churning after hearing and watching the news about the devastation that super typhoon Haiyan did to my home province in the Philippines...**

Tsk, tsk, tsk.

Myself an Albayano, I am most thankful that God spared my province, loved ones, relatives, and friends from undue sufferings wrought by Mother Nature. Who knows what might have been, had Haiyan/Yolanda

---

208   World Vision, "2013 Typhoon Haiyan: Facts, FAQs, and how to help," https://www.worldvision.org/disaster-relief-news-stories/2013-typhoon-haiyan-facts.

chosen to pass over Albay and not Visayas. But then a particular depression of the soul came upon me. I could not keep myself from thinking these "bad" yet profound thoughts:

- Does God love the Albayanos more and love the Visayans less?

- If we prayed to God so that Yolanda changed course, and thus spared us, were we asking to have destruction and devastation come upon other people instead, not us?

- Other global people admire the Filipinos for our resilience in the wake of countless calamities. *Pero mas gugustuhin ko pang sa kanila na lang ang resilience, huwag lang tayong dumanas at daanan ng katakot-takot na kalamidad!* [However, they may have all the resilience they want, just spare us from these horrifying calamities!] And last but not least,

- Why are we getting these calamities in the first place?

Lord, I'm sorry for harboring these thoughts at all, but I am just human, with a limited wisdom and mind that is curious and needing answers. These questions depress my soul.

Thank God, Manoy Apen (Serafin Gaor Escarilla), a friend on social media whom I respect so much for his practical wisdom, gives me the proverbial slap on the face. "It is really hard to fathom the will of our Lord, the mystery behind it. Only HE knew why."

And finally, Fr. Jerry Orbos has these words to say: "Yolanda has come and gone, and has left so much destruction and suffering in its wake. How fragile is our life, how temporary are our earthly dwellings and how small our worldly achievements! May we be reminded that life is short, and that death is certain."[209] ∎

In 2001, I taught Music at St. Mary's Catholic School in Brownsville, TX. There, I wrote music for one of my favorite Scripture passages from the Gospel of John. As the Music teacher, I was in charge of the school's music ministry. In that capacity, I formed a children's choir to enhance our school Masses every Friday. I was looking for liturgical children's songs for the feast of the Ascension, but unable to find anything suitable and to my liking, I made up mine. John 16:20-23 provided the inspiration outright. In it, Jesus talked of his impending death and his promise to return and be with his disciples forever thereafter.

Aptly titled **PROMISE**, the song goes this way:

> You will weep and mourn
> While the world rejoices,
> But your grief will be joy.
> You will weep and mourn
> But I'll see you again
> And your hearts will rejoice.
> And no one will take this joy away from you.
> On that day you will not question me 'bout anything.

---

209   Fr. Jerry M. Orbos, SVD, *Philippine Daily Inquirer,* Moments, *"Beyond 'Yolanda'"*, 11/9/2013. https://opinion.inquirer.net/65083/beyond-yolanda.

> You will weep and mourn
> But I'll see you again
> And your hearts will rejoice
> Then whatever you ask the Father,
> In my name, he will give you.

> *-from* LITURGICAL AND CATECHETICAL SONGS
> FOR CHILDREN, Volume 1 (unpublished)

The entire school community had to sing the song at Mass, not just the choir; so, I had to teach it to my 1st to 5th grade Music classes. One particular girl in the 2nd grade was moved to tears as her class was practicing the song. I approached her and inquired what was the matter. She said in between sniffles that she remembered her father who—I learned later—died a few months earlier. She said the song made her cry.

In 2003, Mrs. Belinda Lerma, the mother of a 4th grade boy member of the children's choir, passed away. I had a professional connection with her; she was the Math Department Head, my immediate supervisor, at Cummings Middle School during my first year of teaching in America, in 1992. She was an active member of St. Mary's parish, and St. Mary's School administrators regarded her demise as an immense loss to the school community. In keeping with this consensus, the school organized a requiem Mass in her honor. As a token of gratitude, I gave her grieving son the privilege to choose songs for her funeral Mass. He chose Carey Landry's **Hail Mary Gentle Woman** and my **Promise**.

A pattern was gradually emerging and becoming obvious. In 2012, the Fil-Am community of Brownsville mourned the death of Ms. Lourdes Victoriano, a respected Fil-Am classical singer, pianist, and music educator in South Texas. Among the songs sung by the Filipino-American choir during her requiem Mass were Sebastian Temple's **Prayer of St. Francis** and Manuel Francisco's **Hindi Kita Malilimutan** [I Will Never Forget You]. They sang **Promise**, too.

A few more funeral Masses crystallized the pattern. If not for Ascension, **Promise** was being sung as a song for the dead.

Why not? If a 2nd grader got so moved to tears by it; if a 4th grade choir member wanted it for his mother's funeral Mass; and if the Fil-Am choir saw it fit to sing to a coloratura soprano's demise—there must be something in the song that's worth the singing. ∎

December 2010 was two days short of its end. In the wee hours of December 30, I was still wide awake, pondering the sad events of the previous day. Five hours earlier, I had attended the funeral Mass for a respectable Brownsville, TX couple, who both succumbed to carbon monoxide poisoning in their sleep. The shock had not yet worn off when, in the dead of night, I received this message via Facebook chat from my friend Joel Ombao:[210]

---

210   Joel Ombao was a classmate in the elementary grades at Sipocot North Central School, Sipocot, Camarines Sur, Philippines. He finished Medicine in the Philippines, and presently resides and works in California.

> **Just to let you know Oti passed away last December 23, 2010. You may contact Mila at 714 496 935. His interment will be tomorrow at 10 AM. Just learned about it tonight, but I will be attending the service.**

Joel's message utterly shook me. Dumbfounded, I replied, "One of us down, and the clock is ticking… Oh God!"

"You sound morbid," Joel wrote back. "But you're right, the clock is ticking…. It started with the good guys… Happy New Year!"

For real, Joel? Wishing me Happy, when Otî is dead!

Otî was Jose Vicaldo.

pril 15, 1975

Dear Jose,

Eight summers of dormancy somewhat make up too wide a communication gap. They could not just make me oblivious, could they? Since another summer is on again, I need to fill that gap. Even if a hundred kilometers away, I want to recall those fond childhood and pre-adolescent days you, our friends, and I had shared. The reasons for this letter's being.

You may wonder: who is this that writes to me and calls me friend?

You called me Jun, a former classmate of yours from Grade 2 to 1st year high. We weren't classmates in Grade 1 (you being in Mrs. David's class, and I in Mrs. Agliam's). We were together, though, under Mrs. Tesorero, Mrs. Palmero, Mrs. de los Santos, Mrs. Baldoza, Miss Rañola, and Mr. Arenillo, from 1960 to 1966. I was a former resident of Sipocot, whose house was just across Main Theater, and whose father was a tailor. I now live with my family here in Daraga, a town at the southern foot of Mayon Volcano.

We moved here in 1967, after finishing my first year at the Sipocot St. John Academy. It was in Daraga where I continued and finished my secondary and college education.

I couldn't get the mailing addresses of my Sipocot acquaintances—then I remembered you. I thought it was a good move to write to you. Even if the address I wrote on the envelope was inadequate or wrong, Mr. Postman could still locate you by just looking at your name. In Sipocot, your very surname rings a resonant bell. So far, the only logical way I know, and I hope it works.

Remember me, do you? If not, I have a few other fond reminders. Help yourself.

1. On occasions, we would find ourselves dashing off after school just to bathe at the *Dakulang Salog* or at that river in Impig [Vigaan River], a distance away from Joel Ombao's house. We'd go there with other classmates or just the four of us. "Us," of course, refers to Roger Bailey, Pablito Pawaan, you, and me.

2. One day in 1965 was no ordinary day for the four of us. It was Pablito's b-day. So, at noon break, he gave us a blow-out at that *halo-halo*[211] stall beside Fang Lee's Grocery and Bakery.

3. At the end of periodic tests (usually on afternoons), we walked the stretch of dirt road leading to the bridge over the "River of No Return" under construction. Naughty schoolboys in their pre-adolescent adventures!

4. One day, Roger and I came to your house for free chicken dung for our garden in Mr. Arenillo's Horticulture. My plants were onions. What were yours?

5. Our class, I-1, won the first prize as best decorated room, Christmas 1965.

6. A day before classes reopened in January '66, Roger, you, and I walked to Mr. Arenillo's house to rehearse a number for an upcoming program. We stayed awhile at St. John's, and there we talked for hours about our Christmas vacation. You told us you had spent it in Nabua, even prided of the place as "the town of professionals."

7. Remember *Marcelino Pan Y Vino*[212] and Mr. Juan Cañezo? And Miss Agregado's sampling of immortal poetic lines. "I envy nobody, no not I / And nobody envies me."[213] Or this:

"It's not the thing you do, dear, / it's the thing you leave undone, / Which gives you a bit of heartache / At the setting of the sun."[214]

8. The four of us (we were so inseparable then) became members of our school's delegation to a Boy Scouts camping in Vigaan. Our troop took a major prize home. Do you remember what we got?

9. And finally, at the end of school year 1965-66, you topped our class, leaving behind Gilda Buangin and Arcádio Morada Jr. with the 2nd and 3rd honors, respectively.

Did I tire you with these details? Invariable friends are just as unforgettable as their shared moments, you know.

---

211   *halo-halo* [Filipino] - Tagalog for 'mixed', also spelled *haluhalo*, "a popular Filipino cold dessert which is a concoction of crushed ice, evaporated milk and various ingredients including, among others, ube, sweetened beans, coconut strips, sago, gulaman (seaweed gelatin), pinipig rice, boiled root crops in cubes, fruit slices, flan, and topped with a scoop of ice cream." Wikipedia, "Halo-halo." https://en.wikipedia.org/wiki/Halo-halo.

212   José María Sánchez-Silva, *Marcelino, pan y vino*. Grafisk (publisher), 1953. ISBN8711088192.

213   Lines from the poem "The Miller of the Dee" by Charles Mackay (1814-1889).

214   See Footnote #167, page 165.

But why have I been mentioning just you, Pablito, and Roger? Understandable—you were my best acquaintances during my stay at SJA, and my last year in Sipocot.

You must be someone great now—an engineer, a doctor, an architect, a scientist maybe. The last bit of information I guessed about you, right or wrong, was that you were studying at the University of Santo Tomas. Here is how I arrived at that guess. In October 1972, during a semestral recess, I shopped for a couple of guinea pigs at Bicol Souvenir in Legazpi City. A man who looked like your father alighted from his truck and talked to the lone saleswoman at the store. I had seen your father during school functions in Sipocot before, so I wanted to greet him, but I refrained. The man's identity got affirmed when the girl greeted him, "Mr. Vicaldo!" From my eavesdropping, I learned she was a UST coed, and she knew you. I concluded you must be in UST, too. With that prestigious school to be in, you must be someone great and distinguished now. [In fact, he finished Engineering from the University of the Philippines, not University of Santo Tomas.]

What did Roger become?

Pablito?

Me? I'm in the noble profession, my foot, holding that proverbial stick in front of my grade-five boys and girls!

See what eight years of non-communication had done? They foment and ferment memories. Then, they draw questions too unbearable to be left unanswered. Last, they create a gap which needs to be filled. Let's fill it, okay?

Good day.

-Jun

Call me desperate and stupid, but I *did* send that letter—to Jose Vicaldo, Malubago, Sipocot, Camarines Sur. Incomplete address, right? However, I wrote my return address on the envelope. The letter might have reached him, for I never received any return-to-sender mail. There was the big possibility, though, that the post-office letter sorter threw it away as routine procedure into the limbo of undeliverable letters. This is courtesy of an inept and inconsiderate *pinoy* postal service and a lazy *pinoy* mail carrier who didn't go the extra mile to help ease someone's longing.

Then in 2009, after 17 years of living in Texas, in the middle of a Music class, I got a call from California from someone who introduced himself as—

"Jose Vicaldo. Do you remember that name?"

But of course! That is one name etched in my brain. I as good as jumped for joy—at last my past was catching up with me!

There was joy and sadness in that first conversation. From him, I learned of the respective demise of Roger and Pablito. Roger was the closest friend I ever got during my elementary years, he being my neighbor just across the street from where I lived. Gradually, though, any sadness gave way to fond reminiscences. Roger's father worked in the local train station, while Pablito was a soldier's son. Maybe he became a soldier himself—I learned later he did. Oti's family owned a poultry farm in Malubago, while mine owned a tailoring shop along

San Juan Ave. The four of us were classmates in school and altogether inseparable. Where one was, the rest converged. For instance, the four of us went swimming in the Vigaan River, in our inglorious "pre-Jewish" nakedness, no exception. Pablito flaunted his private dangler as the most inglorious of the bunch in terms of size. Through our long-distance conversations, Otî and I were spontaneous in sharing these memories, about which we enjoyed talking, laughing, and reminiscing.

In the months following, we kept ourselves in constant communication. He added me as a friend on Facebook. The wires of communication between our revitalized friendship became no let-up hotlines. Through Otî, I later connected with other former classmates, Vic Baldoza, Horace Templo, and Joel Ombao. Later, we likewise came to know each other's family; he married Mila nee Velasquez, a Sipocoteña mutual classmate, while God blessed me with a Camalignon[215] whom I met in Manila. Otî raised two lovely daughters; I raised one. We expounded our respective residences, our occupations, our hobbies. Otî was into photography, while I was into writing, which I thought were pastimes of the extrovert and the introvert, respectively.

Through his artful photos on Facebook, I went along with him in spirit to his travels here and abroad. Photos of his visits to our native land Philippines and our former hometown Sipocot, Camarines Sur, in particular, always tugged at my heartstrings.

Alas, the fraternal joy was not to last. Conversations gradually became few. One day, to my silent shock, he disclosed he had a brain tumor! The revelation sounded as if it was the most natural thing to say; there was nary a tone of regret or apprehension. Wheelchair had become a necessity. His uploaded photos on Facebook showed various phases of medical treatment and surgery. OMG, I prayed, please don't cut our hotlines!

Early December 2010: My phone rang during a Christmas party in Harlingen, TX with the Dimaguiba family, my Fil-Am close friends. Otî was on the other end of the line. "How are you?" I asked. He wanted to know if I have the contact number of Rey Garcia, another mutual classmate from way back. "I'm in the hospital," he said in a light-hearted tone. I sensed something ominous. He wished me Merry Christmas.

December 23, 2010: The Salinas couple of Brownsville, TX slept to their death in their own bedroom. No, not from a brain tumor. Carbon monoxide poisoning.

December 30, 2010: In the dead of night, in the wee hours of the morning, at 12:46am Central Time, Joel relayed the sad news. "Otî passed away… December 23…."

Oh God, Oh God, please… Stop the clock from ticking!

Be still, Jun! "You sound morbid."

 o now, 2015, on Otî's 5th year anniversary, three down, one to go. Roger Bailey, Pablito Pawaan, Jose Vicaldo, Arcádio Morada, Jr. It's driving me crazy, driving the hell out of me. It started with the good guys. And the clock has been ticking.

---

215   *Camalignon* [Bikol] – a native of Camalig, Albay; of or relating to the town of Camalig, Albay, Philippines.

God bless Roger.

God bless Pablito.

God bless Otî.

And God bless me. ■

Caleb came out small in his condition but turned out big in our perception. He appeared too soon, sooner than ready, sooner than expected. His presence was brief, but he will stay. He will live in our hearts, in many people whose lives he touched, for a long, long time to come. Knowing him has become a source of food for the soul in our own spiritual journey towards God. Caleb is—was—just a baby! This is my way of expressing how he and his family, from June 15 onward, had made me and others see how to be divinely human and humanly divine.

Oh, I'm sorry, but truth is I never met Caleb in life. I only met his dad, his mom, his grandparents, his clan on June 20, during a celebration in his honor, his own funeral, at Sunset Funeral Home. But that's going too abruptly into Caleb's story. Somebody should tell his story from the beginning. And there's no person who can do the job better than his own mother, from her Facebook posts.

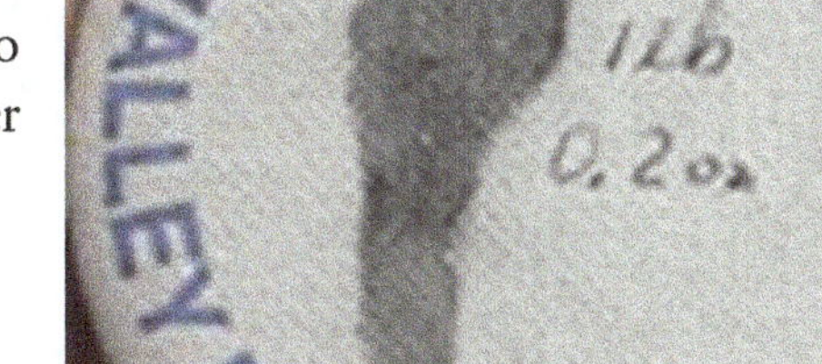

Ali Cepeda Martinez

June 15

Baby Martinez was born via emergency C-section today. Please pray for our baby. We trust that God has a plan for his life. I opened my Bible while in my hospital bed and this is the first verse that I saw. "For you have been my hope, Sovereign Lord, my confidence since my youth. From birth I have relied on you; you brought me forth from my mother's womb. I will ever praise you. I have become a sign to many; you are my strong refuge. My mouth is filled with your praise, declaring your splendor all day long." (Ps 71:5-8 NIV)

Ali Cepeda Martinez

June 16

Meet our son, Caleb Andrew Martinez. We chose to name him Caleb because it means "wholehearted" (Numbers 14:24) and Andrew means "man, warrior." Andrew was the disciple who helped his brother follow Jesus. He brought the little boy with fish and bread to Jesus, along with many other people he brought to Him by serving as a disciple.

We thought it was fitting for our little fighter, who we pray brings many people to Jesus. Please keep praying; he is so tiny.

The little fighter never had it easy. Yes, life is tough, but his fight was tougher. How could it be any easier if he, flesh and blood and organs and all combined, was just a little over 1 pound? When I was born myself, my family told me I was 6 pounds, within the normal 5 to 10. But the overwhelming love and affection of his family and people around him compensated for or even exceeded what he lacked in normal development.

And me? I am not even his parents' acquaintance, just a friend and co-worker of his grandma. Except to pray, I couldn't help in any other way. Yet I don't remember any other time when I prayed for someone I remotely knew as intensely as when I offered my prayers to God for Caleb that night.

Ali Cepeda Martinez

June 16

Update on Baby Caleb—We just found out that his doctor is arranging for him to be airlifted to Driscoll Children's Hospital in Corpus tonight. Brian will be going with him and I'll be headed over as soon as I'm discharged from VBMC. Driscoll saved my brother Daniel's life 24 years ago and his nephew is a fighter, too. Please pray for peace and guidance for everyone involved. "I prayed for this child, and the Lord has granted me what I asked of him. So now I give him to the Lord. For his whole life he will be given to the Lord." (1 Sm 1:27-28 NIV)

Ali Cepeda Martinez

June 16

Another update on Baby Caleb. The team from Driscoll came and evaluated his condition. They feel it would be unsafe to transport him without being able to monitor his blood pressure. (The goal is to be able to monitor his BP by performing a surgery to open an artery in his arm.) Caleb's doctor is fighting hard for our sweet son. He will try to put in a temporary line to hold him over until he can get the surgeon. Please pray for his doctors and nurses, and for wisdom in this situation. Please also pray that they can find a blood vessel that they can use to monitor his BP. (Here's picture of Caleb's daddy reading "Prayers for Boys" to him.)

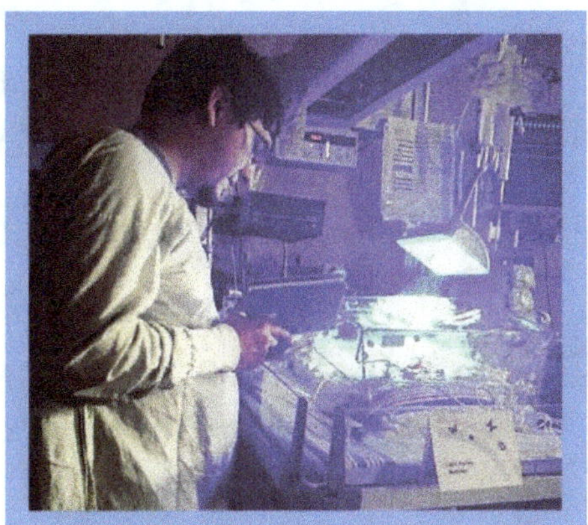

Ali Cepeda Martinez

June 17

Please pray for our sweet baby. Our doctor is fighting so hard and has said that Caleb is a fighter, too. Our doctor is still fighting, but they are running out of options. Please just pray. We know that God is in control.

Baby Caleb's travails continued. The difficulties persisted.

Ali Cepeda Martinez

June 17

Both doctors came to evaluate his case. They're concerned enough to not perform the surgery. They'll monitor and evaluate his kidney function for the next 3-4 hours. We may have to make some even tougher decisions soon. Please pray for God's peace for everyone involved in whatever is to come. He looks just like his daddy, except he has my nose. Our sweet Caleb is so beautiful.

The ordeal went on, but not for long. "God doesn't work on our timetable. He has a plan that He will execute perfectly and for the highest, greatest good of all, and for His ultimate glory."-Charles R. Swindoll

Ali Cepeda Martinez

June 17

We were able to hold our sweet baby, Caleb Andrew Martinez, this morning. He was sleeping in our arms when he opened his eyes in Heaven. He lived outside of me for 42 hours and he fought for every single second. We are so thankful to all of you who have heard about our sweet boy and have prayed so fervently for him. Everyone who cared for Caleb at VBMC with such gentleness and love for him; for that we are also thankful. We pray that our son's life will serve as a reminder to all who hear of God's love and faithfulness, even through the most difficult of circumstances. His name means "wholehearted servant of God" and we pray that many will follow Jesus through our son's legacy. We will always thank God for blessing us with our precious son and will forever praise Him for both the 23 weeks and 42 hours that Caleb was with us. I am convinced that neither death nor life, neither angels nor demons, neither the present nor the future, nor any powers, neither height nor depth, nor anything else in all creation, will be able to separate us from the love of God that is in Christ Jesus our Lord. (Rom 8:38-39NIV).

I read the sad news, and I slumped in a chair. Then guilt enveloped me. Look, I scolded myself. Not a tinge of heartache despite such loss, only praise and thanksgiving in the mother's words! Don't you see such trust in God as the family manifests? To grieve is human, but to transcend grief into something positive is humanly divine. Or divinely human.

Ali Cepeda Martinez

Yesterday

In our hearts, you all are forever a part of Caleb's Story. The day we found out we were expecting Caleb and each day since, our prayer has been that our child would serve God every day of his life. We never imagined that his life would be so short, but we don't want his story to end. We hope he touched your life such that, ultimately, you will come to realize or reaffirm that this hope we are clinging to is not just a coping mechanism. God is real and His Word is true. Because of Jesus Christ, we will see our son again. Brian and I would no longer have a wish to continue living if we didn't feel God's presence sustaining us as we try to heal, one breath at a time.

We will be having a celebration to honor Caleb's life on Friday, June 20 at 1:00 pm at Sunset Funeral Home in Brownsville, TX. A private interment in San Benito, TX will follow.

Life is here for a reason. "I will not die an unlived life. I will not live in fear of falling or catching fire. I choose to inhabit my days, to allow my living to open me, to make me less afraid, more accessible, to loosen my heart until it becomes a wing, a torch, a promise. I choose to risk my significance; to live so that which comes to me as seed goes to the next as blossom and that which comes to me as blossom, goes on as fruit."
-Dawna Markova

Baby Caleb's life on earth may have been short but remarkable, because through his family he has touched many people deeply. His mother's words overflow with so great a spiritual richness that even his short life transcends into deep and immense prayers of faith, hope, and love. Her faith in a wonderful God is so great such that it emboldens us who may not have the same to work for it. His family's love for him is so overwhelming such that we, who never had the chance to touch him in life, could not but experience his radiant warmth. The family's hope and positive outlook amidst the pain and emotional darkness of these past three days inspire and enlighten us. So touched, I thank them for letting us be a part of the family in spirit and enriching our lives.

Baby Caleb Andrew, you are like the mustard seed. So small in your condition. But you are a big fruitful tree in our perception. You are the seed planted in us to grow, blossom, and bear fruit. ■

In the spiritual scheme of things, life is everlasting. Life goes on and forward, from mortal to eternal—interrupted and dichotomized by death in the transition, and then life goes on anew. People come and go. We want to keep those we love from moving away, or at least delay their departure from mortal life. We want them with us longer, if possible. But sad to say, that's not the way life goes. The hereafter waits for everyone. Life is eternal.

Either we ourselves leave, or we witness others go. Death is the way of all flesh. A day we live is a day closer to the grave.

On June 4, 2017, a family friend, the respectable Bella Luna, lost her battle to cancer. Manang Bella and her sisters Manang Pura and Manang Lita, teachers all, have been a part of my family life, especially my daughter Carmela's childhood. From the time my batch of Filipino teachers came to Brownsville in 1992, Manang Bella and her sisters have made us feel at home, far from our homeland, by being themselves—hospitable, compassionate, caring; they hosted a welcome party for us new teachers. (See page 74.) Manang Bella would always come to my daughter's birthday parties starting when Carmela was two. When Carmen, my wife, had to leave for New York, Manang Bella and her siblings came to our house and sent her off with comforting words and "spending money" to spare. Whenever you met them—in church, in gatherings, in the mall, wherever—Manang Bella would always acknowledge your presence, and even make *beso-beso*[216] with you. She was a serious-looking but very endearing lady. Hers was a stern but wonderful life.

Manang Bella worked for a long time at Russell Elementary School in Brownsville, TX until her retirement a few years ago. Her students, their parents, and her co-workers loved her as a teacher. During her wake and funeral Mass, many of them came and expressed their sentiments about her demise. "You reap what you sow" was the common refrain from Manang Bella's life as an educator. She was strict, yes, but she cared and motivated her students to use their full potentials. She drove many of them to success.

At the funeral rites for Manang Bella, her surviving family chose the Fil-Am choir of Brownsville to do the singing. Along with known funeral "mainstays" **On Eagle's Wings** (Michael Joncas), **Here I am, Lord** (Dan Schutte), **Huwag Kang Mangamba** and **Hindi Kita Malilimutan** (Manuel Francisco, SJ), the choir sang **Promise.** I sang with the choir, too. When the family asked me to be a pallbearer, I said yes without hesitation. If only I could do something more, I—on behalf of my wife and daughter who were at the time in New York—would gladly volunteer. It's the least thing I could do for a wonderful person who Manang Bella was.

---

216   *beso-beso* [Filipino] – the practice or form of greeting family, friend or acquaintance by kissing the cheek (and oftentimes the other cheek too); cheek-to-cheek kiss.

Her interment fell on June 13, 2017. That night, the moon was yellow and waning gibbous. But the moon was beautiful. Bella Luna. ∎

The first time I met Manang Ray was in 1992, the year 25 Filipino educators, including me, arrived in the Rio Grande Valley from the Philippines. She exuded life, vitality, eagerness, enthusiasm, curiosity, openheartedness, humility, comeliness, and grace, everything in one worldly pack. Newbies in America, most of us found teaching posts in Brownsville, TX, where she was a Math teacher herself. Manang Ray and her husband, Manong Ros (see page 73), were among the few compatriots who took it upon themselves to welcome us in the name of *bayanihan* and Filipino hospitality. Knowing that we were undergoing a stage of culture shock and homesickness, the couple invited us to a party at their home.

Between the two, Manang Ray was more outgoing and outspoken than Manong Ros, who mostly kept to himself. But among my first impressions of her was that she was a person who could touch anybody's heart, by her intrinsic simplicity and humility. She was so simple in her own natural way that some people might easily forget or disregard Manang Ray's educational capacities and qualifications. (She had a master's degree in Education, a Texas certification in Mathematics, and a license in Tax Preparation, among others.) Some people could disdain her at one moment, then realize with guilt that her childlike innocence and humble viewpoint don't make her any lesser person in God's eyes. Honestly, I had been "some people" innumerable times before, and I don't think I am ever the only one. Repeatedly, I'd realize that Manang Ray was just that—a ray of sunshine in an overcast world. She is an uncomplicated person in a complex world. She is an ever-smiling person in an angry world. She is a loving person in a love-hungry world.

That's simple, incomparable, unforgettable Manang Ray.

The last time I met her was in January 2019, my last year in Brownsville before moving residence to Woodside, NY. It happened inside the Adoration Chapel of St. Mary's Catholic Church. We had not seen each other for a couple of months now. A few weeks earlier, she got hospitalized for a particular heart condition. This time, entering the Adoration Chapel, she walked with a cane, in calculated pace but still full of life and enthusiasm. She didn't see me as she entered, but after she finished praying at the front kneeler and was about to leave, she recognized my presence and silently walked towards me. Then she extended her right hand to mine and, in a moment of cordiality, squeezed my right hand as a welcome-I-had-not-seen-you-for-a-long-time gesture. She left as gently and silently as she came.

That simple gesture of cordiality from Manang Ray I will fondly remember and treasure for the rest of my life.

I moved to New York on February 27, 2019. Getting used to life in the Big Apple took a long while. Hardly settled in, I heard the unsettling news on March 27. Raymunda Alibin, my most simple and humble compatriot, crossed over the Great Divide and met her Creator. ∎

Farewell, Friends! Your mortal images and memories, how our paths crossed and how we touched each other's lives, will stay in my heart. With your loved ones, we send you off in grief, but we'll rise from it, in Jesus' promise of eternal joy. With your love and splendid memories, we see you go.

When my time comes, when I go, I hope they sing my song **Promise**, too.

Everyone goes, sooner or later. Even Jesus, who became one of us, had to go. But he promised to come back. He made sure that his disciples understood his promise to be with them forever. He would never abandon them. They would never be orphans. They would not grieve for long.

He dies and gloriously rises back to life. But again, he has to leave, to sit at the right hand of the Father in heaven. Well, worry not, because he promised to send us his Paraclete.

He did.

He is with us forever. ∎

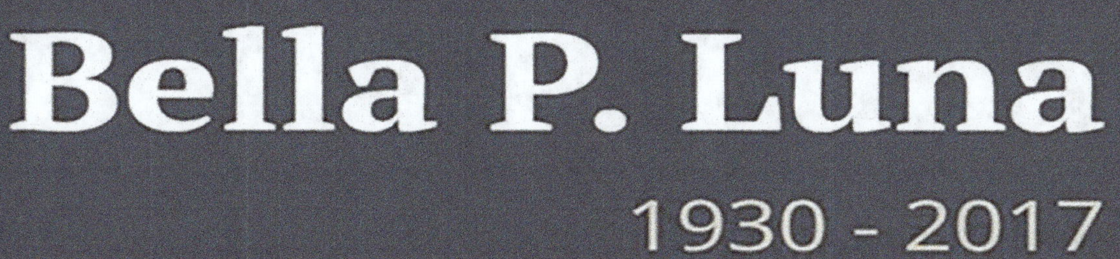

The stern but endearing Bella, well-loved by her students and colleagues, worked for a long time at Russell Elementary, Brownsville, TX.

Otî, my childhood classmate and friend, of Sipocot, Camarines Sur, Philippines, and Fullerton, CA.

Manang Ray's innate simplicity and humility, touched everybody's heart.

35
FANATICAL
A parent-parishioner raves and rants about Music

October 29, 2003

Dear Msgr. Gus[217],

The peace of Christ be with us!

Because of the delicate matter about which this letter expounds, I choose to remain incognito. I am a parishioner of St. Mary's Church and a parent of St. Mary's School. This parishioner attends church every Sunday, and I very often celebrate with our students during their Friday Mass. I therefore know whereof I speak.

This is an effort to compare the music ministry in our Sunday liturgy (10:45am Mass) and our Friday liturgy (10:10am school Mass). The parish music ministry plans and executes our Sunday liturgies, and the school's religion and music departments do the Fridays, I suppose.

Both of them are excellent, the first one serving the parish at large, and the second, serving our school community. Our Sunday musicians sound seasoned and professional. Our school musicians, students all, are a joy to watch and listen to.

If one goes to the Sunday Mass, one notices that there is a minimal connection between the readings or theme of the readings and the songs we sing. The responsorial psalm is seldom based on the psalm of the day (I read the missalette). For the past three Sundays, as an illustration, the cantor has been singing HOLY IS HIS NAME by John Michael Talbot (every choir has its favorite, I guess). Frequently, during the Communion, the choir sings meditative songs in a hurry or songs that may be classified rock and roll style, distracting people from the solemnity of that part of the Mass.

During the children's Friday Mass, on the other hand, one cannot help but be moved by the spirit by which the liturgy is celebrated. Our children's participation is enormous and inspiring. Entrance songs are really invitations to come and celebrate. Responsorial psalms are very novel and exceptional (they are

---

217   Monsignor Gustavo Barrera, pastor of Mary Mother of the Church Parish and St. Mary's Catholic School until 2007, in September of which he was assigned as pastor of Our Lady of Sorrows Parish in McAllen, Texas. He forwarded these letters to me.

composed by the school's music teacher!) and very faithful to the psalms of the day. The Communion songs are always meditative and prayerful. And the recessionals always make you feel motivated to follow God's word and attend the children's liturgy next Friday. The music is mostly based on a theme or the readings of the day.

And the music interpretation! Well, I don't know if other parents feel the way I do, but every time I join the Friday Mass, I come out of the church feeling so alive and so exhilarated. When we sing to God we pray twice, and our kids more than accomplish this by their singing and their instrumental performance. The lowly recorder—that annoying instrument your child comes home with and practices *ad nauseam*—has become a sweet music maker. Handbells (how the small kids play them is our heart's delight) are simply angelic and amazing. The xylophones, the percussion instruments, yes even the drums, add up to an atmosphere that is both solemn and inspiring, prayerful and inviting. Our Friday music ministry planners need to be congratulated for a job always well done—they more than accomplish their job!

Now, my point is, our Friday liturgy bunch of musicians needs to be seen and heard by our parishioners as well. We need, too, our Friday liturgy planners to make our Sunday Masses more thematic and vibrant. I am more than sure that if our school musicians and liturgical planners can make our Friday masses such powerful and effective celebrations, they can also make our humdrum Sunday Masses inviting and extraordinary.

This may be wishful thinking, but I don't think this is impossible. A once-a-month schedule is a good start. The parish should strike a deal with the school regarding sponsorship of Sunday Masses once every month. I'm pretty sure that St. Mary's School will be more than willing to sponsor such. Besides, it's a good way to advertise the school, isn't it?

Well, I hope my wishful thinking becomes a reality. I know I am not alone—there are many other parent-parishioners who think the way I do.

Thanks for giving time to consider this letter. And more power to you!

Yours in Christ,
A Parent-Parishioner

January 25, 2004

Dear Msgr. Gus,

Our children have made it again! And this parent and a lot more are ecstatic about it!

I am referring to our St. Mary's School students' performance during the opening mass for Catholic Schools Week today. Wow, they were so commendable! Their presence made this Mass totally different from those of the previous 2 weeks with the Parish Choir. I have been in these three liturgies, and can't help but compare and criticize—again!

If you remember, I wrote last October, though incognito, to convince you to give our school choir a chance to sing in the 10:45am Mass at least once a month. It seems, though, that I—speaking alone—was not convincing enough or that you didn't think that our children really deserved such a privilege.

To be fair to Joe/Gracie [music director and cantor, respectively, of the Parish Choir] and company, their musicianship is excellent. Only their planning is not. They seem to be contented with singing [the same songs] over and over, two or three weeks in a row, regardless of weekly theme or readings. Take the last two Sundays as examples. (Ask for their mass song lists for the past two Sundays, to verify.) To my analysis, Joe and Gracie, being professionals and busy with their respective personal jobs, cannot spend more time than they usually give to rehearsing their choir and introducing new music. And if their music ministry is *gratis et amore*—that is, no payroll involved (I'm not really sure about this), then the parish actually cannot demand more than what they are already doing.

On the other hand, there is the school choir with the accompanying children's band, which can altogether offer a fresh sound, far from the repetitiveness of our parish choir. They may not be the best sounding children's choir in town. What sets these children apart is not the quality of their voices, nor the virtuosity of their playing, but the relevance of their repertoire to the scripture readings of the day. They plan their songs, obviously, to fall under one unifying theme, governed by the readings. The responsorial psalm sung today, penned by the school music teacher, is the exact one found in the missal for January 25. (How the teacher does it, coming up with a song for every mass the school celebrates, is totally incredible but, happily for us, true.) It is creativity at its best—novel and fresh, complete with cute instrumentations of the rhythm-band kind! (You should see and hear three little girls as they played cymbals, temple blocks, and [cabasa]—a Latin American percussion instrument with a scratching sound, to accompany *One Bread One Body!*) Yes, the children also sing old songs in school liturgies now and then, but even the old mass songs they sang today (*Go Tell Everyone, One Bread One Body*) were beautiful and appreciated in the light of their adherence to the readings. The Communion songs were really meditative and prayerful, enhancing the theme and solemnity of the time. And, oh, the bells! When they played the offertory song, *Make Me a Servant*, with those bells interspersed with choir singing, the Church seemed to have transformed into a place of heaven. No compliment could be better than this!

No use complimenting, though, if I am the only soul raving. So, I am forming a group of parents-parishioners who think the same way that I do. In due time, we will express our intention openly to the Parish Board. And in due time, I will expose my identity to give flesh and blood to my ravings. In the meantime, I say: Please give our school children a chance to vivify our Sunday Mass with their beautiful music! Please make it possible.

Yours in Christ,
A Parent-Parishioner

ay 16, 2004

Dear Msgr. Gus,

So you thought I was not there. So you thought I did not see our children perform during your 25th anniversary [as a priest].

Way before the opening song (old lyrics, new upbeat melody by our Music teacher), I was there, seated among hundreds of [your] relatives, friends, and well-wishers. I imagined the boy soloist as you yourself, at the onset of puberty, heeding the Lord's call: "Then I heard the voice of the Lord, saying 'Whom shall I send? Who will go for us?'" And you answered, "'Here I am, Lord,' I said; 'Send me!'" Goosebumps were all over me; I have never seen and heard a more dramatic introduction to an entrance song! There's not a song in recent memory or in the Parish Choir's repertoire that would have been more fitting and appropriate to the occasion than that one from the book of Isaiah.

The responsorial psalm, accompanied by marimbas, recorders, and 1,001 percussion instruments, is remarkable because it is lilting and full of enthusiasm—and faithful to the psalm of the day. (On the other hand, today is the third Sunday in which the Parish Choir has sung its favorite song *Holy Is His Name*—can't they think of more appropriate songs to play and sing? Or are they just too lazy to plan something else? I suggest they could just read the psalm from the lectionary, if they are planning to sing the same song next Sunday. Please!) Anyway, on your anniversary mass, our school choir had a very novel way of expressing your mission as a priest, to *Go Out to All the World and tell the Good News!*

I think the major highlight of our school choir's repertoire that evening was **Pescador de Hombres**. We've heard and sung this old song before, but now it had more meaning and "flesh" to it. It became so new, so solemn, so meaningful, and so emotional many oldsters in the crowd were teary-eyed as they sang with the choir. That is the exact mood I expect and always witness during Communion every Friday and the few times our children have been invited to sing on Sunday. (I wish I could say this regarding our Parish Choir; all they sing at Communion are redundant recycles sung in unbecoming tempos!)

Their other songs were as remarkable. **Servant Song**, **I Am the Bread of Life**, **Happy the People You Have Chosen**, **Proclaim**!—most of these, I understand, were composed by the school's Music teacher. Remarkable, not because our school choir is a first-class choir (which it is not) but because of proper planning, relevance, and hard work. To come up with a list of appropriate and relevant songs for a celebration is a feat you can't accomplish through sloppy planning. And to execute that list satisfactorily requires hard work. Which leads me to the question: What if it were the Parish Choir that planned and sang at your 25th anniversary Mass? I hate to even think about it.

And ho- ly, ho- - ly, ho- ly is his name… (It's a melodious and meaningful song, Lord, but forgive me for hating to even think about it now! Blame it on Joe and Gracie.)

It is now 16 days after your anniversary Mass. If I were so enamored of our school choir, so ardent, so fanatical, why did it take me this long to tell you about them? Well, honestly, after the Mass, I was as much exultant as quizzical. Exultant, due to our children's A-performance. Quizzical: why, despite this being your event, did very few children attend? The children's choir used to have 40 members, but only 15 showed up that night. What used to be 4 pews of recorder players was then only 1 pew! What used to be a bunch of school musicians was then only a measly 4 individuals! What happened? You are the school boss—don't they like to share your joy on your anniversary?

And so baffled, I embarked on a little sleuthing myself. In casual interviews, I asked some students, some parents, and some teachers. Gradually, the answer emerged. The answer lies in this question: If St. Mary's can persuade and "force" its students and teachers to attend events such as Bike Rodeo, why can't it persuade them to sing and play instruments during the Boss' anniversary Mass?

Things fell into place. I have been advocating for more school choir participation (remember my October and January letters?) long enough to be heard, but it seems mine is a lost cause. No matter how good our school choir and musicians are, they seem not good enough to sing on Sundays in the school's name. Now I realize why. If this were a sports activity, the school would ardently advocate for it. But no, this is Music, a second-class subject in St. Mary's; this is Music, a sissy subject for most parents. So, with apologies to you, Msgr. Gus, very few school children came to your event.

It's a pity because it would have been a great time for some apostolic exhortations. Priesthood is a vocation, and surely during your anniversary you would talk about vocations. Definitely, you would not find it very useful to talk about vocations to a congregation of oldsters (me included). Definitely, you would want children to hear you—the more, the better. The school choir and musicians are children—and so, inviting the St. Mary's children's choir was aesthetic and apostolic at the same time. But no, this was Music time, not sports. Sorry.

My admirations for the school choir/musicians and for the efforts of the school Music teacher (you should keep that guy in your employ) won't diminish a bit. I would like to let them know that at least this parent fully appreciates their work. I will remain their No. 1 advocate, their No. 1 fan. May God bless them and enable them to keep up their good work.

And more power to you, Msgr. Whom will you ask to sing on your 50th year anniversary?

Very truly yours,
The Parent-Parishioner of [a] Lost Cause ∎

36
UNCOUTH
"We" includes everyone

istory is a wheel. It repeats, it repeats, going in patterns, moving in circles. Well, nothing profound there, absolutely nothing to cause you nosebleed. Oh, wait, I beg your pardon: because it's a wheel, history can knock you down and run the hell over you. There, the nosebleed—or worse!

Throughout my schooling, I hated repetition and memorization of facts and figures—basically what you do in History, right? This guy named George Santayana said that "[t]hose who cannot remember the past are condemned to repeat it." So, I would spend hours trying to memorize events and dates and personages to keep up my grades in order not to literally *repeat* History. History, the school subject, is a pain in the neck. I mean, the head.

Worse, whether you dig it or not, history is a shadow, the shadow we call Past. And because it's a shadow, history follows you wherever you go. It hounds and haunts you. Even while you're on vacation!

To illustrate, I zero in on the Chinese. You'll soon see why.

According to history, between 4500 and 4000 BC, agricultural progress in the Yunnan Plateau in China pressured and drove indigenous peoples to migrate to the island now known as Taiwan. Then, by around 3000 BC, with their unique language, they began migrating towards the Philippines. There you go!

Long story short, the Chinese have been a significant part of the Filipino way of life. You crave *pandesal,* then go to your friendly neighborhood Fang Lee bakery around the corner. Your Tatay needs tailoring supplies for his business, then go to your friendly neighborhood Zhang Min Haberdashery. You need to fly to Manila from your Legazpi City domain, then go book your flight via Philippine Air Lines by Lucio Tan or Cebu Pacific Air by John Gokongwei. In the crowded and humid metropolis, you cool off inside SM Megamall in Mandaluyong, Manila; this 3rd biggest shopping mall in the world is owned by Si Chì-sêng, or Henry Sy. Hope you notice that Fang, Zhang, Lucio, John, and Henry are Filipino—and Chinese!

I had taught elementary grades in Xavier School (San Juan, Manila), run by the Jesuits and populated by all-male Filipino students with Chinese ancestry. Scores of these Filipino-Chinese students have constantly emerged as prestigious, productive, and patriotic members of the Philippine society here and abroad. When I migrated to the U.S., I found out that many former students have earned their niche and success in their own fields of specialization in many parts of the world.

We perceive the prevalence, if not dominance, of the Chinese around us in whatever way, shape, or form. I am a rock if I don't feel the influence of the Chinese in my midst.

269

Meanwhile, in 2013, under the leadership of President Benigno Aquino III, the Philippines filed an arbitration case at the Permanent Court of Arbitration in The Hague (the Netherlands) against China. China had earlier been claiming that it has indisputable historical sovereignty over the entire South China Sea within its nine-dash line.

Official maps published by the Chinese government showed the nine-dash line running proximate to the Palawan group of islands and several provinces in Luzon, overlapping with the Philippines' Exclusive Economic Zone (EEZ). Through this purported nine-dash line, China has surreptitiously occupied several islands within the zone. The Philippines' stance, therefore, is that China has violated our sovereign rights under the United Nations Convention on Laws of the Sea (UNCLOS).

According to UNCLOS, an island controlled by a country is entitled to a "territorial sea" of 12 nautical miles (22 kilometers). The country likewise has the right to the island's EEZ whose resources—such as fishery stocks—it can exploit, of up to 200 nautical miles (370 kilometers).

China has long maintained that both the UNCLOS and the Permanent Court have no bearing and jurisdiction on the case. It has refused to take part in the arbitration, and insisted on various occasions that it never could acknowledge whatever verdict came forth from The Hague.

The Hague set the verdict for release on July 12, 2016.

On July 1, my family of three flew home to the Philippines. On July 9, we were on the last leg of our tour of Luzon, Philippines' main island. *We* were my wife Carmen and me, our daughter Carmela, plus our respective siblings and their spouses, 22 people in total. From Manila, we chartered two vans that took us up north to Vigan, Ilocos Sur, veering southward to Baguio City, then back to Manila. Before finally getting to our home province of Albay, we stopped for a day at Villa Escudero Resort in Tiaong, Quezon, "where Filipino history and culture come to life."

At the Villa, you see and taste Philippine country life firsthand. Among other features, you ride on a carabao-driven vehicle as a native musician plays a guitar and sings Filipino songs. A river runs through the Resort, so you enjoy a leisurely paddle on a bamboo raft on its still water. You satisfy the lure of artifacts and antiquities in the Escudero Museum, one of the largest of its kind in the Philippines. You partake of Filipino foods at the Waterfall Restaurant with the strange sensation resulting from wading in the water while you eat. And you immerse yourself in the pageantry, the pomp, and color of Filipino cultural heritage through the Resort's song-and-dance extravaganza, "Philippine Experience Show."

Towards noon on July 9, a large tourist bus full of Chinese nationals arrived at the Villa. By then we had finished eating at the Waterfall Restaurant, and while walking around the place, we learned that the cultural show was to start at 2 o'clock. Since we were a large group—22, if you remember—we went early to the venue for the first-come-first-served seats.

The venue was a large roofed pavilion that doubled as a canteen, but without walls. A few tourists had now occupied several front tables, and people were trickling and filling up the place. Our group occupied two long tables near the stage, choice seats indeed. There was a large floor space between us and the stage, so we were looking forward to a fun-filled, unobstructed viewing.

A few minutes before the show began, into the pavilion strutted the Chinese nationals. Of course, since the pavilion was now nearly full, the vacant seats left for them were not ideally located, either at the back or the far sides. We noticed two half-naked male Chinese, each with protruding tummy above tight black swimming trunk. Part of the Chinese contingent, they strode back and forth in front of us, surveying with obvious interest the big vacant space between our tables and the stage.

For a while the two Chinese disappeared from circulation, but after a few minutes came back with the manager of the place in tow. From our vantage point, we could see that the foreigners were telling the manager something, and he appeared at a loss for words. Finally, as if allowed, the Chinese walked to their posts at the back of the pavilion, then hauled their table and chairs to the vacant space in front of us!

Hey, hey, hey!

My wife Carmen stood up and complained to the manager aloud. "This can't be! This is not right!" she said in her characteristic fiery manner. My daughter Carmela stood up, too, and seconded the motion. My two feisty ladies were standing up and fighting for our rightful unobstructed place!

Shades of history being a wheel? Or a pain in the neck? Or a shadow that always follows you?

Loud oral altercations between the Chinese and my two feisty ladies ensued. The Chinese were undeterred. Carmen turned to the manager. "You have the authority to drive them away from this place!" she said. To which the bashful manager replied, *"Sinabihan ko na po, pero hindi po kami magkaintindihan!"* [I told them, but we could not understand each other!]

After which Carmen issued forth a profound tirade: *"Pilipino ka sa sarili mong bayan. Bakit mo hinahayaang apak-apakan ka ng mga banyaga?"* [You are Filipino in your own land. Why do you allow these foreigners to trample on your rights?]

The Filipinos in the audience, who were waiting for the show to start and whose attention was now upon the Filipino-Chinese commotion, collectively clapped their hands. It was the sweetest, most glorious racial sound!

Again, the manager talked to the foreigners. At last, the two Chinese hauled their table and chairs and moved away—just to the side, not to obstruct our view, but still in front!

Carmen and Carmela got appeased. Or did they?

The cultural show started with a sensational opening number. It showed through music and dance the primeval story of the first (Filipino) man and woman. How artistic!

But then the Chinese were laughing. Loud! Laughing at what? At this unique presentation of our cultural beginnings? They laughed again. They were mocking our culture!

"Shush!" (That's Carmen.)

Simultaneous with:

"Shut up!" (That's Carmela.)

Then we heard the sweetest, most glorious racial sound of clapping one more time.

The Chinese shut their mouths at last. They never so much as made a disturbing sound after that. Good, because had they made another nuisance—my wife told me later—Carmen would have overturned their table on their face!

On July 12, the Permanent Court of Arbitration in The Hague ruled in favor of the Philippines against China over the territorial disputes in the South China Sea. It ruled that China has "no historical rights" based on their "nine-dash line" map.

The Chinese had their tails between their legs? No way! It was our own President, Rodrigo Duterte, who kept his silence, tied our own hands, and coyly maintained that China is a power that should not get intimidated.

What more can I say? It's history, folks! ■

ometimes, age is not a reliable source or gauge of good manners, let alone wisdom. My wife and I were in the middle of a queue in front of the Philippine National Bank of Baguio when this old lady came along and started a commotion. The old lady wearing a thick make-up, lavish trinkets and baubles, and a flamboyant air was cutting the line. She tried to insert at the beginning of the line.

"Senior citizen *ako!* I'm a senior citizen!" she said as defiant stares met her.

"Senior citizen *din ho ang asawa ko* [My husband is a senior citizen, too]," my wife Mameng politely said, pointing at me. (OMG, was I put on the spot! Thank you, dear!)

"*Balikbayan ako, galing sa* New York, United States!" the old lady said with her nose still up in the air. "I'm a repatriate from New York, United States!"

So?

"*Galing din ho kami sa* States, *sa* Woodside, New York," Mameng said. "We came from the States, too, from Woodside, New York." I could have added, "And Brownsville, Texas."

The lady backtracked but continued grumbling yet loudly.

She never stopped grumbling, even as she was retreating down the line. So, my wife saw the need to vent her own tirade. "People who come from the U.S. know how to take turns and wait in line. In the U.S., you go to public places, and there's discipline. They show courtesy and respect for others. Not to swank, blow their trumpets, flaunt their entitlements, contemn people, and expect preferential treatment!"

The overbearing senior citizen met her match. Did I hear any more grumbling after that? ■

rarely pay any attention to friend requests on social media from people with unfamiliar names, but lately one guy's name sounded unusually unfamiliar. So, I wrote the guy a message: "Hi, Abdou. I received your friend request. However, I would like to know first why the sudden interest in me. What made you want to be friends with me? How did you come to know my Facebook account, and where are you based? Are you in any way involved in the Christian ministry? Thanks for giving time to answer these questions."

Abdou Konteh replied, "yes my friend i just see Ur timeline that's why i like to add u we can be a good an honest friend an i am Abdou. I am from the Gambia the smiling coast of west Africa an i will like for u to be my good friend as well an am i welcome?"

Me: "Most certainly! Tell me more about your ministry. Regarding me, I am involved in the music ministry of my local church, Mary Mother of the Church Parish."

AK: "an i hope that we will be good friend as well. Oh okay my friend for me i am here with my family but now i have lost my family since i am 6 years old. An i am school also before but now i am not in school my friend an i like to go back to school as well my friend. But i don't have who will responded me to go back to school. An i am here alone with my grandmother an my grandmother is a old woman now my friend. That's why i cam here for looking a friendship from people who can responded for us as well my friend. An thank u for asking my condition an i am a Muslim as well my friend an meh god bless u as well my friend. An meh god give u long life an Ur family as well okay my friend an u are welcome to read these message okay?"

I paused and sensed something cooking in Gambia, Africa. I must have radiated my hesitation. "????," Abdou wrote back. Time to quit the chat for now. But before I logged out of Facebook and shut off the computer, I wrote a message to the African.

Me: "God bless you too, Abdou!"

Five days later, at nearly 8 in the morning, my android notification blared: "okay my friend u are always welcome"

It was from the African, or whatever the entity was. I didn't even know the gender. Why bother?

Each person has inherent, inalienable dignity, I reminded myself, so let me call it "he." Past noon, **AK** followed up: "hi"

OK, I told myself, let's give him the benefit of the doubt. Let's go along for the ride.

Me: "How are u doing, Abdou?"

AK: "oh my friend i am not doing good as well here today"

Me: "Why?"

AK: "because my friend we dont have food at home to eat"

Me: "What's happening to your government? What are your leaders doing? Do they know your problems?"

AK: "oh yes my friend they no our problem bit they dont like to help us as well" / "an my friend i will need ur help as well"

Me: "In what way?"

AK: "i will like for u to send me some money through western union"

(*Biglang tumaas ang kanang kilay ko!* My right eyebrow slanted upward.)

AK: "please just try ur best for me is just any amount u can my good friend. God is the one who can pay u an for me i will here praying u as well my good friend"

Whether prudent or paranoid, my next move was to find ABDOU KONTEH's profile using the search engine on FB. In front of me flashed not one but 49 accounts with same such name, not counting the variations Abou and Konte. But the Abdou that was trying to befriend me—and asking for money via Western Union—had the profile picture of a black African child and his playmates. For friends, he had a handful of Caucasians and non-blacks with Asian or European sounding names. "Did he dupe every single one of these people?" I asked myself.

At once, I accessed my FB security settings and blocked the Gambian, or whatever he is. Call me bigot, racist, or judgmental, but I don't intend to fall victim to a potential scammer. One can't be too careful online these days.

But then, this possibility: what if he is telling the truth? What if he is a badly impoverished citizen of an impoverished African country? What if he is the man who, walking from Jerusalem to Jericho, met a band of robbers who divested him of his belongings and left him half dead? Am I being the priest, or the Levite? Am I a teacher preaching good neighborliness and yet passing up the chance to be the Good Samaritan in this poor African case?

Only God knows if I am right or wrong. Similarly, God's loving eyes see the real Abdou, whatever he is! May God help him and bless him. May God forgive me for my indiscretion, if at all. ■

omebody unfriends me, and I should have been offended, but I am not. I'm a social turtle, slow to friendship and sensitive to such negative feedback in my cyber social life. But I believe his reason to dissociate should not bother me.

My former friend is a fellow educator in Texas. We were both emigrants through the auspices of the same recruitment agency many years ago. We both underwent similar rigorous testing, preparation, and cultural orientations before coming here and immersing ourselves in the American public school system. Our respective résumés enabled us initially to work in the Rio Grande Valley, though later on greener pastures beckoned and led us to separate ways. He moved to Dallas, while I stayed put in Brownsville, TX. After several years, we met again on Facebook, and everything was going well—until my friend unfriended me.

What did I do to deserve such repudiation?

Well, more than any reason, it started when I wrote to my friend a PM. In cyber lingo, PM translates to private message:

> Hi, Habas. I hope this reaches you in your good and reasonable self, and that the friendship between us, no matter how superficial and social-media-oriented, will still prevail despite this message.
>
> Because I knew you were an educated person, I made friends with you. I made friends with you because I thought you were an excellent writer and that in you I found a kindred spirit. That's until a few weeks ago, when I discovered that *The Sunday Website of St. Louis University* is your favorite haunt. I discovered you copy things from renowned people on that website and pass them off as your own.
>
> Just a few minutes ago, I chanced upon your posts on my newsfeeds and got dismayed. Why? You copied snippets of Eleanore Stump, Gerald Darring, and Fr. John Foley (*Comfort, The Things That Hinder Us, A Long Long Time*) without mentioning them as your sources.
>
> Sometimes, in our want to be more appealing as writers, or in the presence of more splendid and profound ideas expressed by other writers, we are tempted to plagiarize. It happens. Honestly, I do likewise copy quotations from that website once in a while; experts and savants in their fields populated the site. But even if I do, as a matter of courtesy, I always mention the website or the particular writer as my source. Don't you think it's right for us to attribute intellectual works to their proper owner?

Not only once have I tried to comment on your posts. Not only once have I wanted to use sarcasm to ask you where you got your ideas. I itched to directly assail you and expose your unjust claim of others' intellectual property, but what good could that do? Not only once have I tried to tell on you to our mutual FB friends, but what good could that do?

Today was the last straw, and this time being December in the season of Advent, I felt I had to write you this message as a friendly reminder. Don't worry. No one else needs to know. That's why I chose to just PM you.

If by this honesty you see me as being arrogant and self-righteous, then I apologize for being so. If by this confrontation you get slighted and offended, then I apologize too for being an asshole to you. You can unfriend or block me, that's fine. I could take that. What I cannot take is knowing that, despite what's going on, I choose to be a silent, complacent, and plastic friend to you.

That's not being a friend in any measure.

Good day, and may the light of Christ be in us during this Advent.

I could only guess what transpired in the mind of Habas after reading my message. I remember him as a soft-spoken, music-loving family man who always fulfilled requests for vocal solo on karaoke sessions during Filipino-American gatherings, events, and parties. Over a couple of hours after sending the private message, I received this reply:

Thank you for the reminder, Mr. Morada. It was never my intent to claim those posts as my own. I am not guilty. Bless you and your family.

And in February, when I looked at my circle of FB friends, Habas was nowhere around and I could not access his website anymore. My so-called friend had unfriended me; to him I am now a *persona non grata*. Did I have it coming? Did I deserve what I got? Am I a lost cause? ◼

My next-door neighbors, the house on my left, are, to say it with compassion, uncouth. They don't own the house; they only rent it from Dodong and Jessica, engineer and nurse, a Filipino couple. A few months ago, they found a greener pasture and a larger, plushier house elsewhere. Thus, they needed renters to their former house to recoup their investment.

Back to my neighbors.

As soon as the large family came in, two or three years ago, the house that Dodong and Jessica built and maintained in fine and spic-and-span condition downgraded. My new neighbors always parked their cars—often reaching 6 vehicles—in the driveway, along the curb, and on the front lawn, balding it in due course. The children would throw their trash everywhere except in trash cans, transforming the space around the house into eyesore. Their wayward trash, of course, often found their way in my vicinity, especially when the wind blew in our direction. Expressive graffiti from paint sprays formed little by little on their front brick wall, showing over-artistic teenagers among the brood. And of late, I was mowing my part of the lawn between their house and mine, when somebody in the family opened the front door. A surge of indescribable stench came out of the house straight to my nose. The stench as good as made me swoon. No exaggerating here.

I tried to call Dodong or Jessica but didn't reach any of them; teachers, engineers, and nurses just didn't have a convenient, common time. I wanted to ask if they knew how filthy and decadent their rented house had become.

Then I recalled a story I read somewhere a long time ago. It's of an old mysterious man who lived by himself in a ramshackle house in a congested part of town. Every morning, the man so common and uninteresting in looks, would go out of his house, position himself in the same corner near the train station, and beg. Day in, day out, for 20 years.

In the meantime, his neighbors wondered. His house was filthy and decadent, and a horrible stench came forth from it. When at last they could stand the smell no more, they complained to the police, who at once came to investigate.

What the police found inside the house was beyond anybody's wildest imagination and expectation. No, not the smell, which came from rotting food and garbage. It was the sight of small bags upon small bags of money that the mysterious man had collected over the years laying strewn all over the house. On the floor, on top and under or inside furniture, in every nook and cranny, lay monetary bonanzas. The house was a treasure trove! The beggar was a rich man!

Every police in town waited with bated breath for the man to come home. When at last he arrived, they told him about the offensive smell from his house. They asked him, too, why he still needed to beg since he was a rich man. The man just went inside the house and locked the door. In the morning, he went to his post near the train station and continued to beg.

Well, we could call the man filthy, uncouth, or other terrible names, but for sure, he had what most of us rarely have—commitment. He might not have grand plans or noble dreams and expectations for himself, but he knew how to focus on what he needed to do. When he died a few years after the police discovery, he turned out to have a few relatives in another town. Lucky them—they inherited the wealth the beggar man had accumulated.

Time to learn from this. You bet the disciples could learn a thing or two from the mysterious beggar man—if they had not done so yet with Jesus' pronouncements in this Sunday's gospel reading. In part, it reads:

> As they were proceeding on their journey someone said to him, "I will follow you wherever you go." Jesus answered, "Foxes have dens and birds of the sky have nests, but the Son of Man has nowhere to rest his head." And to another he said, "Follow me." But he replied, "Lord, let me go first and bury my father." But he answered him, "Let the dead bury their dead. But you, go and proclaim the kingdom of God." And another said, "I will follow you, Lord, but first let me say farewell to my family at home." To him, Jesus said, "No one who sets a hand to the plow and looks to what was left behind is fit for the kingdom of God." (Lk 9:57-62)

When Jesus said "Follow me," he was in effect telling his disciples to spread the Good News of salvation to everyone—*with* commitment. There must not be *any* temporizing. The original disciples did their job till the end of their lives. He was passing this mission on to a new generation of disciples, and those whom he calls to such ministry will not necessarily have an easy time of it; thus, the need to focus on the job. The need to do it with one's whole heart. The need to do it with faith, with trust and confidence in God's aid and providence. The need to keep John the Baptist, the staunch proclaimer of the Word, in mind. Remember to spread the Good News with commitment. Remember to share the Good News without fear.

A tall order for everyone, but everyone's reward is great.

 t may not have yet sunk in, but we are *everyone*. "We" includes you, me, my wife Mameng, my daughter Carmela, the Chinese in our midst, the overbearing senior lady, and Abdou Konteh, the presumed African. "We" includes my uncouth neighbors who, for all we know, may be hiding their own trove of riches in Dodong and Jessica's house, waiting to be discovered. "We" even includes Habas, my copy-paste-deny friend. No surprise here, we all are the generations to whom the Good News has been told and retold. Just like the long-lost relatives of the beggar man who find themselves richer by association, we inherit the riches and blessings given to us by a loving, merciful Father God. We are heirs of God's kingdom no matter how we, one time or another, appear uncouth in men's eyes.

We are the next generations of Good Newscasters. The richness of our inheritance we bequeath upon the new generations of God's children who need to hear and know the Good News as we did. With our inheritance, with God as our portion and cup, comes a tall order—and a great responsibility, indeed. ■

37
MISCELLANEA
Some serious, sidesplitting, scampish stuff

Life is like a box of chocolates. You never know what you're gonna get."

That's his mom teaching Forrest Gump a practical lesson on life. Well, I am no fictitious Forrest, as I am a bona fide flesh and blood. But I believe she is so Solomonic in her sumptuous wisdom, especially applied to… my dogs, Valentine and Azkal! Walking the dogs is like a box of chocolates—I do not know what I'm going to get. Literally.

Or if I'm going to get anything at all. Lucky days and leaner days intertwine. Depends on whether people are too careless to mind their belongings, too rich to worry on misplaced valuables, or too organized to fidget on excess or clutter. One man's trash is another man's treasure. However, I'm no garbage scavenger, garbage collector, or trash fetishist, so I say, "One man's junk is another man's treasure." Even then, I do not walk my dogs to search for junks. I just walk *to walk* them. If I see your junk and it's for the taking, who am I to pass up the chance? But if your name and address were on your junk, bet your bottom dollar I'd be knocking at your door to put things where they should belong.

I walk my poodle and schnauzer two times a day, early in the morn before work, and late afternoon, after work. In the hundreds of times I have walked these guys around my neighborhood or beyond, I have accumulated scores of things picked up along the way. I have stooped to pick up everything worth picking up, which could be of any use.

Everything, so far, includes:

- an empty wallet for men
- another wallet for men with $100
- countless pennies
- 7 nickels
- 3 dimes
- still-usable buttons
- 6 pirated DVDs with Chinese subtitles
- 3 Tejano music CDs
- a rosary

- an orphaned gold earring
- countless caps of soda bottles with Coke Rewards[218] code
- a $5.00 bill

  and (*brace yourself)*

- 2 condoms! (Unused, unopened, untouched, in their square packets)

No, I have yet to pick up a piece of string… and I shouldn't take the cue from Guy de Maupassant even if I turned blue.

Oh, Guy was the author of the classic short story "A Piece of String," which I read a long time ago in my English Literature class in high school. It's regarding Maitre Hauchecorne, a French peasant on the road to destruction. As he went to market one day, he saw this piece of string on the road. He picked it up, by force of habit, for future use, an act seen by a malicious enemy, Maitre Malandain. It so happened that on that same day and on the same road, and around the same time, another man lost a pocketbook containing money and business papers. Malandain saw this coincidence as an opportunity to malign his enemy, so he pointed to Hauchecorne as the one who pocketed the lost. Of course, he denied it, and insisted that what he picked up was just a piece of string. Even when later, the real finder came forward to return the missing pocketbook, the psychological harm persisted. That he was a liar, that he was the rogue, that people did not believe him—these haunted Hauchecorne for the rest of his life, up to his grave. Just because of a piece of string.

The piece of string was Hauchecorne's undoing, his ruin, his destruction. Well, just for fun, and considering the list of stashed items above, what could be *my* most possible undoing?

I know what you are thinking. No, I did not find those two condoms at the same time. The first one I found on a warm summer morning just before dawn. Azkal was relieving himself on a curb near an electric lamp post when a glistening plastic, square in form, caught my eye. It was pink, with Durex trademark, and read "1 natural rubber latex." *Wow*, I said to myself, *poor boy misplacing this! And poor girl taking the risk!*

Reaching home, I took out the thingy from my pocket and tore the pink plastic packet to see the content. (To be honest, of course, I knew how it *looked* through pictures, but I wanted to see how it looked firsthand. You are green-minded if you think I wanted to find out how it *felt* firsthand by putting it on where, by tradition, you wear it!)

Anyhow, the second one I came across in the fall, just around twilight. This time, it was golden plastic, with "Lifestyles—RIBBED PLEASURE" written on the packet. What pleasure is that? Upon reaching home, I inserted the "golden lifestyle" in between the decorative fake flowers in a wicker basket on top of my coffee table in the living room. I guess I wasn't that much curious anymore about how it looked and felt after that earlier encounter with the natural rubber latex!

Meanwhile, in December, my wife Mameng came home to Texas for vacation and laparoscopy. If you are family, you know how obsessive-compulsive she is. Every corner and crevice inside the house do not stand a chance being untidy or disorganized in her presence. Thank God, the laparoscopy procedure limited her movements and activities. So, for months, *Lifestyles* stood undisturbed amid the flowers, the idiot in me forgetting I ever placed the incriminating object there. Or else it could have been my undoing! I could only imagine the inquest that could have followed, if she laid her eyes on the embodiment of the so-called ribbed pleasure!

---

218   A rewards program sponsored by Coca-Cola Co. which was phased out in 2017.

It's around 6:00 pm now. Valentine and Azkal get agitated. They can sense the time to go. OK, boys, life is like a box of chocolates. Let's find out what we're going to get this time. Or if at all. I hope not a piece of string or another condom. Let's go! ■

From afar, they lay visible, yet unrecognizable. They stood near the curb on Venice Street, a few feet from an electric lamp beside a grassy vacant lot in my neighborhood. The dark-brown rectangular object appeared leaning on top of another object, which was turning up red-and-white, as I and my dogs Valentine and Azkal approached. Since this was early Saturday, just before dawn, no cars were up and running yet, let alone people. The street was empty, except for myself and the two dogs.

As we got closer, the objects became more discernible. There they were: a 12-can box of Dr. Pepper atop a 12-can box of Coca-Cola! *Hey,* I asked myself, *what are two boxes of sodas doing in the street on an early morning like this?*

Because it had drizzled in the night, the street was damp and the boxes themselves had droplets of rain (or dew?) on their surfaces. I deduced that the boxes might have been standing there for some time now. Upon closer examination, I saw that one end of the Coke box got deformed and torn where the Dr. Pepper box was leaning; the Dr. Pepper box itself was bent in the middle. I surmised that during the night, the two boxes might have fallen undetected from a moving vehicle, landing in the current spot, one on top of the other. The impact of the fall might have caused the deformity in the Coke box; and the impact of Dr. Pepper's fall on top of the Coke might have caused Dr. Pepper's bent shape.

The moral quandary of the moment reared its head right away: Should I be a finder keeper? What should I do with these two boxes of "sinful" beverages, proven anathema to health-conscious people? (I don't have orthorexia[219], but I don't crave for soda either.) The original owner had not yet realized their loss, for nobody had come looking for them; otherwise, these boxes should not have remained in the street untouched and unclaimed until now. Or should I leave them there for others to claim?

After a moment of indecision, I hauled the boxes at last, lifting them together as one piece with extra care. The damp cartons were still strong enough to hold their respective contents intact, but for how long? I trudged on, inchmeal, because I knew that any miscalculated step could send the bunch of soda cans falling altogether back onto the street! Compounding the problem was the fact that I had Valentine and Azkal pulling on me! At normal speed, it could take us five minutes to walk the distance from that point of Venice Street to my house. This time, however, it took us over 10 minutes to reach the threshold of my house!

In Greek mythology, Pandora unleashed the evils into the world by opening the Box. In the darkness before dawn today, did I unleash any evil from my own Pandora's boxes?

What should you have done? What was the righteous way? ■

When I was much younger, from as far back as I can remember up to when I was thirty-something in the Philippines, asthma had been my constant companion and bane.

---

219   orthorexia – morbid obsession for eating healthy foods only.

Growing up as a toddler in Sipocot, Camarines Sur, in the 50s, I was a constant visitor of the town pediatrician. Tatay or Nanay went with me during those trips. Little by little, though, the pressure of their work, the frequency of my asthma attacks, and the impossibility of cure swayed my parents to rely less and less on doctors—and more and more on over-the-counter remedies such as *Asmasolon* and *Marax.*

Nights were nightmares during your bouts with asthma. You coughed, your chest felt tight, you got a shortness of breath, and you wheezed when you exhaled. To lie in bed was out of the question; otherwise, when I did, coughing became harder, wheezing louder, and chest felt tighter. As a result, I often slept while sitting with my head on a table or reclining on a rocking chair inside my mosquito net. Imagine me on the rocking chair inside the mosquito net! I did not enter school till I was 9 years old, and when I did, being absent because of sickness was often my excuse. As a result, the malady took a significant toll on my schooling.

Asthma had defined my lifestyle. Physical activities, including games and exercises, triggered asthma attacks, so I shunned sports. I was a finicky eater, because the wrong food (especially the sweet or cold) could start the asthma fire! More indulged in less-active sedentary work, I grew lanky. Family and friends considered me as a late-bloomer, and my self-esteem sank. When I could not sleep, when I sat so hapless and helpless because no *Asmasolon* or *Marax* was on hand—I was living in a dichotomous time.

My early years up to young adulthood were a time of suffering as much as a time when I learned, or taught myself how to mull, compose music, and write. They were my worst of times, but likewise my best, because of asthma. They were my primitive era, as well as my civilization. My Dark Age, as well as my Renaissance, my Golden Age.

Through the asthmatic nightmares, I suffered and endured while seated alone in the dark of nights. With only a *gasera*[220] for light, I waited for *Asmasolon* to take full effect and the wheezing and coughing to subside, counting written pages instead of sheep. But from the anguish and the tribulations came forth what I now consider my personal triumphs. Most of my poems, essays, letters, short stories, a one-act play in Filipino, two operettas, and a cantata, and other handiworks came at a great price. Or they were the price my nightmares had paid me, which otherwise I would not have gained if I did not experience them in the first place.

When I emigrated from the Philippines to these United States in 1992, and lived in Texas near the Rio Grande, I took with me a box of *Marax.* Wonder of wonders, *Asma mia* stopped! I didn't bother to know why, and I don't want to know. The fact is, for twenty-nine years now, I've had no serious bouts with my long-time friend, *Asma mia.* So, I thought I've outgrown her. The box of *Marax,* unused, was forgotten. Until tonight.

Tonight, I retired at 10 o'clock, but a shortness of breath and a tightness in my chest awakened me at around 11:30. Dreaming, I thought I was. But no, it was the nightmare of my youth beckoning! I was wheezing. My chest got tight. And I had to sit right up on my bed.

It's now 2:00 am. I'm still wide-eyed as an owl. I'm coughing. Wheezing. Still unable to sleep. I am not ready for this, and no *Asmasolon* or *Marax* on hand. I'm still waiting for the asthma to subside. There's Facebook with which to while away the time; at this wee hour of the morning, I am not alone or lonely online. But I need to get some sleep.

I remember my *Marax* tablets in my trove of bric-à-brac. Hey, should I look for the long-expired tablets and swallow one? *Marax* has been waiting there for many years now! The asthma remedy of my youth may still be effective, who knows, just dormant all these years. I need to sleep. Music classroom at Villareal Elementary is beckoning. Work waits, and I need to work.

---

220   *gasera* [Bikol] – gas lamp

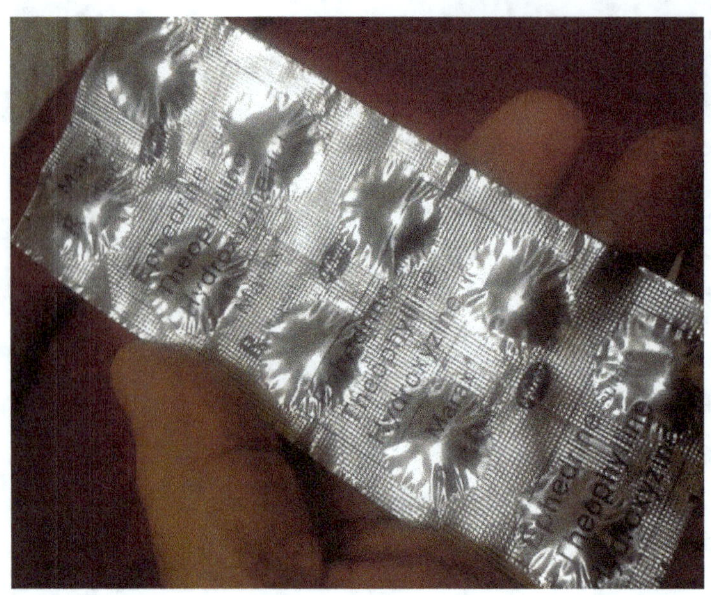

A quick Google search for *Marax* told me that the manufacture and sale of ephedrine theophylline hydroxyzine (more commonly known as *Marax*) had long been discontinued in the U.S. The Food and Drug Administration banned the use of ephedra in all medicinal preparations in response to mounting evidence of adverse effects and deaths from its use. *Huh?*

I found my box of *Marax* and yanked a pad of tablets. The five pads in the box were bought in 1992, all 50 tablets of which expired in 1994. What the heck! Desperate for immediate relief, I tore off and without hesitation gulped a tablet.

By golly, it still eased my lungs! ■

axing nostalgic, on board the Bicol Express. We go to the Legazpi City Philippine National Railways (PNR) Station at around 4:00 pm, and board the Bicol Express for its 5:00 pm departure. Thereupon it hurtles its way through the towns of Albay (Daraga, Camalig, Guinobatan, Ligao, Polangui); Camarines Sur (Bato, Nabua, Iriga, Baao, Pili, Naga, Pamplona, Libmanan, Sipocot, Lupi—*I must look for my sister Merl's and my brother Otê's house when the train passes by Colacling*—Ragay, Del Gallego); then it winds its way through Quezon and Laguna, before at last reaching Tutuban, in the heart of Manila, at around 6:00 am. The trip covers a distance of more or less 500 km, taken in around 12 hours of travel through rugged tropical terrain.

Except that I'm not taking the Bicol Express for real. It is in actuality the Amtrak Maple Leaf Train from Toronto, Canada, to New York City! That's a 12-hour trip, too, but over a distance of—take note—875 km.

Carmela and I have had our very first enjoyable Canadian vacation, courtesy of a couple of friends. Our host, Alex Mendiola, a Filipino-Canadian, drops us off at Toronto's Union Station at 7:00 am on the dot. The morning rush-hour is on, as humanity of various nationalities comes to and from the heart of Canada's biggest city by Lake Ontario—in calm, polite, and well-organized manner. Any traveler can see no such irritating hustle and bustle as they can experience in similar transportation hubs as Tutuban, Araneta Bus Port in Cubao, or even Grand Central in New York.

Carmela and I board the 2nd coach of the Maple Leaf Train waiting by Gate 16 of the terminal, as stipulated in our tickets. We find our seats by 8:10 am, but I notice my cell phone is nowhere around me! Departure time is 8:20! I panic—what is life without my cell phone? And I can imagine Mameng ranting! A train attendant is standing guard nearby, so I ask him if I can go look for my phone, which I presume I misplaced somewhere near the Amtrak ticket booth.

I run, but actually not knowing where to go. Station personnel standing by the escalator ask where I am going, and I tell them my predicament. "Is this it?" one of them says, as he shows me a cell phone in his hand. "Somebody found this and turned it in a few minutes ago. Said he found it on a bench beside the Amtrak ticket booth. There's no name on the phone, so I hoped somebody comes and asks for it. Here you are! You should be more careful about this thing. Tell you what, go to settings of your phone, and there you should write your name on display. That way it's easier to trace you back as owner in case this happens again."

This is the most welcome homily I've ever had in my life! "Oh, yes, thank you, sir!" I say, as I run back to the 2nd coach where my daughter has been waiting, as worried as I've been, for my return.

Who was the gracious finder? How did they know where and to whom to turn it in, considering the countless personnel inside the terminal? How did they know its owner took Gate 16 out of 17 gates? By now I realize this miracle can only happen through the help of my guardian angel, my guardian saints, and/or the Holy Spirit! I don't have the answers to the mystery, but for this alone, I have an ample reason for which to praise and thank God! It starts our journey on an emotional and spiritual note.

Maple Leaf leaves at 8:20 on the dot, whether every booked passenger is there. Carmela and I occupy seats with unobstructed windows in the middle of the coach. The train hurtles on its tracks in comfortable smoothness. From Port Chester, her workplace, Mameng calls my cell phone and asks where we are now, and how the trip is going. I tell her we just left Union Station a couple of minutes ago. I don't mention the surreal cell phone incident, but I describe to her how happy and satisfied we are with the amenities, comfort, and overall environment inside the train.

I tell her seating is airplane style, with spacious leg room, forward facing. We can recline our seats to a more sleep-conducive position. Luggage racks are overhead, and under the seats are spacious rooms for miscellaneous personal effects. In one bottom-seat compartment, I put my bag of groceries (which we bought earlier in Toronto so our tummies won't complain during the 12-hour trip). In the other bottom-seat compartment, I place a box of a dozen Tim Horton donuts, the gracious "pabaon" of my former student Peachie and her hubby Jun Sta. Ana. She was my student at St. Agnes' Academy in the Philippines. The couple lives in Toronto.

In the wall near the window are power outlets through which to charge our cell phones and electronic devices. Wi-fi is available once the train reaches the mainland United States, we are told. I plug in my laptop and intend to while away the time doing Facebook and other online stuff.

The train goes through the most fascinating sceneries in the American northeast. It slithers southwest to Niagara Falls, and stops at US Immigration and Border Protection Office before entering Buffalo, NY; here, border guards lead us inside a building where stern Customs officials scrutinize every passenger's passport and demand satisfactory answers to their immigration questions. After the individual interrogation, they next ask us to return to our seats, whereupon the train continues on its way due southeast, across upstate New York.

The train has a dining coach, a Café. It serves burgers, pizzas, hot dogs, wraps, sandwiches, salads, coffee, soft-drinks, and other beverages, nothing much more. For lunch, I order two pepperoni pizzas, which turn out to be 6-inches in diameter, microwaved for 3 minutes, for $6 bucks each. "Do you want something more, honey?" the white old saleslady asks. (Why are white folks so accustomed to calling you *honey* or *sweetheart*?) "No, ma'am!" I say, as the bag of groceries under our seat flashes in my mind.

Mountains covered in pine, oak, and beech come into view, as farmlands appear with barns and grazing cattle. Innumerable lakes and waterways appear near our windows as the train passes through towns with Native American Indian names.

By the time we reach Syracuse, a white woman with huge luggage comes in and positions herself in front of a black couple, who seat right across Carmela and me. The bulky luggage of the newly boarded woman occupies much of her leg room. The white conductor tells the woman to put her luggage in the baggage compartment near the entrance to the train. The woman looks at him with hostile eyes and says, "No way! The train is not even full. Why should I put it there?" Conductor says, "Then let me help you put it upon the overhead rack." The woman still declines. The conductor leaves as he shakes his head.

Another conductor, this time black and big-bellied, comes and repeats the same imperative to the woman, which she again declines to do. The black conductor is not about to go his merry way without resolving the problem, so he himself puts the enormous luggage on the overhead rack, then leaves. After which, the woman issues a mouthful behind his back. He turns around and darts back to the woman.

We are captive witnesses to this public spectacle with a racial undertone. We hold our breath as we expect a tense confrontation. The guy, however, just stops in front of her, not uttering any word, looks at her with piercing, scolding eyes, then leaves. The scene stuns us. What patience and self-control! Indeed, why use an eye for an eye and a tooth for a tooth?

Throughout this time, I have been trying to access the internet through the so-called wi-fi that the train supposedly has. But I can never open Facebook or *Inquirer.net* for my daily dose of social media and Philippine news; the sites just keep on buffering. I guess it's because so many people on board the train are online, using their laptops and their phones at the same time. It takes me forever to go online! Grudging, I decide to work offline. For want of something to do, I run Microsoft PowerPoint and Corel Photohouse, and edit pictures for school use back in Texas.

Mameng calls again, and we talk in Bikol. The white lady moves to the vacant seat in front of us. A while later, she reclines her seat, not to sleep, but to tell me I talk so loud and that I disturb her! This is in full hearing of Mameng, so she cuts our conversation short. Instead, she texts, "Just apologize, don't answer back, coz it's your fault. I'll talk to you tomorrow."

"I'm sorry!" The white woman doesn't show any sign she acknowledges my apology.

I see the black couple right across from us, taking coffee and a sandwich for lunch. Putting out my box of Tim Horton donuts, I say to the husband, "I hope you don't mind, but I saw you having coffee, and this may be an excellent combination." I show them the donuts. "You will do me a great favor if you take a few, to go with your coffee!"

The couple, who will later alight at Yonkers, partake of a donut each, although with hesitation at first. In the end, they are so thankful to me that they shake my hand and give me a gratuitous smile before disembarking later in the journey.

By the time the train runs along the bank of the Hudson, it's dark. New Yorkers say that traveling on this part of the state in the fall is such a feast for the eyes due to the changing colors of the vegetation. But it's currently July, no use crying over this missed opportunity now. The train stops at Poughkeepsie, then a few minutes later, the black couple disembark at Yonkers after smiling at us and waving goodbye. I wave back and reciprocate the smile with a smile. Before long, the Amtrak Maple Leaf Train enters the bowels of the New York subway system and stops at the Penn Station, into the heart of Manhattan. ∎

My friend Donna Belle had a not-so-proud moment the other day. I read her status post on Facebook before I drove to work. She was driving 55 on a 40-mph road, so a police officer on motorcycle apprehended her. The police officer, however, only gave her a warning, maybe after finding out that Donna Belle was a medical professional. This considerate act saved her $200, the price of a speeding ticket. As I read her post, I smiled in gratitude for her police benefactor. Then I went on my merry way to work.

Well, I did not see my own not-so-proud moment coming. Past noon, my 3rd-grade choir noticed something.

"Mr. Purple, there's a hole in your pants behind you!" said the first child.

"Huh?" At once I groped behind me, searching for the hole.

"Na na na na boo boo! We could see your underwear!" The next girl sang her taunt in jest.

I tried to cover the hole with my hand. "Too late, it's green!" said another girl, cracking up everybody.

"Wait, hold on!" a boy said. "It's a mistake—everybody knows it's always purple!" Another round of laughter.

"Boys and girls, you're having fun at my expense!"

This time, everybody laughed, including me. I had a nervous laugh. I was thinking: When I placed my denim pants into the washer last weekend, there wasn't any hole there. The over-efficient machine might have worked even more so that it made the half-inch hole in the corner of the right back pocket.

"Do you have a jacket, Mr. Purple?" said Heather Tellez, my girl Friday in the 3rd-Grade choir. "You can wrap it behind you and tie the sleeves at the front, and nobody will know there's a hole."

"Except us!" The girl, who noticed the hole first, was making a mountain out of a hole-hill!

In fact, nobody laid eyes on any underwear. I was wearing my Villareal Elementary teal spirit shirt, tucked in, and that was what showed through the hole. This was the real thing:

That's a purple underwear I was wearing! I was afraid they might discover the boy was right!

"OK, thanks, boys and girls! You're the best!" I said. "But remember, it's our secret! If everybody in school learns of this, I know who spread it."

"Our secret, Mr. Purple!"

Oh, I love you, boys and girls! I wasn't smarmy. ■

Nowadays, it may be so much more convenient and easier to mistrust people than to find goodness in them. Losing trust in people has become as commonplace and involuntary as breathing. Mistrust is so widespread we forget that goodness still exists and amazing creatures out here in our world still answer to the Christian call.

I had an experience with such a creature at Wal-Mart sometime ago. On that day, I thought of treating myself for having finished writing my Christmas program script by buying items I'd not had for a long time. Ice cream, soda, crab legs, and Texas toast topped my grocery list. After shopping and loading the groceries into the car, I shoved the shopping cart aside and drove home. It took me no time to arrange the items in my fridge and pantry, after which I slumped on the living room couch and turned the TV on to while away time.

Then my phone rang. The secretary at Villareal Elementary School was on the other end of the line.

"Mr. Purple, are you forgetting something?" she said.

"I don't think so."

"Think again!"

"Well," I said, at once becoming pensive. "I'm afraid I don't know."

"It's past 5 pm, and I am supposed to be at home," Ms. Janie Cortez said, in half-jest and half-reproach. "You are a very lucky guy! Somebody just turned in your black belt bag to the Office. You come pick it up, can you?"

I stood dumbfounded. Damn belt bag! My on-the-go mobile depository! That's where I put important, handy belongings. Driver's license, credit cards, social security card, insurance cards, passport—in short, everything that pointed to my personal identity! "How on earth…?" I said, with a mixture of wonder and embarrassment.

"Well, a lady had called earlier figuring out if there was still somebody in the Office. She said she was coming to turn in a lost belt bag. I asked the caller, 'Whose bag?' She said, 'Mr. Purple's.'"

The lady caller further told Janie that she saw a woman pick a black belt bag from one of the unattended shopping carts in the parking lot at Wal-Mart. Her presence there at that exact time was providential—it might have prevented the woman from keeping the belt bag for herself; she was to take it aside into her own car, if not for the lady caller's prompt arrival at the scene. She approached the woman. For humanitarian reasons, she suggested to the bag finder that they both looked inside the bag for any ID to trace the owner. "I know this guy," she said, after rummaging in the bag. "He is my niece's former music teacher at Villareal Elementary!"

"So, here is the bag in my Office!" Ms. Janie said. "How soon can you come to retrieve it?"

Faster than lightning, I flew to Villareal. As soon as I got hold of my belt bag, I cried well-nigh in appreciation and gratitude. Finding out that everything in the belt bag was intact, I vowed to be more careful—and never to doubt goodness in the world. ■

he airport attendant manning the X-Ray machine at Harlingen International Airport pressed the stop button. She pulled out a laptop bag and asked, "Is this yours, Sir?"

This was December. I was on my trip to New York—Harlingen to Houston, then Houston to LaGuardia Airport in New York—to bond with Mameng and Carmela during the Christmas break. My good friend and neighbor Nap Tesorero took me to Harlingen right in the afternoon of the last school day at Villareal Elementary. I thanked him, wished him and his family a Merry Christmas and a happy New Year, and waved him goodbye just before I checked in for my Southwest Airlines flight. Then the X-Ray machine…

Nodding, I was told to follow a Hispanic lady in blue airport uniform to a cubicle, where she began the proceedings by enumerating my rights and what not to do. "Don't touch. You can only look as I make the search."

What did they see on the X-Ray that triggered this search? "You have shoes in your laptop bag," she said.

"My foot!" I thought.

She ran white circular wipes on my shoes, then inserted them at this machine detector, which dinged. Right after the ding, she made a loud announcement (I didn't know to whom in particular). "Negative!"

What was she looking for in or on my shoes—traces of drugs? Traces of bomb powder? They wouldn't find any. Only *alipunga,*[221] my foot!

"What are these doing in your laptop bag?" the Hispanic lady in blue asked.

"Well, I didn't have any room for them in my checked-in luggage. They, in particular, make the whole thing suspicious?"

She didn't answer, and I was too busy fixing the things in the bag she disarranged.

Moral: Shoes and laptop bags don't mix! ■

The fish is more often caught by the mouth. And so is the Filipino. Oh, no, don't misunderstand me; this is not a racist rant. Though not a fish, I am myself a true-blue Filipino, who had lived in Texas for 27 years before moving to New York in 2019. This is just poking fun at our labial idiosyncrasies, mine included. After all, Filipinos are a happy people, and humor is inherent among us, even at our own expense. This goes without saying that since the following incidents happened for real, I have taken much care to protect identities and their privacy.

"What happened to your bff?" a Caucasian nursing-home co-worker of Ms. Kuliglig asked for her fellow *Pinay* nurse's whereabouts. "I heard she called in sick this morning."

---

221   *alipunga* [Filipino] – athlete's foot, *tinea pedis*; used here for humorous effect.

"*Shh*, not so loud…she went to the bitch," Ms. Kuliglig said in a low voice.

The co-worker gave a confused look. *"Huh?"*

"You know, to relax and unwind," Kuliglig said, still in a hushed tone. "The soft breezes and the gentle waves on a walk at the seashore have a relaxing effect. She's been over-stressed lately. So, she went to the bitch."

"Oh, I see!" the Caucasian nurse understood. Did you?

A friend got on a bus in Houston, TX, and found himself in a dire predicament. His pennies fell from his coin purse as he was rummaging for enough quarters for his fare. He exclaimed, "My pinnies!" The African-American female bus driver gaped. My friend's repeated exclamation ("OMG, my *pinnies!*") did not help bail the awkward vibes out of this situation.

Watch out for your pinnies, folks!

A newly arrived Ilocana[222] in Texas ordered Kentucky fried chicken. "What do you want to go with it?" the African-American attendant asked.

"Sows, please," the Ilocana said.

"I beg your pardon?"

"Sows, please." The Ilocana repeated her demand without batting an eye and with a hint of impatience.

"I don't…" the attendant said, but in a flash of wisdom, came back and gave the Ilocana a small container of their signature KFC dipping sauce. Maybe, just maybe, this dipping sauce will do for *sows*!

It was the last straw. The Ilocana showed her displeasure through her voice. "Just give me ketchup!"

Ah! Ketchup, not sows, coming up, ma'am!

Who can better introduce one's OFW daughter than a visiting *Nanay?* During a Fil-Am party in which the emcee asked Nanay to talk, she said, "My pamily comes prom Nobeleta, Cabite, Pilipins. We hab a bery close-knit pamily. My late husband's name is Josep. We hab tree children: Pilemon, Mon por short, an accountant; Estepania, Pan por short, a teacher; and my youngest, who is here wid you, Berginia, Bergie por short, she is a…" Bergie's friends and acquaintances drowned Nanay's sentence with their applause.

They know, *Nanay!* Bergie is a nars, and you dislike f and v.

And then:

"What do you want to eat on Christmas Eve?"

"Hum," is the straight-forward answer.

"What do you mean?"

"I want to eat hum on Christmas Eve for a change. With *queso de bola* and fruit salad besides."

Okay, then, let's eat hum and, while at it, rejoice and sing a Christmas carol. Be cautious, though, as to how to read the letters hidden by #. "D#ck #e halls wi# boughs of holly! #a la la la la la la la la!"

Ayos![223] ■

---

222   *Ilocana* [Filipino] – a female native of northwestern Luzon in the Philippines; male counterpart is Ilocano.
223   *Ayos*! [Filipino] – (expression) Good! Just fine! Alright! Oh, yeah!

38
VERNAL
They color life and make it less humdrum

*ANGKA!!!* In the urban jungle of New York sometime ago, Mameng, Carmela, and I came upon this tropical fruit tree in the Steinhardt Conservatory of the Brooklyn Botanic Garden. It was worth the collective scream!

(At first, I wanted to write "Filipino fruit tree," but googling *jackfruit* wilted away the nationalistic notion; hence, the more eclectic phrase tropical fruit tree. Why, I'll shout it out later.)

With fondness and longing, we call it *langkâ*—with that circumflex that shows the characteristic glottal stop of our native tongue.

There is nothing to be said that my *kababayan,*[224] insular or overseas, do not yet know about the langkâ of our Motherland, Philippines. For the sake of my non-Filipino friends, however, I must give info on this species

---

224   *kababayan* [Filipino] - compatriots.

without sounding vain or repetitious. Know that, *kababayan* or not, you are doing me a great favor by tolerating my indulgence in nostalgia and throwback mania. I guess one perk of aging is that you are more inclined to hark back to the hick of the past than forward to the heck of the future.

Anthropologists believe jackfruits were first cultivated in India. Grown in tropical countries in Asia, Africa, and even in the Americas, langkâ is prevalent in the Philippines but—*sigh!*—it is considered as the NATIONAL FRUIT OF BANGLADESH! (That's the shout-out.) *Huh*? Can you believe that? Can you shake that off?

Langkâ is usually yellowed (ripened) and eaten raw, but people in many parts of the world love to eat cooked green immature jackfruits as well.

As a teenager in Daraga, Albay, Philippines, I liked plants, especially the trees that grew in our small front yard. Among others, we had **lanzones** (*Lansium parasiticum*), **cacao** (*Theobroma cacao*), **chico** (*Manilkara zapota*), and **langkâ** (*Artocarpus heterophyllus*).

I loved to climb up the old langkâ tree, especially in summer when its stem and branches were sprouting with fruits. The pungent aroma of a ripening langkâ, redolent from afar, was always an irresistible invitation to particular 6-legged bugs to wreak havoc on the fruit; it was likewise an enormous temptation to the unauthorized 2-legged species to cart the fruit away when you were not looking. Ripe jackfruits are not only lavish in odor; they're sizeable, too—jackfruit trees bear the largest fruits in the world, weighing up to 80 lb. and reaching up to 3 feet long. You can never hide undetected if you are a ripe langkâ.

Each fruit has many banana-like bulbs that contain the numerous seeds and the flesh that surrounds each. Only the flesh and the seeds are edible. The ripe yellow flesh is super sweet, while the seeds taste like chestnut when roasted or boiled. The flesh is an essential ingredient in Filipino snack delicacies as *ginatan,* and *halo-halo,* among many others.

What a feast we had every time there was ripe langkâ from our front yard! The oldest among us usually took charge of cutting up the large fruit into smaller manageable segments; then the other siblings helped themselves to the yellow bulbs and gobbled them up till done or till somebody complained of stomach- or tooth-ache. In the end, it was always a chore getting the hands rid of the persistent aroma and the sticky sap that the fruit excretes. A swipe of petrol did the job.

Green immature langkâ are as sought after as the ripe. We peeled the green fruits and cut the flesh into small thin pieces before cooking. My mother would boil the pieces in coconut milk, garnish with shrimp paste, dried/smoked fish, or pork trimmings, then spice up the concoction with *siling labuyo.* Here in the U.S., I can imitate that procedure, using canned green jackfruit from Thailand. But I can come nowhere near the flavor of the fresh green langkâ that *Nanay* used to cook and serve on our dining table at home.

I'd been told that the old langkâ tree of my youth is not there anymore. Along with the cacao, lanzones, and chico, the langkâ tree had to be cut off to give way to a *sari-sari* store which my elder sister Piping built in its place. Progress crunch, economic boost. Isn't this the way of the old, preempted by change?

So, when we saw real honest-to-goodness *Artocarpus heterophyllus* at the Steinhardt Conservatory of the Brooklyn Botanic Garden, we gasped and straightaway posed for posterity with the langkâ tree in all its glory. But is this the langkâ of our Motherland, or the *kathal* of Bangladesh? Who could find fault with the excessive exclamation points of my opening word? (Look all the way to the very first word of this narrative panel.) Who could blame me if I reminisced? Hysteria taken over by historia, these words on the langkâ are the mute, solemn, and irrefutable testament of the endearment. ■

*adya na kamo, magkaranta kita!* [Come, let us sing!] Better yet, let's sing a Bikol song I composed in my youth, on the *ficus pseudopalma*, more popularly known as *lubi-lubi*. The lyrics stemmed from my experiences as a child on our farm in faraway Taloto, Camalig, Albay.

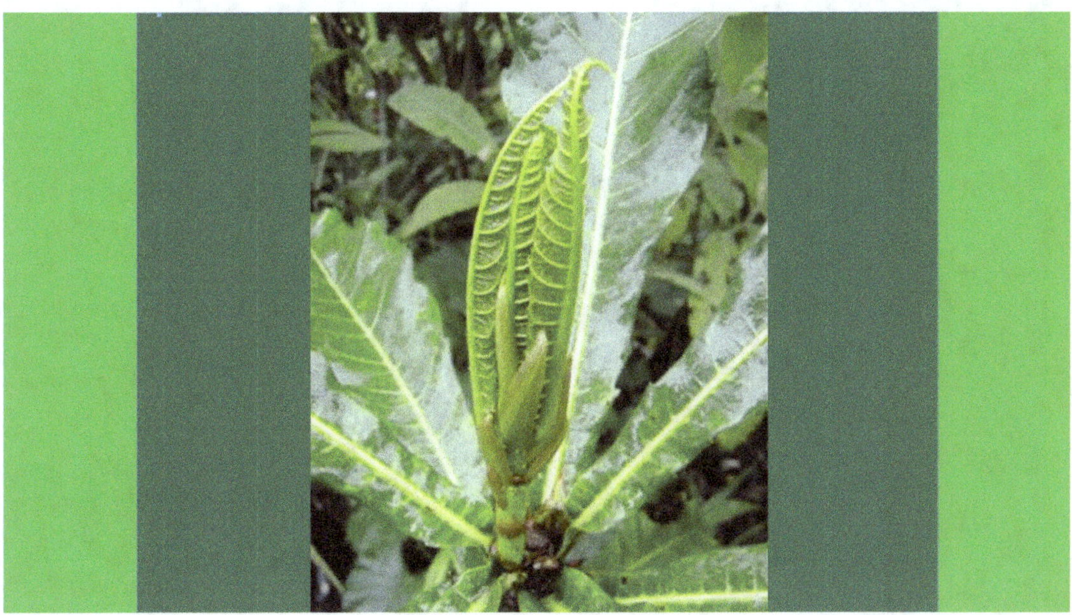

Lubi-lubi is a plant endemic to the Bicol peninsula. It lives in the wild but can be found even in urban areas, sometimes as ornamental plant. It stands like a coconut tree, and on its crown is its sought-after edible young shoots. My mother used to cook a bundle of these shoots in coconut milk garnished with shrimp paste, dried or smoked fish, or fresh-water shrimp (plenteous in the river that ran through our farm); with lubi-lubi around, you had an inexpensive but sumptuous dish!

My siblings and I usually would go into the woods and coconut groves around our *payág*[225] and return with a bagful of lubi-lubi shoots. Sometimes when a lubi-lubi's bud was still very young, we refrained from plucking it to save it for the next time around, to let it grow more mature. But the next time you came by to pick the bud, it might no longer be there; someone else with the same goal plucked it ahead of you!

That is the story narrated in the song.

Friends and acquaintances, however, conjectured I was writing and singing in metaphors for my love life. Comparing lubi-lubi to a maiden, they implied I was an admirer of this maiden from a distance, among many who desired to win her hand. They said that it was clear I did not make the right advances at the right time; another guy won the maiden for himself over me and my inaction. They said the lines *"Iba an nakinabang, siisay nakabangraw, / Nagpudo sa bulong-panunaw"* pointed to these implications.

Well, that's the beauty of a creative work; it is always open to interpretations, which may sometimes be more striking and colorful than the original meaning of the composer. A creative work is likewise open to misinterpretations. In all honesty, I wrote **Lubi-lubing Paladan** as a poem/song while I was in 6th grade going to freshman in high school in Sipocot, Camarines Sur. On the cusp of adolescence, at thirteen, I did not write adult topics from firsthand experience. With **Lubi-lubing Paladan**, I believe I was literal and still way before the threshold and throes of romantic love.

---

225   *payág* [Bikol] – a farm hut.

♪♫LUBI-LUBING PALADAN♫♪

from AKO BAGA IKOS: Songs From My Youth *by* Arcadio Morada, Jr.

1

Ako nakahiling sa dalan	Once, I saw along the footpath
Poón lubi-lubing paladan.	A blessed lubi-lubi plant.
Sakóng tinandaán ta ini babalikán	I noted its location, intending to come back
Pag-abot kan tig-orogbosan	When the bud would appear.

2

Nagka-ogbós ini, nagdahon	Soon, the bud and young leaves emerged
Sa kababantay kong haluyon.	After my long wait.
Langkág sa daghan ko, noarin pupudoón	I was eager and impatient as to when
An ogbós sakong gugulayon.	To pluck the bud for food.

3

Tará ta pagsulnóp kan mainit na aldáw,	Just as the warm sun set,
Ogbós ta nawarâ, kinua ni siisay daw.	The bud vanished, gotten by someone.
Iba an nakinabang; siisay nakabangráw,	Someone else benefited; who saw
Nagpudô sa bulong-panunaw?	And plucked digestion's cure?

4

Alagad huli ta paladan	But being blessed,
Ining lubi-lubi sa dalan,	This lubi-lubi by the footpath
Paglaom sa daghán, sa liwat tig-ogbosán:	Gives me hope for the next budding time:
Daí ko na luluya-luyahan![226]	No more weakling, I will be more alert! ∎

My foreign eyes never saw such beauty till, on my first March in America in 1993, I beheld the abundance of life and colors of spring. To think that I didn't even live in a more temperate zone in America but in the semi-tropic *tipotex*. Yet spring was gorgeous here, if not more lovely, as anywhere else in these United States. It might sound unconvincing, but never mind. In the semi-tropic *tipotex* city called Brownsville, on my 25th vernal equinox in Texas, spring gently but surely reared its head and made its mark. Here were stark signs.

GOIN' BANANAS. Time and time again, I would rarely see a standing banana tree in the aftermath of winter. (Bananas are herbs, but we are so accustomed to calling them trees the misnomer sticks.) So now that winter 2016 was past, which wasn't that cruel and wintery, my backyard was goin' bananas with three individuals flaunting their blossoms! My calculations pointed to May or June for bacchanalian days of *baduyà*[227] and *turon*.[228] Of course, mine are no match for those long and robust plantains in U.S. supermarkets imported from Guatemala, Costa Rica, or Ecuador; but I can settle for my backyard banana as they contained potassium just as well, and gratis at that. As Mameng would say in Bikol, *"Sagin sagin ka pa, batag man sana!"* [What's in a pretentious name? A banana in whatever shape or form is still *Musa!*] Whatever!

I missed the *tundan*[229] and *lakatan*[230] varieties of dessert bananas at home. They're so indigenous, for I've not found them anywhere else. I've not savored their exquisite tastes for about 20 years now! And, of course, who could not miss the *saba*[231] of home? Compared to imported U.S. plantains, *saba* is shorter; however, it remains to my tongue the most delicious cooking banana in the world.

My backyard banana trees said, "We are not your *saba*. Take us or leave us!" Of course, I took them! Otherwise, I would not have my *baduya* and *turon* bacchanalia in June!

---

226   Amoradajr, "Lubi-lubing Paladan," audio-file, 3:57min, https://soundcloud.com/amoritis/lubi-lubing-paladan.

227   *baduyà* [Bikol], or *maruyà* [Filipino] – banana splits coated with batter and fried till golden.

228   *turon* [Filipino] – banana (of the cooking variety) wrapped in eggroll wrapper and fried.

229   *tundan* (or *latundan*) [Filipino] – *Musa sapientum.*

230   *lakatan* [Filipino] - *Musa acuminata* (AA Group), most popular dessert banana in the Philippines, much more expensive than the *tundan*.

231   *saba* [Filipino] – *Musa acuminata × balbisiana* (ABB Group), cooking banana used extensively in Philippine cuisine.

❦**MANGA MANGO**. Philippine mangoes, specifically the carabao mango,[232] are so golden, aromatic, succulent, and luscious. I mean the distinctly Filipino ones, as those cultivated in Guimaras or Zambales. Without doubt, these are the sweetest mangoes in the world. At the flea market in Olmito, TX, I saw boxes upon boxes of Ataulfo mangoes being referred to as Manila mangoes and looking like real Philippine mangoes. How, for heaven's sake, they got Manila attached to their name when, in actuality, they come from Mexico, is beyond me.[233]

Mango is a tropical fruit tree, impossible to cultivate in temperate countries. But in Texas, with its semi-tropical climate, it may be welcome to grow. Well, not so welcome, because there poses an annual threat: it can get frigid in winter here, too. So, when your mango tree is infantile, the casualty rate is high.

On Christmas Eve 2004, it snowed in Brownsville. Folks say it only snows here every hundred years thereabouts! As a result, a young Philippine mango tree which I bought from the local nursery and planted in the backyard a few months back, languished in the snow. Well, not totally, because in spring a new stem grew from the part that was not "snow burned." Sad to say, in 2008, it succumbed to another bout of devastating winter.

Then in 2010, Manay Marlene Aranda gave us a foot-high mango seedling, which we planted in the backyard right away. Succeeding winters were not so harsh, so the tree thrived. By 2014, it looked as if it had gotten a greater adaptability to the annual chill.

In 2015, my mango bloomed but only had ONE fertilized flower, meaning ONE fruit. Unfortunately, even that one fertilized flower did not thrive. It left me nothing but hope.

Spring 2016 saw an incredible bounty of mango flowers. They bedecked the two-meter tree with its own flowers so that you could barely see the leaves. Yesterday I mowed my backyard lawn, whereupon I noticed so many bees a-flirting with the blooms.

[Fast forward to April, the lanky mango tree flaunted over 30 fertilized pistils. In May, little kidney-shaped mangoes with their green shiny skin posed as great temptation to be eaten raw and immature, garnished with sauteed *bagoong alamang,* but I did not oblige. By the last week of June, 21 golden, aromatic, succulent, and luscious mangoes swayed by the gentle breezes from the Gulf of Mexico. I took a video of them and forwarded it to Mameng, who said she couldn't wait to savor them. When I woke up one morning, 5 of the largest ones got plucked and stolen away in the dead of night. My prime suspect was my next-door neighbor whom I spotted sometime casting covetous eyes on my *Mangifera indica!* Well, I picked and packed the remaining 16, and hurried off to Woodside, New York. Mameng said they tasted so luscious!]

❦**GRAPE NA, FRUITS PA!** An overpowering fragrance emanated from my backyard early this morning, catching my attention as I was to walk Ash and Valentine around the neighborhood. The very sweet odor came from my lone grapefruit tree, every branch or twig of which had flowers galore from the lowest point of the foliage up to its crown. By November, most of these fragrant white blooms would become luscious ruby red grapefruits, ready to harvest.

The very amiable and kind-hearted Abel Gonzalez gave us the grapefruit seedling as a gift shortly after we had our house constructed at Pompeii Street in 2004. Less than two feet when planted, it was so well adapted to Texas weather and soil that, in less than three years, it grew up slightly taller than me and bloomed.

---

232   *carabao mango* [Filipino] – a variety of *Mangifera indica,*
233   Ataulfo mangoes are said to have originated from the Philippines, reaching Mexico through the Manila Galleon Trade of the 17th century.

It produced 6 grapefruits for the first time, and every year thenceforth, it kept adding up its bounty. In one particular year, 2015, we harvested 75 luscious ruby red grapefruits from our lone grapefruit tree! It was so astonishing to see how such a small tree could produce so many fruits! Because of the weight of the fruits, the slender branches contorted and the fruits practically touched the ground.

The hope that spring brings was nowhere more explicit than in this God-given tree in my backyard! We thanked the Lord for this abundance.

And last but not the least...

MARANGO MORINGA MALINGA MALUNGGAY—Gosh! The shoots were sprouting all over my *malunggay* tree in the backyard. My American neighbors didn't care because they knew nothing of this tree. *Moringa oleifera* in scientific circles, it has many known nomenclatures. *Drumstick tree, golden shower tree, horseradish tree, benzolive tree, kelor, marango, mlonge, moonga, nébéday, saijhan, sajna* or *Ben oil tree* are enough reasons to say it's not native to the Philippines! In fact, many countries in Asia, Central America, the Caribbean, South America, Africa, even in the Himalayan foothills, and Pacific Islands claim moringa as its home. You can't find moringa in Iceland, of course.

It is taking root in the United States—courtesy of denizens like me of tropic origin who long for the *ginataang malunggay*[234] which Nanay used to cook at home. Moringa is not only an excellent source of food. It is likewise a veritable drugstore of herbal medicines. It's not referred to as Miracle Tree for nothing: the leaves, pods, fruits, flowers, roots, and bark of the moringa tree are useful in more ways than one. And I've read somewhere that *malunggay* has seven times more vitamin C than oranges, and four times more calcium than milk; scientific studies showed *malunggay* has four times more vitamin A than carrots, three times more potassium than bananas, and two times more protein than milk. Whoa!

Say what you want, though, but I don't mind those benefits. What I hold of proximate importance is having *ginataang malunggay* mixed with squash and garnished with a couple of crabs on my table. Dinner time!

Spring comes, spring brings hope, and hope springs eternal! ∎

---

234   *ginataang malunggay* [Filipino] – moringa leaves boiled in rich coconut cream.

39
TOUCHED
How did I do?

First thing every Sunday morning, "Bow down to the Lord, splendid in holiness." (Ps 96:9a) So, I've just been to St. Mary's Church where Monsignor Gustavo Barrera called everyone in attendance "salt and light" of the world. It's not much of a presumption, I suppose, to put myself in the fold. I don't know if I deserve such inclusion, let alone Msgr. Barrera's accolade or admonition, and I pray to God I do, but these I know:

At my age, I must have touched others' lives, this way or that way, in vague, insignificant, deep, or large measure. I must have possessed a few God-given gifts that made my immediate domain and niche somewhat better, nicer, more colorful, or more wonderful in which to live. If the opposite is true, if I have made it stale, ugly, forbidding, or uninspiring with or without my knowing, then I apologize. If I have lacked compassion and charity to make my dealings with others unsatisfactory and unpalatable instead of savory and satisfying, then I apologize. With extra perseverance and caution, I will go on using my God-given gifts not for personal aggrandizement but for the good and service of others.

I have been a teacher my entire life, and will ever be so. Not just a few students throughout my teaching years have come forward to tell me, in oral or written form, how my example or a particular lesson guided or changed their lives. Of course, on these occasions, I pat my shoulders and bask on the laurels. But I caution myself, too. The best praise my students can ever give me is when they themselves continue to add flavor to the lives of others, as I might have given flavor to theirs. The best praise they can give me is when they themselves pass on to others the light that I passed on to them. We strive to not lose our flavor. We strive to not stifle our light or put it under a bushel basket. ■

Stanley Tan is a name etched in my memory, not only because he was such a well-behaved, cute, oh so adorable student in one of my Christian Life Education classes. One day, during my last year as a CLE teacher in Xavier School (Manila), the fifth-grader approached me and asked an intriguing question offhand. "Cher," he said, "why did you move to CLE from Science and Math?" Other students before him had asked this same question of their "former" Science and Math teacher. Stanley, though, was the very first and the youngest, who slammed the question—with a bomb—into my face.

So, I gave my usual answer: "Why, is there anything wrong with that?"

Stanley shrugged his shoulders and said, "Nothing, Cher. Only that Science and Math are more fun." Then the bomb: "I see you teaching CLE, I see a Pilipino teacher teaching Chinese!"

I laughed at the joke, then realized that the joke was on me.

Stanley may not remember this conversation anymore, or wonder if it ever happened at all. To this day, his postulation comes up whenever I teach. It's been both bane and boon, curse and charm, injunction and inspiration. It keeps me on my teacher's toes and always poses my eternal teacher query at day's end:

"How did I do?" ■

I remember with fondness my first-year high school English teacher, Mr. Eustaquio Arenillo, back in 1965. In 1975, I bumped into him during a seminar-workshop we both attended, held in St. Agnes' Academy of Legazpi City, where I was in my second year of teaching. After exchanging pleasantries, at once I recounted fond memories of him as the teacher who taught me the art, skill, and analytical technique of diagraming. If you know how to diagram a sentence, you know as well what part of speech is each word in that sentence, and its proper use.

"This, Sir," I said, "accounts for much of my sense of grammar!"

"*Aha*, did I at long last produce a fellow stickler!"

I smiled. "I'll take that as a compliment. Matter of fact, Sir, I regard you as a positive influence for which I will be so grateful, for the rest of my life."

"I am elated; thank you!" he said, as he held my right shoulder.

When at the end of the seminar we parted ways, I made sure he knew my belated appreciation of him through a heartfelt handshake and a hug. That was the last time we ever met. God knows I treasure that moment over four decades ago when a handshake and a hug confirmed to a former teacher his influence on my growth and development. ■

Through the years, though few and far between, I have had my share of humble glories as a teacher myself. Take the other day, for example. Facebook notified me it was Clark Alejandrino's birthday.

I greeted him, of course, more by force of FB habit than by fond association. To be honest, his name only rang a faint bell as a former student at Xavier School in the 1980s. Passaging time has rendered our connection even hazier. Bits and pieces of more recent developments on Clark, however, thrilled and made me proud of him in an enormous way. I learned of late that he earned his Ph.D. in East Asian environmental history at Georgetown University in Washington, DC not so long ago. At the time of writing, he just gained a prestigious seat as a faculty of Trinity College in Hartford, Connecticut. Still, Clark liked my dull birthday greeting. "Thank you, Mr. Morada! I can still sing your Apostles song."[235]

"Apostles" is one of those catechetical/instructional songs that I have composed through the years as a religion teacher in various Catholic schools in the Philippines and the U.S.

---

235   Arcádio Morada, Jr., *tagaalbay*, "Apostles," YouTube video, 1:36min, https://youtu.be/gJ6qFum8me4.

♪♫ **APOSTLES** ♫♪
from CATECHETICAL SONGS FOR CHILDREN *by* Arcadio Morada, Jr.

Special friends of Jesus,
A-P-O-S-T-L-E-S
Ten and two, chosen few.
A-P-O-S-T-L-E-S
Simon Peter and Andrew,
Philip and Bartholomew,
James and John and Matthew
Most of them loyal and true.
Then the others were Thomas,
James, and Jude Thaddeus,
Simon the Patriot,
Judas Iscariot.
They were all dear to Jesus.

No, Clark, thank YOU! You have made my remembrance and my teacher's perspective clearer! Without knowing it, you have just made my day. You have just given me another humble glory and a tremendous sense of fulfillment. ■

ad, you're all smiles and vibrant, as if a teenager who has just seen his crush!" my daughter Carmela said, as we walked around downtown Toronto, Canada. The weather was perfect as I strolled, oblivious of the rush-hour pedestrians and traffic. "Watch your steps, Dad! We are not in Dreamland!"

Those among us in my age bracket know this feeling. Those among us who are educators know this feeling. It is the feeling associated with hearing from former students how you were as their teacher so many years ago. It is the feeling associated with listening to them recall moments you shared with them, both bittersweet and humorous, waiting to be told.

I've just reunited with two such students right before the Toronto downtown stroll. How I love and cherish—and will do so for long years to come—talking and reminiscing with Peachie and Gina today! The last time we saw each other as teacher or students of St. Agnes' Academy (Legazpi City) was in 1978, before I left Bicol for employment in Metro Manila. Thirty-six years ago!

That is why I am "all smiles and vibrant" today.

I was their Math and/or Music teacher. Gina remembers how she loved to "May I go out, Sir!" and stayed in the school comfort room [restroom] for the next 15 minutes of my Math class! Peachie loved Music. *"Pa-Peachie-Peachie pa.* Call her Tua, Sir!" Gina taunts, from Peachie's first name Perpétua. "She's too old for Peachie!"

Tua was in my Daragang Magayon choir. "What Ever Happened to Magayon" was an operetta I composed in 1975, shown in St. Agnes' Academy in 1976. At my age, because of Facebook or progressive dementia, I am partial to everybody associated with this operetta. That explains the extra fondness for remembering Reycelle,

Jimmy, Ronald, Philip, Evelyn, Irene, Marisan, Angel, Sheila, Tessa, Tua (FB friends altogether), or any other member of the cast and choir. If given the chance, I could spend the whole day reminiscing with them!

Gina did not aspire to join the choir. "I didn't have the voice," she said. She excelled in other things. Being "pasaway" [see Footnote #49, page 27] in a somewhat joking manner was one of them. She loved to argue out of things, as in physically out of class, to escape your lesson. Math, she hated much. She'd do things with humor and carefree clumsiness. Wonder what she *did* become? An engineer!

The river of life may be shallow or deep, stony or smooth, narrow or wide, short or long, but it sure takes you to your unquestionable destiny. Gina may not incur nosebleed upon reading the foregoing platitude, but her hearty laughter surely will give a lot of meaning and dimension to it.

Gina is the happy-go-lucky kind, and Tua the sweet and refined. They still are. They both have families of their own now. Gina married a Canadian, and Tua a Filipino from Bulacan. Both appear successful as far as where the river of life has taken them. I enthuse to know what they have become!

Gina and Tua delight in seeing me too, as much as in meeting my addition, my *bitbit,* my daughter Carmela—oh, they adore her and say so! They are nosy about Carmela's status, her love life, her studies, her passion. They express their willingness to know developments in her artistic undertaking in New York.

Four hours flitted by so fast, with Tua's husband, Jun Sta. Ana, and Risa Navera-Slonim, another former Agnesian, joining the reunion over brunch at downtown Toronto's **Hot House Restaurant & Bar**. When the time to say goodbye came, we promised to keep in touch, and to see each other again in the future. They wanted to meet Mameng, my wife, too. And please, next time, could we stay reminiscing longer?

Thanks for the memory, Gina and Tua! Until next time... ∎

Angelo Benares is another student out of thousands I had had in my 14 years at Xavier School. We have been friends on social media. Once, he wrote on his Facebook timeline as he flashed a picture of Julie Andrews in her iconic movie: "Never grows old. I distinctly remember being Gretel's age when I first watched the **Sound of Music**... now I'm the age of Captain von Trapp."

ME: Not even close to how I feel, Angelo. When I first watched it and heard "the hills are alive" in 1965, I was energetic Kurt then. Now I'm older than the Mother Superior, who just sings because she's too old to "Climb Every Mountain."

ANGELO: Hahaha, will get there one day, too! Stages! I remember getting so bored with the song "Something Good"—now it's one of my favorites. ☺ Music was always a big part of your classes, Sir.

ME: Are you ready for a long rejoinder? Enjoy it or not, here is a long story. Indeed, there was music in my Xavier School classes, especially in my Christian Life Education, for which I usually composed and sang my own materials. There was a dearth of CLE audio-visual aids then, despite the LRC.[236] (I don't know if you still remember my song SACRAMENTS, or GO AWAY, SATAN—to name two of them.) Embarrassing to say, I didn't finish school as a Music teacher. I don't have any Music degree, either. Though I liked music so much that I wanted to try teaching it. *Kapal ng apog!* It so happened that in the1980s, there arose an opening for a Music teacher in Xavier grade school, in partnership with Ms. Teresita Fainsan, who was the department head. I said to myself, "Why not?" So, I insinuated to her my intent. One day, she called me aside and asked

---

236   LRC, Learning Resource Center, the Xavier School library.

me to play the piano. Somewhat embarrassed, I told her I was not an instrumentalist; I could only play the guitar. She must have raised an eyebrow. Then she asked me what method, if ever, was I to use—Kodaly or Orff? Embarrassed again, I knew nothing of those terms at that point in time. Ms. Fainsan might have raised all her eyebrows in dismay; she might have been saying, "*D'yan ka na lang sa* CLE!" [Just stay in CLE!]

I did stay in CLE for almost a decade, until 1992, when I finally left XS for the States. Here, they consider Music as lesser in importance as, say, Reading, Math, or even PE. In fact, they call Music teachers "support" staff. And you could be a Music teacher so long as you're elementary-teacher certified. My chance to penetrate the realm! To make the long story short, I've taught Music for the rest of my professional life in the States, until my retirement in May 2018! Never been happier in my entire career than when I started teaching Music! Audacious and cocky, I could have been, and I might as well have been singing "I Have Confidence" with Maria. I vowed to impress those children; in time, they will look up to me, because I have confidence in me!

There goes my autobiographical vignette. *Ha ha ha...* thanks for your indulgence and time, Angelo! ∎

he barged, making no sound, into the Music Rm at the most inopportune situation—my nap time. In an instant, I roused to a sitting position behind the teacher's desk where my head had rested on two small pillows before the intrusion. I gaped at the apparition before me, but then recognized right away who the intruder was.

Isabella!

The persnickety. Outspoken. Unabashed singer. Closest to my Music teacher's heart. Translation: my favorite singer in the choir.

Today being the last day of school, there were no Music classes, and I was not expecting anyone, not even my favorites or any other member of my choir. But here she was.

She'd been with the choir since 1ˢᵗ grade. She always got meaty solo parts in our school musical shows. At present, she was in 3ʳᵈ grade. With three such shows every year (Christmas, Texas Public Schools Week in March, and End-of-the-Year), I had given her nine solo times so far. And there was more to come.

Give her the hardest song, and she sings it without effort, like a pro. Give her an irreverent song and she sings it to a T. Make her sing any religious song and she'd do her pious best. She is gorgeous and prankish, imitative of Miley Cyrus, as much as she is serene, dainty, and graceful as the Virgin Mary. Onstage she oozes with confidence, as if it is the most natural thing for her to do and the most natural place for her to be. In short, she is a very promising singer. When she sings, I can imagine the youngish Lady Gaga, Katy Perry, or Taylor Swift.

"I have something for you!" she says, her face as vibrant as ever.

She hands me a gift bag, which she places on top of the teacher's desk, and urges me to open it right away. "It's something to write on, like a journal. And there's a card." I hesitate. "Come on, Mr. Purple!" she says. Damn shyness! She herself is not prone to shyness, and shy people, to her, are intolerable. Still somewhat uneasy, and embarrassed, for having been "caught" napping by someone, albeit during my off-period, I take the gift out of the bag little by little.

A blank book!

(So, she wants me to write. I need that. My eternal writer's block is over, thanks! Right away I write—I make the 1-inch-thick journal's first entry, of course, entitled **Isabella!** The opening line says: "June 2, 2016: If for this alone I am asked whether to rest... or resign....")

"You shouldn't have bothered," I say. I reach for the card at the bottom of the bag. "Love & Gratitude," the front page says. I turn the page, and the message blares before my eyes. *"Mr. Purple.... You are the most detirmined teacher ever! Because of that youv turned me into a confident girl I am! Thank you for everything! I love you—Isabella."*

Now, I will be a hypocrite if I say I am not touched. Such manifestation of student appreciation and gratitude may come few in a teacher's life—or at least in my range of experience. But when they do come, it's heaven. If for this alone I am asked whether to rest from burnout or retire altogether, I say I am inspired to teach further on for the rest of my life.

Love you, too, angel! Keep it up, as I keep myself alive, for I will be the very first one to buy your very first CD album. ■

he little boy waited till the last minute. This was my last day at Villareal Elementary School. Javier and the rest of the 2nd-grade class knew that I was not coming back for their Music class next year.

"Mr. Purple, good luck!" Jacqueline said.

"Happy retirement!" Samantha said, teary-eyed.

"You won't have a headache," mischievous Pedro said, "because you won't see me no more!" And just before I dismissed the class, Javier came up to me and bear-hugged me! Then he gave me a piece of paper he was holding in his hand. Unfolded, the paper outright broke my heart. ■

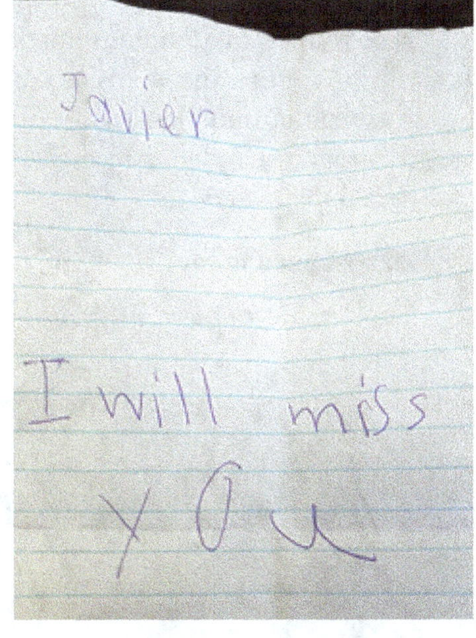

The initiators were Ashley and Dana, 4th Grade members of the **Singing Hawks**, our school choir. They had to plan and do it right under my nose, intending it to be a secret and a surprise. The initial plan was to make a card, to be autographed by all the choir members and teachers (who were willing or available to sign). A designated choir member would then hand me the finished card, poster-size, during the last day of the school year, the very last time we would be together as a family in school before my retirement.

Since choir membership was across the different grade levels, the job was gargantuan for Ashley and Dana, considering there were 60+ choir members. The two had many responsibilities as conscientious students, and they could only do this additional responsibility before the first bell, during their vacant periods, and after dismissal.

Then the girls had to choose five, on behalf of the entire choir, who are willing and brave enough to do the corny stuff. Aned, Domenick, Gilberto, Viridiana, and Aylin took the job.

Dismissal on the last day of school was at 12:00 noon. At about 11:50 am, while I was taking keepsake selfies with students in the school playground, from out of the blue Ashley and Dana came up to me and admonished that I needed to go with them. They said the Principal's Office wanted me, because somebody was looking for me. A little dismayed by the interruption, I grudgingly walked with them towards the school's back entrance. Through the glass door, I noticed the five choir members standing in the middle of the hallway with their backs to us, all still. As soon as we opened the door, they sprang into action.

Aned turned around, exposing a placard that said **We**, followed by Domenick's that had the picture of a ♥. Gilberto's turn exposed **You,** while Viridiana and Aylin had the words **Mr Purple** after their consecutive turns.

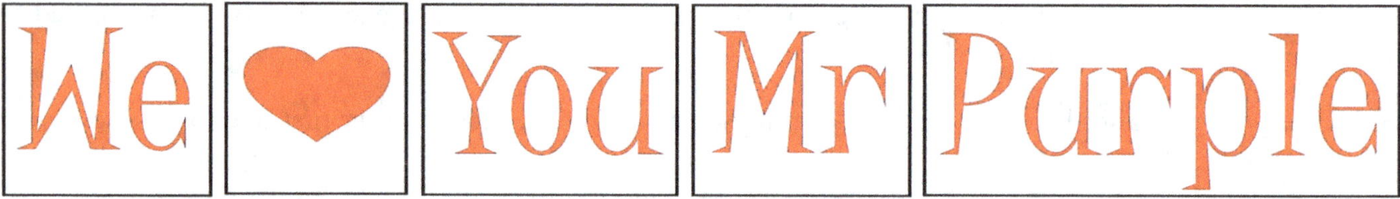

Then the five altogether ran toward me and hugged me. Along with Ashley and Dana's, seven pairs of arms were enfolding me all at once!

The whole situation flummoxed and overwhelmed me. My first reaction was to cringe at the corniness of it all. I realized that the words or the message might have been simple, or worse childish, but it now struck me as heartwarming and memorable. The poster-size card materialized from out of the blue, and someone (I could not recall who) handed it to me. All I was conscious of was saying, "I love you, too, guys! You're awesome! You're making me cry!"

Tears welled in my eyes. I said to myself, "I will remember this, and you guys, for the rest of my life!"[237] ∎

<u>Mr. Purple</u>

A teacher takes a hand opens a mind and changes a heart. Thank you for believing in me and making a difference.
Ava Herrera

---

237   Arcádio Morada, Jr., *tagaalbay*, "Last Day," YouTube video, 17:37min, https://youtu.be/KRYCFC5UJgI.

40
REVERSALS
Full circles and changes in the offing

re you into poems? Many people are, and it's OK if you are not, because poetry is its own language, sometimes intemperate, often incoherent, most of the time alien. I was myself lured into poetry way back in high school, courtesy of my English teachers. I dabbled in poetry as self-expression.

One of my early poems, shown below in its entirety, is a poem entitled **Poem**. Redundant, *duh*, but who cares? In it, I tried to define what, to me, is a poem.

> *A paradox*
> *A skeleton of words with flesh of feelings,*
> *and fibers full of enlivening bloodstreams*
> *A poem is a skeleton*
> *with flesh and blood.*

A further random check at my trove of unpublished poetry came up with the following quatrains from my youth with no rhyming scheme. Uninteresting... but wait! As I was reading the entire poem now as an adult with supposedly more learning and experience, I could only blush with embarrassment and glee. In a fit of adolescent humor, more in keeping with my little understanding of the meter in poetry, I wrote these quatrains half a century ago.

The quatrains in question are of a poem entitled **Changes**, written in 1972, which was a significant year on various levels. The Watergate scandal, the terrorist attack at the Munich Olympics, the imposition of martial law in the Philippines—these were among the many big and noteworthy events of that year. On a personal level, that year my sophomore self was languishing in the Bicol University College of Education, taking up a course for which I had supposedly no affection or calling. Why I was there at all is a long story by itself (which I've taken great pains to describe and rationalize in **Diaspora**, page 29). However, it was likewise the year I realized I wanted to write—and that, by several indications, I could write. Something rekindled the flare of writing prose or poetry, first nurtured in high school. Of course, the flair for writing might not have been necessarily there. And I will not be any presumptuous as to say I was, at that point, already a *writer* in its genuine sense.

Which brings us back to **Changes**. The mood of this poem begins lightheartedly and ends darkly—with an expletive at that. Fifty years ago, the world was young and so was I. Using non-rhymes and pseudo-rhymes, I wove adolescent angst in this poem of 5 stanzas. The first and third lines contain 8 syllables, while the second and fourth lines, 6. I must have enjoyed writing it, let alone learning how to apply the 8-and-6-meter scheme.

From my vantage point of 71 years, I look at it with a smile on my face. I am satisfied. This little poem or its author may not have amounted to something big, but I view it now with pride for myself just as well.

1

Upon a rock, beside a creek,
I fondly set my throne;
The humming birds, the murm'ring stream
just filled my heart with joy.

2

So jocund still, I chimed a song
that filled the atmosphere.
It seemed the birds, the stream, the air
all wanted me to sing.

3

But, O my fate! Large clouds so dark
had gathered up above.
The atmosphere of jollity
in gloom was left to stay.

4

Then songs to sigh, not songs to try,
became a part of me.
Love birds I knew now sang regrets
of their forsaken love.

5

The murm'ring stream—O wretched stream—
now stunned by flooding roar.
Beneath the shade, I cried, "All things
are like the weather—*Damn!*"

There was this rich man who lived a life of luxury, "dressed in purple garments and fine linen and dined sumptuously each day." Outside the door of this rich man's house was a poor leper named Lazarus who waited every day hoping to eat "the scraps that fell from the rich man's table" but to whom the rich man showed no compassion at all.

But fortunes come, and fortunes go. Lazarus died, and in time, so did the rich man. Lazarus went to heaven, while the rich man went to hell.

What a reversal of fortunes!

From the netherworld, the rich man saw Lazarus occupying a special place beside Father Abraham in heaven. In his agony, the rich man cried out to Abraham to please send Lazarus with a drop of water to cool his tongue and lessen his "torment in these flames." Abraham said no. Then, the rich man asked Abraham to at least send Lazarus back to earth to warn his brothers to repent so as not to join with him in hell. Again, Abraham said no. "If they will not listen to Moses and the prophets, neither will they be persuaded if someone should rise from the dead." (Lk 16:19-31)

Damn! ◼

Ican't recall who first thought of the getaway. After four decades, I am not even sure of the exact date. Maybe my fun-loving colleagues at Xavier School conceived and cooked it up in March 1980, just before the school year ended. Somebody must have said, "Let's go to Bicol!" Or something to that effect. And I might have said, "W-w-why not?" Or something to that effect. So, at the start of Xavier summer break in April 1980, off dashed Osang Angeles, Mel Valdez, Alice Ignacio, Cleo Perez, Oli Carluen, and Ophie Rey to Bicol. The collective intent? To spend a 5-day vacation with my family and me!

Mel, Oli, Ophie, and Osang, with Neil (Mel's niece), were to take the bus, while Cleo and Alice, the train. Whether by bus or train, going to Bicol was a 10-to-15-hour affair. As a Bicolano myself, I had taken these means of transport at least once a month. For them, though, it was a novel idea: it was to be their first-time long trip to Southern Luzon via Pantranco bus or the Bicol Express!

Their vacation destination was First Park, Daraga, Albay. Wait, that name sounds foreign. I should fool no one.

First Park is a first-class subdivision in my hometown of Daraga. No, we weren't *in* the subdivision. My residence was *along* the outskirts of the subdivision, in a misnomer of a place called Mapiña.

I might have worried somehow. Why and how had anyone talked me into agreeing to be host to this summer getaway? I had little to offer. First, my family didn't own a more presentable place in which to stay. Second, my family didn't own any guesthouse or exotic haven with amenities that could satisfy my guests' tastes and cravings for balmy rest and relaxation. I mean, our house in Mapiña was OK to my family, for we'd known hardships and poverty as far back as I could remember. But it was a whole different story, with city-bred ladies billeted in our house! It might humiliate—and embarrass—them.

Our semi-concrete house, which started building up in the early 1970s, was forever unfinished. Tatay was a tailor who had known better days. With business plummeting in Sipocot, Camarines Sur, where he had established a tailoring shop, my family had to move to Mapiña in 1967. Misfortune struck again when a fire broke in the neighborhood, starting from our next-door neighbor's house; it turned our less-than-a-month-old house and most of our belongings, including my father's tailoring paraphernalia, to ashes. Although I was contributory to my family's finances because of my employment in Xavier School since 1978, I had two other siblings in college; so, leaner days were upon us and hardships beckoned harder than ever. That was why the semi-concrete house, with its foundations laid a decade ago, was still a work in progress and had no finishing touches sooner in sight. This was the context facing my lady guests, and it was unflattering.

Our house wasn't anything to drool about, much less vaunt.

(Tatay, Nanay, and our house)

But they had been insistent and excited. So, *halá, sige!* [238]

I forewarned my parents and siblings about our guests. They asked, "What should we do? What are the things to prepare? Are they *delikada?*" [239] I said, "Just the basic things. Just be natural. You don't have to fuss. You don't have to shrink. They will understand." But at the back of my mind, I was dreaming: "Transform our house into Mayon Imperial Hotel. Red carpet and live band for welcome. Limousine and catering services on hand!"

The Morada household, as per instruction, was as natural as natural could be when the ladies arrived. Tatay, Nanay, and my siblings were to do their daily chores without fuss and inhibition. There was going to be no disruption of the normal household activities and routines. Our bedrooms were, literally, little to crow about. Visitors or no visitors, if someone needed to defecate, they had to be instructed to use the outhouse, the only toilet amenity we got. If they needed water, our artesian well never ran dry. No fuss.

Soon after their arrival, I introduced the ladies to my family. Our guests and I worked together as Grade 1 Team at Xavier School. Cleo and Oli were English teachers, and Osang was PE. (Alice was Cleo and Oli's friend from the English Department.) Mel taught Christian Life Education, while Ophie did Art. I did Math and Science. Neil, not a Xavier colleague, just came along with Mel for the ride. For extra camaraderie and fun, they banded themselves for this trip. With the ladies' varied tastes and persuasions, and with me at the helm, my family and I hoped to make their stay satisfying. How? We were to treat our guests with respect and hospitality, and without pretensions. We were to treat them to the simple provincial life.

---

238   *halá, sige!* [Filipino] – Go ahead!
239   *Delikada/o* [Filipino] – delicate, fastidious, picky, fussy.

Simple provincial life was eating *laing,*[240] *pinangat,*[241] *tinaguktok,*[242] *molido,*[243] *Bicol Express,*[244] pilinuts, or other uniquely Bicolano delicacies. Simple provincial life was sipping homemade hot chocolate taken from the cocoa tree in our front yard, or homemade coffee harvested from the coffee grove at our farm. Moreover, simple provincial life was sharing meals at the table without using spoons and forks; the hands were the best utensils especially when eating *tuyô,*[245] Guinobatan *longaniza,*[246] or *badê na sibubog,*[247] with *kamatis, sibuyas,*[248] and *sinanlag.*[249] If they wanted to have a few sips of alcohol, we could use *lambanog.*[250]

We slept under mosquito nets made from abaca woven by Nanay. We cooked our meals using firewood from logs which Tatay gathered from our farm. No, we didn't own a car, so we relied on public transportation for mobility. We didn't have a telephone line. Whatever the season, our house had no air-conditioning system. There was only one toilet bowl, no sink in the outhouse, no toilet paper, and no running water; you had to fetch it yourself from the artesian well. There was no water heater for the bath, but who cares? Pumping water and taking your bath in the open, by the artesian well as you pumped, were both sexy and extraordinary. You couldn't do that in Manila, could you?

At first, simple provincial life was harsh or limiting, but in due course, the ladies acclimatized fast. They were too civil and prudent to complain. Things were turning exciting and enjoyable.

Days passed as if a whirlwind. On the third day, Tita Irms (Irma Paycana of the Xavier Pilipino Department) joined us. A Bicolana herself, Tita Irms was visiting relatives in Camalig, Albay, and came by to see how my guests were doing. She even chartered a jeepney to make moving around easier and brought packed lunches for our sightseeing tours.

Thanks, Tita Irms!

Another day, and the ladies wanted to visit our farm. Our farm! What did they want to see on our farm? Thinking they were out of their minds, at once I wanted to sing an old song learned in elementary. *"Come, come and see my farm, for it is beautiful / El perrito goes like this, Ruff, ruff!"*

"Let's go!" they said.

On our farm they were to see and hear not only *el perrito,* but also *el gatito, el patito, el burrito, el chanchito, y el NPA!* Oh yes, they might also chance upon the NPA[251] reconnoitering! Our farm was deep in the hinterlands of Camalig, where the hills rolled wild and the NPA roamed free. Our farm, at Nágkasuî, was amid NPA country!

"Let's go!" they said.

---

240   *laing* [Filipino] – dried taro leaves, *apáy* in Bikol, in small pieces, boiled/cooked in coconut milk with shrimp paste, chili peppers, and a garnishing of pork.
241   *pinangat* [Bikol] – a dish of shrimp paste, coconut milk, chili peppers, and onions wrapped in taro leaves cooked by boiling.
242   *tinaguktok* [Bikol] – fish (tilapia) boiled in coconut milk, with tomatoes, onions, and chili peppers.
243   *molido* [Bikol], see Footnote #25, page 11.
244   *Bicol Express* – a stew of pork, chili peppers, shrimp paste, onion, ginger, and garlic in coconut milk; named after the train that plied from Manila to Legazpi City in Albay in olden days.
245   *tuyô* [Filipino] – dried fish.
246   *Guinobatan longaniza* [Bikol] – a kind of sausage mainly of pork fat, made in the town of Guinobatan, Albay.
247   *badê na sibubog* [Bikol] – dried round scad.
248   *kamatis, sibuyas* [Filipino] – tomato, onion.
249   *sinanlag* [Bikol] – garlic fried rice.
250   *lambanog* [Filipino] – distilled liquor made from coconut or nipa palm sap, derived from *tubâ* (palm toddy).
251   NPA – acronym for New People's Army, Filipino armed communist guerrilla group.

To reach Nágkasuî [literally, "forked"] you had to travel sixteen kilometers by rickety jeepney from Camalig town to a far-flung *barangay* (see Footnote #5, page 8) called Talôtô—Tatay and Nanay's place of birth. Only one jeepney plied the road; so, you engaged in a game of "catch-me-if-you-can" to reach Talôtô. During the wet season, the road was more clay than gravel, but since this was summer, the going was easier. What made the entire trip cumbersome for the uninitiated was the trek from Talôtô to Nágkasuî, a four-kilometer ordeal over treacherous hills and footpaths strewn with weird-shaped limestones.

"Let's go!" they said.

To reiterate, we owned no luxury guesthouse anywhere, more so on our farm. There was just a *payág* (see page 291), devoid of luxury, standing on top of a hill in the middle of nowhere, in Nágkasuî. If it could be a consolation, around the *payág* stood coconut palms, pili trees, and other fruit trees for the picking. Down in the valley on one side of the hill were our coffee grove and intermittent patches of abaca. On the other side of the hill ran a river, which was our fishing, swimming, and laundry hole altogether. A spring oozing from limestone rocks beside the river was our drinking water fountain. For my family, these were modest luxuries, more than enough to get by, but for our city-bred guests?

"Let's go!" they said.

So off we ventured to Nágkasuî. The group had fun while trekking the 4-kilometer path, especially when Oli stumbled after stepping on a limestone rock, which she later called *talabá*.[252] At the farm, we enjoyed farm-fresh *buko*[253] flesh and juice, bathed in the river, and ate other fruits in season.

And we stayed on the farm for the night. The *payág*, a structure around four-by-five-meter in dimension, of creaking bamboo floor and *sawali*[254] walls, accommodated 10 people that night, packed like sardines! I couldn't imagine how the likes of Cleo and Alice survived! What I know was that everybody did. *Walang sisihán!*[255]

Thank goodness, no NPA came by to reconnoiter. I was afraid to think of what might have happened, had they chanced to come. Maybe one of them could have run amok, shouting, "A feast of lovely ladies! *Yahoo!*"

Whew!

Back to Daraga, we toured around several of Albay's places of interest on board Tita Irms' chartered jeepney. We visited Cagsawa Ruins. We climbed up the hill where the baroque Our Lady of the Gate Parish Church stood, overlooking Mayon Volcano, Daraga town, and its environs. The jeepney negotiated the serpentine road halfway up the volcano to the Mayon Resthouse, where we enjoyed the panoramic view of several coastal towns of Albay and the Pacific Ocean. We then proceeded to Tabaco, then Tiwi, and marveled at Naglagbúng Hot Springs. We went swimming at the Reyes Beach Resort in the coastal town of Santo Domingo, Albay.

Our daily itineraries wearied the ladies, but never diminished their enthusiasm. There was still time to go discoing at the Mayon Imperial Hotel with my brother Jose, my brother-in-law Ely, and me. Another lovely, humid evening, four shy Daragueño[256] lads, emboldened by bottles of San Miguel beer and gin, treated the ladies to a traditional *harana*[257]; the ladies obliged by singing a few songs themselves. These ladies were game,

---

252   *talabá* [Filipino] – oyster.
253   *buko* [Filipino] – young coconut.
254   *sawali* [Filipino] – flattened bamboo strips, twilled and matted.
255   *Walang sisihán* [Filipino] – literally, "no blaming"; expression used in win or lose situations.
256   *Daragueño* – a native of Daraga, Albay, Philippines; female counterpart is Daragueña.
257   *harana* [Filipino] – serenade.

they were cowboys. I mean, they were a bunch of cowgirls always willing to do whatever, and ready for the hardships and challenges of the ride!

But even good things got to end. So did this trip. Thenceforth, the ladies went back to Manila, and I in May, during which we met together again to do our summer work for Xavier School. Then, a few years would see us—me, Osang, Mel, Oli, Ophie—grow families of our own. Cleo, Alice, Ophie, and I would migrate to the United States. Osang would go to Canada, and Oli to Australia. Mel and Tita Irms stayed put in the Philippines, although the grand dame of the Pilipino Department would move from teaching grade school to high school in Xavier. To date, she is now retired, as are Cleo and Alice, who are back to the homeland. I am now retired, too. Meanwhile, I write memoirs. I was pensive the other day and began writing about that Bicol getaway four decades ago.

Voila! I have come full circle.

ver four decades overdue, this piece of my mind ought to have reached sooner those wonderful ladies who visited. I know it took me far too long—41 years to be exact! But I felt compelled to write what I ought to have said to them in person so long time ago.

Putting my cards on the table, I declare I was a hypocrite if I never hoped this trip to dematerialize. I was a hypocrite if I never felt aghast at the conditions which, because of my familial state of affairs, I made them undergo and endure. I was a hypocrite if I never wished I were rich so they could have been more satisfied and comfortable. Every inconvenience, discomfort, and ordeal they experienced, I could have minimized or prevented from happening had I been more forthright with them at the start. Before they even crossed the threshold of that bus or train that took them to Bicol, to us, I should have been more persistent and emphatic in my disclosures and warnings. At the end of that trip, it was but expected and natural to hear any of them say, *"Buti pa hindi na lang ako sumama!"* [I shouldn't have gone!] *"Akala ko kasi..."* [I thought...] Or this: *"Sa huli ang sisi!"* [Regret is always at the end!] They being such good friends with good breeding, I never heard them complain. At the end of that trip, it was possible they had this or that impression of me and my family. Whether their impressions were good or otherwise, this I have to say:

I apologize for the inconvenience, discomfort, and ordeal, ladies. The four-kilometer trek and the packed sardines in the *payág*, among others, come to mind. I apologize for my lack or ignorance of logistics that made your visit anything but wholesome and enjoyable. I have never been a very effective/efficient leader/organizer. But this I say with prudence and honesty, the invitation to come and share a vacation with me and my family came from the bottom of my heart, even if at first there was a bit of hesitation. Whether you liked the outcome or despised it was another story. Again, I apologize.

And the simple life my family lived—this I won't be ashamed of, or apologize for, not at all. There is always grace in being poor. ■

r. Purple," said one of the 2nd graders as we were walking towards the Music Room during their Music period. "Want to try this on and find out how you look?"

The cute girl showed and handed me a fake mustache, one of those self-adhesive party supply novelties that's great accessory to any fancy costume.

"*Shh,* quiet!" We were walking down the hallway by the assistant principal's office and towards the 4th and 5th grade classrooms. "Classes are going on, Andrea. Behave."

So, she whispered. "This will look good on you!"

Her classmates snickered. Dominic cajoled, though in a suppressed manner. "Come on, Mr. Purple! Try it on, please!"

I pretended not to hear him, but at the back of my mind, "Why not! Just so you'd see, I'm not that kind of guy you think I am!"

You think I'm a music geek. Too bad! You think I always prefer and conjure a serious image. Too sad! Worse, you think I'm too old for such things as Andrea's toy mustache. Worst, you think I don't know how to socialize with your age group or play along with you. Think again!

Just then I remembered a segment of an old poem by Lewis Carroll in his book **Alice's Adventures in Wonderland**:

> "You are old, Father William," the young man said,
> "And your hair has become very white;
> And yet you incessantly stand on your head—
> Do you think, at your age, it is right?"

Looking at the selfie taken a few minutes later inside the Music Room, I repeated the young man's question to myself: "At your age, is it right?" ∎

ow this. You couldn't miss my house at Pompeii Street on account of this flaming-red mailbox. Or at least, from afar, that was how it might have appeared to any passer-by in our neighborhood. On closer view, actual bougainvillea shrubs growing from two flower boxes on the sides of the mailbox bedecked it with red blooms. I had trimmed, fashioned, and trained the branches to form an arch over the mailbox, taking years to fulfill. (Sorry for the amateurish outcome, but that was what I, a horticulturist and landscape artist *not*, could only muster). Over the years, I sometimes stood from a distance, looked at my handiwork, and said with glorious satisfaction, "Not bad!"

"You won't miss it." That was often the motivation I gave to anyone looking for my house. "Look for a red bougainvillea arch over a mailbox…"

At the outset, I bought the shrubs over ten years ago from a local nursery as two small potted plants, each a foot tall. Mameng uttered the first dissenting opinion and ominous foresight. "Why *that* plant?" "Why not?" I said. "It's acclimated to sub-tropical Texas."

As days passed, however, when the thorny plant, little by little, flaunted its deep red color almost year-round, the disagreement might have diminished, if not vanished. Even Maura and Napoleon, my neighbors across the street, might have developed a somewhat favorable impression of the red arch, or a live-and-let-live stance towards it; I had never heard them speak ill of it, let alone complain. It was the very first view that met their eyes every time they opened their front door, day in, day out.

It was obvious I had learned to love and nurture the shrubs (or were they bushes or vines?), despite the thorns and stubborn branches. After all, they're one of those things that God sent to add color to my humdrum house and life. Alone working in Texas while my wife and daughter struggled in New York, my bougainvillea arch was a welcome and enjoyable diversion from weekday drudgery. Besides, it amused me no end to hear the friendly mailman say I trimmed the arch so nicely. A bonus usefulness was the arch as a deterrent for the punks who often vandalized and destroyed the neighborhood mailboxes in the dead of night. Not this mailbox in a bougainvillea arch.

ne day, however, I needed to let the arch go—along with it, the enhancing color, the years of nurturing, and the joy it had given my soul. The shrubs had outgrown and abused their usefulness. The shrubs had grown too big for comfort. Like cancer cells destroying the body they live in, the roots cracked one of the concrete flower boxes in time, threatening to jeopardize and destroy the entire setup.

The phrase "root cause" took on a new level of significance. Who might ever imagine that a foot-tall potted plant with pin-sized roots would one day crack a stone?

There's a time for nurturing; there's a time for destroying. Over ten years of growing and caring did not end in one fell swoop. The only machete I had was not up for the job of chopping the resilient stems. Thus, I had to cut the foliage first. Even then, I might have appeared too pathetic and miserable such that a neighbor came to my aid and offered their pair of pruning shears. Thank goodness, it made the job so much easier.

Because I was not wearing gardening gloves, the thorny branches pricked my hands, as if in retaliation.

It took me an hour to finish the job. I was emotional, stressed, and hurt. It was a hard decision, but it was time to let go.

I was sure it was for the better. It was time for healing and liberating. The shrubs and the arch are now but fond memories. It pained to realize that once upon a time, one mailbox along Pompeii Street feasted with

red bougainvillea—which made looking for my humdrum house easier. It pained to realize that my house became more humdrum and emptier because of their demise.

In 2019, it was my house's turn to let me go. I had to leave Brownsville, Texas, in favor of Woodside, New York. I didn't need to worry. Nobody along 62nd Street ever had a mailbox as flamboyant as that which I had at Pompeii. Not a mailbox in a red bougainvillea arch. Not in a million years! ■

 **L**eavin' Old Texas, or plain **Old Texas,** is a traditional cowboy song. I first encountered this in the 1970s as a student at the Bicol Teachers College in Daraga, Albay, Philippines. The song was one of the part-singing pieces in a music textbook with brownish and frayed pages. I chanced upon this old book in an obscure, seldom visited corner of the BTC library. Old, still usable, and useful.

Since I could sight-read written music, it was love at first sight. The song possessed a melancholic quality that so touched the sentimental person in me. In the quick passage of time, I became a teacher of various subjects for 18 years in the Philippines and 26 in the United States. Twenty-three out of this 26 I spent teaching Music. Forty-four teaching years later, **Leavin' Old Texas** remains my most favorite western song that has ever existed and the saddest dirge a cowboy has ever sung.

> **I'm going to leave old Texas now**
> **They've got no use for the longhorn cow.**
>
> **They've plowed and fenced my cattle range**
> **And the people there are all so strange.**
>
> **I'll take my horse, I'll take my rope,**
> **And hit the trail upon a lope.**
>
> **Say adios to the Alamo**
> **And turn my head toward Mexico.**

One day in March 2018, I had my spring concert, featuring Villareal Elementary School **Singing Hawks**, my children's choir. "Your swan song," Mr. Pablo Leal, my principal, said after the show, describing the whole affair. One of the production numbers in the show was **Old Texas**, of course.[258]

The cowboy song and I had come full circle. I never realized it; the journey started from that obscure corner of my college library in Albay, to this humble, high-performing elementary school in Olmito, Texas. Melancholic **Leavin' Old Texas** had gotten applicable to me. It was hard to deny that a *leavin'* was happening soon.

Melissa Shafer, the emcee, announced it at the end of the show. "This will be the Singing Hawks' last concert with Mr. Purple!" she said into the microphone. "He is leaving us soon—he's retiring!" She then asked me to come up the stage and join the choir. Whereupon, my fave soloist, JoSaleen Cisneros, sang **Wonderful World** to me, then the children and I shed a tear or two (or more). This was altogether unexpected, and I loved Melissa, JoSaleen, and the entire gang for it!

"Why leave now, Mr. Purple?" Jadelynn Cortez, co-emcee, later admonished. "Why not put it off for another year, till I'm 5th grade and leaving the school, too? Please, please!"

Sorry, Jadelynn. Huge reasons. I've gotten too old for comfort. Spirit is willing, but the flesh has gotten weak. Hypertension, aching joints, floaters in both eyes, enlarged prostate, incontinence, getting tired dyeing my hair black every so often, degeneration or loss of hearing and other faculties causing increasing inability to keep good classroom management. It's no wonder Mr. Leal had been getting after me as an eagle to its brood these last two years. And more than ever, I want—*er...* need—to be with my family in Queens, New York.

Oh, yeah! New York—not Mexico. ■

---

258   Arcádio Morada, Jr., *tagaalbay*, "Leavin' Old Texas." YouTube Video, 3:51 min, https://youtu.be/28rSjFH0qE4.

October 26, 2017. *All dogs go to heaven*, the movie says, but does heaven have any restrooms? For my dear Azkal is heaven-bound, in his old age of 11 years. I will never ever forget you, Ash, my boy. Together with Valentine, you have given me so much naughtiness where there was Valentine's grouchiness, playfulness where there was Valentine's indifference, gray where there was Valentine's white. I could only imagine how much you suffered: your skin flaked and peeled, your hair came off, you peed so much more than usual. I wanted you to stay, but I too realized I had to let you go. Now I wonder how Valentine, or even I, will get along without you. Goodbye, Ash! Goodbye, sausage! Goodbye, Azkal, you rascal! I will miss you.

ecember 20, 2018. You should have told me, little old Valentine. I wish you could. Was this just a nap, or were you by then feeling something wrong within yourself on this last selfie with you? Were you hurting, just plain lethargic, or just wanting to lie comfy on me as I drove you to your guardian's house? You should have been expecting this; every time I'd be away on long trips, it was customary to put you under Norma Hernandez's care.

You appeared lonely as I hoisted you up to my arms and laid you in the passenger's seat before we drove away from our house at Pompeii Street. Did you sense I was going to leave you again, to her care? I talked to you as if I was nuts, before I sat in the driver's seat and cranked the car. You needn't worry, I assured you, because Norma was very fond of you and, through the years, had learned to love you as much as I had. Then, without my telling you, you jumped on my lap and snuggled. Full of love, I petted you.

Little did I know it was the last time I was to ever pet you as you slept! And little did I know it was to be your last slumber on me!

I flew to New York to be with my other beloveds—Mameng and Carmela. I did this like clockwork in July and December; we ought to be together as a family separated most part of the year by Carmela's schooling, Mameng's work in New York, and mine in Texas. This meant for those few days of the year, you needed to get by without me by your side. Between them and you, you got an edge because I spent the rest of the year with you.

Once again, our togetherness in New York always called for joy and celebration, especially in December, while you spent Christmas in Texas with Norma and waited for my return in January. In the meantime, Mameng and I were preparing for Jesus' birthday in our Woodside, NY apartment when the phone rang. Norma was calling from Brownsville and broke the news.

She said you looked just fine yesterday. This morning, you were less mobile and did not touch your food.

Past noon, she had to break the news to me. Valentine is heaven-bound. Gone for good. On Christmas Eve.

In a few hours, the Christian world rejoiced over the nativity of Jesus. I was celebrating, too, but Jesus knew and understood that in this dark niche deep in my heart, a genuine sadness seethed because of your passing, dear little old Valentine.

I wonder how the young girl might react if she saw herself with me wearing her toy mustache. I knew her as bubbly one moment, shy and reserved the next. Andrea's in ninth grade now, 2022, around 15 years old. That's about fifth of my age. Do the math.

Four years ago, to this day, I planned to sell my 1997 Honda Passport, which I originally bought for over twenty grand. It had been in good running condition until one day in 2017, when it finally conked out on me. In effect, it said, "Hold on, I'm now gonna slumber still, never to waken. I'm too old for your comfort!"

A Mexican car dealer expressed a willingness to buy the SUV. He offered this measly sum, which was not even commensurate with the price of four new BFGoodrich tires mounted two months earlier, before the vehicle refused to run. The Mexican could buy it, he said, for $300—take it or leave it. My friend Jose Bok Amacio, Jr. sympathized. He said, "Depreciation!"

Unless you are wine, real estate, antique paintings, or furniture, the old depreciate. Poignant fact of life.

Sadness came in a row. Two days before the $300 trade, I commemorated the first anniversary of Azkal's forced deportation to the Humane Society.

Azkal was my Schnauzer, nicknamed Ash, who had followed me home as I was walking my poodle Valentine one morning in 2010. (See **Ark**, page 106.) A check with the vet later showed that Ash was around 4 years old at that point in time. So, by 2017, Ash was 11 years old, ancient indeed in dog years. It was no wonder that in October of that year, the old dog could no more control its bladder; it urinated profusely at undesignated and unaccustomed places inside the house, at close intervals. My friend Editha M. Lane described it succinctly in one word: incontinence!

Incontinence is the bane of the old.

A few of my acquaintances opined that consigning the old dog to the Humane Society was a smart and right move. Doing so could relieve me of the responsibility of taking care and providing for the medication of the dog in its old age. Because I was myself working and providing for my own needs, Ash was a significant burden on my shoulder; it was but right to take the old dog to the Humane Society. As if the Society is the eventual depository of the old, the infirm, and the dying!

Which got me thinking in jest: Was Ash American? I was thinking of a parallel. Americans consign their elderly to nursing homes. For most Americans, it's the most humane thing to do.

I am not most Americans. Well, I'm lucky to be a Fil-American. I have a choice. God willing, I'm retiring in the Philippines, where I grew up, where family is priority, where culture and tradition have no room for nursing homes. We don't dispense with the elderly; nursing homes are not very common or non-existent where I came of age.

And who says I'm old? Or incontinent?

Andrea, the young girl, might say, "Mr. Purple, you're retired! Me and my class miss you!"

Miss you too, young girl! I say this in earnest.

True, I'm retired, but *kalabaw lang ang tumatanda!* Now, this is smarmy! ■

amalig was as sleepy a town as ever when I arrived on February 16, 2020, so provincial and idyllic, especially with Mayon Volcano's majestic presence gracing the landscape. As always, my lodging and accommodations were at this spic-and-span uninhabited house of the Monsalves, my late in-laws, near the center of town. Egal, a cousin of Mameng, was waiting for me; she commissioned him to be my *alalay*, assistant, and help for the duration of my stay in the Philippines, from February till August. She thought maybe I could use some help to monitor the ongoing construction of our Dream House in Barangay Cabagñan, three kilometers away, which started two weeks earlier. This was to be our retirement house, one of the fruits of our labor in America, a humble showcase of our American Dream. Mameng and I planned to repatriate for good in 2023. We had high hopes for a coming full circle soon in Camalig.

Twenty-four hours earlier, I boarded the AirTrain in Jamaica, New York, for JFK International Airport. This middle-aged Filipina on board, two seats away from me, recognized the *kababayan* (campatriot) in my person. She was the only passenger on the train wearing a face mask, the blue surgical kind. Maybe thinking of charity, she slid near me and offered a face mask she pulled out from her purse for my use. With this compassionate act, she then relayed some alarming news. The media downplayed it, she said; that nearby Elmhurst Hospital had so far documented several people infected with the novel coronavirus and casualties were mounting by the day. These were Chinese nationals who visited their relatives in Wuhan, China, in December. She couldn't be too careful, she said, thus the face mask.

I accepted the mask, put it on, though with slight embarrassment, and gave her thanks. We talked for a while more before we disembarked and parted ways into JFK, where hardly anybody was wearing any mask. I took mine off, feeling as if an outcast. Once inside the Philippine Airlines plane bound for Manila, the alarming news from my anonymous benefactor on the AirTrain preoccupied my mind. I wore the mask and seldom took it off till the plane landed at the Ninoy Aquino International Airport in Manila sixteen hours later.

At the NAIA, precautionary measures against the novel coronavirus were in place, posted in strategic places around the airport, apparently not enforced in their strictest sense. Passengers of flights originating from Hong Kong or other places in China had to wear mandatory face mask; but many were walking without it for reasons only the airport personnel knew.

From local news, I learned later that the first documented death from the coronavirus in the Philippines happened in San Lazaro Hospital in Manila on January 20. A Chinese woman, on vacation here, unwittingly carried the virus from China. (Did I hear Wuhan?) Just two weeks before my arrival, on February 1, the second documented Philippine death from the now-emerging pandemic occurred. The male companion of the woman who first died from the coronavirus, who was also a Chinese national, got infected and died from the scourge that was now getting global attention as COVID-19.

he Monsalve house where I'm staying in is a semi-concrete old house built in the 1990s when my in-laws, Pa Catalino and Ma Emerita, were still alive. It sits with two other houses on a property bequeathed by Ma Emerita's well-off forebears, on Barangay 5 in Camalig población. They had the common yard paved in concrete, while a concrete fence encloses the three houses, each owned by a sibling of Mameng. The house at the rear is her sister Yaya's. The entire right side of the perimeter belongs to her eldest

brother Badong, and her single younger sister Nene manages the house on the left but doesn't live there. That's why Mameng and I always stayed in this house whenever in town, as I do now.

It is well into March. The Philippine government has imposed a nationwide lockdown from March 15 because of COVID-19. The lockdown shutters business establishments, disables public transportation, prohibits social gatherings including church activities, imposes curfew, and restricts traveling from one province to another. Going from one barangay to another, though allowed, requires a barangay pass. Armed with such a pass, Egal and I continue on our daily routine of walking to the construction site at Cabagñan to check, even if no work is in progress.

The lockdown has banned construction activities. The local and national economy is at a standstill. Today, returning to our lodging at Barangay 5, I notice a common, yet profound, scene. Midway to the top of the concrete fence, there grows this shiny, delicate weed with vibrant heart-shaped and glossy leaves. Now's the dry season, so it has not rained for a long time. How does this living thing outsmart and defy death, and stay full of life despite the lack of water and the preponderance of the sun?

I take a close-up look at the plant and ask, as if a nitwit. Apart from prayers and meditation, and of course writing, I can't think of a better and more productive task to do at the moment. Because of COVID-19 and its offshoots of lockdowns, quarantines, curfews, social distancing, and other such things, our personal worlds have become tinier. We become wary of other people's presence, and every other person is a suspect carrier, including family. It has confined us inside our homes, which have become our tiny worlds for over two weeks now, with no end in sight. So, move around as much as and as long as we want within our own tiny world. That's what I'm doing when I spot this plant. Get the camera and take a snapshot. Voilà! A conversation piece is born, and I ask the question. How does this thing outsmart and defy death?

This was two days ago. Yesterday I had diarrhea and slight fever. Egal panicked and called Mameng in New York to inform her right away. This must have given her so much cause for worry. COVID-19! Aghast, she directed Egal to buy Diatabs and any fever medicine from the local drugstore pronto.

This morning, thank God, I am free of diarrhea and fever. I look for the delicate weed with vibrant, heart-shaped, and glossy leaves growing midway to the top of the concrete fence, but it's not there! Who might have plucked the helpless thing from its niche? Did Egal, Yaya, her husband Leon, or anyone in Manoy Badong's family play God by snuffing out the life of that green and resilient living thing? I ask Egal, and he shakes his head. No use approaching the others; they might construe my asking as needful of psychiatric attention. They might even laugh at me for drooling over insignificance. I wax emotional, go to my room, and write.

We learn from experience how adaptive and adjustable earth's creatures are. They have coping mechanisms. The plant with heart-shaped leaves growing on the dry concrete fence exhibited that fact. Human beings show that as well. But whosesoever hands snuffed the life out of that resilient plant might as well be the pandemic that besets us humans now. In the long run, we realize that, no matter how resilient humans are, we are as vulnerable. That's life.

The global human statistics of COVID-19 to date are staggering. As of October 2022, about 630 million COVID-19 cases and 6.6 million deaths since China reported its first cases to the World Health Organization (WHO) in December 2019. All because of that travel-hungry virus from Wuhan!

I am still alive. I have yet to see my Dream House done, one humble showcase of my American Dream still unfulfilled. God willing, I intend to stay alive as long as it takes. But the poor plant is missing. If that is not poignant, I don't know what is!

The plant in question? *Peperomia pellucida*. Not *Homo sapiens*. That's my scientific name. I'm a more resilient and smarter species, so I will survive. ∎

eet Pampu, the chocolate mongrel. She is our new housedog. Her not-so-feminine name is nick for *pampulutan*, literally, something meant or intended for *pulutan* (see Footnote #32, page 16). She's just over one-year-old; that, too, is how old our new house is. When construction workers were laying the foundations of the house in February 2020, Nestor, a stay-in hired hand, took it upon himself to bring a mongrel puppy to the construction site. Nestor stayed in until the completion of our house in December 2020. The puppy has stayed in as our guard dog thenceforth.

At the start, the workers jokingly gave her the name, and her supposed destiny. But it was not to be. For she has grown to be a remarkable dog, with neither ticks nor fleas, nor *asmod* (stinky dog smell). Her fur doesn't shed, and best of the list, she's turned out to be an excellent guard dog. They only reared and geared her for the slaughter and the table (as *pampulutan*) on their after-work drinking sprees, but fortunately, they've allowed her to live onward.

Her domain is our house-and-lot property, my and Mameng's retirement home, in Cabagñan, Camalig, Albay. Pampu is an efficient alarm system by herself, for she automatically barks at anything that moves and makes a sound coming around and inside her territory, especially at night.

I have become very fond of Pampu. Without fail, she wags her tail and comes near me whenever I call out his name. She enjoys being stroked on her underside, especially under her rear legs, which she automatically opens up for the stroking. She has become as dear a pet dog to me as Valentine and Azkal were. In my life, those beloved pet dogs are two big shoes to fit in, but Pampu looks like getting at it with flying colors. ∎

COVID-19 was not even a germ of an idea yet when we started planning for our retirement house. I lived in Brownsville, TX, and had just retired from teaching. Mameng still worked in New York, as did Carmela. Our daughter had just begun a relationship with Alfred Molina—not the movie star, though just as good-looking—and, therefore, no Adam June Molina yet in our lives. Mameng and I thought it was high time for us to think of retiring for good in the Philippines. With my retirement lump sum and our collective earnings, we could start building up our Dream House.

We had expressed our intention to people, not just kith and kin, who could help turn our dream into reality. During our homeland trip in July 2019, we brainstormed and approached people with know-how. Our niece-in-law, Sheilah Nuyles, agreed to make the design. Before returning to New York in August, Mameng and I completed the ultimate plan, in close collaboration with Sheilah. We signed a contract for a "Proposed Two-Story Residential Building" in an 800-square-meter lot in Cabagñan, Camalig, Albay.

Mameng and I formed a consultative and brainstorming "council" with nephew Rizen Raposa and niece Donna Nolasco-Almario, to iron out concerns that might come up. We appointed Engr. Lee-Vincent Alcantara, a Daragueño, as our Builder-Contractor. With the public relations expertise of Juby Nolasco, Mameng's youngest sister, acquisition of the necessary permits and pre-construction documents was a snap. By December 2019, the construction of our Dream House was all set to go—but so, too, was a looming threat from China. Asymptomatic travelers infected with the novel coronavirus from Wuhan, China, preempted the start of our construction and, worse, unwittingly spread a new global scare.

Construction was in hectic progress when I arrived in Camalig on February 16, 2020. Because I was well into retirement, I had the time to see to whatever needs arising in the construction's course. I was barely a month on active watch of the construction from the sidelines when the World Health Organization (WHO) declared the coronavirus or COVID-19 a global pandemic in March. Governments around the world, including the Philippines, imposed lockdowns and quarantines to stop the spread of the disease in its tracks. The lockdown banned all social assemblies, stopped operation of businesses, and halted all construction activities as they involved people's mobility and assemblies.

Restrictions eased up by May 15. After a two-month hiatus, construction could now restart at full gear. Meanwhile, by June, Egal and I, with Mameng's concurrence, of course, scouted for and canvassed household materials supposedly subject to the homeowners' preferences. We had a grand, exhausting, but enjoyable time selecting what we thought were the right furniture, tiles, faucets, toilet bowls, bathtub, countertops, paint colors, color schemes, etc. Our guiding norms: minimalist and simple. No to the ornate, no to bold and vivid colors.

Mameng originally planned to join with me in Camalig in July, in conjunction with her one-month vacation from work. We were to return to New York together in August. Because of the pandemic, however, she had to re-book her flight to December and return by January 2021. I, too, had to re-book my return to New York from August to January to coincide with her return flight.

Construction careened from August to December, propelled by the ready availability of funds on our side and the precision and efficiency of the building contractor. Eight-million thanks we ought to accord Sheilah and Lee! By Christmas 2020, one humble fruit of our labor in America was ready for God's benediction. ∎

The Architect's (Sheilah Nuyles) drawing of our humble Dream House

Our Dream House as of this printing, now being touted in town as The White House

The Philippine government, through its Inter-Agency Task Force on Emerging Diseases (IATF), announced on March 20, 2020, the ban on religious gatherings starting March 22. Cabinet Secretary Karlo Alexei Nograles said the IATF would give more details on the ban in the next few days, "particularly as regards Masses and worship services and religious gatherings." The ban disallowed large crowd gatherings, including worship services. Nograles said that this was "part of stringent social distancing measures designed to prevent the spread of... COVID-19."

Directly and adversely affected was the holding of Eucharistic celebrations in churches. The government ruling likewise limited the holding of weddings, baptisms, and funeral services.

In the months following the ban, people resorted to celebrating the Eucharist in the comfort and safety of their homes, through TV, radio, and the internet. Most churches broadcast their Masses and devotions, hoping to reach the faithful and give them a choice that addressed both health and spiritual concerns. In April, restrictions on worship gatherings eased up, allowing limited attendance in churches for Eucharistic celebrations. The Church and other establishments followed strict rules on social distancing.

Circumstances, therefore, prevented me from celebrating the Eucharist as often as I might have wanted during the pandemic. To provide for my spiritual needs, I have resorted to praying the Holy Rosary more often daily. "More often" means *twice* daily, first thing in the morning and last thing at night. Praying the Rosary is a devotion I have learned to practice early in life.

"The Rosary of the Virgin Mary, which gradually took form in the second millennium under the guidance of the Spirit of God, is a prayer loved by countless Saints and encouraged by the Magisterium. Simple yet profound, it still remains, at the dawn of this third millennium, a prayer of great significance, destined to bring forth a harvest of holiness. It blends easily into the spiritual journey of the Christian life, which, after two thousand years, has lost none of the freshness of its beginnings and feels drawn by the Spirit of God to 'set out into the deep' (*duc in altum!*) in order once more to proclaim, and even cry out, before the world that Jesus Christ is Lord and Savior, 'the way, and the truth and the life' (Jn 14:6), 'the goal of human history and the point on which the desires of history and civilization turn.'

"The Rosary, though clearly Marian in character, is at heart a Christocentric prayer. In the sobriety of its elements, it has all the depth of the Gospel message in its entirety, of which it can be said to be a compendium. It is an echo of the prayer of Mary, her perennial Magnificat for the work of the redemptive Incarnation which began in her virginal womb. With the Rosary, the Christian sits at the school of Mary and is led to contemplate the beauty on the face of Christ and to experience the depths of his love. Through the Rosary the faithful receive abundant grace, as though from the very hands of the Mother of the Redeemer." [259]

I prayed the Rosary this morning, December 25, 2020, as customary. Since today was Friday, I was to meditate on the Sorrowful Mysteries. But wait... today was Jesus' joyous Nativity. A question sprang up—should I better say the Joyful Mysteries instead?

Am I violating any rule/law, written or unwritten? Which one is right, which one is proper? I remember having asked these same questions before. December 25, 2018, fell on a Tuesday, pointing to the Sorrowful Mysteries, so I posted this dilemma on social media. Catholic friends were quick to weigh in on the matter.

"I believe Joyful is more appropriate, for today is the most joyful day, the celebration of the birth of Jesus Christ," Editha M. Lane said. Edith and I belonged to a special group of friends in Brownsville, Texas. We called ourselves the Dimaguiba Family.

"Jun, I prayed the Joyful Mysteries for Jesus' b-day! It is not a violation. It is just proper for the occasion," said Edna Royo, classmate at Mother of Life Center.

"It's àpropos," Doming Litong, former colleague at Xavier School, said.

"No violation or offense, Jun," Lorenza Dalida Miro, another classmate at MOL, said. "I prayed the Joyful Mysteries, too. What is important is we go into meditation and are one with Jesus, Mary, and Joseph in our journey towards redemption from sin."

---

259   Apostolic Letter *ROSARIUM VIRGINIS MARIAE* of the Supreme Pontiff John Paul II, https://www.vatican.va/content/john-paul-ii/en/apost_letters/2002/documents/hf_jp-ii_apl_20021016_rosarium-virginis-mariae.html#fn1.

My friend Loida Mondragon from Dallas thereabouts had a few things on her mind about the matter at hand. "Those are just suggested days. If one can pray all the mysteries within a day, on any day, then there's nothing wrong with praying the Joyful Mysteries on a Tuesday [or Friday]. Remember, too, that before the Church added the Luminous Mysteries, by tradition we prayed the Joyful Mysteries on Monday and Thursday. Now, the Joyful Mysteries got moved to Monday and Saturday to give way to the Luminous Mysteries on Thursday. I don't think that the Church set in stone the schedule on when to pray particular mysteries. In fact, nothing in life is static as shown in the evolution of the Holy Rosary throughout the centuries. What's important is using the Rosary as a path to contemplation as we develop our relationship with God."

"Prayer is prayer," said Josefa Florence Culanag, another former colleague at Xavier School. "There's no [Church] law that says you can only pray a mystery according to its designated day."

I appreciated my friends' views on this matter, and I agreed with them.

But, brothers and sisters in the faith, please allow me now just the same to make modifications in the way I pray the Rosary. This change is quite different from the conventional way of praying the Rosary—so different that I may incur the ire of the traditionalists among us if they learn of it.

Let me clarify that this change is personal, and in no way do I impose it on others. I find wisdom in this change, so I want to share it with others, anyhow.

First, I want to stick to a fixed schedule for the Mysteries of the Rosary. By tradition, the Church has promulgated four Mysteries—significant events in the life of Jesus and Mary. In my proposed change, each day of the week has its corresponding Mysteries. Since the Church has established only four sets of Mysteries, I need to add three more sets. From where do I get them? From the most authoritative source, of course—the Holy Book, the Bible. The change should be Bible-based.

What could be a suitable topic or subject for the mysteries that I wanted to add? Oh, I have given this question much thought for a considerable time. At first, I had the general topic "the teachings of Jesus" for consideration; later, I realized from personal experience that I have learned of Jesus' teachings mainly through his parables and miracles. Therefore, I came up with *Wondrous*, *Allegorical*, and *Instructive* Mysteries. **Wondrous** Mysteries deal with the larger-than-life and most extraordinary signs/miracles that Jesus performed. **Allegorical** Mysteries are the parables. *Instructive* Mysteries are Jesus' core teachings. Since there are many miracles and parables to choose from, I did not make the final list through *eeny-meany-miney-mo* or random selection; rather, I based it on the firm belief that I learned about Jesus through these particular miracles or parables. Unlike the traditional mysteries, **Wondrous**, **Allegorical**, and **Instructive** Mysteries are not timeline-based. And let me reiterate: the choices are personal, for my personal use.

Second, an important feast or solemnity celebrated by the Church on a particular day preempts the change. For example, my aforementioned dilemma: if Nativity falls on a Friday, which points to the Sorrowful Mysteries, then Joyful Mysteries take the place of Sorrowful. For another example, August 15, 2022, falls on a Monday. Monday points to Joyful Mysteries, but August 15 is the Feast of the Assumption, one of the Glorious Mysteries. Therefore, in 2022, I meditate on the Glorious Mysteries when I pray the Rosary on August 15.

Third, I use SET A in my morning prayer, SET B at night.

Here now is the "little" change I propose for myself on the Mysteries of the Holy Rosary and when to meditate on them. This change only takes effect and stays with me. If ever someone reads about this change, please know that it is only incumbent on me, and I am not imposing it on anybody. The Catholic Church has nothing to do with it. I own up to this change and so deserve whatever criticism or commendation it may incur.

JOYFUL MYSTERIES
Monday

1. Annunciation
2. Visitation
3. Nativity of the Lord
4. Presentation of Jesus in the Temple
5. Finding of Jesus at the Temple

WONDROUS MYSTERIES
Tuesday

A
1. **Healing the Deaf** (Mk 7:31-37)
2. **Opening Eyes of the Blind** (Mk 10:46-52)
3. **Curing the Demoniac** (Mk 1:23-38)
4. **Cleansing the Leprous** (Lk 17:11-19)
5. **Healing the Paralytic** (Mt 9:1-8)

B
6. **Great Catch of Fish** (Lk 5:1-11)
7. **Calming of the Storm** (Mt 8:23-27)
8. **Feeding of Five Thousand** (Mt 14:15-21)
9. **Walking on the Water** (Mt 14:22-36)
10. **Raising of Lazarus** (Jn 11:1-46)

ALLEGORICAL MYSTERIES
Wednesday

A
1. **Sower** (Mk 4:1-20)
2. **Mustard Seed** (Mk 4:30-34)
3. **Good Samaritan** (Lk 10:29-37)
4. **Salt and Light** (Mt 5:13-16)
5. **Rich Man and Lazarus** (Lk 16:19-31)

B
6. **Unforgiving Servant** (Mt 18:23-35)
7. **Tenants** (Mk 12:1-12)
8. **Wedding Feast** (Mt 22:1-14)
9. **Lost Sheep** (Mt 18:10-14)
10. **Prodigal Son** (Lk 15:11-32)

LUMINOUS MYSTERIES
Thursday

1. Baptism of Jesus
2. Wedding at Cana
3. Proclamation of the Kingdom
4. Transfiguration
5. Institution of the Eucharist

SORROWFUL MYSTERIES
Friday

1. Agony in the Garden
2. Scourging at the Pillar
3. Crowning of Jesus with Thorns
4. Carrying of the Cross
5. Crucifixion/Death of Jesus

INSTRUCTIVE MYSTERIES
Saturday

A
1. **Praying** (Mt 6:5-15, 7:7-11)
2. **Greatest Commandment** (Mk 12:28-30)
3. **Golden Rule** (Mt 7:12)
4. **Rich Young Man** (Mt 19:16-26)
5. **Beatitudes** (Mt 5:3-12)

B
6. **Bread of Life** (Jn 6:48-59)
7. **The Way, The Truth, and The Life** (Jn 6:48-59)
8. **Washing of the Feet** (Jn 13:12-15)
9. **Vine and Branches** (Jn 15:5-17)
10. **Judgment of the Nations** (Mt 25:31-36)

GLORIOUS MYSTERIES
Sunday

1. Resurrection
2. Ascension
3. Descent of the Holy Spirit
4. Assumption of Our Lady
5. Coronation of Our Lady as Queen of Heaven and Earth

My Rosary is now full circle. You saw it here first. ■

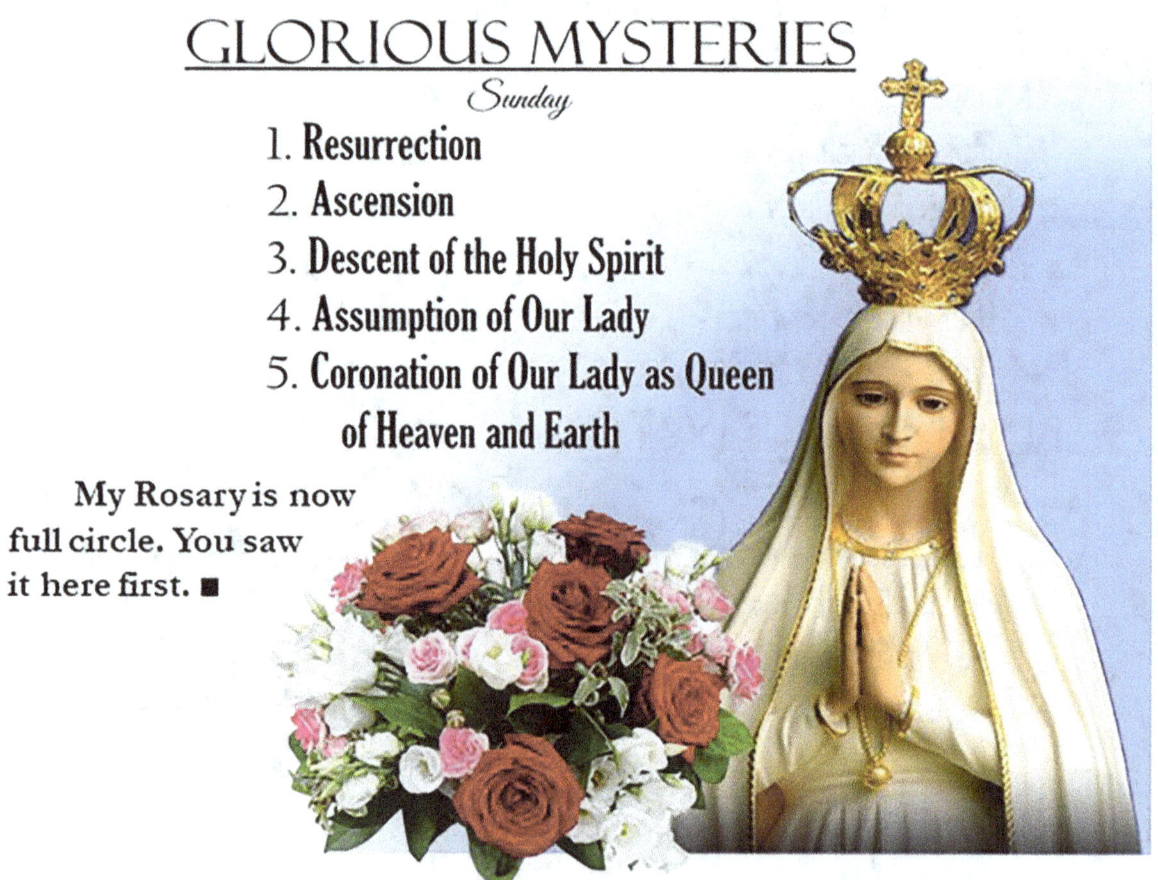

41
SILVERADO
Twenty-five years in a nutshell

oy was in the air. "OMG!" Rogie Legazpi exclaimed. "That's all I can muster to say!" Joy was in the offing. Joy was at the outset when I coined the name **Silverado** for the Facebook group of Filipino teachers—including Rogie, me, and 23 others—who came to Texas in August 1992. I formed the group as a rallying point towards our 25th year reunion in August 2017. Yes, it had been that long!

Rogie scratched his head vis–à–vis the name choice, but on second thought realized that "that's in reference to the no-man's-land terrain of So[uth] TX." Indeed. And more. To me, the context of the name was plain yet subtle. **Silverado** was a 1980s Western that showed a group of unlikely heroes saving a nefarious town from lawlessness.

Unlikely heroes, or likely villains? Batch 92 came to America not to save it from whatever, per se. I could speak with conviction on behalf of the Batch, as I was a part of the whole enterprise myself. I don't assume we came looking for greatness or the stuff of legend—that is trying to be noble yet renders us presumptuous. In pragmatic terms, we came to earn the almighty dollar, and in ideal terms, to make any difference as teachers that might present itself along the way. We came to earn our keep while contributing any change, no matter how infinitesimal, in the educational system of Texas in particular and the United States in general.

We sprang from the length and breadth of the Philippine archipelago, flying to Texas in staggered groups. *Edith Derrada, Eleonor Felicilda, Emee Cabañero, Ester Mejia, Gwen Delfin, Jane Lorenzo, Judith Cunanan, Leilani Olaires, Lillibeth Reyes, Lorna Patiño; Maria Oropesa, Maribel Reyes, Nancy Martirez, Nemia Bagtasos, Perly Andres, Rolita Liwagon, Rose San Diego; Adlai Saniel, Arcádio Morada Jr, Armand Ramones, Ernesto Ibarra Jr, Eugene Mangsat, George Doloroso, Rogie Legazpi,* and *Vic Sinining.* We were not just exotic names, but experienced professionals, civil servants, and educators in our beloved homeland. Of the Batch, 14 were married, their respective families left behind in our homeland (Adlai, Arcádio Jr, Emee, Ester, Eugene, George, Jane, Judith, Leilani, Lillibeth, Lorna, Maria, Perly, and Rose); and 11 were single (Armand, Edith, Eleonor, Ernesto Jr, Gwen, Maribel, Nancy, Nemia, Rogie, Rolita, and Vic). In the course of 25 years, the statistics would show changes, whether expected, unforeseen, or unwanted, for the better or worse.

For most of us, the journey began with this Palm Sunday announcement at the classified ads section of the Manila Times in April 1992. Ms. Becky Grajo, who owned a recruitment agency for nurses in the Philippines, joined forces with Ms. Florita Tolentino of Omni Consortium of Houston to enable employment of Filipino teachers in Texas. Omni Consortium was a conduit for the recruitment of Filipino teachers for the Rio Grande Valley. Quite enticing in its drabness, the ad urged teachers—and other professionals with at least 12 Education units—to take and pass a competency test in order to qualify for a working visa to teach in Texas. An opportunity of a lifetime!

325

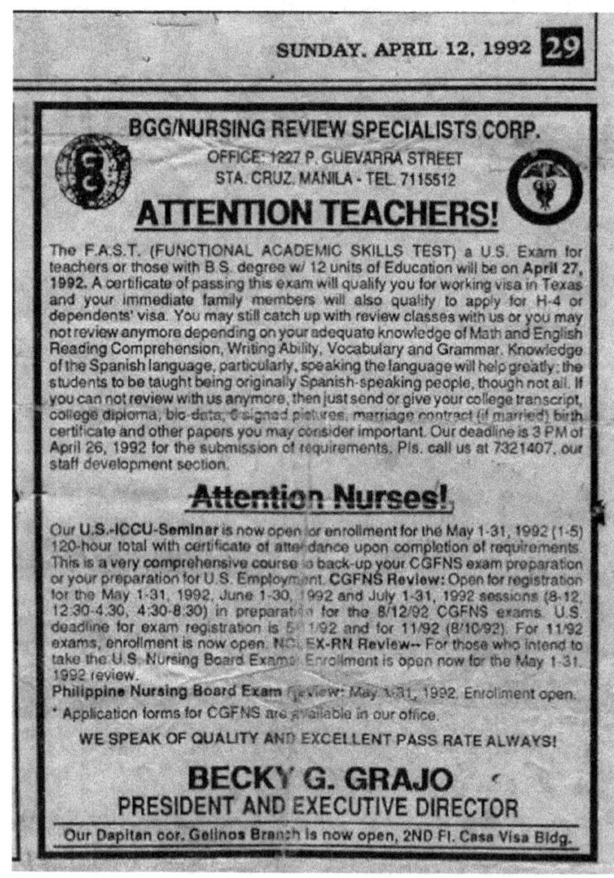

I needed no prodding. Right away, I turned in the requirements and paid $100 for the F.A.S.T. In May, the results were out. I resigned from Xavier School (my employer) in June, effective August 1, 1992, without regard for the certainty of the whole situation.

Certainty was on my side, thank God! Omni Consortium was legit, Mrs. Tolentino a certified and duly authorized recruiter. Everything was legal, and on August 18, 1992, I and 17 other Philippine professionals bade farewell to our respective families and flew to Houston, TX. There were other departures before and after ours, adding us up to 25 teachers in total. Thus, the future of Batch 92, for the next ten years at least, looked foreseeable. America, elusive land of milk and honey for many of our countrymen, was now at our fingertips, under our noses, beneath our toes. For all the 25 teachers of Batch 92, America was now within our grasp.

A picture of meek lambs herded into the Promised Land, the 25 of us shifted gears to the Rio Grande Valley from Houston. We found first residence in several units of the Borders Apartment in the city of Brownsville. Most got employed at the Brownsville Independent School District and a few at the neighboring Los Fresnos Consolidated Independent School District. As we inched to our 2nd year, because of immigration and personal issues, the exodus to other school districts began, which disbanded and dispersed the original group.

Our families joined us shortly to settle down in Texas. In 25 years, as fate goes, our children have come and grown, finished their U.S. education, and given a handful among us their grandchildren. But reality bites. Of the 14 married teachers who left the Philippines in 1992, three (George, Lillibeth, and Leilani), estranged from their respective spouses, later found new loves and remarried. Of the 11 single teachers, six had American-brand marriages (Eleonor, Ernesto, Maribel, Nemia, Rogie, Rolita) and grew families of their own; but, sad to say, two have thereafter gotten divorced (Eleonor, Maribel). The paths we have taken for the past 25 years have been diverse, interesting and, in reality, unforeseeable.

One of us has bitten the dust. *(Eternal rest grant unto Eugene Mangsat, O Lord, and let perpetual light shine upon him.)* We don't know the whereabouts of Vic, Gwen, Edith, Nancy, Ester, and Maria. Those who are still in the coop, alive and kicking, are now scattered from the East to the West Coast, from Texas to Chicago. A few are now retirees, and many are "retireables".

We who have stayed put in Brownsville (and Harlingen) TX held a Grand Reunion on August 11-13, 2017. The venue was at South Padre Island, roughly 25 miles northeast of Brownsville, at the Gulf of Mexico. Of course, we would have wanted everyone to come. However, just how grand the reunion would turn out, did not depend just on attendance, but mostly on the mindset and attitude we brought into it. The attendance was disappointing; we didn't have a quorum (only 9 out of 25 came!). But we who came could say in confidence that the joy we shared, in that short and fleeting togetherness, more than compensated for what we lacked in number. We who came shared colorful only-in-America experiences. It was a grand time venting out and recounting happy and sad life histories. Likewise, we rekindled old friendships and camaraderie. For sure, joy was in the air.

There was enthusiastic joy in the planning and anticipating. Judith Cunanan, our indefatigable unwritten-and-unofficial leader since Day 1 (August 18, 1992), always the epitome of grace and elegance under pressure, took it upon herself to coordinate the whole affair. She formed the core group, conducted meetings for brainstorming and planning, and arranged for the venue of the reunion, among other tasks. I was to be the unofficial historian, while Eleonor (Ely) Felicilda-Scheiber and Maribel Reyes-Colglazier provided coordination.[260]

The venue was a rented condominium at 131 East Aries corner Gulf Blvd, South Padre Island, TX. The island itself was a fond getaway during our first years in Texas, forever occupying a niche in our hearts.

There was ecstatic—short of insane—joy in the arrivals, seeing each other in the flesh for the first time after 25 years. Screams of joy, especially Emee's, demonstrated the feeling so well.[261]

There was deep joy in reminiscing about the good old days, especially experiences in our past workplaces. We still laugh at Vic's "reclaiming" anecdote, no matter how many times we'd retold and heard it in the past.[262]

There was regal joy when, retelling a classroom experience, Emee became Queen of the Jungle. This occurred when a 5th grade student said, "Philippines is a jungle, right? And you're the queen." He began describing the jungle and the beasts, putting teacher Emee in an unpleasant light in front of her students. Blood boiled in her head, but restraint and good sense turned the sticky situation around via her rejoinder that gave us, her listeners, not just a small measure of pride. She said, "Oh yeah, I may be the Queen of the Jungle, but I'm the queen of this classroom, too. So be nice and do your job!"[263]

I had overkill joy in cooking the *pinoy* goodies assigned to me to prepare beforehand: *turon, pork adobo, laing,* and *balisungsong*.[264] Miscalculations due to overexcitement! In my joy, I overestimated quantities. It had been days past the reunion, and I was still consuming the left-overs. No sooner end in sight. This is in stark contrast to our grand plan for the next reunion. We set our sight to 2019! [Sadly, it didn't materialize.]

There was filial joy in knowing and interacting with Ely's brood, especially the adorable Suzie. We were so proud of Ely for how she had managed raising up three smart kids on her own. Ely is a single mom who divorced her American husband. She had many reasons, the most valid being the guy's inaction and lack of initiative to find a job during the entire duration of their marriage. We prayed for more blessings for her family in the coming years.[265]

There was compleat joy when Nemia, the "baby" of the Batch, arrived on the second day. Along with Rogie, she was the youngest among us—25 years ago. She was turning Golden in September, and what would that make the rest of us?[266]

---

260   Watch on YouTube: *tagaalbay*, MARIBEL, 2:59min, https://youtu.be/E-t9W-zKeFY.

261   Watch on YouTube: *tagaalbay*, FEASTING ON "Mani ni Maribel," 0:36min, https://youtu.be/Se2uvPoyRmI.

262   Watch on YouTube: *tagaalbay*, RECLAIMING, 1:41min, https://youtu.be/NIt6jPWzN5Q.

263   Watch on YouTube: *tagaalbay*, QUEEN OF THE JUNGLE, 1:04min, https://youtu.be/NPnTHG0xuOY; and EMEE, 0:54min, https://youtu.be/I6h5n0sgegM.

264   *balisungsong* [Bikol] – steamed ground rice or cassava in banana leaves.

265   Watch on YouTube: *tagaalbay*, ELY, 2:17min, https://youtu.be/7rGQeRO_2pQ.

266   Watch on YouTube: *tagaalbay*, NEMIA, 1:08min, https://youtu.be/9pIcfvKVERI.

There was nostalgic joy in watching videos of past memorable moments together. Especially our 10th year anniversary. If Lani was *estariray* [star of the show] then, everybody was *estariray* now, without doubt. Video clips taken throughout the event, uploaded on YouTube, were testamentary to this.[267]

There was gambler's joy in playing Maribel's *Loteria*, none other than good old Bingo using Spanish terms instead of the usual numbers. $1,000,000 was at stake, courtesy of the President of the Philippines, Rodrigo Duterte. *Kidding!* But, fake news aside, Rose showed how it was to win. *El camaron… la chalupa… el gallo… la estrella… la corona—eeeeeeiiiiiii!* [268]

There was melodious joy in singing to our hearts' content during the karaoke hour. In every *pinoy* party, there sure is karaoke!

There was pure joy in playing Rose's *Christmas in August*, knowing that her giveaways came from the generosity of her heart and her pocket. But her heart and her pocket weren't the only things with which Rose was generous. Her total dedication to her craft—as a kindergarten teacher all these years—was common knowledge and unquestionable.[269]

There was teary-eyed joy as we browsed through Lani's old picture album together and laughed at how young and goofy we used to look. What better way to retrace paths we had taken than through those frozen memories in rectangles?[270]

There was naughty joy in trying to figure out where, how, and what everyone else was doing at the moment. *Quo Vadis,* Ernesto Jr, Armand, Rogie, George, Vic, Adlai, Perly, Nancy, Maria, Ester, Lillibeth, Jane, Edith, Gwen, and Lorna. To be honest, guys, we didn't make fun of you just because you were absent! Oh yeah, we might have had fun at your expense, but who was to blame? Next reunion around, attend!

There was priceless joy just by walking on the beach. So was by listening to the sound of the surf at the Gulf of Mexico. And more so by watching the sun come out of the horizon till, after a few brief minutes, it was full blown. The scene we usually regarded as too commonplace became this memorable because we were together. It was one sunrise we may never forget.[271]

There was immense joy in watching Lani dance at Clayton's Beach Bar. She attested it was her first time doing so in a public place like that. Don't you wonder how the verve overcame the nerve! She's retired from teaching for several years now.[272]

There was joy and satisfaction in eating together, and at night, snoring together. My much-anticipated *Snores Symphony* with Rose and Lani might not have pushed through, but it was fun to know that I was not alone snoring the night away. Lani was doing crescendo in F sharp, I was decrescendo in A flat, and Rose was C natural. Now, whatever musical key Rose was in, she always had the right pitch. In fact, Rose has always been the role model, be it singing, or making your cheeks impeccable, soft, and lucid![273]

So, there was flawless joy, especially among the ladies, in learning Rose's health and beauty "secrets"—her *Perfectio* skin rejuvenation treatment, her turmeric therapy, and her lipstick tattoo, topping other things. They were a hit and in high demand. Vanities, ladies, never grow out of style.

---

267   Watch on YouTube: *tagaalbay*, LEILANI, 1:08min, https://youtu.be/gx33d5QT7_8.

268   Watch on YouTube: *tagaalbay*, LOTERIA, 1:44min, https://youtu.be/HCN2BuNi7zs.

269   Watch on YouTube: *tagaalbay*, ONE DEDICATED TEACHER, https://youtu.be/PySePBdHGnk.

270   Watch on YouTube: *tagaalbay*, OUR FIRST YEAR IN A CAPSULE, 1:47min, https://youtu.be/x26yXBvPrH0.

271   Watch on YouTube: *tagaalbay*, SUNRISE FOREVER, 2:16min, https://youtu.be/qKV0A7tNpI0.

272   Watch on YouTube: *tagaalbay*, VERVE OVER NERVE, 0:16min, https://youtu.be/zL5Ve4snI8o.

273   Watch on YouTube: *tagaalbay*, ROSE, 3:06min, https://youtu.be/hggAAJLFCWI.

There was heartfelt joy in going back to your first place of residence and employment in Texas. Borders Apartment… BISD… LFCISD. Sure, unpleasant work experiences might have abounded in these environs, too. Yet it was heartening to think that, once upon a time, you walked through that gate and that hallway. That's the school library, the cafeteria. There's the Faculty Lounge. Never forget, too, that once upon a time your very name they emblazoned at the door to that classroom.

There was tearful joy in hearing Rolit and Ogie (Judith's hubby) square off for the best joke ever. Ogie's jokes were hilarious, rendered more so because they came from a shy, soft-spoken, and gentle man; but, of course, Rolit's jokes won hands down—told in her inimitable and innocent countenance and Visayan accent. Tita Rolit, *ang tita ng bayan* [everybody's beloved auntie], has always been popular among us as someone who vivifies our funny bones with her one-liners.[274]

There was grateful joy in announcing the **Silverado Alay-Kapwa Award**, which goes, of course, to Ogie and Judith. If any couple deserved our gratitude, it's them. The time, money, or effort they spent and exerted for us was tantamount to our reunion's success. So, our toast for joy, peace, and happiness was likewise a token of our gratitude to this unselfish couple.[275]

Last, there was hopeful joy in the offing. The future might be unfathomable, but together we vowed to meet again in two years. We were not getting any younger. If we were to do it in five, ten, or 25 years, it'd be a more formidable struggle to raise a quorum. Who knows what the future holds?

Rose and Rolit flew back to New York, Emee to Maryland, Nemia and Lani to Houston, while Judith, Ely, Maribel, and I got back to the rigors of our daily life in the Rio Grande. The reunion was over, but the ardor stayed quite a while. **Silverado**, the FB page, and Messenger remained hotspots for chats.

Nemia writes—

My daughter and I were talking about the reunion. I told her we will have our next reunion in two years instead of in another 25 years. She asked why.

Sabi ko [I said], "How old do you think I will be in 25 years?"

So she added my age mentally. She said, "Mom, you will be 75."

Sabi ko, "What about if someone is already 65 now?"

Sabi niya [she said], "Oh, no! Someone will be 90!"

I said, "See, we have to do it again sooner than later."

---

274   Watch on YouTube: *tagaalbay*, BISAYA MAN GID, 2:36min, https://youtu.be/Dy7RM1QBZDQ

275   Watch on YouTube: *tagaalbay*, THE TOAST, 1:15min, https://youtu.be/ZuMFBilEhvw.

Of course, Nemia is telling her daughter subtly that the mathematics of age is inversely proportional to the statistics of convenience and mobility. (This statement, entirely my own, may give us nosebleed, but I refuse to reduce it to simpler terms—for our peace of mind.) Everybody knows that. So, Lani says in cheerful denial, "Tell her Tita Lani doesn't know how to count, *kaya pretend na lang.*" [Tita Lani will just pretend she doesn't know how to count.] In the same vein, Emee says, "Tell her Tita Emee has stopped counting and stays at her current age, regardless." Ely chimes in with a scary foreboding. *"Kaya nga, we have to do it habang nakakalakad pa tayo."* [That is why we have to do it while we can still walk.] In silent response, I engage in wishful thinking. "In 25 years, I intend to walk without a cane or a wheelchair, God willing!" But Judith, in all honesty, says, "Tell her Tita Judith will be 94 in 25 years!"[276]

Guys, let's coordinate more closely and plan more diligently for the next reunion. Remember, in 2 years! This time, we should work for more attendees; contact as many members of Batch 92 as we can, search for them in all the nooks and crannies of these United States and beyond. Venue should no more be down south at the tip of Texas but northeastwards—at Rose, Rolit, and Emee's domain—New York or thereabouts! In the meantime, while waiting for that special day in our collective life, here are a few servings of chicken soup to savor in the next two years.

- "In everyone's life, at some time, our inner fire goes out. It is then burst into flame by an encounter with another human being. We should all be thankful for those people who rekindle the inner spirit." (Albert Schweitzer)

- "I cannot even imagine where I would be today were it not for that handful of friends who have given me a heart full of joy. Let's face it, friends make life a lot more fun." (Charles R. Swindoll)

- "Remember that the most valuable antiques are dear old friends." (H. Jackson Brown, Jr.)

- "Every parting is a form of death, as every reunion is a type of heaven." (Tryon Edwards)

And last, an anonymous quote (courtesy of my friend Puring Quindoy, a Xavier School colleague and New York teacher-retiree now based in Arizona), our mantra:

- "Friendship is a promise made in the heart, unbreakable by distance, unchangeable by time."

See you! God bless us all! ■

Standing L-R, **Eugene Mangsat, Ernesto Ibarra Jr., Armand Ramones, Rogie Legazpi, George Doloroso, Arcadio Morada Jr., Perly Andres.**

Seated L-R: **Eleonor Felicilda, Emee Cabanero, Judith Cunanan, Leilani Olaires, Maribel Reyes, Nancy Martirez, Rose San Diego, Maria Oropeza, Ester Mejia, Nemia Bagtasos**

Not in the picture: **Edith Derrada, Gwen Delfin, Jane Lorenzo, Lillibeth Reyes, Lorna Patino, Rolita Liwagon, Adlai Saniel, Vic Sinining**

SILVERADO, Batch 92

---

276   Watch on YouTube: *tagaalbay,* JUDITH, 2:14min, https://youtu.be/fdFVFozHKRE.

42

CHIMERA

Dream becomes a Monster to outlive

"Mr. Purple!" A male voice startled me, uttering the moniker by which I am known in these parts for the past twenty-six years, from 1992 through and beyond my retirement in 2018. *These parts*, of course, means Cummings Middle School, St Luke's Catholic School, Incarnate Word Academy, St. Mary's Catholic School, and Villareal Elementary School.

Presently, I had been rummaging through the candy aisle at our neighborhood Walmart looking for jelly beans when the voice broke my concentration and directed my gaze to its source. In front of me was a thirty-something Mexican male, pushing a half-filled shopping cart.

After a moment of hesitation, I recognized the guy. "Mauricio Guerra!" In front of him, I stood still, gasping in awe and concealed resentment. "Is it really you?"

"I can't believe you still recognize me!" Mauricio said in his Hispanic accent, beaming a likewise excited grin. "After all these years!"

Yeah, after all those years! This chance meeting happened in 2012, exactly 20 years after he and I sparred as Student and Teacher in a special Math class at Cummings Middle School. In my first year in America, on my first day of school, that Math class of 13 Mexican migrants included this guy who's calling me Mr. Purple now. Teacher could hardly teach in *español*, and Students could hardly learn in *inglés*; so, Teacher's classroom management went kaput. This Student became one of countless others who made Teacher's life a helluva roller coaster ride.

In Greek mythology, a fire-breathing creature called Chimera can give us the chills: a lion with a goat's head protruding from its back and with a snake for a tail. A three-headed monster! You know what, Mauricio, when I came to America decades ago, I never expected to find that three-headed monstrosity in my midst. I had my own personal Chimera!

Lion was America, everything that it stands for—the geography, the people, the culture, the institutions, even the American Dream, inhabit the head of that Lion. Goat was everything psychological associated with my longing for home—my family, my relatives, friends, the Filipinos, and the Philippines inhabit the head of that Goat. And Snake? Students and the school, in which they are, inhabit the head of that Snake.

Listen, Mauricio, you look so pleasant now, so amiable, but you were Student once. You interacted with me, learned from me, idolized me, called me names, challenged me, insulted me, mortified me, loved me, harassed me, upset me—and yet remembered me! You made my years in America so colorful, provocative,

331

hateful, arduous, hellacious. There had been scores upon scores of you and your likeness such that I could write a book just cataloging your names. I could recoup battalions of you in my decades of teaching in America.

At first, I desired to slay my three-headed Chimera, using every power and ability at my command. But then I realized the futility of fighting such monstrous entity. In actuality, I could never overpower my Chimera. I learned the hard way that taming and getting along with the monster was much more helpful to me. I learned to cushion the monster's blows, or altogether avoid getting struck, to smoothen the rough scratches inflicted upon me by its claws, and to blunt their sharp edges. As a defense mechanism, I learned to brush up on my weaknesses, to raise and play my own game. Above everything, I learned to throw caution to the winds—for my own sake.

Therefore, my Chimera has altered the course of my life in America, and my entire life. I am the product of every experience I have had with my Chimera, the repository of every knowledge and wisdom I've gained from my Chimera; I am the accumulation of every failed or fulfilled dream or aspiration for and about my Chimera. When the day is over, I can without equivocation say that my Chimera has fashioned me, to my liking or not, into what I am now.

So, Mauricio, when you wonder why I still recognize you "after all these years," my simple explanation is, I can't and won't forget. I should even thank you—

or the helluva roller coaster ride which you and my Chimera as a whole have put me (and the rest of my batch of Teachers) on, I thank you. It takes much effort and unburdening to say this. It is painful, frustrating, exhausting, mind-boggling. But here is a chronology of that ride anyhow:

- August 18, 1992—We, my group of 18 professionals from the Philippines, arrive in Houston TX, marvel at the sights and sounds of America; at the same time, we sense the slam-bang beginning of an ardent longing for home. Lion amazes us, while Goat casts its insidious shadow upon us.

- August 19, 1992—In the morning, Raul, son of Ms. Florita Tolentino who's responsible for our migration to America, accompanies us to the Social Security Administration Office in Houston. This is an important step we have to take. Here, each of us applies for a number. Henceforth, Lion keeps track of us through our individual numbers, our identities.

- August 20-21, 1992—*Manang* Sarah Boyles, Tolentino's cousin from Surigao in Mindanao, Philippines, leads us to a tour of downtown Houston, window-shopping in big malls like the Galleria. In the evening, most of the group fly to the Rio Grande Valley, except five: Ernesto Ibarra, Ester Mejia, Maria Oropesa, Nancy Martirez, and myself. The following day, Manang Sarah takes us to NASA, America's famous center for its fascination with science and space. We continue to gloat and salivate at Lion's good looks and magnificence.

- August 23, 1992—On this Sunday, the remaining five fly to the Rio Grande Valley, our final destination in Texas. The compassionate Mr. Abel Gonzalez, Ms. Tolentino's right hand in the Valley, meets us. He says that we are off most schools' hiring timeframe, but just the same, he assures us of jobs. The next day, he says, he will take us to various school districts in the Valley. The law of supply and demand is in our favor, Gonzalez says. He prefers to take most of us to Brownsville Independent School District. Snake leers at us.

- August 25, 1992—On this Tuesday, I get hired as Math Teacher at Cummings Middle School, Brownsville ISD; most of the other Filipino Teachers get hired on or around this date, too. We have two workdays for "psychological and intellectual" preparations, as well as making our physical environment, our classrooms, ready for the opening day of classes, on August 31. Snake is coming upon us!

- August 31, 1992—Today is a Monday, during which I first meet my Math 7 classes. At 1:00 pm, you, your classmates of Mexican migrants and I first meet eye to eye. All of you can read, write, and speak English—*not!* I spend an agonizing thirty minutes trying to figure out what your names are and how to say them. *Mi nombre,* I introduce myself while stabbing my chest with my index finger, *Morada. Como se llama?* One girl is Citlali, a boy is Cuauhtemoc, a boy and a girl are both Guadalupe, and you are an annoying and garrulous Mauricio when I first meet you today! To think that you, talking in your mother tongue, are in this English-speaking Texas, United States of America!

- September 14, 1992—On this Monday, a Student in another Math 7 class explodes a stink bomb in my room while I am teaching. Pandemonium! Ms. Estella Aguirre, Principal, comes over and tries to fish out the perpetrator/s. No clue. No snitch.

- September 22, 1992—On this Tuesday, somebody sneaks and sticks a freshly chewed gum on Teacher's seat while I am teaching. Without my knowing, I sit on it. Of course, I am stalled for a brief, embarrassing moment. When at last I stand, everybody is in stitches, for the gum sticks to my behind, or my behind sticks to the gum. It may not be the worst humiliation, but I am most humiliated just the same. Later during the day, somebody's Post-it notes find their way to me, revealing who the culprit is. Do you remember Lyka Cantu? For being so innovative with her gum, I love that girl with every bit of my heart! That's an irony.

- September 25, 1992—I receive my first paycheck from Lion's personification, Uncle Sam, net amounting to ₱44,240. I am told that you young Mexicans excel in Math at heart; *aver,* knowing the prevailing dollar-peso exchange rate, compute my net salary in dollars. That is tantamount to my blood, sweat, and tears teaching you, Snake! Snake is relentless and formidable; so, equal pay for equal work.

- September 25, 1992—Same day, I reserve a ticket for Manila in secret. Nobody else knows, not even my wife Mameng in Manila. Not my immediate roommates Rogie Legazpi and Adlai Sañiel, and certainly not Ernesto Ibarra, George Doloroso, and Eugene Mangsat; they occupy the second room of this two-room apartment we migrant male Filipino Teachers rent. I guess everyone is preoccupied with their own concerns to even notice I am struggling against my Chimera—and losing!

- September 27, 1992—I come to my senses and cancel Continental Airlines flight reservation IWR2CH for Manila set for September 30, over a cone of Rocky Road.

- September 28, 1992—Feast of Lorenzo Ruiz, first Filipino saint and patron of the Overseas Filipino Workers, I send a letter to Mameng with the assurance: "Don't worry about me. With prayers, I will survive." I may as well have said, "I'm taming—and learning to live with—my Chimera!"

- October 25, 1992—I say to my wife, "It will take time till I fully attune myself to the American situation." Many things still depress me. Work. Homesickness. Disgusting Americans and *kababayan* alike. And mean Students whose only business in class, I suppose, is to disrupt and corrupt normalcy. My Chimera has reared its ugly heads to the hilt! "But rest assured, I will cope up, promise." I say this so as not to make Mameng worry, although deep in my heart I am nowhere near accomplishing it.

- November, undated, 1992—Josie Basco, former colleague at Xavier School, Philippines, leaves job and takes flight, to nobody knows where. Grapevine is abuzz with irreverent gossips that Teacher could not endure Students, third-grade non-readers, half of whom are non-English speakers. I wasn't the only Teacher upset by the Snake!

- December, undated, 1992—Maria Oropeza, one among the Teachers who arrived with me on August 18, resigns, *err*, gets terminated—because Student, having been not granted permission to go to the restroom, pees his pants and his school stuff. Whether on purpose or by accident, only Student knows. Of course, the parents go to the proper authorities *pronto*, whereupon they offer two choices: fire Teacher, or they will sue the school. It's a no-brainer. Teacher has to go.

- December 21, 1992—Vic Sinining, another Teacher in our batch, leaves for Seattle, WA, at the start of the Christmas break. He never returns in January or forevermore. [Wonderfully, Vic rose from the ranks and became a U.N. diplomat, and now resides in Africa as a top educator!]

- December 31, 1992—My roommate Adlai's family, wife Ely and two kids, arrive in Brownsville from the Philippines. They bear the good news that the U.S. Embassy in Manila erstwhile approved their visas with no cinches. This bodes well for my family's visa application. I am expecting my wife and Dimple's arrival soon.

- January 4, 1993—One after the other, two Christmas cards with cut-out pictures of Mameng and my Dimple have arrived last December 31 and today. I am overjoyed, the same feeling I exude every time I receive something from home. This time, what my wife sent me was to me extra special. She has taken great effort in looking for those cards with the right messages and cutting out and pasting on it her and Dimple's pictures. To others' eyes, what resulted was as corny as could be, but to me it was a novel way of greeting me a Merry Christmas and a Happy New Year. It is enough to drive away my Christmas nostalgia and depression.

- January, undated, 1993—Two of my roommates have resigned from their teaching jobs, Rogie Legaspi and Eugene Mangsat. Know that these two are excellent Teachers, Mauricio, but I presume nasty Snake gets the credit just the same for this uncalled-for turn of events.

- February 2, 1993—Mayon Volcano's eruption is big news in the States. I worry for my wife and daughter, who live in Camalíg, a town at the foot of Mayon. CNN shows footage of the eruption. I get to see Mayon on American TV, as well as Our Lady of the Gate Parish Church in Daragá, Albáy. My mother and my siblings live in Daragá town, as proximate to Mayon as Camalig. There was even a Eucharistic celebration shown on the video footage, and I recognize not just a few familiar Dragueños in the congregation. Goat casts a sidelong eye.

- February 14, 1993—A bleak Valentine, with Mayon eruptions still happening. As I wake up and turn the TV on, CNN video footage shows death and destruction from landslides and lahar, in an unnamed *barangáy* at the foot of Mayon. The video further shows the iconic Cagsawa Ruins vis-à-vis families mourning at a requiem. Nostalgia, worry, and despondency beset me. Maybe everything that's happening is a way of saying my family has to hurry to come to Texas. I am worried to the max. Goat casts a frantic eye.

- March 27, 1993—On this Saturday, Mameng and Dimple arrive from the Philippines. At long last! With my family beside me, I now have a formidable weapon and shield against loneliness. Goat better watch—and keep—out!

r. Purple, Mr. Purple!" Mauricio, garrulous and prankish as ever, bellowed as he interrupted my stream of thoughts. I came around and gasped. "Please meet my family." Before me was a Caucasian lady with two kids in tow, a boy and a girl, around the ages of 7 and 5.

"This is my wife, Carol, and our two lovely kids. Hey kids, meet my former Math teacher when I was in middle school. He was very fond of me!"—he gave me a wink. "Carol here is from Houston, and we met in college. We both work in one of those oil refineries in Houston, and we just came here to Brownsville to visit my Mama. You know when our firstborn child José Luis was born, my Mama she was the one who strongly suggested the name in honor of her own papa; now she's very fond of him and wants us to come visit every so often. So, when our girl was born, Carol said, now it's my turn to give the name. I said, sure, and she gave our baby girl the name Jennifer in honor of whomever. What a cute name and a cute girl, my Jennifer, don't you agree, Mr. Purple?"

Indeed, the Mauricio I knew, whose gab was the boon of his mates but the bane of the Teacher. "Of course, Jennifer is so very cute and sweet!" I said, without flattery. "You're such a lovely family, Mauricio and Carol."

"Thank you, Sir!"

"So, Carol, I knew your husband as a student, but how is he as the man of your house?" Now it was my turn to give Mauricio a wink.

"Oh, Mr. Purple," Carol said, "Mauricio is the perfect husband for me, the best role model my children can ever have!"

Beaming, sensing something cooking up in my head, Mauricio said, "I see what you're thinking, Sir. This Mauricio in front of you is no one else but, and not any different from, the Mauricio you knew—only transformed. Like the moon, Mr. Purple! I underwent phases, too, changing and becoming. I believe the Mauricio you met in school was just changing to and becoming the next phase of his life. Middle school was just a phase, and I am now the better for it."

I was awestruck, to say the least. Wide-eyed, gasping while standing still, it took me a long time to process his utterance. It wasn't exactly revolutionary new but, I realized, certainly striking and profound. At last, I said in half-jest, "Since when have you become such a philosopher, Mr. Guerra?"

He philosophized on the moon's phases. In the world of reptiles, they undergo ecdysis, or in simpler terms, molting or shedding the skin. In my adverse focus on Snake, for a long while I forgot the moon goes through phases, and Snake molts!

Mauricio wanted to know my preoccupations at the moment, what I did after Cummings. I gave him my two decades of work history in a capsule: "Since Cummings, I've taught Music." If I stayed in Math, my brain cells could have long gone haywire. Music is a breeze. Less accountability, less pressure, more color, more culture. The stuff I enjoyed doing—and getting paid besides. And Choir. That was why, a few minutes earlier, I was looking for jelly beans, a weekly treat for my Choir.

"It was such a pleasure meeting you after 20 years, Mr. Purple!" Mauricio said as he chased after Jennifer, who had taken a few pieces from the chocolate section and was next to unwrap one. "I hope we meet again someday!"

After several more pleasantries exchanged, goodbyes said, and hugs done, I proceeded to Walmart's personal care department and got a pack of Revlon hair dye for my graying hair. I got home from shopping that day refreshed and exhilarated.

Pleasure was mine meeting you again, Mauricio!

Three years later, in 2015, I needed to change my financial institution and went to this Texas bank to open a new account. The thirty-something bank personnel who attended to my needs, was a charming and very accommodating lady, with a dignified bearing and a pleasant voice and disposition. Tools of the trade, I supposed. She could be mistaken for one of those *mestizas* in Mexican telenovelas, gorgeous enough to be a Miss Universe finalist. She looked at me without batting an eyelash, then read my application form in silence for a while, after which she opened her desk drawer, as if searching for something. When she found what she was looking for, she turned back to me.

"Mr. Purple, my peace offering!" she said, flashing a smile, as she slid a packet of Wrigley's Doublemint Chewing Gums on the desktop toward me. "My stay at Cummings had been a colorful one, and you were one of those who made it so." And then the *coup de grâce*: "Don't you worry, sir—there's no gum in your seat!"

I glanced at the lady's name tag. It read—*L. Cantu.*

Lyka Cantu!

For a moment, this Teacher's world stood still. Full of intent and reason, my face gave the lady the warmest, most heartfelt smile I'd ever flashed. Indeed, Snakes molt, and school is just a phase. Like Mauricio. Like the moon, Mr. Purple!

Snake, thank you.

Goat, thank you,

Lion, thank you.

Thank you, my Chimera.

And, *oh*, hugs and kisses, my Guardians. In your presence and guidance, I've lived to tell the tale!

From Teacher—with love. ♥ ∎

Appendix A

MUDFISH

Ah, could my anguish but be measured and my calamity laid with it in the scales...

-Jb 6:2

apiña is an itch at the southern foot of Mayon Volcano. That's a figurative, or figuratively literal, way of describing our village whose name in Filipino means "pineapples aplenty." For our village at the foot of Mayon neither grows pineapples nor corns—only people who covet any fruits of value but realize sour grapes are more abundant and affordable. You can't be too willing or satisfied scratching it off, it being an itch at the foot. Just a kilometer from Daraga town proper, Mapiña connects two ways to the national road, along which the town's commerce and education centers abound. The two ways are the asphalted road of First Park Subdivision, and a footpath winding along and passing over the Golden River.

Puri and I often followed the first way to school. We were freshmen in a local Catholic university which gave us free half- and full-tuition as high school salutatorian and valedictorian. But today, during the lull of an October rain, we walked the other way.

Golden does not always mean precious. Case in point is the Golden River being the constant object of offensive sighs and saliva, courtesy of passers-by and itinerants. Its tributaries are the town's sewers and canals, and on its banks stand unscrupulous outhouses in precarious overhang. These outdoor toilets pour golden dregs into the mudfish-inhabited water, concocting a mixture repugnant to the noses and eyes of unaccustomed humanity.

The recent rain had stirred the murky mixture, emitting a nauseous stench. I pinched my nose tight, but Puri walked on with an invisible shield from the malodorous.

We spotted a shoal of mudfish fingerlings undisturbed in a small segregated pool on a sandbar. Neighborhood children might have made the refuge. We stopped at the mid-bridge. I contributed to the pollution by spitting. My saliva landed on a drifting slab of wood, producing a faint splash loud enough to pierce my eardrums and heart.

As he gazed at the fingerlings, Puri broke the silence between us with his husky voice. He said, "I want to write a story on mudfish."

A surprise this artistic craving was not. As former editor of our high school organ, Puri once said, "I want to write my swan song. Then I'll endow it to someone who understands me." I said, "I won't accept any piece grim and mawkish."

I asked, "What on mudfish interests you?"

"Mud," he said, as he looked at the fingerlings. "The dirty life."

Feeling as sorry for them amidst the dregs and stench, I said, "How pathetic!"

"Just the expression I expected."

"Sympathy," I said, "is the mother of affinity."

"Affinity, the mother of sympathy," he said. Again, he turned to the fingerlings. "The most pitiful creatures on earth, aren't they?"

"You catch them, put them in a clean pond, and they won't be pitiful anymore," I said, without thinking.

Puri looked into my eyes. "I mean," I said, "what if those young mudfish, instead of being forever in that cruel environment, were in a clean and placid pond?"

"You're attempting to narrow the impossibility gap."

"A clean pond isn't possible?" I asked.

"Of course, possible. Though, mudfish are not for clean ponds."

Our eyes met in mutual repudiation. I felt he was making a fool of me.

"You mean mud is eternal," I said.

"You said it."

"The basic rule in the universe is change."

"Better to change *your* concepts."

"Consider evolution."

"Darwin didn't know mudfish," he said. "Mud is eternal—and universal."

"Don't be naïve, Puri. Mud is subjective and conditional."

"Mud is unconditional forever!"

I could not have that. I resumed walking, more annoyed than defeated, and he followed. A natural spring by the river bank, Mapiña's primary water source, was on our right side, and ahead of us was an ascending flight of concrete steps. Prodded by my ego, I said, "Mud is not a quicksand. If the mudfish themselves tried to leap out of the mess, they could."

"Fail they will," Puri said with conviction.

"Why?"

"Because they ought to live and die in their natural environment." He paused for a moment, during which he shrugged his shoulders. I was reaching my boiling point.

"Never hope," he said, "that God will spare mudfish good lives. This is not being sacrilegious."

By now, dead infuriated I was. Two people have their longest distance between two points, and at this moment we reached ours. *Dear mudfish,* I soliloquized. *God has blessed you with enviable, sturdy life. You can live through conditions and circumstances few other species can withstand!*

"Puri, have you ever read the Book of Job?" I asked, with the veins in my neck standing out as the primeval earthworms in Paradise.

"I know its content," was the flat answer.

"For goodness' sake, learn from it."

"Why should I?" he said. "Job was a moron turned idiot!"

We arrived in school twenty minutes late for our Theology 1 class. Fr. Felipe de los Santos, the university chaplain and our professor, had started his lecture and was fuming mad, as usual, at the entire class. He was not keen on latecomers; we entered the classroom and sat at the back as unnoticeably as we could. The old priest banged on the professor's table, set aside his dark goggles, and continued his tirade.

"Listen, young men! You are a scholarly lot, but the most impassive creatures I've ever met!

"With what are you so bored?

"Why enroll in this course? Because it's in the curriculum? No, because you want to be happy. You want to live with life. You want freedom from principles that paralyze the mind.

"I hear the murmurs. You are giving me an adverse sign. What you want is materialistic happiness, not spiritual.

"Young men, I offer you this piece of advice: never be materialistic, lest your conscience became impotent, your power of reason perverted, and your whole life rougher than rough. If matters are the center of your life, then you don't live it; they live your life for you.

"Be human enough. Aspire to be godlike. Recognize faith in the Infinite Power. Otherwise, man is a paralytic, living in uselessness, or a viper, living in guile!"

Amen, I said to myself, living in shame.

Puri himself looked pale after the session. "I'd better transfer to another school and shift to another course," he said as we strolled around the sprawling campus lawn on a free period.

"Your ambition," I said, "is to be an engineer." Among the local schools, ours was the only one that offered engineering.

"The shoes don't fit."

"Purisimo Buendia, you are a brainy fellow!" I was stating a fact. Though I topped our graduating class in high school, he placed second not because he was less intelligent, but because I was more outgoing and sociable. "I don't believe any academic course can bother you."

"Theology does."

"Theology!"

"Makes me sick."

"Why?" I asked and pouted, with knitted brows. "Boring?"

"Abstract."

"It is understandable."

"Inconceivable."

"Indispensable."

"I can't tackle it."

"You don't have to tackle."

"I can't swallow it," he said. "Makes me puke. Next week is our final exam. See me walking out of this mess."

"You are impossible! This is no mess. Theology tests are just a click of your fingers."

"Answering the final exam is the height of conformism," he said. "I cannot be party to nonsense."

"Even if giving a few answers means passing the course?" I said. "Look, Theology should speak to your heart and head."

"Save your sermon for the dumb," he said.

"It's in your best interest."

"I am not a turncoat."

"As your friend, I am not asking you to be. Give to Caesar what belongs to Caesar, and to God what belongs to God—for your sake."

"You"—his voice jumped an octave higher—"can tell me not to change course or school, for friendship's sake, but it's not your business to rid me of whatever dignity and self-respect I may still have!"

"Oh, please!" I said. "The problem is you've got too much pain in your heart! Rid of your plastic sentiments!"

Granted. Things may be plastic, but not Puri's right fist, nor my face. I fell on the lawn with a thud resonant of bruised flesh and dignity.

"Not even you," Puri said, still in falsetto, pointing his index finger at me, "not even you can talk me into changing the color of my skin!" He then strode away.

Unbelievable language, coming from someone fraternal! Stupefied, I could not get on my feet.

The whole time, other strollers had scampered around to help. They just wanted to stare at my sorry state, as if for entertainment. The janitor who was keeping the campus lawn trim was around too, mad at my having scratched his carabao grass. An irate security guard appeared and asked me, first, if my white polo-shirt got begrimed; second, how much it hurt; and third, how come I sprawled supine in the grass.

My God, I prayed, *please help me find a handkerchief to dab on my nose!*

It was bleeding.

The Theology 1 final exam came too soon. I thought Puri cut class, but he came and sat in the farthest corner of the classroom. Despite Fr. de los Santos' admonition that we must try our best, Puri just stared at the test paper. From the corner of my eyes, I saw him write something on his answer sheet. He might have nixed his helluva plan, whatever. Everybody appeared to have finished the exam. Could it measure what it purported to measure?—It could if we feigned that the Chinese never started writing 0 for nothing. For even as the answer sheets passed to the front, everybody figured out that someone wrote nothing more than his name to satisfy very easy, fundamental Theo questions.

A. As a Christian student, what are the 3 aspects of your life? *Blank.*

The papers then reached Fr. de los Santos, who was sitting behind the teacher's desk in front of the class. Browsing, the good Father must have come upon a noxious paper because he took off his dark goggles and directed his eyes, in amazement, to where its idiotic owner sat.

B. What are the four kinds of acts of piety? *Blank.*

"Mr. Buendia, why are you so impassive?" the Reverend Father asked, with his characteristic fervor. "You've never been active in class, you've never done well in your quizzes and mid-term exam, so you must have made up for it. Don't you belong to this class of geniuses?"

C. What are the popular and technical names of 10 prayers studied? *Blank.*

Puri reddened. Everybody was in deep silence, but far from being bored. Someone was on the brink of his worries.

D. Give the six needs: first 3 of the body & next of the soul. *Blank!*

Mustering guts, Puri stood up and said, "Father, why include Theology in the Engineering curriculum?" He looked as if gritting his teeth.

E. Give the six enemies: first 3 of the body & next of the soul. Goddam devil—*blank!*

"Young man," Fr. de los Santos said in a helpless undertone. "This is a sectarian school."

"Offer it," Puri said, "as an elective, if not as silence."

"Caramba!"

The Reverend Father stood up and stared at his young opponent, as if trying to look for credibility. There was a tense silence.

"The best instruction is not in words," Puri said, with heavier resentment and sarcasm.

"You are very demanding, young man," the Father said. "Elective! What do you think of Theology course, controlled by students' vanity? Silence! Silence is tolerance, and we cannot tolerate youth to be misdirected. Our job is to redirect."

"By grading the faith of the gullible, the complacent, the pretentious?"

At last, the lethal accusation of his adversary toppled the Father's patience. "Shut your erroneous mouth!" he said, as he banged the table, attracting the students outside to swarm by the jalousied windows and open doors of our room. "We are not grading but testing the strength and the endurance of your faith!"

"In 1521, Spaniards colonized Philippines with Cross in hand but with gold in mind. There's a modern-day parallel."

"Jesus Christ!" Fr. de los Santos said, his fury in his sped-up words. "You prove yourself, Buendia. Don't tell me this behavior is academic freedom. This is license! You are harboring ill-gripes against me, against the Order, and against the Administration. You'll be glad this happened!"

Fr. Felipe de los Santos, his Dominican cassock bustling in the air, left the classroom in a jiffy.

The Committee on Discipline sprang into action. As the guardian of campus morality and academic excellence, it conducted a quick but thorough investigation of the case of Fr. Felipe de los Santos against Purisimo Buendia. The Committee found the defendant guilty and approved his expulsion. Puri's name headlined the October issue of the school paper. Everyone scoffed at the worst example of campus behavior.

Mapiña gave him everything from plain laughter to ludicrous invectives. No other resident had ever given such ignominy to its name!

His parents refused him the privilege of tending the family's vegetable stall at the Daraga market. Confronted with questions, Nicolas Buendia said, "The surname doesn't make the man!" Or acted he didn't need to hear questions no more.

My own feelings? God-awful. I mean, you realize every person has their wilder moments. If I were a critic, I could rave that the most poignant part of Rizal's *Noli* is the Damaso-Pia bed scene. Make me a courtroom judge—I will throw the gavel out of the window.

His swan song ended with the people he knew and who knew him corroborating his undesirability. But our story didn't.

One morning in March, my mother asked me if I wanted a new handkerchief since my favorite one had seen better days. I said it had sentimental value. But then she was no simple person to convince, because after I had consigned it to her for laundering, she declared she might have misplaced it somewhere, that it was missing. Since she could find better handkerchiefs in the market, she volunteered to buy a new one for me.

"Thanks, Nanay. Don't bother," I said. If I never had another handkerchief for the rest of my life, I'd give thanks. If ever I needed one, I could just use my underwear.

With my afternoon classes as pretext, I left my arctic home. Instead of going to the Theology 2 Engineering class of the university chaplain, I bought a ticket to a second-run movie whose title I did not care to know.

The humid, bed-bugged movie-house—oh, what a snug place in which to sleep! It was dark—I mean, *night*—outside when I awakened. Night, boring or insomniac sometimes, is a period, while darkness is a mindset. Night is nature's way; darkness, man's.

I wanted to stay longer inside the movie-house, but it was wiser to be *in* the house. House meant that place to pass the night sleeping in bed without having eaten a Pavlovian supper. And home is where the house is. So, I slapped my cheek and wished to spend the night under a Mapiña roof, because home was where lay my heart, and parents were home.

"Waiting for you," a husky voice says at the bridge over the Golden River. There may not be any shoal of mudfish fingerlings or pool or any sandbar somewhere beneath us, but I'm sure from whom the voice comes.

"H-h-h-how's life?" I say. The first time we talk in months.

"As usual," is the flippant answer.

As usual!

"Always sordid and rough," he says, with a smile akin to a snicker. "How are the classes?"

"F-fine."

"Looking forward to when you'll be Engineer—"

I cut the statement short. "You've waited for me?"

"Someone sometime left this in the spring." He draws something from his pocket—my handkerchief! "I ought to know it's yours. I got reason to talk. For the last time."

"What do you mean *last*...?"

"I'm leaving."

"Where headed?"

"None of your business," he says. "Just need to hear the punch and the bloodstains didn't cost us our friendship."

I retrieve the handkerchief from his hand. "We are always friends."

"After five silent months," he says.

"I am always," I say, with the condescension of a child explaining the word *"truly"* to his retarded brother.

"Maybe, but that's just one less person ganging up on my immoral me. And don't say I'm delusional. Morality seeps deep in my marrow."

"Morality is relative. If ever people hate you, they misunderstand."

"Sympathy is a useless emotion," he says, maybe to make me as calm yet arrogant as he is. "You don't deserve my company."

"You are just your old, impossible self," I say. "Don't you have feelings nicer than self-pity? You are a part of my life."

"You'll find better friends—people without plastic sentiments."

A long, long, long reproachful silence. Inside myself brews what is to be my eternal remorse. Outside, wild goosebumps are feasting. *Our Father in heaven, holy be your name, your kingdom come...*

"Once," Puri at last breaks the silence, "I told you I'd write a story on mudfish, remember? Here, the manuscript of a failed life." He hands me a thick bundle of papers, which I get with reluctance. "But I haven't yet surrendered. I still believe in God, the Father Almighty, Creator of heaven and earth and wealth, poverty, injustice—"

"God has done no injustice to you!"

"Here we go again!" he says, his breath shuddering and deepening into a sigh. "Want to continue on your way? Home must be waiting by now. Glad to be on my way, too."

"Tell me, Puri," I say. "How can I make you call off your plan? If you must, leave in the daytime, at least."

"There may be wisdom in darkness."

"There is time to change your mind, Puri," I say. "Believe me, you are going towards a life of sure uncertainties."

"Mudfish is mudfish," he says as he walks away. In one moment that will haunt me forever, he disappears into the bleak darkness beyond. ■

Appendix B

THANKSGIVING FEAST
PROLOGUE

SETTING:	In the Datu's Courtyard
CHARACTERS:	Magayón
	Datu
	Rajah Buhawen
	Dawani
	Daliwawa
	Gayang/Narrator
	Advisers
	Guests
	Guards
	Warriors
	Tribesmen/Women
	Dancers

#1. PRELUDE—"*Kaidtong Manga Panahon*" [In the Olden Times]

NARRATOR: (*offstage; begins with the first repetition of the PRELUDE. As Narrator talks, PRELUDE repeats as many times as needed.*) Many, many years ago, when even your great great grandparents had not yet lived, there was a famous Malayan tribe of people in this our wonderful, tropical land. Far and wide, this tribe was known, because its datu had a beautiful daughter named Magayón. Many sultans, maharlikas, rajahs, datus, and lakans from both near and far lands came just to woo her and vie for her attention. They showered her with the gifts and tributes they could afford to bring.

(*Curtain opens on a tribal feast. The Datu's courtyard, lavishly decorated, fills with people, elders/advisers, guests, tribesmen, women, and children in their finest attires. Low bamboo tables on rear center stage, forming one long table, are set with varied fresh fruits and foods by the tribeswomen. The Datu sits at the center. On both sides of him are his advisers, while other tribesmen/warriors sit or stand here and there. A few seats are still unoccupied; these are for the guests who are to arrive one by one. A gong is sounded as personages*)

Rajah Malumay of Karilaya

Sultan Karim of Tawalisi

Datu Lakay of Katandongan

arrive, each offering bigaykaya, *gifts and tributes to the Datu. Guard announces each arrival. The last guest to arrive is* **Rajah Buhawen of Panay,** *who enters with his nose up in the air, but offers his gift to the Datu just the same. The guests gradually fill up the vacant seats. PRELUDE ends.)*

DATU: Honored guests of our beloved land, welcome to all of you! We open our hearts to thank dear *Gugurang,* our supreme and compassionate God, who has given us this season's rich harvests of meat and grains. Come and enjoy this evening! *(Everybody claps hands in jubilation.)* And now, I beg for your attention! May I present to you my daughter—Magayón!

(Everybody applauds and stands. Magayón, in her fine attire, enters, followed by her two maids-in-waiting, Dawani and Daliwawa. She sits beside her father. While the applause is on, a cacophony of men speaks offstage. MAGAYÓN THEME starts.)

#2. MAGAYÓN THEME

VOICE 1:	Oh, she is beyond compare!
VOICE 2:	*(whispering)* Lovelier than the prettiest flower!
VOICE 3:	She has stars in her eyes!
VOICE 4:	Roses on her cheeks!
VOICE 5:	Pearls in her teeth!
VOICE 6:	And the blackness of the night in her hair!
VOICE 7:	Oh, what a beauty!

(MAGAYÓN THEME ends.)

DATU:	Let us begin the celebration!

#3. LET'S DRINK TO LIFE! *(Cast, with Chorus)*

1. (DATU)	For the plants and animals that live to serve us;
(ADVISER 1)	For the meadows and the mountains green;
(ADVISER 2)	For the rains that surely give us life abundant;
(ADVISER 3)	For the earth that raises everything we want;
2. (GUEST 1)	For the grasses of the fields that grow to feed us;
(GUEST 2)	For the birds and fishes large and small;
(GUEST 3)	For the scores of gentle deer and then the wild boars;
(GUEST 4)	For the flowers and fruits that we enjoy, of course! *(gobbles up a banana; everybody laughs.)*

(CAST/CHORUS) Refrain:

Let's drink to life, life, life!

Let all our hearts overflow with jubilation!

This is a most fitting time for celebration!

Let's drink to life, life, life!

3. (ADVISER 4)	For our families who care for us and love us;
(A WARRIOR)	For our friends and enemies as well.
(BUHAWEN)	For the stinger of the bee, as well as honey,
	Tears and laughter, ever part of you and me!
4. (DATU)	Even for the ants and fleas that bite and hurt us;
	Even for the things we may not like.
	(slow and emphatic)
	Earth is full of goodness and abundant blessing;
	(accelerating)
	Let us keep on thanking God for everything!
(CAST/CHORUS)	Repeat Refrain, then CODA.
CODA:	Let's drink to life, life, life!
	Let all our hearts overflow with jubilation!
	This is a most fitting time for celebration!
	Let's drink to life, life, life, life, life, life, life!

(Right after the song, indigenous music fills the air. Everyone sits; the banquet starts. While the partakers eat, dances regal the feast. The guests may give their dance offerings, their dancers dressed in costumes suggestive of their places of origin. Curtain closes at a suitable time during the feast, cutting it short.) ∎